TOLTECA

K. MICHAEL WRIGHT

Platinum Imprint
Medallion Press, Inc.
Printed in USA

DEDICATION

For Eslabeth: faith shall never die.

Published 2006 by Medallion Press, Inc.

The MEDALLION PRESS LOGO
is a registered tradmark of Medallion Press, Inc.

Printed in the United States of America

Library of Congress Cataloging-in-Publication Data

Wright, K. Michael.
   Tolteca / K. Michael Wright.
      p. cm.
   ISBN-13: 978-1-932815-46-7
   ISBN-10: 1-932815-46-5
   1. Toltecs--Fiction. 2. Tula Site (Tula de Allende, Mexico)--Fiction.
   I. Title.
   PS3623.R554T65 2006
   813'.6--dc22

                                        2006012342

10 9 8 7 6 5 4 3 2 1
First Edition

ACKNOWLEDGEMENTS:

I would like to thank my wife, Carrie. Without her talent as a writer and editor, her perseverance and dedication, *Tolteca* would never have found the courage to be what it needed to be.

TOLTECA

K. MICHAEL WRIGHT

PART I

SON OF THE MORNING

CHAPTER ONE
ONE REED

The Island Named Paradise, the Eastern Sea
The Toltec year One Reed, the season of the quetzal—May 455 AD

When night had grown long, and the fires of the village had died, Topiltzin, alone, climbed the high cliffs at the sea's edge. With warm salt air in his lungs, he knelt and searched the stars before dawn swallowed them. At least the skies had not changed. He had never been certain how far they had traveled through this ocean before reaching the island; but he knew at least that these were the same stars he had studied from the Hill of Shouting when he was young. Through all the years of his exile, Topiltzin had watched this sky. He had carefully tracked the path of the Blue Stars against the horizon. He had marked the days.

He was old—fifty and two years, the same age his father would have been when Topiltzin left for his last rubberball game in the Southland so many years ago in Tollán. Topiltzin's skin was aged; his beard, long and white-gold; the tangled locks of his hair along the sides were silvered, but his eyes were still a steady, sharp, blue ice as they searched the face of the sea.

Topiltzin heard a rustle, and turning, he discovered Paper Flower had followed him. She was there, suddenly beside him. That was her way, jaguar eyes, silent, a soft wind you did not notice until you felt it lightly brush your skin.

When Topiltzin had died his first death, when the Lord of the Shadow Walkers had slain him, Paper Flower's had been the first face

1

he had seen from death's abyss. He was certain death had already tasted his flesh, accepted it, and Topiltzin had nearly slipped away forever—there seemed no reason to remain—but when he looked back one last time, he saw her. She had been dabbing at his blood with a wet cloth, and when she realized he was watching, she gasped, startled. Glancing at her now, Topiltzin remembered that moment so clearly—her face that first time, how it cut against the acid blue of the sky behind her—her sharp features, her raven hair, the small lips, her eyes, quick, tender. In that moment, it had been as though Paper Flower reached across the quiet of death, touched Topiltzin's heart, gently, softly . . . and brought him back.

One score years and four had passed, yet she looked this night more beautiful than ever; her jet hair was now silvered in streaks that played in the moonlight. They had grown old here, upon this isle of the sea. They had born children beneath the white sun. They had laughed, they had wept. Life had played itself out in measured breath, and now Paper Flower was a part of him, their flesh one flesh. There was now a little of Topiltzin in the eyes of Paper Flower, and she in his, a warmth, a knowing touch, a tenderness almost like a wound.

Topiltzin turned back to the horizon. It was there, the talisman, the Morning Star. It ran herald of the sun, and Topiltzin knew she had traced its path as carefully as he had. He knew how she had feared this particular dawn for many years. They simply had never spoken of it. Yet it had come in the night like a thief, and now it was as though the future were kneeling there with them, as though part of what they were had already become memory.

"The Son of the Morning passes through the house of the Raven," Topiltzin said. "This is the year One Reed."

She quickly brushed aside silent tears, as though irritated with them. "Is there no way I can touch your heart?" she whispered.

Topiltzin kept his gaze upon the horizon—partly because he did not want to see her tears, he did not want to break. He had broken inside over the past few days many times and now he was determined to be strong and so he kept his gaze on the sea, the face of it, like blue leather, rippled with the rose of dawn. "You *own* my heart," he said, quietly.

"And yet you are going to leave."

"I have no choice in that, Paper Flower."

"You have choices. Choice is what you gave us that day on the beach when the Lord of the Shadow Walkers came for our souls. It was your gift to us, but also, it was our gift to you. We gave you life, we offered you choice, and now comes the moment you must choose. Choose between us and your ghosts, Topiltzin."

He sighed, finally turned to her. Paper Flower's eyes searched his, angry. He touched her cheek, but she pulled back. He could sense her anger, but all he felt in response was sadness, far, a sadness that just watched. "Somewhere," he said, softly, "love is marked—all we have shared—as love could ever be."

She shook her head. "No. Not this time. You speak with a silvered tongue, my prince, but there are no words to make this pretty."

Another tear crossed her cheek. Topiltzin reached to catch it, but Paper Flower angrily brushed his hand aside.

"You want to take my tears? You could. You could take them all if you wished. It is a simple thing to take them. But if you do what you are thinking, Topiltzin, then I shall keep these tears." She waited for a response and when she didn't sense it forthcoming, she turned away sharply, slipping over the steep side for the climb down.

"Wait! Paper Flower!"

He reached for her, but she was too quick, and she did not look back. For a time he stared after her, sadly, but then he turned to look again at the sea and forced the sting of sadness away. There was no time for it; there could be no weakness in him now. These many years, Topiltzin had listened to the silence that carried across these waters, but what was more, what he could not turn from—he had also listened to the screams. Perhaps that day on the sand—long ago in the land of Tollán, when he had faced the Shadow Walker— perhaps he had cheated death. Topiltzin had taken these years like a thief, but now it had turned, time had curled about the earth in full circle. The dawn sun would mark the Bundling of Years. It was time to return to Tollán.

⌇⌇⌇⌇⌇⌇⌇⌇⌇⌇⌇⌇⌇⌇⌇⌇⌇⌇⌇

Paper Flower crossed the white sand of the beach beneath the cliffs. She had first started toward her hut; but knowing Topiltzin would come later, she decided he should find it empty. He should get used to empty; empty was his choosing now. She had loved him these many years, full and rich and with all her heart, and their sons and daughters, they were like sparkling jewels. She had tried to teach him to forget, but she had failed, and in failing to reach Topiltzin's heart, it seemed she had failed in everything. Her sadness was as endless as the sky this night.

She made her way to the wide, half-moon beach where the sand glittered as though diamonds might have been tossed. It was one of the most beautiful places she had ever known, and there were memories here—good memories, cherished.

Near a shelf of blue rock that curled fingers against the dark, ancient stone of cliffs, she slid onto one of the ledges and sat back, searching the curl of the waves for an answer, for comfort, for anything they might offer.

He had been a good father, Topiltzin. When his sons, born of thirteen queens, had grown old enough to touch manhood, Topiltzin started to train them. Paper Flower watched as their children first played mock games, wrestling for control of hillocks or groves of coconut trees; and in the beginning, she had smiled. It seemed the games built strength and courage, teaching them well. They laughed as they struggled in mock battles; but as they grew older, Topiltzin's sons carried shields that were as well crafted as any she had known in Tollán. They fashioned deadly spears and bows that could sink their oiled shafts deep into the trunks of palm trees; and not long after, the laughter—their innocence and youth—started to leave their eyes. More and more the peaceful valleys of the island they had named Paradise filled with the chilling echoes of the Flower-Song, the words the ancient heralds had given war in the Land of the Reeds. Then she knew; she realized what he was planning. Topiltzin was going to return. And he was going to take their sons.

CHAPTER TWO
THE GREAT OLD ONES

The next morning, the Bundling of Years

They waited, naked but for breechclouts, staring down the west wind into the Emerald Sea, which now lay glittering warm beneath the midday sun. Somewhere far, this sea air had whispered off the homeland, and Topiltzin let it fill his nostrils, touch his blood.

With him were his three eldest sons, tall, muscled, with ropes and tackle hung over their shoulders. They awaited the coming of the great ones, the Voyagers of the Deep.

Sky Hawk, his third-born, pointed seaward, excited. "There, Father!"

Topiltzin searched. It was a moment before he saw the whale surfacing, an arch of its slick, gray back peeling out of the green sea. Topiltzin lifted his fist in the air, and from below, from the beach, conch shells sounded. His daughters, gathered upon the white sand, sang to the sea beasts. They would lull them with the song of virgins, bring them close. The emerald drums sounded a steady, rhythmic beat.

Turquoise Prince, Topiltzin's firstborn, the son of Paper Flower, lifted off the black rock as though he were kin to eagles, spreading his arms. Watching him, Topiltzin felt that he might easily soar, touch the clouds, steal fire from the sun. As his arms lowered into the dive, he spun, dropping into the water sleek and smooth, his white-gold hair streaming before he vanished into the sea below, soundless.

6

TOLTECA

The next to dive was Huemac, Topiltzin's second-born. Huemac was not agile; he was muscled and heavy, which had always surprised Topiltzin because this was the son of the shy, waif-like Jewel Twirler, his youngest queen. Huemac did not dive; he leapt from the Cliffside with a warrior's scream and dropped through the sky like a stone. Below, the sea seemed to swallow him. Huemac's blood was rich, fevered; spawned of passion, his dark eyes could sometimes chill with the very whisper of the night sky. Of all his sons, Huemac was the fiercest warrior in the games.

The third to dive was Sky Hawk, smaller than the others, but fleet—quick. Sky Hawk had a zeal for life that seemed to have no bounds. He was swift, always the clever one, the sly one, always with a joke, always the one to make them laugh. Sky Hawk's lithe, muscled form parted the waters below perfectly, and when he surfaced, he swam with strong, swift strokes, sure of his target.

Topiltzin now lifted his own rope and equipment and laid them over his shoulder. For a moment, he turned to gaze down at the beach. He raised his hand, spreading fingers in the sign of the word, and there were cheers in answer. Below, the sons and daughters of Topiltzin danced as once children danced in Tollán. They danced with feathered veils trailing in streamers, holding between them the tendril of the flower cord as they wove in circles. Topiltzin's seed among the High-Blood of the Chichimec women had produced haunting visions—faces, sharp and lean; deep, almond-feathered eyes.

When Topiltzin turned and dove, he heard the drums' pace quicken to a hard, rapid trill. Age had stolen his quickness, but he could still feel the kiss of the west wind before the sea swallowed him, and when he broke surface, he swam with a steady stroke.

Through the waters, far ahead, he saw Sky Hawk briefly. How fast he had reached his target! He rose from the waters riding the back of a great gray-mottled whale, holding tight, both hands coiled in ropes that were anchored to the whale's flesh by barbed hooks of fishbone.

7

Topiltzin and each of his sons would choose a whale; each would take a Great Old One into the deep this day and return with its flesh.

When Topiltzin could feel the cooler currents of the ocean stream, he stilled. He waited; only sea and sky were about him. It did not take long. Soon Topiltzin could feel the waters pressing before the Old One as it came, parting the sea before its face. He called to it, *Come, come, great one. We will dance. We will sing the moon down into its lair.* He lifted the heavy ropes and tackles from his shoulder and started them spinning above his head, around, around. When he let go, they splayed outward, skimming the blue waters, just as the shadowy form emerged from the deep.

The great beast broke surface, its nose spearing into the center triangle of ropes. Topiltzin let the giant's weight pull the ropes taut, let the slipknots tighten over the beast's snout. Riding its back, Topiltzin drove a spike into the flesh with a mallet and quickly looped a rope about it, then winched it, anchoring himself to the beast's side. He gently moved one hand over the skin. Soft skin, like a woman's.

When the whale dove, Topiltzin kept a firm hold, clinging. The ropes, constricting the air-spout, had cut the animal's breath short. He would not dive long. Beneath the waves, as the beast descended, Topiltzin continued to crawl over the body slowly, mimicking a gnat, an ant. Shafts of sunlight spilled through the emerald water in streamers. A school of silverfish scattered as though the beast were blowing through snow. The Old One did not feel him; Topiltzin was but an irritation. Topiltzin's lungs thirsted for air, but he quieted them, whispering calm. Only when he could stand no more did he suck from the airtight shark bladder.

They dove still deeper, until the sun could no longer reach them. Gliding swiftly though the shadows, Topiltzin wondered who might be watching as the Prince of Tollán rode the sea beast. He closed his eyes, stilled all movement, saving breath.

The Old One finally ascended, swiftly upward until it burst

through the surface, going for air, and now Topiltzin moved quickly. He slammed the thick pine slug into the whale's air hole and wedged its barbed anchors into the flesh. Bloodied froth boiled about its edges. Small jets of warm seawater hissed out of splits in the skin as though to erupt, but it was useless. The more the Old One struggled to blow the plug, the deeper the hooks sank into the smooth skin. The whale could no longer get air.

The Old One heaved downward, diving, spiraling into the dark. The sun retreated into the world of sky, and the waters grew sullen. The whale twisted first one way, then another. Topiltzin hugged the flesh, calmly, waiting, ropes coiled about his arms. As it weakened, Topiltzin drank its power, taking the strength of the beast. It was a spiritual touch, something beyond the whisper of flesh; it came pure and silvery. The blood of dying was the richest blood of all.

They broke through the surface furiously, again ripping downward, twisting, rolling beneath the sea.

Forgive me this, my friend, he whispered from his heart. It had to be that he took the beast's breath, for Topiltzin would need all the strength he could gather. The coming days were fire waiting, a burning. Time was marked in the Heavens, in the Star Skirt of the sky. He was going to return. Topiltzin, the Blue Prince, would return once more to touch the earth of Tollán.

A terrible wail came from the throat of the beast. Mournful, it cried to its brothers. It was dying. No air, dying. It sang to them, that a prince of men had taken him, the Old One, the voyager of the dark waters. It bade them farewell.

Surfacing for the last time, the whale rolled to one side, gently washed by the sea. Topiltzin lay, spread on its skin until the canoes reached them. There were four sealskin boats moving swift and light upon the waters, palm-wood oars flashing. Lines were tossed; briarwood hooks sunk into the gray flesh. One of his sons called to him.

"Father, are you all right?"

Topiltzin lifted his hand in the sign of the word. His children then worked the oars, and they towed the whale back to the island.

Long ago, when he had first seen the island of the eastern sea, he had given it a name taken from the plates of gold, the ancient words from the Land of the Red and the Black. He called it Paradise. First-Life. Its mighty cliffs, the deep green lush of vegetation, the pearl-white sand of its beaches—they had seemed then to know the secrets of life.

By the time the boats approached the shore, night had fallen. The sky was proud, and the shore had been sprinkled with stone fires. From the sea, Topiltzin rode the carcass, kneeling. Seeing him return, his children cheered; they ran forward, splashing through the surf. Topiltzin slid off into the warm sea. He strode toward them, waist-deep, reaching his arms out as they crowded about him. The drums echoed away into the night. Winches were anchored to palms, and the beast was pulled onto the shore.

Two others were already being harvested. Turquoise Prince and Sky Hawk had both brought in great gray whales. But it was long before Huemac returned. His ropes had snapped, and Huemac had almost been lost. The canoes had searched, but had not found him. Long hours later, Huemac had swum back alone in the sea of night. Weary, head low, he finally wandered up the beach. Seeing him, Topiltzin rushed forward and took his son in his arms. Several of Huemac's sisters gathered about him as well, but he would look at none of them; he only stared at the sea, his dark eyes angry.

"I am sorry, Father. I lost the Great Old One. My anchor rope broke loose of its tie. I have failed."

Topiltzin turned him. He looked carefully in Huemac's eyes and smiled, squeezing his shoulder firmly. How he loved this one! "Take heart, my son. We have seven; we are ready."

"But one of them was to have been mine!"

"Huemac, we leave as one. We have no possessions. We have

only each other, and you are very close to my heart."

"But Father, I failed, I . . ."

"You have failed nothing," Topiltzin said firmly. "It is in Tollán that we shall be tried, not here. This is but a lingering, a waiting. Come, fill your heart! Take rest. Sing this night."

At first Huemac resisted, but Topiltzin then spun him backward with a laugh and Huemac stumbled off balance. One of his sisters caught his hand as she was passing and pulled him into their dance despite his mood.

The children of Topiltzin danced and sang, for this would be the seventh boat, and this would mark the time of new beginning. His daughters wove the flower tendrils and sang the song of the midnight star.

Topiltzin watched them for a while, but then turned away and strode alone to the far edge of the first boat. This boat had been completed eight days ago. On the skin of its underbelly, his daughters had used blue dye to paint the image of a poppy seed. He smiled, but the smile slowly faded. When he noticed a shadow against the hull, he turned. He was surprised to find Paper Flower.

"Elder sister," he said, "I had guessed you would have no more words for me."

Her dark eyes studied him carefully. Of all his queens, she had easily outwitted him these many years. She had listened to his stories; she had watched him teach his sons the mock battles—but she had continually warned him of this dream. She had never shared it. When his sons had completed the first whale-ship, Topiltzin had asked her to give it a name, and she had. "Nightmare," Paper Flower answered that morning without pause.

She stared at it now with even greater foreboding. She sighed. "Topiltzin, I'm worried about Huemac."

"He will be fine. He is dancing with the others."

She shook her head. Topiltzin glanced briefly toward the shore fires. Huemac was indeed no longer among them.

"He has gone into the jungle," Paper Flower said. "Alone."

"Find his mother. Send Jewel Twirler to speak with him."

"It is not Jewel Twirler he needs. He needs his father, Topiltzin."

Topiltzin glanced at her. "There will be time enough to teach him."

"Where? In Tollán? And what are you going to teach him there? Terror? How to walk the night in fear?"

"Paper Flower, you do not understand . . ."

"I understand more than you know." She stepped in front of him, where he could not look away. She took his face in her hands and forced his eyes to meet hers. "We are here!" she gasped. "We are love; we are light. We are *life*! Do you not see us?"

He started to speak, but as it often was with her, he could find no words.

"You understand many things, Topiltzin; in so many ways you are strong, you are without equal. But this dream of yours: why do you not see that there is nothing left back there? Nothing left in that place but darkness!"

"This is why I must return. How can you question it? I must return to help them find light once more."

She turned his shoulder roughly and pointed to the beach. "Look, look at your children! They memorize every word you speak; they sing your every song. They follow you as though you were the sun itself. You search for your ghosts, your Nephalli, the Many Dead, yet you do not even see your own children. How is it, Blue Prince, that you are going to help anyone find a path when you leave this island blind?" She touched his cheek. She spoke sadly now. "I once believed you were a god, the very soul of the Tolteca. Then I discovered you were only the Prince of Tollán—merely a king. Finally, as time wore upon us, I understood what you really were. You were a man—no more. Be that for us! Be a man. They have no need for the Son of the Morning! These, your children, they need only a father."

He stared at her troubled, and finally she lowered her head.

"What is the use?" she sighed. "You do not hear me. I stand right in front of you, and yet it is not my voice you hear. It is *his*."

"His?"

"You don't hear your daughters sing; you don't even hear your own God any longer, Topiltzin Nacxitl. All you hear now is the Whisperer, and when you return, when you go back there, that is what will be waiting for you—*Him*—the mirror that shines dark against the sun." Her sharp eyes deftly searched his. "You do this, you take your sons on this vision quest, and you will leave our hearts and all we were behind you. If you wish to think about your journey, think on that. There is no quest; there is no glory, but there are many, many hearts on this island that love you more than the sun."

She turned away and he watched her walk along the shore, tingling. He wanted to follow; he wanted to tell her his head was screaming, that he was falling, sucked into the ground by the heaviness of what was coming. He wanted to plead with her, explain that he needed her heart and her love now more than ever. Part of him knew she would make this stand—she had to, she had to be the voice that spoke for her children. He loved her beyond loving, but he could not grant her this, he simply could not.

He had come here to pray, to touch the first ship and find meaning, but now he only ended up staring at the line of the shore against the moonlight. As the whales had been slaughtered, their blood had run back to the sea, and now the tide's foam washed scarlet in the moonlight. The sky understood. Yes, Paper Flower was home, she was truth and light and all that was good in the world. Yet this world was not his, nor could it ever be. Topiltzin's world was bearing even now upon him in blood fingers that stretched across the western sea with a single, unforgiving promise.

CHAPTER THREE
NIGHT SONG

For the longest time, Obsidian Snowflake merely watched him—Huemac, still wet from swimming back, his hair tangled about the handsome face. She could see such sadness in his eyes. On the beach, there were celebrations, and the singing and laughter even reached here to the darkness at the edge of the jungle, but surely everyone could not pretend it wasn't coming, that the count of days was about to pull their entire world into the sea.

For the longest time she wanted to go to him, but instead she just watched. He had been sitting there for a full degree of the moon now, just sitting, staring out to sea. She wanted to believe that perhaps his heart was as heavy as hers, that he was thinking of tomorrow, that he would soon be leaving. But Obsidian Snowflake guessed this wasn't why he was sad. Huemac was troubled that he had not brought in one of the Great Old Ones. He wasn't thinking of her. In fact, after tomorrow, it would be many years, very many years before he ever realized that he had left her behind.

His chest was bare and it stirred her—not that she hadn't seen his chest before, but always she marveled for such power seemed to breathe in those muscles. When matched with his heart and the fire of his blood, they crafted the perfect warrior. If only they had also crafted the perfect man. She finally stood. He had instantly turned. She knew he would spot her quickly—his senses were as keen as any predator's. In the games, he was unmatched. It was why they called him Stone Hand; he could toss his brothers like they were leaves. Huemac had even created the razor-swords of edged obsidian sharpened as scalpels. Seeing the dread swords for the first time, many of her sisters had laughed, but Obsidian Snowflake had not laughed. She had noticed the glimmer of the razor sharp obsidian knives that ringed the wood like teeth, and she had watched as Huemac cut through saplings, leaving their milk to drip down the severed trunks, and it left her prickly with fear—for what if the bark were flesh and the milk were blood?

She slowly walked over to him, searching his dark, intense eyes. She then just climbed up to the rock and sat beside him, turned to stare out at the waters, the way the ripple of the moon laid against the leather skin of the sea. Finally she spoke.

"I thought to craft something, some small thing to give you to take on your journey, but nothing I made seemed able to hold my heart, so finally I just relented. I guess all I can craft for you to take with you is my memory."

He stared at the sea a long time before saying anything, his brow heavy. He was angry. When he got angry like this, there was little use in trying to speak with him. Huemac would always be difficult to love.

"This is the Night Song," he finally said, "the Bundling of Years. We are not to think of leaving this night, remember?"

"That is all foolishness, Huemac. I am supposed to pretend you are not leaving tomorrow? Why should I not pretend as well that the sun will not rise in the morning or that the ocean will just run away from the shore so that the boats have nothing in which to sail? I cannot be foolish like my sisters." She pulled her legs up to her chest and curled her arms around them. "What about you? Be honest with me . . . what do you feel, this night?"

He took his time in answering. "I failed him."

"Our father?"

"Yes."

"I think not, Huemac. You worship the sand that touches his feet; you know all his songs by heart; you carry his stories with you everywhere you go. Almost you are he, so how could you fail him?"

"My brothers both brought in Great Old Ones this night."

"Of course, but do you really think that matters?"

"Yes! Everyone is watching what is done this night. How could it not matter?"

"Because you are going to give our father much more than the skin of a whale. You will take his songs of warriors and kings, and you will bring them to life, just as if you were a god. Don't you realize, Huemac? You are the fire Topiltzin takes with him to the sea."

"How would you know these things, Obsidian Snowflake? You are just a girl."

She stared a moment at the far line of the sea, its white curl against the night sky. "I know a lot of things despite being a girl, and I know how pointless it is for you to brood this night or to stare at the sea for hours, because you could not give him more, Huemac. You could not!" *You give him what you will never give me!* She cried out in her heart, but then she calmed herself carefully—she was not going to leave him with tears this night. "So let it go, think of other things right now."

"What other things?"

"Perhaps think that with the morning you will never see me again."

Hearing that caught him off guard, and he just stared at her, blinking. "Of course I will see you again."

"How? I cannot build ships from the skin of the Old Ones. How will you see me again?"

"I don't know how, but I will. I have to! If I thought . . ." He paused. He then did something very unlike Huemac. He took a long breath and let his heart into his eyes. So few people would ever see this side of him, and for Obsidian Snowflake, it was so rare that it immediately brought a mist of tears to her eyes. The great Stone Hand that lorded over the mock battlefields was suddenly gone, and all that remained was the tender heart of a young boy. The Huemac she loved.

"If I thought I would never see you again, Obsidian Snowflake, then I could not live. I could not even follow my father. I would just die. Therefore, I will not think it, and so it will not be. No, I will see you again."

"Tell me more lies, Huemac. Say you will never leave at all—not really, not in the smoke of your heat. Tell me that in your heart, time will just stop turning and you will never forget me, and that we will always be together there, in that place, a place known of stars and written of in the Heavens where love is spoken. Would you say that to me, Huemac?"

"I do not have words like you have, Obsidian Snowflake. But yes, I will let my heart speak these things. Yes."

She touched his shoulder. It was muscled like rock, like stone with a soft skin, sweated. "Then here is my gift to take with you," she said softly. "I give my heart to your memory. What that means is that your memory alone shall own my heart—in all of time—and no one else. And you are leaving with the dawn, forever, and so it will be that no one shall know my heart again."

"I cannot let you do that."

"You cannot stop me because already you have taken it—gone when first I saw through your eyes, when first I saw that part you show to no one else."

"What do you mean? Of what part of me do you speak?"

"The part that waits behind your stone eyes, the part that hides, that watches back afraid."

"I am not afraid. There is nothing I fear."

"I think there is, Huemac, but your secret is with me so you do not need to worry. It is not wrong to be afraid? Who can look into the dark of night and pretend they fear nothing? Only liars do that. You could never be a good liar."

He stared at the sea for a while, his lips tight; and when he looked back, his brow narrowed and his eyes grew serious. "If you are going to do this with your heart, Obsidian Snowflake, then I will do the same. I will never give mine as well. Not to anyone. Not in all of time."

She shook her head. "You cannot say that to me."

"Of course I can! You can say it; why wouldn't I be able to say it as well?"

"Because you could be king—someday a king. A king must share his heart with his people or else he is nothing."

"King or not, my heart will belong to you alone because I so swear it this night on my blood, and I do it from the same place you have spoken, so it is no different."

Obsidian Snowflake turned back to the sea, holding her legs tight. She didn't let Huemac see the tears in her eyes. She didn't want him to see them, and so for a long time she just sat next to him, silent. The far sound of the waves from the shore and the drums of the night songs on the beach were the only sound.

Then she said, quietly, "Tonight, Huemac, can I lay with you? Not to bind as girls do to half-brothers, not in that way, but just to touch, that our skin may touch through the night, that we can always remember the touch because for so long all my heart will ever know will be your memory."

"Yes," he answered, as quietly as she had asked.

四回四回四回四回四回四回四回四回四回

After the Night Song had ended, when the thirteenth hour of night turned and the fingers of dawn reached from beneath the earth, the Bundling of Years was complete. It was the Empty Time, the time that lives past the night, yet before the dawn.

On the beach of Paradise, Sky Hawk still worked, crouched on the frameworks of the last ship. He had spent the night working the thick oil paste deep into the gray skin. It wasn't necessary; the ships had all been sealed earlier. When his brothers had left for their huts, they had called to him, but Sky Hawk just smiled and told them to go on without him, that he would work the oil against the seams a bit longer. Once alone, he felt a kind of quiet settle. He could feel the Great Old One's courage as he worked the skin. He could almost sense the pathway from the touch; he could almost picture the shores of Tollán, a land he had never seen, and the thought of it, the thought that these ships understood their path, stirred him.

Sky Hawk paused a moment and leaned back on his haunches. He looked down between the wooden slats and noticed how the ship rested on bloodstained sand. He knew that his father's songs were myth and poetry, but the truth of them was that there had been war for eight hundred years in Tollán.

He noticed with a start that he was not alone. Turquoise Prince was standing below, watching him. He and Turquoise Prince shared the same mother, and yet they were so different, it often left him wondering.

"It is late, little brother," Turquoise Prince said when Sky Hawk met his eyes.

"Past late. It is early now. A true believer can see the dawn already."

"A true believer. I suppose that is how you have spent your night then, not sleeping, but still dreaming."

"And what about you? Why are you not asleep?"

"I tried. It was useless."

"Of course—this is why I just kept working. These ships will not last more than ten days at most, but the more oil and the better it is worked, the longer they will swim."

"Ten days. What land are we going to reach in ten days?"

"We've spoken of this before, Turquoise Prince. If you do not want to trust in our father, then I will keep faith enough for both of us. God will move his hand and we will cross these waters."

"You speak as though it is easy for you."

"I'm certain it will not be easy for any of us."

"It seems easy enough for him."

Sky Hawk paused. He glanced down at Turquoise Prince, who watched back through his bright, quick blue eyes. He was firstborn, eldest brother. He was a skilled warrior, almost the equal of Huemac—both intelligent and perceptive, yet he had never learned to feel beyond his own touch.

"Some things we should not question, elder brother. Some things we should just trust by virtue of our heart."

"Sky Hawk, you are such a romantic. Do you not realize we are leaving in ships fashioned of whale skin for a shore no one has seen in twenty-four years, a shore that is forgotten, unknown? And when we reach it—if we reach it—there will be fifty of us. Fifty, with half of those barely old enough to lift a weapon. What is our father going to do with an army of fifty warriors who are mostly children? I know you believe in the songs, but not all of us can be dreamers; someone has to look in the face of the dark. If we ever reach this fabled Tollán, I fear that what waits for us there will not be poetic."

"Oh, it will be poetic. There is as much poetry in a storm as there is in a blue sky. But that aside, think, Turquoise Prince. Think of this: we have explored every rock on this island. What is there left to discover? Even if we scale the highest cliff—what more is there to see? Yes, the sky is rich, the land is bounteous, but here the shore always has an end. We will ever be no more than we are now."

Turquoise Prince looked away, sighed. "Very well, Sky Hawk. Make an army out of boys and prophecy of pain, but I you tell we shall bleed, we shall die, and none of it is going to be as pretty as the songs they will write of us. I suppose you intend to keep working until morning's light?"

"Yes."

Turquoise Prince nodded. He pulled his cloak over his shoulder. "I will see you when it comes then, little brother." Turquoise Prince turned to walk down the sand alone.

CHAPTER FOUR
FAREWELL TO PARADISE

The ships were made of whale skin, dried and stretched taut, well oiled. When the morning sun hit them, they glimmered on the beach like dark jewels. The hulls were built of whalebone and the hearts of palm-wood. They were shaped after the manner of the reed ship of Tikal that had brought them to Paradise so long ago. When that ship had sunk, Topiltzin and the thirteen Chichimec women had been left adrift on rafts. The sun was killing them, and two of the girls were near death when Topiltzin spotted the island. He stood, calling, pointing, drawing them out of their death daze, lying on his belly and paddling with his arms.

Now, in the rose-haze of dawn, Topiltzin walked where the whale-ships were gathered upon the beach. He could not quiet the feeling that it was already over, that all the words had been written and he was only walking through memory's shadow. It was still the warm season, yet there was a chill cutting through the sea air that bit hard and turned his skin pimply. He paused at the last ship, the seventh. Most of his sons were resting for the voyage, but here he found Sky Hawk still on one of the wooden platforms, rubbing down one last bare spot of skin. Topiltzin had ordered the ships sealed against moisture, for he had not forgotten it was rain that finally pulled the reed ship of Tikal into the sea so long ago. Rains had lashed at them two whole nights. Some of the girls had asked him to call down the Heavens and stop the rain from falling. Back then, they still believed Topiltzin was a god.

Sky Hawk paused and glanced down. Seeing his father, he

smiled. His smile was taken sight unseen from his mother, Paper Flower, both her smile and her sparkling eyes.

"This one is finished," Sky Hawk said.

"It was finished last night."

"Yes, but it is always best to work the oil hard into the stitching." Sky Hawk nimbly dropped onto the sand, wiped his hands on a piece of weft. "Besides, I wanted to watch the sun rise once more over Paradise."

Topiltzin nodded. "And how was it?"

"It seemed the sky understood."

Sky Hawk gave Topiltzin a quick, knowing gaze, fully aware of the burden his father carried this morning. "I will check the stores one last time," he said before sprinting away.

Topiltzin watched him leave. Unlike some of his sons, Sky Hawk seemed to understand that to feel the spirit of a fire one must also taste the pain of a burn.

Topiltzin touched his hand against the hull of the whale-ship. Many times, he had listened to the Great Old Ones at sea. He used to spend hours off the island at night, on wicker rafts, lying face-up to the stars, listening to them. They were such fine singers; and yet their song was always sad, mournful, as though they knew some secret men would never understand, and that was the song he felt now—the whispered promise.

𝖇𝖉𝖇𝖉𝖇𝖉𝖇𝖉𝖇𝖉𝖇𝖉𝖇𝖉𝖇𝖉𝖇𝖉𝖇𝖉

Turquoise Prince walked along the sand, searching for his mother. It was almost time to board the ships; he even feared he might not find her and he wanted just this final moment with her, so he quickened his pace. He could not shake the knot of fear inside him. He had felt it for days, a cold, gripping fear. It was his secret, he spoke of it to no one, but it left chilled fingers down his back. It almost seemed that shadows were watching, as though someone was waiting with ice-like confidence.

22

TOLTECA

He drew up before a group of children near the southern edge of the beach, and he waited there for his mother to see him. She was kneeling to tie the bodice of his little sister's best-painted dress, and it was his little sister, who was named Plume Gum, who saw him first.

Seeing Turquoise Prince, Plume Gum ran past her mother and leapt into his arms. His other brothers and sisters gathered around him as well.

"You look like a warrior," Plume Gum said, touching the shoulder pad of his armor.

"Well, I am only your big brother, Plume Gum. Besides, how would a little girl like you know what a warrior should look like?"

"From Father's stories, of course. Mother says you are to sail on the seventh ship, the one that bears the standard of the White Eagle."

"Yes, I will."

"You must tell me, when you see me again, what the very deep of the ocean looks like, what color it is, and what fishes are there."

"I will little one, I will."

He gave her a squeeze, thinking how she didn't really understand that he was sailing into the deep of the ocean, that she would never see him again. Though that sadness choked him, he did not let it register on his face; he just smiled as he lowered her to the ground, then stood and looked to his mother.

Paper Flower's eyes were firm and cautious this morning. Unlike the night before, there were no tears this time. She was resigned.

"Run along now," she said to her children. "Go up the beach. I will join you."

Little feet padded along the sand. Alone, Paper Flower looked him over and gave him a half-smile. "I've seldom seen you in the cloak with all your weapons. It's startling how you look like one of them."

"Them . . . you mean the Tolteca?"

She nodded and the smile slowly faded. "Time is so thin, Turquoise Prince," she whispered, desperately holding back her tears.

He stepped forward and pulled his mother into a tight embrace.

23

She sighed heavily against him, shaking, but he could tell she was determined not to break, not to cry.

"I will honor you, Mother, in all I do. I will carry your strength to this other shore, and when we are there, I will not let anyone forget the light, the truth, the way we have been taught. Though the four winds scream on all sides, I will see to it that the center is held."

She stepped back, her hands on his shoulders, her head lowered. "I almost don't want to tell you this, Little Prince," she said, using the name she had called him when he was a child. "But you look so much a king that I wonder if it's selfish to want to keep you. If you were to rule in that land, it would, I suppose, become a better place." Her dark, almond eyes searched his carefully. "Take my love and hold it to your heart!"

"I will, Mother."

"And promise me one more thing, Little Prince."

"Anything . . ."

"Watch over him!"

"I promise."

"Tell him someday that I could never hate him. I can't surrender my heart this day; it is just too hard in me. But when you are there, in that land, on a day that is far from this, tell him I shall always love him. Tell him that. And know I will always love you as well, my boy, my son, my little one—always and ever." She squeezed his shoulder. "Come. You must give me the strength to walk up the beach."

He curled his hand about her arm, and they turned toward the boats, which were moving now, slowly easing backward toward the sea.

With dawn's first full light, the ships were lowered to the water's edge by their lashings. The smooth hides glistened, slippery, and as the first waves smashed into their hulls, they crested easily, as though the great whales were returning to the sea.

TOLTECA

Topiltzin's wives gathered, also his daughters, and those sons who were to remain behind. All of them gathered at the sea's edge, solemn. Most of his daughters wept, quietly, restrained. The night before, as asked, they had celebrated, but with the morning, the laughter and singing had ended. With the morning, they wept. They had known only each other, only this, the island, the endless days of sun and warm green waters, the song, the dance, the night, rich in stars. No ill had ever befallen them; none had died; none had even been sick. It was as though the island had become its namesake, the garden where first God's finger had touched to form the children of men from the earth and the maize stalk.

Once the ships were in the deep water of the reef, held only by single tethers to the island, Topiltzin knelt in the sand before his women to tell them goodbye. How he had loved them all, each in a different way, each with a different love. He lowered his head a moment, tried to gather strength. When first he looked up to them, his voice was calm.

"I wish I could explain why this must be done, but I can only say that something speaks as though it has been written against my soul, and I have no choice but to follow. I take your sons, and all I can know is the same voice that calls for me speaks for them as well. But I will leave you a promise that . . . if I am able, if the stars allow, I will return.

"I have searched my heart for words to say goodbye, but as Paper Flower has told me, there are no words for this. I cannot say goodbye, nor can I ask that you ever forgive me, but I can say I will always love you, each of you. Forever." He finally looked to Paper Flower. "Time in all of time," he said quietly, his eyes on hers. "And those are not just the words of a silvered tongue, Paper Flower; it is what I feel."

Unlike her sisters, there were no tears in Paper Flower's eyes. She watched Topiltzin carefully, but her gaze was unforgiving. "Promise you will never let them forget who they are," she said at length.

"I promise that."

25

"You have taught them courage. You have taught them how to fight, how to sing, even, I suspect, how to die. If you are able to find the pathway home before it is too late, Topiltzin, teach them that as well."

"I will teach them all I can, all my heart can know, Paper Flower."

"Then there are no words left," she said. "The morning has come. You have chosen. Go. Leave us, Prince of Tollán. Return to your ghosts."

He stared at her a moment longer, his heart breaking. He paused long enough to meet the eyes of each of the others, then stood and turned toward the ocean. His heart shattered; it broke into pieces and seemed to fall about him in shards. He would never forgive himself, he would now forever be marked unforgiven—but there was no choice.

The ships were waiting, settled into the deep, oars poised. From the prows, those sons who had been named shield-bearers lifted their standards high. With a shout their voices called across the morning; they were strong, they were determined, they would follow their father into fire if he asked. They were the sons of To-piltzin. With a chill, Topiltzin realized that on the prows of seven ships, the seven heralds of the Tolteca flew once more in the heart of the morning.

As he started for them, Topiltzin felt something touch his shoulder and turned. He had hoped she would ultimately give him her blessing, and he turned, hopeful, but he found it was not Paper Flower who had touched him; it was Jewel Twirler, the youngest of his wives. Her eyes were red from crying through the night. She carefully took his right hand and slipped something into it, then curled his fingers about it tightly, squeezing with her own and though her eyes were damp with tears, there was also fire in them, promise, determination.

"In the days that come," she said, her voice now weak, but strong. "If my heart is of use, let this be your light. Keep it close, for you, for our sons, and remember—I am here, Topiltzin! I wait for you." A tear ran quick. "Because *you will return!*" her voice whispered, but in sworn oath that was also a command.

Topiltzin touched her cheek and turned swiftly. He strode toward the ships and did not look back; he would not let them see him break. The crest of a wave hit his chest as he reached the tether of the lead ship and coiled one hand about it, letting his sons pull him upward as the oars of the ship dipped and pulled them into the deep.

◙◙◙◙◙◙◙◙◙◙◙◙◙◙◙◙◙◙

The fifty sons of the Topiltzin left the island of Paradise on the day of the Serpent in the year One Reed for the land of Tollán.

Only when he was deep into the sea, when it was impossible to turn from their path, only then did Topiltzin open his hand and look on what Jewel Twirler had given him. It was a small seashell. On its surface, in bas-relief, she had carefully carved the cross of the Morning Star, the talisman of the Serpent Plumed—the signet of his father. True north.

CHAPTER FIVE
THROUGH THE BLUE-GREEN SEA

They had been swallowed deep not only by the sea, whose waters had darkened, but also by the night, into a sky that bore no stars. Topiltzin had ordered the covering skins drawn taut and lashed to their staying pins, and not much time had passed before a light rain pelted them, drumming tiny fingers, murmuring. All about, they could feel the restlessness of the sea pressing against the oiled skin of the ship. Topiltzin's seven ships were connected with long, entwined ropes, umbilical cords that bound them, and through them he could almost feel the others pressing through the seas with him.

In the belly of the lead whale-ship, Topiltzin had affixed a lamp stone, hollowed carefully, filled with oil, and its flame illuminated the bone ribs of the ship that curled about them. Many of his sons were artists and had worked the bones into arched coils of sky serpents, great winged beasts with gaping jaws. In the shadows etched by the pale flicker of firelight, they undulated, seeming to move. Smoke lazily drifted through the hole in the top covering, into the rain. There was a strange calm, as though they were protected. Perhaps they were. Perhaps the Heavens watched, cared for them—led them through the ocean's path, as once it had the ancestors.

The whale-ship lurched suddenly, and a bit of the oil lapped over its serpent trough and spilled across the polished stone base in tiny rivulets of flame. But the faces of his sons were unafraid, for they were no strangers to the sea. They were the swiftest rowers and the strongest swimmers. In Paradise, they had lived from the abundance of the sea.

28

TOLTECA

Across from Topiltzin, on the far side of the ship, leaning back against the keel bone, he noticed one son, Moan Bird, the second-born child of Jewel Twirler—Huemac's younger brother. Moan Bird's face was a shadow of his mother's; her eyes were there, wispy, tender eyes, as if they would remain forever young. He heard her whisper: *Because you will return!* Topiltzin had tucked Jewel Twirler's seashell into his belt pad. Of his women, only Jewel Twirler had offered to forgive him.

Moan Bird was weaving a soft song with his reed flute. It spilled into the belly of the ship almost like a tear. His sons had left everything: their brothers, their sisters, their mothers—and the voice of Moan Bird's flute was for them one heart. Never had they complained or asked for a reason. Topiltzin had spoken, and they had obeyed. They waited in the belly of a whale, swallowed into the dark of the sea, lost from stars and Heaven, left with only shadows of the faces of all they had loved. All would be memory now, and Topiltzin knew well how memory could sting.

Topiltzin eased back in the wicker throne his sons had fashioned for him in the stern of the whale's belly. Much of the throne was of whalebone, richly engraved with the image of the Serpent and the Eagle. His sons had never seen an eagle, for there were none in Paradise, but the artisans among Topiltzin's children had somehow seen through his own eyes, images as mythical to them as the ancients of Xibalba were to Topiltzin. Not only had they carved the eagle, but also the pelican, the King of Birds; and the swift one, the stag of the hills; even the rabbit, small and quick thinking.

Huemac was seated beside his father, to his left. He had been named Swift Sky at birth, but now was called Huemac—the Great Hand—because of his strength and his prowess as a warrior in the games.

Huemac seemed to have taken little from his mother, Jewel Twirler, except his height. He wasn't tall, but he was weighted heavy in muscle, with broad shoulders and thick arms that sometimes reminded Topiltzin of his own father, Sky Dragon. His brow was heavy, his eyes solemn. Of warriors, he was like the stout tree against the wind, for he would withstand his brothers, toss them as though they were stones.

Huemac laid his head back against the smooth whale hull and half closed his eyes. Topiltzin had noticed a girl watching Huemac closely as they left. Of his daughters, he knew this one for her keen intelligence, her quick eyes. She was called Obsidian Snowflake, and Topiltzin guessed that her image was haunting Huemac now.

Huemac noticed his father's eyes. He offered a stern face, a brave face. "Father," he said, where all could hear, "give us a song. We are into the sea now—sing us again the days when you were young and walked with the sons of the Tolteca, the Sons of God."

Topiltzin paused. These gathered here, in this boat, were his firstborn. He had given them the eagle staff, the highest division of warriors next to the Sky Dwellers. A Sky Dweller was born only of battle, after the change, the taking of first blood, and all were selected from the Eagle Knights. Topiltzin wondered often what had become of them, the named proctors of his father. Surely they had cut a deep, hard swath through the Shadow Walkers.

His sons were watching him, waiting, but Topiltzin only shook his head. "I am growing old with such stories. I get lost in them. It is time we had a new singer." He gazed about at them. "In Tollán, they chose singers from among the strong, the warriors, for it was believed all poets were first warriors by blood."

Topiltzin's eyes came to rest upon Turquoise Prince. His son's eyes, though a rich blue, were cut with the sharpness of a predator, an ironic gift of Paper Flower's blood. In his own day, Topiltzin had placed little stock in birthright, yet his son seemed to have been born a prince—and he could sing. Turquoise Prince could sing with a voice that carried across the morning and touched the next day.

"Sing to us, Turquoise Prince," Topiltzin said. "Let the words of our fathers deliver us as we move through the blue-green sea."

At first Turquoise Prince just stared at the fire. Moan Bird had stopped playing the reed pipe, and all waited. At length the boy looked up and Topiltzin marveled at the hard edge of light that shone in the dark blue eyes. Turquoise Prince looked directly at his father, as if they were alone in the ship.

"It is said," Turquoise Prince sang, "among the stars that look down, among the clouds that sweep the sky, that once there came upon the face of the land those who were called the Sons of God. And they were us, and we were they. We came through the mighty dark, the great deep. In times men have forgotten we came, we crossed, and we passed through from the Land of the Red and the Black. Our God went before us, and we were his sons, therefore we followed.

"And we landed there in Panatela, which is to say our home, for thus it was spoken, for thus it had been written. In that time we followed the singer whose name was Ehecatl Nephalli, the Father and the Wind; for it was the Wind that had led us, Ehecatl, Ahman-om-Amen; and it was His voice that went before our face, sweeping the way. And so it was done. It was spoken: the name of God.

"And it came to pass, in time we journeyed; we crossed the mountains and the wastelands. We took our women, our children, and our sacred writings, our metal castings and star knowledge, and we walked, we came to that place called *Tomoanchan*: Zarahemla. There were many then, by that time, in that day, descended of four sons, brothers, the four corners of the world, both light and dark, both water and air, both earth and sky. Of these four, we were the Nonaloca, the wise, the artisans, the warriors, the judges and the priests, the givers of law, the speakers of truth. Where we went, there followed lightning, there spoke thunder. For we became dragons, kings, and conquerors, lords of all we knew . . ."

Turquoise Prince paused then; he eyes shifted, and he stared distant; and for a moment, Topiltzin thought he would not finish. He had not said a word since they had sailed; his eyes were swallowed in a far, sad pain, but then he looked up; he gazed at each of his brothers in the ship.

"And so we will be once more," he finished.

Huemac then leaned forward. "Yes!" he added, almost a shout, and he curled one hand into a fist. "Now sing, my brothers! We shall let them know who comes through the sea this night!"

At that, everyone, including the firstborn of Topiltzin, sang together. All but Turquoise Prince, who now only watched the flame and would no longer meet his father's eyes.

The sea bathed itself in morning sun, and Topiltzin stood at the prow of the lead whale-ship. To either side were appendages, anchored to the hull, hollowed-reed canoes with latches for oars and thwarts for six rowers each. The stroke was kept by a hollow jade drum, beating slow, rhythmically, as though it were the heart of the whale; and the wide fan oars lifted, dipped, lifted, and pulled through the dark waters. They were far, deep into the sea; the water was colder here, darker, almost purple. The world had become sky and water, stretched against the horizon.

Topiltzin's other ships were scattered to either side, all loosely connected by feathered rope, seven ships, seven caves through the waters. Each held the signet of their squadron on bamboo poles, richly painted. One bore the image of the Serpent, another the Puma, another the Shark, a fourth the Seashell, a fifth the Wind Sign, a sixth the silvered wings of the Hawk, and foremost, in the center was the ship of the firstborn, bearing the standard of the White Eagle.

Something caught Topiltzin's eye, off the prow—dolphins, backs arched, following the ships, laughing with the beat of the oars. There were times when he would have thought this an omen, a sign, but it seemed that signs had bled out of him long ago.

Below, in the center of the lead ship's belly, Huemac kept the oar beat, giving the drum resonance and a strong heart.

Turquoise Prince stood beside Topiltzin at the prow, searching the waves. The winds tangled his white-gold hair and played out the feathered mantel Paper Flower had woven for him with such care.

On the back of the cloak, his mother had painted a Blue Eagle, and feather-workers had given it brilliance—arched, dark talons, white tail feathers, and tightly knit blue breast feathers. Its eyes were glittering inset jewels, now blue, now black. Whether knowingly or not, Paper Flower had crafted her son a dragon cloak.

"Forever, Father," Turquoise Prince whispered, gazing over the sea, "only water, wherever we look. How do you know direction?"

"There were seafarers who would ply their ships from Tikal in the south, past the neck of land and then to the open ports of the Sea Kings of Anáhuac. They did not sail far from the coastline, but once past the neck, it was always swifter to circle into deep sea—away from the coast. There they would find the dark waters, the stream that moves through the ocean, and it always brought them home. This beneath us is the dark stream. It always moves west to east."

"Then, in a way, you know how close we are?"

He wondered. He knew they were holding to true west, and he knew that Tollán would eventually rise from the ocean to greet them. During that first long-ago voyage, when he and the thirteen Chichimec women were adrift in the reed ship of Tikal, Topiltzin had been so near to death that the days upon the sea were now only a lingering, far memory.

"More than a day, fewer than twenty," Topiltzin finally answered. "But I feel something, the air, the sky, the way the wind sifts past us . . . I think it will not be long. I think the shores of Anáhuac are not far."

"What will happen when they see ships bearing out of the eastern sea? Will they gather to welcome us?"

"We come as kings. It is we who will welcome them."

Just then, behind them, Moan Bird's flute began to whistle in time with Huemac's solemn oar beat. It seemed amusing at first, for Huemac's oar beat was never meant to be music, but Moan Bird somehow made it so. Topiltzin smiled and Turquoise Prince, despite his seriousness, had to chuckle.

"He is a strange one, Father. I sometimes wonder why it is you bring him among your Eagle Knights. He seems not the warrior."

"There are many kinds of warriors, Turquoise Prince. Moan Bird will give us spirit."

Turquoise Prince laid the edge of his cloak back over his shoulder as the wind ruffled its feathers. The angle of his face, the cut of his blue eyes, they reminded Topiltzin a moment strongly of Paper Flower. She had sent along the courage of heart in this boy, someone to watch over them all. The firstborn of Paper Flower had indeed grown strong and tall, but Topiltzin would always remember the child, the fat little boy with his shock of white hair who would never stay near home, who always wandered the seashore striking terror into his mother's heart. How many times had they given up Turquoise Prince as drowned in the sea?

When night came, they left the ship open to the sky, for it was warm and there were stars scattered.

His sons passed among themselves yellow fruit, sliced into strips. Perhaps it was the stars, so clean and perfect above the night sea; perhaps it was the calm, warm wind that eased them ever west—but they had lost the melancholy of the night before. They laughed; they talked among themselves. Some stood and danced. The children of Topiltzin had always loved to dance. Even these, the firstborn, began to sing and clap, and the dancers among them leapt and spun.

Topiltzin had to laugh, watching them. Their mothers had given them this—a bit of madness. The sea would smile to think that warriors danced in whale-ships beneath the eyes of the stars.

CHAPTER SIX
LANDFALL

On the eighth day, it was there—land. From the third ship, which carried the Wind Sign Knights, Sky Hawk blew the conch shell and waved his arms, shouting for his father. Sky Hawk pointed. His voice was far, but carried across the waters sharply.

"It is there! See, Father! There, we have come!"

Though he searched, Topiltzin could see nothing, only the endless space of water, and even Turquoise Prince beside him shook his head.

"Sky Hawk," Turquoise Prince muttered, "he has eyes like his name." Still, Turquoise Prince continued searching and then smiled. "But he is right, Father. There, you see, that is land. Yes! Look!"

He directed his father's vision. Topiltzin's blood stirred quickly. At first, it was only a dark line, like the sliver of the last moon, shallow upon the horizon of the sea.

Huemac's drumbeat quickened. "Harder!" Huemac shouted. "Row for land! For Tollán!"

The feathered oars lifted and fell in powerful strokes. They almost soared. The blue waters peeled back from the edge of the prow. It seemed to Topiltzin that the land came to them. It seemed to spread its arms across the sea, growing, reaching to the north and the south. Land. Surely, these were the sacred shores of Anáhuac. Topiltzin lifted the conch shell to his lips and let it call to the sky, answered by each of his sons' ships in return.

They were coming. The gods should know. The day and the hour should be marked. He would return on his birthday in the year One Reed, as he vowed he would the day Paper Flower had brought him back from his first death. He had promised himself that, in the Bundling of Years, he would return to his homeland on the day that he was first given unto it. One Reed was the mark of the warrior, held in the house of the east, the yellow sun, the white sun. It was a good year to have been born, a good year to return.

From all the ships his sons gathered, crowding at the edges of the prows, searching the land that drew upon them. The rope tethers were dropped away, and the ships now raced forward under full oar. Huemac's powerful drumbeat surged, pulling the ship of the first-born into the lead and the rest now followed in a staggered line.

A bird circled, a cormorant, and Topiltzin looked up, he met its eye. Perhaps it would know him; perhaps it would understand.

They came through an opening of land and into a wide bay where the water was as still as a mirror, waiting quiet, and there was only the sound of the oars lashing to their drumbeats as the sons of Topiltzin watched, hushed and breathless. Paradise had been an island; always there was an end to it, always the curl of water taking every horizon. But here, both to the north and south, the land stretched away forever.

Topiltzin's ship made landfall. The prow lurched and slammed into the soft sand, cutting it for a moment as though it were parting sea, then coming to a halt. Turquoise Prince took hold of the prow railing, but it was Huemac who leapt out first, splashed into warm water, and staggered onto the beach. He lifted his arms in the air and he danced, spinning in circles, his hands in fists as he screamed at the sky.

◧◩◧◩◧◩◧◩◧◩◧◩◧◩◧◩◧◩◧

Topiltzin had all the ships drawn onto the beach. The long canoes were cut from their bamboo lashings. Once the ships were grouped together, he ordered them disemboweled of their supplies: weapons and quilted armor of cotton and maguey fiber, shields and ensigns, seeds, dried fish and fruit, and sharkskin bags of wine.

Many of his sons could not contain themselves, and some sprinted down the length of the shore. They turned rocks over, they tasted the dirt, studied the great fronds and palm plants even though these were not much different from those to be found on Paradise.

Topiltzin himself walked up the shore to a high spot where he could look beyond, west. The land was flat and rolling, just tangled sea brush, but there was a smell here, a remembered smell. He had a sense of where he was. This was the land north, as he had hoped. If they had made landfall to the southward, in the heartland of *Tomoanchan*—Zarahemla, they would have found swamps and wide rivers, marshes. If they had landed on the southern neck, the black cone of Cumorah would have marked the sky with its calm breath of smoke. Here it was arid; the sand was gray and the sea brush squat. This was certainly Anáhuac, the Land of the Sea Kings, the place where the manatee swims. He had been here once before. Not only had he played the rubberball game in the City of Skulls, which lay not far north, but once, when he was young, he had walked these very shores with his father.

His sons scared up a flock of gray fowl that hooted as they took to the sky, wheeling. Sky Hawk came up to him on the knoll. The others were all over the beach below, searching it as though they might find treasure.

"The ships are ready, Father. I have grouped them as you asked. The canoes are cut loose."

Topiltzin nodded. "Coat the skins in fresh oil—don't rub it in, just coat them."

Sky Hawk paused, but only for a moment. His eyes had caught Topiltzin's. He understood the meaning, he was too cunning not to have guessed, but Sky Hawk hadn't flinched. He nodded, then turned and sprinted for the beach. Topiltzin wondered of him, his spirit was so strong. Never once had he questioned Topiltzin, but always his eyes were reserved, suggesting he understood more than anyone what waited for them. He seemed almost a seer. Perhaps he suckled the spirit of his grandfather.

Alone, Topiltzin walked farther, beyond the crest of the knoll, until he was out of sight of the ships, until the sound of the sea was muffled. The ground here was hard and windswept. He searched the horizon, though he wasn't certain for what he sought, and, in fact, he had never done such a thing as he was about to do. When he last stood on the soil of Tollán, he lived by the fire of his heart and that seemed enough. Now he needed something more.

He remembered once, standing near a fountain of crystal-white water, keeping out of sight where he could watch his brother, a priest named Sky Teacher, pray. Sky Teacher had been alone in a clearing, and he had opened his hands, palms spread. He had closed his eyes. It seemed his brother's face had taken in light and Topiltzin almost expected to see something appear or to hear the air whisper in answer, but there was nothing. The only sign of God was his brother's face—calm, quiet, as if he were with a friend.

Now Topiltzin paused, taking a deep breath of the warm, dry air. He remembered none of the sacred words or even what his father had taught him of this when he was a boy, so Topiltzin simply opened his soul; he just let his feelings out, a simple thing—a feeling something like: *Save us. Protect us!*

He waited for an answer—perhaps a voice, perhaps a feeling like wind touching. But there was nothing; there was only the sun on his face, only the distant call of cormorants, only the smell of the sea brush. Perhaps that was all there was to it, praying—just a feeling of the sun, the answer of birds. Perhaps men simply walked alone, and God was no more than the smell of sea brush. Topiltzin briefly let his fingers pass over the notch in his belt where he had sown Jewel Twirler's seashell, what she had called the light of her heart.

━━━━━━━━━━━━━━━━━━━

When he returned, he found his sons had assembled. The whale-ships had been pulled onto the sand, free once more from the water, gathered. They were ragged, even with their fresh coats of oil. Perhaps that God had delivered them here at all was testament enough of prayer, answer enough. Though they could be made strong again, certainly seaworthy enough for a return to Paradise, Topiltzin knew the path needed now to lead only to Tollán. There could be no hesitation, no weakness.

He motioned for Turquoise Prince who sprinted to his side.

"Your bow, Turquoise Prince."

Turquoise Prince slowly pulled the bow off his back and offered it.

Topiltzin curled his hand about the grip. "Select a resin-laden arrow."

For a moment Turquoise Prince paused, wind playing out his yellow hair. The others watched, concerned. Huemac stepped beside his father, narrowing his gaze on his brother, but Turquoise Prince ignored him, keeping his eyes trained on Topiltzin as he pulled an arrow from his quiver. Topiltzin took the arrow and notched it loosely in the bow's string.

"Make fire," he commanded.

Turquoise Prince now stared back, concerned.

"Did you not hear me?"

"I hear you," Turquoise Prince said. He turned, lifted his satchel from his belt, then knelt and laid out his pack. He took his fire stick and drilled the spindle. "Tell me, Father," he said as he worked, "the morning we left—when you told our mothers you intended to return to them—did you already know you were lying? Or is it something you've just now decided?"

The smoke flared, the tiny flame invisible in the sun until Topiltzin touched it with the tip of the arrow. The arrow hissed as the resinous powder ignited.

"Whatever my words or even my thoughts," Topiltzin said, "Paradise must now become a memory."

Instead of using it, Topiltzin handed the bow and arrow to Turquoise Prince.

At first he hesitated, but then Turquoise Prince lifted the bow and flaming arrow from his father's hand. He tightened his jaw, watching his father a moment longer, then sneered and turned, moving so suddenly and so quickly, it didn't seem he aimed at all. The arrow soared into the sky, dropping from a high arc to vanish amidst the ships. It seemed at first nothing was going to happen— that he had missed. The ships were still, huddled together, the waves behind them lapping. Then, slowly, the arrow's fire spread across the skins like spiders crawling. The pitch caught hold and soon burned hot. The saltwater on the skins left a line of black smoke that Topiltzin knew would been seen far from this shore.

⌘⌘⌘⌘⌘⌘⌘⌘⌘⌘⌘⌘⌘⌘⌘⌘

When the sun was mid-sky, Topiltzin and his sons, now filling twenty long canoes, rowed into the mouth of the river beyond the isthmus and entered the land called Tollán. Behind them, the line of smoke from the ships had slowly inked across the sky, almost like a finger lifting. The sand and sea-grass knolls quickly gave way to lush green fronds and trees along the banks. This river was wide and would easily take them inland through the mangroves. His sons wore full battle attire: the quilted tunics of knitted cotton, the breastplates of interwoven feathers, rich in the colors of their ensigns. Their hair was tied in war braids with trails of crimson cotton and some, the strongest, bore green and blue feathers that hung against their left shoulder. Shield-bearers covered the rowers with long shields whose brightly colored feather fringes trailed in the green waters. Every other canoe bore a signet, tall and proud, taken from the stern posts of the whale-ships. Topiltzin's, the first canoe, bore the signet of the White Eagle. If any were to see, if any had marked the finger of smoke left in the sky from their landing and had come to peer through the thick mangroves that lined the river, they would know; they would understand that here returned the Turquoise Lords, here returned the Sons of Light.

CHAPTER SEVEN
BLOOD OFFERING

Deep into the land, swamp cypress and the long, broad palms of wind-feather plants swallowed the river. Topiltzin stood in the stern of the first canoe, and he watched the shadows along the riverbank carefully. He knew they had been followed, almost as soon as the ocean fell from view and the river delta narrowed. Yet he hadn't seen movement, not even a shadow stir. Whatever followed was silent—it merely watched, and that left Topiltzin strangely uneasy.

At sunset, they reached a wide bay of the river that forked. Topiltzin recognized this fork in the river, the quiet of the trees here, and he remembered how with the dawn, the river always misted until it was almost a fog. He ordered the canoes drawn up, and his sons unloaded supplies. He had Sky Hawk oversee the building of a camp in the clearing near the riverbank. His sons worked quickly, each knowing his separate task; everything had been rehearsed many times on the island. In the center of the camp, they built huts of reed mats. He had taught them how to swiftly cut and lash the fronds, how to seal the tops with thick mud. In short time a defensible camp was laid out, as good as any division of Tolteca warriors would have done. Their weapons were stacked in bundles. At the camp's perimeters, ramparts of dirt were upraised. Sound traps were laid as well. If the traps were tripped in the night, they would make sounds only ordinary, the snapping of dried reed, the rustle of leaves, but they would single any approach. As Topiltzin watched his sons move with skill and purpose, he felt a slight shiver. It was as though he had stepped back in time and was once more watching the armies of the Tolteca in the field.

Any army coming from the eastern sea would have been intercepted by now—and yet they had passed through unchallenged. Topiltzin wondered of it, the quiet, the eyes that just seemed to wait and watch.

When night came, the sky was cloudless and the moon cast a full, watery light. The Star Skirt glittered like a celestial umbilical cord above them, twisting white and blue. It was a good night for first offerings, and Topiltzin ordered that the ritual seedcakes be laid out, along with the sharkskin bags that held the purest wine, the wine of the century plant. He then had his sons gather in a semicircle near the banks of the river. The firstborn were closest, the others spread to either side. Turquoise Prince brought his father a reed platform with a painted mat. As Topiltzin knelt on it, Turquoise Prince motioned the others to kneel as well and Topiltzin looked over his sons. Topiltzin had never spoken of covenant, and in fact, he wasn't sure how to speak it. It was as though he was trying to read signs from a book whose language he had long forgotten.

"We will now do as the Tolteca did in times of war, in their cities and in their temples. We will take covenant. When the Tolteca did this thing, in those days when they still walked the path of the ancients, no power withstood them, and even armies as terrible as the night trembled at their coming.

"The words of covenant are not something I remember, but what is important is that we understand they were spoken in memory of the singer, the Serpent Plumed. It is said that though he was a god, he walked among us as a man. Therefore, we give unto his memory our best seedcakes, our finest white wine, that it becomes like his flesh and like his blood, for that is how the ancestors taught, and that is how it was done in Tollán. Let each of you bear witness in your heart—make testimony there—in that place where rests the smoke and the spirit of your soul—that you honor him, that you do his word and his will."

He paused a moment. They watched with interest and even

reverence. Topiltzin had never taught them covenant because he had never believed himself worthy. On those days when such things were taught in the Calmecac schools of Tollán, Topiltzin would often be found spearfishing on the lakes of Tollán. That was all well because it was Sky Teacher who had chosen to walk the path of priests. Wherever he was, Sky Teacher was still the true singer of Tollán and, ironically, all these young spirits had to guide them was the rogue, the ballplayer, the wanderer—Ce Acatl Topiltzin Nacxitl.

᧝᧝᧝᧝᧝᧝᧝᧝᧝᧝᧝᧝᧝᧝᧝᧝᧝᧝

Before he had retired to his hut, Topiltzin walked the perimeters of the camp, searching for the eyes he sensed were following. Yet he saw nothing. The trees were silent as though the land here were virgin. But a feeling inside of Topiltzin whispered past fear—a feeling of emptiness, as though he were dead, as though the moment his foot had touched the soil of Tollán, he had become dried flesh and hollow bone. Alone in his hut, his fingers traced his wound—the old wound of his first death, the scar left of the one they called the Smoking Mirror. It cut through the side of his beard. It left hard, mottled skin up the edge of his cheek past his right eye to the temple. It halved his face. Since the day on the beach, he had never seen himself in any reflection, and he did not know what the scar looked like, but each time he touched it, he imagined himself a monster.

When finally sleep took him, it was harsh and troubled, turning into a nightmare that at one point awakened him. He drew up, startled and sweating, and realized he might have cried out, for he turned to find Sky Hawk kneeling beside him.

"Father? Are you all right?"

Topiltzin composed himself. He nodded.

Sky Hawk wore full armor, the thick cotton mantel, a net-cloak over one arm, a helmet carved of whalebone in the image of an eagle, wings spread. In one hand, he clutched his atlatl, already loaded with a dark, polished dart. Topiltzin remembered now. Sky Hawk had been on watch. Topiltzin noticed, through the doorway of the hut, that the night sky had turned a dark blue. Dawn was not far.

"Father, many of the sound traps have been sprung," Sky Hawk said calmly. "An army approaches." There was no fear, no alarm in his voice; he could have been reporting the approach of rain.

Topiltzin was not surprised of the news. He took Sky Hawk's wrist and stood, then stepped out of the hut. Turquoise Prince and Huemac where there, waiting.

"Every thing is prepared," Turquoise Prince said.

"You should have awakened me sooner."

"They come slowly," Sky Hawk said. "They are not night seekers; they will not attack before dawn. We decided to let you rest. Huemac has spread word carefully."

"How many come?" Topiltzin asked.

"Perhaps two hundred," Sky Hawk answered. "They have gathered throughout the night, from the north."

"How are they attired?"

"They are naked but for loincloths. Their bodies are painted. Many of them have their hair knotted and wrapped about their heads like women. A few are armed with spear, others with bow and arrow, but most carry only clubs of stone and wood. Many are barefoot, and there are those, Father, who are wholly naked, wholly exposed."

Topiltzin lifted his crimson cloak and looped it over one shoulder, tying it in place. "We must alert the elder of each division."

"This has already been done," said Huemac.

Sky Hawk helped Topiltzin draw on the breastplate of cotton closely overlaid with peccary leather.

"The firstborn are ready?" Topiltzin asked.

Huemac nodded. "As planned, Father."

"The Serpent and the Puma Knights?"

"I have had them fan out along the river's edge."

"The Wind Sign Knights?"

"Wide, to the left."

Topiltzin nodded. He stared a moment, surprised. He felt something clawing at him, yet the eyes of Turquoise Prince were calm and focused, and the eyes of Huemac were fierce. Sky Hawk, if anything, seemed more concerned about Topiltzin than fearful of the coming battle. There was no trace of fear or hesitation in any of them.

Sky Hawk placed a steady hand on Topiltzin's shoulder. "I leave now to command the Seashell Knights in the rear guard, but I will see you again when this is finished."

Sky Hawk turned and sprinted for the trees. Topiltzin was startled to realize that it was his sons who were giving him strength—not what he would have guessed on the eve of their first battle.

Huemac pulled on his helmet and gazed through its grizzly mask. He had fashioned a helmet in the shape of a human skull, with its temple bones flared in spikes of hardened obsidian and the plated jaw opening about his face.

"When we engage," said Topiltzin, "remember the signals. At the sound of the first conch shell, we will turn on them in fury. But with the second, if it sounds, we will give them mercy."

"We remember, Father," Turquoise Prince said.

"Everything," Huemac added, slapping his fist to his shoulder, the salute of a Toltec warrior. "We stand ready."

"Good, then," Topiltzin said, curling his fingers through his shield straps. "I believe these are the hills of the Mixteca. They are cowards and poor fighters, but it is almost certain we are outnumbered."

"Numbers do not matter," Huemac said. "As you told us on the island, the battle always rests with God, and surely this hour belongs to us—for we are Tolteca."

Topiltzin nodded. "Yes . . . yes, you are."

Turquoise Prince stayed near his side as Huemac moved among the others, whispering quietly. Topiltzin slowly lifted his moonsteel sword and slid it through his hip sash, its edge against his thigh. Topiltzin had kept the moonsteel alive only with seal and whale oil. Even then, the sea had eaten pockmarks into the once-polished surface. He lifted the quiver of atlatl spears and dropped it over his shoulder.

It was so quiet. The morning mist of the river drifted through the camp undisturbed and lazy. He searched the shadows of the trees, but saw nothing; there seemed not even shadow, as though the lingering dark opened to emptiness.

Ready and armed, the firstborn now gathered about Topiltzin, keeping themselves hidden behind the palm fronds of their huts.

Turquoise Prince quietly took position on Topiltzin's right. He nodded that his captains were ready. Huemac returned to crouch at Topiltzin's left, watching the jungle through dark, calculating eyes. You would not guess, looking in those eyes, that Huemac had not tasted battle; his gaze held the cold acceptance of a seasoned Slayer.

Topiltzin glanced to Turquoise Prince and spoke quietly. "Let it begin."

Turquoise Prince lifted his hand in a fist—a signal to lay the trap. In the center of the camp, some of the firstborn moved about in full view. These few were not armed. They made it appear as though the morning meal was being prepared; fires were lit, breakfast cakes outspread. Behind the shelters of their huts, the rest of the firstborn crouched fully armed, preparing for battle. Spears were quietly loaded into troughs. Leathered hands curled tightly about the hafts of the razor-swords. The razor-swords were fashioned after the swords of the Tolteca—after Topiltzin's moonsteel blade. Topiltzin did not know the crafting of metal, and he had first trained his sons only with the spear and atlatl. Yet it was Huemac who had one day brought to the games a wooden sword whose edges were ringed with a circle of obsidian blades honed to the cutting edge of scalpels. Huemac had calmly walked forward and with a piercing scream, he halved the trunk of a young quaking asp with a single, well-placed backstroke. In time, Topiltzin's sons had mastered the deadly weapons with grace and speed. On this day, the sword's teeth would finally be tested against flesh.

"Why is it they come sneaking?" whispered Turquoise Prince,

calmly scanning the trees. "Why not offer us welcome instead?"

"Their world is fear and darkness. They are weak. Welcome comes only through strength."

As dawn curled through the trees and the mist of the river lifted, the assailants started to close on the camp, quietly. Here and there, Topiltzin finally caught movement—shadowy figures inching ever closer, thinking they were surrounding the camp, unaware their movements had been carefully tracked throughout the night.

Topiltzin noticed Huemac's hand clench and re-clench the smooth, sharkskin handle of his razor-sword. The image would haunt him. And for a moment, Topiltzin wondered if this were wrong, everything he had done, all that he had taught them, all his plans, all that he had hoped for—somehow terribly wrong.

Topiltzin turned. A howl went up as though a coyote had screeched, and the assailants leapt from the trees, rushing the camp from three sides. Some came dancing, twisting, others screaming, wild and crazed. The first huts and tents were empty, and these were being slashed, torn, and thrown aside. Topiltzin stood slowly. At his flanks the firstborn rose, fanned out, taking position. Protected by their large shields, they now stood in plain sight, grouped in the center of the camp like targets.

Huemac hissed through tight teeth. "Come, welcome death."

Seeing them, the assailants instantly closed, running, howling. It appeared that the few Tolteca shields in the center of camp were about to be overrun by hungered wolves, closing on all sides but the river. Spears had already begun to *thud* like insects against the firstborns' shields.

"Brace for it!" Turquoise Prince shouted, easing his weight onto his back heel and setting his shoulder into his shield.

The initial shock slammed into the shields of Topiltzin's firstborn. The attackers smashed with clubs, stabbed with spears. Nothing from this point on would be practice and Topiltzin feared for each of his sons, but the shields of the firstborn held the line as though they were veterans. Nowhere did they panic, and when

Turquoise Price called retreat, it was slow, methodical, organized—just as they had been trained. The firstborn were slowly pulling back toward the river, and with the feigned retreat, the assailants grew confident; the chiefs among them howled. Sensing weakness, the onslaught surged, the ferocity of the blows became fevered. It was no longer predictable; things could turn.

The firstborn were outnumbered as much as seven to one; there was no margin for error. Though the other divisions waited at the edges, they made no move. The firstborn had to hold the center until the enemy was drawn deep.

At Topiltzin's left, Huemac hissed bitterly between his teeth. A spear had gotten past his shield and lashed the cotton armor of his shoulder pad. Though he almost drew his sword, he instead used his shield, slashing its edge across the attacker's face, cutting through the nose. As his sword, Huemac's shield rippled with obsidian razors.

"Easy," Topiltzin cautioned.

Huemac held back, but he was snarling. He seemed to be taking each bludgeon as a personal insult.

Topiltzin could see his other sons holding back with difficulty as well. In places, the reinforced shields of the island's hardwood had begun to shatter.

"Hold!" Turquoise Prince shouted above the din. "Hold your lines!"

Topiltzin heard a scream, somewhere from the left. He winced—fearful. Even one loss would be too great, for behind every shield was one of his own sons.

"Steady," Topiltzin warned. "Mark your brother's flank!"

From the far right Topiltzin noticed a Toltec shield in the mud, trod beneath the bare feet of the attackers. He was thankful not to see a feathered mantel beside it. The break must have been closed, just as he had taught them. Fortune was still with them, but it couldn't last much longer. Each step back now came at measured cost. At any moment, he could lose one of his sons. But if he turned too soon, he would lose more.

Turquoise Prince had to grab a brother beside him and throw him back as a shield broke in the center. Turquoise Prince had exposed his right, and Topiltzin swiveled, bringing his right elbow into a throat, dropping the assailant. Everywhere, the front was weakening.

Huemac roared as a spear broke though the face of his shield. With a savage half-step, he kicked one of them in the chest. Topiltzin remembered that Huemac's sister had spent weeks crafting his shield, and now its center was shattered. Huemac was furious.

"Hold!" Turquoise Prince screamed. "Keep your pace!"

"Let us at them!" Huemac howled in pain.

"Wait for it," Topiltzin commanded.

The hammering against Topiltzin's shield seemed madness now, relentless. Some attackers in the rear were even clawing over the shoulders of their comrades to get at the firstborn. Huemac was snarling through his teeth as he blocked blow after blow. An edge of Topiltzin's shield splintered. Another blow rocked him, but he continued stepping back. Topiltzin felt his heel touch the soft bank of the river.

"Now!" he screamed.

Turquoise Prince lifted the conch shell, blowing, but Huemac hadn't waited, he first crushed the face of an attacker with the front spike of his broken shield and then ripped his mace from its shoulder thongs and waded into them, bringing the weapon heavily from side to side. He was literally splitting heads as he went. Topiltzin swore beneath his breath, for he had to press hard to keep pace with Huemac. Topiltzin kept his shield tight against his left shoulder to cover Huemac's flank. He used his right arm to wield the moonsteel Tolteca sword in sharp upper thrusts to the hearts and guts of any who stepped in his path.

Behind him to the right, Turquoise Prince moved with power and determination, slicing his razor-sword across a chest, back-stepping to lance another's throat.

Topiltzin had to step over a head that had been severed so cleanly from the shoulders it didn't seem even to spill blood.

Finally, from the trees along the riverbank, the archers and slingers of the Shark Knights let loose their bolts and stones. The missiles cut like hail into the attackers, dropping them everywhere.

The attack was shattered almost instantly. Many of the assailants turned to flee, but there was to be no retreat; Sky Hawk and the Wind Sign Knights had already fallen upon the flanks. The attackers were now dropping weapons and scrambling desperately to escape the terrible razor-swords, the darts, the arrows honing in like insects, the slinger stones that cut with balls of spiked obsidian able to slice through to the bone. They were being slaughtered on all sides. Some managed to break through the lines and leap into the river, swimming for their lives, but most of them were simply dying. The slippery feeling of blood against the soles of Topiltzin's sandals struck a far memory. For an instant, it all came back to him: the rich, sweet-sour smell of sweat and blood and panic; the screams of horror; the give of flesh against his sword.

"Father!" Turquoise Prince was screaming. "Sound the conch shell! They have dropped their weapons! Father!"

Topiltzin reeled a moment, blinked. "Yes," he stammered, reaching for his belt, but Turquoise Prince had not waited; he ripped the conch shell away and lifted it himself, blowing with all his might, once, then twice, the second a long wail that cut through the sound of battle.

A few moments longer the razor-swords of the firstborn continued to rip flesh, but then, seeing swords being lowered, the front line paused and drew back.

All except Huemac. He seemed not to have heard. He was using his razor-sword with awesome skill, and in the few seconds that Topiltzin watched, Huemac cleaved through an arm, opened a throat, then a chest, spinning, his sword a blur, whipping blood.

"Huemac!" Turquoise Prince screamed. Still Huemac didn't turn. One last swipe disemboweled a last warrior, leaving the guts to spill like snakes dumped from a basket.

"Huemac!" Turquoise Prince shouted again, this time seizing Huemac's backplate and spinning him. "The signal has been given!" Turquoise Prince shouted in Huemac's face. "Lower your sword! Now!"

Huemac snarled and backhanded Turquoise Prince, staggering him. "You will not issue me orders!"

Turquoise Prince regained his balance and looked at Huemac, enraged. He ripped off his helmet and cast it aside. He started at Huemac, but Topiltzin quickly grabbed his shoulder.

"Enough!" Topiltzin shouted. "Both of you—enough!"

Huemac stared at Turquoise Prince with hands in fists, but made no move.

Turquoise Prince paused, looking about himself—looking at all the bodies. "Dear God," he whispered.

Everywhere, bodies littered the ground about the firstborn. The dead were thrown as though a wind of knives had struck them, the ground splattered with blood and body parts—heads, bowels, arms—and all of it seemed to have happened in a matter of seconds.

Turquoise Prince knelt to pick up a weapon. He studied it and looked at Topiltzin. "It's a shovel," he said, standing. "What have we done here, Father?"

"We had no choice," Huemac growled.

"No choice!" Turquoise Prince shouted back. "Did anyone notice they were fighting with shovels and fishing spears? For gods' sakes, these are farmers!"

"Farmers that tried to kill us in our sleep!"

"But still farmers! And we have just slaughtered them like gutting children!"

"Enough," Topiltzin shouted once more. He looked first to Huemac, then to Turquoise Prince. "One thing to learn of blood— once spilled, it cannot be reclaimed."

"Blood," Turquoise Prince said. "Is this the ink the Tolteca used to write their songs, Father?"

"Innocents fall, Turquoise Prince. They die every day. Sometimes they die because they were standing in the wrong place, and sometimes because they make mistakes. Those that lie here guessed we were simple prey. It was a deadly error. Enough pity. You are the eldest son; show it."

Turquoise Prince stared back a moment longer. "Fine," he swore, tossing his sword in the dirt. He crouched to wrench a dagger from his boot. "Take your daggers and move among the wounded," he shouted. "Spare any that you can, but deliver the rest our mercy."

Turquoise Prince then lifted the head of an attacker who knelt still trying to hold in his bowels with both hands. He thrust the dagger quickly through the man's heart and laid him back into the mud.

Topiltzin listened as moans and cries were snuffed out one by one. Few could be saved. The razor-swords of Huemac had a way of cutting flesh in rich, wide swaths, like flaying meat for cooking, and the blood ran in gutters to the riverbank. Topiltzin wondered what he had unleashed. Even the mighty Sky Dwellers of Tollán had not left a battlefield drenched with such horror.

He looked up to find Huemac had remained at his side. Huemac was staring at the survivors—the attackers in the clearing who had survived the battle. Hemmed in on all sides by the sons of Topiltzin, they were now prostrate.

"Do you see this?" Huemac said. "They put their faces in the dirt."

They were chanting, desperate. Topiltzin guessed it was some kind of prayer.

"Do you know what they're saying?" Huemac asked.

Topiltzin listened carefully and realized he did indeed recognize the tongue. They were speaking Quiché, the language of the Maya, and they were chanting the same phrase repeatedly. It left him shocked. He had not heard these words spoken in twenty-eight years, and they now left a shiver down his back like ice fingers walking. It was the name of his father.

Sky Dragon! Spare us, Sky Dragon!

CHAPTER EIGHT
LEGEND AND FLESH

Topiltzin found his way alone to the top of a mound. It wasn't a natural mound; it was a tomb, an ancient death mound. If the scrub and scant dirt were cleared, there would be cut stone—a mansion of the dead. There were many such tombs here, just north of the river.

He glanced back through the trees, making sure he was alone. He lowered himself to one knee. He dropped his helmet to the side and set his fist against the dry dirt.

Hearing his father's name spoken in the tongue of the Quiché-Pipil had shaken Topiltzin to the core. It pierced a memory that was all but forgotten. He hadn't thought of his father in nearly thirty years.

"Father," he whispered to the windless air.

As at the beach of their landing the day before, the only answer was the touch of the dull, white morning sun.

♦♦♦♦♦♦♦♦♦♦♦♦♦♦♦♦♦♦♦

When Topiltzin returned, walking across the sands toward the river, he saw that his sons had gathered the surviving Pipil near the riverbank.

"What are we to do with them, Father?" Huemac asked, seeing Topiltzin had returned. Huemac grabbed one by the hair, wrenching his head back, but the boy did not react, his eyes remained closed. "This is all we get from them."

Topiltzin looked down on the Pipil and spoke to them in Quiché.

"Who among you is eldest?" His words were a little broken, for he had not spoken the language of the Mayan priests in many years. The Pipil stirred, but no one answered.

"Who among you is eldest?" Topiltzin repeated more sternly.

Though numbered in the hundreds when they had come for battle, they were fewer than half that number now. Some exchanged glances; there were quick whispers. Finally, one stood. He was no more than twenty years. Compared to Topiltzin's sons he was small, only reaching Huemac's shoulder. He kept his head lowered, refusing to meet Topiltzin's eyes.

"My lord," the boy said, as though ashamed, "I am eldest here."

"What is your name, boy?"

"Ocpop, my lord."

"Why have you Pipil done this? Why come by night with weapons, seeking our blood?"

"We . . . we were afraid, my lord."

"Afraid of what? We have not harmed you."

"We saw the smoke; we knew you had gathered on the riverbank, and we believed you were sorcerers, my lord. No one had then seen your cloaks or the featherwork of your shields. But from this river, sorcerers have come in the night. They come seeking our children. We feared for our children, and this is why we attacked."

Topiltzin tightened his jaw. "And where are the Tolteca? Why do they not protect you?"

Ocpop looked up, startled, though being careful not to meet Topiltzin's eyes. "My lord?"

"I asked of the Tolteca. Why do they not protect you?"

"My lord . . . you . . . you are Tolteca. Pity us, my lord! For we did not realize! We did not see until it was too late!" He was whimpering now. "Forgive us . . . spare us, honored Great Lord."

Topiltzin noticed the looks of his sons. They would not understand the priest-tongue, but they would understand the word Tolteca, and all of them were watching the exchange with interest.

"What makes you think we are Tolteca? Why say this? Have

you seen Tolteca before?"

"No, my lord."

"Never?"

"Only images of you . . . we have beheld the images."

"What images?"

"Carvings. The stone carvings . . . they can be found in the south."

"The south . . ." Topiltzin said, puzzled. Tollán was due west and to the north.

"The mountain that is shadow. The Mountain of Burning. There are many flat stones in that place, and on them are carvings, warriors, dressed as you, some with beards. Tolteca. Some call you the Stone Warriors, but many remember you as the Tolteca."

Topiltzin felt a shiver. The boy was speaking of Cumorah, the killing fields of the deep south.

Topiltzin looked to Turquoise Prince, who stood in the center of the Pipil, his cloak wrapped about his shoulders, eyes dark and troubled. Turquoise Prince had not missed his father's reaction.

"Turquoise Prince, tell your brothers to strike camp. Gather your weapons and equipment for the march."

Turquoise Prince nodded and turned. "Prepare to march!" he shouted. His brothers followed him toward the camp, all but Huemac, who remained behind, standing in the center of the Pipil, still prostrate before Topiltzin.

"Go with them, Huemac."

"I do not leave you, Father."

"It is all right; these Pipil will not harm me."

"Perhaps. But I will stay here nonetheless."

Topiltzin stared at Huemac a moment. Huemac folded his thick arms over his chest and stared back with resolve. Topiltzin sighed.

"Ocpop, tell your brothers to lead my sons to your village. Have them send runners ahead to tell your elders to make ready for us. We are tired, for we have crossed the sea. We seek rest and food—your people shall be well rewarded for their charity."

"My lord," he said. He motioned to the others, speaking quickly.

They began to dismount. The boy turned back to Topiltzin, his eyes still lowered. "They do as you ask, my lord. Is there anything else?"

"Are you a good runner, Ocpop?"

The boy paused, still careful not to meet Topiltzin's eyes. He half nodded. "I am, my lord."

"I want you to run for me, Ocpop—run west and north. Cross these plains until you reach Tollán. You know where the city lies?"

"Tollán?" The boy seemed puzzled at first. "I . . . yes, yes, my lord, I know of this city."

"Good. Tell any you see that the Dragon has returned from the east. Let them know I am coming."

The boy nodded, looking uneasy. "Yes, my lord."

"I will speak with the elders of your village, and if you return quickly, I will see that you are remembered. You are a brave lad, Ocpop. Now go, run, and do as I ask."

Ocpop turned and sprinted along the side of the hill. Topiltzin knew it would be a long run through the flatlands, sometimes even dangerous. He watched the boy until he turned out of sight beyond the burial mound.

Topiltzin walked down the knoll toward the camp. Huemac joined him.

"That boy, why did he run away?" Huemac asked.

"He wasn't running away. He runs for Tollán."

Huemac glanced behind with interest. "Tollán? Will your people come searching for us, then?"

"Perhaps."

It was late afternoon when the army reached the villages of the Pipil. The main village bordered a manmade, shallow lake still being maintained and harbored several *chinampas*—islands planted in squash, corn, and beans. There was a scattering of reed huts, clusters of mud brick and thatch buildings, and dominating the community, a raised platform large enough to contain a marketplace and two minor temple towers, none of which was the work of the Pipil, who now occupied the area.

Topiltzin had been here before. He remembered a ball court lay to the north of the shallow canal that harnessed the river water to create the *chinampas*. The Mixteca who built this city were lowland craftsmen who had followed the Tolteca in the days when they expanded to their northern empire. The Mixteca used ochre to fire their pottery a deep, almost metallic red. It had been highly prized, even in Tollán. They were also known for the stiff peccary armor they harvested from domesticated herds. During the market days of the Mixteca, merchants would gather from all parts of the empire, from the ocean shores of Anáhuac, the southern lowlands, even Tollán.

Now the people occupied scarcely half the houses. Near the market center, the main palace was uninhabited. Its once brilliant wall murals were now bleached by sunlight, leaving them cracked and peeling. Even though some of the villagers were living in tents on the outskirts of the village, the palaces of the Tolteca—easily the finest buildings in the area—had been left empty. The entire municipal plaza was slowly being reclaimed by the earth as sand and scrub swept over the red, polished stonework.

The people here were desperately poor. Their children were naked; their women were plain; their men were worn and broken by the earth. Word of the bloodshed at the river would quickly spread westward; it would fulfill its purpose, but he wished they had at least engaged an outland garrison, even a merchant city, anything but this, plodders. Simple plodders.

Word of their coming had obvious effect. The people of the village had left their huts and tents and now lined either side of the old Toltec roadway that led to the market plaza—the only one still maintained. The villagers watched the sons of Topiltzin coming out of the plains with awe and wonder. There were old men, boys, and women with tired faces and vacant eyes who clung to desperate children. They were clothed mostly in loincloths or simple maguey tunics and skirts.

The sons of Topiltzin came in divisions, each division with its standard-bearer, who bore the feathered ensign of his unit strapped to his back where it rode high in the airless wind. Not one of Topiltzin's sons had fallen. They had emerged virtually unscathed from the morning's battle.

As they closed on the village, though most of the villagers came out to watch, Topiltzin noticed that others had scattered. In the distance, a column of dust marked their path. They had fled due north, straight into the high desert. It looked to be a harsh season here, hot and dry; the deserts would likely claim most of them before they could reach the great red river that bordered the unknowable lands of the far north.

Near the plaza, Topiltzin lifted his fist in the air, and Turquoise Prince ordered the army to halt, his command echoed by each division captain. Topiltzin watched as the village nobles hurried forward to greet him. They were dressed in their finest, but it was a sad sight; even their best tunics were time worn and thin. The central figure, who must have been their chief, wore a simple brass diadem and a trail of weary quetzal feathers that fell over his left shoulder. Not a fat Mayan elder here, just a thin old man, his hair matted and uncombed. He wore an obsidian lip plug. The chief and his entourage were the only ones to draw close. Just as Ocpop had done, they kept their eyes averted from any of the Tolteca; once a few feet away, they dropped to their knees.

A half-circle of the firstborn surrounded Topiltzin. Turquoise Prince, on his right, watched the villagers, troubled. Huemac stood at his left, one hand always on the hilt of his razor-sword.

"Why do they do this?" Turquoise Prince whispered.

"They have seen your standards, your shields. They understand you are Tolteca."

Topiltzin gestured to the leader with an open palm. "Please," he spoke in Quiché, "tell your people there is no need to bow before me.

Tell them they can stand. Tell them they can look into my eyes."

The old man, shriveled and bent, nodded, but no one stood, and neither did he raise his head. "My lord," the old man said, "Honored Sky Dragon, my people dare not. They fear they will be burned if they look into your eyes."

"Then be an example to them, old man. You be the first. Stand up, look into my eyes."

Slowly the chief looked up. He winced against the sun, which was to Topiltzin's back. He shaded his forehead. He looked at Topiltzin, then Turquoise Prince, but when he looked at Huemac, he gasped. He laid a hand to his chest, quivering. His face went white. He now addressed Huemac, bowing until his head was pressed to the roadway.

"Forgive me, my lord."

Huemac looked back, startled. "Is he talking to me, Father?"

Topiltzin nodded.

Huemac stepped forward. "You speak to me, old man?"

"He won't understand you, Huemac."

But the old man did understand. He answered Huemac in broken Nonaloca. "I remember you, my lord, Honored Sovereign, Great Sky Dragon."

Huemac's mouth fell open. "He . . . you . . . you believe I am the Sky Dragon?"

"My lord . . . do you not remember? I was with you in the far south! I was with your armies in the passes of Manti, where the blood of the Hundred Hands was shed! I was one of our lord's attendants. Do you not remember me?"

Topiltzin knew of the Battle of the Hundred Hands. It had raged for seven days. The Sky Dwellers of his father had been locked in battle until there was no wind left in them, until their legs were weary, their arms tired of killing; but in the final hour they had turned the armies of the Southland—first they turned them and then they slaughtered them. Six thousand had been slaughtered, their bodies scattered across the plains beyond the narrow passage.

The jungles ran with blood.

Topiltzin now looked carefully at Huemac. Of course he had noticed it before, but this time the resemblance left a shiver—the locks of black hair, sweaty from battle, the broad shoulders, the heavy brows, the strong forehead. A young, powerful Sky Dragon in his prime.

"Father?" Huemac said, noticing the look.

Topiltzin turned back to the Pipil. "Look up, old man."

The elder paused to carefully look up.

"Do you honestly think the Sky Dragon would not have aged since the Battle of Manti?"

"I . . . I would not know of such things, but is not the Honored Sky Dragon a great wizard, a God Speaker? Could he not do anything he wished?"

"Pipil, this boy is not the Dragon, he is my son. It is not so amazing that he would look like his grandfather. I am Topiltzin, the Blue Prince of Tollán. I am no wizard, and I have aged as much as you since the Battle of the Hundred Hands."

The old chief was shivering as if cold, but he finally comprehended. "You . . . you are Topiltzin!" he whispered, astonished. "Topiltzin Nacxitl, the four-legged?"

Topiltzin nodded.

"Topiltzin, the ballplayer! Yes! We know of you! Topiltzin. Everyone remembers you. You played once in Bonampak, my home village."

"Many times in Bonampak."

"It is an honor to see you, my lord."

"What is your name? What am I to call you?"

"I am called Turtle Walks Quickly."

"I am honored, Turtle Walks Quickly. These with me are my sons. And Huemac here, the image of his grandfather, is Lord of the Eagle Knights."

The old man bowed and bowed again before Huemac. Huemac lifted a brow, amused.

"We are deeply sorry that blood has been shed," Topiltzin continued. "The warriors of your village fought nobly, but they did not realize whom they had attacked. We cannot bring back your fallen, but the Tolteca have not come to spill your blood. If anything, these sorcerers you mistook us for—they can now fear us. But between our people, elder Turtle Walks Quickly, between the Pipil and the Tolteca, let there be peace."

"Of course, of course! We welcome you, Honored Lord Topiltzin Nacxitl, Serpent Plumed."

Topiltzin tingled. In his day, no one would have called him Serpent Plumed.

"My village is here to serve you," the old man continued. "Whatever you need, whatever you ask, it is yours."

"Food and rest is all we require," Topiltzin said. He glanced at the plates and bowls of gold and silver trinkets, probably taken from the wives of these chiefs that morning. "These you can return to their owners."

The old man stood. He spoke to the others in quick Pipil-Quiché, the tongue used to do business. The plates and bowls of jewelry were quickly removed. Along the roadside, slowly, carefully, the people stood up, murmuring, still frightened, but finally they were looking at Topiltzin and his sons in wonder.

Topiltzin noticed Huemac turn to find a small, brown child who had stepped from behind his mother to gaze up at him with wide, brown eyes. Huemac narrowed one brow and the boy quickly scampered away. Huemac laughed aloud.

Topiltzin smiled, turned back to the chief. "Lord Turtle Walks Quickly, we are weary. My sons and I have journeyed far. If you would show us to your village . . ."

"Of course, of course, Lord Topiltzin. This way, this way."

As Topiltzin followed the old man toward the village, most of the villagers stepped back, murmuring, watching him pass in awe, but a few, carefully, tremulously, reached to touch his robe. Topiltzin found one little girl back-stepping so quickly to keep pace with him that she nearly fell. He bent down and swept her up, onto his shoulder. This finally lifted their fear. They at last flocked about Topiltzin and his sons, and as word spread, more and more came out of their huts.

The market plaza had quickly been made ready. By the time the sons of Topiltzin reached it, there were flute players, drums, singers, dancers. Most of the lyrics were ritual, a pale imitation of the songs of Tollán and Zarahemla. Topiltzin told his sons to mingle, to do their best to put the villagers at ease. As the sun reached late day, mats were set out, and the women brought clay plates of food and large gourds of white *pulque* wine. Topiltzin seated himself on the red painted mat that had been provided him, along with Turquoise Prince and Huemac. He tried to relax, to keep these people at ease, but he couldn't stop thinking about what the old man had called him, that he had referred to Topiltzin as Serpent Plumed. For a breathless moment, the memory swept him. The sudden caw ripped through the air, the jungle below, distorted through its eyes, rushed past, bathed in a dark hue of blood. Topiltzin quickly focused himself, pulling out of the spell, but only slowly did the market plaza bleed back into his consciousness. He looked around, worried that someone had noticed, but Turquoise Prince only looked at him with a sigh.

"These people," Turquoise Prince said. "They dance, they sing, and yet we slaughtered their sons and brothers."

Topiltzin tried to relax. "You must let them sing, Turquoise Prince. Smile, reassure them. And why shouldn't they sing—their feared sorcerers, the dread dark, will no longer seek them."

"Why is that?"

"Because it knows we are here. The dark will now come seeking us."

"Should we fear the dark?"

"If I did not know better, Turquoise Prince, I would think you were your mother."

Huemac grunted a half-guffaw. He slapped Turquoise Prince on the shoulder and grinned. "Father is right. You worry too much, Turquoise Prince."

"I suppose you'd have me happy and stupid, like you."

"Of course. To help you along, I insist you taste this *pulque*. Here, do it. Drink."

Turquoise Prince stared at Huemac a moment, uneasy, but Huemac shoved the gourd in his face, and he finally took it. He sipped, but Huemac demonstrated how it should be done properly, letting it spill down his chest. Topiltzin chucked.

Servants brought a large, decorated clay plate of roasted duck. It had been prepared carefully, with a rich tomato sauce, but Topiltzin knew the price this meal would cost the poor of this village. He smiled to the servants, but then waved his hand.

"Take this away. Give it to those villagers over there, the eastern edge of the plaza, the poor ones."

One of the servants tried to protest. "But . . ."

"And when you are finished, come back with the food you give your women and children—maize and chili peppers, beans, no more than this."

The head servant still hesitated.

"Go. Do as I ask, Pipil. Bring all my sons common food."

They nodded, scampering. A thin, bent woman whose hair reached past her waist and bounced as she walked took the duck elsewhere.

"Why have they taken it away?" Huemac asked. "The bird looked well prepared."

"It was, but to these people, it is precious. My father taught the Tolteca that, to lead a people, one first must serve them. Sky Dragon would labor in the field with the common plodder, ply his canoe alongside the workers of the *chinampas*. He lived as his people lived. There was a day, long ago in the Southland, in the

63

cities of Zarahemla, when the Lords of the Nonaloca began to use their people as slaves. That was the beginning of the blood wars. We will not let something like that happen. We shall never suckle the common people, Huemac."

Directly before them was the main temple. Unlike much of the city, it was in some repair; the sweep stairway that led to the summit had been kept clean, and the limestone was mostly intact. It wasn't in its prime, though. A deep cleft, a crack from an earth tremor no doubt, snaked up one side; but the rest, facing the plaza, had been cleaned and maintained. From the roadway, Topiltzin had noticed the temple platform still had its temple house with a shadowy doorway where the sacred fire burned. This had once been the Temple of the Creator, and the dim light of the fire meant there were still priests in this village. He wondered when they would make an appearance. Though the elder chief and his nobles were here in the plaza, not far from the mat where Topiltzin was sitting, Topiltzin had yet to see a priest.

Most of the Pipil's singers were girls, and their gentle song warmed Topiltzin. He thought a moment of the laughing faces of his daughters, their bright eyes, the way they had perfected the dance of the flower tendril. If only he could have brought them all—his sons, the younger ones, his daughters, even his women. Topiltzin had no way of knowing what waited for them here, and he would never have allowed innocents to voyage through the unknown deep.

The servants now returned with plates of maize and tortillas, chili peppers and beans. It was far from common; it was the finest they could prepare. Topiltzin nodded, smiling, and ate quietly.

As dusk drew near, the villagers' fears seemed at last to have softened, and the Pipil had begun to talk among themselves of ordinary things, perhaps forgetting Topiltzin understood them. They were speaking of the ceremony being prepared. Priests were coming. He was hopeful. The village leaders were all descendants of midland Maya; but if the priesthood was still practiced here, it would at least be a comfort. When at last Topiltzin saw the priests approaching them, his heart sunk.

The priests wore cassocks and hooded cloaks. These were far from plain white cotton robes worn by the old priests of the Calmecac; these had been blackened. Those with dropped-back hoods had dark hair that was matted and wild. When they were close, Topiltzin noticed there was a smell to them, something almost nauseating. In Tollán, the tenders of the Creator would never have gone unwashed.

One of them stepped forward, half bowed before Topiltzin. Only his eyes were visible beneath the shadow of his hood. "My lord," the priest said, "we have heard that you are Topiltzin, the Bird-Serpent who comes to us from the east. Our God whispers to us that we must bring you offerings."

"Have I not made clear that I seek no offerings here?"

"If we were not to honor you as our teachings ordain, the people would wonder, my lord. As much for them, as to honor you, is it important we bear testimony that we, the penitent, acknowledge who now walks among us."

If the nobles of the village and the people had feared to look in Topiltzin's eyes, this priest did not share their apprehension. Beneath the cloak, black eyes watched him with something of a proud disinterest. It reminded Topiltzin of a Balam priest, though he wasn't sure this was even a Maya beneath the hood. Behind the priests were sub-attendants in gray robes, along with two female servants.

"Very well, Priest," Topiltzin said uneasily. He wanted to tell them to wash themselves and return when they were clean, but he did need to assure the locals in this place that he came in peace. He would have to put up with unwashed priests for now.

The priest nodded. He lowered his head and quickly whispered words that Topiltzin did not recognize—and that puzzled him. Why did the priest not speak Pipil? There was something else about the words; it was a language he had heard spoken, and though he could not place it, it left a distinct feeling of unease.

Looking around, he noticed that although his sons were still relaxed, eating and drinking, a quiet had fallen over the people of the village.

The priest turned. With the attendants at his heel, he walked up the sweep of stairs toward the summit of the temple tower. Other dark-robed priests coming behind lit the stone lamps that were set at intervals along the stairway. The lamp oil was laced in cinnabar and quickly burned white. It was near dusk, and shadows were long, giving the temple definition, carving its angles in sharp light. The shadow of the stairway seemed to undulate against the smooth side of the tower in the image of a serpent.

Topiltzin drank some of the *pulque* from a clay mug. He now realized why Huemac had remarked on it. It was strong—not a wine for food, but rather the type found in taverns of the lowlands. No wonder Huemac liked it; it was wine for falling down, and his sons had not tasted anything like it before. In Topiltzin's day, it would have been considered dishonorable to offer such wine to a Toltec lord. It was not a wine of kings; although, when he thought about it, it was the kind of wine to which he and his ballplayers were accustomed. Perhaps that was fitting.

When the dark-robed priest reached the platform edge at the top of the temple, he lifted his arms, baring his palms to the dying sun. Below, in reverence, the dancing and singing ended, and even Topiltzin's sons stopped talking as a quiet swept the plaza. The priest began to chant, a prayer song. It was again the strangely familiar guttural language. Listening, it suddenly struck him. Topiltzin remembered. He had heard this prayer once before, deep in the lowlands, in the jungles, where a sacrificial offering had been performed prior to the playing of the rubberball game.

Topiltzin stood, panicked, but it was already too late; it happened too quickly. They had lifted one of the female attendants, a young girl with long, glistening dark hair, onto the altar stone. Her skirt and blouse were ripped away.

"No!" Topiltzin screamed.

As though the high priest were in a trance, unable to hear, his butterfly knife flicked, spilling blood. He worked expertly. Topiltzin could not see the body of the girl; he felt an icy chill as he saw the priest's hand rise into the sky. In it was the girl's heart, held against the dying sun.

Topiltzin threw his head back and screamed, as the leopard screams in the forest, his hands in fists. His sons, everywhere, were instantly on their feet, weapons drawn.

The Pipil scattered in fear, crouching, hushed.

Topiltzin lifted his finger to the temple. "Huemac! Take the temple now! Seize them!"

Huemac and a squadron of his brothers rushed past Topiltzin, leaping the stairs two and three at a bound.

Topiltzin grabbed Turquoise Prince's arm. "Have these Pipil surrounded! No one leaves the plaza! Plodders, women, children— hem them in! Now!"

Turquoise Prince spun on his heels, shouting to his brothers. Some of the Pipil screamed as the sons of Topiltzin drew weapons and closed about them, sealing off the plaza. Those beyond the plaza fled into the desert.

Topiltzin ascended the temple stairs, his hand on the hilt of the moonsteel sword. When he reached the summit, he was breathless. Huemac and his captains had the priests on hands and knees, heads lowered, the tips of spears and razor-swords poised at their necks. Topiltzin stared at the body of the girl. The stone had arched her back, and the blood that poured across her breasts was rich and glistening. Her eyes were still open, staring upward, silent.

Topiltzin then looked at the bowed head of the high priest. His cloak had fallen back; his hair was thickly matted, tangled. He finally recognized the smell. It was the rot of dried blood. Here, on top of the temple platform, where the eternal flame of the Creator should have burned, the same smell was rampant, and looking down he realized the stone of the platform was caked in blood, aged by the sun, cracked in places like dried mud.

He turned to the temple house. Flies circled, and the smell

coming from inside was stifling. From the shadows within, a flame burned in the stone altar; but behind it was a veil of dark mesh. Behind the veil, a seated figure was watching Topiltzin.

"Stay with the priest, Huemac."

"Yes, Father."

Topiltzin stepped into the temple house, past the stone holding the oil lamp with its flickering light. He grabbed the thin, mesh material of the veil and ripped it down. The smell hit him with such strength he nearly gagged. For a moment, he could only stare. It was an idol, made of wicker, sitting cross-legged, watching him. The idol's head was a skull, painted in glowering swaths of light blues and red. The eyes were not hollow; they were fitted with white stones inset with irises of turquoise and black pupils of obsidian. They looked so alive, it seemed they might blink. Topiltzin's gaze was then drawn to the idol's foot. One foot, the left, was missing. In its place was a round, shining obsidian mirror. With a shudder, Topiltzin realized who this was. Perhaps Topiltzin had survived that day on the sand so long ago, but Topiltzin was just a man. The Smoking Mirror, apparently, had now become a god.

Topiltzin snarled and stepped forward to rip the idol from its pedestal. The idol's body was light, made of reed, weighted only by its jewels and quilted cotton clothing. Topiltzin lifted it above his head and walked out into the red, dying sun until he reached the edge of the temple platform. Below, the Pipil were prostrate, shivering, ringed by the deadly razor-swords of Topiltzin's sons. Topiltzin screamed and flung the idol into the air. The Pipil shrieked. Some of them covered their heads, as though the Heavens were falling. The idol slammed into the temple steps and rolled, scattering jewels and attachments. The golden ear pinged off a stone corner and went spinning, glinting in the sun. The skull, already brittle, shattered. When the broken wicker bundle rolled into the plaza, the Pipil screamed. Only the dreaded razor-swords could keep them from breaking.

"You, Pipil, hear me!" Topiltzin cried, his voice echoing. Everyone below froze, the villagers trembled, some of them covering their heads as if he were going to throw more gods down on them. "This thing—this idol in your temple—it has no flesh; it hears none of your words; it tastes none of the hearts you have offered it! No more! No more will you offer blood! Your priest-craft is ended this day, for I am Topiltzin Nacxitl, son of Sky Dragon, and I bring a new covenant!"

He glanced to Huemac. Huemac and his brothers still had the priests at swords' edge. They bowed so low beneath the obsidian blades that their foreheads were pressing against the stone.

"Deliver them their heads," Topiltzin commanded.

Huemac did not flinch at the order. He gripped the lead priest by his matted hair and screamed as he ripped the razor-sword back, severing the neck in a quick, clean cut. He stepped forward and flung the head into the sun, hair whipping. The screams below equaled those that had sprung up at the idol's destruction. In moments, all of the priests were beheaded; heads were hitting the stone plaza like melons. Huemac then, one by one, kicked the bodies over the steps; they rolled, gaining momentum, arms and legs flailing as they bounced.

"What now, Father?" Huemac asked quietly.

Topiltzin glanced at his son. Huemac's fiery eyes were dark and unflinching. If he was filled with dread, it did not show.

"Take the body of this girl. Bury her, with her heart. Then, gather the chief and the tribal elders. March them up here and have them cleanse the walls of this temple. They will understand your tongue. They do not speak it commonly, but they will remember the words of the Tolteca. Slay any priests you find among them." Topiltzin paused. "This place sickens me." He looked down on the naked backs of the people bowed before him. "Have Sky Hawk send our supplies to the west, there, by that far hill—erect camp. We will not spend the night in this place."

Huemac nodded. He turned to the altar stone and, with a surprising gentleness, lifted the body of the girl in his arms and quickly descended the stairs of the temple, his brothers following.

Topiltzin noticed that fresh blood now mingled with the layers of dried blood, seeping into the cracks. How long had he been in this land—but a day, but a sunrise—and already the constant sight of blood was eating at his soul.

The obsidian mirror that had been the idol's foot lay broken on the temple platform, and when Topiltzin glanced down he saw his scarred face reflected, shattered, splintered. He did, indeed, look the monster he had concocted.

CHAPTER NINE
THE NEPHALLI, THE MANY DEAD

S moking Mountain, one half of the twin peaks that bordered the Land of the Lake beyond the plains of Otumba, rose majestically into the sky. The second mountain, White Woman, to the north, was capped in snow most of the year. Between them lay the passage west, and from its summit, one could look down upon the Valley of Tollán. It would be there: the crystal blue of the lakes would shimmer; the green *chinampas* would mat the valley floor. Tollán would glisten, as though there were jewels scattered; the gold sheath of the temple would run liquid against the sun. Tollán would be there, like a pattern of stars on the plains of Otumba.

In the last few days, Topiltzin had pressed his sons in hard march across the flatland of the eastern plains. Twice they had passed ruins. The first was a satellite garrison of Tollán, where there had once been a fine ball court, painted rich red and blue, with smooth, almost perfect walls. Like the desert that was taking it, the garrison lay broken and windswept, and the nearby village was crumbling as though insects were dismembering its stones, its stucco and mud brick slowly moldering. The trees that once had been here, the great oaks and willows with their weeping leaves, the fields of cocoa that had been so carefully cultivated with irrigation canals fed from the mountain streams—all were gone. The cocoa trees had become mesquite; the willows had become rabbit bush and cacti.

The very face of the earth had changed. It was as though the creators had swept their hand across the ground, and in their shadow, the earth had twisted and cracked. The green trees and vines had shriveled; the mesquite and bramble had begun to crawl, and most of all . . . the people had vanished. The Mixteca, the Olmeca, the barbarian wanderers of the Northland—there was nothing here but lizards and snakes coiled beneath rocks. At times, Topiltzin and his sons would see no one in days of walking. Other times they would spot small groups of hunters, people whose skin was baked dark from the sun, people who scurried away like rabbits into the dry, empty plains, sometimes in such panic they left their belongings. Topiltzin came upon a camp in which a large kettle still bubbled with sage grass and grub roots, and there was gourd pottery, corn grinders with corn powder scattered, even water jars. All possessions were deserted when the people fled in fear. He had hoped his coming to be greeted with cheers; the roadways could have once more been pelted with flowers as the ballplayer returned.

Food was getting scarce. Each morning Topiltzin sent his archers and slingers to hunt whatever moved, to bring back lizards, even moles that scampered. These were scarce, however. The land was parched and empty.

When Smoking Mountain and White Woman finally came into view against the horizon, majestic in the distance, Topiltzin took heart. He remembered a village near, but when Topiltzin and his sons reached it, they walked through solemnly, gazing in awe, for it had been swallowed by great cacti and aloe plants that were taller than men. Everywhere they had grown, as though the people had died and their spirits had rooted into the earth and produced the tall, wide leaves. Topiltzin had juice taken of the plants, for the water skins were nearly empty. His sons also found wild onions and blue corn. Among the rubble of the town, he determined everything had been abandoned many years ago and was still in place, as if waiting for someone to return. A film of dust and dirt covered everything in gray. Plates were still stacked upon shelves. One table held platters with the hardened remains of round bread cakes and cups still waiting for an evening meal, now covered in sand, hard as stone.

TOLTECA

Topiltzin was reminded of his age as he ascended the mountain passes. This was the warm season, and the sun was high. In colder seasons, snow and ice could choke the mountain roads, but now they were pleasant. As they ascended, the air cooled from the blistering heat of the plains. At last, there was greenery. The foothills were scattered with wildflowers, many of them in full bloom, and the air was sweet. An eagle circled overhead at one point, and many of Topiltzin's sons had called out, pointing. There had been hushed silence when the eagle had cried, its call echoing. They had always drawn eagles, crafted them in paint and stone, but never had they seen one until now. Indeed, it warmed Topiltzin to see the bird in full wing across the blue sky, for it seemed the valley floor had been taken by insects, the scorpion and the fire ant, the beetles and the crawling things. It seemed all noble beasts had died.

Higher up, near the passage between the twin summits of Smoking Mountain and White Woman were tall, ancient pine, resinous and sweet. There had once been a well-worn road here, kept open even in the cold seasons, winding its way from the summit to the valley like a ribbon. It was now barely discernible beneath the overgrowth of wild grass. Topiltzin had to pause; his legs ached. He had been eager to reach the summit, but the harder he climbed, the farther it seemed to grow; and now, near the top, he simply had to rest. His sons gathered about him, many of them marveling over the plants and the great mountains, particularly Smoking Mountain, which loomed above them to the south, a mist idly washing from its cone leaving a thin shadow against the sky. Topiltzin sat on the grass, leaning back against a tall pine. Turquoise Prince brought him a sharkskin of wine, and Topiltzin drank lightly and laid his head back against the tree.

Turquoise Prince squatted beside his father, searching the peaks of the mountains. "This is Smoking Mountain," Turquoise

Prince said. "And to the north, that peak we saw, that was White Woman."

Topiltzin nodded.

"Then we are close. Tollán must be there, just beyond."

Topiltzin closed his eyes. He felt weary enough to pass out if he allowed it. He was surprised when he felt his son's hand touch his shoulder; and looking up, he saw Turquoise Prince watching him, concerned.

"Father, if . . . if things are changed, if they are not as they once were, you must remember that you still have us. We have followed; we have come with you, and you will not be alone this day. And not just us, for with us walk the blood and spirit of our mothers. Remember that."

Suddenly tears stung Topiltzin's eyes. One fell free across his cheek, along the line of his scar. A cloud drifting had been snagged by the mountain's peak, and it settled about them with a sweet mist.

"My face," he whispered, looking to Turquoise Prince. "What does it look like to you?"

"Your face?"

Topiltzin nodded.

Turquoise Prince paused a moment, then said, "It looks like the face of a king to me, the face of our father. It is courage and spirit."

Topiltzin half smiled. "You lie as well as I do," he said. He stretched out his hand and let Turquoise Prince help him to his feet. Topiltzin paused to take a deep breath into stinging, weary lungs. His head was light, his vision for a moment gray.

Turquoise Prince nodded to one of his brothers who brought a freshly hewn staff of raw wood. Turquoise Prince handed it to Topiltzin. "We have fashioned this for you from a fresh tree limb. It will help steady you. The climb was steep, Father. Even I am winded."

The staff had been sanded smooth and was as tall as Topiltzin. He took it, nodding. "Thank you."

Turquoise Prince stepped aside. They were near the summit. Just beyond, the valley would open to view.

TOLTECA

"It is decided among us," Turquoise Prince said, "that you should be the first to look upon the valley of your birth. Therefore, we will linger, follow just behind."

Topiltzin looked over his sons, gathered to either side of the passage, watching him with expectant, concerned gazes. Why did he feel so alone? He looked finally to Turquoise Prince and remembered the eyes of Paper Flower as they had watched him leave Paradise. *Nothing is left back there but darkness.*

As Topiltzin walked the passage to the edge of the summit, he felt the cool air of the cloud kiss his skin, and he let the smell of pine and wild grass fill him, bleeding memories. Memories quick and scattered.

⌘⌘⌘⌘⌘⌘⌘⌘⌘⌘⌘⌘⌘⌘⌘⌘⌘⌘

Topiltzin stood there, for the longest time, staring numbly, his skin cold beyond the sting, as though his lungs had forgotten breath. The valley spread below him like a laid-out cloak. The lake was a stain of blue, the ground a mosaic. Tollán lay beneath him. It was there, still, quiet . . . dead. The Pyramid of the Sun had been stripped of its gold. The inner plaza, the palaces, the temples were a darkened husk; they had been burned. No fire breath drifted from hearths; nothing moved from the inner buildings. Only the wind. The River of Cleansing that once ran through the city was a line of dry sand. The only life below was on the outer edges of the city, where tents and shacks of squatters were littered like debris.

After a moment, his sons gathered about him, and all gazed upon the fabulous city of legend. The stories they had heard since they were children, the songs and poems—there it lay, like a husk of corn trampled in the field, broken, stiff in the sun, stripped of its color.

"We will go down," Topiltzin said. He gripped the staff and began the long walk. Below, the squatters of the outer barrios were already fleeing, taking up their precious things and running for the desert with their dogs and children.

K. MICHAEL WRIGHT

𐄂𐄂𐄂𐄂𐄂𐄂𐄂𐄂𐄂𐄂𐄂𐄂𐄂𐄂𐄂𐄂𐄂𐄂𐄂

As Topiltzin walked among the ruins of the outer barrios, where once the shops of the obsidian craftsmen had swelled with the noise of the workers—hammering, laughter, calls of the vendors—only the wind stirred. Darkness gazed from doorways. As he passed a crumbled stairway, a squatter, naked, peered from behind a slab of stone with frightened eyes, then turned and ran, bare feet padding. Topiltzin walked in long strides, using the staff to keep his pace. His sons merged into the city behind him, among the buildings, spreading out, searching. They didn't follow him into the center, but lingered in the outskirts. Topiltzin guessed that was Turquoise Prince's doing, letting Topiltzin go into the heart of the city alone.

Topiltzin stopped before a stairway that crisscrossed three stories of apartments. Much of the stairway lay in broken slabs. This was the artists' barrio. The wall murals, once so brilliant and mesmerizing, were now bleached by sun and dimmed by rain. It was almost unrecognizable, but Topiltzin still remembered this place. Before him was the apartment that had been the home of Mud Puppy Soldier. It was here Mud Puppy had taken his wife; here he had hoped to raise his first child. Topiltzin stared, sadness through him like a spear. He moved on, past houses whose outer limestone had fallen away, leaving a skeleton of rotted foundation plaster. He made his way among streets difficult to recognize until he reached the inner citadel.

Topiltzin slowly crossed the main market plaza. The splendid red stone that had once glistened in the fires of the celebration of the Night Butterfly were now dull and worn. Dunes had formed of drifting sand. Bramble had wedged through cracks.

He reached the palace plaza and paused. It was blackened. Fires darkened the murals, the paintings, the wooden lintels, and sculpture of the Palace of the Lawgivers. The splendid Avenue of the Blue Stars lay in ruin. The troughs of the many fountains were choked with sand. To the north, the Pyramid of the Creator was left with its lime plaster slipping off like skin shedding from the bones of the dead.

Topiltzin circled. Everywhere, buildings were blackened, the stonework smashed and crumbled. The earth had begun to wash over the great citadel of Tollán, like a sea rolling in slowly, swallowing it.

Topiltzin finally cried out. He dropped the staff, falling to his knees. He screamed with fists clenched, his back arched, his eyes tight, his face lifted to the Heavens. It was an animal scream, a primal cry, and it echoed in the silent, hollowed shells of burnt-out buildings.

⸎⸎⸎⸎⸎⸎⸎⸎⸎⸎⸎⸎⸎⸎⸎⸎⸎⸎

Huemac was amazed. There was a shadow of fear in him, but mostly amazement. It wasn't as though they came, more like they had grown from the soil, hundreds of them. Huemac had been careful; he had left scouts at their flanks, watching as his father went deeper into the city, and yet these people had somehow surprised them completely. How could no one have seen them coming? How had they gotten this close without warning?

Huemac leapt atop a crumbled stone wall, crouched, holding his shield at his side. But these desert people, they were not attacking. They just watched, quiet. These were not the poor, wretched creatures Huemac had been convinced were the only inhabitants of this land of Tollán. No, these were very different. Warriors. They had cold, dark, fearless eyes. They were lean and sinewy, muscled. They carried spears and stone hammers, long knives of flint; some even held shields of deerskin and peccary hide.

"Take up arms!" Huemac shouted. He would have used the conch shell, but that would have signaled Turquoise Prince, who had followed their father to the inner city. Whatever its outcome, this battle, Huemac would keep for himself.

His brothers were swift. On the island, drills such as this had been practiced many times. The sons of Topiltzin instantly formed a frontal line of interlocking shields. Yet the desert people did not move; they did nothing; they only waited, watching. What amazed Huemac was even with the painted shields and weapons of Topiltzin's sons glistening, there was no fear in the eyes of the desert warriors. Huemac was impressed. A smile curled across his lip.

Sky Hawk leapt upon the wall and crouched beside Huemac, one hand forward like a cat.

"Look at them!" Huemac whispered. "Just look!"

"How many, Huemac? How many are there?"

Huemac only shook his head. "They must number close to a thousand!"

"But we just walked here!" Sky Hawk blurted. "There was no one! There was no sound! Where did they come from?"

Huemac felt strangely calm. If they had meant to attack, the sons of Topiltzin might very well be scattered and bloody. They had come for something else.

Huemac dropped from the rock and stepped through the front of the shields. His brothers parted to let him pass through, and with Sky Hawk at his flank, he walked into the clearing between the feathered Tolteca shields and the desert warriors. For a moment, he wondered if these perhaps were remnants of his father's people. He then realized the cut of their eyes, their faces. These were Chichimeca, as their mothers.

"What are you going to do?" Sky Hawk whispered at his side.

Huemac slowly raised his hand before the warriors. "Welcome them," he said. At first, his hand was a fist, but then, slowly, he opened it in the sign of the word that his mother had taught him long ago.

Seeing this, one of them stepped forward and lowered his head toward Huemac in a gesture of respect. Huemac guessed this one might be their prince—a tall, sinewy youth with a deerskin cloak and eyes that could swallow the night. This one lifted his hand and his fingers spread to return the sign of the word.

"What is your name?" Huemac asked, speaking not in Nonaloca, but in Chichimec.

"I am named Second Skin."

"And I am named Huemac."

"Strong Hand," the prince interpreted. His dark, predatory eyes calmly scanned the row of feathered shields. "It is true then," he said. "The Tolteca have returned."

Huemac nodded. "Yes, it is true. Who are you people, and why have you come from the desert?"

"We are called Nomads, those that have no home. A runner came many days ago. He said the Tolteca walked again in this land and that they would come here, to the place once called Tollán. When our elders heard these things, they sent us the swiftest youth. We come to find the one called Topiltzin Nacxitl, the Serpent Plumed. We have come to serve the Son of the Morning."

Huemac felt himself shiver. He glanced aside to Sky Hawk. "Get Father," he whispered.

For hours, Turquoise Prince rested on his haunches, watching his father. Topiltzin could have been stone out there, kneeling, head bowed, for he had barely stirred.

Turquoise Prince felt a knot in his throat as a tear fell across his cheek. How long, how many nights had Topiltzin gathered them about the shores of Paradise or in the crags of the cliffs that overlooked the Emerald Sea or among the fires of their courtyards and told them of this place, his blue eyes sparkling with memory— the wonder of Tollán. How the Tolteca were Lords of the Blue Stars, voyagers, more than flesh, but possessing the blood of gods. Seeing Tollán—even though it had been hollowed, gutted, stripped like a whore, its temples burned and its palaces swallowing sand—even then it whispered majesty. Its splendor was now a ghostly pall. But there had once been a Tollán! The fabulous beings that had lived here, who had built this place, certainly they had been nothing less than Sons of Light. It was all true. Everything his father had told them. Once it had all been true!

PART II

TOLTECA

CHAPTER TEN
THE BALLPLAYER

The Valley of Otumba (Mexico), the City of Tollán
The year One Death—421 AD, twenty-five years earlier

At night, a thousand fires burned in Tollán. Torches dipped in cinnabar created a soft, alabaster glow that lighted the streets and canals and could paint the edges of stars. From the Hill of Shouting, Topiltzin could see the city spread over the valley floor, glittering in an image of the star skirt of the sky. The city had been built following the patterns of the night sky at summer's zenith.

Topiltzin often came alone to the Hill of Shouting. It was rich with memories of his father, the man whom his people called Sky Dragon. When the Blue Prince lay on his back, staring up at the night sky, washed in splendor, he always remembered the night when the Dragon had shown a young Topiltzin the Home of the Gods. "Look, my son," the Dragon said, lifting his great hand to point direction. "The small cluster there, almost hidden in the star stream of the sky, hanging like grapes. Those are the Blue Stars. It is said that there rests our home, whence we have come, whence we have journeyed and to which we all must someday return." The young Topiltzin had stared in awe, feeling a shiver down his spine. The moment had ever remained in his memory. The Blue Stars did indeed *seem* like home. This night they shone like a cluster of crystal grapes hung in the sky.

Topiltzin, the Prince of Tollán, had come to the Hill of Shouting this night to ask the Blue Stars for strength. In the past days he had felt weak, not of muscle or sinew; in these he was well honed, hardened. Topiltzin's weakness was of the heart. It was the cold, quiet ice of fear. In the past nights, it had come upon him like sudden rain, a fear that had no face, a fear that spoke no words, a fear that simply waited.

The season of the games was upon him. Tomorrow, the people would gather, the nobles from Cholula, the Lords of Anáhuac, even the strange, somber Maya. They would come to witness the rubberball game. More specifically, they would come to see Topiltzin play it. For seven years, the Turquoise Lords of Tollán had ruled the courts of the rubberball game. In the four corners of the world, none had conquered the Lords of Tollán, and Topiltzin was their captain. They were feared, and they were champions. The fame of Topiltzin had reached the east coast, the mountains of the narrow passage, even the steamy jungles of the Southland. It had even ascended the cruel, stone steppes of the highland merchant cities. Everywhere he was known. Everywhere they cheered the Blue Prince of Tollán. Yet here, on the night before the first game of the season, the nameless fear that had dogged him the past few days closed like a cold, stone hand.

His father and his brother, the priest, were much closer to God than he was. They could lift their voices, and God would listen. He would answer. At times, Topiltzin swore he could see the very breath of God spill down upon the brow of the Dragon. It had never been so for Topiltzin, and if the Blue Stars offered sympathy this night, it was unspoken. He closed his eyes, his hands curled to fists, and for a moment—for only a moment—the Blue Prince let his heart wish that he could look again upon the weathered face of his father, that he could look into those stone-gray eyes and let them take his fear.

Topiltzin stood and lifted the deerskin bag that held his ball equipment and pulled its sling over his shoulder. Just beyond, a wide stream dropped over a sheer edge to a deep emerald pool hollowed out of rock. He stepped forward and dove. When he surfaced, he swam the cool waters of Tollán's northern lake until he reached its western shore, where a rubberball court had been carved out of the ground. This was not the court where the games would be played tomorrow, but one built by ancient hands, long before the Tolteca had come to the Valley of Otumba. When Topiltzin first found it, it had been almost unrecognizable. Wind had scattered dunes over its surface, and the sun had bleached color from its stone. Once swept clear, it had proven surprisingly smooth. It was a perfect place to practice, for it lay outside the city, in the wastelands. Tollán's lights did not reach here. Her people never came here. His only audience would be the stars, his only light their light, and such was the way of the rubberball game that it was better played by intuition, by the *feel* of the ball's direction and speed, rather by trusting the sight of it.

Topiltzin knelt at the ruins of the court to untie the deerskin satchel. It was said that the rubberball game had begun in the time of the creation of the world, when old gods ruled; a time so distant no one knew any longer the names of the people who had created the game. They had become the Many Dead, yet one could still see their cities, their ruins, mounds of earth and crumbling stone. One could go there, to the south and east, where the thick river deltas bred caimans and the cypress boughs swam in slow waters. There one could find ball courts so ancient they had eroded into the earth like a stain.

Topiltzin drew on his kneepads and the wide-belt harness. This equipment was only for practice. It was plain, unadorned. For the games, his belt was inset with turquoise, the knee guards ringed with quetzal feathers. He actually preferred to wear this unadorned equipment, but those who came to see the Turquoise Lords of Tollán play, came for splendor and glory.

Topiltzin dropped down into the center court with bare feet, holding the rubberball. For a moment he paced, stretching out the tendons of his legs, his arms, bouncing the ball off the steep sidewalls, warming it. The game was never played with the hands, only the knees, elbows, buttocks, and hips. His muscles warmed,

Topiltzin threw the ball high and crouched. When it dropped, it leveled off his right hip. The solid *pong* echoed in the chamber of the court, and Topiltzin circled, directing one hard, narrow shot off his elbow and a second off his knee. He rolled, spinning, and brought the ball close to the center marker of the wall, using his buttocks, keeping them tight.

In the games, when Topiltzin played, cheers would erupt like thunder down the side of a mountain, flowers would rain upon the court, and often the people would rhythmically chant his name. Such sounds seemed to whisper about him as he worked the rubberball, its weight humming, until his muscles burned with sweet pain.

He finally caught the ball in his hand, then dropped back, damp from sweat, his lungs stinging. He was twenty and seven years. He was prime. Tomorrow would be the first game. When they came to see him, to cheer him, they would not be disappointed. Whatever fear haunted him had crept into the shadows of his mind. Perhaps it waited somewhere, on haunches, like a cat; but for now, it had become easy to ignore.

He let the ball slip out of his fingers, watched it roll into the center court near a faint skull that had been painted, long since bleached by sun and rain. Over this, to his sudden astonishment, moved the shadow of someone standing above. Topiltzin looked up, startled. A girl stood on the opposite side of the court, at its edge. Watching. From his angle, she was only a silhouette, an image of long, dark hair, a whisper of a light skirt tossing in the evening wind.

"You play well, my prince," she said. Her voice was soft, moist, and unfairly feminine.

"Do we know each other?"

"I know you," she answered. "Whenever you play, I come early, long before the games, to make sure I can be near the edge, to make sure I am close enough to see your eyes. You have blue eyes."

"You are certain?"

"Most certain."

"And what color are your eyes?"

"Black, like a hawk's. Like jet."

"Perhaps you should come closer, where I can see them for myself."

"You would not want to look into my eyes, Blue Prince."

The wind lifted slightly. Her hair played out, and the far glow of city light behind her seemed to make it shimmer.

Topiltzin struggled to dismiss the growing feeling of disquiet she seemed to intensify. "How long have you been there?" he asked.

"Nights without number I have waited here. But this night, my prince, we come. My people come—for you. And nothing will ever be the same."

She tossed something. It drifted to the ball-court floor, and Topiltzin stared at it, curious. When he looked up, she was gone.

He instantly leapt forward, over the wall, and searched. Up here was only flatland. The lake glittered quietly, undisturbed, bordered by a field bearing the crippled shapes of cocoa trees. Beyond, before the outermost barrios of Tollán, were the tents and mat houses of the poor; and before them, a long stretch of scrub and brush. There was no place she could have traveled that quickly, but she was gone. She had simply vanished.

Topiltzin calmed himself. He turned and dropped back into the court, walked to its center. Near the rubberball lay a black rose. When he picked it up, he was surprised to find that it was not real. The petals were artificial featherwork. Suddenly, what had seemed a smooth stem bristled with a thorn that sprung from its side to sting him sharply. Topiltzin pulled back, ripping a gash in his middle finger. Blood rose in beads and trickled between his fingers. Topiltzin looked over his shoulder, expecting her perhaps to be there, looking on the joke she'd played, but there was only the night, only a wind that played.

He tucked the rose into his hip guard and picked up the rubberball. He pulled himself out of the court but felt suddenly queasy, even a little drunk. He looked at the cut on his finger and tasted it— it was more than blood. Topiltzin had just been poisoned.

CHAPTER ELEVEN
THE SHADOW WALKERS

The Garrison of Utzlampa, in the far jungles south of Tollán
That same night

They came, like scattering wolves, through the jungles at full run, silent. They came, weapons clean and glinting, the stone axe sheathed in copper, the thrusting spear hard-edged. They came whispering swiftly through the trees, like wind in the night.

Soaring Hawk did not hear them at first, even from where he stood upon the stone ramparts of the southern fortification wall, half crouched, his weight on the staff of his spear. He did not hear them until it was too late, but then, that would not have mattered. The coming of the Shadow Walkers to Utzlampa was like the shadow of a mountain falling over a stone.

Soaring Hawk had been ordered earlier to keep night watch over the battlements. From the south shores of the east sea, merchants were coming through with a shipment of coral, and they had sent a messenger earlier to report they would travel, even through the night, to reach the safety of the garrison.

"Something follows us," the messenger, a small-built runner, had told Coriantun, the garrison's commander. "Something comes, bearing from the south."

Soaring Hawk was standing beside his captain, and he remembered Coriantun skewering his face. Coriantun was a stone-faced Maya who had wrought such carnage in his day he became known as Terrible Red Hand.

Coriantun spat to the side and said, "From the south? There is nothing south of us but naked heathens who eat bugs. The only thing to come bearing upon you from the south would be your own shadow."

"Nevertheless, good captain, my lords have requested an escort of your garrison to see them safely in from the coast."

Coriantun chuckled. "It would take more than your lords to get my men into that jungle, particularly at night. You would not perhaps consider parting with a bit of this fine coral, would you?" Coriantun did not wait for a response. "Of course not. Sell your mother first, eh? This I will do: I will post night watch on the garrison wall. No more."

"But, Captain, we will be overwhelmed! We—"

"No more." Coriantun had black, predatory eyes, and he trained them on the messenger with expected results. The messenger bowed, then turned and sprinted into the trees to the south.

The garrison of Utzlampa, some fifty-five men, was stationed this far south because no one wanted them elsewhere. As a high judge had told Soaring Hawk when he was sentenced to Utzlampa after a night's brawl in the streets of Bonampak that had ended in blood, "You may be useful in war, but otherwise you eat filth. Therefore, I will send you where filth is abundant."

As it turned out, Soaring Hawk did not much mind the jungle. It was thick, heavy, always a noise to it, night and day, a stink to it. The serpents were long and wide as a man's waist. The monkeys sometimes howled at night like women being raped. He had once stood eye to eye with a black leopard, lean and shiny, looking into its slit, green eyes. It had regarded Soaring Hawk with calm lack of interest as it rested on a rock ledge, tail dangling. Few men had seen black leopards and lived.

Soaring Hawk was called Scarred One, for he bore countless wounds of battle. He had fought all his life. He was born into combat. In his village, it was custom that as male infants were brought from the womb, still bloodied, they were lifted into the air by one foot and sealed by oath as warriors.

Therefore, it was when Soaring Hawk heard the coming of the Shadow Lords to Utzlampa, he did not bristle with fear, only curiosity. He had learned to measure the strength of an enemy by the weight of their footfall as they advanced. When he listened this time, when he knelt close to the ground, he heard the rumbling of the earth, as though the jungle itself moved toward them. There was no number to this sound.

Soaring Hawk lifted the oval shield off his back. He brought the conch shell to his lips, sounded it, and cast it aside. It clattered across the stone, and he did not believe there would be further use for it. He was trembling a bit, but not with fear, for Soaring Hawk had never feared battle. He trembled, rather, with anticipation, for he could feel them now. He could feel the earth beneath his feet as they came, and in his mind, he saw them, full run, swift through the trees.

Behind him, within the garrison, Coriantun broke from his hut, pulling on a quilted cotton breastplate. He was only a short distance from the fortification wall upon which Soaring Hawk stood. For a moment, Coriantun paused and seemed to sniff the air with his ugly face. He screamed a war cry, a rally, and leapt onto the stone battle-works beside Soaring Hawk. Coriantun set a copper-sheathed hardwood dart into the trough of his silver-handled atlatl—his spear-thrower.

"Whore's blood, Scarred One," Coriantun whispered as he shifted his weight onto the balls of his feet, his thrower angled, "what could that be we hear?"

The garrison's warriors were assembling, leaping onto the battlement, taking position along the ports of stone that oversaw the jungle. There was a clearing hewn out of the forest just beyond them, painted dull in moonlight, and suddenly warriors broke into this clearing like a wave spilling through the trees. As they came, they started singing a steady, growing chant which built to a scream.

Soaring Hawk felt his skin shiver as if a breath of ice had passed. He stared in awe, for never had he seen anything like them. They did not look human—something else. Perhaps they were the fabled *werejaguars*, for they almost seemed to come leaping, flying, with dark bodies painted silvery black and weapons glinting. They looked to be shadows moving with the night.

"We shall meet our God this hour!" Coriantun screamed, shifting his weight back for the throw. "Let us look Him in the eye and spit!"

Coriantun spun and whipped his dart into the air, launching it from the oiled shaft of the spear-thrower. The short spear soared swiftly and straight, dropping one of the oncoming warriors. The body vanished beneath the others, trampled.

The Shadow Walkers were close now, close enough for their faces to be seen. Many were painted to appear white and skeletal.

Soaring Hawk launched his own dart, singling out a powerful lead warrior who was coming hard, screaming, his face painted in a red-white grimace. Soaring Hawk's dart took out the runner's neck.

As Soaring Hawk brought another dart to his thrower, an arrow tore through him. It was quick, almost soundless. He might not have noticed it but for the tug at his shoulder. Another then *whunked* into his thigh and anchored there, tight, quivering in his muscle. Soaring Hawk launched a second dart, taking its mark.

Arrows ripped at the fortification causeway, whispering all around, clattering against the stone. Beside him, a javelin slammed into Coriantun's shield, breaking through the wood, its tip grazing his cheek. Coriantun did not finch. He answered with a defiant scream. "Come, you fine bastards, come taste my spear!"

Soaring Hawk cast aside his dart thrower and lifted his sword. He had carried a heavy, moonsteel weapon for seventeen years. His sword arm could barely hold it; the arrow had severed too much muscle in his shoulder. He had to use his left hand—not his best, but still capable. The Shadow Walkers leapt onto the parapet. Many of them vaulted high, through the air, spinning, their energy peaked to frenzy.

Soaring Hawk's sword ripped though a muscled stomach. Their screams sounded like the cries of jungle cats. Soaring Hawk could see their eyes. There was no fear; they were black, vacuous. Soaring Hawk understood he was about to die, but there was no fear in him, either. He had been ready to die many times before this.

Soaring Hawk fought with fury, taking throats, stomachs, chests, slaying until his sandals slipped in the blood on the causeway. He was amazed, for they could have killed him ten times. Instead, they danced about him, wearing him out as he fought, feeding him their flesh and cutting him with small razor slashes from thrusting spears tipped with obsidian and fishbone.

Now Soaring Hawk shivered, for Coriantun was screaming. They had cut off his sword hand, but they had not killed him. Instead, they had slammed him to the stone of the causeway and bound his arms tightly behind him. They then lifted him high, and he struggled furiously as they carried him off, screaming, red-faced, the veins in his neck taut.

Soaring Hawk was fighting without breath now. One of them almost had him by the arm, but furious, Soaring Hawk screamed and kicked him back, then shore off his head. He circled, crouched, slammed his blade into a kneecap, sundering it. They were all around him, everywhere, dancing, jabbing at him, and Soaring Hawk had no strength left. His arm was numbed and heavy. One of them grabbed his hair from behind. Soaring Hawk lost his balance and felt himself hit the stone floor of the causeway. He was turned, and his arms were wrenched back, tied tightly. They lifted him above their heads and heaved him over the fortification wall, where he was caught by other hands and soon was being carried at a run.

Soaring Hawk realized that the Shadow Walkers had not slain any of the garrison's soldiers, but that all of them were being carried along while he was bound and lifted high. Then, for the first time, Soaring Hawk felt true fear. It cut into him, through him. It flushed into his cheeks, seized his chest in sudden panic; his breaths came in short gasps. He knew what was going to happen, but he did not let himself scream. Coriantun might scream, but the great Soaring Hawk would never scream.

CHAPTER TWELVE
NIGHT BUTTERFLY

In Tollán, Topiltzin staggered through the alleyway of an outer barrio of the city. It was late, and though the fires of the street lamps still washed the alley in a dim glow, there were no people. The tenant dwellings, stacked three stories high to either side, were quiet. Topiltzin was sweating. At one point he collided with a stone roof column and twisted, off-balance, and dropped to one knee. The ground spun. Topiltzin lifted his arm and stared, amazed. In the hour it had taken him to come this far from the ancient ball court, the poison seemed to have crawled up to his elbow, leaving his lower arm swollen, fat and purple. He could no longer curl his fingers. The pain was a dull, maddening ache, itching as though ants were running.

He forced himself to his feet. Despite the deserted streets, he knew this was the eve of the festival of the Night Butterfly. Just beyond, the plaza of the marketplace blazed with light, leaving a halo against the sky as though the city were burning. There, merchants would be setting up pavilions, laying out reed mats, and getting their wares ready for market, which would begin with the dawn.

Topiltzin pushed himself in that direction, staggering like a drunk, sweat blurring his vision. He held his arm as though it were detached from him. By the time he reached the stairs leading to the north plaza, he was not only out of breath but weak to the point of fainting. He leaned against a stone pillar to gather his strength. Only after a moment did he realize what the pillar was. It stretched into the sky like a finger jutting out of the white limestone finish of the plaza, black basalt. It was the Serpent Plumed, feathers laid back against the skin like scales. The base formed the serpent's head, mouth gaping, its fangs shimmering, backlit by the plaza's firelight. This was the Dragon—the image of his father's breadth and power. Here, in Tollán, Topiltzin's father was seldom referred to any longer by his priest name. Here he had become the Sky Dragon, the terror, the Wrath of God—the Serpent Plumed.

Topiltzin tried to swallow, but his mouth was dry as cotton. He became dimly aware of a line of Mayan servants filing past him toward the plaza. They were hunched over, carrying heavy loads of cocoa beans suspended from headbands looped over their foreheads. Topiltzin was in the shadow of the serpent pillar, and none of them noticed him. This was the northwest end of the marketplace where the Maya always gathered. They journeyed for months from the jungles of the Petén, over the highland passes, bringing their wares to the markets of the Night Butterfly. In the week of the celebration of the butterfly, a merchant's entire fortune could be made or broken.

Behind the train of carriers came their master, walking high and proud, wearing gold ear pendants and a rich mantle of quetzal feathers. He was a wealthy merchant, a High-Blood Maya of the lowlands, not often seen this far north. He had the mark of royalty, borne only by those of the house of the ancients: a purposely misshapen head, rearing upward, cone-like, to a peak. It was a status symbol of wealth. Young lords, when still infants, were placed in wooden vices that molded the pliable bone to an apex. It was considered a great honor, something Topiltzin could never fathom. But then, he would never understand Maya. They left him with a feeling of mistrust—too mystical, too inhuman. But they *knew* medicine. The finest physicians to be found anywhere were Mayan.

Topiltzin reached an unsteady hand from the shadow and jerked the high merchant inward when he passed. The man gulped, taken completely by surprise. Topiltzin awkwardly turned him about and slammed him against the stone pillar, holding him by his cotton-silk tunic.

"Do you understand Nonaloca?" Topiltzin said, his voice a dry growl.

The man nodded, but by the look on his face, Topiltzin could have been a demon's apparition.

Topiltzin paused to take a weary breath, hanging his head a moment before he could look up. "I need a physician. You understand?"

The man stared, blinked. Topiltzin was trembling from weakness. He pulled the Maya closer, where words could not be mistaken. "A physician . . . take me to a physician." Topiltzin gritted his teeth as a wave of pain and nausea washed through him. "Now!" he snarled.

The look in the Maya's eyes changed. He seemed for the first time to actually *look* at Topiltzin, and then to the swollen arm Topiltzin held against his chest. Near the wrist, a vein had split like a seam bursting. Blood trickled slowly.

The Maya finally responded. He lifted Topiltzin's good arm and laid it over his splendid quetzal mantle, helping Topiltzin to walk. Once out of the shadows, the merchant shouted a quick Mayan tongue. The baggage carriers, still bent over and plodding toward the market area, now stopped, amazed. Several of them eased back and lowered their packs. Topiltzin was far above them as they gathered, but soon he was being carried at a run. His head fell back, hair dangling in sweated knots. The pretty girl's poison was certainly potent. His stomach was tightening as though a winch was being twisted.

They had apparently recognized him. He caught only bits and pieces of their Mayan chatter, but one had called him *the Prince*, and this caused even more excitement. As though out of a dream, Topiltzin noticed several Mayan women running after them, veils of their robes trailing, their bare feet soundless.

They soon came to a halt, and Topiltzin was lowered onto a reed mat. The prince managed to pull himself into focus and ease down onto one knee. By now, he had attracted a whole gathering of

Chontal-Maya, all waiting with concerned faces. More surprising was the physician. Directly before him, seated cross-legged, was an old woman. She was Mayan, with leathered skin and white hair so light and fine it stirred, even in windless air. She watched him without expression through opaque eyes. A witch—they had brought him to a witch.

"He is sick," the merchant said. "It appears he has taken a festered wound."

Topiltzin lifted his swollen arm. His skin felt like it was burning, peeling away.

The old woman reached out, searching with her hands, seizing his fingers. She was not using her eyes. They remained fixed and dull. She was blind. Yet that did not stop her from quickly finding the gash left by the poisoned thorn. The witch bent over, laying dry, thin lips on the wound to suck—hard. Topiltzin hissed at the quick sting of pain. She rose up, tasting, and spat to the side. The dull, whitish eyes seemed to look right through him.

"Poison," she said in Toltec-Nonaloca. Her voice was husky and raw. "There is poison in you, Prince of Tollán."

"Get it out." It was all he could say. It was difficult just maintaining consciousness.

She nodded, slowly. "This can be done. But tell me, Topiltzin Nacxitl, do you have faith?"

Topiltzin winced, his head about to burst. "What?"

"Do you *believe*?"

"Believe . . . in what?"

"In truth, in light, in the sky!"

"I'll believe anything you want. Just take this damned poison!"

She chuckled, turning his hand palm upward and clasping tightly. Baring a long nail, capped in razor-sharp obsidian, she cut a quick incision into his arm, from the inner elbow to the wrist. The pain was white-hot, and Topiltzin snarled between tight teeth. His eyes teared.

"Sweet virgins," he whispered.

She then slashed sideways, across the wrist at its nodal point, forming a cross. The cuts were straight and clean. Bloodied pus burst from the incisions; he could feel it spill out like warm water rushing.

Suddenly her fingers were in his mouth, craggy, the skin like old leather. She shoved something mushy beneath his tongue. When he began to gag on the stinging, bitter taste, she clasped her hand over his mouth, pulling his head forward.

"Suck of it, then swallow!" she commanded.

Topiltzin tried, but almost heaved before he could get it down. When she released him, he broke out in a spasm of coughing.

"You are killing me, old woman!" he stammered.

She cackled. She lifted the misshapen lid of a gourd container. Wriggling, wet things were within, and her fingers deftly fished out a hairy worm. Topiltzin could not believe his eyes as he watched her slip the worm into the folds of the incision she had made. It wriggled furiously as she closed amazingly strong hands over his arm and squeezed.

"For the love of God," Topiltzin moaned as pain jolted through him. Within the incision, he could feel the worm burst open, and the witch quickly mashed in the pulp with hard, merciless fingers. Topiltzin dropped his head back, biting down on his lip. He nearly passed out. Sweet pain pulsed through him in waves while the witch continued to work the pulp up the length of the incision. When he finally looked down, he was surprised to find she had also wrapped his arm in a mesh of maguey fiber and was smoothing it over with some kind of white paste that smelled like a dying marsh. It dried quickly, leaving a stiff, mud crust that tightened against his skin like a hand clasping. She squeezed his fingers into a fist and wrapped them in place, then tucked his arm against his chest.

"By morning it will be numb. You will not feel the arm for two days. But if you have faith, then it will surely heal."

A strange kind of euphoria was swimming through him, an effect of whatever she had made him swallow. It melted his pain, leaving him dizzy-warm. "And if I have no faith?"

TOLTECA

She gazed at him calmly through the opaque eyes. "Is it not spoken of those who have no faith that surely they shall die?"

Topiltzin dug into the side pouch of his belt. "Your medicine is good, old woman. Your sayings do little for me." He tossed four silver coins onto the mat, more than one would pay a physician, let alone a witch. Yet she paid no attention to the clatter of the coins. She continued to bore into him with her blind, vacant eyes.

"Do not play the rubberball game this season!" she suddenly hissed. "Do not journey to the land of the *ceiba*, Topiltzin Nacxitl. A shadow comes! A Mocker whose face is darkness!"

Topiltzin actually shivered. Perhaps it was how her eyes pierced, or the drug she had given him, or the chant-like way she had spoken, but her words cut through him. It was as though she had reached over and slapped him.

He drew back, maintaining composure, and stood to leave, suddenly anxious to be out from under the gaze of those white eyes. The moment he was on his feet, blood drained out of his head, and Topiltzin's vision grayed out. He felt himself falling, and the last thing he remembered was the sound of the old witch cackling with amusement. She had known he was going to pass out.

⁂

Topiltzin slept—the witch had given him a dream.

In this dream, the dawn sky was bleeding over a flat horizon. Wind sifted dry earth, like fingers moving. Topiltzin and his brother both strained against headband load carriers, the same that the Mayan servants had used to carry cocoa for their master. Yet this load was not cocoa. Topiltzin and his brother were dragging behind them the great basalt image of the Sky Dragon, and a meandering track had been left through the dirt.

Topiltzin and his brother, whom the people called the Teacher, had been born on the same dark night—twins. In the dream, they were young, no more than seven or eight, the age of first innocence

99

when it had still been so hard to tell them apart.

Topiltzin's brother worked mightily against the ropes and headbands, straining with all his might, his blond hair matted in sweat. He seemed to fear something and kept looking over his shoulder. Then Topiltzin saw them. Jaguars were coming from the south, coming hard at a panting, dead run. Their paws were quiet, resembling the padding of dull thunder. Dark clouds boiled out of the sky, spreading shadow.

Topiltzin felt a wave of panic and pulled with all his might against the ropes until he was clawing on hands and knees. Yet the jaguars overcame them, tearing into the basalt dragon. Clean, white fangs ripped the dark stone as though it were flesh, and blood spilled richly upon the sand.

His brother screamed, falling to his knees, and Topiltzin watched, stricken. It all seemed to freeze in the image of a jaguar lifting its head, a shredded chunk of stone-flesh in his mouth, blood whipping. The words of the witch whispered against the dry wind: *"A Mocker whose face is darkness."*

CHAPTER THIRTEEN
FLESH EATERS

Soaring Hawk watched breathlessly between the hard wooden bars of his cage. He was within sight of the Temple of Ut-zlampa.

Toltec captives were being led up the wide limestone stairs of the temple. They had been drugged, and they walked willingly, slightly off balance with hands unbound. Drums beat a hollow heartbeat all about them. There were moaning flutes and windpipes, a mockery of song, like wind through narrow rocks.

The warriors of the Shadow Walkers wore armor of thick cloth with a chain net of bronze links woven into the fabric. They carried bronze-sheathed weapons: spears, axes fashioned of stone, maces with hard spikes. They were lean and powerful, ribs showing, muscles sinewy.

Among them, brought to witness the ceremonies of midnight, were the high priests and noble Lords of Cobá and the southern cities that lay along the coast. These Maya were treated like high kings. The Chichimeca had assembled the Mayan nobles before the temples on mats, where maidens with bared breasts and oiled bodies waited upon them.

Soaring Hawk thought he recognized one of the Maya, the Lord of Tikal, who was called Parahon. Soaring Hawk had once hired out as a mercenary in the jungles just beyond Tikal, which was still a free city of the Southland, and he could never forget the haughty face of the chief high justice, the Lord Parahon. Soaring Hawk could guess what Parahon was doing here, three weeks' march from his precious Tikal. He was selling his people to the Shadow Walkers for his own skin.

Soaring Hawk had tried to pull apart the tight, leather binds of the cage, but they were melted to the wood, hard as rock, adhered with some kind of cement. He could only watch, crouched, naked. The cage was not tall enough to stand in.

When the first victims reached the top of the temple, they were lifted into the air and slammed over a stone that had been erected on top of the temple tower. The stone was arched and rose to a point against the victim's back. When the body was stretched over it, a robed priest stepped forward and lifted an obsidian knife. For a moment, there was only the sound of the fires flickering. The knife made a swift slice through the chest, and the priest deftly ripped free the heart, snapping tendrils of tissues and vessels. He held it high, squeezing, letting the blood fall onto his face. The body was lifted and slung onto the steps of the temple, where it rolled, *thudding* off the stone. Below butchers were waiting. Axes flashed and obsidian knives worked quickly. The thorax was opened like it was a crab shell being split. The guts and vitals were scooped out. The neck was severed, and the head was affixed to the end of a spear and paraded about by a naked maiden whose body was painted as a leopard. The victim's legs were divided up, and runners carried the hanks of thigh to the fires.

From then on, bodies continued to roll down the steps, one after the other. The white stairs of the temple's tower, which before this had only felt the pad of the bare feet of Nonaloca priests, became drenched with blood.

Soaring Hawk felt a cold, biting fear knotting in his stomach as he watched the thighs, the upper arms, portions of the ribs and back, all sectioned, all being turned on spits over great fires not far from where the Mayan nobles were gathered. Some of the Maya watched with undisguised horror, but others offered feigned smiles, nodding to their hosts appreciably.

"Oh, mother of gods!" someone cried from another cage. Soaring Hawk turned to see Wolf Feather weeping. The younger warrior looked to Soaring Hawk with reddened eyes, horror-stricken, his face pale as he began frantically, hopelessly trying to wedge loose a bar of the cage.

Soaring Hawk pressed back against his cage as one of the heads paraded past, eyes watching him, blood spiraling down the staff of the spear.

Now the dark priests were coming for the line of cages where Soaring Hawk waited. As the warriors were pulled from their cages, many thrashed and screamed. He saw one, a man named Blood Gut, pulled from the cage by his ankles while he attempted to hang onto the bars. His fingers were pried loose. Screaming, his head was wrenched back by his hair, forcing him to kneel. They made him drink from an urn, pouring the liquid down him until he began to choke. He was dragged toward the temple.

Soaring Hawk could taste a lurid panic swimming in his gut, crawling out along his skin. He watched the fat Lord Parahon of Tikal, seated cross-legged on his mat, his elongated head turning slowly, looking down as meat was brought before him. Parahon did not hesitate; slowly and deliberately lifting it, looking to his hosts, he began to eat, as though this were pheasant or turkey, just roasted, still dripping with fat.

Soaring Hawk lost control. He began wildly thrashing against the cage. He dropped back against one side and tried to kick out one of the bars. He kicked until the soles of his feet bled, but it was useless. He told himself that he would not be taken. When they opened his cage, he would slay them, break necks, tear into them. Yet, morbidly, he could almost feel himself being eaten. He looked down at his own thigh, sweated, smeared with blood from the dawn's fighting, and a tightness in his chest threatened to steal his breath.

The cage door was ripped open. In his panic, Soaring Hawk saw only faces beyond the cage, sharp-edged faces of High-Blood Chichimeca, narrowed, with dark eyes and straight black hair. They seized him with stone grips by his ankles, jerking him forward.

Soaring Hawk attempted to fight, but was thrown against the cement of the plaza. A knee mashed his face to the side, holding him down as they lashed his arms to a pole.

He was then turned over, and a priest, above him, lifted an obsidian knife and deftly, quickly, cut off his penis, his testicles, grabbing them and slicing through with a quick stroke. He saw those pieces of himself being dropped into a clay urn that was heaped in flesh and tissue, a collection, like grubs, like maggots in blood. A dead shock had swept him. He wasn't being drugged like the others. He found himself oddly remembering his mother, when he was only a boy, their dwelling in Tollán, the way she would stand on the terrace early in the evening and call him home from the streets.

He was being carried face upward, and the sky spilled over him, the stars bouncing as he was carried. Something different: they were going to do something different to him. He wasn't being taken to the stairs of the temple tower, but past it. It would be over soon, he kept telling himself, whatever waited; it would be over soon.

As he was carried past the Maya, he caught sight of one fat Chac priest sitting on a painted reed mat, fat drippings smeared over his plump cheeks, chatting idly with the Chichimec beside him.

"My God, oh my God, oh my God," Soaring Hawk heard his own voice pray, as though it were someone else's. He was being taken alive to the fires. One of them was a great pit, whose coals had been burning all day. He had noticed this pit from his cage. It was like a lake of white-red liquid, swimming with a light film of fire running over its surface. At the edge, the heat wafted against him in waves. A priest was over him, near enough that Soaring Hawk could smell him, rotting. The priest's eyes were filled with a strange, terrible power. He quickly smeared Soaring Hawk's head with some kind of gel. He could taste it against his lips, aloe and cactus pulp. Was it a drug to ease his pains? No! They were smearing his head in cactus pulp, greasing it in lather. He squinted his eyes, for everything was blurry now.

TOLTECA

He was hoisted aloft, and the staff to which he was affixed was thrust into the fiery pit. He screamed out as the watery fire seared his flesh, boiling through his skin. His voice choked in spasm as he jerked uncontrollably. They turned him. Facedown, he could see waves of heat swimming out of the rippling fire. Yes, they had coated his head to keep him alive, conscious. Even though the aloe was hot, bubbling, dripping, it kept his head from bursting. Turned again, he saw his chest ripple as fire washed over it. The skin split, curling back in charred boils.

Soaring Hawk bit into his tongue, shearing it, gnashing from side to side, until blood flushed his mouth. He sucked it down, into his lungs, gagging, choking, until his body heaved in convulsions, and he began to drown. Then, finally, horror mercifully sucked him into darkness.

CHAPTER FOURTEEN
THE RUBBERBALL GAME

Topiltzin opened his eyes. It was midmorning. Waves of heat washed through the open portico into the palace room where he lay. He had no idea how he had gotten here, or who had brought him to the palace. At least the pain and nausea of the night before had been muted to a dull ache.

He rose slowly, testing himself. His arm was numb from the elbow down. The old woman's wrappings had hardened like a shell. He slammed his wrapped fist into his palm, and there was strength in the blow—no pain. He stretched out his limbs then walked, naked and sweaty, to stand at the open, third-story plaza that looked down upon the city.

Tollán was laid out before him like flayed skin. Throughout the night, merchants had been preparing, and now it was high market. People swarmed among the huts and pavilions, which were set out resplendent in color: blues and crimsons, quetzal greens and unspotted whites.

From here, he could also see the tents of the penitent that bordered the southern walls of the city. On this, the eve of the Night Butterfly, the annual pilgrimage to the waters of the Bird-Serpent reached fever point. Thousands had come, swelling the city to twice its size, and priests plied among them in search of souls. Despite their efforts, by day's end the pious would be overwhelmed by the celebrants—the drunkards, the gamblers, the whores, and most of all, the rubberball game.

Realizing Topiltzin was awake, the servants were scurrying. Four of them quickly appeared in the room, picking up his sleeping mat, bringing breakfast, setting out his clothing. Three were native Chichimec women. The other, Dark Feather, was an old man, withered and white haired, who had once served Topiltzin's father.

Other than the servants, Topiltzin lived alone in the great Butterfly Palace of the Nephalli kings, even though it had more than a hundred rooms. In the past, they would have been filled, but his father, the Dragon, was gone. He no longer dwelt in Tollán. It had been almost a year since his father had vanished into the western deserts. No one knew any longer if the Dragon would ever return. There were those who said he had ascended to Heaven and lived now at the right hand of God. Topiltzin was yet to give his father up for legend, but when his father had failed to return to the city after six months, the prince had emptied the palace of all magistrates and governors—all the leeches. Since there were only two blood descendants of the Dragon, Topiltzin was the only member of the royal house still in residence. His brother, the priest, seldom came to the palace. He made his home among the people and the godless, here one night, there another, the next in the forest or the hills or the desert. They called him the Teacher, and he was likely this moment somewhere in the outskirts of the city, pressing among the tents of the pilgrims, bringing them the word and the light.

In a way, the palace had become something of a tomb. The only kings within it were those who rested below, in the damp chambers of the ancestors, wrapped in oiled cloth and seated against the walls, waiting for God. As for Topiltzin, he did not number himself among kings, living or dead.

"Dark Feather," Topiltzin said, and the old man turned, but did not look up. The native Chichimec servants clung desperately to old ways. They still would not look directly into the eyes of Toltec royalty, as they would not have looked into the eyes of their own lords, who once ruled this land.

"How did I get here last night?" Topiltzin asked.

"*They* brought you, my lord. Sleeping, you were brought."

"Who brought me?"

"Maya. They laid you upon the steps of the palace, and they disappeared into the night. They said nothing. We found you to be well—merely asleep—so we brought you here, my king."

Despite his efforts, since his father's disappearance, Topiltzin had been unable to persuade these people that he did not intend to be their king. They had all but crowned him.

"Dark Feather, I am *not* your king."

Dark Feather only nodded and continued his task of rolling up Topiltzin's sleeping mat.

"This is the eve of the Night Butterfly," Topiltzin said, growing inpatient. "Stop this, all of you, and go celebrate." The servants did not immediately respond. They attempted to pretend not to have heard.

"Stop!"

Now they hesitated with dismay. Topiltzin sighed.

"Go to the markets. Go buy things, dance, find sex. Get drunk. Celebrate! Now! Go!"

They blinked, heads still bowed, then started out of the room.

"Everyone!" Topiltzin screamed after them. "Tell all the servants this is a day of fat-tongued celebration! Anyone not celebrating will be whipped!"

The last two women now broke into a run, holding up their skirts.

Alone, Topiltzin poured a drink from the wine gourd the servants had left. He paused a moment, staring at his own reflection in the tall, smoked obsidian of the wall panel. Shaggy hair falling over his shoulders, lean and muscled, he looked much the way he felt—angry and potent.

Topiltzin tied on a painted-deerskin breechclout and a wide snakeskin belt. He tied a scarlet warrior's band about his head. From the ends of the band hung bright green Quetzal feathers, which he dropped back over his shoulder. The feathers were the mark of a warrior and could be earned, even for a prince, only by a kill in battle.

TOLTECA

Topiltzin stepped through the enormous shadows of the palace's front columns of dark, carved mahogany, imported from the jungles south. When he started down the wide, lime-coated spillway of steps that led to the Avenue of the Heavens, the sun fell hot and white upon his body. It was welcome. Naked but for his breechclout, he let sun seep into his skin, his still aching muscles, his chest, his thighs, baking the remnants of pain and nausea. He intended to play the rubberball game that night. All that was left was to sweat out the last of the pretty girl's poison.

He passed through the market in the same area he had visited the night before, but there was no sign of the witch. The marketplace was a hive of activity. Avenues had been formed between the mats and pavilions of the vendors—tiny streets, well trodden. From beneath brightly colored awnings, merchants waited with grinning faces, eager for coins, beans, gold tubes, quetzal feathers—it really did not matter how one bartered.

The crowds seemed to grow thicker as Topiltzin edged his way through them. There were performers near a turquoise mat. On their backs, they spun-painted and carved logs with bare feet to the delight of gathered onlookers. Fire dancers were spinning, twirling high to the heavy beat of a jade drum and flute.

Topiltzin stopped mid-stride. A Maya had suddenly stepped directly before him, blocking Topiltzin's path, offering a wide, stupid grin. His inner teeth had been filed down to spiked points. Maya believed this was becoming, but it looked more like decay to Topiltzin. The man had emerged from a bright blue-green awning ringed in a tassel of Quetzal feathers. In the sun to either side of it were large reed cages housing plump little brown dogs, all of them now roasting in the sun, peering from their cages with suffering eyes, tongues drooling feverishly. The Maya looked on Topiltzin with delight, his long hair unwashed. Brazenly, he clasped a calloused hand on Topiltzin's shoulder.

"Ah! You are the prince! The prince has come to the market-place! I know you! Why, you play the rubberball game!" He turned to shout across the small avenue where several women and an old, withered man sat beside baskets of tomatoes and chilies. "Look here! This is the Prince of Tollán! It is the Turquoise Lord of the ball court, it is . . . ahhh!"

Topiltzin had seized him by the throat. "Listen to me, you febrile toad, one more word, and I'll put one of these fat little dogs down your throat. You understand?"

The man nodded. Topiltzin continued to clutch him by the front of his robe; he glanced to the cages, narrowed his brow.

"Just why is it you bring these little dogs to market? It would not be, by any chance, for blood offerings, would it?"

"No, oh, no, my lord, it is well known that this is the city of the Dragon. The Lord Sky Dragon denies the shedding of blood! It is not allowed! No, my little dogs, they are a delicacy; they are a fine sustenance, my lord, why, look on them! I've fattened them, plumped them; they are for feasting! They . . ."

"Are for altars."

"No! Forbidden! Not for altars; not these, no, never, never. No."

"What is your name?"

"My lord, I am Ah-Kin-Na-Ahau-Pech-Chan."

In his head, Topiltzin translated. He came up with Sun-Priest-Mother-Lord-Tick-the-Younger, which sounded perfectly ludicrous. Topiltzin let the man loose; he had a smell this close. The prince looked a moment at the cages, piled on top of each other, stuffed thick with the small beasts. Most were reduced to simply existing beneath the heat.

"Tell me, Sun-Priest-Mother-Lord-Tick-the-Younger: Have you ever heard that on market day, particularly on the feast of the Night Butterfly, if a slave were to escape and manage to reach the edge of the market plaza before his master could catch him, then that slave went free? Have you heard of this custom?"

"My lord, the Dragon forbids the sale of slaves here in Tollán!

There are no slaves here at this market. For years now, no slaves."

"Yes, but these are in the southern quarter of the Petén. After all, the Dragon's voice is no longer heard in southern Petén. Is that where you come from? The Petén?"

"My lord, I am from Chiapas, from the lowlands, from Tollán-Zarahemla, near there, my lord. I am a refugee of the wars; I have fled the Petén."

"Still, just down the river from you, toward the highlands, just through the jungles, there you would find a market for flesh. True?"

"I . . . I would not know, my lord. I seldom go downriver. Wars. Too many wars now. No one travels downriver."

The Maya swallowed, watching through tremulous, bloodshot eyes. Too much corn mead the night before.

"Listen, my friend," Topiltzin said, circling behind one of the cages, "since I am prince here in Tollán, just for today, I will cause this custom, this law once held for slaves, now to be applicable to little dogs. What would you think of this?"

"But . . . dogs, my lord? As slaves?"

"Think of the sport it could provide, running for their lives to reach the plaza perimeter! And if they reach it—freedom! At long last in their miserable little dog lives. Freedom! This is, after all, a festival. A celebration. True?" Topiltzin was now shouting.

"True?" he screamed.

The Maya, terrified, half gestured a nod. "Then, let us celebrate, by God!"

Topiltzin ripped the top cage open and spilled it. The Maya screamed, gripping his hair with both hands as little dogs tumbled over themselves out of the cage, rolling between his legs. Hitting pavement, they instantly scattered, little dog feet padding, scrambling. Seized in panic, the Maya lunged, but his dogs broke in every direction at once, as though they understood perfectly Topiltzin's game.

"Be quick, Sun-Priest-Mother-Lord-Tick-the-Younger!" Topiltzin urged, ripping open another cage. "The quicker you are, the fewer little dogs will reach the edge of the plaza and become free men!"

The merchant was screeching Mayan tongue too rapidly for Topiltzin to decipher. He had to pin two little bodies against his legs, but they were slippery with the Mayan's sweat and managed to wriggle loose. Topiltzin dumped another cage open.

"My lord! Please! Ah! Oh! In the name of God! Please!"

"In the name of *God*?" Topiltzin said, spilling out another one. "What God would that be? The Chac god? Maybe? Or perhaps the toad god—the goggle-eyed one?"

"My lord! I am Nonaloca!"

"Then so must be these little dogs!"

Topiltzin kicked open the last cage and turned. Dogs were tearing off madly in all directions. Onlookers were laughing, pointing. Several nearby vendors were thrown into chaos as little dogs stampeded food baskets and tortilla mats. As Topiltzin left, the dog seller was pulling out his own hair.

Once free of the markets, Topiltzin walked quickly, striding through the barrios and then the dusty air of the obsidian grinders and on, through the tents and reed huts of the poor, until he reached the flatland that led to the northern deserts. Here he ran at a good, steady pace, letting the sun heat his muscles. He would run until he had sweated out the poison, until his blood was cleansed and quickened.

The sun eased low in the sky over Tollán. Shadows had grown long, for the celebrations of the Night Butterfly were about to begin. Crowds gathered about the ball court. From the one-story speaking platforms, which were scattered throughout the city, singers were heralding the song of the ancient battle of the sun and the nightwind—the battle that would soon be enacted on the ball court of Tollán. Fire-tumblers came dancing, spinning to the reed pipe and turquoise drum. All was being made ready for the rubberball game.

TOLTECA

Topiltzin stood in the antechamber of the cavern of Zuyuva, which lay beneath the Temple of the One True God, as attendants strapped on his equipment. First was his wide, tasseled breechclout, which bore the signet of the house of Nephalli, the reed bundle, for Topiltzin was a direct blood descendant of Ehecatl Nephalli, the first grandfather who had crossed the seas in his great reed ships.

Topiltzin's hair was braided and tied in warrior's crimson silk. Seven quetzal feathers fell across his back, representing the seven years the Turquoise Lords had ruled the ball courts. About his calf, the attendants placed brazen shin pieces, ringed with turquoise feathers. About his left thigh, they tied the talisman of the cross, the signet of the morning star, the light of terror. Then, about his hips, they placed a yoke made of tapir hide, wrapped and stained mirror-black, the inner edges gilt in gold. The breastplate, a white crystal disk painted in an image of a halved conch shell, was lifted, and the leather straps were tied back beneath his shoulders. The plate's spiraled chambers were in semblance of the seven paths through the sea taken by his ancestors.

Topiltzin's knee guards were of polished leather, his armguards reinforced with brass studs. His cloak, floor length, which he would wear as he walked to the ball court, was crimson, and on its back was a feather painting, a brilliant red-green sky serpent, the Wrath of God. They lastly placed the headdress upon him; it bore a relief of the Butterfly Dragon wrought in white gold.

He nodded, and the attendants scurried, leaving him standing near the eternal flame that burned in a hollowed ring of white stone. Now his players assembled the four soldiers of the Tolteca, known upon the ball courts as the Turquoise Lords.

First came Mud Puppy Soldier. As he walked down the dark of the cave, he lifted his hand, gloved in black leather, studded with swirls of jade about the knuckles. He spread his fingers in the sign of the word. Mud Puppy's long brown hair fell tangled about his shoulders. His eyes were dark like stone, like obsidian, for his mother had been Chichimec, a Nomad, and her blood lent a proud, sharp edge to his face. Yet in truth, Mud Puppy was gentle, softhearted. Only on the ball courts did he become the jaguar. Of the four, only Mud Puppy had taken a wife, who was now with child. Mud Puppy grinned when he was near the fire. He and Topiltzin clasped each other in an embrace.

"My brother," Mud Puppy whispered.

Topiltzin stood back and held Mud Puppy at arms' length.

"You look well, Mud Puppy—well fed, healthy. This wife of yours must treat you properly."

"She does. And you, my prince, you also look well. I have longed for this—seeing you again. It seems many seasons have passed."

"You have swollen this woman's belly; that is what I have heard. Is it true?"

"You must meet her, see for yourself."

From the cavern came an echoing scream. Topiltzin and Mud Puppy turned. Beating his chest in rhythm as he walked came Rattle Eagle, the Stone Breaker. He strode toward them, fists sounding *thuds*, his blood-red cloak flared wide. Rattle Eagle was huge. He was not quick, but he could stop thunder with his fist. His hands were clad in jaguar skin that was wrapped in ties that crisscrossed his muscled forearms. On his elbows, which could strike like stone maces, were cups of moonsteel, well dented from use, fashioned of the same metal that formed the dreaded swords of the Tolteca. When he was near enough that the fires of Zuyuva ran liquid across his chest disk, Rattle Eagle screamed again at them, a furious victory cry, lifting his fists, shaking them. He then stepped forward and swept Topiltzin into an embrace. Topiltzin was tall and well built; but Rattle Eagle, whose arms were like the trunks of a *ceiba*, dwarfed him, lifting his feet off the ground.

"Topiltzin, Blue Prince, you calumniating bastard, have you been well, my friend?"

"I have."

Rattle Eagle then slammed a large palm on Mud Puppy's shoulder, knocking him a little off balance.

"And you! I understand you have impregnated a woman! Well, by God, that is good. We should, all of us, do this. We should all take a pact, Topiltzin, a covenant for each of us to impregnate at least one young woman before the next cold season arrives, at least one woman each, in order to keep apace of Mud Puppy."

Mud Puppy grinned proudly.

Last came Coyotl. He was of noble lineage, as Topiltzin, his father having been a high Lord of Cholula and his mother a princess of Zarahemla, born of the old bloodline of the Nephalli kings. But Coyotl's parents had both died when he was young, killed in the mountain passes by highland thieves, and he had been raised by his grandfather, a crazy old priest who chose to live in the wild, and his grandmother, who some said was a witch. They had taught their young scion strange ways, and for this reason, perhaps, Coyotl was not as other men. As his namesake, he was something of a lunatic, just a little crazy. Coyotl had once told Topiltzin that he had no place among common men, among tillers of the earth, and also no place among the proud, the noble, and neither had he place among the poets, warriors, or priests, and so he played the rubberball game.

Coyotl paused before them, grinning, his skin brown, well baked by the hot sun. He was prone to spend his time in deserts or highland mountains. Seldom did he sleep beneath a roof. Standing beside Rattle Eagle, he looked no more than a young lad, for Coyotl was not tall, but he was very quick. He had shorn his hair off but for stubble. Through his nose he had placed a crystal plug, a tube that encased a small, crimson feather from a proud macaw. Coyotl had lost his left eye in pitched battle in the jungles, and when last Topiltzin had seen him, he wore a ragged patch over the scarred tissue. Now, in the orbit of his skull, rested an eye-crystal. It was made of polished white coral with a plug of obsidian to resemble the pupil; ringed about it were flecks of blue jade forming the iris. It was an odd choice, for Coyotl's other, human eye, was a dark brown.

Coyotl wore little body armor for the game. Instead of a hip guard, he wore only a snakeskin belt, and for gloves only wrappings of black leather. His loin-clout had no insignia; it was only aged deerskin, frayed about the edges.

Rattle Eagle sneered and slapped one arm about Coyotl, hugging him tightly.

"By God, here he be, the little throat-cutter! Good to see you, Coyotl. Good you are not yet dead. I have missed you!"

Coyotl had a way of grinning out of one side of his face, and he did this now, slapping Rattle Eagle's cheek. He then embraced Mud Puppy like blood kin. Finally, he turned and set his good eye on Topiltzin.

"Brother," Coyotl said warmly.

Topiltzin embraced him. The little warrior looked dirty and half starved, but it warmed Topiltzin to see his friend once more. Topiltzin stepped back.

"Tell us, Mud Puppy," Topiltzin said, "who have we as vanguard for the rear courts?" He was referring to the auxiliary players, the goaltenders, who were chosen from among the youths. Each year, they were handpicked and personally trained by one of the Turquoise Lords. To be a goaltender was considered a great honor, for only the valiant, proven as warriors in mock battles of the Calmecac schools, were chosen.

"Good, strong young blood," Mud Puppy reported. "I have chosen them carefully—orphans this year, all of them orphans. They were eager, Topiltzin. I have put muscle beneath their young flesh during the dry season in the courts of Colhuacan. They are quick. They wait now above."

Topiltzin gazed at his three comrades. If he could name reasons why he played, why each year he returned to the courts, one of them would be found here, in the eyes of his friends.

"Then we have come," Topiltzin said. "The Turquoise Lords have gathered once more. Let us begin! Let us conquer! Let us play the rubberball game!"

TOLTECA

They were gathered, the people. Many had come to see the rubberball game in the great court of Tollán on the eve of the passing of the Night Butterfly. The sun was now low. Braziers and holy fires had been lit.

People lined the edges of the ball court. They had gathered upon the tables and sweep-stairs of the mighty sun temple. They were perched atop the high walls of the marketplace and even the roofs of the palaces.

Nearest the court were the nobles. Stands had been built of wicker and reed, and upon them sat the Lords of Tollán and the Highborn of Cholula. There were also great merchants from the highland cities: Sea Kings of Anáhuac; and, from the Southland, Mayan Sun-Priests and Jaguar Priests, heads deformed, robes and cloaks splendid, gold glittering.

Slowly, from the eastern end of the court, a heavy stone doorway rumbled and slid back. The four Turquoise Lords of Tollán emerged from the caverns of Zuyuva. They walked forward, flanking each other, and Topiltzin lifted the rubberball, painted black and gold, high in his fist. The crowds erupted in a roar. The people of Tollán could have been welcoming gods, such were their cheers. Topiltzin noticed, from the corner of his eye, children who had managed to creep beneath the spectator stands to the edge of the court where they gazed at him in awe. He turned to one and smiled, and the boy's face visibly paled.

In the center court, Topiltzin and his three soldiers stopped. Behind them, the three youth selected by Mud Puppy, who had been waiting in the wings, fell into rank across the width of the end chamber, where they would guard against the rubberball's fall into Toltec ground. The goaltenders were clad in short, turquoise-blue cloaks, leather breechclouts, and thick leather hip pads. They were allowed to touch the ball only with their hips.

The chants abated, and there was a pause as the stone door of the western court shifted, rumbled, and opened its passageway. The first game on the eve of the Night Butterfly was always played against Cholula, Tollán's sister city to the southwest. Because they were the visiting team, the Cholulans emerged from the west, the night end of the court. The four Cholulan soldiers wore dark crimson cloaks and breast-shields of white, polished obsidian. They were tall, powerful warriors. The foremost of them was named Scarlet Macaw, and he was their captain. His mark was his proud, red hair, which he never wore braided, but always left free in the wind, falling regally over his shoulders. Topiltzin had faced him before. Two years ago, Scarlet Macaw had nearly put the rubberball through the stone ring and would have defeated the Tolteca. Topiltzin had blocked it at great cost, and his side still bore the scars left by the blow of the heavy rubberball.

A silence settled. Everyone now waited for the movement of the sun—for the precise moment of dusk, when the great orb slid beneath the earth in the western sea. The crowds made no sound. The sun-keepers knelt at the upper edges of the two steeply sloped court walls; it was there the carved-stone ball-rings had been inserted in the high center of each wall, north and south. The sun's shadow fell from the rings' images. From the top of the north wall fell the image of Mictlan, death grinning, holding the ball-ring. To the south was the image of a rabbit, crouched. The sun painted their shadows diagonally, both perfectly aligned, for the eve of the Night Butterfly always came upon the equinox of the harvest.

As the shadow-images of the ball-rings fell past the top edge of the court walls, the Sun Crier sang out. The games were played at the very edge of day and night. The crowd erupted as Topiltzin threw the rubberball high into the air, straight up, soaring.

As the ball dropped, Topiltzin spun and slammed it off the edge of his hip protector into the steep, sloping north wall. The rubberball game of the Night Butterfly had begun.

Coyotl ran forward, dropped into a rolling spin, and crouched center-court, where he always waited, for only Coyotl was quick enough to take the center. Rattle Eagle moved back, deeper, watching for his time, careful. He would know his moment.

Topiltzin and Mud Puppy moved in against the Cholulans to work the ball, to keep it humming, to burn it into the far west wall, to score the first *kill*, or point. They worked in harmony, they knew each other's ways.

It was once said that in Xibalba, the Lords of Death had played the rubberball game in the night house of the sun, when it swims in death's sea. The Death Lords had spoken prophecy to the children of the Tolteca, that should they play the rubberball game there in Xibalba and lose, for then their sun would forever be swallowed beneath the earth, into the caverns of night. The sun of the fourth age of men would then end, and all who were upon the earth would too be swallowed so new life could bleed from the wounds of death. When Topiltzin played the rubberball game, in his mind, in the heart of him, he always played it there, in Xibalba, against the house of Death. For this reason, Topiltzin had become lord of the rubberball game—for his people, that the Tolteca should never be forgotten.

Topiltzin now moved like a cat, honed and quick, sometimes spinning into the air, leaping, sometimes dropping low, sliding along the cold cement of the ball court. The sound of the ball in his ears was like a heart beating, it was like blood flowing, fueling him, as it was kept in constant motion against the cement. Sweat coated Topiltzin, leaving him slippery.

In the beginning, while the players were strong and not yet winded, no kills were scored; the ball did not breach either teams' goal barriers, which marked the east and west ends of the rectangular court. Those who had scored the most kills at the end of a degree of the sun would win the game—unless the ball was to be driven through one of the stone rings on the top center walls. In that case, the game was instantly over, for to score a kill through either ring was to win the game. But that was very difficult to do. The rings were high, and the rubberball was nearly the exact size of the ring.

To drive it through took great force and perfect alignment.

The ball was kept in hard play, swift, always humming. At times, when it caught the torchlight, it seemed like a comet spinning past.

Soon, however, the Cholulans tired, and then came the moment to score. The rubberball had curled off the slanting wall at an angle to the Cholulan's court, and Topiltzin leapt high with his arms tucked tight and his head down. He met the ball in a perfect deflection, striking it with the edge of his hip protector. He sent it from him like a shooting star.

Topiltzin then dropped onto the cement and stilled—frozen, watching. He could not believe what happened next. A young, dark-skinned goalkeeper of the Cholulans dove to block. The youth was large, well built, his dark hair flying as he leapt, arms outstretched. He had trained all summer for this moment, and now he hurled himself into the ball. Scarlet Macaw had screamed at him to let it pass, but the boy took Topiltzin's strike into his gut. There was a dull sound as the heavy ball sank into soft flesh.

Topiltzin was stunned. The blow threw the Cholulan youth. He slammed into the stone wall of the rear court. As he crumpled, the ball rolled away from him, leaving a smear of blood. The boy had been unable to keep it from passing the goal line.

The crowd screamed, and the score singers called loudly. Flowers were thrown as the first kill of the Tolteca was cheered. This time, the "kill" had been literal, for the youth did not get up.

For a moment, the screams of the crowds echoed numbly in Topiltzin's ears. The game was forgotten, and he stared at the body where it lay, crumpled. Scarlet Macaw was at the youth's side, but the boy was already in convulsions. Topiltzin could hear the gods of Xibalba whisper, laughing together as they ascended, for it was said the Lords of Xibalba always came to welcome the souls of ballplayers.

Now Scarlet Macaw walked slowly toward the center, ball held high in his fist. The boy had been carried to the side, curled in death spasm.

When they were close, Scarlet Macaw looked for a moment on Topiltzin, the ball poised for the throw. Except for his dark and fiery eyes, there was no emotion in the Cholulan captain's face.

Scarlet Macaw threw the ball. It spun in a high arc and dropped. A Cholulan soldier sent it into play off his thigh, where it would leave a heavy bruise. The legs of ballplayers were always bruised and scarred, which was the cost of not catching the ball just right; sometimes they were left crippled.

Coyotl flashed past Topiltzin, spinning, and sent the ball back toward the west, the night-goal.

The blood of their fallen fired the Cholulans. They fought like panthers now, and Rattle Eagle moved closer, ready to aid his teammates. At one point, the ball hummed along a sidewall, near the stone ring. If the ball went through the center ring, it was endgame; the one who had sent it won for his team. Seeing the opportunity, a powerful Cholulan leapt to slam the ball into the high stone circle, but Rattle Eagle leapt, too, then twisted, ramming his elbow-guard into the Cholulan's chin. Topiltzin was near enough to hear the Cholulan's teeth shatter. Rattle Eagle was not called the Stone Breaker for nothing. The ball rebounded off Rattle Eagle's knee, and Topiltzin caught it with his buttocks to send it hurtling toward the western goal. The Cholulans now had only two goaltenders left standing, making the shot easy. Topiltzin centered the ball between them, and though they both leapt to block, it *whunged* against the cement wall of the west end, and the Turquoise Lords scored another kill.

The cheers were deafening. Roses were thrown into the ball court.

The Cholulan soldier whose teeth had been broken by Rattle Eagle knelt a moment, unsteady. Then, slowly, he stood, swallowed his pain, and came forward. Though blood spilled from his mouth, he just spat to the side. He leveled a hard gaze at Rattle Eagle, who grinned back. His elbow guard—once again—was splotched with blood.

As the night drew down from the sky and the court filled out in firelight, the Cholulans continued to play hard, driving, never weakening. They brought the ball heavy and quick, so fast, so solidly that if it hit anywhere but on a hip protector or a knee guard, it would maul the skin. Topiltzin was once forced to rebound it off his thigh, leaving sweet pain. Glancing down, he noticed pimpled beads of blood squeezing out of the bruised muscle.

Scarlet Macaw tried to rub out Topiltzin. The Cholulan captain brought an elbow into Topiltzin's side, hard into the ribs. The ball was driven toward the east goal, but one of Mud Puppy's goaltenders saved it, dropping low and letting his hip guard absorb the blow.

The crowd's roar continued. Sometimes it seemed a steady sound; at other times, it would erupt in convulsions.

Then the moment came for Topiltzin. Coyotl set up the ball, angling it off his rattlesnake hip guard right into Topiltzin's path. It was a shot they had used many times. They had practiced it for years. Topiltzin saw it coming, swift along the side, angled at a perfect spin. Scarlet Macaw also had seen it and was closing on Topiltzin in a hard drive, but Mud Puppy came out of nowhere and collided with the Cholulan with a sound like stones cracking.

Topiltzin ran up the steep side, twisting, somersaulting. In midair, he caught the rubberball on the notch of his hip guard and drove it toward the center ring. He heard it sink through the stone hole with a dull *ponk*. There was no other sound like that, and to Topiltzin it was music, an intoxicating drug.

The crowds leapt to their feet as though possessing one mind gone insane. The cheering was like an earthquake. Part of the wicker stands collapsed, spilling startled, rich lords into the crowds.

Topiltzin tried to land on his feet, but a Cholulan slammed into his side, burying a shoulder into Topiltzin's rib, even though the game had ended. They hit the edge and slid along the cement. Topiltzin, furious at the knife blow of pain in his side, grabbed the hair of the Cholulan and slammed his face into the stone.

Topiltzin came to his knees, his body riddled in agony. The crowds were chanting his name. Roses and other flowers were falling like snow into the ball court. There was a carpet of petals growing on the stone floor. Mud Puppy and Rattle Eagle seized Topiltzin by an arm and a leg and lifted him high, holding him up to the crowds, who broke into chanting, many with fists in the air.

"Blue Prince! Blue Prince! Blue Prince!"

The Lords of Tollán were once more conquerors. Topiltzin had defied the Death Lords of Xibalba. He had given the Fourth Sun promised life; he had again nourished the mighty Tolteca.

Then he saw her: the girl, laughing, dark eyes dancing. She was the same who had poisoned him. He had not forgotten the face, the high set of the proud cheekbones, the long, silk-black hair. Balanced precariously by the arms of Mud Puppy and Rattle Eagle, he only saw a moment of her before he was tossed higher. When he looked back, the girl was gone, but Topiltzin felt his skin shiver, even in the midst of the crowds' adoration, for in her place was the old woman—the witch. Topiltzin wondered: could she have been a shifter? Then, perhaps in answer, Topiltzin's saw the old woman fade to shadow. She seemed to melt backward into the crowd.

CHAPTER FIFTEEN
THE PRIEST

There had been fat-tongued celebration. After following the dancers, the singers, after drinking and smoking tobacco from clay pipes, the ballplayers of Tollán took up residence in a large tavern hall, rich from the produce of the recent market. However, before the drinking of the *pulque*—the white cactus wine—began in earnest, Mud Puppy bid his brothers farewell.

"I go home to my wife," he explained to a questioning Rattle Eagle.

"But Mud Puppy," Rattle Eagle cried, "do not go home! Bring her here. With us! We will welcome her, treat her as one of us, as a brother."

"That is what I fear, Rattle Eagle," Mud Puppy replied, laying a hand on Topiltzin's shoulder as he left.

Rattle Eagle stared after him with narrowed brow. "We have been insulted!"

Coyotl offered an explanation: "I think what Mud Puppy means is that women do not go in much for drinking until their heads swell and for cracking skulls and pulling out tongues in tavern brawls. They like to stay at home, burn copal, make tamales."

"Gods . . . glad I am not one—a woman, I mean."

"So are we all, Rattle Eagle."

The three ballplayers feasted on shell food, roast duck, tamales, rats in tomato sauce, winged ants in savory herbs, maguey grubs with chili sauce—all chased down with cocoa mead.

After they had eaten, Coyotl pulled out his new false eye and spun it on the reed mat. It came to rest staring at Topiltzin. The back of the eye had been carefully worked with veins of bloodstone for realism. Rattle Eagle and Coyotl were, by this time, both well sodden with *pulque*.

Rattle Eagle leaned forward. He prodded it with his finger. "What is this? Where have you found this eyeball, Coyotl? Explain."

"I stole it."

"You stole it? From whom?"

"A demon—an idol of a foul temple that lay deep in the stinking jungle. It is the eye of Mictlan."

"Tell me how this is so!"

Coyotl was all too happy to do so. Topiltzin guessed he had been waiting all night for someone to ask. "I was with vanguard mercenaries, watching over salt merchants in the Petén. A Gadianton death squad attacked them in their sleep. Most were killed, quickly and silently. But I sprang to life and slew ten of them before they could bring me down. Perhaps they were impressed with my prowess, for I had littered parts of their bodies about me like a butcher! Whatever the reason, instead of killing me, they carried me off to a city of red stone, and there they put me in a cement box. In the deep of night, I wedged it open with my toes and escaped. I was about to flee, when a thought took hold of me . . . almost as though it were not my own. I felt compelled to scale the side of their great red temple."

"Why?" Rattle Eagle demanded. "These were motherless, lecherous thieves! What could you wish of their temple?"

"I knew their idols had crafted eyeballs of the finest gems. I wanted one. So I clawed up the temple's dark side, like a spider. When I reached the top, I found there an old priest, tending the fire. His back was to me. He was a godless sorcerer, so I broke his spine like tinder and dragged him into the temple house. It was lit inside by small braziers, flickering, all dim."

Rattle Eagle's face had taken on a glow of utter fascination. He hung on every word.

"To the back was a dark cloth hanging, and behind it, shadowy, a figure. It could have been a man, sitting there, watching me. My hand trembled as I reached for the covering cloth, and it was cold, Rattle Eagle, cold. I could see my breath. Slowly, I drew aside the cloth, and . . . there he was! He was made of wicker, but for his skull, which was human, wrapped about with leather for his flesh. He was draped in robes and hung with rings, ear pendants, all coated in dried blood that caked over him. It made him stink. Yet I had fixed upon his eyes: black crystal obsidian inset with turquoise. The finest merchants of Zarahemla had no match for this! I filled myself with courage, stepped forward, and ripped the idol's head off!"

Rattle Eagle actually gnashed his teeth.

"Then I tore out the left eye of the demon! It sparkled; it glittered there in my hand. I ran through the jungles two whole days without turning back. Only later, when I was sure I was alone, only then did I test it in the hollow of my own eye socket. It was a perfect fit. The demon and I might have shared the same mother, so perfect was the fit of it."

"But demons," Rattle Eagle interrupted, "they have no mothers, Coyotl."

"Not true, my brother . . . even the worst of us have mothers. Is this not so, Topiltzin?"

"Legend would have it so, Coyotl. But since demons are not born of flesh, their mothers can be nastier than ours."

"A good point! So then, there I was," Coyotl said, twirling the glass eye about so it looked in Rattle Eagle's direction, "feeling the fit of it in my head, when suddenly I happened to look in the direction of the fire . . ." Coyotl paused for effect. Rattle Eagle waited in hushed anticipation. "And I realized, feeling my skin grow cold, that I saw through this eye! I saw the very mouth of the underworld; I saw demons dancing, with high steps, leaping in the firelight! And I screamed and tore it from my head."

"You lie!" Rattle Eagle shouted. "He lies. Again he lies!" Rattle Eagle pounded his fist on the mat. "Topiltzin, is this not a lie? Demons offer no vision through glass eyeballs!"

TOLTECA

Topiltzin sighed. "There are no demons, Rattle Eagle. No devils, no demons, only the mescaline and peyote. If Coyotl would just stop drinking, perhaps he would no longer have such terrible visions."

Coyotl chuckled.

Rattle Eagle narrowed his gaze. He pointed his square finger at the orb. "You . . . you put this thing in your eye hole! How can you do that, Coyotl?"

"I will show you." Coyotl picked up the crystal orb and deftly popped it in. He rotated it until the pupil gazed fixedly at Rattle Eagle. "Watch." Coyotl made it appear as though his eyes were looking out either side of his head, like a lizard.

Rattle Eagle wrinkled his face, consoling himself by draining his gourd mug of *pulque*. A serving maid moved in to refill it.

Coyotl was grinning, but the grin faded when he noticed Topiltzin. He reached over to tip Topiltzin's gourd mug slightly, looking inside. "You have not been drinking, Blue Prince. As I think about it, you have not even been talking. One would think we lost the rubberball game. Is something wrong?"

Topiltzin gestured with a wave of his hand. "Nothing, perhaps it is just the poison still in me." There were, actually, no effects of the poison left, other than the image of the old woman's face Topiltzin could not seem to shake from his mind.

"Poison?" Rattle Eagle asked. "What poison?" There were beads of wine on his thick beard.

Topiltzin displayed his arm, still wrapped, even though the cast had been shattered near the elbow and was frayed about the edges. "I was poisoned just before the game."

"By God!" Rattle Eagle slammed his fist against the mat with a dull *thud*. "Who did this? A Cholulan? Let us go out, find him, break his nose, tear his ears from his head."

"It was a girl—a very pretty one, actually."

Rattle Eagle looked stricken. Apparently, that a girl had done this left him speechless. Overcome, he could only shake his head, sadly, and drink heavily from the refilled mug.

127

Topiltzin stood. "If we are to depart tomorrow for the Southland, I must try to sleep this off."

"Women," Coyotl muttered, "that is why I never trust them. They will poison you every time."

⌐⌐⌐⌐⌐⌐⌐⌐⌐⌐⌐⌐⌐⌐⌐⌐⌐

The palace was empty, hollowed-out, lifeless, and as Topiltzin walked through the antechamber, his sandals echoing on the hard floor, he couldn't shake the feeling, the turn in his gut, that something was wrong.

He made his way to his personal chambers, and there paused to look over the city, its low fires pale against dawn's first light. He poured water into a basin and brought it to his face. From the polished obsidian mirror panel of the wall, Topiltzin's image gazed back at him in pale smoke. With alarm, he suddenly realized that over his shoulder another figure was watching, silently. Topiltzin whirled, startled.

His brother stood with quiet calm, his blue eyes looking not much different from Topiltzin's own in the mirror, only these were lifted from the smoke of the obsidian. Perhaps that was fitting. Topiltzin's eyes often clouded in the heat of passion, but his brother's were always clear. The people called him Sky Teacher and if, with their father's departure, they had made Topiltzin their king, then they had also made his brother their Dragon Speaker, their seer. When the Blue Prince was younger, he had often pondered how it was that his brother was so perfect, so chosen of God.

This night, his brother wore long, white robes—the simple robes of a priest—and a gray, cowled cloak. His long, golden hair fell freely over his shoulders. There had been a time, in their youth, when no one could tell the two of them apart. It was often joked about among the nobles, among the women, how much they were alike. The years had burned something into the face of Topiltzin, a hardened edge, and to his brother's they had lent a certain weight of calm that seemed to smolder in the dark blue eyes. No longer were they identical.

"I thought I was alone, Sky Teacher," Topiltzin said.

"You no longer use my priest-given name?"

"Why should I? I am no longer a priest. I am a ballplayer now."

All the Tolteca were given a birthing name by the priests, one that was spoken in the ancient tongue of the ancestors, but only the high priests and seers used them any longer, and high priests in the streets of Tollán were thin these days. Topiltzin also had a priest-given name, but it had been so long since anyone had spoken it, he no longer remembered its correct pronunciation. That occasionally bothered him.

Sky Teacher walked slowly to the open terrace to stare over the city. "I understand the Turquoise Lords are victorious—again."

"We will always win. And you? Have you saved many hearts, brought many souls to the waters of the Serpent?"

"My victories rather seem to pale before yours. The Tolteca would much prefer to sing, to dance in the marketplace with their Blue Prince. I was walking today, and it seemed I had managed to gather a following, young girls . . . maidens. When finally I turned, they said, 'You are he!' They wanted to touch my robes—to touch the great ballplayer, the Turquoise Lord." He turned, smiled. "Something of a disappointment, I must admit."

Topiltzin smiled back. Sky Teacher walked past him, laying his hand on Topiltzin's shoulder, warm, assuring. There was strength in Sky Teacher like stars, like the sun and moon.

Sky Teacher looked over Topiltzin's mural-painted wall. "I understand you are to leave upon the morrow for the mountain passage, to play the ballgame in the Southland of the Petén."

"Yes," Topiltzin answered.

The mural was of reed ships and a wide ocean curling with white water. The borders of the mural were inset with seashells and pearls. It depicted the first crossing, the coming of the ancestors. The prow of a reed boat cut the waters in a harsh spray, and at the helm, tall, proud, stood the ancestor, Ehecatl Nephalli, from whose loins had come the kings of the Nonaloca—kings, as well as warriors, priests, artisans, beggars, whores.

"I hope you have not come to warn me of shadows like the others," Topiltzin said.

Sky Teacher continued to gaze at the mural. "People are warning you of shadows?"

"I have been told—by mystics—that this is not a good season to travel to the land of the *ceiba*. Something about prophecy. What have you read in the stars, my brother?"

Sky Teacher turned, slowly, and for a moment, there were no secrets between them. "You have always read the stars as easily as I. I bring no futures. I have but come to say farewell."

Topiltzin felt his skin shiver. Sometimes Sky Teacher's eyes were almost as painful to look upon as were their father's. Like the eyes of Sky Dragon, they seemed to bleed truth.

"As for the skies," Sky Teacher added, "one does not have to journey to the land of the *ceiba* to find shadow. We have fine cities here in the Northland, but we have skies as well. Ours are no brighter. The native calendars name this the year One Death; perhaps that overly stirs the imaginations of prophets and mystics."

"Perhaps."

Sky Teacher smiled. He had a smile that had not changed in twenty years, the grin of a boy still innocent. He clasped one of Topiltzin's hands in both of his. "Good luck on your journeys. It is possible there is more to your rubberball game than most people comprehend. However, I would like you, this time, to remember something . . ." Sky Teacher broke off for a moment, then continued as though it were nothing. "Remember we will always be brothers, and that you, no matter how long or how hard you try to outrun your own shadow, shall always know *who you are*."

The priest stood back, jaw clenched tight, hands squeezing the hard muscles of Topiltzin's arms, and left. There was a soft sound of his bare feet across the outer foyer; after a moment, there was only silence.

For an instant, Topiltzin almost started after him, but restrained himself. Their paths had been drawn so differently it almost seemed to be something ordained by God. Perhaps, of the two of them, one had to have taken the bad blood, the fire and fury. One had to have taken rage in order that the other be pure.

🮕🮕🮕🮕🮕🮕🮕🮕🮕🮕🮕🮕🮕🮕🮕🮕🮕🮕🮕🮕

Dawn had come. Shafts of its rose light spilled through the portico. Topiltzin denied the feelings that threatened. He assured himself he knew nothing of vision, or prophecy—that he was only a ballplayer. Nonetheless, he knew, as he stood there, that he would never see his brother again. He also knew he was looking on Tollán as it was, splendid and gilded, for the last time.

🮕🮕🮕🮕🮕🮕🮕🮕🮕🮕🮕🮕🮕🮕🮕🮕🮕🮕🮕🮕

When he slept, Topiltzin dreamed another dream; only this one had not been induced by witches' poison. It was a dream of long ago, a sliver of time lost. It was a time when Topiltzin was a boy, no more than four, riding upon his father's shoulders, when Topiltzin's hair was still white and his eyes still sparkled with wonderment. Sky Dragon was walking down the Avenue of the Heavens, toward the temple, and already he had gathered followers. It was always that way; wherever he went they came, just to see him, just to be close to him. It was said in those days that Sky Dragon had seen the face of God, but to Topiltzin he was simply a big man with wild graying hair and a thick beard and a wide grin.

"Faster!" Topiltzin had urged, and Sky Dragon had half chuckled.

"What do you mean—faster?"

"Faster! Go faster, Father!"

"With you on my back?"

"Yes, yes! Faster!"

Sky Dragon shook his head and ran. "Better hang on, Blue Prince!"

Topiltzin had rocked back, almost losing balance, but then he had grabbed hanks of Sky Dragon's long hair in both hands. With Topiltzin clinging desperately, bouncing on his big shoulders, Sky Dragon ran down the causeway; both chuckled, father and son, while the followers pursued. It was such a wonderful sound, Sky Dragon's laughter. It was something Topiltzin had only heard when he was young, when the world was rich, quick, and alive; for in later times, when the shadows, the wars, and the prophecies began to unfold, Sky Dragon no longer laughed. How Topiltzin missed that laugh. How he missed that big, smiling face.

Then Topiltzin found himself awake, in the dark of his room, light spilling over the portico from the city, and he stared upward at the stone ceiling. He realized there were tears in his eyes. "Father," he whispered.

CHAPTER SIXTEEN
THE MERCHANT

The Ancient City of Zarahemla, Deep in the Petén

Thirty days' journey to the south of Tollán and twenty days' journey from the garrison of Utzlampa, in the verdant heart of the Petén jungle, lay the fabled, ancient city of Zarahemla. At the city's southern border, near the banks of the river Sidon, a Toltec captain named Scorpion was making his way along a worn, stone pathway.

Scorpion was weary. He had been seven days in the swamps of the Petén, west of Zarahemla, fighting, sometimes waist-deep, in dark water and blood. He was captain of a squadron of Toltec warriors who had been sent to ward off a wave of deadly highland Maya who called themselves *Itzás*, which meant "water wizards." It seemed the Petén wars had become more and more senseless since the Nonaloca had withdrawn from the lowlands seven years ago. Whole governments now rose into power and were overthrown within a month. In fact, the current Zarahemlan government that had requested Toltec aid forty days ago was due to fall any moment. Assassinations had begun in earnest, and the chief high judge was found two days ago hanging by his feet, disemboweled in the public market plaza. Scorpion's tour was almost certain to end soon, at which time he would be free of the lowland jungles, along with their sweat, rain, and bugs. He was ready to go. After this, he would welcome the dry, baking heat of the northern plains. Then came the note from Hueloc.

Hueloc was a large, corpulent merchant, sometimes wealthy, usually broke. When Scorpion had first received the message, scrawled on a bit of bark, that Hueloc had an offer and would meet him at dawn, Scorpion had tried to talk himself out of going. In earnest, he had tried. Nonetheless, here he was, feeling an uneasy gnawing at his gut as he made his way toward the Mayan tavern Hueloc had specified. Three times in the past, Scorpion had been coaxed into joining Hueloc in business ventures. The last one had nearly gotten him killed. He had, in fact, lost two of the fingers of his left hand when he was caught and tortured by highland thieves.

When the tavern fell into view, cloaked in an evil, hovering morning mist that was nearly overgrown by jungle, Scorpion almost turned back. That would have been wise. Instead, he assured himself he would simply listen to Hueloc's proposal (which more than likely involved a scheme to make them all "ugly rich"), and once Hueloc was finished, Scorpion would leave, calmly refusing to have anything to do with it. It would be simple. It might have been simpler not to go at all, but Scorpion was possessed of a morbid curiosity, fueled somewhat by the memory of the messenger who had delivered Hueloc's note the night before, a young Chichimec woman with night-silk hair and hypnotic eyes.

Scorpion stepped into the tavern and paused for a moment to survey it. It was nearly empty. Scattered about on reed mats was a collection of old men, Maya, drinking their early morning cocoa and boiled maguey mead from wart-encrusted gourds. There was a sick, sweet smell to the place, and the air was stale in blue smoke from cigars and tobacco tubes. The murmuring was in thick Mayan tongue; Scorpion understood only pieces of it. In Zarahemla, Toltec-Nonaloca was seldom spoken any longer.

He peered through the blue fog of the tavern. Hueloc occupied a far corner, seated on a red mat, looking like a great hairy frog. A young girl was squeezed under his thick right arm. Hueloc's face bore a certain harshness to it, a little like he had been hit with a flat stone when he was a child, the nose leveled out, the eyes beady and sharp beneath heavy brows. He had a thick black beard and long, wildly frayed hair.

Seeing him, Scorpion again felt a strong urge to leave. In fact, he did step back, retreating, but Hueloc had spotted him and raised a fat hand.

"Scorpion, you old whore!" he screamed in his hollowed, rusty voice. "I have been waiting! Over here! Come!"

Scorpion curled his three-fingered hand in a fist and walked slowly among the reed mats of the tavern, cursing between his teeth and promising himself, once more, that he would just listen and leave.

The girl Hueloc hugged against him looked to be no more than fourteen. She smiled shyly through green eyes when Scorpion paused before the mat.

Hueloc gestured. He was seated cross-legged, wearing a purple cotton robe and multicolored maguey cloak. The robe was open at the chest, where stiff hairs protruded. Hueloc, as well as being the fattest man Scorpion had ever met, was also the hairiest man he had ever known.

"Sit your buttocks down, Scorpion. I suspect you could make use of a drink. I happen to have some here with me."

"I had no doubt," Scorpion murmured. He sat slowly, careful not to seem in the least bit interested in anything Hueloc was going to say, but aggravatingly curious, nonetheless. It was true that nine times out of ten, Hueloc's ideas ended up costing him—in time, in money, or in body parts. But then, he could not deny they always had potential. Once he had proposed building reed boats to conquer an island in the sea. "Sooner or later we'll reach one, and by the blood of gods', we'll become holy kings and lie about eating strange fruit. We'll each have fifty wives. What do you say to that, Scorpion? You have to admit . . . there are possibilities. With your sword arm, and my handsome face, Lord, but there would be possibilities . . ."

Hueloc looked Scorpion over, shaking his head. "In truth, my brother, you look bad. You look to have been dragged down the road and trampled by pig-tapirs. Been fighting virile heathen in the bush?"

"It is not important how I look. What is this about?"

"This is my woman. What do you make of her?" Hueloc squeezed her. She batted her soft, green eyes. She had a scattering of freckles across skin as white as *pulque*. Her hair was red-brown.

"Are you certain she is not your daughter?"

"Not that I know of, but then, I have not questioned her on the matter. Little bint . . . I just love her." He released her and leaned forward, shoving the hollowed-gourd mug across the mat toward Scorpion. "Drink. You will need a drink."

"Why?"

"Because of what I am about to tell you." Hueloc brought a paper-wrapped cigar to his tiny lips. Despite his wide, stone-like face, he had small lips that seemed wholly buried beneath his thicket of mustache and beard. He lifted a burning stick from the fire and puffed madly. Scorpion decided it was perhaps not a bad idea to take a drink. The *pulque* was so strong Scorpion almost gasped, but he would sooner draw blood than let Hueloc think he couldn't take strong drink, so he drank full, then, his head spinning, set the gourd back onto the mat. Hueloc chuckled low somewhere in his enormous belly, then shoved the cigar at Scorpion.

"Here. Smoke."

Scorpion shook his head, but Hueloc kept the end of the cigar pointed at his face. "It is special," Hueloc promised.

Scorpion sighed, took the cigar, brought it to his lips, drew in a small puff, and exhaled it.

"Now I will tell you something, Captain," Hueloc said, snatching back his cigar. "You and I, we are going to be rich! This time, it is certain. Ugly rich! By God and whores! So rich, I plan to erect for myself a turquoise bathhouse. Stock it with maidens."

All of Hueloc's ideas began just this way. It was almost a ritual— how rich they were going to be.

For a moment, Hueloc seemed to vanish in the smoke of his

cigar. "This time, we will not fail. Listen, old friend." He leaned forward. "I know . . . I am aware, in truth, that I have led you—on occasion—down unfruitful paths. What is one to say? Even the great must at times err."

"Let us talk business, Hueloc. I do have other matters to attend."

"You do? What would they be? Got a few bints of your own lined up in the forest? Got a bean game?"

"What is on your mind?"

Hueloc puffed thoughtfully. "Since these recent wars down here, Scorpion, have you noticed anything unusual?"

"Blood? Carnage? Villages burning in the outland?"

"That is hardly unusual; after all, this is Zarahemla. We burn villages as entertainment! Gods! Think, Scorpion."

"Just talk to me, Hueloc. Get to the point."

"Very well. Have you noted that the entire west-south trade route has been severed? I have. No one can get through the Petén but by gods—Great Sky Dragon, his holy self. Yet the Dragon is currently off somewhere in the desert; either that or he has ascended to Heaven and sits on the right hand of God, breathing fire. Probably he's dead and rotting in the earth with his ancestors. Wherever he is, with the trade routes cut off, the only substance that gets to Tollán from the south is salt, since they just route the salt out along the coast in rafts. So, I have been thinking, the good nobles of Tollán and Cholula have painfully learned to do without certain items for some months. Thus, there exists a high market demand for these certain items. And there is one item in particular, I would wager, the great nobles of the north would pay *very* highly for—if there was an offer."

Scorpion nodded. "And just what would that be, Hueloc?"

Hueloc grinned beneath his big beard and reached over with thumb and forefinger to shake a wedge of the girl's cheek so tightly he left marks.

"If I recall," Scorpion said dryly, "by edict of Sky Dragon, the Tolteca cut off your hands at the wrists for transporting slaves—women in particular."

"But Scorpion, the Dragon is gone! Remember? Vanished! No longer present. He has left one son who is a godless player of the rubberball game, and another who is a common, barefoot priest. The situation is, well, ripe like dark fruit."

Scorpion shook his head. "No. No, not me. If you try to sell Zarahemlan women, you'd just as well cut your own throat. Things have not changed up north that much."

"I am not speaking of Zarahemlan women."

"What . . . women, then?"

"Chichimeca, pureblood. I speak of southern Chichimec maidens with dark skin, silken hair, and bodies firm and supple. The jungles south, in the swamps of Utzlampa—why, they just bloom with them—maidens and bananas everywhere."

"And how are you going to get these maidens?"

"Thieves! Remember them? The Highlanders?"

Scorpion covered the missing fingers of his left hand, although Hueloc had already glanced at it, arching a brow. Two years ago, when Scorpion had been captured trying to steal quetzal feathers for Hueloc, it was highland thieves who had cut off his fingers one by one.

"In the City of Jaguars," Hueloc continued, "they have hunters who bring in the finest female flesh in all the jungle. I have noticed their pavilions are as common in the lowland lately as the huts of salt merchants. Of course, thieves could never get their women over the northern passages to Cholula. The Tolteca would simply cut off all their heads, for they are at war with one another. But you and I, being Toltec ourselves, we could pass through the mountain garrisons as easily as we can walk. Who would stop us? And the women? They would just be women saved from the eternal damnation of their young, virgin souls. Freed from the clutches of sorcerers! Brought by us to receive the sacrosanct word of God and be cleansed of iniquity—we would be heroes."

Hueloc studied Scorpion carefully now, his narrow eyes waiting. Scorpion told himself this was the time to tell Hueloc that he refused to have anything to do with such an absurd idea. Instead, he stared back stupidly.

"I need two hundred men," Hueloc pressed.

"Impossible."

"Necessary."

"I lost seventy men on the banks of the Sidon ten nights ago. Seventy! For gods' sakes, how do you expect me to find merchant-warriors in times like these?"

"Warriors walk the streets. Recruit them. You are a captain, are you not? Simply do not tell them it is a merchant venture. Tell them you are going to invade the heart of the highland cities in a special, secret mission. Appeal to their patriotic zeal."

"Hueloc, were I caught in a time of war taking able men for a venture in women-flesh, do you realize what they would do to me? And you?"

Hueloc leaned forward and took a long drink of the *pulque*. Beads of it rolled along his beard. "It would seem prudent not to get caught, eh?" He leaned back, setting one great hand on his belly and using the other to toy with the red-brown hair of the girl. "We will be rich," he said contentedly, "ugly rich."

Scorpion had a headache. It was possibly from the strong *pulque*, possibly the cigar, but more possibly from listening to Hueloc. He *knew* this would happen. He should have stayed away; he should have spent the day at camp.

"What is your capital?" Scorpion said.

"Let me worry about that."

"This much involved, my very skin on the line, I think not. What is your purchase capital?"

"I have none. In fact, I am destitute, poor as a chili farmer. I lost everything but the girl wagering over a bean game. When I learned you were in Zarahemla, I determined that we would be able to help each other. I help you out of being killed in the stinking jungle, and you help me out of being poor."

"I suppose you plan to steal these women—from highland

thieves. If I recall, the thieves tend to frown upon stealing—from them, that is."

Hueloc sighed. "To be honest, I do have an idea of how to raise a bit of capital, but I am just not certain I should share it with you. I suggest you trust me."

"I would sooner trust a puma."

Hueloc shrugged and produced, as if by magic, a tied roll of deerskin from his robes. He pulled off the tie and snapped it out with a flick of his wrist. Scorpion stared at it. It was a faded map, drawn in a certain glyphic style Scorpion remembered having seen in ancient runes near the coast.

"That's a map," Scorpion said.

"This map is special."

"So are my buttocks."

"Graves."

"Graves?"

"Tombs, Scorpion. Tombs! I got this map from a dead man, a godless tomb-robber who had lost all his hair to a disease and whose skin was black like old leather. He was an ugly man, but a good grave-robber."

"And what makes you think this map is authentic?"

"Because the poor bastard died for it. Would you die for a map if it were not authentic? I say to you, no, you would not, because, despite the dull look on your face, you are not as stupid as you appear to be, Scorpion."

"I suppose you killed him."

Hueloc leaned forward and narrowed his brow. "I may be a drunken idolater, I may be a gambler, I may even let wind from my buttocks in the marketplace, and I might, on occasion, be a thief, but I am *no murderer*. My mother taught me principles, by God! It just so happens this tomb-robber was killed by a cutthroat, dark-livered Mayan trader named One-Leg-Dog-Macaw. I did kill One-Leg-Dog-Macaw, but that was not murder, it was God's justice."

"I almost hesitate to ask what might be in these graves other than bodies."

"This map is a copy of one found carved upon a wall of the runes of Xibalba." Hueloc's fat finger mashed down a red mark stained onto the map. "That is near the Chiapas. It was once some manner of Jaredite ceremonial center. The tomb-robber had in his maguey sack ten or twelve small carvings of pure jadeite."

Scorpion shifted his jaw. "If you can get your hands on Xibalba jade, why bother with women-flesh?"

"Aw, well, as it appears, there is but a handful of tombs. We should dig up enough to make us look well placed, but not enough for a turquoise bathhouse stocked with maidens. I happen to know the Highlanders drool for Xibalba jade, and for them, women are cheap. We will stir their greed to fever pitch and hope they are still as stupid as when last we visited. Of course, I assume you do not harbor reservations about cheating a few thieves."

He was obviously never going to let Scorpion live down the loss of his fingers. "This will never work," Scorpion said without conviction.

Hueloc smiled, drew a great breath of smoke, and blew it in plumes out his nostrils. "I have things planned to the smallest detail. All you have to do is to keep my hair on my scalp and my entrails tucked warm inside my belly. Or perhaps you would prefer waiting until they send you home, honor you for your years of service with some flatland in the far north where nothing grows but rock lizards and yellow weed." Hueloc grinned and nudged the gourd bowl of mead. "Have some *pulque*," he urged. "We'll drink! Celebrate! Soon to be rich, both of us—rich as Lords!"

CHAPTER SEVENTEEN
THE WARLORD

Deep in the Jungles of the Petén—the month Flaying of Men (sixty days after Scorpion's meeting)

A mist shrouded the camp of Xiuhcoatl, the Fire Serpent, Lord of the Tolteca-Chichimeca. They were known collectively as the Slayers. Centuries ago, when the Tolteca migrated to the north, leaving the jungles of Zarahemla, the Slayers had stayed behind. As the true believers of the One God became fewer and fewer in the Petén, the Slayers alone remained followers of the Word. They warred against all who invaded their jungle, they fought until they no longer had cities, until their villages burned and their temples decimated, until they were but roving warriors— predators without home. They were the final remnants of the Old Empire, and they had warred for five centuries.

꧁꧂꧁꧂꧁꧂꧁꧂꧁꧂꧁꧂꧁꧂꧁꧂꧁꧂

Blade Companion was making his way through the camp of the Slayers to intercept a Mayan Lord who had quite suddenly appeared from the jungles, complete with his train of servants and a squadron of soldiers.

Blade Companion was not one of the Slayers; he was not a Chichimec warrior, but was Tolteca, a high captain of the Dragon Lords—Sky Dragon's personal bodyguard. For a season now, he had been commissioned to travel with the Slayers—to fight with them, to live with them, if necessary to die with them. This was in token of the kinship of the Dragon and the Tolteca-Chichimeca, who were known among Blade Companion's people as the Sons of Helaman, after their ancestors. At all times, there were among the Sons of Helaman a detachment of Dragon Knights, twelve captains, all Tolteca warriors of proven rank.

Thus far, Blade Companion had seen the famed Slayers of the Fire Serpent attack only once, and the memory of it was still with him. They had assembled silently among thorn forest at the crest of a hill, well hidden. They blended into the shadows. Unlike the Tolteca, who came with plumage and brilliance to battle, the armies of the Fire Serpent were without color. Their weapons, even the silver glint of the moonsteel Tolteca swords they carried, were smoked dull and gray. Their armor was darkened leather, reinforced with dull brass and copper, stained and worn.

The day Blade Companion had seen them in combat, he first had to wait long measures of the sun, nearly the whole morning. The Slayers lingered, silent and without movement, until a column of highland Gadianton thieves wandered into the valley below their hill. The thieves were fat from the plunder of a naked city. There were prisoners, women and children, and in the vanguard, back-carriers where hunched over, laden with jade and gold.

When at last the Gadiantons were directly below, there was a single motion given of Fire Serpent's first captain, a lean, cunning killer named Obsidian Sword. In sudden breath the earth trembled. The Slayers descended at full run, coming deadly, like a jaguar dropping on its prey.

The highland Gadiantons, no common warriors themselves, were taken without warning. They attempted to quickly form frontal lines of interlocked shields, but it was a panicked move. The atlatl-darts of the Slayers were launched from handheld throwers. Their points were hollowed out so that when they were thrown, spinning, they screamed like eagles. Many of the darts had been coated with resinous pitch, and when set ablaze, came like flaming serpents. The atlatl-darts decimated the hastily formed frontal line of the Gadiantons, and by the time the Slayers closed for combat, the Gadiantons had been thrown into panic, scattered and bloodied. Like a field being harvested, they were systematically slaughtered. It was over in only moments.

When first he saw the Mayan Lord he had been sent to intercept this day, Blade Companion immediately surmised this was at least one of the four *cătun* keepers, a Balam priest. The Mayan stood immobile in the steam of the jungle, arms crossed, waiting like a molded statue.

Aware of whom he approached, Blade Companion made his way with bearing. He had respect for the Maya. They were savage fighters when they sought to draw blood. Blade Companion knew they seemed docile at times—even foolish. They had a fanatic penchant for counting, they were haughty and proud, hoarding their money in treasure houses, and they possessed disgusting habits of sex and food. Yet, in a tight moment, in deadlock combat, the sight of a division of Mayan warriors coming through the jungle at full run was indeed welcome balm—or terror—depending on whose side they had taken.

When he reached the Mayan lord, Blade Companion bowed, gesturing with his hand to his heart, and stood and waited. The Balam priests of the Maya considered language with barbarians quite beneath them. To any but the initiated to the mysteries of the Balams, the high priests and judges would speak only in signs. Blade Companion was Nonaloca-Tolteca, and a priest in his own right, trained in the Calmecac of Tollán, but he understood the Balam would consider him no more than a savage.

This close, Blade Companion quickly assessed that the Balam was most probably a governor. In fact, Blade Companion's first guess was that he was none other than the great Parahon, whom the Tolteca called Stormy Sky. Parahon was the Lord of Tikal, which was the primary coastal city. The governors of these conglomerates were highly valued, powerful allies, especially in times such as these.

For a moment, the Balam merely gazed upon Blade Companion with disgust. He then made quick signs with his hand. He indicated he wished a private conference with the mighty Fire Serpent. To have given Fire Serpent the epitaph "mighty" was impressive coming from a *cătun* keeper. The Maya had always said the White Lords and their vassals were strangers in this land, and would one day be no more than memory. They, however, would always remain—until the skin of the earth rolled up like a scroll in the last and terrible cleansing of God.

"What is the reason you have come this deep into the jungle, Lord Balam?" Blade Companion asked in lowland Mayan, carefully enunciating each syllable in respect.

The Balam signed quickly. With eyes as cold and empty as a stone carving's, and merely for the presence of the Fire Serpent, he explained his reason. He then folded his arms. He was one of the nobles of the lowland steeped in the traditions of the ancestors, and his head reared backward from the forehead, the top of it hung with quetzal feathers. One effect of the disfigurement was that the eyes became stretched into slanted slits. With such distortion, it was impossible to tell if a Balam priest was laughing or crying, angry or drunk.

The Balam wore the proper plumage of a Mayan Lord. His wide, tasseled breechclout was painted in glyphs; his wrists and ankles were garnished with bracelets of turquoise and silver; his robe was feathered silk; gold fell from him everywhere. His adornments tinkled when he moved.

Blade Companion bowed and motioned a direction. "My lord. I will escort you to the Fire Serpent. My name is Blade Companion. I am a high captain of the Dragon Lords of Tollán, and Lord Sky Dragon's personal emissary to Fire Serpent. Welcome, then, to the camp of the Sons of Helaman."

The Mayan, whose expression did not change in the slightest, tipped his head slightly forward, which was all the acknowledgment Blade Companion expected.

"May I ask," Blade Companion said carefully as they walked, "from where you have journeyed, and of your name, that I may properly present you to the Honored Fire Serpent?"

The Maya signed quickly: I am Parahon, chief high lord, Sun-Priest and Spokesman for the Jaguar of Heaven-Born Zuyuva. You may present me as such.

Blade Companion felt a shiver. He had guessed correctly it was Parahon. Heaven-Born Zuyuva was the formal epitaph for Tikal. For the chief high judge and Balam of Tikal to have come this far into the jungle was almost unthinkable. It would have taken him weeks to find Fire Serpent, even if scouts had been guiding him, for the Slayers seldom camped in the same area more than seven or eight days.

For Parahon to do this could only mean crisis, and crisis for Tikal was crisis for Tollán.

Thus far, Tikal had been too powerful to attack. Even the Gadiantons left her alone. Her strength lay not in military power—she had relied for centuries on a skeleton of warriors—but rather in commerce. Both the Tolteca and Gadiantons, and even the Dark Lords of the heretic *Itzá* Maya who now ruled much of the Petén, all depended upon the trade routes that fed through Tikal. For this reason, though mindless bloodshed raged in the lowland, Tikal and her sister cities of the coast remained a neutral zone. Foodstuffs, obsidian, salt, and tobacco all still passed through the river ports of Tikal, where they then plied the seaways up the Yacatan to the northern deltas of the Sea Kings of Anáhuac. Tikal's health was life and death for hundreds of thousands. Any threat to her freedom would mean not only war, but also devastating famine. The entire world would rock on its foundation.

The Slayers in the camp watched silently as Blade Companion passed, giving the Mayan and his richly attired train of baggage handlers a hardened gaze. Parahon, naturally, ignored them completely. The Balam walked with his head high, his eyes fixed straight ahead. The camp of the Slayers was an adornment of death:

moonsteel weapons, worn shields, and skulls. Skulls were affixed to the entrances of tents, mounted in wicker racks, piled in mounds. Some, those from the latest battles, still had flesh clinging to the bone, with eyes shrunken and withered. None of this seemed to have the slightest effect on the Mayan. He could have been strolling through a marketplace. Blade Companion was at least impressed with his grit.

The quarters of the Fire Serpent were in the center of the camp, surrounded by the tents of his high captains. Fire Serpent's wind-circle tent was a weathered gray, indistinguishable from the others about it, except by his personal guards—muscled warriors who were never far. Fire Serpent's first captain, Obsidian Sword, and a squadron of guards now approached Blade Companion, eyeing the Mayan with suspicion. Obsidian Sword was the Fire Serpent's right arm. He was tall for a Chichimec, his skin was dark, his eyes a fired black, his hair braided in the manner of the Tolteca, tied in crimson cord. His face was severe, even savage. He was a bred killer. At forty and seven years, he had become a hardened, edged weapon, bearing the very countenance of his name.

Blade Companion took Obsidian Sword aside. The Mayan waited, assuming a look of indifference. Blade Companion said: "This is the governor of Tikal, and he has traveled through the heart of the jungle, alone with twenty servants and an armed escort, just to see Fire Serpent."

"From Tikal?" Obsidian Sword sneered, wincing one dark eye. "A Mayan governor? Impossible! It is a trick."

"I think not; he seems too authentic. And I have heard of him, Parahon, Stormy Sky."

"He comes here, to the jungle? What madness is this?"

"He has stated that his words are for Fire Serpent alone. Whatever they might be, they should at least prove interesting."

Obsidian Sword looked past Blade Companion, his gaze narrowed.

Blade Companion sensed Obsidian Sword's rising irritation. In battle, Obsidian Sword was calm and calculating, he made swift, accurate decisions, ruled by no other passion than the kill. But in personal matters, his temper flared like fire in wind at the slightest provocation. "I know these people," Blade Companion pointed out. "I have handled them before."

Obsidian Sword shifted his narrow jaw and turned. He stepped through the flap of Fire Serpent's tent. Seven warriors, the Fire Serpent's shield-bearers, encircled Parahon and his four baggage carriers. If any of the Maya were to make a wrong move, they would be cut down before they could blink. The *ennui*-filled Balam waited calmly, his lids half closed.

Obsidian Sword stepped back into the sunlight. He held the tent flap open, and nodded to Blade Companion.

Blade Companion motioned to the Balam. "Most honored one, my captain will see you now."

The Mayan inclined his head slightly and walked forward. Fire Serpent's shield-bearers closed in behind, preventing Parahon's attendants from following, but that seemed to matter little; Parahon did not even look back. This troubled Blade Companion. In other circumstances, a Mayan Lord would have insisted with stone-headed determination on attendants. Never would a Balam have walked into the tent of a common warrior without servants to sweep the way. The fact he did not even protest alerted Blade Companion that Parahon was a little desperate, perhaps a lot desperate. Blade Companion followed him in, growing ever more worried.

With the tent flaps closed, the Balam paused, then slowly lifted his gaze and looked upon the Fire Serpent. Blade Companion watched Parahon closely, for though the Mayan had managed to walk through the camp of the Slayers unaffected, he was now facing their king, a legend in the land of the *ceiba*. Amazingly, the Maya still did not flinch; he still offered a gaze as though he might be looking at a servant or a chili merchant. Blade Companion had heard it said the high Balams were so arduously trained, for so many years, they literally transcended worldly matters. Perhaps there was merit to such tales, for truly this Sun-Priest had stone nerves.

Clay braziers burned low with aged coals, fire flickering over their surface, giving the tent an unearthly glow, like a dying sun. The skin of the tent, on the inside, was stained red, as though it might have been soaked in blood as part of the curing.

Fire Serpent was seated on a wicker throne, something he never did unless he was receiving emissaries, and even then, Fire Serpent was half reclined, more sprawled in the chair than seated. He was forty and two years, but age had not yet affected him. His body was hard, lean, and muscular. His eyes were fierce, and his handsome, narrow face bore the high cheekbones and severe cut that was the mark of High-Blood Chichimeca. His skin was the color of red earth and his hair was night black, long, falling over his shoulders. He wore only a loin-clout and a sword, its scabbard tied to his thigh with leather straps. He gazed at the Mayan with cold scrutiny. Fire Serpent's countenance never failed to remind Blade Companion of a jungle cat, his ease, and his calm, restrained savagery.

"Fire Serpent," Blade Companion said, "I offer Parahon, Sun-Priest and Spokesman for the Jaguar of Heaven-Born Zuyuva."

"A Sun-Priest from Tikal?" Fire Serpent said. "Here, in the godless jungle? Is this not somewhat unusual, Lord Parahon?"

"Captain," Blade Companion cut in, "the Balam does not speak with the uninitiated, that is, those who are not trained as priests. The Lord Parahon will communicate with us by signs, however. I can interpret."

"That shall not be necessary," Parahon said. His voice was amazingly high; it might even have been a woman's.

Blade Companion turned, startled. The narrow, slitted eyes of the Mayan caught his only briefly.

"What I am about to say needs no sign. It should be spoken, as men to men. I come not as a priest, not even as a high judge—I come as a man."

Fire Serpent offered no response. He waited. The Balam dropped all pretense; his body was relaxed, his head no longer attempted to see above those around him, and amazingly, he even looked down.

"Two seasons of the moon's turning before this, on the night Seven Flint, I was taken captive from my palace. They came unbidden, unheard, and my guards, my servants, did not even realize I was gone until the next morning. I was bound and carried in a covered wicker litter by runners who never seemed to tire. When at last I was allowed out of it, I realized I was far to the south. I was in the garrison village of Utzlampa. I was then greeted by my hosts." The Mayan lifted his gaze, first to Fire Serpent, then to Blade Companion.

"They were Shadow Walkers."

There was a moment's silence—only the soft flicker of fire running over the coals of the brazier. Although there seemed little variance in Fire Serpent's expression, Blade Companion could see his eyes spark, he could feel the body of Fire Serpent tense, coiling. Both Fire Serpent and Blade Companion had heard the name Shadow Lords.

"Explain this," Fire Serpent said calmly.

"One of them came forth. He was as broad shouldered and tall as any Tolteca. This one, he was their prince, their young king, for all of them bowed before him, all averted their gaze when he strode past. Though he was dark skinned and Chichimec, this one's eyes were blue, like skies at mid-sun. He told me that his people were those who were called the Shadow Walkers, that they had come, had traveled for many seasons, that they had crossed the great wilderness and the narrow neck of land, that they had descended from the mountain spine of Panotla. He named a lake, whose bottom holds the dark of the universe. He called it Aztlán."

Fire Serpent stirred. He eased forward in his chair. Blade Companion felt his breath short. All these things were known. There had been an invasion of the Shadow Walkers only once in the past, nearly two centuries ago, and still the legends of it were sung over fires. The Shadow Lords had nearly extinguished the Nonaloca-Tolteca in a desperate battle that left dead strewn upon the earth of Cumorah until it was like the carcass of a fallen beast.

TOLTECA

"He told me also they came numbered as are the stars," Parahon continued, "that there was no number to his armies, that they were as the sands of the earth, as drops of rain upon a lake. He then made an offer, a demand. He told me I was to hereafter pay devotion—oblation—to his God, and that in his God's sacrosanct name I was to lay open the gates of my cities. If I were to do this, I was assured, my people would be spared. They would be allowed to live as slaves and whores of the Shadow Lords. They then offered us . . . communion. To consummate our covenant."

"Communion?" Fire Serpent posed.

The Mayan nodded. "I first believed this offering to have been the flesh of Tolteca warriors, for these Shadow Lords sacrificed them in pits of fire and upon the temple tower of Utzlampa whose steps ran rich with blood. One of the governors of the southern cities—and many had been brought to this . . . this celebration—one refused to eat. He was Lord Moon-Priest-the-Elder, chief high judge of Uxmal, and they struck off his head. The rest of us ate. We ate carved, roasted flesh, its taste . . . sweet. They sang, danced, they sacrificed, long into the night, and their wine was thick, mixed in blood. Then this lord, their king, he returned, he came before me once more, and he inquired if I had liked the meat, the flesh offerings. Because his warriors surrounded me and Lord Moon-Priest-the-Elder's head lay not far from where I sat, I answered that it had been acceptable. It should have been, he told me, since it was the flesh of my own daughters. He had fed me my children! Moreover, he smiled, his lips tightening as he leaned forward to clasp my robes. He whispered to me, promised, that if I were not to honor him, to pay tribute of flesh, to appease his God, that he would swallow my cities like stones in the sea, that he would roast me over darken flame until the juice of my face trickled down my throat. I was given two cycles of the round to decide—sixty days. Fifty have been spent finding you."

Fire Serpent stared a moment; his eyes narrowed. His fist had tightened over the arm of the throne. His gaze shifted to Blade Companion, but Blade Companion had no words, no counsel.

"Have you any true indication of their strength?" Fire Serpent asked.

Parahon shook his head. "They move like wind. No scouts have returned to speak of them. Once I was back in Tikal, it was as though they had never existed. But for the taste in my mouth, I might have believed it was all a dream."

Fire Serpent tightened his jaw. "Did they speak the name of their God?"

Parahon paused, blinked. "They called him . . . Mocker."

Blade Companion noticed Fire Serpent wince at the name. Centuries ago, the ancestors of the Chichimeca—Fire Serpent's ancestors—had worshiped the Mocker, the Night and the Wind. The name was a far legend, a distant echo of Fire Serpent's past.

"If such numbers come against you," Fire Serpent said, "as the stars of the sky, what do you believe I can do, Parahon? I am only nine hundred. Hardly the sands of the earth."

Parahon did not answer for a moment, he but stared at Fire Serpent with cold eyes. Then he said, "I do this for my people, for Tikal, for the cities of the coast, even for the Nonaloca. I come to you. What you do, Fire Serpent . . . that is for you to decide."

For a long while, Fire Serpent studied the Mayan, silent, his dark eyes lost in thought. He stirred finally, lifted himself from the throne. "Then I thank you," he said quietly, offering his palm in the sign of the word.

Parahon swallowed, inclined his head, and started to leave, but he paused just before the doorway of the tent, and looked back. He almost did not speak further, he almost held his breath, but then his eyes darkened and he said, "Lord Fire Serpent, I will pay any amount, any sum you demand if you but slay this blue-eyed prince who would feed me the flesh of my daughters." The last words had been choked. "Anything you name! Take his heart, Fire Serpent! Drink his blood!"

Fire Serpent stared back, affected. "I do not proffer my services, Lord Parahon. But I will consider your request."

Parahon steeled his gaze, inclined the tip of his head once more, and left the tent. Blade Companion started after him, but Fire Serpent lifted his hand.

"He is a Sun-Priest, a seer and prophet, I am certain he can find his own way back to the jungle. Stay with me."

Blade Companion relaxed. Fire Serpent was staring absently at the flame of the brazier. He ran a hand through his night-black hair, pulling it back from his cheek.

After a silence, Blade Companion spoke softly, his voice sounding far away. "What do you intend to do?"

Fire Serpent looked up slowly; his jet eyes bore into Blade Companion. "Have a drink. Would you like to join me, Captain?"

"Only if it is strong."

"It is," Fire Serpent assured him, filling two gold goblets from a clay urn.

CHAPTER EIGHTEEN
THE BARTER

The Highland Mountains of the Gadiantons—south and west of Tollán

It had taken Hueloc two full seasons of the moon to reach the highland mountains of the Gadiantons. The rains had begun in earnest, and nearly every afternoon they were pelted with sudden downpours that left them soaked through and the ground steamy. It was after just such a rain he found himself wondering if things were not different here in the highlands. He was walking with four Toltec bodyguards through a plush valley surrounded by peaks and deep green grass, and there was nothing out of the ordinary—except the feel of the place. It was as though a shadow had been drawn over the mountains, though not a shadow he could see—the sun still split streamers through the gray clouds—but a shadow he could feel. Something was making his skin crawl.

Hueloc had for many years known the king of the thieves, a grizzled bastard weathered of gluttony named Nine Monkey. They had something of a working relationship, and after three months of travel, through jungle and muddied mountain roads, Hueloc was looking forward to Nine Monkey's bathhouse and servant women, who were always balm to the eyes. He had left Scorpion and the two hundred Toltec warriors on a plateau well away from the City of Jaguars and set off at dawn with high hopes. As a precaution, he brought along four of Scorpion's own shield-bearers.

The highlands were a volcanic ridge that formed the spine of the western coast. The City of Jaguars was pivotally located. To the southeast, the mountain range melted into jungles rich in obsidian. Directly east were gorges whose cliffs notched like fingers into the lowland rain forests of the Petén and the plush cities of the Maya. North, the spine of the mountain curled about the edge of the sea, then eastward to deposit itself at the very doorstep of Tollán.

But something was different about the highlands this time. The thieves of the ancient order of Gadianton had ruled here for decades, and that was the first thing Hueloc had found troublesome: there were no Gadiantons. As he came close to the city, well into the thieves' domain, he should have been intercepted by guards who watched the road from garrisons nestled in the rocks and mountain peaks. Yet no thieves came. The only warriors they encountered were patrols of Chichimeca. Someone, something, had taken the weathered, greedy faces of the thieves and replaced them with Chichimec warriors, with body armor of bronze and silver netting, who roamed in squadrons like packs of coyotes.

Scorpion had given Hueloc four Butterfly-Eagle Knights—large, brutal bastards. Beneath their cloaks, which the Butterfly Knights kept wrapped about them, they positively bristled with weapons, but Hueloc still felt a quiver of uneasiness. Thus far, for some reason, the Chichimeca they encountered ignored them other than a curious gaze or two. But the closer they had gotten to the city, the thicker became the dark warriors, looking ever more deadly. It was like walking into a lair of serpents. As they passed, Hueloc heard one group talking among themselves, and for a moment paused. They spoke a tongue Hueloc did not recognize, and this stunned him. As a trader he prided himself on knowing every language uttered in the four corners of the world. He continued on, reasoning with himself that the mountain had for nearly a century been a nest of killers—perhaps this new strain were simply foreign mercenaries hired by Nine Monkey. That would make sense. With the wars in the Petén, thieving had become a dangerous business. But where were the ill-clad, dirty-haired Gadiantons? Where were the dice games, the whores, the squalid markets on the outskirts of town?

When the City of Jaguars finally unveiled itself and Hueloc and the four Tolteca walked beneath the high stone gateway of the city's outer wall, Hueloc stopped short, holding up his hand in signal to the Tolteca. For a moment, he stood dumbstruck. The city was a hive of Chichimeca, they were everywhere—lean, bred killers. There were *no thieves*!

Hueloc winced at the sight of the city's temple, feeling fingers crawl down his spine. The temple was not far from where they stood. Built by Nonaloca priests when the city was founded by the Tolteca centuries ago, it was a small mountain of white limestone finish, a replica of the temple tower of Tollán, only smaller. Hueloc had always marveled how the sweep of stairs had shivered to silver with the dawn, but now they were a stark red-brown. His first impression was that they had been painted, but then he realized the color and the bitter smell permeating the air were of the same origin—blood. The temple stairs were literally sheathed in blood, leaving the limestone facing blackened and scaly.

Twenty or more killers suddenly surrounded Hueloc and the Tolteca. A dozen or so obsidian spear tips were leveled threateningly. Behind Hueloc, the four knights drew together and tensed, ready at any moment to draw weapons, spill blood, open flesh.

This was *not* part of his plan, and Hueloc muttered a curse into his beard. He had planned this entire venture down to the smallest detail. Everything was to unfold very smoothly! As he had explained to a distrustful Scorpion, "Nothing can go wrong, absolutely nothing at all." Now he could feel the Tolteca getting ready to die, and for a moment, the tension in the air was as thick as the smell of blood.

Hueloc was greatly relieved when a Gadianton was shoved forward—at last, a vile thief! This one was a breed of Mayan, Toltec, and Chichimec blood, an ugly man really, but welcome. Hueloc noticed a warrior prod the man with his spear tip.

"They want you to tell them who you are," said the breed.

TOLTECA

Hueloc offered everyone a broad, merchant's smile. "I would be honored to do so. I am Hueloc, the merchant! I have come to seek conference with Nine Monkey. I have some very unusual jade which should interest him greatly."

The breed stared as though Hueloc might have been totally insane and carefully spoke the twisted language Hueloc had heard earlier. Amazingly, the breed was translating! Something very odd was at play here. Hueloc then noticed the dogged expression and pale skin on the man. He was a prisoner! The first thief Hueloc had seen all day, and the man was a slave. The lead warrior, a handsome Chichimec with night-black eyes and silken hair, gave Hueloc a dead-cold look and motioned direction with his sword.

As Hueloc and the Tolteca walked through the streets, escorted by the squadron of warriors, he was thinking this all had the fit of a bad dream. He entertained the possibility he might actually be back in camp, fast asleep, dreaming. That would explain the skull racks: as they passed the base of the temple, there fell into view rows of skulls mounted one above the other on wicker stakes, all drying in the sun. Some still had sufficient skin on them that Hueloc was finally able to surmise the whereabouts of a majority of the thieves. They were being used for wallpaper—a temple decoration. The racks surrounded the base of the temple on all sides, and the stink of putrefying flesh was stifling. A kind of sick panic crawled up Hueloc's skin, but he choked it back.

Hueloc eventually found himself deposited in the Hall of Lizards, once the palace of old Nine Monkey, but Hueloc was now losing all hope of seeing the sly, toothless grin of the king of thieves. The palace looked quite different these days. The murals had been replaced with strange, somehow malevolent zoomorphic images, and the front façade had been sculpted into a red-stained sun disk.

Scorpion's Tolteca flanked Hueloc to either side, fully alert. If they were unnerved, they did not show it; their faces could have been cut from stone. Of course, Hueloc expected no less. These were Butterfly Warriors, blood and carnage were ordinary fare for them; they had not even reacted to the skull racks. Hueloc was certain they were fully prepared to die at any given instant. He, however, was not.

Hueloc watched numbly as what must certainly have been a High-Blood Prince was carried from the palace's inner chambers into the light. Hueloc had been hoping for a thief, any thief, any Gadianton in charge here would have been acceptable, but instead came a Chichimec prince, borne in an ornate, wicker litter by muscled servants. The prince was cruelly handsome, confident, with that certain cunning only the merciless seemed to acquire. He came accompanied by a virtual army of servants, mostly young maids, so beautiful they left Hueloc's mouth dry. The maids prepared the prince's throne, laid finely woven pillows on it, laid a leopard skin over the seat and arms. They swept the floor before him as he stepped from the litter and regally lowered himself into the throne. They fanned him with great palm leaves.

The prince was young. How young, Hueloc was not certain, but too young to have gained his stature by prowess. This was a blood dynasty Hueloc was witnessing, a hereditary prince, in marked contrast to the kings of the thieves who had always proven themselves first in bloodshed, then in treachery.

A mat was laid before the throne, and at a motion from one of the servants, Hueloc seated himself upon it. He nodded and smiled at the prince. Hueloc could not remember ever seeing a Chichimec so handsome or dark skinned, his face lean, chiseled, and sharp. His eyes were blue! Astonishing. Hueloc had never seen that before in a Chichimec—sky-blue eyes ringed at the edges in silver. The effect was haunting; Hueloc imagined he could be looking into the eyes of death.

"I am told you wish to barter," the prince said, "to trade goods." He had a rich, deep voice, resonant until it almost seemed to echo, and he spoke a careful Nonaloca. Hueloc could detect only a trace of accent.

For a moment Hueloc stared, amazed. He was thinking the

prince was so finely honed he could have been a scion of the gods—it was amazing. He pulled himself into focus. He was about to engage this High-Blood bastard in a challenge of wits, and he had to be at his best. He calmly produced from his belt a deerskin bag, loosened the ties, and let the contents scatter over the red-stained wicker mat.

He and Scorpion had found the stones only after a full season of the moon searching through jungle thick as soup. The map had not been as promising as it appeared. Yet here they were, the finest pieces of Xibalba jade Hueloc had ever come across, seven ancient finger-sized figurines. They were meant to look like samples, but in fact, this was all the jade Hueloc had. Fifteen ungodly days of digging in mud and rain, all for seven pieces.

Watching the High-Blood Prince's eyes as he gazed over the scattered carvings, Hueloc felt a flicker of loss of faith in himself. The prince could not have appeared less interested. He did not look greedy at all. Something else drove him. Yes, something other than greed fired the passion of this cunning bastard, and Hueloc shuddered at his guess that it was blood—the blood of innocents.

These are just more thieves, he told himself with reassurance. *Better looking, more deadly, more numerous than the old thieves, but thieves all the same.*

The prince's lightning eyes, looking unearthly, shifted to study Hueloc with all the interest of a cat pondering which leg to rip off first.

"You are brave, fat man."

Hueloc grinned. No one, after this, could ever deny that. Hueloc was treading in a snake pit frought with deadly vipers. Brave was indeed a fitting word.

"And," the prince added, "Tolteca. Are you not, bearded one?"

Hueloc spat to the side. "Blood only," he replied with disdain. In the highlands, Tolteca was never a favorable title.

"A hard thing to dismiss, blood," the prince said.

Hueloc shrugged.

The prince motioned and a servant quickly retrieved one of the figurines. The prince fingered it a moment, held it up to the light.

"What are these?" he asked.

"Figurines. Of the ancients. These are treasures, my lord, from the very tombs of Xibalba."

"Xibalba?" The prince glanced to his servants, one of whom, Hueloc realized, had a familiar cut to his face. It was the same ugly breed that had met them at the gate.

"Xibalba is a fable," the breed said, his voice slightly tremulous. "It is a land . . . a place, O Lord, where dwell the ancient ones who have no name, the Many Dead, the buried."

"How appropriate," the prince mused.

Hueloc wondered why it was appropriate, but decided not to pursue the matter.

The prince leaned forward. "We speak then, Tolteca, of the land called Desolation?"

Hueloc was stunned. Not one called Xibalba *the land called Desolation*. No one, that was, but the priest. Hueloc had been born of goodly parents, well off, and had been raised in the sacred Nephalli city of Zarahemla. There, as a youth, Hueloc had been sent to the Calmecac schools, where he was taught the language of priests. In the books of priests, the runes of Xibalba were called Desolation— but nowhere else. This prince, though he was lordly and wellborn, was certainly no priest, Hueloc would bet his very buttocks on that. Nine Monkey, the old Gadianton, would never have known that word, and in fact, by his expression, the breed had no idea what the prince was talking about.

The prince smiled, watching Hueloc carefully, and added, "The land of the Jaredite."

Hueloc, numbed, nodded. Who was this Chichimec? Where had he come from . . . and *who* had taught him? "Yes," Hueloc responded calmly, "they have been called that. On occasion."

"Tell me, fat merchant, what could have become of these ancient people that they were all destroyed? That they warred in pride and blood until they are no longer known among the living? That they have become the Many Dead?"

"I am neither priest nor scholar, my lord. I could not speculate," Hueloc said, anxious to change the subject, "but I can tell you this: they were amazingly good with jade."

"Yes," the prince acknowledged, carelessly tossing the figure back onto the reed mat where it grinned, fang-toothed, at Hueloc. "And, since they have been destroyed," the prince continued, "since they are no more, such pieces as these become of even greater value. Am I right, fat merchant?"

"Enormously greater."

The prince eased back and stared gravely at Hueloc a moment. "I'm curious," he said, "how is it you have the courage to come here to my city, plying trinkets as though this were a market plaza."

"As I mentioned, my prince, I am not Tolteca beyond blood. I go where I please. I do not interest myself in politics, except where they determine profit."

"I see . . . then perhaps you are not as courageous as you are greedy."

"Yes . . . ah, precisely."

The prince chuckled. Hueloc grinned back warmly, but he felt a cold chill from those eyes, the way the silver rings at the edges seemed to make them glow like braziers.

"You seem quite at ease." The prince's eyes narrowed. "Perhaps you know something I do not, fat man."

"Which is?" Hueloc ventured, cheerfully, choking on a rising feeling things were going to get ugly any moment now.

"Why I should not roast your fat flesh slowly over fanned fires, or perhaps boil you, or pluck out your eyes and feed you your own testicles. Why should I barter with you, when it is vastly more facile to just cut your throat?"

"My lord, there is a simple reason. It is this: I can deliver more stones, hundreds more, enough to fill a temple! Why, this is merely a sampling." Of course, that was a lie, but Hueloc was quite adept at lying when the situation required it.

The prince tilted his head. "And . . . where are these stones of yours? Your companions have them tucked beneath their cloaks, perhaps?"

Hueloc shifted uneasily. Scorpion's warriors did not flinch at the reference. "Good Prince, if I were to explain where I have put my stones, then there truly would be no reason you should not feed me my testicles, which I have little desire to consume. But let me say this: some of these pieces are most remarkable, like none I have ever seen, the finest, purest jade, exquisitely carved."

"Then why do you not take these stones to the Tolteca? Should they not make you a rich man? Why bring them to me?"

"Women." Hueloc took a breath and grinned.

"Women? I do not understand." The prince glanced to his advisors, but they could offer no explanation.

"You see, my lord, in the Northland there is a Great Lord who rules . . ."

"Honored Sky Dragon," the prince said, quite clearly, and again pronounced as only a Nonaloca priest would say it.

"Yes . . . er . . . Honored Sky Dragon. Before Honored Sky Dragon became king of the Northland, there was a fair trade in flesh. The kings of Cholula, it is said, had nearly a hundred female slaves in their court. Of course, the owning and sale of slaves was banished by Honored Sky Dragon. However, since the king of Tollán no longer rules, well, women flesh acquires a somewhat greater potential profit base than stones of Xibalba."

The prince stared at Hueloc with glazed eyes, almost as though he had not heard. "Honored Sky Dragon no longer leads his people?"

"Not . . . not for more than a year."

"How could this be?"

"You have not heard, my lord? It was after the Battle of the Hundred Hands. The Tolteca slaughtered seven thousand Mayan warriors, all of whom had been in forced retreat. The king's Dragon Knights, incensed with blood fever, overtook and slew them. It is said that the rivers ran with blood. The Dragon wept. He cursed his own warriors and left them, abandoned them in wrath, never to return."

"Where did he go?"

"No one knows. Into the deserts. Into the sea. Into the sky." Hueloc shrugged.

The prince suddenly rose from the throne, attendants scattering as he did. For the longest moment, he gazed upon the smoky veil of sunlight streaming through the open columns of the palace, standing perfectly still. He then looked to Hueloc, but his eyes had hardened. His look seemed to be fired with blood.

The prince asked, "How many?"

Hueloc hesitated, confused. "My lord?"

"How much women flesh are we talking, fat merchant?"

"Forty. I was hoping for forty. Young ones. Virgins. There is, ah . . . they have this penchant for virgin flesh in Cholula."

"Do they? The Nonaloca? A penchant for flesh?"

"You seem somewhat familiar with the Nonaloca, my prince, but in truth, they are not as they once were."

"No?"

"They have become, err, shall we say, more relaxed in their ways."

"Why? Have not their priests taught them well? Has not their prophet chastened them properly? How could this be that they would trade in women flesh? That they would fall prey to blood fever, the mighty Lords of the Nephalli?" The prince narrowed his brow. "Are they no longer the true followers of God?"

"Yes . . . and no. What I mean to say is—"

"They have fallen. They have become . . . stained."

"Perhaps. Who could say?"

"That is a pity. When a people like the Nonaloca, shining as the sun, jeweled as the stars—when such a people fall, it is like the falling of a great tree in the forests: all can hear it. And many will come for the carcass of the fallen, to gather kindling against the coming dark."

"Actually, my prince, the Tolteca still wield a heavy sword."

The prince paused, again lapsing into a distant stare. "Virgins?"

"Hopefully. Yes. Virgins." Hueloc cursed himself. The man had unnerved him considerably. It was getting difficult to concentrate.

"And how will you know they are so? How will you ascertain you are not being fooled?"

"The point is that they *appear* to be virginal. It is the appearance that has import, not the verification."

"I see." The prince seemed to lapse again; his eyes glazed. Hueloc found himself waiting in absolute silence, ignored. The attendants of the prince kept their eyes lowered, fixed on the ground. None of them stirred. For a moment everyone present might have been—all of them, Hueloc included—so many statues gathered in the great hall.

Finally, Hueloc said, "Are you interested, my lord?"

The prince shifted, looked at him with detachment. "Why not?" he said. "Yes, fat merchant, virgins for stones! You amuse me. If nothing else, it does have a certain poetic appeal. How do you wish to make this exchange?"

"Two days march north; along the mountain passage, I will meet you with my men. There is a plateau where the river drops in a great waterfall. The gorge below splits into three heads. It is called the Valley of the Thrice-Headed Serpent. I will have the stones of Xibalba with me."

"And I am to have forty . . . virgins ready to exchange for them?"

"Handsome ones." Hueloc permitted himself a smile. "The prettier, the better."

"And should I arrive with these pretty virgins, and you with your stones, what will prevent me at that time from plucking out your eyes and slitting your throat from one of your ears to the other?"

"I shall trust you as a man of honor."

The prince grinned. Thank God he had a sense of humor. "I will be there," he said, and left. He strode into one of the chambered rooms of the palace, his attendants scurrying after, leaving Hueloc with a certain chill when he should have tasted sweet victory, should have been rejoicing in his windfall good luck. Instead, he was simply grateful to be out from under the predatory gaze of those eyes. He breathed a sigh of relief and stood quickly, snatching up the figurines and ramming them back into the deerskin bag.

"Let us shed ourselves of this godless place," he said, stepping past Scorpion's warriors, who followed soundlessly at his flanks.

CHAPTER NINETEEN
TOLTECA

In an antechamber, the man called Smoking Mirror watched as the fat merchant and the four Tolteca made their way up the crowded city toward the gates.

"Have them followed," he said quietly, and one of his captains turned and soundlessly left the room.

It had been a long time since Smoking Mirror had seen a bearded Toltec, and these with him, his soldiers, they had to have been none other than the famed Butterfly Warriors, prime fighters of the Tolteca. Utzlampa had been stocked with dogs. The mountain stronghold he had taken four days ago had been held by primitive inbreeds. He was getting closer. He could smell them, their spirits in the air—eagles. He could tell just by the eyes; the Butterfly Warrior's never flinched, even when he, the Smoking Mirror, looked into them, probing, searching. There was no fear. Fear had been bred out of them. He noticed now, as the fat merchant hurriedly made his way toward the gate, the Butterfly Warriors carefully flanked him, still at the ready. He smiled. It was true, then. It was all true!

When he had first heard the fabulous stories of the old man, Smoking Mirror had thought them just more legends of the great ancestor Ehecatl Nephalli. He had heard such legends all his life. It was said the great stone cities of Aztlán's shore were once crafted by the hand of the Nephalli, during a time when the four brothers had emerged from the sacred cave. Indeed, they rose there, somber and magnificent—stone and legend and the *huaca* of the Nephalli were as old as the lake. The old bearded one had come among them, the priest, and the Teacher as he had asked them to call him. Smoking

166

TOLTECA

Mirror at first had him thrown into prison and there he would have let him rot, but the priest had no fear of prison, no fear of his captors. Even after days of starvation, there was something in his eyes. Something gave him strength far beyond his old, brittle bones.

Smoking Mirror had him brought to the palace, and there, for months on end, he listened to all the old man could teach, hanging on every word. The fabulous Nephalli Tolteca, who honored their ancestors, who never lied but always answered yeah, nay, they were blessed with great riches and knowledge. They were skilled in all the trades, the arts and artifices: feather-workers, feather-gluers, scribes, lapidaries, carpenters, stonecutters, masons, potters, spinners, weavers; fashioned they the sacred emeralds; fashioned they the precious turquoise; smelted they both gold and silver and moonsteel, the sacred, hidden metal of the ancestors. They knew how to write and kept sacred books deep beneath their great temples. They charted the paths of the stars and the Heavens. And they understood there were many divisions of the Heavens and that there existed, there dwelt, One True God and his consort, who ruled over the twelve Heavens and the common people were created there, from thence came their souls, from the blue start, the grape cluster of the sky. The Tolteca were righteous, they were not deceivers, their words were clear words; they did not lie. They addressed each other as the lord, my elder brother, the lord, my younger brother. And what fired Smoking Mirror's interest the most were the stories of their king, who was a sky speaker known as "Sky Teacher", a man who had seen the very face of God, who heard God's words and breathed them down upon his people—seer, prophet, law giver— *Honored Sky Dragon.*

Smoking Mirror could still remember the old man's eyes glowing with light as he told the stories, eager to teach him and his people the path, the way, the only road to Heaven. His words had made Smoking Mirror shiver as though he were cold, for by the old bearded one's eyes Smoking Mirror knew he spoke truth. Just as the people he described, he told no lies.

In the end, when he had the old man flayed alive, Smoking Mirror watched those stone-gray eyes carefully, waited for them to flicker with terror, but it did not happen. All the old man had said to him as he died slowly, his skin removed, the red muscle of his old body slowly drying with unimaginable pain—all he had said was, "I forgive you, my son." That had left Smoking Mirror filled with astonishment. He had been forgiven!

CHAPTER TWENTY
BLOOD GATHERERS

Topiltzin wondered if perhaps he was lost. It hardly seemed possible—he knew this country well. In past years he had journeyed many times into the southern lowlands, and he had never gotten lost. This time, the lowland seemed to have changed. In the past month, he had felt a growing apprehension the closer he got to the land of the *ceiba*. Now, having crossed over the mountain passages and the first marshes into the actual jungle, it was more than a feeling—it was a presence. Something here was different. It seemed the sky was different; it seemed shadows had taken greater countenance. Now Topiltzin stood before a torrential river he was certain had not existed the last time he had come, and for some reason, this river possessed malevolence. Staring at it, he could picture fiery waters cutting into the earth, uprooting trees, tearing away undergrowth, ripping through the limestone bedrock as though the Creators themselves had cut it with a sword edge. The river ran quick and dirty; its path was a scar through the jungle. *This was the beginning*, he thought. He stared across to the other side. The witch's face of darkness—whatever it turned out to be— waited there, just beyond. Topiltzin felt almost as though he were looking into its eyes.

Behind Topiltzin, coming single-file through a jungle path toward him, were the other ballplayers, including the three young goaltenders recruited by Mud Puppy. Behind them were six baggage carriers laden with equipment, and a squadron of mercenaries Topiltzin had hired six days earlier.

The southern lowland was divided from the north by a narrow

mountain passage that rose between thick coastal swamps. The ballplayers of Tollán came this far south each season, because in the land of the *ceiba* the ballgame had begun, and here it was still played with a reverence and intensity that bordered on religious fervor. In the Petén, ballplayers died to win the game, and women wagered their children on the outcome.

Rattle Eagle was the first to reach Topiltzin. He drew up beside him, sweating from jungle heat, and stared stupidly down at the torrential waters, narrowing his brow. The river cut directly through the jungle path they had been following, severing it.

"You are not lost, are you?" Rattle Eagle asked. He looked up when Topiltzin didn't answer. "Gods, Topiltzin, you are not lost!"

"Call Tarantula," Topiltzin said.

Tarantula was a Toltec captain, once a Dragon Knight. Topiltzin had hired the dark-eyed captain and his squadron of mercenaries six nights ago, after a particularly terrifying dream that daylight could not wash away. Tarantula and his men had been wandering the Northland between wars. There were many such men, hungry, lean, scarred from battle. Since the Dragon had abandoned command of the military, whole armies had dissolved into roving groups of mercenaries, hiring out to the highest bidder—sometimes even turning on their own merchants for plunder. Tarantula was a man Topiltzin knew by name and reputation for his cold blood.

Rattle Eagle turned and bellowed out in his thunder voice, "Hail! Tarantula! Up here!"

Soon Tarantula appeared from the jungle, moving swiftly past the others. Topiltzin noticed his sword was drawn.

Mud Puppy Soldier drew up beside Topiltzin with a questioning glace. Mud Puppy had been withdrawn for the whole trip. It had apparently pained him to leave his woman, fat with child. Topiltzin wondered also if Mud Puppy shared any of the dreams or premonitions that had haunted him the past weeks. But the rubberball game would not wait for dreams or even childbirth, and Mud Puppy had too long been a ballplayer to stay behind. Now Mud Puppy stared at the river in amazement. He knew this part of the jungle almost as well as Topiltzin; they had traveled it together many times.

Tarantula was a grizzled veteran with an ugly scar disfiguring his lip and lower chin. He paused next to Topiltzin and gazed down at the waters calmly. He had stone-gray eyes and a bald, hard, almost pointed head. He was simply too ugly to have been anything other than a warrior. In his right ear was inserted a jewel ornament, a tube of white obsidian, in the manner of the Chichimeca. He wore a battle-scarred peccary-skin tunic and bronze, chain-net body armor. A thick-bladed moonsteel knife was strapped to his back in a sheath of rattlesnake skin. A bundle of atlatl-darts was lashed to his left thigh. Over one shoulder hung a hardwood buckler with a painted deerskin covering.

"This river, what is its name?" Topiltzin asked.

"This river has no name, my lord. This river was not here a week ago. It did not exist."

"How can that be? You have fought in these jungles many years—do rivers often spring up out of nowhere?"

Tarantula stepped a little closer to the edge. "Not this size of a river," Tarantula said. "Not that I have ever seen. I would say this is sorcery."

Rattle Eagle gasped, but Mud Puppy half chuckled. "Sorcery! Sorcerers make rivers?" said Mud Puppy.

"Here, in the jungles, they do a lot of things."

"How do we cross it?" Topiltzin asked.

"I will have my men fashion a bridge of *liana* vines and wood. That should take no more than a few degrees turn of the sun. However, if I may say so, my lord, I would guess there is a reason for the river."

Rattle Eagle's eyes widened.

Again Mud Puppy snorted. "A reason? And what would that be?"

Tarantula gave Mud Puppy a cold glance. "Someone does not wish us to cross."

"For gods' sakes, who would not want us to cross?" Mud Puppy demanded. "There are only villages beyond, nothing of worth. If you ask me, good captain, this is nothing more than runoff of melting snow. There is no need to involve sorcerers in this."

"It does not snow here."

"Then it has been raining. Excessively."

Tarantula nodded. His eyes were calm. He was the type of man whose expression would change little, even with his throat opened. "Whatever you wish." He thrust a square-jointed finger north. "I and four of the others will venture into that thicket of trees for material. I will leave two warriors with you." He departed.

"Captain," Topiltzin said.

Tarantula paused, turned.

"You are not, perhaps, a little ill at ease."

"No, my lord, I am not ill at ease. I am home." He studied the trees beyond the gorge. "Less than a year ago, I fought no more than a stone's throw east. They came out of these jungles like vermin, their heads were shaved, their bodies painted, they were naked. They bore crude weapons of stone and fish bone arrows. We slew so many we could not walk over the bodies; they were piled that high. The stench was intolerable. If I were not a sensible man, I might even think I smell it now. But I have no ill ease. This is the jungle. Perhaps you mistake caution for apprehension. I will gather the material for the bridge, my lord. And if, by chance, there is trouble, sound the conch shell." He bowed and turned, motioning four of his men, walking into the thicket.

"You ask me," Mud Puppy said to Topiltzin, "he is as likely to cut our throats as anything we might find in the jungle. We should have kept to the coast, inland past the delta."

"Tikal lies directly south and west," Topiltzin said. "I do not intend to waste my days swatting mosquitoes and avoiding caimans in the coastal swamps. Besides, Mud Puppy, we are not here to fight. We are ballplayers!"

"So then," Rattle Eagle said, troubled, "you trust this Tarantula?"

"If I did, he wouldn't be worth his pay."

TOLTECA

Rattle Eagle looked about. He was chewing on a wedge of sugar cane he had cut from a patch growing to the side of the road. "Where is that little scurrile bastard Coyotl? Have we lost him?"

"He left some time ago," Mud Puppy answered. "He said he would catch up with us later. He was muttering something about mushroom plants."

"Mushrooms again," Rattle Eagle grumbled. "Fed them to me last time, made me stupid, made me nearly lose my normal mind."

Topiltzin walked along the edge studying the ravine. Below the top soil, the waters seemed to have cut straight through the white rock, almost as though it was an incision. Its waters were rushing madly, brown as chocolate broth.

Strangely, Topiltzin lost his apprehension. Something waited, something breathed on the other side of that river. So be it. Anything was better than remaining in Tollán. The past year he had gone nearly mad in the city, weighted with its magistrates. With Sky Dragon gone, the people implored Topiltzin to make decisions. He was asked to lay his seal upon endless papers and counts of beans, of stone, of wood, of gold, surveys of people, formulations of law. He needed this. He welcomed fear.

"Mud Puppy," Topiltzin said, and the ballplayer drew near. "Have this cook of yours prepare us some food; we should have lunch."

Mud Puppy studied Topiltzin a moment, curious. "Are you all right, Blue Prince?"

"Why? I look ill?"

"No, you look . . . content."

"I am hungry. So is Rattle Eagle. Is this not so, Rattle Eagle?"

"I could eat," the big man said, biting off another chunk of the cane.

Mud Puppy nodded, a bit puzzled, and walked back toward the baggage carriers.

Rattle Eagle slowly edged closer to Topiltzin. He motioned to the river. "You . . ." He paused, a little uncertain. "You agree with Mud Puppy, then? About the rainwater? That this is not the work

173

of sorcerers?"

"No," Topiltzin said.

Rattle Eagle nodded. He took a deep breath and slowly released it. "Ah."

Having crossed the ravine on a wobbly bridge laid down by Tarantula's men, they were soon following an old road that was once a prime trade route to Tikal. It was somewhat overgrown with bush; the jungle was rapidly reclaiming its own. Tarantula and his men had gone ahead of them, clearing a pathway with their broadswords.

At one point Topiltzin paused, curious. Branching off the main road was a well-worn path that curled into the jungle. Shadows were dark and the undergrowth seemed almost to be alive, to shift, whisper. Topiltzin stood transfixed. The others had paused behind him. Tarantula and his mercenaries were ahead, cutting frond. Looking back, seeing Topiltzin, Tarantula motioned his men to pause.

"I do not like this look in your eye, Topiltzin," Mud Puppy said, drawing close and glancing down the pathway. Dusk was drawing deep shadows already, and the pathway looked almost like a cavern into the thicket. "Topiltzin?"

Topiltzin crouched, peering deeper. Tarantula had started back toward them. The baggage carriers waited. Rattle Eagle, to the side of Mud Puppy, watched Topiltzin with a worried look.

"Something is in there," Topiltzin said.

"Of course," Mud Puppy pressed, "this is godless jungle! It is full of *things*!"

"Yes . . . but this has been waiting—for me."

"What! Blue Prince, listen to reason. If we do not keep moving, we will not reach the clearing of which Tarantula spoke. You *do* want to get out of this jungle before nightfall?"

Tarantula reached them, glanced down the pathway. "Is anything wrong?" he asked.

TOLTECA

"We are going in there," Topiltzin said, standing.

Mud Puppy swore between his teeth. Rattle Eagle gasped and glanced to the pathway as though it were the mouth of a beast.

Tarantula gazed down it with a puzzled look. "Why?" the mercenary asked.

"Something . . . draws me."

"The jungles here are often dangerous, my lord. This pathway is leading west and south, deeper into the Petén. There are swamps beyond, more wide rivers, I—"

"Bring your men, Captain. We are going in."

Topiltzin did not wait for further response. He shifted his buckler back on his shoulder and started into the jungle, one hand set upon the hilt of his sword where it was thrust between the leather ties of his belt.

"What of the rest of us?" Mud Puppy shrieked.

"Do whatever you please." Topiltzin started to run. "Captain!" he shouted. "Double pace! There is little time!"

In a moment, Topiltzin was out of sight.

Tarantula circled his sword, shouting in a harsh, worn voice, and the mercenaries swept past Mud Puppy, moving down the pathway at a calm jog after Topiltzin.

"Gods," Mud Puppy hissed. He glanced at the baggage carriers, then to Rattle Eagle, who had not moved and still regarded the narrow pathway like one might regard an opening to the underworld.

"Mother of frogs," the big man muttered, worried.

Mud Puppy paced a moment, then turned and grabbed his sword and shield from the side of his pack carried by a servant. He strapped the shield over his shoulder.

"What are you doing?" Rattle Eagle asked.

"I am going in."

"You are following them!"

"Not without regret." He lifted an atlatl and a bundle of throwing spears and turned to the three young goalkeepers. They were huddled together, looking a little puzzled, but lacking the experience to be afraid. "You three goaltenders, you move on, and you baggage carriers also—keep on according to the map until you reach the ridge of the Tikal hillocks, free of the jungle. Set camp."

The eldest youth nodded somberly, and immediately embarked. The others fell in line behind him.

Mud Puppy looked to Rattle Eagle, then upward, scanning the horizon. It was almost dark. Seeing the sun being swallowed by jungle, bleeding as though wounded, he began to wish he had stayed in Tollán. His wife, Seven Flower, had wept when he left. It was not that she meant to discourage him, for often in one summer's journey Mud Puppy would return with enough jewels and mantles to satisfy their needs for the entire year. Still, she had wept, laying a hand over her swollen belly. Now Mud Puppy quietly wished he had stayed behind. He could be lying near his wife, cool in their lower dwelling of painted cement walls. Instead, he was with madmen. One lunatic, Coyotl, had vanished in a quest of what he called "*Teo-nanácatl*, tiny mushrooms that grow here," and the other lunatic, Topiltzin, had grown more and more unpredictable the farther they got from the Northland.

He noticed Rattle Eagle watching, concerned. The big man was so often like a child.

"What about me?" Rattle Eagle asked, as though he feared the answer.

"You should follow, go with the goaltenders—but then we might lose Coyotl altogether. Someone needs to wait for him."

"You are saying you want me to wait here—for Coyotl?"

Though Rattle Eagle's look was deeply troubled, Mud Puppy nonetheless nodded, and without looking back, plunged into the thicket, feeling a little like the jungle was swallowing him.

Rattle Eagle watched Mud Puppy vanish with dismay. He started to take another bite of the cane, but only stared at it numbly. Things had gone terribly wrong. Crossing the river, he had felt his skin crawl, for it was a river made by sorcerers, and the bridge was narrow—the ropes and lashings threatened to burst. Now the jungle was waiting just to eat him. In the past, when they had journeyed to the southern lowlands to play the rubberball game, it had always been a time of celebration, of drinking the *pulque* and laughing as the night fires of the camp burned low. It had never been like this, sorcerers' rivers and dark trails that promised misery. He hated the thick of the jungle, and worse, it was fast getting dark. He had been left to wait, alone, in godless bush, all because Coyotl wanted mushrooms.

"Where are you, you little frog?" Rattle Eagle grumbled.

Coyotl ran through the thicket. Occasionally a frond, a branch, slapped him. Already the sky, the smell of the air, the earth against his feet—already they had undertaken a warm glow. He had eaten the mushrooms less than a degree of the sun before and already he was feeling his skin tighten. These were potent! He had a bundle of them wrapped in a banana leaf and stuffed into his belt pouch. Coyotl planned to mash them up and put them into the tortillas tonight at camp. That way, they would all be ugly drunk by moon-fall, and the night would be grand. Mushrooms that grew in the jungles of the *ceiba* were the sweetest, the quickest to seize hold of flesh and mind. Coyotl had eaten only a tiny bit, and his skin all over was tingly. He ran at an easy pace, reasoning he would catch them well before sundown.

He knew this jungle as well as he knew the streets of Tollán. He had fought here when he was younger, and many times he had traveled the trade routes as a vanguard mercenary. Thus, when Coyotl, in the shadows of dusk, dropped headlong into a fast-moving river, whose waters raged like a torrent released of Heaven, he was taken wholly by surprise. There had never been a ravine here before, he was certain, and he could not believe what had happened until he was sucked under muddied currents, half dazed by a blow to his head. He struggled to keep to the surface, but the undertow was powerful, and he might have drowned but for a passing chunk of deadwood to which he clung. When he realized a waterfall was the sound in his ears, roaring, and that just ahead the torrents seemed to drop off the very edge of the earth, he frantically tried to swim for the side, but the current was too swift. He gulped a breath and hoped he falls were not nearly as deep or as fierce as they sounded. He felt the hard rock bed of the gorge brush against his back as he surmounted.

When Topiltzin broke through, into the clearing, he half paused. There was a small settlement here; several thatch huts had been built about the edge of a wide river that pushed through the jungle so slowly movement was barely discernible. One of the huts was ablaze, fire greedily lapping up its side, curling over the top where thatch billowed in thick gray smoke. Several of the villagers lay scattered on the red dirt, dead—more than dead, dismembered. Here lay an arm, or a thorax missing all parts. Even the hardened Tarantula drew up, startled. A wooden fence of peccary piglets had been broken open and the little beasts were rooting about for food—finding it plentiful. One was dragging entrails through the dirt as another gave chase. These were fresh kills. Whatever had happened had just taken place. One of the villagers, an old, leathery man whose legs had been hewn off at the hips, was crawling toward the river, leaving a swath of blood in an unsteady trail.

It was this Topiltzin had felt. Almost as if the village had cried out to him. As he had drawn closer, it was as though he felt the dying. There were times such feelings had struck him in the past. Once, when he was playing the rubberball game in a city of the coast, he had rushed to the edge of a river without knowing why. Something, some force, had simply pulled him there. He stood on the rocky bank, staring, numbed. He had arrived moments too late to save a small child who did not even scream as a caiman took it in its mouth. A family of coastal natives had been gathering mollusks, and the great lizard must have come so fast, so silent, it was only noticed by the splash when it returned to the water. The father had screamed, breaking into a run, pulling a flint knife from his belt, diving after the beast. Topiltzin stood watching, feeling helpless. The native had reached the caiman and man and beast churned the waters in struggle. Blood seeped outward like a stain. The caiman bobbed, floating on its back, the gut slashed open to the neck. The father, weeping, carried the limp, bloodied form of his small son back to the beach. They hadn't even noticed Topiltzin, and they left, whimpering.

Topiltzin had fallen to his knees on the sand, stricken at the smell of death left upon him, stricken he had felt it so strong, and he wondered what force had pulled him there too late to help.

It was a similar feeling that struck him now, that left a sickening knot in his stomach.

A woman screamed to the side of him and Topiltzin spun, tensed, sword drawn. She was virtually dead. Her stomach had been opened in a wide, razor slice, and the vitals spilled between her fingers despite her efforts to contain them. She inched toward him on her knees, muttering the same thing repeatedly. It took him a moment to catch the tongue; it was ancient Mayan, Mulekite, spoken only in the jungles.

"My babies. My babies. My babies." She was pointing toward the river. Then it struck him. Mayan villages always teamed with children—happy, naked children. Yet there were no bodies of children; the slain were all adults.

Topiltzin shivered and searched the jungle. The thicket was pocketed in shadow. It was close to dark, and he felt the urge to somehow command the sun to linger.

Tarantula, beside him, winced at the woman.

"They have taken the children." Topiltzin gazed over the wide, slow river. "We are going after them. Kill that woman, for God's pity, and follow me." Topiltzin strode forward, and broke into a run.

Tarantula motioned and one of his warriors lifted an atlatl from his back and with a flick of his wrist planted a hardened, moonsteel dart through the woman's sternum with a hollowed *thud*. She jerked, mouth agape, and dropped forward. The warrior kicked her over, freed his dart, then he reloaded it, now bloodied, into the trough of his spear-thrower.

The river was slow and shallow when Topiltzin waded through. At the deepest point, it came no farther than his waist. On the other side he paused, realizing the killers might not be so easy to follow. He waited for Tarantula to reach his side. Tarantula searched and pointed his sword. A narrow path had been cut into the now darkened forest. Topiltzin started forward, but Tarantula gripped his arm.

"In order that you know, that you are aware, my lord, if we go in there . . . it is unlikely we will return alive. This is *their* land now. *Their* jungle."

"No, Tarantula, it is God's. I intend to go in, and I intend to return. We are Tolteca! They are but carrion. We attack, full run."

The other mercenaries gathered at the riverside. Tarantula looked into the jungle, tightened his jaw, and motioned with his sword. He broke into a hard, powerful run, and Topiltzin fell in beside him. The others came behind, weapons drawn. Three of them, at Topiltzin and Tarantula's flanks, ran with thrusting spears angled forward, readied for the kill, anchored in notches of their belts. Tarantula ran with his sword arm crossed against his chest, the blade of his sword pressed near his cheek. Branches and fronds of the jungle whipped at them as they ran.

The sun was being swallowed and darkness was closing. Ahead—how far he could not be certain—Topiltzin could hear cries, screams. This time, he would not be too late.

Mud Puppy stumbled past the bodies, through the smoke of the village, somewhat numbed. He had almost caught up with Topiltzin, but now lagged. Nowhere in his expectations had he considered he would be walking into a war zone of the Petén. Mud Puppy had never been trained as a soldier. He had been trained in the Calmecac as an artist, a poet—as a singer in the festivals; and, on his own, he had trained as a ballplayer. Even though his given name was Mud Puppy Solider, he had never known combat. But he urged himself courage and continued, ignoring the sting of fear coursing his veins, because Mud Puppy would follow the Blue Prince anywhere, even into death, which he had little doubt was precisely his direction. Coyotl had once told him there came certain moments when you stepped forward, when you died, when your blood spilled and your spirit ascended. For each man, stars marked such a moment by their movement in the Heavens. It was something already written, already spoken. There comes a time to die.

Mud Puppy struggled out of the filth-ridden banks of the river, plunging into the jungle darkness. First he stumbled, but soon broke into a hard, breathless run, sweat stinging his eyes. He thought, for a moment, that ahead he could hear the cries of children. They came like birds calling, like an ordinary thing, as though there might have been merely dancing, celebration.

Rattle Eagle stood immobile. He almost dared not move. Of all things, of all places, Rattle Eagle hated most the jungle. It crawled with serpents, it whispered with insect voices. He breathed in steady, controlled breaths, searching slowly the gathering gloom. His eyes seemed to say to him, look, scurrying things, and over there!—a serpent as large as a man's waist, coiling, no!—there, over there, the green, slit eyes of a leopard. The skin of his side flinched; something was crawling up it. He bristled, glancing, then screamed and slapped his hand, smashing something with a soft *crunch*. It left a black-red blotch, a few remaining hairy legs.

"Godless, bloodsucking bug."

How could things have gone so wrong! They had been singing as they marched over the mountain road. They were cheered when they passed through the town of Colhuacan. Children had run out, showering them with flowers, running alongside with idiot grins. The season of the rubberball game had begun as it always had. It was one of the few times when Rattle Eagle was well fed and not lacking for coin. It was one of his favorite seasons.

This jungle was not only humid, thick in moss and insect vermin, but he had the ill feeling that the sky—not from clouds or haze—but just the sky itself had somehow grown darker. It was as though the farther they went into the Southland, the deeper they descended into the earth, as if they were passing into the bowels of the underworld.

Now night was closing.

When Rattle Eagle heard movement coming through the bush toward him, his mouth half opened to cry out, but then he tightened his jaw, narrowed his gaze, and spat to the side. He slowly drew his heavy moonsteel sword and took a warm grip of the leather-wrapped hilt. Rattle Eagle's sword had been fashioned especially for him by his father, who was a guildsman of the sacred moon-metal mined by the Tolteca from the far north. The sword was well weighted, thicker than most swords, hardened, double-edged with one edge serrated for ripping. It had a kind of personal feel to it, and now it drank his fear and fed him stone courage.

The sounds were closer—voices, not animals. Animals did not laugh and speak. These were men coming toward him; and here, in this jungle, in these days marked of a bloodstained moon, they were most likely not going to be friendly. But Rattle Eagle preferred men. Animals of the jungle he did not wish to entertain. But men—men he could slay. Rattle Eagle slipped his arm through the straps of his buckler and lifted it from his shoulder. He stepped back, easing himself slowly into the bush, between huge, damp fronds, and waited. They were coming from the south, along the pathway.

He saw them, perhaps twenty. They were warriors, mostly naked except for some body armor of leather and copper, some helmets. Weapons bristled, mostly spears with dark, obsidian tips. When he noticed the head of one of Mud Puppy's baggage carriers bobbing along on the tip of one of these spears, he felt a cold stab of pity for the three young fools who had come to play the rubberball game with the Prince of Tollán—for certainly they were all cold dead and drained of blood. Rattle Eagle felt his sword arm tingle, ready, felt his hips ease a bit lower, into a crouch. Slaying time was near.

Topiltzin could see the glimmer of fires ahead, burning through the red blood of a dying sun, leaving the jungle in eerie flicker. There were drums beating, keeping pace, all about. Just beyond, a clearing had been hewn into the jungle; the trees, the undergrowth—all had been burned.

Topiltzin sickened, for the screams were those of children, even of infants. They seemed to call to him, as though they knew he was coming, as though they could feel the Prince of Tollán near. He ran faster, dizzy with rage. He broke away from the other warriors. Only Tarantula managed to keep at his side.

Topiltzin curled both hands about the hilt of his sword. Tarantula growled, his teeth clenched, his eyes fired.

When the clearing fell into view, the flood of vision that fell upon Topiltzin's eyes seemed enough to blind him. Images of it, flashes of it, he would remember the rest of his life.

A squat temple had been erected of mud and dried adobe, painted red. Bodies were littered about its square, fat base; and atop it, a face seemed to hover above an altar. The altar was a slab of stone, and on it a small body squirmed, back bent, arms flailing, but in death spasm, for the priest lifted a small heart as though it were a tomato, and bit into it, letting the blood spill across his chin and neck. The small body was then rolled off the altar stone. It bounced over the steps of the temple platform. Topiltzin realized he was screaming, that in rage and fury tears were suddenly stinging his eyes. The bodies about the base of the temple, littering it, were small bodies—children, scores of them.

Warriors were everywhere, the entire clearing literally crawled with soldiers, and though Topiltzin tried with all his strength to reach the temple platform, where yet another victim was being lifted by arm and leg, though he began to slay, soon he and Tarantula's Toltec warriors were surrounded. The Tolteca were deadlocked in struggle, outnumbered five to one.

Topiltzin used his sword in heavy, furious strokes, slashing, thrusting, ripping. Beside him, Tarantula tried to guard the prince's flank, screaming. The captain's sword moved like the flicker tongue of a serpent.

"My prince!" Tarantula screamed when Topiltzin separated from them, wading into the warriors of the clearing. "Topiltzin! Wait!"

Topiltzin fought blindly, driving toward the temple, cleaving his path with powerful strokes of his moonsteel blade. He had no idea how many there were. They were Chichimeca, hard, lean, hair shorn, bodies painted in stripes. They wore little body armor, and fought mostly with thrusting spears and maces. To his right, from the corner of his eye, he saw one of Tarantula's men go down. The mercenary had been caught in the side by a thrusting spear that broke through the skin of his back, and when he screamed, dropping his buckler, he was jerked forward, and they fell on him like wolves on a carcass.

Rattle Eagle waited, careful, hidden—silent. He could have been a stone carving resting there in the forest, aged and stained with rust. They came laughing, speaking a scurrile tongue that Rattle Eagle had never heard before. He noticed one of them, a young warrior, wearing a breechclout of leopard skin. The warrior's head was shorn but for a streak of plumed hair down the center. He wore chest and abdomen armor of leather plates. On one arm, he had fashioned a human jawbone, still bloodied, that had been cleaned of skin and muscle and set in place as though it were an armband. Over his back a square, feather-tasseled shield was hung, and from his belt dangled two fresh scalps. One of the scalps was of light orange-red hair. It was the hair of one of the goaltenders, the one who had been so excited the morning they left Tollán that he had danced, clapped, sang to himself. Rattle Eagle also recognized their baggage, their ball gear, wrapped in deerskin, now mounted on the back of a large, ignorant-looking barbarian, who wore a loincloth without a breech cover as though it were a diaper for an infant. This one, this large bastard, lifted his head back, laughing, and Rattle Eagle winced, noticing that all his teeth had been filed to resemble the pointed fangs of a caiman. The big warrior carried in one hand a stone mace with copper-sheathed spikes. Most of them carried spears—one or two had longbows strapped over their backs, and Rattle Eagle noticed at least one Toltec sword.

They were coming close now. Two of them, younger ones, were spinning about, high stepping, dancing and singing in their vulgar tongue, with laughing faces. Rattle Eagle realized the red about their mouths and chin was blood; they had been drinking blood. This was some foul manner of feast.

"So be it," Rattle Eagle whispered into his beard.

The heathens were near, close to the pathway Topiltzin had taken, and Rattle Eagle let rage fill him. He just let it spill into his blood.

He stepped directly in front of them, and those to the front halted, stunned at the suddenness of Rattle Eagle's appearance. Rattle Eagle grinned.

"Good morrow, you preying, scurrile-tongued, shit-eating bastards. Prepare now to meet your master, the Filth-Eater of Hell!" he screamed, muscles flexing, and leapt forward.

Before a breath was taken, he had slain three. The first he slew with the serrated edge of his sword, opening the chest like splitting a crab shell. The second, he cleanly and simply beheaded with a deft stroke, the chin snapping with a pop that sent the head spinning. The third he thrust through, so deeply he had to set his boot against the man's chest to retract his blade.

One of them screamed and ran, a base coward. Fear struck all of them, but the others still attacked. For a breathless moment, Rattle Eagle found himself moving very quickly, deflecting the angled thrusts of fine, sharpened copper-sheathed spears, but the pathway here was narrow, and they could not outflank him. Rattle Eagle continued to slay, letting them in close enough for ripe killing. He grabbed a wrist, jerking the body into his blade like skewering a fish. He lifted the man by the front of his leather armor and heaved him, sprawling, into his comrades.

Then they all started to flee, scattering madly to either direction, even leaping into the trees, screaming. It was a moment before Rattle Eagle understood why: Coyotl was coming at them from the opposite direction, coming low and swift, circling like the wind, slicing flesh in hissing strikes of his razor-sharp sword, spinning past all attempts to stab him with spears. When they ran, Coyotl leaped up. The little ballplayer was nearly naked, and his body was pounded in bruises and cuts, but he screamed and ran after two of them, like a man possessed.

Rattle Eagle found himself once more standing in the jungle alone. Coyotl was insane. He had always been a little insane, but since he had obtained his demon eye, he had become dangerously insane.

Rattle Eagle walked over and lifted the shoulder pack filled with their equipment: the shin guards, the elbow guards, the rubberball. Their only motive for coming to this godforsaken jungle was to play the rubberball game! It would be very disappointing to Rattle Eagle if all they were going to do was fight parasitic barbarians. He pulled his buckler over his back, shouldered the equipment, turned, and started down the path Topiltzin and the others had taken. He heard screams from the jungle behind him, and guessed it was Coyotl taking his mark. Not long after, Coyotl stepped out of the trees before him, smiling, his sword sheathed.

"Killed a few shit-eaters, did we not!" Coyotl said, breathless.

Rattle Eagle glanced down, noticing that in Coyotl's belt were looped two scalps, still dripping blood.

"Why those?" he muttered.

"They took scalps! Thus, so did I. Where are the others? Why are you alone?"

"I do not know where they are. They left me to wait for you. The baggage carriers and the youths—the three goalkeepers—they are slain."

"I gathered as much when I found their bodies back there in the roadway. It looked to have been swift slaughter. I must admit, my big friend, I was pleased not to have seen your face among them looking upon the Heavens with dull eyes."

Rattle Eagle grunted and continued on, trudging forward.

Coyotl fell in beside him. "Do you not wonder, yourself, what had become of me? And where I have been?"

Rattle Eagle glanced aside. Coyotl looked to have been dropped off the edge of a mountain. When first he had seen Coyotl, he was naked but for a loin wrap. Now he had clothing taken from his victims. He had on a foul leather corselet of barbarian body armor, and had looped a tasseled deerskin breechclout through his belt.

"It was frightening," Coyotl said, strapping on sandals, hopping first on one foot, then another, keeping up with Rattle Eagle. "Sometime I will tell you of it." He fished into a pouch of his belt and pulled something out, held it up. Rattle Eagle stopped to look; he squinted. At first, he thought they were two eggs—round, white, bloodied, in a transparent fish-tissue pouch.

"Alligator eyes," Coyotl said. "Magic!"

꩜꩜꩜꩜꩜꩜꩜꩜꩜꩜꩜꩜꩜

Topiltzin took a wound to the shoulder. A jagged club with razor-sharp fish bones embedded in the wood sliced a ripping gash through his skin, but he did not feel it, and the attacker before him grunted when Topiltzin's sword slammed almost to the hilt through his ribs. At the same time, he rammed the front spikes of his buckler into another warrior's face. Above the screams of killing all about him, he could still hear the cry of another child, this one old enough to be screaming her mother's name.

"Nooo!" Topiltzin shouted. "Lord God, give me strength!" But the child's scream was abruptly cut off. Topiltzin's vision was blurred in tears. His sword slammed into a wooden shield and lodged there. He tried to rip it loose, but it was jammed. Within a moment he fell back, twisted, and he would have been slain had not Tarantula thrown himself forward to deflect a spiked mace blow with his shield. To Topiltzin's right, another of Tarantula's men dropped, slamming into the ground, a stone axe having shattered his skull.

Topiltzin ripped his long knife from its sheath where it was tied to his calf, threw his buckler aside, and seized the fallen sword of the Toltec. He leapt forward, the sword in one hand, the long knife in another. He sliced open a face in a quick slash. He again separated from the others.

"No, Topiltzin!" Tarantula screamed. "Keep to my flank!"

But Topiltzin no longer cared. If God meant him to die, then such was about to be ordained, for he could not stand to hear another child's scream. He drove into a warrior, lifting the body on the tip of his sword and casting it to the side. He slashed the knife across a neck, tearing through the windpipe. He drove steadily forward now, toward the temple. He lost the knife, jammed in the chest bone of a warrior, and gripped the hilt of the moonsteel Tolteca sword in both hands, slashing in heavy blows. A razor-tipped spear ripped across his side, shearing away a chunk of his leather armor.

Topiltzin reached the steps of the small temple and leapt forward, taking the thin, narrow stairs two, three at a time.

Tarantula and four remaining Toltec warriors reached the bottom of the temple and turned sharply. Using the temple base to guard their backs, they locked shields in a frontal defense. The remaining savages literally threw themselves forward in frenzy. Tarantula screamed when a spear shaft sunk into his side, tearing through his plated leather armor, but he didn't fall; he continued fighting, leaving the small thrusting spear lodged in his side.

The priest saw Topiltzin coming. He looked up, his face bloodied, his eyes flamed, and he roared at Topiltzin, not a human voice, not a man, but the snarl of a leopard. His teeth looked fanged, and they dripped blood. The sorcerer looked down at the girl he held pinned to the stone with one hand. Her legs were kicking, her arms flailing, small nails swiping at the bloodied skin of the priest's arm. The priest raised his white obsidian blade of rippled stone. Topiltzin hurtled forward, clearing the last of the steps, leaping, almost in flight, high, spinning, as he did when he played the rubberball game, a scream tight between his teeth. He cleared the altar stone and struck the dark-skinned priest hard in the face with a round kick. He heard the jaw crack, teeth shatter. The priest's head was knocked to the side, his gnarled hair flung back, and with a grunt, he went over the back edge of the temple.

The girl dropped off the stone and crouched. The sacrificial knife clattered across the top stone of the temple tower. Topiltzin leapt over the edge in pursuit of the priest.

Tarantula and the others held off the last of the dark warriors. The Tolteca were hard pressed, wounded, all of them, blood spilling through them. A knife sheared open Tarantula's cheek to the bone, to his teeth. He fought on, screaming through his own blood, his arms weakening from wielding the sword. He had lost his shield and fought openly, slashing. Then, from the trees, falling upon the dark warrior's rear flanks, Mud Puppy Soldier came at full run.

▦▦▦▦▦▦▦▦▦▦▦▦▦▦▦▦

When Mud Puppy reached the sacrificial clearing, he was without breath, numbed in fear. Then, just as Coyotl had described, it no longer seemed to matter. There were bodies strewn in a path leading to the two-story temple tower that had been crudely erected there in the woods, and it seemed Topiltzin and the mercenaries of Tarantula had hewn their way through a forest of warriors, felling them to either side.

Tarantula and three of his men were still alive, fighting furiously, but he could not see Topiltzin.

Mud Puppy may not have ever faced battle, but he was a good hunter of waterfowl, and as he ran toward the mercenaries he lifted his atlatl from his back, setting a fire-hardened mesquite dart into its trough. He told himself this would be no different from hunting with his father on the lakes of Tollán. He dropped from a full run to a crouch, knees sliding in bloodied dirt, and brought the spear-thrower over his head in a circular motion. It hissed and clicked as he released the trigger and let the dart fly. The atlatl dropped one of the painted warriors from behind, burying into the flesh of his back. Mud Puppy reloaded the thrower, locked it, took aim, and killed another. One of them noticed him then, a hard, fierce-looking savage with black stripes painted over his body and face. The warrior turned, screaming, and rushed Mud Puppy, throwing a copper-sheathed axe. Mud Puppy ducked the heavy whisper of the axe, spun the atlatl hard and put a shaft dead center into the warrior's chest, buried up to its dark feathers. The man's feet slipped out from under him and he went over on his back.

゠゠゠゠゠゠゠゠゠゠゠゠゠゠゠゠゠゠

When Rattle Eagle and Coyotl reached the slaughtered village, they first slowed, then stopped. Rattle Eagle winced, horrified. The sky was dark now, although the clearing was still well lit by burning reed and thatch huts.

Coyotl stared at the dismembered body of one of the villagers. "You see this?"

"Yes . . . I can see."

"Blood Gatherers," Coyotl said.

Rattle Eagle narrowed his gaze. "What do you mean?"

"This is the work of sacrificial priests. Blood Gatherers. Sorcerers who go before the coming of an army to gather strength from the blood of innocents. These are Shadow Walkers, Rattle Eagle."

"What . . . are Shadow Walkers?"

Coyotl swallowed. "Prophecy," he said.

Rattle Eagle stared at the dismembered body pieces. He almost asked Coyotl what he meant by prophecy, but he did not really want to know, so he didn't ask.

Topiltzin sprinted after the fleeing priest. The man was powerfull he ran like a leopard, swift through the trees, dodging, shifting. He was quick, but the Rubberball Player was pursuing him. When the priest realized he was about to be overtaken, he spun about, lifting a sword. It was a heavy Tolteca sword, the moonsteel darkened. The priest took stance and gritted his teeth, snarling, again the voice of a cat, nothing human in it. His eyes seemed to be lit against the shadows. He seemed to actually swell in size as Topiltzin closed.

Topiltzin slammed his sword into the wizard's with a ringing clank, ripping past him and spinning about. He was met by amazing strength. The priest attacked, his blade coming in swift, deadly arcs and for a moment Topiltzin was backtreading, blocking blow after blow. One met the tang of Topiltzin's sword, cracking its center, and Topiltzin was left with only a hilt. The Blue Prince dropped low, as he did to catch the rubberball, and the priest's blade hissed over his shoulder, whipping at the leather tassels of Topiltzin's shredded armor.

Topiltzin shot forward, into the wizard's legs, lifting, heaving the man into the air. Incredibly, the priest did a nimble somersault and landed squarely on his feet, then without hesitation whirled, his blade hissing. Topiltzin leapt back, but the blade sliced neatly through his leather breastplate, deep enough to leave a thin jet of blood. The next blow came so near Topiltzin's neck he could feel the kiss against his skin. Topiltzin slammed into the trunk of a tree, off balance. It took all his power to spin away, every muscle in him firing at once. The death thrust of the sorcerer's blade took a sliver of Topiltzin's skin from the shoulder and lodged into the tree too deeply for the priest to withdraw it quickly.

Topiltzin took his moment. Dropping his hips low, he drove his elbow solidly into the priest's face. Any normal man would have fallen. Nevertheless, the sorcerer snarled his cat hiss and seized Topiltzin by his breastplate.

Topiltzin was unable to believe he had been thrown. He struck the limb of a tree so hard it snapped with a *crack*, and Topiltzin hit the ground, his air sucked away.

The priest turned, took hold of the hilt of the sword and wrenched it free, flinging chips of fresh wood. His head swiveled like a serpent's on his neck and the arm came up, over, and flung the heavy sword as though it were merely a dagger, whipping it from the wrist. Topiltzin, half numbed, forced himself to tuck and roll, shielding his face with his arm. The blade slammed into the earth very near his face. He took hold of the hilt and ripped it out, then vaulted to his feet.

The wizard was directly before him, as though he had materialized, and before Topiltzin could lift the sword, the priest slammed a back-fisted blow across Topiltzin's jaw. The Blue Prince almost lost consciousness, but in reflex, even as he staggered, he brought the sword in an overhand arc. The blade slammed through the priest's shoulder. The wizard's arm fell to the side, dropping onto the ground like a chunk of meat.

The sorcerer moaned, stepping away, and Topiltzin closed for the kill, but was met by a kick in the gut, so well placed it staggered him off balance.

Topiltzin dropped to one knee, breathless, once more close to blacking out. The wizard stepped back from Topiltzin; his eyes fired and his hair seemed to swim about him like serpents. With a sound like breaking twigs, first a bloody sprout emerged, then, amidst flexing and crackling, a reddened, muscle-heavy arm yawned from the stump and sheathed itself in bloodied skin.

Topiltzin struggled to his feet, chilled, sickened. The wizard hissed, bared his teeth, and leapt forward. He came like a cat springing. Topiltzin screamed, shifted his weight back, and brought the sword sideways in a heavy arc. This time the neck of the priest gave way with a *chunk* and the head spun free, hair whipping wildly. The shoulder of the wizard still rammed solidly into Topiltzin's chest and he was thrown back, the sword knocked loose.

Topiltzin was again on his knees, doubled up. His chest had caved in, and he heard at least one rib crack. He sucked painful air, holding his chest and looking up.

The sorcerer's body was still standing, in the dark, shadowy mist of the forest. It fell onto its back, shivered a moment, and lay limp. Blood drizzled from the clean cut of the neck stump. Topiltzin waited, chilled, but despite his prowess, the priest apparently did not possess the ability to generate a new head.

CHAPTER TWENTY-ONE
JAGUARS

Before they moved on, Coyotl and Rattle Eagle searched the massacred village, dreading the discovery of Topiltzin or Mud Puppy, but, in fact, there were no Tolteca, only simple villagers. Rattle Eagle had paused over the body of a woman whose flesh had been removed, wholly. The body sat, propped against a mud hut, red veins glistening over musculature, mouth agape, eyes white and staring outward, a dull film over them. She seemed to be staring at *something*.

"Why? Why this, Coyotl? Why do such a thing?"

Coyotl winced, feeling a chill deep in his bones. Long ago, his grandmother had told him of the high sorcerers, the flower-weavers. He pulled Rattle Eagle aside. "Listen to me; these are plodders, a village of plodders—"

"Dead plodders."

"Exactly; therefore, they are past our concern. But Topiltzin is not among them. Now think, Rattle Eagle, where did he say he was going?"

"Here. Into the bush. That was all he said."

Coyotl searched. They could have gone in any number of directions. Night had already fallen, and for some reason it looked thicker than usual; it looked to be swallowing the stars, for the stars seemed to have no light. They seemed merely ice in the sky.

"Tell you this much, my big friend," Coyotl said, "I have a distaste for open jungle at night. I think we should find shelter, quickly. The evening star is shining. My grandmother told me never to sleep in the open beneath the evening star. We could get lost in the jungle.

194

Perhaps we should stay here."

"No," Rattle Eagle said flatly. "I would rather be lost."

"But—"

"You stay here, Coyotl. Sleep with her, if you like." He gestured at the skinned woman. He started toward the edge of the village.

"Wait." Coyotl hurried after him. "Rattle Eagle, I have seen men go into the jungles at night and never return. We need shelter!"

Rattle Eagle glanced to the sky. "Against the evening star?"

"We can just clear out a hut."

"No. Not here." Rattle Eagle paused, staring at the river, wide, mud brown, moving thick as corn soup. "That way," he said. "We will find shelter across the river." Rattle Eagle continued.

Coyotl glanced back once more at the flayed women, remembering the stories, the prophecies, the legends of the Shadow Walkers, then turned and hurried after Rattle Eagle.

They waded into the river. Its waters were warm and sticky. Coyotl feared looking down, and he cursed the mushroom now coursing his skin, for he could not shake the impression this had somehow become a river of blood, thick, near clotting, and even though he kept his eyes averted, it seemed to glisten in dull moonlight. He paused. An arm floated past them.

"Gods," Rattle Eagle muttered, staring at it, "what is happening here, Coyotl?" He turned, looking into Coyotl's one eye.

"Killing," Coyotl said, moving on. "Nothing new to the jungle."

"But, killing like this? The cutting up of parts? Skinning a woman like she was a peccary?"

Coyotl was silent. No. Not that kind. The jungle was harvesting new horror. They stepped out onto the bank and Coyotl, shivering, glanced down, expecting his legs, his breechclout, his sword, all to be sheathed in blood, but found only dark water, here and there bits of leaves.

"Seems to be some manner of trail leading in there," Rattle Eagle said, pointing.

Coyotl noticed a path leading into uninviting darkness, the

jaws of a monster. The trees even seemed to curl over one another like a gaping mouth. He noticed tracks, he knelt—Tolteca sandals. Topiltzin had gone in there. But how far in Coyotl could not guess, and nightfall now drew dark shadows. "We will wait here, near the river, until morning. At first light, I will track them."

"Why wait?"

"Because I cannot track at night. Now, let us construct a covering."

"Covering?"

"Against the rain."

Rattle Eagle glanced upward. "There is no rain, Coyotl. There are not even any clouds in the sky."

"I speak of the rain of the evening star. It will send down sliver serpents."

"Sliver serpents?"

"Worms that eat into your brain. You can hear them, eating, inward—but what can you do?"

"You believe these things, Coyotl? Worms? From a star? That seems somewhat difficult to digest."

"It is not you that will be doing the digesting. We need a roof over our heads. My grandmother never told me lies."

Coyotl glanced back across the river. The village clearing was like a scar amid the trees. Not that long ago, this was forest. They had slashed it, burned space for their crops, threw up their wicker huts, erected their drying sticks, planted their corn, fenced in their domestic fowl and peccaries. At the end of the year, they would have moved on, the jungle would devour the sunlight, leaving no trace of the village—as it would do now, feeding on the blood-rich soil.

Coyotl saw a slight opening through a thicket, and started through. "Just follow me, Rattle Head."

"You call me that again I will rattle *your* head, you little frog."

The opening was a small animal trail that led to a small clearing along the shore of the river.

Coyotl cut fan-fronds and tied them together with strips of bark. Rattle Eagle gathered moss for bedding, and in no time they were beneath an awning, propped against the thick, bowled trunk of a willow.

There were animal sounds all about. Coyotl could identify some: monkeys, macaws making occasional screeches, and a memory struck him. Once he had been in a village, not far south of here. It had a market plaza and two midsized temples staffed by thick-eyed Mayan Nonaloca priests. Coyotl had been sitting on the edge of the plaza, a jar of *pulque* between his legs, smoking a rolled cigar, when he realized there were birds talking to him. They were sitting in a tree just above him, about three of them, macaws, speaking to him as though he were perhaps a visiting relative, mocking him in thick Mayan-Chichimec.

"Hungry," Rattle Eagle complained.

"I will gather food in the morning."

"I thought we were going to find Topiltzin in the morning."

"We will find Topiltzin and then we will gather food; or, if you prefer, we will gather food first and then find Topiltzin."

"Good enough, but what about now?"

Coyotl glanced at him. Rattle Eagle seemed almost in pain.

Coyotl sighed. "Wait here."

"Where are you going?"

"To a flower festival, to dance a frog dance with young girls, have sex with them afterward."

Rattle Eagle narrowed his gaze.

Coyotl crossed back through the blood river. It was still a young night, he told himself, and nothing unnatural would be likely when the night was so young. The sort of things his grandmother talked about all generally occurred after high night, after midnight. He searched the village quickly. At a grain bin, he stuffed several ears of corn into a maguey cloak he had snatched off the ground. Pausing, he noticed that inside a hut, tortillas had been left on a squat wooden bench, near the burnt-out hearth fire. They were neatly rolled, fat tortillas shaped like butterflies, some like spiral stars with four points. He looked around before he realized no one was going to mind if he took a few.

As he made his way back through the river he held it all against him, bunched up in the cloak, like he had great, gourd-squash breasts. He had once met a woman with such breasts, enormous; she nearly had to carry them about, and the Maya of her village wanted ten *senum* from him just to have sex with her, as though she were a goddess, perhaps.

When Coyotl returned to the small clearing, Rattle Eagle sat up. He watched as Coyotl squatted and began unloading the contents of the cloak.

"This is from that village," Rattle Eagle muttered.

"No, it is from the coast. I bought this food at market from coast dwellers. I would have gotten some fish, but I was worried it might rot before I returned."

"How can we eat dead people's food?"

"Simple: we place it into our mouths, chew it up with our teeth, and swallow it into our bellies. Our bellies do all the rest. Here, some young corn."

Rattle Eagle took it—he hesitated, but took it. He began munching, slow at first, then a little quicker. At one point, he paused. "I have been thinking, Coyotl. I have been thinking about the game. We . . . we are not really going to play the rubberball game this season, are we?" Rattle Eagle had brought the equipment for the rubberball game along with them the whole way, holding it high above his head when they crossed the river, and it now sat off to the side in its deer-hide carrier. He gazed at it while stripping a second ear of corn of its husk.

"Why not?" Coyotl said. "We have played in the City of Thieves when the passage was closed off to Tolteca. We have played in Cobá when war raged among the swamps. Men may die, cities may burn, but there will always be the rubberball game. It is separate from people's differences. I think that is why I like it so." The tortillas were well made; the corn was young, sweet, and crisp. A few tomatoes, a few chilies—this might have been a meal worth enjoying. Rattle

TOLTECA

Eagle tossed corncobs into the bush. He wadded up a tortilla, stuffed it into his mouth, and chewed with fat cheeks.

"So . . . 'ell me . . . what purpose in . . . in"—he swallowed—"in cutting off that woman's skin? Um? Tell me that, Coyotl, for it seems to make no rational sense."

"What? You believe the world to be rational? Once, when I was young, my grandmother told me that the earth we walk upon, that this is our pain, our suffering. We have been sent here, to this world, because we are damned. We are dependent, all of us. This is our penance, a place of fear and terror. Those of us who manage to reach Heaven are able to escape. But those whose hearts are darkened. . . this is their dwelling forever. So you see, this life, this flesh, it is not Paradise, nor was it meant to be. To live forever as men live would mean to live forever in fear."

"Your grandmother told you this?"

"She was a witch."

"Your grandmother was a witch? You have never mentioned that before."

"I suppose I do not mention it often, but when it comes to such matters as this—godless things—having a witch for a grandmother lends me a certain advantage. One should always make use of any advantage he has, that is what my grandfather told me."

"Was he also a witch?"

"No. He was an opal merchant."

"Married to a witch?"

"Yes."

"But . . . would not that be awkward—being married to a witch? What if she got angry?"

"She was a good woman, Rattle Eagle, a fine woman, a kind woman. She did not cut off people's fingers for burning in spells or that sort of thing."

Rattle Eagle stuffed a second tortilla in his mouth and seemed to swallow it without chewing. "So then, what did your witch grandmother tell you about the flaying of women?"

Coyotl paused. He almost did not say anything more. "She said there once came a people to the land of Nomads, led by sorcerer-kings. These people, they came from a place far to the south, a place of mighty mountains, a place they called the lake of the earth mother—Aztlán. These sorcerers, they believed that by draining the blood of innocents they would obtain for themselves power. Therefore, they sent Blood Gatherers ahead of their armies, and these ate the hearts of their prey, and the prey they most cherished where those of white skin, for they hated all Tolteca. In those days, our ancestors, the people of Zarahemla, gathered at the mountain Cumorah, and there they engaged the sorcerer-kings and their warriors in a terrible battle. When it ended, the sorcerers either were killed or driven off. It is foretold they will return in power and terror. They are called, by the ancients, the Shadow Walkers, for they walked the *night and the wind.*"

Rattle Eagle stared into the distance, troubled. "What have they to do with that woman?"

"No other sorcerers I have heard of practice the flaying of skin, only the ancient Shadow Walkers of Aztlán."

"What then does this mean . . . if these Shadow Walkers once more roam the land?"

"Perhaps no more than we will have to hunt them down again and destroy them. Or perhaps it means our day has been marked in the skies, and is known to God. Perhaps it is no less than prophecy."

෴෴෴෴෴෴෴෴෴෴෴෴෴෴෴෴

Later, despite Rattle Eagle's predictions, it began to rain, light at first, but as Coyotl well knew, rains never stayed light in this part of the world. Soon the Heavens spilled like torrents, and Coyotl was thankful of the shelter overhead. There was enough ache in his bones, and enough exhaustion, that he fell into a dark, troubled sleep. Thick dreams came, like a fog, like someone had been there, making them, manufacturing them, a dream sorcerer, a night-wind.

Then he awakened.

It had been deathly quiet—no birds, no monkeys, no macaws, just dull, dead silence, and amidst it, suddenly, a deep gurgle. At first he imagined it to be Rattle Eagle's snore and was reaching to shove him when he froze, his breath caught. It was one of those times in one's life when things converge in a numbing shiver. Perhaps it was the dream wearing off, perhaps the very darkness, but what he saw at first looked to be jaguars, circling, closing about them, at least ten or twelve of them. Yet jaguars never hunted in packs. He realized they were armed, and it seemed they lifted, they rose onto hindquarters, and became men—warriors wearing polished mirror-disk breastplates. He had seen such disks before, carved, as these, with rays swimming out from the center. The Shadow Walkers had come, and Coyotl's chest jumped. Their hair was braided. Most carried Tolteca swords, burnished dark, and others held thrusting spears, readied for death strike.

One of them threw back his head and screamed, howled at the night, veins in his neck taut.

Rattle Eagle awakened, instantly starting to his feet with a snarl in his throat, his hand upon the hilt of his sword, but Coyotl gripped his shoulder, roughly pulled him back. He wasn't certain why, for perhaps unleashing Rattle Eagle on them would bring death, and these were certainly flesh eaters. Death seemed a good choice. Yet, Coyotl had the strong sense, almost whispered in his ear, that he *must* live—for the sake of Topiltzin. It was a spiritual kind of knowing, unexplainable, but he understood the feeling; it struck deep chords.

Rattle Eagle paused, crouched, still ready to leap forward.

"Stay alive, Rattle Eagle . . . for me, stay alive, my brother."

Rattle Eagle breathed heavy, but let his hand slip from the hilt.

CHAPTER TWENTY-TWO
ESLABETH

Sky Teacher closed his eyes, resting his head against the trunk of a willow. It was the rainy season, and when it was not raining, the sun would crack the ground of Tollán. The natives once said that in the hot seasons, the breath of the stone giants spilled across the earth; and without the rains, the earth scorched like the skin of a beast roasting over coals.

Sky Teacher had come alone into the east hills of Tollán, far enough from the city that there was only the sound of waters running from hill-fountains and birds among the trees. The trees here had been preserved. They were all that was left of an ancient forest. It was said the valley had once been thickly wooded, but now it appeared as barren as the womb of an old woman. The Tolteca had harvested the last of the woods, perpetuating the cycle begun by the land's native Chichimeca. The Valley of Otumba was a desert but for the lakes that nestled the entombed city.

Sky Teacher knew in his heart that the end had come upon the Tolteca. The words of the prophets had foretold this day. The Old Ones, the grandfathers, had looked far, hundreds of years into time, and had seen his people here, living on the edge of a bloodied sword.

Yet it was more than prophecy that left Sky Teacher's heart heavy this day; it was loneliness. Sometimes Sky Teacher felt so alone, it ached. He missed Topiltzin. The Blue Prince had been gone a full two seasons of the moon. By now, he would have crossed the mountain passage that divided the north from the southern lowlands.

Sky Teacher almost wished time could shift, could return to the days when they were younger, when he and Topiltzin would travel each season with their father to the coast. In those days, there had been no loneliness. Back then, very often, the Dragon would laugh. He would run with them, he would dance. Once, Sky Dragon had fishermen take them all to sea in a great dugout tree belly, with muscled rowers, and there they waited for the Old Ones to come—the whales. Soon they appeared, their humps curling, the rowers plying the waters with powerful strokes to keep pace. Topiltzin had leaned over the edge of the dugout, screaming with excitement, and Sky Dragon was forced to grab his son's arm to keep him from falling into the sea. Sky Teacher could still hear Topiltzin's young voice echo: "Let us ride one! Come, Father, let us climb onto their backs!"

The Dragon had laughed, pulling Topiltzin back, kneeling beside him. "We could not breathe beneath the waters, Blue Prince! Why, we would be swallowed into the depths of the sea!"

To this day, Sky Teacher could still remember the look in Topiltzin's eyes. For Topiltzin had not heard anything his father said—he was already riding the humped backs of whales into the kingdoms of the sea!

Sky Teacher smiled warmly with the memory. There had never been anyone quite like Topiltzin, and Sky Teacher was going to miss him badly.

His eyes flicked open as suddenly he realized there was someone before him. He had been so lost in memory he had not heard the approach. It was the boy, Temictal, an elder student of Sky Teacher's from the Calmecac School. Temictal stood waiting, patient. He probably would have stood there hours without speaking. Sky Teacher shaded his eyes, and Temictal half bowed. Temictal was tall and pale, and his short-cropped hair was never tame, but rose from parts of his head stiff and unruly, giving the impression he was always nervous.

"My lord, I did not mean to disturb you, but . . ." He paused, uncertain.

"It is all right, Temictal. What is wrong?"

"The wife of a nobleman, a woman of Chalaco, has journeyed

to Tollán to see you. When I tried to explain you would be back in only a short time, she utterly broke down; she fell weeping to the floor, begging that we find you immediately. It concerns her son. I would have waited, perhaps until evening, until you returned, but she was in great distress. So much so that I pitied her."

Sky Teacher stood, gathering the folds of his cloak, and began walking. "We will return, Temictal."

Temictal quickly fell in beside Sky Teacher. As they rounded the hillock pathway, the Valley of Tollán spilled into view, its north lake glittering in sunlight. Its painted walls looked almost alive.

"Tell me of this woman, then," Sky Teacher said as they walked briskly toward the lakeside.

"It would seem, my lord, that her son was always devout, always a good son, but of late he was visited by dreams. To rid himself of them, apparently he went into the hills and consulted a sorcerer. The boy was missing four days, and when finally they found him, he was mad. They have brought him to Tollán in a cage."

"Who has brought him?"

"The mother and her one daughter. They hired a porter to carry the boy's cage on his back."

"How old is this boy?"

"Four and ten years. No more."

"And have you seen him, Temictal?"

"I have, my lord. In all truth, in honesty, it was not the woman, but the sight of her son that pressed me to seek you. I had him taken to the palace. I felt he was unclean, therefore I did not wish to bring him unto the temple."

Sky Teacher walked a moment in silence. Temictal was a somber lad. Among Sky Teacher's students, Temictal was the wisest, the most levelheaded. He was only ten and seven years, but was already so much a priest that Sky Teacher had pondered sending him forth to teach the word, even at such a tender age. He glanced aside at the boy, and Temictal looked back worriedly. He was plainly frightened.

"Has anyone else seen this boy?"

"No, my lord. I was careful no one other than I knew of this. I was not certain why, but I felt I should be prudent."

"Keep it so."

"Yes, my lord. There is something else—I helped to carry the cage to the palace myself. The boy attacked me through an opening of the cage as we ascended the palace steps. He seized my wrist, and . . ."

Sky Teacher glanced down. Seeing Temictal's wrist, he felt, for the first time, real concern. The skin of Temictal's wrist was lacerated as though it had been savaged by fungus. In spots, it was bloody, with white pus. Sky Teacher paused and took Temictal's hand.

"You must have this tended, Temictal. When we reach the city, you will go to the house of the physicians."

"But, my lord, you may need me."

They had reached the lakeside that ringed the north of the city, and Sky Teacher raised his staff, motioning the attention of a canoe. Many canoes plied the waters of Lake Tollán, moving deftly between its large, squared, manmade islands—the *chinampas*. Each island was bordered by willow trees whose roots anchored the plots of land into the fertile bed of the shallow lake waters. From the mountains, they formed a pattern of squares that covered nearly the entire lake. Each island bore crops year-round. They also formed canals constantly active with canoes ferrying squash, beans, tomatoes, and potatoes to the city. The canals fed directly into the central market plaza of Tollán.

"My lord . . ." Temictal said carefully, sitting across from Sky Teacher as a muscled rower pulled them swiftly across the dark blue waters, ". . . how could such things as this be? That a mere boy should become consumed by dark powers?"

"Where there is light there must also be dark, Temictal. And though we seek always the light, there are times when the dark seeks us."

"It is said the old sorcerers of the woods can cause malevolent spirits to possess them, walk about in their skin, look out through their eyes, and that from this they drink power. Is this, then, what has happened to the boy—a spirit has taken his skin?"

"Did it seem so to you?"

Temictal nodded gravely.

As they crossed the lake, a dull sun danced off the waters. Singing drifted from one of the *chinampas* where young women were picking cherries.

Sky Teacher was struck with a far memory. It was of battle, in the pitch of jungle, in the deep of the Petén many years ago, when Sky Teacher had been a young warrior. He had found himself alone after a fierce, deadly fight. He was wandering, bloodied, weary, and lost, when suddenly he stood face to face with a high priest, one of those who called themselves Sun Speakers. The priest wielded an axe, and he had pressed Sky Teacher with amazing strength, even cutting him across the stomach. Sky Teacher drove home a death thrust, through the man's heart. The priest had not died immediately; he stood, he shivered, and something came out of him, through his eyes, his mouth. It screamed, something almost human but lacking face or parts. It knocked Sky Teacher into a stagger, soaring wildly into the thick trees of the swamp.

Later that same night, Sky Teacher sat across from his father in the king's tent, hearth fire burning low. The Dragon had been staring into the flame, weary, as often he was when there was great slaughter. Combat seemed to drain his father of spirit—not blood, not flesh—but spirit. When Sky Dragon's hard, gray eyes finally lifted, Sky Teacher asked much the same question as Temictal.

"Father, tell me how a sorcerer can have such power? How does God allow this, that demons may possess a man?"

Sky Dragon had replied calmly, without ceremony. "Remember something, my son, remember this: Dark can never stand against the light. Should it try, it will assuredly be destroyed; for such is matter, such is the earth, the Heavens, the stars in their course, the sun in its shining. Of such things, of such powers, neither fear nor tempt them. Offer neither wonder nor pride to the face of the dark."

TOLTECA

Sky Teacher now stared at the young, frightened eyes of Temictal and offered a calm half-smile.

"There is nothing to fear, Temictal. Do not be troubled."

"Are you certain you will not need me, my lord?"

"I am certain."

When they reached the wharf of the marketplace, Sky Teacher thanked the rower with a nod, and stepped out after Temictal. He pointed Temictal west, toward the government houses. "Go. Take yourself to the house of the physicians."

"But, my lord—"

"Have your wound tended. Think no more on these things, Temictal. I will explain them to you another day."

Temictal stepped back, bowed, then started off for the physicians. Sky Teacher waited calmly, and when Temictal predictably paused to look back, shooed him onward.

Sky Teacher made his way slowly toward the palace. The sun against the golden sheath of the temple seemed almost to be melting it, as though the golden skin might slip and spill, molten, into the streets.

An old woman with wild gray hair, missing teeth, lowered her head when he passed. "My lord," she whispered, and Sky Teacher set his hand on her shoulder before continuing. He nodded to others who met his eye. His brother, Topiltzin, would have drawn a crowd moving midday along the Avenue of the Heavens. The people would often gather here just to see if the Blue Prince might come out of the palace. But Sky Teacher drew only a curious gaze or two, perhaps a whisper.

When he reached the steps of the palace, he calmly walked up them, letting peace into his thoughts . . . *neither wonder nor pride.*

At the great oaken doors, servants ran to meet him and dropped almost immediately to their knees.

"Up, please, up, up," Sky Teacher said, purposely meeting each of their eyes when they stood. "I have explained, have I not, that you need not bow to me? I am not your king, and even if I were, the Dragon would no more allow you to prostrate yourself than I would. Now, where are they, the woman and her daughter who were brought here by the elder youth?"

The old man, Sky Dragon's manservant, spoke first. "My lord. Within the chamber, my lord."

Sky Teacher nodded and set a hand on the old man's shoulder. "Go. Be about your business. They have come to speak with me in private."

The servants nodded and scattered. The great doors were quietly closed as Sky Teacher entered.

Sky Teacher found the palace far too arid, far too depressing. When he was in the city, he stayed in the Calmecac, the school for youths. Sometimes he would stay in the Temple of the One God, but never in the palace. It had become a lonely, sullen place. He walked slowly and serenely through thick, polished wooden portals leading to the reception hall. There, against the far wall, were gathered two women and the cage. The cage was fashioned of bamboo bars, with wicker side panels that enclosed it, all drawn tight. The older woman, the mother, approached when Sky Teacher neared. She examined him carefully.

"You . . . you are the Dragon Speaker?"

Sky Teacher smiled. "We have no Dragon Speakers here in Tollán any longer, good woman, only priests—here and there a prophet. I am Sky Teacher, the son of the Dragon."

She was instantly on one knee. "Ah . . . my lord, my lord, it is so kind that you would come so quickly, so . . ."

She paused as Sky Teacher set his hand warmly on her shoulder. He lifted her arm, urging her up, and looked quietly into her eyes. "Fear no more, woman. Your grief already has been too great. Take comfort." He brushed aside a tangled strand of gray hair that had clung to a dried tear on her cheek. He looked past her briefly at the daughter, and was startled. He had not expected such beauty. Her eyes flicked away from his glance. Her hair was a rich, pale red, her skin as white as clouds. She kept near the cage, almost touching

TOLTECA

it. Sky Teacher *felt* her spirit. Even here across the room, he was touched with its purity. She remained so close to the cage because she loved the person within. Even if he was mad, she loved him.

Sky Teacher walked slowly toward them. Near the cage he heard a snarl, perhaps a whimper, a desperate sound.

He looked back to the woman, then the girl. "I will speak with your son, with your brother. I will leave it to you if you wish to stay or not. If you desire, you could both wait beyond, in the antechamber."

The old woman shook her head. Sky Teacher needed no answer from the girl; she would not have left even if he had ordered it.

He stepped forward and unclasped the front lock of the wicker side panel, then threw it open. The boy scampered back, as far as he could, pressing himself against the far edge of the bars, staring at Sky Teacher in utter terror. He was breathing in quick, short gasps.

The girl started forward, but Sky Teacher held up his hand, urging her back.

The youth was dressed only in a loin-clout. His body was scarred with lesions. On his face were boils, some of them broken open. He began slapping at his face with one hand, then he stiffened and his eyes rolled into the whites, his teeth tightened in a grimace.

"Priest," a harsh, washed voice hissed, "you have no face here. Your God is weak! Your sun has no heat, no fire! You are dead, Tolteca! Nephalli! All of you, walking corpses. The beasts shall feed on your filth. Already the stench of you fills the earth."

Sky Teacher had not reacted in any way. He stepped forward, closer. The boy's head now shook back and forth; his body shivered, violently. Sky Teacher lifted his right hand, palm bared, fingers spread. It was the sign of the word. Sky Teacher spoke with peaceful certainty. "Leave this boy. In the name of the great Father, by the word of the Son, through the spirit of the one Mother, the Light Whose Name Is Splendor, depart."

There were screams. It was not as he had witnessed in the jungles; there was no shadow being this time, no form or substance, but he did feel something come against him. It was like a harsh wind. It seemed to try to shear his skin as it passed, as though it bore claws. It twisted the folds of his cloak and pressed his gown against him. And it smelled—the raw, angry smell of the boy's festered wounds. Then it was gone.

The boy stared through brown eyes, a boy's brown eyes, troubled, but human. He glanced quickly to the girl, then to the woman.

"Mother," he whispered.

She started forward and wept.

"Come forward, boy," Sky Teacher said quietly. "Come out of the cage."

The boy crawled to the door and climbed out. He was shivering. Sky Teacher laid his hand against the boy's face, on either side. The skin was warm, feverish. Sky Teacher closed his eyes and let forth his spirit, let forth a simple, healing prayer, whispered from his heart. He then stepped back, and took the boy's hand, urged him toward his mother.

"Take him to the waters of the temple," he told her. "Tell the priests there that I have sent you. Have him washed. They will treat his lesions; the healing should be swift." Sky Teacher unclasped the shoulder broach of his cloak and laid it over the thin, bony shoulders of the boy. "Seek out no more sorcerers, boy," he said, sternly. "There is little wisdom in seeking light in the bowels of a darkened pit."

"Yes, my lord . . . but the dreams. I could no longer bear them . . ." He looked up. "What if they return?"

"If you cannot bear your dreams, then open your eyes. Look upon the Heavens, the moon against the sky, the stars where they glitter, the sun in its brilliance. In all these rests the face of God. Look upon them and take comfort. But speak the Light Whose Name Is Splendor, and fear not."

The boy nodded and bowed.

"You may leave the cage," Sky Teacher said to the woman. "I suspect you will have no need of it on your journey home."

"Thank you, my lord, oh, thank you." She stepped forward

and attempted to kiss Sky Teacher's hand, but he withdrew it, lifted her face.

"That is not necessary, good woman."

She stared at him a moment, her eyes searching. "You are . . . you are all they say you are," she whispered. She turned, her arm about the boy, and the two of them started away, the boy limping slightly.

The sister bowed when she passed Sky Teacher. "I also thank you, my lord," she said softly. She had not met his eyes.

"Have you . . ." He paused, surprised he had spoken—for he did so just to stop her, just to see her face again. "Have you a place to stay? Until your return?"

She hesitated. Her eyes were a warm, feather green. Before, they had been hidden from the light. "We have bedding, my lord, and the nights are warm."

"Yes. They are warm."

She smiled, bowed again, started to turn.

"However . . ." he said, and paused, watching her face. It was as though he had known her before. It was more than that, more than memory. He *knew* her—those same eyes, that face, this spirit—he had known her before. Of that, he was certain. "I . . . I was wondering . . . if you have food. It has been several days walk, and—"

"My lord, you are most kind, but you have done enough for us, more than we can ever repay. And yes, we do have tortillas and corn, and we have enough cocoa beans to purchase our needs. I thank you, my lord." She bowed, started once more after the others.

"I don't believe I even know your name," he said, stepping forward slightly, out of the shadows of the corner, where the flicker of the braziers fell across his face.

She paused, uncertain. "I am called Star Skirt."

"Ah . . . yes, but have you been named also of the Nonaloca priests? Have you a birth name?"

She nodded. "It is spoken, in ancient tongue, Es-la-beth. But none have ever called me by my birth name that can I remember."

"Do you know what it means?"

She shook her head.

"Oath of God."

She smiled. "In that case, my lord, I would be more comfortable with Star Skirt. That is merely a night sky."

Sky Teacher grinned.

"And you, Sky Teacher, do you have a bright name?"

He nodded. "Perhaps another time," he said, stepping closer, just a bit, even though her reaction seemed almost to back away.

"I know I am making you nervous," he said carefully, "but if you would . . . just one more question."

She nodded.

"Would . . ." He paused, not quite believing what he was about to say, and indeed, the words seemed to come from someone else than himself. "Would you marry me, Eslabeth?"

Her mouth parted, she blinked, startled. There was no answer, only a slight gasp. He could have been a specter standing before her. He walked closer, until he was close enough to touch, until she could see into his eyes, and he let a part of him spill through, as he rarely did. He felt his skin shiver, watching her, for yes, she recognized him. She must have; the look on her face lost its fear, her eyes almost seemed to mist. Then she looked down. She brushed a finger quickly over her eye.

"Forgive me, my lord . . . I . . ." Her words died.

"No," he said softly, "it is you who must forgive me. These are times like none before. Days are swift now. Perhaps it is not entirely unwise to act on impulse. Impulse may be all that is left us. At least consider my offer, Eslabeth." Her eyes lifted. He smiled gently. "After all, you will be in the city at least another day. If you wish, merely leave. If, however . . . if you feel otherwise, but send for me. Go there, to the Calmecac, the school of the priests. They will know where to find me." He slowly knelt before her, on one knee, lowering his head. He lifted her hand, and kissed the middle finger softly.

He stood, looked deep into her eyes, then turned and left her, walking swiftly through the antechamber. Once he was alone, he fell back against the wall and gathered his emotion. Speaking to Eslabeth had left him far more shaken than confronting the demon.

"Topiltzin," he whispered to the empty room, "it seems now that you are gone I am left with the burden of being a lunatic on my own. Would you could witness, my brother, that we are not as different as you might believe."

CHAPTER TWENTY-THREE
THE EXCHANGE

Hueloc stood waiting in the pale sun. It was there, in the sky, he even felt its heat upon his skin, but it seemed muted, shadows seemed bolder. Some men might have thought it sorcerers' work, but Hueloc placed no credence in mysticism, be it of good or bad blood, even though he had once entertained the prospect of becoming a priest. As a young boy training in the Calmecac of Zarahemla, he would watch the calm, dignified Nonalocas. There did indeed seem to be light in their eyes. But it was all so much easier to believe then, being young, caring of nothing further than the sun on his dirty skin and beans for supper. Now, age weighing upon him like a crust, he cared only of one God—avarice and greed. Of course, the priests of his youth would have explained to him, carefully, how such thinking could entrap his soul. This was a godless world, and there seemed little time left. So he might as well make himself rich, gather some women to have, buy a fine villa, and—most important—build a great, steaming bathhouse with walls splendid in turquoise, and mesquite to flavor the steam. Hueloc would sweat there like a Great Lord. And he would grow old, filthy old, his skin could rot, his bones become brittle, he would forget faces, names, and finally he would die, spittle on his lips, but at least, by God, he would have suckled life.

He paused now—someone coming.

Hueloc had chosen a position near the very edge of the mountain, where a white-blue river of virgin water first split into three heads between jutting rock mounds, then dropped off the end of the earth. There was a distant, far rumble below. To stand at the edge and look down, it appeared the blue water fell in three long, silvered ribbons to vanish in dense, green-pocked jungle. If anything went wrong here, Hueloc had planned an escape—straight down the cliff beside the falls, then like a salamander he would slither into the jungles and find shadow. He had even scaled the sheer face of the cliff the night before, painting rocks in red ocher to mark a pathway.

But nothing would go wrong. The exchange would go smoothly. The Tolteca would kill the proud bastards who had sucked the blood out of Nine Monkey, and Hueloc, the Tolteca, and the forty virgins would take a leisurely journey down the old merchants' passage to the Northland of Tollán. They would occasionally stop, make camp, sing, see if the virgins could dance, have fat tortillas stuffed with lizard meat.

The clearing before Hueloc was a half-moon plateau of the mountain passage, part of the old road. There had once been a fine inn here, an old fat woman always waiting with beds, maguey wine, and oily tortillas. There was only rubble left of the buildings, but the Plateau of the Thrice-Headed Serpent was so fitted to his purposes that engineers might have constructed it. A thicket bordered the north ridge behind Hueloc, tangled with willow, dogwood, thorn— and Scorpion's two hundred Tolteca. They were waiting, crouched behind trees, rocks, tucked into shadow, all well hidden. Some lay on their bellies, weapons close, like vipers. This would be one deadly afternoon.

Hueloc had himself donned an expensive mantle for the occasion. It was one of his finest, a Dragon Lord's cloak. The shoulders were ringed in brilliant scarlet feathers. A cotton and feather painting spilled across the back in a splendid image of the plumed Sky Dragon. It had belonged once to a warrior, a high captain, a knight of the Butterfly-Dragon Lords, and the featherwork was simply magnificent, black, red, turquoise, quetzal green, falling in regal folds to the ground. The Dragon Warrior who owned it had been quite drunk, and willing to gamble over a game of vanilla beans, which Hueloc was very good at when he wished to be. One side of the mantle was dropped back over Hueloc's shoulder, to free his sword arm. But the other carefully cloaked the spring-loaded atlatl clutched in his left hand. He had loaded the spear-thrower with a shiny, moonsteel dart with barbed tip. He had chosen it especially for the proud, savage, High-Blood Prince. If he had known the prince's name, he would have etched it into the shaft—it was that promised. Over one shoulder Hueloc had also looped a square, painted wooden shield. His hair was braided, as a warrior's, tied back with crimson ribbon, quetzal feathers hanging. In fact, he very well might have been a Dragon Lord standing there, large and woolly.

The High-Blood Prince came. He was carried high in a litter by four muscled warriors. He sat eased back in the litter's chair, calmly regarding Hueloc as he approached. Hueloc had about him, in open view, seven warriors. One of them was Scorpion, positioned just to his right, within distance of a whisper. Hueloc did not wish to appear weak, but at the same time he meant to appear inviting.

A trail of servants accompanied the prince. His litter-bearers were huge, muscular, almost grotesque in their stature. This Chichimec was far too regal, far too noble. He seemed almost a Toltec. It was going to be a pitiless shame to kill him.

Between Hueloc and the prince lay a stone bridge, spanning the swift, silver river, another remnant of the old merchants' road. It was wide and well built, but still, only seven, eight warriors abreast could cross it. Beyond the bridge and the river, back toward the south, was a heavy thicket of trees. Hueloc was aware those trees might conceal a few warriors, but he did not believe the prince would bring many—he was too proud. Even if he did, Hueloc reasoned, the river was ample barrier, and would provide his two hundred Tolteca rich opportunities to mete out death with missiles.

Hueloc forgot all about such matters when he saw the women. Girls, more properly, for they were young, all in their early twenties or less. They were like a gathering of flowers, coming along the pathway toward the river, surrounded on all sides by lean, deadly-looking warriors. Hueloc saw the glistening of their silken hair, long, straight; he saw their dark skin, smooth; he saw the light airy movements of their skirts, their blouses. Ah, they were beautiful. Often Hueloc found High-Blood Chichimeca to be the most beautiful of women, and this was precisely what he hoped would be the opinion of many a rich merchant in Cholula. The girls looked to have been handpicked. Hueloc counted heads quickly: seventeen, eighteen, nineteen. Nineteen pretty, dark-haired heads, which was not forty, but then, who cared, for they wore cotton dresses of colored print, light, airy, flowing. Those dresses could probably sing. Hueloc grinned, happy.

"See there, Scorpion," he whispered, "I told you not to worry. The prince is a man of his word."

"He looks to be a man of his word. He also looks cunning enough to have us for sport. Those trees beyond the river could conceal enough prime warriors to harvest us like a field of dry corn."

"Relax. He will bring along a death squad, a few shield-bearers maybe. No more than that. He is too confident."

The prince, the women, the gathering of warriors guarding them, all crossed the bridge. Hueloc had positioned himself far enough away that crossing the bridge was necessary. The prince was playing right into Hueloc's game. Nothing was going to go wrong. It was a good day, a fine day, for the sun was high and the air was clean. Hueloc was going to be rich.

When he was a stone's throw distance from Hueloc, the prince held up his hand and the litter-bearers came to a stop. They continued to hold him, like stone carvings sweating in the sun. The prince regarded Hueloc from beneath a canopy of crimson weft, seated in a fine, gold-encrusted wicker throne. To either side of him, Chichimec warriors fanned out, maybe thirty in number, all of them naked but for painted bodies, loin flaps, mirror ornaments strapped to their chest, and weapons. All of them bore Tolteca swords, but the moonsteel had been darkened, blackened by fires, until it was like night. Hueloc liked the look. He would have to remember to have some metal wizard burnish his own sword that way. The warriors surrounding the prince were nimble, muscled, and powerful as leopards. He guessed they were swift and deadly, almost certainly the prince's only escort. Their naked flesh was begging to be riddled with moonsteel darts. The day was looking brighter. How could he have imagined the shadows to be so threatening?

The girls gathered to the left of the prince, close back by the river. They were standing silent, in a huddled circle, masked by warriors. The warriors near the girls would make a difficult mark. They would have to be taken without harming the women-flesh. Hueloc had hoped for at least thirty girls to cover any losses. With this small number, he could not afford to lose a single one of them. But then, Scorpion had two score of Eagle Archers concealed along the upper ridge for just such a purpose, lying on their bellies, longbows yawning with moonsteel arrows. It would be like spearing fish.

"I hope you have chosen your archers well, Scorpion," Hueloc whispered, at the same time smiling, bowing toward the prince.

Scorpion did not answer. He stood behind his great, oblong wooden shield, as did the other six Tolteca who were in the open area surrounding Hueloc's flanks.

The prince had come dressed as his warriors, naked but for a painted breechclout and a circular mirror device strapped to his chest. Circling one knee was a tassel of red-black macaw feathers. He bore no weapons. His hair was unbraided, and in the wind of the pass it rippled over his shoulders. He was certainly a handsome bastard.

"Fat merchant!" the prince said in greeting. Hueloc could have sworn his eyes sparkled—glittered, like lightning-blue stones in the sun. "I see you have friends with you this time."

"A simple precaution, as you have taken."

"Indeed. We do not seem to wholly trust one another. So, then, where is your jade?"

"It is close . . . nearby." Hueloc motioned at the women. "I count only nineteen—a bit shy of our agreement."

"It was a matter of quantity or quality. I decided that a man of your . . . distinctive taste would prefer quality. Have I guessed wrong?"

"I cannot be certain until I see them more clearly. Your warriors are in the way."

"Yes, they are. Show me your jade, and I will have them move aside to give you a better view."

Hueloc turned. "Scorpion . . . show him the jade."

A moment later Scorpion looked back, startled. "What?"

"I said show the bastard his jade!"

Scorpion swore between his teeth, then turned to one of his men and motioned with his sword. The warrior understood. He turned and sprinted toward the thicket of trees that concealed the Tolteca.

The prince watched calmly, and it troubled Hueloc that his expression seemed one of amusement. There was a mocking half-smile on the handsome lips.

When the captain reached the trees, he turned and lifted his shield, and his voice carried cleanly as he shouted the command to fall out. Tolteca spilled forth, quickly forming a solid, vast semi-circle of locked shields and bristling spear tips, curling to either side of Hueloc. Two hundred prime warriors now looked out at the prince and his small gathering from beneath ornate helms. To Hueloc's flanks, bowmen dropped to a crouch, throwing aside their shields, and trained the tips of obsidian arrows directly at the prince's head.

"You have very little time to ponder this, my prince," Hueloc said, curling his hand tightly about the haft of the atlatl beneath his robes. "What I wish you to do is to send the women forward— without their companions. Do so now, quickly. Any hesitation, any delay, and my archers will pin your head neatly to the back of your wicker chair. Do we understand each other?"

"Perfectly. Does this mean, then, that you have no jade?"

"Oh, I have a bit more jade, just enough to open up your chest, you highbred shit-eating bastard."

The prince smiled. He motioned, but the warriors about the girls only tightened, closer, hemming them in. In seconds, the trees beyond the river blossomed with an offering of Chichimec warriors that soon spanned the length of the plateau. There were hundreds, four or five times the number of Hueloc's Tolteca. Archers sprinted forward quickly, dropping to their knees at the riverbank, pinning shafts to their bows. In moments, a virtual harvest of arrows bristled to either side of the stone bridge.

"Good God, Hueloc, we're all dead!" Scorpion whispered beside him. "He's got more than six centuries of men. Lord God, but we are dead!"

"Not dead yet," Hueloc hissed. He realized the prince was chuckling.

"It would seem, Fat Merchant," the prince mused, "we both have had the same idea in mind. Tell me, then—you seem plausibly intelligent—what should we do at this point?"

Hueloc glanced to either side. He met Scorpion's eyes briefly, narrowing his gaze. He turned to the prince and sighed. "I suppose, Highborn . . . we should die."

Hueloc ripped the atlatl from his robes. Dropping to one knee, he screamed and brought the weapon over his head, flinging the dart with all his weight, centering on the chest of the prince. Arrows exchanged in deadly flight, and from that point on it became difficult to figure out exactly what was happening. Chaos rained down upon the Plateau of the Thrice-Headed Serpent.

Hueloc rolled in the dirt, arrows whizzing. One caught him in the side, white hot. He rolled over it, snapping the shaft, wedging a sizable wound in his flesh. Just behind him, two Tolteca dropped like stones as arrows took deadly mark. One of them was Scorpion. A dark-feathered shaft had sunk into the visor opening of Scorpion's helmet and he staggered back, dropping his shield, never really knowing what had killed him.

The prince had tried to dodge, but Hueloc's atlatl-dart *whunged* into his chest mirror, sundering it, and the Highborn fell, vanishing behind the wicker throne that was instantly riddled with arrows, hitting like a swarm of insects pinpointing.

The prince's shield-bearers had been pretty, naked and splendid to behold, but they were slaughtered like fattened offerings in a merciless rain of darts. Near the women, however, the warriors fell carefully; they were being picked off one by one.

Hueloc sprung to his feet. One part of him urged him simply to flee, to make good his escape, but another part reminded him that if he did, he would be penniless and possibly hunted by Scorpion's men—or the High-Blood's—whichever of them managed to get off the plateau alive. The warriors of the dark Prince were coming at hard run, screaming, drums were sounding, conch shells called from deep within the trees—more of them. There were possibly thousands back there! Bridge rafts of wicker mats were being thrown over the river. They were going to pour down upon the Tolteca like a landslide.

Any normal soldiers might have fled, but Hueloc knew these were Tolteca, warriors supreme. The first duty of a warrior was to die, and the Tolteca were excellent at dying—merchants were not—neither, for that matter, were virgins. Hueloc sprinted forward, motioning with his sword. "Save the women!" he screamed, and a squadron of Tolteca came at his side. They needed no explanation, they understood. The women, among all the souls on this plateau, were the only innocents. They must be saved. Tolteca warriors had an innate, unwritten sense of heroic honor; it was something burned into their minds like fire tattoos.

There were still enough warriors surrounding the women to offer battle. Hueloc almost lost his arm to the first who leapt forward, sword slicing. Hueloc blocked with his wooden buckler and brought his sword up low, angled into the man's pelvis. The warrior cried out as he was heaved backward, blood spewing between his legs. The Tolteca with Hueloc then bore in like heavy caiman, slashing, thrusting. There was brief, savage fighting.

"Run!" Hueloc screamed at the women, who were huddled together, frozen in fear. "To the waterfall, run! Now! Or you'll be killed in the crossfire! Run!" He grabbed the nearest of them and threw her forward. She staggered and broke into a run. Others followed, Hueloc shoving them along. "Quick, or you'll be killed!

The falls! Run to the edge of the falls!"

They ran in a wavering column. One dropped, an arrow taking her from behind. She sprawled in a flurry of her colored skirt, and her hair frayed out. Pitiless. Hueloc seized a fallen shield and held it over his shoulder to absorb missiles, running after the girls, urging them speed. No Tolteca followed. The squad of them who had run to reach the women stayed behind, engaged in combat, and were methodically hewn down by missile fire from across the river. God, but they were noble sons of whores, Hueloc thought as he ran.

The prince's warriors poured over the stone bridgework, more over wicker bridges, and they came like a flood onto the plateau, everywhere dropping from Tolteca missile fire. The Tolteca braced, readied themselves. There would be battle like gods flailing; there would be pomp and blood. Hueloc almost wished he could stay and watch.

An arrow *whunked* through Hueloc's shield. Another sank into his side from the back, biting. Hueloc half stumbled. He almost went down, but kept running. He passed two more girls as he ran, both of them dead, sprawled out. The rest made it to the edge.

The Tolteca were moving forward in a line, shields locked, preparing to meet the overwhelming number of warriors fast advancing into their front.

Here, at the far edge of the gorge, Hueloc was barely out of arrow range. He cast the dart-ridden shield aside and pointed downward with his sword, screaming, "There is a pathway of rock marked in red stones! Follow the red stones! We have to climb down! Now! Move!" He grabbed a tender arm and shoved one of them forward, careful to keep hold of her lest she slip. She met his eyes, and for a moment Hueloc was taken by her beauty, by the piercing raven stare. She went willingly, carefully over the side.

"The red stones!" Hueloc shouted in Chichimec. "Follow the stones! Move quickly, and do not look down! Just look for the stone in red!" He fed another over the side, guiding her arm. The pain from his back knifed though his ribs. He wondered how bad it was going to be. He had two shafts in him somewhere, which were two more than he had calculated. The descent to the jungle floor was narrow and precarious; for a moment he wondered if he was going to make it alive. He led another one over gently. "The red stones," he said quietly in her ear. Her hair brushed across his face as she passed. They had some kind of perfume, all of them, something flowery that came into his nostrils like a fragrance of Paradise lost in hell.

As he led the last of the girls over the edge, he tallied the count—sixteen. They'd lost three getting to the cliff edge. He started over the edge himself but stopped, for movement had sent paralyzing blows of pain through his midsection. He noticed one of the girls had turned and was looking back at him, mouth agape.

"Go on!" he shouted. "Keep moving! And don't look down!" He glanced at his side, just under his elbow. The obsidian tip of the arrowhead was there, bloodied, having passed through his back. It was mostly skin, he told himself, but pain seemed to promise an organ or two had also been snagged. He chose not to ponder the fact he might slowly bleed to death in the jungles from internal wounds. The pain of movement with the shaft in him, however, was simply unbearable. Hueloc rammed his sword through his belt loop and took hold of the arrow's tip with his fist, then jerked outward, as straight as he could. It only came halfway, and Hueloc screamed, his guts rippling in spasm. Still screaming he wrenched at it again, then once more, finally freeing the shaft, leaving a considerable hole in his side. He tossed the shaft, which was coated in a sticky sheen of his own inner blood. He almost fell. There was a momentary grayness, a fading of sound, and he nearly fell over the edge of the gorge unconscious. It would have ended there for Hueloc, the Great Gut, plummeting like a soggy rock and exploding somewhere below, but he pulled himself sharply into focus, the image of his body hitting earth like a melon, stinging him to full consciousness. He turned to start down the pathway and noticed the girl was still there, still staring at him in silence.

"Why are you waiting!" he shouted. "I told you to move! Go! Go!" He stepped over the edge. The sweat in his eyes almost obscured the painted rocks. He could barely move his right arm, and even though the shaft was out of his side, it still sent spasms of pain through him whenever he twisted in a certain direction. At such moments, it became difficult to cling to the edge. He wondered if this was perhaps his last adventure. He wondered if indeed Hueloc was going to die an ignoble death. Then he felt a hand from below carefully guiding his foot. He glanced down, amazed. Blood splattered over the rock, but he eased his weight onto it. He then concentrated directly on the face of the cliff before him, and let his feet be guided by the soft hand of the girl.

"I get out of this one," he whispered to the rock, breathless, sweat beading down his face, "I will be famous. They will sing of me in ages to come. Hueloc, the Great Gut!"

There was a precipice, a ledge on the face of the mountain that offered no further footholds. The cliff did, in fact, curl beneath itself, gouged out, forming a sheer drop to the pools of the waterfall. Hueloc had decided the night before that the precipice could well hold thirty women—and himself. By the time he reached it, he was utterly exhausted. He was losing too much blood; it was just dripping out of him warm and sticky, and Hueloc's head was swimming in that feeling that comes with blood loss, a drunken feeling but lacking weight. Blood had soaked a huge blotch of soggy red through the tough leather of his body armor. He paused, leaned against the face of the cliff a moment, panting, dizzy. Pain, like a serpent wriggling in his belly, had churned to nausea. From the corner of his eye, he realized they were all watching him, sixteen young, virginal Chichimec, all staring at Hueloc with a mixture of fear and awe. Hueloc sucked down his weakness and turned, offering them his most stoic gambling face. One, a small one who was not wholly Chichimec, for she had reddish gold hair and freckles, stared at Hueloc's hand where it gripped his side, fingers bloodied and glistening.

"Sorry, my ladies," he said, "but I have been wounded. Therefore, I bleed. Not a pretty sight, but we have no time to deal with that now." He kicked a coil of hemp rope over the side. He had secured it to a rock where it uncoiled and hung, swinging over the pool of the waterfall. He glanced up. The roar of the falls beside them left no clue as to what might be happening up there, but whatever, it had to be grim. He peered over the edge below. White water fell, boiling into a pure blue-green pool. It looked something like a gem.

"Over the edge now, down the rope. Then we . . ." Suddenly, words failed him and he stood, staring numbly at the faces that looked back. Warm, young girls, certainly not one of them older than twenty, and the youngest, the small freckle-faced one, could have been fifteen. Up until this point, they had been, in the mind of Hueloc, simply merchandise. It startled him to realize they were so tender, that their faces looked upon him with all the quiet virtue of the undefiled. He shivered, and perhaps it was the blood loss, but the shiver went all through him, and actually made his body quiver. One of them pressed forward, a girl who appeared to be the eldest, an unfairly beautiful girl, with long, almost silvery black hair and perfect, glittering almond eyes.

"My lord . . . are you going to faint?" she asked in refined Chichimec.

He brought himself into focus. "Do not be concerned. I am fine. Well. I feel good. When you reach the end of the rope, just drop into the pool. Can you all swim?" No one suggested they couldn't. "Then let us begin." He touched the eldest, the shocking beauty, on her bare shoulder. Her skin had a wondrous soft sheen to it. "You first."

"I am called Paper Flower, my lord."

"Paper Flower. You can help the others reach the shore as they come. Quickly, now, we must be quick, the sun is nearly slipped beneath the world, and above we may only guess that the Tolteca are hard pressed."

Paper Flower stepped over the edge and started down hand over hand. Hueloc realized, watching her climb, that not only was she unfairly beautiful, but somehow, by some twisted sense of justice, God had also crafted her with intelligence.

Hueloc waited until she was near the end, then ushered another, helping her over, holding a soft, tender arm.

"Quick, quick! As swift as you can!"

He wasn't entirely sure of the hemp. It seemed good rope, but he had bought it at last thought, and the seller was suspiciously unclean. Because of this, he let no more than three down at a time. He kept looking up, seeing only the falls, only water, only sky. Yet he sensed something, as though something was about to curl over the edge and snake downward. At one point, stunned, he saw a body sweep past in the white water of the falls.

He turned. One girl was left, only one, the small one, the freckled one, and she was pressed back against the stone, shivering. He motioned to her.

"Quick, quick, come, girl."

She glanced at the rope and shook her head. Her eyes were near tears.

"It is easy! Trust old Hueloc. Why, the mountain face we have just climbed down was far more frightening than this."

She again shook her head.

"What is it you fear? The height?"

She shook her head.

"What then . . . the water?"

She paused.

"You fear the water? You cannot swim?"

"No," she whispered weakly.

"Well . . . listen here, I am certain the girls below will help you."

She shook her head. Hueloc cursed beneath his breath and glanced down the rope. The last of them were dropping off into the pool.

"Very well . . . come with me. I will not let you drown, I promise."

She regarded him with caution. He raised his hands, gasping. "I am

TOLTECA

Tolteca! Can you not see! Here, look on my beard. A Toltec beard! Nonaloca, all my ancestors, my father, my grandfather. In addition, as you know, a Toltec cannot lie. I will not let you drown. You have my word. My cousin, he is a priest."

The girl started forward, cautiously. Hueloc leaned over, grunting with pain, and lifted the rope, coiling it about his stomach.

"Hang onto my neck, just wrap your arms about my neck, and hold on tight. I will do all the rest." She started forward. "Come, quick! Quickly!" Hueloc turned, kneeling. Her small, birdlike arms wrapped tenderly about his neck, pinning his beard against him, and her feet coiled about his large midsection. Hueloc started down. Pain gnashed at his side with each hand length, and he could feel blood spilling over his leg, dropping away into the waters. But her weight wouldn't have mattered that much—she was light as a bird. He imagined that if she fell she would probably float like a feather. He then felt a jerk. He looked up, gasping. Above, near the precipice, the hemp had begun to uncoil, fraying out. One strand had broken.

"Ah, sweet mother of frogs," Hueloc hissed, now sliding down rapidly, hand over hand, the rope burning his legs where they were wrapped about it. Another jerk, a second coil snapped. The rope now dangled by a single strand of hemp. "Lord God, do not let this young innocent die. Do you hear me? Do not do this!" The rope snapped, and, screaming, they both dropped in freefall.

CLUCLUCLUCLUCLUCLUCLUCLUCLUCLU

Paper Flower gasped, seeing the two of them, the big Toltec waving his arms as though he might be trying to fly, and the girl, the small one called Jewel Twirler, dropping beside him. When they hit, a great plume of water erupted.

"They will need help!" Paper Flower shouted to the others, who were gathered at the edge of the pool, showered by the mist and spray of the falls. She dove headlong and began swimming.

After a moment, the two broke surface, the great man gasping, struggling. He was not a very good swimmer, but before he started for the shore he searched about and reached out a big hand for Jewel Twirler where she flailed at the water, gasping. Soon he was limply stroking, barely staying above water, dragging poor Jewel Twirler with him by a fist of her hair. She was flogging the water, terrified, but the Toltec kept her above the surface. When Paper Flower reached them, she pulled the Toltec's big arm over her shoulder and began a sidestroke for the shore. Shortly, others helped, buoying him up. He pulled in Jewel Twirler and held her close. When they reached the edge, he rose and staggered out of the water, carrying Jewel Twirler, then set her down on the rock. She looked up at him with adoration, as though he might have been a god. Paper Flower knew the girl was a bit lacking (in the past days they had been together, she had spoken perhaps twice, both single words: yes, no). The girls gathered on the rock, and the big Toltec paused to wring out water from his great, feathered dragon cloak. He seemed not to notice that blood was spilling freely from his wound, that his skin was pale, and that his eyes did not look entirely focused when he gazed over them, taking a deep breath.

"Ah! Yes. That is done. We made it alive. Hah!" He grinned, slapped his chest, and lost consciousness, slamming onto the rock. His big body bounced and rolled back for the waters. He was pulled back by several girls who knelt over him. Paper Flower peered into his face. He had a handsome face for a fat man—quite dignified. She glanced down at his wound and winced. It was hard in him, but perhaps it had caught mostly fat.

"Strip him of his armor and lay bare the wound," she said to the others. "We must stop his bleeding or he will die. Quickly, find kava root, palm leaves. Tear your skirts for bandages. We will need sticks for a fire drill. Let us pull him into the shade."

She took hold of one arm and began tugging. His weight, limp as he was, was enormous, like a great fish cast upon the shore. They had been given an odd savior, Paper Flower thought as they dragged him along in jerks.

CHAPTER TWENTY-FOUR
THE SMOKING MIRROR

Smoking Mirror stood, angry, heaving the dart-riddled litter aside, hissing through clenched teeth. He had been unconscious—this he could not believe. The fat man had actually struck him so hard in the chest the mirror plate was cracked through the center. He ripped it off and flung it aside.

Before him, on the Plateau of the Thrice-Headed Serpent, the last of the Tolteca were dying. Toltec feather shields and mantles littered the ground among their fallen. They had refused to run; they had instead chosen death. They were, indeed, all they had been spoken of by the old missionary, but the end was near for them. Captives were being taken. The last of the Tolteca were so wearied, so heavy from battle and the death of their brothers, they were weak enough to be stripped of weapons, pulled down, and bound. They were carried by runners to waiting cages. There would be offerings this night—none other than the blood of the mighty Lords of Tollán, the so-called Sons of God. Strength would be suckled.

They had needed this. Smoking Mirror had not expected it, admittedly. It still numbed him that he had not seen through the eyes of the fat man and so much had gotten past him; but this first taste of Tolteca flesh would fever his men. Many had feared the stories, the legends of the bearded ones. It would be good for them to know the Tolteca died as men die, that theirs was but the flesh of men.

He had traveled far from the home of the lake mother's tit, and here in this land, past the treacherous narrow passage where the jungles took many of the weak from disease, they could no longer turn back. Yet the whisperer had promised him; and this, the first offerings of the Tolteca, was assurance. The youth of Aztlán, as had been promised, would now feed off the gold, the cities, and the children of the Tolteca.

Smoking Mirror remembered the night the whisperer had first come into his head. It seemed, even in his mind, he had only just then stepped from the desert, spawned of the sand and his only mother, his only father was the whisperer. At first, the Old Ones had mocked Smoking Mirror, whom they called Auca, he who has no home. But the whisperer had always shown Smoking Mirror his true path. He was the messenger. For a time he was only the wanderer and his followers were few; but as they became more deadly, others followed, others came to hear. Word of who he was spread and the whisperer made it known that he had brought them the flower and the song—that he alone of all the ancients could awaken the ancient heart of Viracocha. Sometimes Smoking Mirror talked to them himself, and other times he let the whisperer speak through him, stand in his flesh and speak openly to them, and when any looked in the eyes of the Smoking Mirror when the whisperer was in his flesh they would fall to their knees in fear. Word spread quickly and once the suckling had begun, they came; they believed, and each who tasted the whisperer's meat became filled with power and vision.

At first there had been only the two thousand youth of the mountain passes, but as they swept through the valleys and let terror walk before them, more came, until they were four thousand, all youth, all filled with the prayers of the Night and the Wind.

In that time, Smoking Mirror had not yet understood where the whisperer was telling him to go. Then the Mocker brought him the old man, the bearded one, the penitent missionary, and as the missionary spoke so did the whisperer, as if there were two voices in his ear, and quickly Smoking Mirror understood. He was amazed. This old man, this was the reason he had spawned, the reason he had become, the reason the laughing voice spoke in his ear. He had come for them. Yes, his followers now were many, but his message in the end was for these here, the golden ones, the Nephalli Tolteca. Until now, the voice might have been lying. He was called *Mocker* because he had raised up kings—only to spit on them; and created mighty warriors—only to cripple them. He mocked like children, and if men did not suckle him, he would suckle them.

Now the whisperer had proven his words. The Shadow Walkers would soon drink the blood of the Tolteca, and this would make them more powerful than any hearts they had yet suckled. This would make them omnipotent. It was the very covenant of the whisperer being sealed in sacrament—it was time. He had come and soon all the Tolteca would hear the message he had brought them. The Tolteca-Nonaloca, the fabled Nephalli kings, would now join the Lords of Xibalba; and as the Shadow Walkers drained their strength and tasted the hearts of their women, the legendary Tolteca would fade like the mist of a river before the morning sun. Soon they would become only smoke and vapor, the Many Dead.

"Bring Flower Weaver," he said, but already the shadow-priest, the *nahualli* who was called Flower Weaver, was near, and hearing his name, he stepped close and bowed.

"I am here, my lord."

Flower Weaver was a shorn priest, a sorcerer. His eyes were as black as a starless sky. The skin of his head was smooth and dark. Smoking Mirror regarded him, and Flower Weaver's eyes narrowed.

"I want the fat man," Smoking Mirror said. "Find him."

Flower Weaver stepped back and closed his eyes. For a moment the sorcerer concentrated, his face stone and silent. Then his limbs shriveled and his face withered as though the bone beneath the flesh were melting, and his head just fell inward, empty. He enfolded. He became like shadow, he seemed to curl himself inward. Then he was gone, he had passed into himself. When Smoking Mirror heard the cry of the Hawk from above he lifted his gaze, searching, but there was nothing to see, for the sky was purple and empty. Yet, across the ground fell a shadow, moving swiftly over the plateau.

Smoking Mirror walked slowly to the cliff edge and stood near the waterfall, gazing outward. The land stretched away to the east; like mosses were the trees, like veins were the rivers.

"I am come," Smoking Mirror promised the night. "Hear me, Tolteca; I bring a message to give your sons and daughters, your fair skin and blue eyes. Your God is dead, fair ones, for you have forgotten his face and dishonored his name. Be not afraid, my children, I will bring you a new God, a new sun. Look on me, for I come singing; I come in flower, in song!"

That is what the old missionary had taught him. In the end, Smoking Mirror finally understood why the old man was sent to him. The old man had told him of a prophecy, that when the Tolteca had forgotten the face of their God, in that day they would be destroyed by the ancient seed of their brothers, the two who were cast out, who became the Lords of Aztlán—the lords of the lake, the soul of the Night and the Wind. The day the sun had risen on the face of the Smoking Mirror, the awakening had begun. This was why he had no memories of Father or Mother, why he had stepped from the deserts with no knowledge of his past. He had spawned, he had come only for this; for just as the Night and Wind had always whispered in his ear, he needed no past because he had been foretold from the very beginning of time.

This night, as his words left him, they fell across the land as shadow, a land once promised the fair of the Nonaloca-Tolteca, the Nephalli, the Children of God, the Sons of Light. The words of Smoking Mirror sealed their flesh, much like an offering being sealed upon altars. He had brought a new religion, a new sun, he had brought the Flower-Song, and nothing here would ever be the same.

CHAPTER TWENTY-FIVE
STAR SKIRT

S tar Skirt wandered through the grand market of Tollán as night fell. This was not a festive night. It was not marked on Toltec calendars, not sacred, but only ordinary, only normal, yet there was celebration. There were tumblers, and she paused to watch them: the flute players, dancing as they played, feet kicking high; the muscular acrobats, leaping, spinning, the feathered tassels of their knees and ankles glittering, the rings of jeweled necklaces falling over their breasts, the circles of featherwork radiating from their backs; the women whose skirts spun like the wings of butterflies. The dancers dipped and strutted, flashed into tight spins, leapt with legs stretched and dropped nimbly to the earth. Singers called to the sky and the turquoise drum and reed pipe kept rhythm. Fire dancers came, bearing flame, leaving streamers in the night as they flew.

Truly, the Tolteca were as no other people; truly, God blessed them. Their priest, their young prophet-prince, he most of all. She had been unable to look him in the eye at first, for when she saw him in the palace, walking toward them, barefooted, in his simple robe of white maguey cloth, she felt—aroused. This was a priest, yet he stirred her from somewhere deep. Passion had touched her like a kiss and she had quickly looked away, ashamed.

She had expected something much different. The stories she had heard of the mighty Dragon of Tollán, whose white-gray hair was like a wreath of storm clouds in anger, whose eyes were like mountain stone, whose voice could cause the strongest men to tremble—Sky Dragon, the slayer of the wicked, the redeemer of

God. This *was* his son. She expected him to be clothed as a regal lord, in a great, feathered cloak, or as a Dragon Knight, in rich crimson and black sheen. Yet he came quiet, simple, and for that he seemed more powerful. Something had simply spilt out of her at the sight of him.

Star Skirt had been, all her life, cautious and chaste. She was seldom given to games, and never, that she could recall, had she been so attracted to a man. In fact, men had thus far merely bored her. One, who was named Water Parrot, had pleaded that she accept him as her Lord before he left for the southern passes, after he had been trained to become a knight's vassal, a shield-bearer. He had fought in two battles, and had returned to Chalaco victorious, with his hair braided and one fine quetzal feather hanging from the braid tie, indicating he had achieved bravery, had been initiated as a knight— that he had killed. Now he was to fight with the Ocelot Knights of the passage garrison. The village girls had thrown themselves at him. They had donned their finest apparel, their flower dresses; they had scented themselves, painted their eyes, their cheeks. They had openly and brazenly flirted with him, some of them shaming their parents. But in the village of Chalaco, it was rare that such a man of distinction would be raised from among them. Water Parrot had been handsome, with fine dark eyes and brown hair, and even the shadow of a beard. He was muscular and bore on his shoulder a scar, a mottled gnarl of skin given by some weapon.

Even the governor, who in Chalaco was only an ordinary man compared to the nobles of Tollán, but who, nonetheless, was the richest and most honored of men that Star Skirt and her sisters had ever known—even he had acknowledged the achievement of Water Parrot.

Star Skirt, however, had not painted her face, had not chosen a flowered skirt, but simple white cotton, a simple white blouse with a colored shoulder cloth. She had only once acknowledged Water Parrot, smiling at him from the other side of the great hearth fire that had been built in the marketplace for the dancers. Water Parrot had not smiled back. He had leveled his handsome, angry brown eyes on her with such a look she had pretended to be distracted by her mother.

It was later, when Star Skirt started home with her brother Wolf Feather, that Water Parrot sought her out. She and Wolf Feather had been walking between the houses beyond the marketplace when suddenly both of them paused, startled. Without sound, Water Parrot had stepped from behind a hut. He looked first to her brother.

"Lord Wolf Feather, with your permission, might I speak with your elder sister?"

"Why . . . yes," Wolf Feather had stuttered. Then he fidgeted. "Alone?"

Water Parrot had nodded. Wolf Feather glanced to Star Skirt in question and she had beckoned him. Alone, Water Parrot came forward, looked deep into her eyes, his handsome face, its square, hard features lit dimly by the distant lights of the plaza. He had parted his lips and kissed her, gently. She had yielded, only slightly surprised.

He said, "Star Skirt, let us, this night, go out, beyond into the deserts, and there be alone, beneath the stars, beneath the Heavens. Just you, just me."

She had paused, wondering why, among all the girls in the village—some who were certainly more becoming—he had chosen her. She lowered her eyes, but he touched her chin, lifting her face.

"I wish to be honorable with you, I mean no indiscretion. But I leave soon for battle, and I would wish that we could, that you . . . that it could be considered, Star Skirt, you might one day, perhaps when I return . . . you might become my wife—bear my children. I have watched you for a long time. Before I left Chalaco, before I ever became a Toltec, I watched you, dreamed of you."

She looked into his eyes. Star Skirt, at that time at least, had never considered life with a man. As yet, she was but ten and six years, and her life was as she wished it—her mother, her father, her duties to her household. She had not considered that one day she must become a wife and bear children to a man. The thought of it then, looking in Water Parrot's dark eyes, left her cold. She was surprised at her own reaction, but it came suddenly, and she shook her head. Looking right at Water Parrot, she shook her head and ran. He had turned, startled. She knew this because she saw him from the corner of her eye when she skirted the edge of a far house. Water Parrot left soon afterward, and never returned to Chalaco.

But this day, when the Prince of Tollán had called her of her birth name, the feelings within her, the need, almost, to touch him—they had been wholly opposite what she had felt toward Water Parrot. When he had asked, so simply, so suddenly, to marry her, it left her without breath, as though it were a thing of dreams. She had ended up simply wandering the streets in a daze, down the great avenue of the temples, through the courtyards, and finally here, to the marketplace.

Now, as she stood watching the tumblers, she had the odd impulse to join them, to shout, to spin. Instead, she moved on, made her way past the outer rings of dwellings: houses in cubicles, one on top of another, with their faces painted in wonderful colors. She ventured past the adobe huts, and then past the outlying fields of corn and squash, all flush, ready for harvest—until she finally found her way to the tent, to the fire where her mother and brother waited.

Wolf Feather had his wounds bound in cotton dressings. The lacerations, even the terrible boils that had threatened to peel away his skin, had almost healed. For the first time since the night he left in search of the sorcerer of the hills, Wolf Feather looked to be himself. He offered his boyish grin and stood when he saw her. She embraced him and stepped back.

"Wolf Feather, you look good, whole."

"I cannot even remember the days behind us, only that they were dark. Perhaps I will be well again. Do you think? Do you believe?"

"I am certain, Wolf Feather." She sat near the fire.

"Where have you been, Star Skirt?" her mother asked, stirring a broth of cactus pulp.

Star Skirt took her time in answering. "Merely in the city, in the plaza. There were dancers there, tumblers and singers. It was wonderful."

"I was about to seek out a Watcher, that he should search for you. I was worried. There are evil men in such a city as this, Star Skirt, of the kind with which you are not acquainted. You should be careful, my daughter. But I am pleased you have been enjoying yourself. Are you hungry? We still have warm tortillas, and a vender was kind to sell us beans and chilies at a reasonable price. I could—"

"No, Mother. Thank you, but . . . I seem to have no hunger."

"Is anything wrong, Star Skirt?"

"Just . . . the city I suppose. So much to see."

Her mother eased back. "We are blessed this day. A great blessing upon us. Your father, wherever he is, somewhere in the Chiapas, he would be pleased to know. It would warm him to see us here. But we should rest now. I know it is early, but we must start back in the morning, before the sun. Otherwise, the deserts will be merciless."

Star Skirt only nodded. How would her mother ever understand she was not coming, that she was staying here in Tollán to marry the prince? It was simply madness. It was the fabric of myth, of fanciful tales. Yet it seemed so easy a decision, as though becoming the Princess of Tollán was the most natural thing anyone could do.

CHAPTER TWENTY-SIX
THE SHAPE SHIFTER

Hueloc awoke in a fever. His mind had fashioned for him a twisted dream. He had been in his bathhouse, and the steam was swimming around him warm, with the moist smell of dampened mesquite wood. The walls were of inlaid turquoise, and the roof was covered in stars of halved pearls set in smooth jet stone. Hueloc himself was laid back against one edge, smoking a well-packed tobacco tube, aromatic with fine herbs, blue smoke curling about his face through the moist steam. Then—he began to ache. He looked down. Blood oozed from his gut, from his side. His reflection on the polished jade across from him was shriveling, his face crumpling inward, as though some creature were sucking out the contents of his body through the wound in his side. He realized that parts of him—his liver, his coiled, blue-red entrails, his spleen, his pink yet black-stained lungs—were swirling about in the bubbling waters which had begun to boil. Hueloc was being made into a stew.

He screamed and his own voice brought him conscious, his eyes open wide, stinging. He found himself staring upward into thick foliage. For a moment he could not place anything, not the day, the night, or his purpose. Then slowly, like feeling returning after the sting of cold wind, he remembered.

They were gathered about him in a small semicircle. At first, while still groggy, he thought they were children, little girls, looking at him, all gathered about his feet. He realized they were the women-flesh, grown, of age for breeding and selling.

He sat up, eased out a troubled breath, and pulled a hand over his wound. He felt bandages, wrappings, and beneath them, some manner of leaves or herbs; he could feel them, spongy as he probed with his finger—perhaps moss. The wrappings, he realized with a certain warm reaction, were the very skirts of these girls. They had torn the hems of their skirts in order to wrap him. That moved Hueloc in a strange way. A soft hand touched him, cold against his fevered skin.

"Are you well enough to speak, my lord?" a tender voice asked, and he turned. It was the elder sister, the one who looked unfairly beautiful and was possibly intelligent as well. She would provide some poor fool endless days of torment. He grunted and cleared his voice.

"Yes . . . yes. I can speak, yes. I feel . . . odd. Very odd." He paused. Everything went fuzzy a moment, then drew back into focus. Although the pain in his gut had been seething, writhing, in his dream, it was not nearly as hard now. It was, in fact, muted. He looked at the wrappings in wonder. These were no ordinary women.

"Perhaps, my lord, you feel odd due to the herb we have given you," suggested the elder sister.

"Herb?"

"Yes, you drank it, my lord . . . you do not remember?"

He shook his head—no memories. The last thing he could recall was falling through the air with the little one. He spotted her, off to one side, watching him from out of her freckled face with little fox-brown eyes.

"It is for your pain," another, who knelt to his right, said. He turned. This one had tender eyes, hair tied in long braids that fell over young breasts covered by a flowered, silken blouse. She smiled. Hueloc was compelled to smile back. "You seemed in terrible pain," this one added.

"Well, I do remember terrible pain."

"It is called Dog Wart root," still another spoke, one just in front of him. She was taller than the others were, possessed of long, rich hair that came all the way to the ground where she knelt. The smooth sheen of her thighs made his mouth water. He stared at this one a moment feeling a little drunk, his head weaving slightly to the side.

"Dog Wart root?" he repeated numbly. She had eyes that sparkled, that certainly were jewels, some kind of dark crystals. Gods, but this one, she was so manufactured, she caused a sane man to drool like an idiot. He could sell this one for the price of two bathhouses!

"It is an herb known to reduce pain," said the elder sister, who knelt at his left. Her knees and the tops of her thighs were brown and damp from the falls.

"Ummm . . . ah, yes. It does seem to work." He poked at his wound. "Good of you to do this."

"It is our honor, my lord," said yet another, this one with a silver tint to the long, silken sheen of her hair. "For one so noble, for our savior."

"Sa . . . savior?"

"You came forward," said the elder sister, "risking your very life, taking terrible wounds to deliver us. We are all in your debt, Great Lord. We honor you."

"Ah. Yes . . . well . . ." He took a breath, considered, and nodded. "I did deliver you . . . I suppose."

"Smoking Mirror was to sacrifice us," the one with braided hair, to his right, said. By her position and her bearing, Hueloc guessed her to be the second eldest sister, and he immediately surmised she would make a perfect maidservant. She continued, "Many of our sisters already were sacrificed upon the altar of their temple. First, the priests took them; they were cruelly raped. Then they were stripped and drugged with an evil opiate that caused them to dance and weave as though they were well, as though they were happy. Even though there were tears in their eyes, yet they dance to the bleeding stone. Then they were eaten. We have witnessed, we have known sisters that have been so slain. Had you not saved us, Great Lord, we would also have been led to the altar."

"I see," Hueloc observed. It began to make sense. Smoking Mirror had used sacrificial bait as meat to lure him out. What a dishonest bastard. "This prince, then, he did not tell any of you the reason he brought you to the plateau?"

The eldest sister looked to the others. "I had guessed," she said, "that we were begin taken to perform some manner of sacrifice to their gods, for they have many and varied forms of sacrifice, they seem even to delight in this variety of means by which they cause suffering. When we saw you, some of us, whispering among ourselves, thought at first that you were like them, more Flesh Eaters. Then we saw your skin and realized you were Nonaloca. We saw by your shields and your armor you were warriors of the Tolteca. We were amazed. We wondered what purpose the mighty Tolteca would have in dealing with the Dark Lord, Smoking Mirror. What was it he said to you as you spoke together . . . something about jade?"

"Jade . . . um . . . yes, we had . . . told him, led him to believe, you see, that we wanted him to sell us jade. Of course, we did not actually desire jade. We desired only to kill him and his band of thieves."

"Band of . . . thieves? But they are many, my lord."

"Nonetheless, we were bold. We deceived him, you understand, into believing we desired riches."

"You tricked him?"

"Ah, yes, indeed we did, we tricked that sly, ill-bred bastard good, tricked him like he will not soon forget." Hueloc genuinely chuckled.

"But, what did he hope to gain for his jade? Why did he come?"

"Ah . . . weapons. Yes, weapons. Moonsteel. We lied to him, told him we would trade moonsteel swords and atlatls."

"I see." She paused. "It is odd then, is it not, that he would bring us? What could have been his purpose?"

"Yes . . . well, as it happened, the words he exchanged with me before the battle ensued was that he after all did not intend to give us jade for our moonsteel weapons, but women—you, all of you. He proposed we should have our desires upon you."

The eldest sister looked convinced. For some reason she trusted him. But why not? Against her feared Dark Lord, Hueloc must have appeared a priest glowing with the very light of God.

"You, er . . ." Hueloc said carefully. "You say his name was Smoke Mirror, this High-Blood Prince?"

"Smoking Mirror, and this because his sorcerers bring to him obsidian mirrors through which he views all he desires, through which, it is said, he can look into men's hearts and see their weakness. He is more than a prince. It is whispered he is a son of God, that he has great powers. We have witnessed, we have seen. He is a mighty sorcerer, by my belief. I do not esteem him a god; but mark, he *is* powerful. How did you manage to slay him? How have you done this? Are you also a sorcerer? Was there a spell placed upon your atlatl-dart?"

Hueloc pondered. "No. It was merely moonsteel, Tolteca, which be enough, apparently, to slay vile, godless bastard sorcerers."

"Then you are a mighty warrior," said the smallest one, the little one with freckles. He was surprised to hear her speak. She had the voice of a child. Gods, she was a child!

"A Dragon Knight, by your cloak," the eldest sister said.

Hueloc noticed his cloak had been washed and laid out to dry on the rock. He glanced at it, gestured humility.

"I am Paper Flower," she then said. "I am the eldest sister. We are all from the same valley. Many of us know one another. My village had been raided by demons seven days before. We—"

"Demons?"

"Yes," she assured him. "Demons. Many were animals, who came like shadow and had the form, the eyes, the shape of beasts, but they fought as warriors with weapons and shields. The men of our village, they were Chichimeca, they were great hunters, and many had even fought the Tolteca in the jungles. The demons were terrible to behold. There were also the dark ones, sorcerers, with painted bodies, and they came into our village like a wind, like a terrible storm that strikes without warning. Our fathers, our brothers . . . all were slain, whether by sword or by tooth and claw. Many of them were killed in their sleep, and our houses were burned. They gathered the children, and these, with us, and others like us, the youngest, the fairest of us, all were gathered and taken to the mountain city, which they had conquered and rebuilt. Our little ones, the children they . . ." She paused and Hueloc noticed that her eyes hardened. "They were boiled. Alive. Their screams were long; all night they went on. We wept for them, my lord; many tears were shed for their pain. They were eaten. Others like us, sisters to us, they have also been slain, upon the bloodstones of their temples. All have been slain to feed their God. They have said to us, have told us, through the mouths of their priests, whose breath stinks of blood, that they have come across land and water, they have traveled like wind from high mountains, from the dark lake, the endless lake, which has no bottom and lies there, far, far to the south, in the heights of great mountains. They call this lake the breast of the mother of God, or Aztlán. They have come to slay the seed of the Nonaloca, the Tolteca, those who are of fair skin and fair eyes. They promise they shall slay all of you, my lord, until you are no longer remembered, until you are the ghosts, the many ones, the buried dead. This because your God, my lord, has now abandoned you. Therefore, you have allowed that the Mocker is come, and his power grows each day. Tonight will be the night of the Evening Star, and the Mocker shall come forth and walk the land, he shall stride. He is Mocker, Enemy, the all and everywhere; he is the dark, the wind, the night, the defiler of men."

She paused. All faces, all of them, were riveted upon Hueloc, waiting. He looked around, puzzled.

"Does this not terrify you?" the small, freckled one asked. "You are Nonaloca! Are you not terribly afraid, my lord?"

"Afraid?" Hueloc turned and spat to the side. Then he snarled, bared his teeth at them through his grizzled beard. Their eyes widened, all but the eldest sister's, who now watched him with a careful gaze. He would dread facing her in a wager; she had the face of a stone-cold gambler.

"Then you feel these Blood Priests," the eldest sister spoke thoughtfuly, "that they are mistaken? That they lie, that they build for themselves false prophecies?"

"The day those ill-bred leeching bastards can hew down the Tolteca is the day the crust of the earth shall roll up like a scroll and crush us all like bugs. Bring them on! Godless calumniators." He slapped the hilt of his sword, curled his lip back.

"Nonetheless, my lord," said the eldest sister, "but for you, we would have fed their God, who is evil, who is a demon. Therefore, we honor you. We are your servants. We wish, my lord, to know your name, and how we should call you."

"Of course! My name is Hueloc. Hueloc, the Great Gut."

There were some giggles. Hueloc only raised a brow and they quickly hushed.

"This, the youngest of us," Paper Flower said, motioning the little one, "is Jewel Twirler. You have saved her twice, once from the sorcerer-king Smoking Mirror, and once from the pool where she was nearly sucked into deep water."

Jewel Twirler crept forward and kissed Hueloc's big toe. Hueloc gasped. "There, there, you have no need to do that, little one."

"But it is our custom," explained Paper Flower. "It is how we honor great warriors in our village."

"I see . . . well—custom. I suppose, then, custom is appropriate."

"This is Night Jasmine," Paper Flower said, motioning the tall one with the long hair and perfect thighs whose eyes were painted in blue shade, whose dress clung to her like passion. She crawled forward, knelt, pulling aside her long, night-black hair, and gently kissed his toe. Hueloc felt the urge to weep, just from the poetry of it. Paper Flower continued, introducing all of them, all sixteen, and one by one they kissed his feet, each of them, kneeling. The one to his right, who wore her hair braided and had warm, tender eyes, and who was likely the second eldest, went by the moniker Plume Gum. Hueloc surmised Plume Gum had an honest spirit, unhindered, unashamed. The touch of her lips on his foot was like a sweet, tender breath of morning mist. Hueloc feared he was becoming delirious. He was unable, in fact, to place all of them with their names. Other than Plume Gum, the sincere; Jewel Twirler, the small, freckled one; and Night Jasmine the unscathed dark beauty, the rest were just girl names and sweet buttercup faces. Except, of course, their eldest sister Paper Flower. Hueloc, in the tender passion of the moment, even forgot to assign each a price. Such was his mood.

Introductions completed, Paper Flower glanced skyward, looking worried. "It is fast growing dark. I fear these jungles, for they are *his* now."

"His? Whose?" Hueloc questioned.

"Mocker. He will come."

"Good. We shall give the mean bastard the hard end of my sword and have done with him. Here, help me up, good ladies."

Plume Gum took hold of one of his arms, and Paper Flower the other. A moment, on his feet, he felt the blood drain down into his toes, and the girls faded out, the rumble sound of the falls grew distant, but he slowly came back into focus. He took a deep breath and let it out slowly. They watched him with concern. "See here," he said in a stern voice, "you girls have been paying too much heed to these pagan, carnivorous priests. He spat to the side. "They are calumniating, good-for-nothing frogs! Idolaters! Vile pederasts, all of them, flesh-eating sons of whores. I spit on them." He spat again.

They stared at him, troubled. After a moment Paper Flower spoke.

"Even with Mocker aside, my lord, is it not wise to find shelter? There are . . . wolves in the jungle, are there not?"

"Wolves? In this stinking piece of bush? Hardly. But there are insects that could suck you dry as a gourd drum. Tell you that much."

Hueloc glanced to the sky. By the look of the sun, he reasoned they had perhaps an hour, perhaps less, before there was darkness. But he had already been this way, a week earlier. Just beyond the blue-green pool of the falls, he had marked an animal path that led a short distance south to a sizable village. The village had a market plaza and a temple tower three stories high, and was stocked with God-fearing Nonaloca priests and simple tillers of soil. It was the kind of jungle city-village one came across often in the Petén—Mayan, of course. Maya bred here like mosquitoes. Every so often, a drought or disease arrived, and they would die off by the hundreds; but in a few years they would have all reproduced, raising new broods of brown, sad faces.

"My cloak, my weapons," he said.

They scurried. The small one, Jewel Twirler, tied on his cloak, standing on tiptoe to set it over his big shoulders while another secured the clasp. Night Jasmine, who moved like a well-trained harlot of Zarahemla—where harlots were well trained indeed—brought his sword. If sex were incarnate and given flesh, it would walk and breathe the very image of Night Jasmine. As she turned away, her long hair brushed past him, smelling of flowers, ticking into his bones. Plume Gum, the one with braided hair who had the position of second in command among them, gave him his atlatl. Paper Flower handed him his bundle of moonsteel darts, and he fastened them against his back to the bracket in his belt, looping his cloak over them. They believed him to be a Dragon Lord, so be it. For a time he would behave as one. After all, the jungle would stretch on a bit, and the damned, vile priests of the Highborn had them all so nervous, they were like cats in a canoe.

"We will go, following that jungle trail," Hueloc commanded, motioning. "There is a village ahead, so you need not fear, good sisters, we shall all be well. I have paid an innkeeper to prepare several tents and reed huts for our arrival, and to have us all well fed."

Paper Flower paused. "You mean . . . you knew, beforehand, we would flee into this jungle?"

"Ah . . . ah . . . yes. No. No, actually, it was merely a precaution, you see."

"But I thought you were expecting jade? Why would you have arranged shelter for us if you were expecting jade?"

Eventually, this one would discover him for all that he was. She was the kind of woman from which one seldom managed to keep secrets. He would make a point of selling her first.

"The lodging was meant for me and a few of the captains. We intended to travel through the jungle to Tikal, you see, on secret business. The rest, the main forces, they were to have returned to the passages of Anáhuac. But I do not suppose the innkeeper and tent sellers will mind that I come with women instead of battle-weary warriors stinking of blood."

She looked right through him. She did no longer believe his every word, he could tell, but the others listened with unquestioning eyes. Hueloc motioned to the road impatiently. "Come along now, all of you; keep together, all of us close together." Soon they were walking along the pathway, passing beneath tall, hulking shadows of mangroves whose leaves dragged through the wide, slow-moving river.

"Why did the Smoking Mirror come to the mountain, my lord?" the second eldest, Plume Gum, asked him. "You are a Dragon Lord, schooled of the mysteries. What has brought them?"

"The same thing that brings all his kind—pure and simple greed."

"You do not believe him to be fulfillment of prophecy?"

"The only prophecy he fulfilled is the kiss of my moonsteel dart. Parasitic frog—surprised me, bringing so many warriors. Dishonest bastard. However, by my beard, I am confident the Tolteca put fear in their febrile bones, down to their marrow."

"Those Tolteca are all dead by now, my lord," Paper Flower stated simply as they passed between narrow trunks of willow that lined the pathway to either side, leaving shadows almost as though they were passing through a cavern. The grumble of the waterfall had receded into the distance. Paper Flower looped his arm about her shoulder, helping to walk. She was strong—he would use this as a strong selling point, a strong, young, childbearing woman—best not to let them discover she was a bit cunning.

Hueloc's head was positively swimming with the effects of the Dog Wart root. Paper Flower smelled to him like a field of poppies in full bloom.

"Even the Tolteca would not have lasted a degree of the sun," she was saying. "I know. I have seen them."

"Seen who?"

"The armies of the Smoking Mirror; the ones who call themselves the Walkers, the Shadow Lords. We have seen them, and they are without number. We were upon the mountainside, taken prisoner, ascending the mountain's side toward the City of Thieves, and we looked upon the plains below, where lie the rivers and lakes of Utzlampa. The Shadow Walkers spread like insects over the land, likes ants upon a hill. They covered the earth. Everywhere their fires burned, without number, like the stars."

For the first time Hueloc felt a little alarmed. Was this possible? Such an army had never been seen in the Petén, such an army might even challenge Tollán. Paper Flower was certainly somber. Her position as the elder sister had given her a slight air of authority. He doubted she would lie, and worse, he doubted she would exaggerate. Armies without number camped in the valleys of Utzlampa— somehow, she must be mistaken. After all, even if she were clever, what would she know of armies? She was a woman, by God—gifted, perhaps intelligent, and given fire-passion eyes—but a woman just the same.

"It is your intention that we are to journey to Tikal?" Paper Flower asked.

"Yes."

"But these jungles are thick, my lord, they are wilderness. Do you know the way?"

"Of course. I have a map to guide us right here in . . . in my belt . . ." He paused, patting his hip belt where the map had been lodged before realizing with a quick stab of fear that it was gone. Hueloc was no scout. He knew the jungle, knew a bit of this, a bit of that, but he always had a map.

Then he noticed they were all giggling at him.

"What? What is it?"

"Do you mean this map?" Paper Flower asked, producing it

from her bodice where it had been carefully tucked, nestled between her breasts. She had tricked him, the little bint. Hueloc wondered how a Dragon Lord might respond.

"Ah, yes, there it is." He reached for it, but she slipped it back in, pulling the bodice tight.

"I will keep it safe," she told him.

"Of course, you . . . you keep it safe, elder sister, and warm, well protected."

There was a sudden sound, a screech. Hueloc had heard many an owl, many a hawk as it circled; but this was neither, nor was it an eagle. The *caw* sounded unlike any he had heard; and it pierced him, almost as though it had been directed downward against him, with force. Hueloc paused, startled. It was near dark, but there was still light, and though the trees were misty, vision was still good. Despite the fact Hueloc was almost certain something approached, there was nothing in the sky. Moving over the leaves of the trees, he saw a shadow.

A sudden fear struck Hueloc. He winced. The shadow-thing was growing. He braced himself, even reached for his sword, but the sky shadow came with such swiftness he had no time. It struck him full in the chest, knocking him back, and something sliced open the side of his cheek, even through his beard—a talon. Hueloc had seen a shadow-image, a great bird of prey, with eyes that glistened red and wet. Hueloc was a big man, well weighted, but was thrown back like a leaf tossed. Those girls behind him were scattered. Hueloc hit the trunk of a willow with such force he nearly blacked out. Paper Flower was flung to the side.

Before Hueloc's face, the shadow-thing unfolded out of itself, first from the center, until there stood a man. His head was shorn and his face was painted, and his naked, black-varnished body had only the mouth and eyes look otherwise; they had been circled in red. In either hand, he bore knives of rippled flint blades, and one of them was bloodied. The talon that had struck Hueloc was obsidian, the same that struck hearts from sacrificial chests.

Hueloc sucked in breath against the blow and pulled himself forward, ripping his sword from the belt loop, dropping low into a crouch, and bracing himself.

The priest lifted one leg high, in cat prance, then sprang forward, leaping, moving far too quickly to keep track of. Hueloc barely saved his neck from being hewed by a quick upward block with the flat of his sword that slammed into the priest's arm. The second knife sliced into Hueloc's leather armor, which was thick enough to offer resistance, at least enough resistance to allow Hueloc to ram his knee into the priest's bared genitals. The blow hiked the sorcerer up, lifting him off the ground a bit, and Hueloc shoved him back. Such a blow would have dropped any normal man, any two men. It would have left them a quivering mass on the ground. As Hueloc came forward, his big Dragon sword slicing through the air, the priest nimbly ducked, spinning past him too swiftly to follow.

Gods, this was impossible. Hueloc was forced to leap forward, tucking into a hard roll, the earth jarring him. He quickly turned, coming to his knees.

Throwing one of the girls to the side with a backhand blow, the sorcerer flung one of the knives at Hueloc. There would have been no dodging it. Hueloc blinked death, but one of the girls threw herself in its path, absorbed it. The sound of the blade *thudding* into that tender body sickened Hueloc.

The sorcerer somersaulted; from a standing start he flipped into the air, spinning, to drop directly before Hueloc. Hueloc screamed, harshly, slicing with the sword, and in fact, he had moved rapidly enough that the priest had to back-step, a little off balance, but when Hueloc came for a second thrust, the man lunged forward. Hueloc had to drop his sword, catching the priest's wrist in order to keep the knife from piercing his lung. The sorcerer's other hand seized Hueloc's neck in a grip so tight he felt the nails pierce his flesh. Hueloc went down on his back, then rolled, pinning the sorcerer beneath him. He grabbed the priest's face, sinking his thumb hard into an eye, so hard the eyeball squished out. The sorcerer's grip continued to tighten on Hueloc's throat. Any moment his windpipe would be snapped like a twig from a tree. Hueloc hissed, furious, and bit into the priest's nose, half screaming, shaking his head. He reared back, ripping off the nose. This, finally, had managed to break the tight hold on Hueloc's neck. Hueloc spat the nose back at the priest and it bounced off his face. The man was inhuman. Amazingly, with an unearthly snarl, he heaved Hueloc back, lifting him into the air, tossing him like a stone. Hueloc twisted, landed on his back, and the priest leapt over him, blood flushing out of the hole in the center of his face, and now both hands seized Hueloc's neck with amazing power, squeezing. Hueloc felt his skin splitting open. The body paint had left the man so oily, Hueloc couldn't get a grip. Hueloc started to panic, about to die. One of the sorcerer's fingers pierced Hueloc's skin, sinking into the muscle of his neck, and Hueloc feared, knowing the man's strength, that the intent was to rip his head off his shoulders.

Then he saw the figure of Paper Flower, balancing above her head a rock she maneuvered with considerable difficulty. She brought it down with both hands, uttering a shriek between clenched, white teeth. With a *crack*, the sorcerer's head split clear to the forehead. He dropped forward.

Hueloc snarled and threw the body aside, then pulled himself to his knees. Paper Flower was quickly beside him, as were many of the others.

"Are you injured, Great Gut?" Paper Flower whispered.

"Well, I am not dead," Hueloc muttered, coughing, sucking for air, "but that be the toughest priest I ever wrestled." He pounded his chest a couple of times and slowly got onto his knees, holding his throat.

The sorcerer lay in the bushes, the back of his head exposing the pink tissue of his brains, glistening in a sheen of blood. Hueloc was now finding his breath, but he paused, seeing one of the girls facedown. The sorcerer's knife was deep in her back, buried to the hilt, and Plume Gum, the second eldest, knelt over her.

"She is dead," Plume Gum said, head bowed. "It is White Owl." Tears dropped like rain from Plume Gum's eyes.

"Gods," Hueloc muttered, "little bint . . . should not have done that. Not for the likes of me." He swallowed and walked forward. He knelt over her, ripped the knife out of her back, and flung it aside. He started to lift her.

"My lord," Paper Flower said, drawing near. "We must leave her."

"We will carry her to the village, bury her proper," Hueloc muttered, still trying to lift her, but Paper Flower laid a hand on his shoulder.

"You have lost a great deal of blood. It will be enough for you just to lead us to the village. Also, it is nearly dark, and we must find shelter quickly. We must flee. Already demons come for us. He was only the first."

"That was no demon, girl, that was some filth-eating priest." He looked 'round at them. "Well, gods, we can't just leave her here."

"We must," Plume Gum said quietly.

He saw they were all resolute, even the small one, Jewel Twirler. He stood, wiped the blood from his face and beard, spat to the side a clot of skin still caught in his teeth. Paper Flower came forward and tied another torn piece of her skirt about his bloodied neck. She looped her arm about his.

"Come, Great Gut. We must move quickly, before darkness falls, for with the dark will come the Mocker."

Hueloc half limped, half ran along with her, the others hurrying about them in a group, all of them watching the trees, fearfully. "You . . . you say that as though you have seen him, elder sister."

"I have seen him," she answered, with such a tone in her voice Hueloc actually believed her.

He hurried as quickly as he could, with as little wish to be left in the night jungle as any of the girls. Whatever form this Mocker might take, Hueloc was quite certain he did not wish to discover it.

CHAPTER TWENTY-SEVEN
THE LORDS OF AZTLÁN

On a high plateau of the stone mountains, not far from the City of Thieves, the Shadow Lords had constructed a great plaza. Slaves had hewn it from the earth, fleshed it out in limestone. It was painted red, the color of song, of flower, of dance, the hue of lifeblood. This night, fires burned like stars from a thousand torches. On the first platform of a squat temple was a throne, carved of stone, overlaid in gold. Its seat was lined in the polished skin of a black leopard, and to either side of it rose tall, silver-gold staffs that burned white flame. Upon the throne sat the Smoking Mirror.

Gathered about Smoking Mirror, lowered on one knee and holding their weapons near their hearts, were his seven high captains, the Lords of Aztlán, warriors of the Night and the Wind. They had been given no glory in their land, but the Smoking Mirror had taught them. While they left for the narrow passage north, relegating the Old Ones to their deserts and their dying cities, the memories of Smoking Mirror's lessons regarding their identity and prophecy reverberated within. The Night and the Wind had taught their ancestors in the beginning, and he taught the way once more, everything he whispered to Smoking Mirror, and the warriors who once walked the shadows now walked again.

It had been a year, a year since their leaving, since the whisperer had told them to leave the lake of Aztlán, and had begun the descent. Only the youth had followed, but that was the wish of the Night and the Wind: to let the Old Ones fear the dawn in their crumbling cities; and, as their crops failed and the people continued the dying, it would not matter. The youth, the Lords of Aztlán would take what was always their birthright, what had ever been promised them—the cities found here, in the land north, rich with gold, fields of corn and cotton, and most of all, the Tolteca. Had not the fat merchant and his handful of Tolteca ventured here, tempting him? They had come just as the old missionary had described, forgetting the face of their God, ripe in prophecy.

The seven Shadow Walkers formed a semicircle before him, dark shields glistening in designs: the fangs of the jaguar, the sun disk, the curled serpent with hood flared. His captains waited in silence; they seemed to neither breathe nor stir, waiting as would ones wrought of stone. Then the conch-shell call of midnight sounded. Its long, eerie moan spilled into the sky.

Smoking Mirror glanced up. The Heavens were strewn with stars, like jewels scattered. In the City of Thieves, the priests would sacrifice those Tolteca who had been taken alive from battle—the strongest, those who had held out to the last, fighting like leopards. Already the armies of the thieves, four thousand strong, had joined him. When they understood he brought them a new God, when they suckled the sacred meat, they were filled with *the knowing*. The whisperer spoke in their ears, and their armies swelled the ranks of the Shadow Walkers. Soon, the strength of the Tolteca would become his as well. All that was required of them was to devour the Flower-Song. Already it had begun. The laughing whisper that had led Smoking Mirror since the day he stepped from the desert—the day of changing when he had come to call the children of Aztlán— had told him that this night he would go out to visit them in flesh, that the Mocker would stride, walking the earth and becoming the Night Speaker, the terror, this night.

When the second conch shell sounded, the warriors of Aztlán, now eight thousand strong and gathered upon the plateau, began to beat their shields with their weapons. Some had taken Tolteca swords, but the metal to it, which shown like the moon in brilliance, had been wetted in fire, darkened to a smoky hue. Those who had

TOLTECA

not taken swords carried the weapons of their homeland, of the highland waters, the axe, the mace, the thrusting spear, the bow and arrow. They beat their weapons in unison, a heavy, solid sound—the heartbeat of the Mocker, the *thud-thud* of the Night Axe. With this, their heartbeat echoing, Smoking Mirror surveyed the eyes of his seven high captains, his Slayers.

Smoking Mirror lifted his hand.

"Hummingbird-of-the-Left," he said quietly.

Hummingbird-of-the-Left lowered his head toward his Lord. He wore a blue chest mirror, his cloak was the dark blue of waters, and his shield bore the symbol of the Purple Hummingbird.

"I will send you north," the Smoking Mirror said, "to the passage where the Tolteca have erected their mighty wall, where they protect their Northland, their sacred Anáhuac. There you will go with your one thousand, and you shall bring to the mighty Tolteca Flower-Song."

"My lord." Hummingbird-of-the-Left said quietly, looking up. His eyes smoldered like the eyes of the leopard that waits.

The heartbeat, the *thud-thud* of weapons against shields continued, it lifted to the night sky in adoration, the whispered voice of the Mocker.

"Terror Speaker," Smoking Mirror said.

Terror Speaker inclined his head. He wore a black jaguar-skin tunic and a gray, a cotton mantle interwoven with bright crimson featherwork. His helmet was wrought in twisted, black agate horns, with eagle talons that curled over the temples.

"You shall go on the Hummingbird's right," said Smoking Mirror. "You shall strike terror into their hearts, you shall take your thousand, and you shall devour their cities, their villages. You shall skin their children like taking flesh for tanning. You shall burn them, slowly, that they will always remember you're coming, that they shall not forget the Shadow Walkers have returned to their lands once more."

Terror Speaker's eyes darkened, like obsidian glass were his eyes, sharp, the searching eyes of a hawk as it glides. Smoking Mirror shifted, feeling his skin alive, stinging with night air, swelling with fever. From the City of Thieves, the offerings of sacrificial hearts to the Night and the Wind were feeding him strength.

"Blood Gatherer," he said, and Blood Gatherer lowered his shorn head. One great lock fell from its side, braided and tied with black silk-cotton. On his chest, he wore a polished mirror disk that swallowed light. The numbers of men Blood Gatherer had slain were uncounted. "You shall go on the Hummingbird's left, with your thousand, and you shall descend like a storm that rolls over the land and plucks the eyes of the innocent. You shall bring the terror of *the knowing* to the Sons of God."

Blood Gatherer lifted his gaze and looked upon his king. A smile curled across his lips. Smoking Mirror let himself smile back. It was odd, striking that they were given such strength; it was like water running through them, like smell in the night.

"The rest—Serpent Slayer, Flower Prince, Sun Ray, Departer— you shall be with me, with your Lord, and we will descend from the mountain and sweep clean the jungles, the rivers, the forest places. We shall come forth out of the wilderness and swallow the old cities of the Nonaloca kings. Our friends, the Gadiantons, who have joined their hearts with ours, they shall walk with us, for they are, as we, descended of the ancients of Aztlán. Their God delivers them up, the Nonaloca, offers them, like meat for our substance. Their sun has died; it lies but an ember in the sky, a cinder without heat. They have no sun; therefore we will share with them our sun, that they may again be warm."

Smoking Mirror smiled and he let the whisperer into this flesh and then stood. The whisperer chuckled, this laughing whisper. He was there, with them now, the Mocker who suckles all mankind. Seeing the axe of the Night in the eyes of their Lord, the seven Shadow Walkers stood also, shivering, quickened and as they screamed, the *thud* of the warriors' shields stepped up in pace. The heartbeat of the Mocker grew excited; it swelled, like sex before the climax.

CHAPTER TWENTY-EIGHT
THE MONKEY PRINCE

There should have been lights from the city; they were close enough. Hueloc searched for them as darkness fell. The Dog Wart root had begun to abate, and pain stabbed at him every now and then, rippled through his guts. Paper Flower had been right, he had lost a lot blood and was getting woozy, not from the herbs or the drugs, but from fatigue.

It had been a perfect plan, all of it, so well thought out, so many weeks preparing. Of all his plans, this one had been the most thorough. Yet here he was, staggering through growing darkness with something of a childish nightmare fear, the kind he remembered having when he was no more than a boy living in Zarahemla. Hueloc's father had lived on the outskirts of the city, where he kept great flocks. Sometimes, at night, cats would come down from the hills. He would hear the snarls from his sleeping mat, and his skin would shiver. Hueloc imagined them to be demons, and in his child's mind, they had not been much different from the shadow-priest he had just wrestled. Paper Flower's eyes had not wavered when she described demons attacking her village, and she was levelheaded for a girl. Perhaps, after all, such things did exist. Perhaps demons did walk, striding through the jungles, searching. A branch slapped across his face and Hueloc jerked back so suddenly he staggered and fell to one knee.

Paper Flower was instantly beside him. "Are you all right, Great Gut?"

He nodded, struggled back to his feet. "Fine, good, just a bit . . .

shy of balance. Been a long day, elder sister."

"Where is this city you have spoken of, with the innkeeper?"

Hueloc paused, swallowed. He noticed the others watching—dark almond eyes, long, silken hair. At night, the hair of Chichimec women seemed to undertake an unearthly quality, as though they, above all races, above all women, were blessed of the moon.

"Got to be close," Hueloc said, unable to hide the nervousness in his own voice.

"Then where are the city fires?" Paper Flower demanded. "Why is it we hear only the jungle? Should we not hear the conch shell trumpets of the temple towers calling darkness?"

Hueloc paused, winced, and shifted his jaw.

"Lord Great Gut," she said, her voice taking on a certain edge, "the truth. Are we lost?" She paused, waiting. They were all waiting.

"Impossible!" he said sternly. Hueloc searched the trees. Lost? It couldn't be. He had mapped out the entire route by daylight four days previously. Yet, they had been following an animal path. One animal path looked much the same as another in near dark.

"Hueloc . . ." she warned.

"No!" he shouted. "Absolutely not. Not lost. You think I would let us get lost in the filthy jungle? Ah? Be sucked dry by godless bugs! We are not lost. Trust me." He shook himself, then started forward, staggering a bit, but determined. "There is a small city up ahead of us, by God and whore's blood, and we are going to find it!"

They hurried after him, falling in behind, Plume Gum to his left, Paper Flower to his right. Hueloc realized his own fears had now pushed him into a half-staggered run. He cursed himself. He was becoming unnerved, and this she-bitch Paper Flower, she was responsible. All these stories of her Mocker, the night-wind—gods, but she had gotten to him. As soon as he was within proper civilization, he would sell her—bargain-price, special reduced rate. Hueloc had never feared the jungles. He had walked in motherless veldt thick as soup and had never given a second thought to night demons. Now here he was, actually choking back panic, all the fault of this bint. God should not fashion such women; it was not righteous.

He paused suddenly. A pathway branched off to the right. He stared at it, blinking.

"What now?" Paper Flower asked. "What do you see?"

"By God, woman, will you let me think?" he snarled. He looked to the right, then the left. "You and your vile demon stories! Sweet mother of frogs, you have me so frightened of seeing your leechlike Mocker, I can no longer think straight!"

"Then you are lost!"

"I am not lost!" he screamed, fists clenched. They were all watching him with unbidden fear. He calmed. "This way," he pointed, and continued.

"This city of yours," Paper Flower said, falling in beside him, "is this city Nonaloca?"

"Why? You need a priest?"

"No. But you might, being so worried."

"I will maintain. Be assured."

"It is Nonaloca?"

"Is any city Nonaloca? Hard to tell any longer." Hueloc stumbled on flagstone. He had almost tripped. He paused, slapped a hand out to catch Paper Flower, inadvertently clasping her breast. With the surge of panic that jolted him, Hueloc hardly noticed. They all stopped, gathering tightly about him. Hueloc looked down, not really wishing to see what he was seeing. The pathway they had followed was now lined in flagstones that led to a flight of short steps. The steps were bordered on each side by wide, lush green hillocks. The city was just before them. If they were dogs, they could smell it. Yet there were no lights, only dull, dark shadow.

"Sons of whores," Hueloc muttered.

"What?" Paper Flower pressed.

"You wait here," he said, starting forward. She grabbed his arm.

"No! We stay together. You would leave us, in these woods, in the dark! What manner of warrior are you?"

He pointed, angry. "There is the city! There! You just step up that rise and it is in front of our face! Understand, elder sister?"

She stared, troubled. "No lights," she muttered.

"Ah! You noticed. See here, I knew you were quick, I knew that the moment we met. We should not be walking like fools into what may be a pit of vipers."

"Vipers light no fires, Great Gut. Warriors, however, do light fires. Therefore, whatever waits . . . waits in darkness. The warriors of the Mocker celebrate: they dance, they sing, they drink. But there is only silence beyond."

Hueloc narrowed one brow. He looked to the others. "All right, then . . . together, close. Let us go forth, elder sister, and pray to God."

The girls behind Hueloc joined hands. He paused as Paper Flower, to his right, and Plume Gum to his left, clasped his hands.

Hueloc turned, started slowly up the flight of stairs. The market plaza of Tlacopán fell into view. Although the sun had died, the images offered needed little light to produce effect. The moon, the stars, the wide, white limestone plaza flat open to the sky—this was enough.

There were bodies. Actually, as the plaza fell into view, Hueloc realized they were more *body parts*. They were littered everywhere, and the blood on the plaza was still sticky, still wet enough to glisten in moonlight. He and the girls paused, stricken, huddled close. The temple rose from the plaza on a layered platform. Its base flesh was littered and butchered. It looked like a slaughter of peccary or a deer harvest, sectioned torsos, arms, legs, haunches of meat. Blood had spilt down the steps of the temple towers, and its stone sides glistened in streaks. In one corner of the plaza was a pile of what Hueloc first thought were yellow fruit, until he realized with a numbed jolt they were heads, heaped one upon another. One of the girls started to scream, but Paper Flower motioned and Plume Gum slapped a hand over the girl's mouth, pulled her close.

Hueloc felt sick. Perhaps he was not a veteran of slaughter, perhaps he was not as grizzled as a Toltec jungle warrior was, but he was by no means a stranger to the sword. He was no weak man.

Staring over the plaza of Tlacopán, he was flushed with revulsion. He couldn't take his eyes off a torso that was once a woman. The breasts had been cut away, leaving white streaks of ribs.

Hueloc started to heave. He slapped his hand across his mouth, but it was useless; he had to turn to the side and jettison a stream of vomit. He stepped back, snarling.

"Mother of God, but this is inhuman . . ."

Paper Flower caught his arm, and it was only then he realized he had almost blacked out, almost fallen. It was blood loss caused this, he told himself.

"Breathe slower, Great Gut. Breathe careful, steady."

He complied, taking measured breaths. Her hand, where it held his arm, was squeezing so tight the nails bit into his skin.

"This is not a good place to be," she said, quietly, close to him. "We must find an enclosure—shelter. Quickly, Hueloc, for there is great evil here."

"Evil? No, gods, I thought this was a flower festival."

"You know this city. Show us direction."

Hueloc nodded. He motioned. "This way."

He found his legs and made his way across the plaza. The huts he had secured for them were on the far side of the city, but he had no desire to cross through to reach them. Instead, he remembered the residence of the priests just south of the plaza. He stepped on something, stumbled, and looked down to see a hand, with a woman's slender fingers, rolling from the impact of his sandal. He realized, as he walked, that whatever occurred had happened less than half a day ago. Blood was still moist in spots. He noticed, glancing back, his sandal left foot tracks across the limestone. It was like a moment out of a nightmare, the tracks of his sandals over the white stone.

One of the girls started screaming and Hueloc whirled, his sword clearing his belt. It was the little one, Jewel Twirler, and she screamed even though her sisters were at her side. She had inadvertently stepped into a carcass, and her foot was lodged in rib bones.

"Aw, for God's love!" Hueloc bounded forward, shoving several of them aside, and knelt. He had to reach into the cold torso and snap a rib before he could free Jewel Twirler's leg. He swooped her into his arms and turned, carrying her, walking hastily. She put her arms about his neck, burying her face into his beard. "You just stay calm, little one," he said quietly, "we are going to find shelter, get some rest. What has happened here, it is over, ended. These poor, godless souls, they are past any care of what befell them." He noticed Paper Flower watching him, but when he caught her glance, she quickly averted her eyes.

They reached the priests' quarters—rows of squared, single-story stone dwellings. The outside was rich in elaborate, geometric designs and Mayan glyphs. Hueloc chose the first of them and paused before a black, empty doorway. He set Jewel Twirler down, tucking her into Paper Flower's arm.

"You wouldn't mind that I go in there first, elder sister? Make certain the priests left the place presentable?" he asked her.

"Please," Paper Flower answered.

Hueloc stepped inside. The priests lived simply here. The city was not wealthy enough to acquire tribute like some of the jungle centers of the Maya. There were only sleeping mats, several low, squat tables, wall hangings of woven fiber; and in one corner sat a body, propped up against the wall, eyes open. In the shadows, the eyes were all that stood out, the whites of them, staring at him. He walked forward. It was a priest, still wearing the dark robes and cloaks favored by Mayan Nonalocas. His feet were bare, and his head had not been shorn. Something had broken open his chest. It didn't look to have been cut or crushed; it appeared a giant hand had thrust in and broken the sternum open and outward. Hueloc wrenched a wall hanging from its staves and rolled the priest's body up in it. He hoisted the body onto his shoulder. He glanced around—one last check—then trudged out.

Outside Hueloc heaved the body aside. It bounced with dull *thuds* off the limestone.

"Even the floor has been swept, sisters. This is a safe haven. We will just pretend we are all somewhere else, some fine city. On the coast perhaps, eh? In the morning, after breakfast of fruit and coconut milk, we will all go out, swim in blue-green waters. Come, everyone, inside." He waited by the doorway, ushering them through. Jewel Twirler lingered close to him, her hand clinging to his arm. Paper Flower was the last of the others to enter. She paused briefly in the doorway and offered Hueloc a glance that might have been something of a thank you. As much as he would ever get out of her, perhaps. Someone had hardened this bint like an atlatl-dart over flame.

"Come ahead, little one," he said to Jewel Twirler, putting his big arm about her shoulder and ducking as they entered.

Once inside, Hueloc re-hung the door cloth of thick weave, and to comfort them further, he overturned a table and laid it up against the doorway. There was now only a small, square window that opened to the night. He thought of covering it, but it did allow for a sliver of moonlight. He wandered over to the back wall, feeling weary, and slid down it to a sitting position. Once his eyes had adjusted to the darkness, he noticed that they had gathered about him, once again, in a half-circle. As at the waterfall, Plume Gum had taken position on his left, Paper Flower to his right. Almost directly before him were the glistening legs of Night Jasmine, well exposed where she had drawn them up, hugging her knees, her eyes watching him as though he might be preparing to offer prayer. Jewel Twirler had moved over and squeezed between himself and Plume Gum, and Hueloc inadvertently put his arm about her, pulling her close. He grinned at them all.

"Too bad we haven't got that cooked meal I had planned."

"Not so bad," Paper Flower muttered. "I lost any desire for food crossing the marketplace."

"What if they come back?" asked one of the girls whose name he remembered as something like Azure Tree.

"They have nothing to come back for," Hueloc answered. "By the look of things, they finished all their work and moved on. Probably miles from here." He noticed they took little assurance in this.

"What if we encounter them while we journey to Tikal following your map?" Paper Flower asked.

"Well, if that occurs, then . . . we will run. Like our buttocks are aflame! As fast as we can, eh? Yes?" He chuckled, but failed to elicit any smiles. "Relax! Everything is fine. Everything is well."

Sounds drifted in from outside—snarling sounds. Hueloc actually shivered realizing these were cats, coming for the meat—either that or shape shifters.

"Just some ordinary jungle cats . . . having supper," he assured them. "Nothing with which to concern ourselves." He grinned. Perhaps in deliberate contradiction, a hissing and alarmingly close snarl yowled gruesomely. Several of the girls looked to the doorway, worried. Jewel Twirler inched closer. "Now, now, not to be concerned about them. After all, little sisters, think on it: why should they venture in here and go to all the trouble of killing and eating us when there is meat out there all prepared, halved, and quartered, all but roasted up for them?" He drew a deep sigh and coughed, holding his side. Pain stabbed in jolts. "Ah . . . this wound. Tell me, any of you sisters happen to snag a bit of that wart-root-dog?"

"It is Dog Wart root," Paper Flower said, then nodded to Night Jasmine who crept forward and untied a small pouch looped in her belt. Hueloc stared at length on her thighs. Night Jasmine had perhaps the most wonderful legs Hueloc had ever seen. Night Jasmine drew a length of her long, black hair over her shoulder and took out a piece of root, digging at it with sharp nails, kneading it quickly. She lifted a wedge of it and Hueloc willingly opened his mouth.

"Keep it beneath your tongue a moment. Suck," Night Jasmine said to him, so close he could just grab her. He packed the wedge of Dog Wart root beneath his tongue.

"You know, sisters," he said, calmly, "it is not so unusual to find carnage in the jungles. Things may not be as dark as they appear. There has been war in this thicket for as long as history has been written, at least as long as Nonaloca history has been written. This is a place of war. Why, one day a city will be the realm of the Nonaloca, where high priests sing to God from their temple towers, and next, well, the next the priests are all slain and have their heads mounted on poles and the dark-skinned cutthroat Chichimeca are . . . oh, ahhh, forgot myself here. What I mean is that you are all Chichimeca yourselves. Of course you're different. Not like the others, eh? I was speaking of the . . . the, er, the mean ones."

"We understand your meaning, my lord," Paper Flower said, offering a slight smile.

"Well, slaughter here, in the jungle, in the thicket—it is hardly uncommon."

A fight had broken out among beasts outside, and the screams were particularly unnerving.

"How about a story?" Hueloc suggested. They looked at him with puzzlement. "Something to take our thoughts off . . . ah, off more unpleasant . . . thoughts. I know a good many stories. Like to hear one?" There was silence.

"Yes," Paper Flower said, "do tell us a story, Great Gut. As long as it is proper."

"Proper? What do you mean—proper?"

"Not bloody."

"Oh," Great Gut chuckled a bit, "I thought perhaps you did not want it to be a tale of desire." He grinned wide. "Pertaining to things of passion." He looked 'round at them. "I mean, you are all . . . nice girls, I assume."

Paper Flower nodded. "And may we assume you are also a nice Dragon Warrior?"

There were giggles. Great Gut grinned. "Of course!" he assured them. "Why, I have led a clean life. A virtuous life! A life of chastity. Of —"

"Humility," Paper Flower interjected.

"Humility, yes, humility."

"And honesty," she added, a knowing glint in her eye.

"Honesty above all!" Hueloc insisted.

"He is Tolteca," added Jewel Twirler. "He cannot lie."

"There, you see, elder sister? What more can I add? Now, let me see . . . ah, I have it! Yes. A good story. This is the story of the monkey prince."

"Is that a Lord?" asked Plume Gum.

"No, but it is a monkey who quite nearly became one."

He paused to suck down Dog Wart root juice. It didn't taste bad at all. Bitter enough to make one gag, but considering the warm, soothing appeal of it in his belly, as smooth as honey. He made a quick mental note that when this was all over, he would return and pursue this herb. The name "Dog Wart root" admittedly gave him little clue as to what exactly it was, but as soon as the opportunity arose, he would come back, perhaps with Night Jasmine (the thought of going into business with Paper Flower chilled him), and gather a supply of it. If it could be reproduced and grown from seeds, he would harvest whole fields in secret places, sell it, powdered, in the markets of Tollán and Cholula for enormous profit. He would become fat with wealth. Filthy with wealth. He noticed the girls waiting and cleared his throat.

"Well then, this is the story of Grand Prince, who was, in truth, a monkey, and how I almost became a rich man."

"But . . ." Jewel Twirler said. "Are you not already a Great Lord? Already wealthy?"

"Well, understand, little one, that not all Lords are rich. Some Lords, well, they have their wealth . . . invested. They are in the *process* of becoming rich. That is what you might say of me, that I am almost rich. I have my money invested."

"In what?" asked Paper Flower, watching him very carefully now.

"Ah . . . I . . ." He paused and grinned. "Many things, many things. Who can recall? I would have to consult with my money counters back there in Zarahemla to be certain. Anyway, it so happened that one day I was in the jungles of the far south. We were seeking out opal gems. In the jungle I discovered a rare creature—

monkeys of red hair with idiotic faces. I then and there hit upon an idea. We decided to capture a number of them and return to Tollán. So we did. Since they had learned to come into our camps and steal food, we set traps. In no time, we had twenty young, prime, red monkeys. When my associate and I returned to Zarahemla, we let it be known—in other words, we spread the rumor—that we had returned with monkeys of a most rare and mysterious breed. We led people to believe they were in fact magical, and that they had come from an island in the deep of the waters where they were possessed of a wizard's spell."

"But . . . were they?" asked Jewel Twirler.

Hueloc paused. "Were they what?"

"Magical?"

"Ahhh . . . well . . ."

"You did not lie," Paper Flower posed. "Did you, my lord?"

"Lie? No. No! Of course not. We meant to train these vile little monkeys, to teach them astounding and amazing domestic feats: to sweep floors, to wash up plates, to make tomato tortillas. So, in truth, they were to become learned of wizards, although, admittedly the wizards were me and my partner, who was named Great Otter."

"In other words," Paper Flower injected, "Lord Great Gut was not lying. He was merely deceiving people."

"Yes. I mean, no, no, not at all. Certainly not. Why, in truth, in a way, Great Otter *was* a wizard. Had only you known him, you would not disagree. He was a man particularly talented in working with animals. He even taught birds to speak. He had enormous cages filled with these . . . these talking birds. Talking is an understatement. Gods, but they could unnerve a man, ceaseless squawking, like caged women, mother of frogs, but I nearly wrung their little necks one night. But that is another story, isn't it? The bird story. Not only had he trained birds, but also snakes, if you could believe. He had these small snakes, little green bastards so quick you would be amazed, and he had them trained, you see, to crawl up women's skirts. Ha! Ha! Gods, but Great Otter could get a rouse out of market day . . ." Hueloc had to chuckle a moment, reminiscing.

"I do not understand," Plume Gum said carefully. "To crawl up women's skirts . . . and what, my lord?"

"Well . . . they would crawl up there and . . . and . . ." He paused. "The idea, you see, was to have a laugh, to have sport with them!"

"With whom?" Paper Flower said. "The women or the snakes?"

"Never mind, never mind!" Hueloc cursed a moment under his breath. "After all, this is not the snake story! By gods! Nor is it the bird story! This is the parasitic-monkey story! Am I right?" He glared at them, red-faced. "So. Then. As it happened, Great Otter worked in earnest for months, working, working, day and night. He became obsessed with these vile little monkeys! He was like a man possessed of demons. It was frightening. His skin got pale from never going out in the sun. His eyes, they had dark circles about them, and he took on a deranged appearance. I actually, at one point, you understand, feared for his wits. He told me these were like no monkeys he had ever known, and Great Otter had the acquaintance of not a few monkeys in his day. So you see, Jewel Twirler, Paper Flower, it therefore turned out they *were* somewhat magical. Why, they were so smart that with Great Otter's talents they became amazingly responsible."

"Responsible . . . monkeys?" questioned one of the others. Hueloc tried to recall her name and came up with Flower-Flower, which he was certain was incorrect.

"Yes. One of them, in particular. Great Otter named this one particularly responsible monkey Grand Prince, and this because he was so quick to learn, so impressionable to Great Otter's instructions, that he seemed to be a prince among monkeys. Great Otter decided he would use Grand Prince as an example of what a magical monkey could accomplish, and arranged publicly, on the greatest market day of Zarahemla, for Grand Prince to perform an astonishing feat. Grand Prince was to go to the market and bring back a full bucket of mead. We reasoned, you see, that there were many rich men there in Zarahemla who paid servants to do just such a thing, to walk to the marketplace and bring back fresh mead each morning.

"On the day of the great exhibition, many nobles, many rich merchants gathered just to see, to observe Great Otter's magical monkey. Great Otter had put clothes on Grand Prince: a fine, feather mantle, sandals of peccary skin, and a painted breechclout. Great Otter came out of his house, which was in an upper story of one of the richer sectors of the city; and there, with the nobles and rich merchants gathered below, he loudly proclaimed, 'Grand Prince, it is a fine morning, and I would wish to have mead for my belly! Go forth to the marketplace and purchase from the mead seller a bucketful of *pulque*. Do not let him cheat you, even though he will try, for he is a sly one. Make certain he fills the bucket full before you pay him. Then bring back the mead and we will have a drink together, here, on the terrace.'

"To the amazement of all, Grand Prince took the bucket and leapt over the terrace, starting off for market, walking upright like a demented little old man, sauntering as though he had an ear of corn shoved up his buttocks, proud as you could ask. Everyone followed, watching, whispering, and I was among them, as amazed as anyone else was. Grand Prince swaggered through the marketplace as though he were himself a noble of reputed birthright, carrying his bucket in one hand and three bronze coins tight in the other. He made his way straight to the mead seller, never looking to one side or the other . . . although he did pause once to look upon a female dancer dressed in a colored skirt. It was then I should have realized that something was slightly odd in Grand Prince's attitude, for he gazed on the dancer with a crazed gleam in his eye. Then he just went on his way, and I thought nothing more of it.

"When he reached the mead seller, Grand Prince boldly stepped forth and thrust his bucket in the old man's face, pounding on the mead cask. The mead seller, guessing this was only a monkey, and therefore simpleminded, filled the bucket barely half full. Yet Grand Prince was not the fool he had been taken for; he would not let the coins out of his tight little fist until the bucket was filled to its lip, at which time he paid the seller and started home.

"At this people clapped and cheered. By now, everything was going so well, I was already calculating what profit was to be made. Why, we had over fifteen of these red monkeys, all of them trained to do astonishing feats. One could even go fishing with a string and hook."

Jewel Twirler gasped.

"Grand Prince impressed everyone present that he was indeed no ordinary monkey, that he must have been, in fact, magical. He came swaggering down the street, barely spilling a drop. When several children came out to tease him and call him names, he utterly ignored them. When one threw rocks at him, Grand Prince calmly set down his bucket and threw rocks back until the boy ran away. I remember thinking to myself at that point I was going to be rich, filthy rich, ugly rich. We would soon be selling monkeys to the finest nobles in the land, no palace would be without one, and everywhere the demand would grow. Then, sadly, I discovered Grand Prince had one . . . slight aberration."

"Aberration?" questioned Jewel Twirler.

"Yes, an aberration is a defect, an imperfection. You see, Grand Prince was truly remarkable, and in fact, he nearly reached the house of Great Otter without incident, but then, well, then he saw a painted woman. Apparently, he had not seen a painted woman before, and the sight of one distracted him. She was a harlot, passing through the market. Her lips were painted red, her eyes hued blue and green, and on her cheeks were orange circles. There were large, oval plugs hanging from her ears, and in her hair, which was tinted a bright, fiery red, were trinkets of polished brass. She even tinkled. Her effect on Grand Prince was deadly. He stopped cold, gaping in utter dismay. Perhaps he was confused, believing women to be chaste, or, perhaps he was aroused. Who could say? Who could know? Whatever the reason, Grand Prince began to lose his mind from the sight of her.

"Great Otter had been standing on his terrace, calmly smoking a tobacco pipe, pretending to be waiting for his morning mead, when he realized something had gone wrong. Grand Prince was in the street just below. Great Otter came to the edge of the terrace and began waving his arms, shouting at Grand Prince. 'The mead! The mead! Forget the wench! Bring the mead! We will have a drink, up here, on the terrace!' Hearing him, Grand Prince almost forgot about the painted woman, almost he lifted his bucket and continued on, desirous of having a drink with his master; but then he paused. He looked once more upon the painted harlot, and with that, he evidently lost his wits altogether. He ran, leaping, whooping, and pounced upon the whore, knocking her to the ground where he ripped off her blouse, her skirt, and began yanking out her red hair in fistfuls. The harlot was screaming, fearing, I suppose, she was about to be raped. Finally, a pair of Market Watchers wrested the poor, deranged little fellow off her and bound him with cords of hemp, carrying him away by force.

"Needless to say, Great Otter was disgraced. The people of the city said that his monkeys were, in fact, demons, sent to curse the Nonaloca by an evil wizard. I lost everything, everything. Gods, it was terrible. I was utterly destitute. All our monkeys were confiscated by the court. I understand they were taken to an island and left there to fend for themselves. I picture them even to this day— all of them working away, washing linen, making tortillas, fishing, sweeping up . . ."

There was silence for a time. Hueloc grinned. Several of them smiled back, then one or two began to giggle; and in a moment, they were all laughing together. Hueloc slapped his thigh.

"Ha! Ah? Ha-ha!" He bellowed guffaws. "Sweeping up! The lot of them!" he howled. "Probably the cleanest island in all the sea!" He noticed even Paper Flower laughing.

Sometime later, most of them, exhausted to begin with, had fallen asleep, huddled together about Hueloc on the stone floor. None had used the mats of the priests and Hueloc did not really blame them. Jewel Twirler was curled against one side of him, her head nestled in his shoulder.

Just before Hueloc slipped off into sleep, he noticed that one was still awake, propped against the wall, on watch. Her arms were wrapped around her knees and her eyes were open. It was, of course, Paper Flower. But had he such an elder sister, he thought, he might not have turned into this degree of vile reprobate.

CHAPTER TWENTY-NINE
MOCKER

Hueloc was dreaming. He was at a large table, set with food, and he was indeed starving. The last morsel of food had been the seedcakes he ate before the coming of the Chichimec prince, and they had been swallowed into his belly like drops of rain into a lake. He was so hungry. Here, before him, a great table, one set for lords. Of course, Hueloc was meant to be a lord. When he was a boy, he would go with his father to the marketplace and see the Great Lords of the Nonaloca of Tollán-Zarahemla. The lords were clothed in rich linen, bearing cloaks of the finest artisans worked in feather paintings, and they wore earplugs of jade and belts of gold-and-crimson cotton. Rich lords walked proudly and upright, for they were not only rich, but also well bred. Hueloc's father had been an old man, the twelfth son of a dirt farmer, a raiser of peccary herds, and a harvester of corn and amaranth seed. Sometimes Hueloc would see in his father's dulled, vacant eyes only misery, a lost life, and Hueloc had sworn that no matter the course of his future, he would not destroy the mold of the earth like his father, he would not burn out his youth until his eyes were as dull as weathered stone. He would, instead, become wealthy.

In his dream, Hueloc sat before a table set for nobles, because at last, now that he was five decades in age, now that his skin had toughened and his beard had grown thorny and salted, now, finally, he had become rich. He looked over the table, servants scurrying about, and hunger welling up from his belly, smells filling his nostrils. Then, appallingly, he realized this was no ordinary table. Instead of ripe, plump plums, there on his plate were the eyes of

Jewel Twirler. Instead of side hunks of peccary meat, instead of turkey legs and fine, roasted fish, there before him were the bronze thighs, the calves, the arms, and the torso . . . of Night Jasmine. Hueloc started screaming, pushing away, but his chair was riveted, and the servants, who, it turned out, were not servants at all, but priests painted black, they were holding him, forcing him to eat, forcing Jewel Twirler's glittering green eyes into his mouth.

He sat bolt upright, sweating, gasping. It took a moment to realize where he was, that in fact, the girls were here, and Jewel Twirler curled beside him, her head in her arms, and Night Jasmine lay on her side, hair splayed over the stone of the floor, all of her parts still attached.

Suddenly Hueloc froze, his breath caught in his throat as stabs of panic choked him. He couldn't move, couldn't breathe. In the window before him was the face of the dead priest, the same he had wrapped in a rug and tossed out into the marketplace. Dead, he was nonetheless standing there, staring in at them through the window, his eyes white and blank, his lips drawn back in a lunatic smile, his skin tight across his skull. There was a sound, a *thud*, rhythmic: *thud, thud, thud*, like an axe working at a tree.

Hueloc sneered and spat to the side. He drew himself up, curled his hand about the hilt of his sword. He had lived too many years, had sweated too much of his life out to crawl, livid in fear. He drew the sword and looked directly at the visage. Some calumniating sorcerer had prepared this. Hueloc started forward, fueling himself with anger. "Cut this bastard to ribbons," he muttered. He reached for the cloth covering of the doorway. The figure had turned, following him, the white eyes watching Hueloc's every movement. Hueloc's fingers curled about a corner of the door covering. A sliver of night fell through and with it something literally came against him, a palpable thing, dark, deep, a cold, unfeeling numbness. He noticed, from the corner of his eye, that the figure was moving toward the door. *Thud. Thud.*

Hueloc gritted his teeth. Enough of witchery! He pulled the door cover back even farther, and dark came in like fingers searching.

"Hueloc!" he heard Paper Flower scream. She leapt from her place against the wall and hurled forward, tackling him. They fell to the floor. Paper Flower was atop him, her hands holding down his arms. "It's him!" she whispered. "*Him!*"

Hueloc winced, started to speak, but paused.

"You open the door cover and he is invited in!"

He stared at her, his skin shivering, a sickening kind of feeling washing through him. Seeing he wasn't resisting, she fell forward, and Hueloc held her, shutting his eyes. Hueloc saw through the edge of the door covering, he saw the figure waiting, groping. Then he realized the sound was the demon's chest, opening, slamming, opening, slamming, like jaws. Hueloc hissed, turning to the side, holding Paper Flower tight. Then, slowly, the sound receded.

"Leaving," Paper Flower whispered. "He is leaving."

"Paper Flower, would . . . would you mind, if I just . . . just held you?"

She nestled close, and he held her, feeling the warmth of her. Hueloc realized for the first time that the world he had known had somehow ended. It was as though the sun had died, and a dark veil of prophecy began to unfold, for Hueloc had heard it spoken that such a day would come, that the Fourth Sun of the ancestors would someday end.

CHAPTER THIRTY
THE CAPTIVE

C oyotl had never seen a Chichimec with blue eyes, and this one had eyes that were somehow more than blue. They looked silver, in the dim firelight of the chamber.

The cages were just tight enough that he could not stand. Coyotl remained crouched, backed against the hard, wooden bars. They had kept him caged for days in the squared chamber, most probably beneath a jungle temple, for the stones here were ancient and water dripped constantly. Humidity left the walls milky. The only light was the slow burning pitch of the torches, the only sound the constant dripping. Coyotl no longer knew if it was night or day.

He had been waiting for them to come, for the moment when they would take him, for he knew these were Shadow Walkers, Flesh Eaters, and that he was being spared only for sacrifice.

But this one, this one who came was no priest. By the way he moved, by the way his attendants kept their eyes downcast, this could be none other than the Lord of the Shadow Walkers. The High-Blood circled Coyotl's cage, but the little ballplayer offered only a cold expression; he let nothing through, not even curiosity. There were two guards with the Shadow Lord, both of them lean, edged killers.

The Chichimec paused before Coyotl's cage. He was carrying a head, held by the neck, his hand into its meat, and now he lifted it. Tarantula. The eyes had been ripped out. Coyotl did not react, but the Shadow Lord seemed to expect this. He tossed the head with a flick of his hand. It bounced along the stone and came to rest in a corner of the cavern. Of course they were going to leave it there to rot, something for Coyotl to ponder as he waited in his cage.

"What can you tell me, Toltec?" the king asked in carefully enunciated Nonaloca. This took Coyotl a bit by surprise. The warriors he had seen, even the priests that had come to feed him, all of them had spoken a harsh, bitter tongue, a speech Coyotl had never heard. But this one, this silver-eyed king, he spoke the language of the Calmecac—the tongue of priests. Missionaries! Of course, that was the reason for the smooth Nonaloca; the silver-eyed one had been taught by missionaries. He probably ate them afterward.

Coyotl did not answer. He let his eyes close a bit, like a cat's, bored.

The king nodded and one of the Slayers laid Topiltzin's cloak out on a stone. They had certainly found it among the ball equipment Rattle Eagle had with him when they were captured. Coyotl wondered if Rattle Eagle was still alive. The last he had seen of the big man, they had beaten him unconscious and carried him away bound in hemp. Here, in this cavern, Coyotl had been alone but for an occasional sacrificial priest. They wanted him fatter. They brought food that still littered the floor about Coyotl's cage where he had shoved it, untouched. If they wanted Coyotl as meat, they would have to settle for him being stringy! He was confident at least that he would make a foul meal.

Coyotl did not let himself look at Topiltzin's cloak, and remained bored.

"Who would wear this mantle?" the Shadow Lord asked.

Coyotl tried to stare at him and breathe only stone and cold, but something hidden there, in those eyes, it shook even Coyotl's nerve. This was a sorcerer, and a powerful one, more powerful than any Coyotl had ever encountered. Something reached through and mockingly and toyed with Coyotl's fear. This Shadow Lord, despite Coyotl's gambling face, knew he was scared. The sorcerer would not have missed the slightest tick, the smallest hesitation. Indeed, a half-smile curled as the Shadow Walker lifted the rubberball, turned it in the torchlight, black and gold.

"I know of this game. We play something very similar in the mountains. Here it is called the rubberball game, is it not?"

Coyotl offered no response.

"In Aztlán, we play with sticks." The sorcerer drew closer. His face was sharp and intense; it seemed almost an artist's work, almost perfect. "I will find him! He could not be far. Of course, the jungles are thick, but I am shadow. I cover the earth."

Coyotl watched him leave, his warriors with him. Only when he was alone, when their footsteps no longer echoed, only then did Coyotl shiver. He fell back against the cage and took quick breath.

They had left Topiltzin's cloak on the stone, and firelight played in the feather painting of the sky serpent. Coyotl did not know the future, could not see past this hour, but he could feel it, cold and dark. He tried to calm himself, to shake the dread. He closed his eyes and let his mind wander and he found himself, surprisingly, back in Tollán, in those early days when he had first met Topiltzin.

He remembered one day in particular, the day he had met the Dragon of Tollán. If any one could help them now, it was that old man. What Coyotl remembered most about him was his spirit. The spirit of Sky Dragon had been like looking into the face of the sun; it left him overwhelmed. The occasion had been a strange one, one that had taken Coyotl by surprise. He had known Topiltzin only half a year and that whole time had been spent teaching the prince the rubberball game, though Coyotl could scarcely imagine what the Prince of Tollán could gain by playing the ancient rubberball game of Xibalba.

Topiltzin had arranged to meet Coyotl in the marketplace near the palace at mid-sun and Coyotl had waited nervously. In those days, he did not entirely trust Topiltzin, for the young prince seemed a little crazy—even as crazy as he did, and that truly made him nervous. Coyotl had been sitting against a pillar, baking in the hot sun when Topiltzin arrived, coming up to him, crouching, and waiting for a long time before he spoke. The prince was so handsome he gave the illusion of being a young god. His hair in the sun was almost white, his skin bronze, his eyes a dark, penetrating blue. Coyotl knew of women who had offered sex just for Coyotl to arrange a chance meeting with Topiltzin.

Blue Prince stared distantly, transfixed, as if he were interested in what was happening in the market plaza, though Coyotl knew that was the furthest thing from his mind.

Finally, Topiltzin said, "I have decided."

"Decided what, my prince?"

Topiltzin's dark blue eyes turned on Coyotl and studied him intently. "I will play the rubberball game."

"We have been playing the rubberball game—the entire rainy season."

"I will play it there—in the Southland."

Only professional ballplayers traveled to the Southland to play. What Topiltzin meant was that he had decided to live his life as a player of the rubberball game, leave his royal trappings behind. Coyotl smiled, shaking his head.

"Blue Prince, Blue Prince, listen to me—this is no life for you! Gods, you are rich! You are a warrior, an Eagle Knight. You have all Tollán in the palm of your hand. These people worship you! You are the son of Sky Dragon!"

"It is no use, Coyotl. I have made my decision. I will play the rubberball game. You must come with me now."

"Where?"

"To tell my father."

Coyotl gasped. "This is a joke, am I right? You are toying with me."

"No, you must come."

"I do not think he will take well to the idea, Topiltzin. If I recall—"

"All you have to do is stand beside me. You do not have to speak. Just stand there and hear what is said between us."

"He'll have me thrown in prison! Gods, he'll see what I have done to his son and he'll call the Watchers. I won't see the light of day for the next seven years."

"He will not throw you in jail. And if he does . . . I will go with you."

"Blue Prince, look on me. I am a rubberball player. Do you not see that I am wretched? I have no place among the Tolteca, I am of no worth, and therefore I play the rubberball game. But you are a prince! Women would die just to behold your face! You do not want to throw your life away as I have mine. I had no life to begin with, it was only fitting that I throw it away. But you . . ."

"He is waiting, Coyotl. Are you coming or not?"

Topiltzin stood. Coyotl knew him well enough to understand that when he fixed on something, there was no dissuading him, so he shrugged, pulled himself to his feet, and followed.

Coyotl had never been inside a palace, and he stared in awe as they walked between the large, polished mahogany columns and into the antechamber. Just inside, Topiltzin nodded to a servant who ran barefoot down the hall and returned shortly with a deerskin bag of ball equipment. Topiltzin took it, slung it over his shoulder, and glanced at Coyotl.

"Are you ready?" Topiltzin asked.

"Am I ready? Am I ready? I would rather eat grub worms. I'm the one trying to talk you out of this, remember?"

"Just don't let him scare you."

"What about you? Are you going to let him scare you?"

Topiltzin stared a moment, not answering, then swiftly turned and stared off down a pillared hallway. Coyotl followed, keeping close to Topiltzin's side. He feared that were they separated, he'd be thrown into the prisons for sure because Coyotl did not look anything like a resident of the palace—he looked much more like a thief.

"What if he loses his temper?" Coyotl asked.

"My father never loses his temper."

"Then why bring me along?"

Again, Topiltzin didn't answer. Coyotl knew how the Dragon

felt about the rubberball game—everyone did. It was not allowed in the Northland any longer; at least, not formally. Anyone caught betting on a rubberball game faced enormous fines, or even one of the prison camps in the desert. Coyotl guessed he understood why. In the past years, it had not been uncommon for parents to wager their own children on the outcome of a rubberball game. More often than not, after the game, there was violence and even death. The morning after would typically find a body or two in some alleyway, a big winner in the games, but not in the aftermath. The only place a professional player could earn a living any longer was in the south where the Maya still played the game with fevered relish and the Dragon's influence was only marginal. In the Southland, Coyotl was sure, the rubberball game would always be played.

They ascended several flights of stairs and then walked briskly down another long hall. Light from outside found its way through open porticos and window slits, illuminating the wall panels. One, an image of the Night Butterfly, radiating with all the splendor of the sun rising in the east, positively took his breath. Coyotl forgot himself and stopped to stare, mesmerized.

"Coyotl . . ." Topiltzin said, impatient.

Coyotl hurried after him and they soon entered a large room—the inner sanctum, the king's own chamber. The walls were of obsidian, polished to mirror brilliance. The floor was marble. In this chamber, seated in an ornate chair before a table on which rested large books of brass plates, was none other than Sky Dragon. Coyotl stopped, frozen, unable to go any farther. Topiltzin strode into the center of the room and waited, the deerskin bag over his shoulder.

"Father," Topiltzin said.

Sky Dragon closed the book in front of him and laid a moonsteel stylus beside it. The Tolteca wrote on the plates with the sharpest metals, and they wrote in symbols like birds and painted eyes, crosses and strange lines. These were the symbols of the Land of the Red and the Black. Only high priests could read or write the vertical columns of symbols, but Sky Dragon was the highest of priests, he was the speaker, the elder.

"This is Coyotl," Topiltzin said boldly, "my friend."

Sky Dragon had large, powerful eyes the color of stone, almost white, and when they shifted past Topiltzin to look at Coyotl, the little ballplayer couldn't breathe, for these were eyes that had seen the face of God—or so it was said among the common people. Seeing the Dragon in the flesh, Coyotl believed. This face had seen God! Coyotl shivered as though he were cold. He wished right now he could be anywhere but here. He would burn up for his sins if the eyes studied him any longer.

"I . . . I have made a decision, Father," Topiltzin said.

Coyotl noticed Sky Dragon's jaw tighten, and blessedly, the eyes turned away to look at the Blue Prince. The thorny, gray brows narrowed—he already knew what Topiltzin was going to say.

"I am leaving tomorrow for the Southland . . ." Topiltzin paused, his voice uncertain. He found courage and continued, determined. "I go to play the rubberball game."

There was silence. Coyotl felt his skin shiver as Sky Dragon stood. For a moment the Dragon paused, his hands resting on the table, his head lowered, and in that moment he looked somewhat human, weighted with trouble. He then walked about the table and approached Topiltzin. Coyotl felt himself panic. He had to fight the impulse to run. In the back of his mind, though it was foolish, he could picture the Dragon taking a bolt from Heaven and flinging it. Instead, the Dragon stepped past Coyotl and suddenly grabbed Topiltzin's deerskin bag that held the rubberball equipment. With a roar, Sky Dragon heaved it into the air. It sailed over the portico, vanishing. There was a polished stone table nearby and Sky Dragon took hold of one corner and threw it with a snarl. The stone must have been heavy, yet it sailed across the room as though it were plaster and smashed against one wall. Fruit rolled past Coyotl's feet. Coyotl could no longer breathe or move, but Topiltzin hadn't flinched; he stared back defiantly. A moment later they faced each other and Topiltzin curled one hand into a fist, but all he did was turn away. He calmly strode for the portico. Coyotl desperately wanted to scream, "Stop!" Yet Topiltzin merely vaulted over the portico's edge, leaving Coyotl very, very alone in the presence of the Dragon. Coyotl knew what the Blue Prince was doing; he was going after his ball equipment, as though that were at all important now.

Coyotl swallowed, unable to move, possibly as terrified as he had ever been in his life. Facing Gadianton robbers on a mountain pass paled before this. Sky Dragon was there, right there, looking at no one else but him, and there was nowhere to hide.

"Coyotl," the Dragon said, his voice deep and resinous, like controlled thunder.

"My lord," Coyotl answered, nervously, not daring to look into the Dragon's terrible white eyes.

Sky Dragon paused a moment—he could have been reading Coyotl's thoughts, looking into his soul, opening up his mind like a crab shell. Or perhaps he was about to call the Watchers and have him thrown into the darkest, dankest prison.

"You appear to be a man of worldly ways," Sky Dragon said.

"Regrettably, my lord, I am. Yes."

"You know the Southland well?"

"All too well, my lord."

Sky Dragon drew a long breath and said, "Take care of my son, Coyotl. Keep him alive."

Coyotl shivered. He slowly turned, sweated from fear, but then, amazingly, the old man's eyes softened, they were merely human, they were touched . . . by tears.

"Promise me," Sky Dragon whispered.

Coyotl dropped to one knee and lowered his head. "My lord, you have my word, my promise."

He felt a heavy, warm hand touch his shoulder, he heard the soft pad of bare feet, and only after moments passed did he dare look up. The Dragon was gone, but his presence seemed to linger in the room; and it was strength, a quiet, reassuring, fatherly strength. If ever Coyotl had a father as this, he would never have become the lowly reprobate he was.

Coyotl knew this occurrence was the last time Topiltzin had ever spoken to his father. They had left the next day for the Southland, and the next six years Topiltzin and Coyotl played the rubberball game as though there were no other meaning to life, and the Blue Prince had never, once, motioned his father's name.

Now, pressed against the hard wicker of the cage, Coyotl wondered how it was he was going to be able to keep his promise to the Dragon. Perhaps the Dragon would let him borrow a bit of that power, a bit of his great and terrible God.

He ended up staring at the gouged-out eyes of Tarantula. Something caught his attention. He winced in disbelief and leaned forward. Tarantula's head had one eye, fitted into the bloodied socket—an obsidian crystal with flecks of turquoise—a demon's eye!

CHAPTER THIRTY-ONE
KINDRED

From where she watched, Star Skirt could see the faces of those who had gathered to hear the one they called the Teacher. It was a small gathering. She had heard stories, when she was younger, of how the Dragon would preach from the hilltops and thousands would gather. Here, in the woods west of the city, there was only a handful, a quiet gathering to hear the son of Sky Dragon. Some of them were children, and these sat closest, about his feet, small faces looking up. Star Skirt had known many priests who spoke from the temple towers, who shouted fiery words of prophecy, but Sky Teacher spoke as none of these. He sat cross-legged upon a large, flat rock, and spoke quietly.

"Many are the gifts He has given." Sky Teacher looked into each of their eyes as he spoke. "Gifts of spirit, of kindness. For some, wisdom. To another, that he might work miracles; that he might, by God's hand, by His word, heal wounds, soften hearts. Yet all gifts borne by men, they shift, they move, they have breath only by a quickening, which quickening is the Word, is faith. And faith is belief in what *is*, but what is not *seen*. There are men who will say to you: *Mark! There is only flesh, only what we touch, only what we comprehend with our eyes.* They will tell you fools alone believe in the spirit of the Word. In this, then, let us be as fools. Let us see without our eyes and feel without touching! For then we shall find stars glittering where others see only night, only darkness, and we shall behold the face of God when others see only the sun, only the moon. Now, come forth . . . any who wish, who need that I minister unto them."

She stepped back, even farther into the shadow. He stood and they came to him. One by one, they knelt there before him, and he laid his hands upon them, closed softly his eyes. She could not hear the words he spoke over them, but when the last of them had come forth, they gathered about him, and he raised his palms, offering the sign of the word.

"My brothers, my sisters, blessed are you. Few any longer seek light. Darkness now lures the Tolteca, draws them forth, a dark which is death, which comes to them in the night, a Mocker. Walk therefore with care, each step, each path. God be with you, even the Light Whose Name Is Splendor, which quickens our hearts, which gives us breath."

They began to disperse, taking their children, walking slowly along a stone pathway that led back to Tollán. Some lingered, speaking with him briefly, distant words, a touch, a smile. Then he remained, alone. He stood for a moment staring after them, and there was something in his look, a deep sadness, as though he were seeing them for the last time. He sat upon the rock and lay back, searching the blue of the sky.

She shivered. Star Skirt had never been a follower of priests. Of course, she had performed the rites that had been given her family. She had carried flowers in processions, she had taken the blood and flesh, and she had believed, perhaps, that somewhere there dwelt a god . . . somewhere far, somewhere unknowable. With him, with Sky Teacher, it was different, almost frightening. She feared God might appear just to speak with him. Such was the way he spoke of God, as though, perhaps, He was a father, or merely a friend.

Star Skirt had been unable to tell her mother why it was she remained in Tollán. She had explained only that she wished to stay until market day—two days from now—and would return with one of the many merchant caravans that plied eastward and passed through Chalaco. If she had been more honest with her intentions, her mother might have thought Wolf Feather's madness had simply passed onto his elder sister.

TOLTECA

Though her heart beat quickly, she stepped forward into the light. Slowly, she walked to where he lay, making no sound, moving across the yellow wheatgrass that tufted the floor of the glade, until, amazingly, she was standing over him. His long, yellow-gold hair spilled over the rock. There was a haze of a beard, two, three days' growth, and reddish. His face had a gentle cut, almost boyish. At the same time, the brow gave it a severity, a hardness. She had seen him harden his eyes, when the spirit-thing came from out of her brother, and that face had been stone, and fierce. He wore simple priests' robes. His shoulders were broad, powerful, not at all what one might expect of a priest. If gods were to walk the earth, they would look like this, she told herself. They would even speak like him.

She felt her breath catch. Suddenly, his eyes were open, deep, sky blue, watching her. She stepped back, startled. She had completely forgotten herself.

Sky Teacher sat up. He looked at her somewhat astonished, and he smiled. She bowed onto one knee, and Sky Teacher was swiftly off the rock, beside her, touching her chin, lifting her face.

"You have no reason to bow before me."

"But I do, my lord."

"No, I am only your brother, and you, only my sister."

She nodded.

"And you, Eslabeth, what have you been doing? Have you been hiding in the trees over there? How long?"

"Forgive me. I meant to come forward, but . . ." She sighed, gesturing. "I have never really been one of them."

"Them?"

"The followers of your God."

"My God?"

"Yes, what I mean, my lord, is . . ."

"Sky Teacher . . ."

"Oh, of course, Sky Teacher—what I meant to say was, well, they always seemed so . . . so assured of themselves, the followers in our village. They looked down upon others, they judged all of us, and because of this I disliked them."

Sky Teacher nodded. "Sometimes I wonder any longer if there are any *followers*. Sometimes I believe the only ones who hear are the children. You should remember, Eslabeth, in the future, it is not what is in their hearts that will judge you—only what is in yours. I see, even by your eyes, that your heart is pure, like a child's. If the stones were turned it would be your light and witness that judged them."

He eased back, sitting against the rock. "Eslabeth. I do so like your name."

"Thank you, my lor . . . ah, Sky Teacher. But no one calls me that. I'm—"

"It has been four days. I believed you had returned to your village with your mother. I had given up. I must confess, I was disappointed."

She lowered her gaze. "I thought I would give you opportunity to reconsider. Perhaps the fever of the moment . . . what I mean is . . . perhaps you spoke in haste when you spoke to me at the palace, and if so, then I would understand. You wouldn't have to explain, because, well . . . even the best of us go a little crazy now and then."

"The best and the worst of us." He stared off at the sky a moment, lost in thought, then nodded. "It is true, there was a fever of sorts. But I have no need to reconsider."

"Yes, but . . . how can you be sure? You do not know me."

"But I do know you. And you know me. However, perhaps it is time we learned more." He stood, offered his hand, helped her to her feet. "Let us walk together. It is beautiful here, and far enough from the city that you can no longer hear the vendors calling their wares. I come here often. It seems more holy sometimes than the Calmecac."

They walked together, silent for a time, not toward Tollán, but toward the high, snowy peak of White Woman, shadowy in the distance where it seemed to have snagged clouds from the sky. There was a smell of forest here and the air was cooler than in the city.

"How did you find me?"

"I went to the Calmecac and the young priest, Temictal, he

remembered me."

"And . . . where have you been staying?"

"I still have my family's tent in the outskirts south of the city, with the pilgrims."

"Well then, Eslabeth, speak to me of yourself."

"What would you like to know, my lor . . ." She paused. When he glanced at her, they both laughed a little. "I cannot seem to forget you are the son of the Dragon."

"I am merely a teacher, Eslabeth. There are no lords here."

"Yes. Well, what would you like to know about me?"

"Everything. Barring that, just what comes to your heart."

She paused for a moment. She thought how infrequent it was for her to speak to men, let alone to one man, alone like this. Star Skirt tended to be quiet, to keep her life well guarded. But there was something about him that left her unafraid. Maybe it was the shadow of his God all around them. "I am yet young," she said, "ten and seven years, but I feel—or at least I believe—that I am wise for my years. Our father, a warrior and hunter, has been gone for a long while, so long my mother no longer hopes for his return. We fear he is among the dead. Perhaps because of this I have aged more than my years. I am eldest of my brother and sisters, and have had to care for them."

"How many are there?"

"We are six. Four are sisters; one is my brother, Wolf Feather, whom you saved from madness."

"And how is Wolf Feather?"

"He is healed. When my mother left for Chalaco, he was laughing."

He nodded. "Please continue."

"Actually, there is not much else. I suppose I have led a simple life."

"Few of us lead simple lives, even in quiet villages."

She pondered. "Well, once I slew a leopard."

"Really? On your own?"

"Yes. He attacked our village's flocks at night, and I killed him with a spear-thrower. My father taught me to hunt when I was young, before my brother was born. He said to me, 'Star Skirt, it appears I may not have any sons, so I shall teach you to hunt like a man.' And he did, I suppose, for when there came a leopard down from the hills to ravish the flocks, I took up the atlatl and I slew him by putting a dart through his side. He fell over and was dead."

"Then, besides being an elder sister, you are also a leopard slayer."

"Yes, I suppose. I also make very good tortillas and tamales. I have even sold them at market when we had need of money."

"An elder sister, a leopard slayer, a merchant, and a master cook. You see, not so simple after all."

She smiled. "And you, Sky Teacher? What would you tell me of yourself?"

"Well, I haven't led as adventurous a life as yours, I'm afraid."

"No. You are just the son of the Dragon, the Prince of Tollán, a revered priest known even in the distant hills as the Teacher, and perhaps our future king."

"There, you see? How mundane."

"How ordinary!"

They laughed and his eyes sparkled so. She guessed that he loved to laugh.

"Tell me then, Eslabeth, have you had time to consider an answer to my moment of craziness?"

Her heart jumped. She took a breath and nodded.

"And?"

"I have decided, in my heart, that if you truly wish to take me as your wife, then I shall give myself to you."

He stopped walking, turned to her. Yet his reaction surprised her, for his eyes appeared saddened. He held out both hands and she let him take hers. He squeezed her fingers.

"I am honored, Eslabeth."

"And I am honored also, Sky Teacher."

He smiled, but there was a mist in his eyes. He turned and continued walking, holding one of her hands lightly. She marveled at how his emotions seemed so quick, so unbidden. It surprised her. She had thought priests were much colder, much more solemn, that God would make them that way, press them like stone.

He said, "I surprised even myself when I asked you to marry. I fear it is my own loneliness, my own pain that moves me. As strange as it may sound, I believe I love you. I believe I have always loved you. Does this sound foolish to you?"

"Yes, foolish. But I have heard it said that fools oft see stars glitter where others see only night."

She noticed a small herd of deer watching from the woods, watching calm and unafraid, and Star Skirt imagined that was because they knew him, they felt his spirit and there was no need to flee. When she looked back, she found he was studying her. He smiled.

"Well, then—let it be so. We shall become one flesh, one heart. Even though we steal time to do so."

"Why do you say that we 'steal time'? I do not understand."

"I do not understand myself fully, but time seems quick; I feel a shadow closing."

"What do you mean?"

"It doesn't matter. Not today. Today we have found one another. I would like to believe it was meant to be—that we find one another—even in this late hour. It is not an accident, this. It is why, when we find each other's eyes we seem not strangers, and I recognize you, as though we have laughed before, ran before, as though we shared so many things . . ."

He paused, lost in thought, and Star Skirt shivered because what he said did ring true. She had seen those soft blue eyes so many times, heard this voice.

"It is a memory," he added. "We are kindred, Eslabeth. Kindred can see across time. We are from the same place in the sky, we are the singers, the children of the seventh star, and the winds of the night sky had taught us before. We remember . . . home." He was seeing something, and it almost frightened her, the light in his eyes, as though he knew things, secrets, the names of stars and even how they came to be in the sky, that if she looked deeper into his eyes there was nothing she could not ask.

She nodded. "Do we wait, Sky Teacher? Do we journey together a time before we wed?"

"If it were not for the shadows I see, yes, of course. But time is so thin . . ."

"What do you mean—thin? What are you saying?"

The blue eyes seemed to soften as though he forced something aside, and when they turned on her they were again the comforting, quiet blue, merely human now.

"Sky Teacher?" she said when all he did was stare.

"We will make one journey. There is someone we must find—another singer."

"Your brother? The ballplayer?"

"I wish, but no, no, he is too far south, he is . . ." He paused a second, troubled, but this time shook it off. "We must find my father."

Her mouth parted, she felt a slight chill. His father, who was known as the Wrath of God. "The Sky Dragon?" she whispered. "But I thought . . ."

"Yes?"

"What I mean is, the people say that he is ascended, that he is a part of the Heavens now."

"He always seemed one with the stars, but no, Eslabeth, I can find him. It is a fair journey, due south into the desert land. Unless you have other matters to attend, I would ask that we leave right away. A sudden choice, I know, madness like everything else I've been speaking this day but . . . at least the journey would give us time to learn more of one another. It will also mean a great deal to him to know I have found you. He has always urged me to take a wife." He paused. "But I'm forgetting so much. You, you have family. What of your mother, Eslabeth? It is my guess you have not told her."

"I just couldn't find the words. She believes I remained in Tollán for market day."

"We should send her word. I could dispatch a runner for your village. I would feel better if she knew."

"A runner comes to Chalaco and tells my mother that her daughter is marrying the Prince of Tollán."

He smiled, shaking his head. "A runner comes to tell her she marries a Nonaloca priest, a Teacher of the Calmecac."

"Of course."

"After we visit my father, we will journey to your village, and I will arrange for a simple celebration to be held. This way, it will not be such a shock to her."

"My mother always fancied I would marry a bricklayer, perhaps a tiller of the soil, a herdsman, a man of simple means."

"Then she was right." He paused and leaned back against the trunk of a tree. The shadow of White Mountain was growing long. "Almost dark," he said.

"Should we not begin back for the city?"

"Let the city lie this night in its smells and its obsidian dust. We will start south."

"Now? But . . . would we not have to gather supplies for our journey first?"

"They are gathered already, all the supplies we need. The earth has spent years gathering them."

He took her hand, squeezing. "Eslabeth . . . Eslabeth . . . you wouldn't mind, as we journey, that I keep saying your name over and over?"

"No."

"Come, we can walk during night sky, almost till dawn."

"Will your father be shocked? To see us when we come out of the flatlands?"

"No. I suspect he already knows we are coming."

CHAPTER THIRTY-TWO
THE FIRE SERPENT

Fire Serpent had tracked them for two days. He knew who they were—Blood Gatherers. He crossed their path first as one might cross the carcass left by a beast who'd been mangled and cleaned to the bone. The Blood Gatherers had devoured scores of jungle cities of the Maya, rended their flesh, sucked their blood. Parahon, the Mayan chief high judge, had been right. Something indeed was preparing to move against the coastal cities of the Nonaloca Maya. Blood Gatherers were going before them. Fire Serpent had been intent on reaching Tikal, but now had changed his mind. Before addressing Tikal, he would exterminate this death squad, these flesh eaters. Whatever world, whatever earth hollow from which they had emerged, he would hurl them back.

When they had found the most recent slaughtered village, the Toltec, Blade Companion, had studied the remains carefully. He had even broken a few ribs of carcasses to look into the entrails. He had carefully examined the remains littered about the temples. He had walked the perimeters of the village, searching for signs, before he returned to Fire Serpent in the central plaza. Fire Serpent was already preparing his warriors, taking up arms for pursuit.

"These are Shadow Walkers," Blade Companion had said. "There is no doubt." He held up a polished mirror disc that had been found at the base of the temple. "This is the ancient mark of the Sun-Priests. This must be the work of Blood Gatherers. The main armies cannot be far. If you linger, Fire Serpent, you may well be swallowed by them."

Fire Serpent had never fully trusted any Toltec other than the

Dragon. Though Blade Companion was an able warrior, he was still a white man, bearded, weak.

"What are you suggesting?" Fire Serpent said calmly.

"Perhaps, with your strength, Tikal could resist, at least long enough that armies from Anáhuac could help."

Fire Serpent didn't answer; he turned away.

"It would at least give us time," Blade Companion added. "I will send one of my captains to reach the north passage and get word to the Dragon Lords."

Fire Serpent turned on him, angry. "You believe they would come here? The Tolteca leave Tollán, cross the northern mountains, into the Petén? No, my friend. The Tolteca shall fall back to the Northland—to their own. I am all this jungle has, and you know it."

Blade Companion paused. He didn't argue. Once it might have been different, but times had changed.

"Fire Serpent, what good will you do in the jungles hunting sorcerers? You will leave the high cities open to the armies of the Shadow Walkers like flocks untended. If the blood of this village brings pain to your eyes, think of the same carnage wrought upon Tikal, or Uxmal, or Chichén. Forget this. March for Tikal, Fire Serpent! Pray to God you reach it in time."

Fire Serpent didn't respond, he only gazed at the body of a woman, absent of skin, the bloodied musculature dried brittle. His gaze lifted to meet those of Obsidian Sword who stared back angrily, one fist clenched tight. Obsidian Sword was Fire Serpent's first commander, and he had family who lived here, in this very village, a sister and brother-in-law, a young nephew whose parts, whose flesh, may well lay scattered somewhere on the plaza.

"Without you," Blade Companion continued, carefully, "Tikal will fall. Like a star falls from the sky. They will devour its temples, its children, like wolves upon scatterlings."

"You go your way, Tolteca, I shall go mine. This shall be answered. These priests, these flesh suckers, they shall taste the sting of the Fire Serpent. Tikal is a fat whore, ripe for cutting. She feeds the Tolteca, but she gives nothing to these, the small people, the forest dwellers, the farmers. If the mighty Shadow Walkers were as swollen as their legend, Tikal would fall with or without me. What good would I be in the face of the sands of the sea? But this, this blood here that fills your nostrils, the moans of these innocents, this I will answer. I will give them rest."

Blade Companion shifted his jaw, looked once more over the plaza. "Then I must bid you farewell."

Fire Serpent nodded. Blade Companion offered the sign of the word with his palm, and Fire Serpent returned it. The four Toltec captains left with Fire Serpent's warriors had gathered at the edge of the plaza, and now Blade Companion joined them. They would leave for the north, taking no provisions, carrying only their weapons. They had shed themselves of all but loin-clouts and leather chest armor, for they would run through the jungles, swift, silent. They were good, they were able and cunning warriors, some of the best he had known, but Fire Serpent felt certain none of them would ever reach the north. There had come to the world an age of last breath, of final song, and the funeral drum already kept slow pace. There had been signs in the sky. Fire Serpent had watched them. A comet had blazed, one never seen. Three days, like a coiled serpent it cut over the southern horizon, a herald of the coming of prophecy. They had passed through a field soon thereafter which lay littered with the bodies of swallows, hundreds of them, like stones strewn. Moreover, four nights before, the mist of the jungle had bathed the moon in blood. The sky spoke, it uttered breath, it whispered. The Evening Star of the year Seven Death shone in the sky, like a second moon was its light, showering the earth like rain, and with it there came a shadow, growing longer each day. This had been spoken of---written.

Fire Serpent stared at the temple; it was a simple white-limestone temple built by Nonaloca priests. It was a hill of shouting, a place where once the high speakers came to teach their children, where once was given the law and the covenant. Now it lay stained in a black coating of dried blood. These had been simple people. They raised their crops, raised their children, obeyed their priests, unfolded their lives in rituals of their calendars, in honor of their ancestors. They brought their sacrifices, their first-flocks, their choice crops, their chosen gifts, each season to the priests. They prayed to God, whispering down the rains. Now their blood lay so thick upon the temple it had dried in caked scales like parched earth.

Obsidian Sword drew up beside him. Though his eyes were those of a hawk, cold as night sky, they were nonetheless misted in tears. His hand curled about the hilt of his sword, clenching, un-clenching.

"Perhaps," Fire Serpent said quietly, "God has forgotten these people. But we have not." He looked into the forest, where the Blood Gatherers had left a trail as they proceeded. "Let us take blood for blood, my brother."

Obsidian Sword drew his lips back in a snarl, then threw his head back and screamed. His war cry echoed through the jungle; it went forth, piercing. The Slayers of the Fire Serpent assembled, to hunt.

▨▨▨▨▨▨▨▨▨▨▨▨▨▨▨▨▨▨▨

Fire Serpent's warriors had moved fleet through the jungles, barely resting, swiftest at night, like panthers gliding. If one were to stand amid the trees, to watch them pass, the Slayers would have seemed merely shadows passing, silent and swift. Only twice had they slept, in shade found from midday sun.

They had come upon the sorcerers' camps several times, but the blood priests left few clues. Any but the Slayers of the Fire Serpent would have lost them. The sorcerers often seemed to vanish, dissolve into the jungles. Perhaps these sorcerers were strangers to this land, but they were no strangers to the jungle, they were no strangers to flight.

K. MICHAEL WRIGHT

Now, midday, Fire Serpent was spending most of his energy in the ascent of a volcano mountain peak that reared out of the jungle floor to the sky. The Blood Gatherers had fled straight up the cone of the thunder mountain, into its rain forests, the fog clouds of the sky. As Fire Serpent climbed, clearing foliage with broad strokes of his sword, the air came into his lungs wet and warm. The thick foliage was coated everywhere in an almost satin sheen of lichen.

Fire Serpent's Slayers had fanned out, forming a wedge for the ascent, and were spread to both flanks of Fire Serpent and his captains. Fire Serpent guessed the priests to be perhaps a hundred, perhaps less. A large death squad, but far smaller than an army. He was surprised; he had expected more. Their slaughter, their path through the forests had the strength of five times their numbers. These, then, were prime killers. They smelled of their profession. Fire Serpent had the feeling almost as if he were going against his own men, his own blood, for these were kindred. They were flesh brothers. Yet they were as dark as a pit of the earth.

Fire Serpent and his warriors fell upon the stragglers, those too winded to keep pace with the prime. The death squads had been fleeing, full run, straight up the thunder mountain, and now their flanks were exposed. Here and there, the Slayers of Fire Serpent made swift kills. The Slayers snarled, sang, and pressed as best they could into a run, whipping past fronds, damp limbs, moss.

Fire Serpent saw them—Blood Gatherers, just ahead. Their bodies were painted a darken hue, leaving them like shadows. Some glanced behind, aware they were being overtaken and possibly amazed, for they had been good. It had taken all of Fire Serpent's cunning, all of his prowess, his best men, to hunt them down.

Seeing they were being conquered, the Blood Gatherers broke form and scrambled. Fire Serpent lifted his atlatl and slung it, choosing a strong, muscled back. His red-hue, moonsteel dart *whunked* deep into flesh and the man arched, cried out. The missiles of the

298

Slayers—quick, hardwood arrows, throwing spears, atlatls, and well-aimed flint-rock shrapnel—now whispered. Here and there, Fire Serpent found himself leaping a body.

Then the Blood Gatherers turned.

It was not something Fire Serpent expected; it took him by surprise. Suddenly, the sorcerers screamed—not the panicked screams of fleeing wounded, but the guttural cries of attack. In moments, Fire Serpent realized the trap. Pursued by larger forces he would have done the same—a feigned retreat into steep and deadly terrain, then turning when least expected in shock attack. The main body of the Blood Gatherer's warriors came at Fire Serpent and his warriors with the slope of the mountain to their advantage. They broke through the mist like the earth had opened its mouth and spewed them out.

"Brace yourselves!" Fire Serpent screamed, and dug in.

They hit like stones flung down the hill, they hit with the flicker tongue of Tolteca moonsteel swords, with a rain of atlatl-darts that whizzed through the trees whispery and deadly. Fire Serpent saw one of his captains go down without a sound; he had absorbed a throwing spear into his shield, but a second had torn through his chest, out the back.

The steepness of the mountain had given them ferocious power, incredible speed; they were literally flinging themselves over the tops of his men.

Fire Serpent began harvesting flesh. He lowered his hips, forming a solid stance and digging in. His blade suckled flesh like drinking, like taking sacrament. As they whipped past he took out throats and thoraxes, sheared limbs, and opened stomachs.

Eventually the Death Lords took their mark, and here and there, Fire Serpent felt the sting of a blade, a knife slice, the swift slash of a moonsteel edge.

A warrior collided with him, flying through the air, arms outstretched. Fire Serpent tucked, rolling, then came to his knees and drove what should have been a death thrust into the soft midsection of the man. He saw the face, briefly. It was painted black, eyes and mouth circled in savage red. The man did not drop from Fire Serpent's thrust. Instead, the sorcerer twisted into Fire Serpent with knives flashing. It was surprising he used only knives, flint knives of sacrifice. This was one of their high priests, a flower-weaver. The human blood of death-sacrifice had made him strong. Fire Serpent spun, but the priest moved swiftly. An obsidian blade sliced past Fire Serpent's neck with a whispered promise. By reflex alone, Fire Serpent caught the thrust of a second blade with the front of his buckler.

Fire Serpent took death mark once more, this time taking the sorcerer's thorax. Blood spilled rich, but the flower-weaver still did not drop. Fire Serpent screamed, a warrior's cry, and rammed his sword in below the ribs, lodging it to the hilt, but even this did not bring him down. A second flint blade slammed into Fire Serpent's side, piercing through the moonsteel of his breastplate, through the quilted cotton beneath, and into skin beneath that. Fire Serpent hissed, dropping back, then circled. The sorcerer stood, weary from blood loss, the hilt of Fire Serpent's sword emerging from his naked gut. Fire Serpent then stepped forward, a low snarl against his teeth, and drove a knife-hand between the priest's ribs. Setting his boot against the chest, he ripped out the heart. Finally, the flower-weaver dropped to the moss covered ground and died.

⊡⊡⊡⊡⊡⊡⊡⊡⊡⊡⊡⊡⊡⊡⊡⊡

Later, below, the bloodied warriors of Fire Serpent gathered, wounded, weary. Obsidian Sword, who had taken a wound to the side of his face that still oozed blood, came before Fire Serpent and lowered his head. "My lord . . . seventy-five. We have lost seventy-five."

Fire Serpent shivered. He had never lost that many men. In the twenty-seven years he had fought in these jungles, he had never lost seventy in a single engagement. Obsidian Sword slowly lifted his eyes, reserved.

"We have counted them. They were fifty."

"Fifty!" Fire Serpent winced. "Only fifty?"

Obsidian Sword nodded. "We believe that three of the priests, the high sorcerers, have escaped. They . . . they did not die as men."

Four of Fire Serpent's captains had already gathered, readied for pursuit. They were prime hunters, trackers, with their shields upon their backs, their weapons gathered, their outer armor shed for the run.

"Find them," Fire Serpent said, quietly. He watched the trackers sprint into the forests, already on the scent. He wondered if he would ever see them again.

"What, in the name of God, Lord of Hosts, do we face, my prince?" a commander said.

Fire Serpent took breath. "Prophecy."

"And how do we fight prophecy?" asked Obsidian Sword.

Fire Serpent only glanced at the hard eyes of his chief captain and tightened the binding cloth of his cotton armor against the wound left from the sorcerer's obsidian blade. He pulled on a cloak, brought by one of his shield-bearers, buckling its clasp.

It was nightfall, and they were weary. Some were dying.

As they moved on, seeking shelter, there were few words among them. They sensed it, like shadow falling. They could feel the earth move. They could smell the paths of animals that fled past them in the night. They could hear the silence of the forest when usually it crawled. Something was coming, slowly, ponderously, moving toward them, certain of its path.

CHAPTER THIRTY-THREE
THE GARRISON

On the night he was to die, Four Rabbit found himself thinking of Star Skirt. He was standing watch on the battlements and he wasn't sure why she had come into his mind, but she had, quite suddenly, and he remembered her hair, her soft voice. Star Skirt had broken Four Rabbit's heart. He had determined someday he would return to Chalaco, and on that day he would be so honored, so respected, she could not possibly turn him away. After all, even this young, he had earned the right to bear the standard of Eagle Knight and had even obtained a post at the garrison of the narrow passage, the gateway that divided the Northland of the Tolteca from the Southland of the Maya and the ancestors.

Four Rabbit had undergone grueling training the past six seasons, and he was at the prime of his abilities. In the last weeks, he had completed the tests of prowess that qualified him as an Eagle Knight. They were conducted in the forested jungles just beyond the passage to the south. There, prisoners sentenced to death, murderers of women and children, were given weapons and allowed to run free. Four Rabbit and other young warriors who had reached the level of Feathered Knight would pursue—unarmed and without armor—tracking their prey into the jungle. Four Rabbit had returned with two heads, tied together by their scalps.

On this night, as he walked the battlements, he wondered what Star Skirt would think of him now. Within a few years, given enough campaigns, he would become a Dragon Lord. Perhaps then she would reconsider.

The garrison of the mountain passage was a prime call. During the rainy season, the coasts would swell with rain and snowmelt until the sea of the east nearly touched that of the west. The swamps of the east coast were filled with deadly serpents and caimans, making them impassable, and the mountain road of the passage became the only safe route to Anáhuac. Many a war had raged here. In the past, before the truce of the Ten Thousand Dead, the Tolteca used to sally forth out of the garrison to bring thunder and terror unto the inhabitants below who practiced blood crafts and worshiped mute idols.

This night, however, something was to come against the northern garrison of Anáhuac, and nothing would ever be the same in the land of the Tolteca, for on this night the Fourth Sun would bleed.

Four Rabbit had trained long enough and hard enough that he sensed something long before he heard a sound. Staring over the passage leading south, he forgot all thoughts of Star Skirt and his skin shivered.

He had noticed, taking the watch earlier, the evening star was bright and shining. Some believed that when the star was this strong, it was best to find shelter from the night, for it was called the Killer Star. Four Rabbit no longer believed such tales, but he nonetheless found himself at times trying to stay in the shadow of the parapet where the rays of the Evening Star were not so bright. At first, he thought it was no more than the star's darts that caused his skin to shiver. Nonetheless, he called below, to the watch commander, Water Parrot.

Water Parrot must have felt the same chill, for once he reached the causeway, he searched below with wrinkled brow and assembled an entire division, four hundred warriors. Soon the high ramparts were manned with prime Tolteca, waiting, Four Rabbit among them.

It was late, past the high hour of mid-sky, when they finally came. Four Rabbit did not know who they were for certain, but he had heard rumors in the last few days. Terrified villagers had been fleeing north, whispering of Shadow Walkers.

And Shadow Walkers came, for this was the night the Hummingbird-of-the-Left marched against the northern passage;

and indeed, he came blessed by the Killer Star.

Four Rabbit felt the earth tremble. At first, though his instincts told him otherwise, he believed it was the earth shaker, a quake, but then he guessed its true nature and his face paled a bit.

"Lord God," he muttered.

"Do you hear?" a warrior whispered to Four Rabbit.

"Hear what?"

"Listen . . . singing!"

Four Rabbit listened, breathless. There was singing! Women's voices, and drums.

"Take up arms!" Water Parrot screamed from the parapet tower. His voice was harsh, but there was an underlying quiver in it.

The archers scrambled on the causeway, assembling, quickly dropping to a crouch at arrow ports with bows yawning, moonsteel darts waiting.

The Tolteca spanned the battlements of the gateway. Atlatls were fitted with moonsteel darts. Warriors took hold their swords, their spears, they lowered the visors of their helms, they lifted shields, they braced themselves.

Four Rabbit held his shield over his chest and waited, breathless. He knew what he felt was cold fear, but choked it back, determined.

The first Shadow Walkers he saw in the passageway were dancers. They looked, in moonlight, to be women, dancing naked, spinning, leaping. Others, cloaked in black priests' robes, came behind them, singing. Four Rabbit winced. He had never seen such a thing before. Whispers and murmurs spread through the ranks. Then the dancers and priestesses melted to the sides, and warriors filled the passage. More warriors than ever Four Rabbit had seen assembled. Perhaps it was the rays of the evening star bathing the canyon, but shadows seemed to stir, lift, taking form. It appeared they were coming out of bare earth, that they were rising from the underworld. Soon the entire canyon filled with an incredible army. Towers came, lurching like drunken old men.

Four Rabbit gasped, numb with amazement. His hand curled

so tight about the haft of his spear-thrower, his knuckles bled white. For a moment the army below paused, took breath, and there was silence. Then the Shadow Walkers came at full run, screaming.

Next to Four Rabbit, a warrior fell, an arrow shaft through his neck.

The front of the army opened up, like a mouth gaping, and spewed forth huge, wooden rams. The rams were mahogany trees of the Petén, cleaned of branches, the ends honed to points. Lances were anchored into their sides to form handles, and they were launched by runners, fifty or sixty to a tree. Perhaps fifteen such tree missiles spanned the pass, hurtling forward at a full, heavy run. Atlatls and arrows rained down, but with little effect. The rams struck the walls with incredible force. Many of them broke through, shattering the wooden beams of the gate, blowing out holes in the reinforced earthen works and heavy wood staves.

The battlement causeway, where Four Rabbit was standing, heaved upward as though giants lifted it. Whole sections of it cracked, sundering. It was thirty feet tall and heavily reinforced, but now sections tore free of their lashing and spilled warriors like pebbles. Four Rabbit saw Water Parrot flung from the battlement tower, screaming, vanishing below into the sea of the Shadow Walkers.

Four Rabbit was now filled with sheer terror. He could hardly breathe. Some of the warriors around him launched moonsteel atlatls that were swallowed like slivers in the skin of a great beast, but Four Rabbit could not move, he could only stare, amazed.

More trees were coming. It seemed unbelievable. Huge, spiked rams, warriors carrying them at full run, their many legs like gigantic millipedes as they leapt over the first beams now wedged in place.

Someone screamed, "Run! Abandon the ramparts! We're going down!"

But Four Rabbit had no time to run. As he turned, the rams struck. Their impact sounded a mighty thunder blow. There was snapping timber and a heavy moan, like the ramparts were a living thing, given mortal wound. The causeway heaved upward, whining, and collapsed. Four Rabbit hurled himself outward, screaming. He flailed, midair, then hit the earth so hard his bones shattered like pottery and his skull split like fruit thrown against stone. He was buried beneath a small mountain of earth and rock.

Beyond the gate to the north, the entire first army of the Tolteca, the Knights of the Eagle Lords, came forth, locking shields, weapons bristling. But they were swallowed. Their struggle, savage and furious while it lasted, shearing flesh and spilling blood with moonsteel talons, was snuffed out like a candle flicker. Below, the foothills and plains lay bare for plunder. The southernmost cities and villages of the great Northland Tolteca were sleeping. They lay in the path of the Shadow Lords like naked children.

Prophecy had begun.

CHAPTER THIRTY-FOUR
XIBALBA

Before they came, before the Shadow Walkers surrounded the cave where Topiltzin and Mud Puppy had taken shelter, it began to rain. In this part of the forest, rain pelted from the sky in torrents. Mist and steam washed into the cave, swirling.

Topiltzin had been unable to sleep, even though he was so weary he found it hard to stay conscious. He wondered if any of the others were still alive, the young goaltenders, Rattle Eagle, or the little Coyotl.

Days before, when Topiltzin returned from the forest, having killed the sorcerer, he found Tarantula lying on the lower steps of the temple, eyes closed, breathing slowly between tightly clenched teeth, held by one of his men. The other mercenaries had all been slain. There was only Mud Puppy who crouched, looking winded and bewildered, blood on his sword. Topiltzin found himself wondering if it had been worth it.

"The children?" Topiltzin asked.

"Fled," the warrior holding Tarantula answered, "into the jungles, my lord. They trusted us no more than the sorcerers."

Tarantula opened his eyes, gazed at Topiltzin, then past him, looking over the darkening sky. "Find shelter, Prince. Keep due south. Try to reach Tikal and the coast."

Topiltzin knelt beside him. "What are you telling me?"

"These are Flesh Eaters we have found—Blood Gatherers." He paused, took what seemed a swallow of air. "Where they go, their armies soon follow. The Blood Gatherers go sweeping the way before the warriors. There will be no rubberball game, Blue Prince; there

307

will be no celebrations, no festivals. This year in the land of the *ceiba*, the only harvest shall be death. Keep to the south. Find your way out of these jungles, my lord." Blood trickled from the corner of his mouth, and he spat it out. His chest was mangled; something had pierced the leather corselet, most probably an axe. Tarantula's eyes grew distant. "A pity you are not a priest. Odd . . . but I wish I had one just now . . . point me in the right direction." With that, he was dead, as though he willed it, sent his spirit forth. Tarantula's warrior lowered his head.

"Blood Gatherers?" Mud Puppy said. "Do you know what he was talking about, Topiltzin?"

"He was speaking of the Shadow Walkers," the remaining warrior said. "They are High-Blood kings. They come from the south, past the many waters, past the wilderness, from the place of the ancestors' first landing."

Topiltzin looked about the clearing. It was bordered on all sides by jungle, uninviting, and in the darkness, he was unable to even make out the trail they had used to enter.

The warrior stood. He was soaked in blood, and Topiltzin realized one of his arms hung useless, the shoulder bone shattered. His skin was the hue of death.

"I do not know your name," Topiltzin said.

"Seven Flint."

Blood dripped from his head where splinters of his own skull were caught in the tangles of his hair. The man drew a dagger from his belt, offering it hilt first to Topiltzin. "If you would, my lord," he said quietly. "I cannot follow with you, and I do not wish to be alive should they reach this place."

Topiltzin swallowed. He stepped forward, embraced the warrior, and drove the dagger through his heart, a quick thrust. The body went limp, and Topiltzin laid him beside his captain. He looked to Mud Puppy.

"What of Coyotl?" Mud Puppy said. "And Rattle Eagle?"

Topiltzin looked to the south. "Perhaps we can still find them before morning if we swing west."

Topiltzin and Mud Puppy wandered the thickness of the Petén, searching for any familiar sign, but it all seemed to have melted into tangled growth. By the second day, they were hopelessly lost. That had never happened to Topiltzin. Never before had he been lost in the Southland, but this time somehow the sun was distant, somehow it was hard to know direction, as though his senses were blunted. When they had found the cave in which they finally took rest, they recognized its face, its smooth, shiny black rock. They realized, seeing it, they had traveled in circles.

As evening drew down from the sky, they sat together against the back wall of the cave, weary.

"We are not going to make it, are we, Blue Prince?" Mud Puppy said, staring out at the jungles. "We are being pursued . . . by Shadow Walkers, by prophecy. There seems little chance we will outrun prophecy." He glanced to Topiltzin and looked away. "When I left, she cried. Like a child. I couldn't calm her. I kept saying, it's only a season, only a brief time . . ." He laid his head back against the rock. "What has happened, Topiltzin? We were once kings of all lands, lords of all we saw. What has gone wrong?"

Topiltzin had no answer. He felt only numbness, as though someone had stolen his emotions, his passion. The only sensation left him was pain. Then he thought he understood. It was death, the aura of it, the smell of it. Death's spirit had fallen over the jungle like snow. Death's weeping had sucked him hollow and tired. He closed his eyes.

"We were once kings, lords of all lands," he whispered.

Soon Mud Puppy was sleeping, wearied, lying on his side, and Topiltzin watched the mist swirl slowly in the cave, oddly reminded of the ocean. If ever in his life he had known peace, a time of good memory, it was during the days he had traveled with his father and Sky Teacher along the coasts, among the Sea Kings of Anáhuac. They had been days less dark, and though Sky Dragon had been a stone figure even then, he would often smile, run with them. He had once taken a conch shell from the waters and, using his great sword, halved it, letting Topiltzin stare at length at the inner swirls of pink and white. "Our ancestors came through the sea," Sky Dragon said, tracing one of the curved chambers. "They passed through, as though passing through caves. This," he pointed to the center of the shell, "this is where dwelt our first home—a land of milk, a place of honey."

"How did we know our way?" Topiltzin had asked. "How did we find our path through the sea?"

"Our ancestors but followed the wind of the waters, the hand of God."

"Will we ever go back? Will any of us ever return to this first home?"

"Perhaps . . . perhaps someday we will."

The mist suddenly shifted, and Topiltzin lifted from memory, realizing something was moving past them, just beyond the cave. He saw them, passing—shadow figures moving through the rain. No one needed to explain who they were to him. They had been hunting him and Mud Puppy for seven days.

Topiltzin watched numbly for the longest time, feeling nothing, no panic, not even alarm. He just watched. The rain eventually eased and there was a steam left rising, and through it, the pale fingers of dawn stretched. Still, they passed.

Mud Puppy awakened, sat up with a start, jolting forward, but Topiltzin quickly slammed him back against the rock, holding one hand against him. Mud Puppy stared, breathless. Warriors were slipping through the jungle, shadowy in the dark fog of early dawn. Though they were just beyond, it was still difficult to make them out. So difficult, in fact, it was some moments before Topiltzin realized one of them was crouched, looking into the cave, watching, curious. His face was painted, the eyes circled in white—a sorcerer. Then he seemed to simply disappear.

The shadows stopped not long after that, and there was dead silence: not a sound, no birds, no insects. Mud Puppy crouched, laid his hand over the hilt of his sword.

The forest before them suddenly erupted in flame; jets of it soared upward from staves of resinous wood forming brilliant white pillars. In the light, a High-Blood Prince sat on a gold-encrusted wicker throne. An audience had been prepared for Topiltzin and Mud Puppy. There were warriors to either side of the prince, even more of them deeper into the trees. The High-Blood waited, calm. He said nothing.

Topiltzin stood and walked from the cave, Mud Puppy at his side. The High-Blood Prince looked directly into Topiltzin's eyes. The Chichimec's eyes were a dark blue, hard like diamond with silver-ringed edges resembling the moon's halo. They almost looked painted. He was naked but for a breechclout and breast mirror. His hair was unbraided and fell wild over his shoulders. There were four captains at his flanks. They wore thin, dark metal armor and leather corselets. Many wore breast mirrors. All bore Tolteca swords. The captains held staffs mounted with insignia: the bat, the jaguar, the hawk, and one, a human heart. They were tall for Chichimeca, well boned, muscled; they had the bearing of Tolteca. They reminded Topiltzin of the pureblood warriors of Fire Serpent and others like him.

Topiltzin thought of drawing his sword, trying to take any of them he could, but the number of obsidian arrow tips waiting from the trees would simply annihilate both him and Mud Puppy. Therefore, he eased back, let the torchlight spill across him, and faced the Prince of the Shadow Walkers.

The High-Blood smiled, tipped his head. "I understand the Dragon of Tollán has two sons, one a priest, the other a ballplayer, a gambler. You . . . you must be the ballplayer. I offer greetings, Topiltzin." The face of the High-Blood was handsome, cut in sharp, powerful strokes with high, bold cheekbones. His skin shimmered with dampness, like a leopard in harnessed power. "What to do with the Prince of Tollán?" he mused.

For a moment the silence settled. These warriors seemed

not even to breathe. They were soundless. Topiltzin had never encountered Shadow Walkers, but now he understood their name. The only sound was the flicker of the torches.

The High-Blood said, "I have an idea, a suggestion. You have come from the north to play the rubberball game, have you not? I know this by the ball equipment of your brothers, your friends. We have captured them. They wait in cages. I was going to have them offered up on altars, but then I found among their equipment a silver diadem inset with turquoise, and the cloak of a prince. So I have kept them alive. They wait now in the vanguards of my army. Very well then, Prince, let us play the rubberball game! And for this, we shall play: for souls . . . for hearts. If you win, you may take my head, and thereby send my spirit, my lifeblood, to the dark of the far skies, where dwells no sun, no light."

"And if you win?" Topiltzin said.

He leaned forward. "I shall swallow your people like a fatted offering; I shall drink the blood of the Tolteca—until they are the dead, the ghost warriors, and the forgotten." He paused. "What do you think, then? Do you like this wager? The stakes of our game? Do you accept, Prince of Tollán?"

Topiltzin bowed the same bow that was given an opposing captain before the games. The High-Blood chuckled, and Topiltzin smiled back, but inside he fought a chill that bit deep. He felt he was looking into the face of millennia, of years unfolding, an age of dark and terror like none ever known by the children of men. The illusion struck him that somehow he could hear the whispered screams of dying and torture, of horror unspoken.

In that moment, Topiltzin promised himself that if indeed this was the face of prophecy, all that was warned of the ancients and the prophets—then Topiltzin would first take life from this High-Blood Prince with his silvered eyes. Perhaps that would not stop their coming, nor change the words of the prophets, but it would answer something. It would speak beneath quiet stars. It would, at least, do that.

TOLTECA

The ball court had lain in the jungle centuries, perhaps millennia. It was only a depression in the earth, cracked on one side where a giant yellow tree emerged, roots snaking. To its southern face rose a tall hillock of feathered vine and creepers that once was a temple. The Shadow Walkers cleared it, stripped away the growth, the tentacles, the bramble. They restored the ball court there at Xibalba; they applied lime to the facing of it so it bled white. They painted the centerlines. They erected the rings, which had been carved of stone by the warriors of the Dark Lord. They stripped the front of the ancient temple so it once again looked upon the flesh of men. One could almost feel them—the Death Lords, the ancient ones of Xibalba—coming to see the rubberball game . . . coming, gathering, whispering.

All was now ready.

The Shadow Walkers climbed up the sides of the temple, they lined the edges of the court, they climbed into trees, they gathered all about, thousands of them.

As dusk fell, the Turquoise Lords of Tollán assembled at the edge of the temple, Coyotl, Rattle Eagle, Mud Puppy Soldier, and Topiltzin. They wore the equipment, the harness yoke, the knee guards, the gloves. Topiltzin looked at his companions. He embraced them, first Mud Puppy, then Rattle Eagle who stood shaggy-haired, his eyes hardened against fear, and last Coyotl, who hugged Topiltzin tightly. They turned and walked along the bottom edge of the temple. Its presence behind them was like an ancient sentinel, attentive, silent. The ballplayers of Tollán dropped into the ball court at its eastern end and waited.

There were no goaltenders; none were needed. This game would be won by the sinking of the ball through the center mark alone.

The Shadow Lord came with three captains. Smoking Mirror wore a crimson net-cloak, a leather-and-wood hip yoke, knee tassels of crimson macaw feathers, and his signet, the chest mirror, dark, misty. His three captains were dressed simply; they wore no yoke, only wraps of thick leopard skin, only gloves. Their hair was braided for war. They dropped into the west end of the ball court. There was a hushed silence all about.

The Smoking Mirror lifted the rubberball high above his head, clasping it in his fist, and as he did so, the jungles shivered in the cheers that went up, deafening. The Tolteca walked forward, toward the center mark, and the Shadow Lords moved in opposite.

For a moment, Topiltzin looked into the smoldering eyes of the Smoking Mirror. The Blue Prince calmed himself, he let no emotion through, no feeling, no thought; he let his blood out, he began to pulse, to feel the air through his skin, a thousand pricks, to feel his muscles tighten, coil, relax.

Yet there was no emotion in the eyes of the Smoking Mirror either. The Highborn looked back with a dark, hidden gaze, as though his eyes were glass.

The Smoking Mirror then flung the ball upward, letting it sail into the gray sky. The warriors gathered beat their weapons against their shields and the rubberball seemed to pause, to spin against the doom of the dying sky before it dropped. It could have been that the cheers swelling as the ball dropped into play were those of the Death Lords, the ancient ones of Xibalba, who had become no more than mist in the jungles, no more than the crumbling stone of their cities, for they left no memories, no faces, only pale echoes of what they were. Long ago, their sun had died.

Rattle Eagle screamed, lifting one leg high, then pouncing forward, into them, scattering two of the tall, lean warriors with elbow blows. Coyotl spun to the side, rolling against the smoothed lime wall. When the ball dropped, both Topiltzin and Smoking Mirror went for it, but Mud Puppy spun past, a shoulder block into Smoking Mirror's chest, and the ball deflected off Topiltzin's hip with a *ponk*. Coyotl was already in position to keep its momentum, and twisted, bringing it off his buttocks, into the back wall where it rebounded.

TOLTECA

It began to sing—the ball—it began to fly.

The warriors gathered to watch were beating their shields, stomping their feet against the earth in heartbeat that reverberated through the stone. Topiltzin ran along one side then did an angled flip, somersaulting, his hip-yoke slamming hard, dead center into the ball, sending it like a missile into one of the High-Blood Captains. The man attempted to spin, to drop his hips and meet the ball with his side, but he did not move fast enough and it struck him full in the ribs, buckling him. Even as the man grunted, twisting to the side, Rattle Eagle collided with him, sending the ball off his own thigh and bringing a knee hard into the man's face. The High-Blood Captain rolled across the stone, doubled in pain, bloodied. But he struggled to his knees and stood.

Leaping for a shot, Mud Puppy and a High-Blood collided, midair, with a muffled crunch, then both pummeled into the side stone, the ball whispering past them.

Smoking Mirror came in a tight, spinning leap, and caught the ball off his right hip. It careened at an angle, skimming the stone almost to the center of the ring. It hit only the base of it, but rebounded so hard it struck Rattle Eagle in the shoulder even as he dodged, lacerating skin and leaving flesh mangled in a round, bloodied pocket. Rattle Eagle spun, wincing, and was hit in the midsection by a High-Blood. He swiveled and dropped a downward elbow strike that left a hollow sound against the High-Blood's back.

"Side bank!" Coyotl shouted, dropping so low he sheared the flesh of his shins, skidding along the cement. The ball rebounded off a knee guard, angled in a new direction.

Mud Puppy saw his moment. The angle was perfect; the yawning dark hole of the center marker seemed to open for the ball, like a mouth. He had to take a hard run, then twist, back-stepping. Going up the side in a high leap, he tucked in his legs to maximize the spin.

It seemed for a moment everything was still, everything quiet, slowed, the ball coming, singing, spinning in its black-gold blur.

Mud Puppy would put it through the center marker. It would leave a hollow *thud* sound. Then a shoulder hit him from behind, so hard and so angled that Mud Puppy heard a *crack*, like a dried tree limb being broken. The force of it jerked his arm in spasm. Instead of the ball hitting his hip yoke, it struck him in the side, in the soft part beneath the ribs. If the first blow from behind had bent him backward, this crumpled him forward. He hit the side of the court and rolled.

He lay on his side. He saw the captain that had struck him, a muscled High-Blood Chichimec with piercing, raven eyes. Mud Puppy saw him spin and catch the rubberball off his buttocks, sending it on. Mud Puppy could no longer move. He could not even lift his head and a dead cold panic jolted through him. He screamed, but no sound came from his throat. He had no voice. The High-Blood's foot cracked Mud Puppy's jawbone with a well-timed blow. Mud Puppy's head was kicked back and his body rolled, blood filling his mouth as he slammed into a corner stone of the east side.

Mud Puppy Soldier lay frozen, staring upward at a darkening sky. He sucked desperately for air.

When Rattle Eagle saw Mud Puppy go down, he felt utter fury. Rage swam through him, choking him, and there was a low scream between his teeth as he hurtled forward. He let the ball, which was in reach, go past, leaving it for Coyotl to pick up, or even one of the High-Bloods, he no longer cared—his target was no longer the ball. The captain who had hit Mud Puppy saw him coming. He spun for attack.

With warriors' screams, they collided. The exchange was swift, deadly.

The Highborn buried a knee into Rattle Eagle's gut full-force, slamming all his weight into it. Rattle Eagle shifted, sideways, grazing it off, then brought an arm across the man's neck. He used his opposite forearm against the back of the warrior's head, and at the moment of contact, he twisted, hard, his whole body wrenching downward. Rattle Eagle screamed, driving, using his weight and the force of his run. The High-Blood Captain's neck cracked sharply. Still screaming, Rattle Eagle continued to twist, harder, tightening his grip. He felt the neck muscles shearing, the sinew snapping, the flesh rending, and finally the head ripped free of the torso, clasped in the lockjaw of Rattle Eagle's huge, powerful arms. The weight of the man's body, hurtling in the opposite direction of Rattle Eagle, severed any connecting flesh.

Rattle Eagle continued spinning, dropping his hips into a tight twist, still screaming through his teeth as he flung the head straight into the goal zone, as though it were the ball and he were taking a kill. The head spun, whipping hair, and hit the stone with a crack-bone *thud*, leaving a bloody splatter as it bounded elsewhere.

The Shadow Walkers went insane. The air reverberated with their cries. Rattle Eagle, Coyotl, Topiltzin, all crouched, wary—but the screams were not of anger, nor of panic. It was a familiar sound, the roar of a crowd when a goal is marked, when the ball strikes home. Though they were enemies, the Dark Lords had risen, their cries filling the air as they cheered the great Rattle Eagle.

Rattle Eagle but turned, readied, his mind locking back into the game, stepping past the blood that spit in pulses from the neck stump of the fallen High-Blood.

Topiltzin crouched near Mud Puppy. He placed a hand on his friend's shoulder. Topiltzin's mind had been on the game, and he had thought Mud Puppy was only unconscious, but then he saw the eyes, staring upward. They blinked. They wept. A sudden cry escaped Topiltzin's lips. Tears stung sharp.

Topiltzin took Mud Puppy's head in his hands. "Farewell, dear brother," he whispered, then snapped the head hard to the side. Mud Puppy's body quivered with one quick spasm, then lay still.

Topiltzin stood, forcing away tears so they would not blur his vision. He stilled them by looking into the face of the Smoking Mirror, who stared back with ice eyes.

They gathered at center court, the Dark Lord flanked by two captains, and the three remaining ballplayers of Tollán. Two bodies lay on the court. Blood had pooled about the center mark, and the old, faded stone of Xibalba seemed to drink it, grateful, thirsted. Topiltzin stood directly across from Smoking Mirror; Rattle Eagle took position on his right, sweating, bloody. Coyotl crouched to his left.

Smoking Mirror studied them for a moment, and it seemed, though Topiltzin wasn't certain, a slight smile curled across the handsome lips. Smoking Mirror knelt slowly and picked up the ball, twirled it between his hands, warming it. A hush descended upon the jungle. Night had drawn fingers across the court and torches had been fired. They flickered softly. The shadow of the goal rings wavered on the limestone walls, taunting.

Smoking Mirror lifted his left hand high, the ball tight in his fist. The Shadow Walkers cheered, they began once more to beat weapons against their shields, to stomp their feet in a paced rhythm that shimmered like a quake beneath Topiltzin's feet. The players circled, and Smoking Mirror launched the ball high to even greater cheering. Horns sounded, arrows soared upward into the night, and drums hammered a deep, hollow pace.

Both Topiltzin and Smoking Mirror leapt for the falling ball, colliding midair, hammering each other with hard blows, and it was again Coyotl, hurtling low like a stone, who caught the ball. It fired off his hip into an edge of the court, ricocheting with a hard *pong*.

Smoking Mirror threw Topiltzin back and turned to meet the ball as it rebounded, sending it off his thigh in the direction of one of his captains who had moved into the back court.

Topiltzin was knocked off balance and hit on his shoulder by a jarring blow, but he rolled and was quickly in a crouch, circling for the ball.

For Coyotl, there had been something wrong from the beginning. From the moment they stepped into the court, he had felt his blood cold. But he denied the fear, and when he played, when he moved, his whole mind, his body, became a single focus. He could sense the wind off the ball as it spun, singing. And he was so playing when something suddenly came against him like a slap, stinging so strongly it jerked him out of all concentration, as though shaken from a dream. Coyotl actually staggered, disorientated. Something hit like cold wind, numbing his skin, and he found himself staring full into the silver-ringed eyes of the Smoking Mirror. Those eyes, like crystals, like blue obsidian . . . as though they were the eyes . . . of a demon.

"Demon's eye!" The whispered words echoed in Coyotl's head, and he realized the Dark Lord, the sorcerer, had sent it, for Smoking Mirror smiled when Coyotl jerked in reaction.

A sudden panic swam through Coyotl; he guessed what was happening even before he felt it. He knew the High-Blood had called forth the eye of the idol Coyotl wore in his head. The crystal burned; it was like white powder igniting, sizzling. Coyotl hissed, twisting. Flame crackled, curling, charring the skin about his eye socket. He hit the stone on his side, ripping at his face, but the demon's eye seemed to be melting, it seemed to be sinking back, deeper, eating away flesh. Coyotl screamed, tearing at his face with his fingers. He kept rolling, dimly aware that one of the Dark Lord's captains came for him, but he was unable to roll clear of the sharp kick in his side, cracking a rib as though it had been the bone of a brittle old woman. The next blow came to the side of his head, numbing out sound from one of his ears.

Rattle Eagle dove to help Coyotl, but he was attacked from the side. He was hit so hard his breath was sucked from him, and even though he spun, though he unleashed a powerful elbow blow in response, he couldn't catch balance. Rattle Eagle was kicked in the back of his leg. At first he couldn't believe he was falling, even when he hit the stone. He realized the pain tearing though his leg was more than a sprain, or lacerated skin. The blow had popped his kneecap out from behind like cracking open a coconut. Rattle Eagle rolled, pain rippling, and came to one knee. A figure hurtled toward him and Rattle Eagle twisted sideways and buried an elbow in the warrior's side. He saw Coyotl just across from him, ripping out his stone eye, tearing his own skin in the process, and blood spilled across his face as he flung the crystal. Coyotl was still screaming, but not from pain. The little warrior was now screaming in rage, diving forward, tucking into a tight roll, and surfacing just under the ball, turning in its direction. His face was seared on one side, the skin blackened and bleeding.

Rattle Eagle was hit from behind, the breath knocked out of him, bones cracking somewhere.

Coyotl had sent the ball in a perfect alignment, and Topiltzin saw it coming, saw his moment. It was the setup, the path. Coyotl had seen the angle and had delivered. Even through his pain, even with the blood spilling over his face, he had delivered the ball as he had done so many times in the past.

Topiltzin was already moving sideways up the edge of the wall, gaining speed, every muscle, every fiber alive. The screaming beat of the shields, the drums, the noise was furious, and as he had done before, Topiltzin let it fill him, let it fuel him. He flipped, banking off the top edge of the court, then spun, tight, whipping, feeling the ball stream toward him. It slammed into the notch of his hip yoke, and Topiltzin turned to drive it in, true for the center ring, to send it like a missile being launched. For souls . . . for the hearts of men.

In that very instant, the Smoking Mirror struck him. But Topiltzin did not see a man; he saw a leopard. The full, airborne form of a leopard, black as night, rippled in muscle, snarling, teeth drawn back. Topiltzin's aim was deflected at its very decisive moment, the instant before the impact.

The Smoking Mirror sent the ball off his glistening side, driving it into the wall, where it slammed off the limestone, then *whunked* through the hoop. It was swallowed with that sound, like sucking, like a scream—endgame.

The Dark Lord had taken score.

Now the leopard came for Topiltzin's throat. Topiltzin caught him. Sliding down the steep embankment of the court, they twisted, grappling. Topiltzin felt a claw shear open the skin of his shoulder, slice past his cheek. They slammed into the stone, and Topiltzin was sliding in blood, on his back, hands locked on the throat of the beast. He squeezed, tight, trying to crush the windpipe.

The crowds were screaming, the sound was deafening, a roar like the earth caving in all about them, and the cat was snarling. Yet the eyes of it, the breath of it, this close, were a man's.

Teeth clenched, Topiltzin continued squeezing against the windpipe. He could feel it starting to give. Hind claws sheared open the skin of Topiltzin's thigh like ripping paper, then, suddenly it was a man beneath him, and the shock of it half broke Topiltzin's hold. Smoking Mirror heaved him backward with a leopard's roar. He threw Topiltzin as though the Blue Prince were only a child, then rolled to the side, grasping his throat, coughing. Topiltzin landed hard against the side of the ball court and came to a crouch. Coyotl was instantly beside him.

The warriors, the Shadow Walkers, had erupted in frenzy. All about the edges of the court they were screaming, the drums were hammering a victory song. The ball was rolling past the center-line, forgotten now. For the first time in seven years, the Lords of Tollán had been defeated. Rattle Eagle crouched on one knee, star-ing, numb.

"We're getting out of here," Coyotl hissed beside Topiltzin, seizing his arm tight.

Smoking Mirror rolled to the side, pulled himself up, sucking for air. Coyotl pulled Topiltzin back until they were beside Rattle Eagle.

"I will kill him," Topiltzin swore, but Coyotl jerked him back violently.

"You can have him later!" he shouted above the screams.

Topiltzin glanced at the little warrior, wincing at the sight of his face, charred up one side, blood dripping down the cheekbone. But the one good eye stared back furiously. "We are getting out of here!"

"How?" Topiltzin said.

"The back wall!" Coyotl hissed.

Warriors above were cheering, leaping, singing. One of the High-Blood Captains had dropped down beside Smoking Mirror and was helping lift him.

Topiltzin stared at Coyotl blankly, trembling. Nothing registered. He couldn't imagine what Coyotl was implying.

"Topiltzin, think! If this court is as Tollán's—if the ancient courts of Xibalba are like those of the Northland—then the back wall panel opens to the temple chamber!"

Topiltzin realized Coyotl could be right, for the courts of Tollán were modeled upon Xibalba's ruins. He glanced once more at Smoking Mirror, who was now on one knee, his back to Topiltzin. Warriors dropped into the court about their prince, cheering, beating swords against shields. At Coyotl's urging, Topiltzin backed away.

Seeing their intent, Rattle Eagle forced himself to back away also, using his good leg for support, ignoring the pain in his broken kneecap. He took position on Topiltzin's left.

They were already in the shadow of the temple.

In the frenzy of their cheering, in concern for their injured Prince, the Shadow Walkers had—just for the moment—forgotten the ballplayers of Tollán. As Rattle Eagle stepped past a warrior he quickly, soundlessly in the throng of cheers, smashed in the warrior's windpipe and ripped away his sword.

They were now against the back wall.

Coyotl spun about. Quickly his hands felt the stone, searching for the wall notch that would release the opening mechanism. Rattle Eagle drew up against Topiltzin's left flank.

"This does not look good, Blue Prince," he whispered.

Topiltzin noticed the faces of warriors above them, faces of rage, of insanity. Any moment, they would break. Any second, they would leap down.

"Coyotl," Rattle Eagle whispered. "We have not much time!"

"Just look penitent," Coyotl whispered, searching frantically. "It's here, it's here, it has to be here!"

Smoking Mirror now slowly stood, slowly turned. The cheering began to die. The Shadow Walkers ceased stomping their feet; the thunder beat of their shields stopped. The Dark Lord shoved his captain aside angrily and looked upon the Tolteca. Topiltzin swore the eyes of the High-Blood were fired, that flame ignited them from behind. His teeth, though he was human, still curled in jaguar fangs.

"Take them!" screamed the Smoking Mirror. "Bring them for sacrifice!"

Cries went up. Rattle Eagle grabbed the first warrior to leap from the top edge, taking him by his chest corselet, slamming the sword through his entire body before tossing him aside. He kept the warrior's sword, threw it to Topiltzin.

"Time to cleave some flesh, my lord!" he cried.

Their backs against the stone, Topiltzin and Rattle Eagle took stance, lowered their hips, and braced themselves. A wave of warriors came against them. Rattle Eagle began screaming, his sword driving them back with flesh-eating strokes. Topiltzin thrust, blocked, his own sword drinking blood full and rich. It could have been ended quickly, but the Shadow Walkers wanted the Tolteca alive. To have killed them would have denied their God, it would have been blasphemy, and Topiltzin and Rattle Eagle were making themselves difficult to grasp.

"Here!" Coyotl cried, finding a door stone, the triggering mechanism. He swiveled it out, then wrenched back on it with all his weight, vaulting up and pushing with his feet off the edge of the court. There was a dull *thumm* sound and the ground of the court seemed to shiver, unsteady.

"Filth-eating sons of whores!" Rattle Eagle screamed. There was a flint knife lodged in his side, which he ignored.

Topiltzin slammed his gloved fist into the face of a warrior before him, sliced open the gut of another. A hand seized his left arm, about to jerk him off balance, but Rattle Eagle sheared it off at the wrist.

The wall behind them was rumbling, the old stone was grinding, sliding back with a heavy, aching sound.

"Blue Prince!" Coyotl screamed, and Topiltzin made his way

sideways, sliding tight against the stone. Blood made the court floor slippery. Coyotl had taken a weapon and fought, his sword spinning in a blur. Topiltzin drove steadily toward Coyotl, shearing anything that got in his way. He sliced open the face of a warrior holding Coyotl's leg, and kicked the body back. Coyotl spun into the dark of the cavern. Topiltzin, at its edge, turned toward Rattle Eagle.

For a moment, an instant, the big man met his eyes, and the look that passed needed no words. Rattle Eagle quickly grabbed Topiltzin's arm and shoved him toward the opening. Rattle Eagle jerked, gasping as a blade ripped through the flesh of his side. Arms had seized his neck, his legs.

Topiltzin started forward, but Coyotl grabbed him from behind, by his hair, and wrenched him into the chamber.

Rattle Eagle swung and drove into them, his blade slashing. They came over him like insects crawling over the body of a beast.

The last Topiltzin saw of him, Rattle Eagle was folding beneath the weight, but as he did so, he was driving himself downward— onto his own sword.

The panel opening was narrow. The rock had barely slid open before it wedged itself on its own debris. As Topiltzin slew any who tried to follow him into the cavern, Coyotl pried against the inside trigger stone that would force the wall closed. The trigger stone whined and creaked. It finally broke off, spilling Coyotl into the floor. The huge, stone panel didn't slide closed, it fell closed, off center. The weight of it came against the bodies of warriors squeezing through, crushing bone and flesh. Topiltzin saw a head narrow, the mouth opened in an oval scream before it popped in a spew of blood.

Then there was darkness.

On the other side of the wall, the screams were inhuman, consumed by rage. They hammered against the stone.

Coyotl used an ancient flint drill to ignite a pitch torch that rested in a wall bracket. The pitch was dried and brittle, but the old wood still burned, crackling.

Coyotl paused and pulled at Topiltzin's arm. "We've got to keep going, Blue Prince!"

Topiltzin stared at the stone, its dark chinks flickering in Coyotl's torchlight.

"Blue Prince!"

Topiltzin turned, met Coyotl's eye. Tears fell. He felt heavy. He felt he was betraying a part of himself to leave. Yet he did. He began with Coyotl into the darkness of the temple tunnel.

Silence soon engulfed them, a stale, mold smell of damp rock enveloping. Some of the old tunnels snaked for miles beneath the jungle floor, carved through the limestone rock of the Petén. Some, it was said, had no end, but descended nonetheless to the underworld where dwelt the Lords of Death to welcome any who came.

CHAPTER THIRTY-FIVE
STORM

Sky Teacher sat up, awakened so suddenly the feeling was as though someone had grabbed him, and he fully expected to see someone before him; a figure, dark, tall, waiting. There even seemed a face to it. Yet there was only the night. To his left lay Star Skirt, curled on her side.

"Topiltzin," he whispered. He drew his hands into fists and knelt there a moment, head lowered. "Topiltzin," he whispered again. Somewhere, the Blue Prince was in pain, somewhere his heart had cried out. Sky Teacher eased back. He stared at the stars, remembering how Topiltzin had always loved the stars. Perhaps Sky Teacher should have said more to his brother before they parted, but it had always been that way. Since they had gotten older, they spoke little.

Watching the Blue Stars, the cluster in the sky, a memory stirred of the day Topiltzin had first decided to journey to the Southland, when he had turned aside the advice of their father, of the elders, and had chosen to play the rubberball game. Already Topiltzin was a trained warrior. He had fought in the south and gained enough valor that he wore his hair braided. He wore the crimson net-cloak and two macaw feathers of honor. He wore the thin moonsteel breastplate that was the signet of the Eagle Knights, and Sky Teacher had always thought Topiltzin would become a commander, as the Dragon had once been. Their father had commanded the troops of the Tolteca when he was only seventeen and his victories in battle were still sung of in the marketplace. Sky Teacher was surprised when the young Blue Prince announced he was to journey to the Southland, there to play the rubberball.

TOLTECA

Topiltzin had come to Sky Teacher last of all, just after sunrise. Sky Teacher was in the fields of the Calmecac. Rows of earth waited for corn to be planted the next day. Sky Teacher paused, planting stick in hand, when he saw Topiltzin coming toward him. Waiting at the edge of the field, he noticed Coyotl, the little warrior. Topiltzin stood for a time, looking over the fields, saying nothing. Sky Teacher noticed his eyes were near tears, but Topiltzin was holding them back. In a way, Sky Teacher understood why this was happening. It was something against the Dragon. When Topiltzin was a boy, white haired and laughing, no two had been closer than Sky Dragon and his beloved Blue Prince. Topiltzin had looked upon Sky Dragon with a kind of awe, the kind reserved for heroes, for legends and gods. Yet as Topiltzin grew older, something changed between them, something unwritten and unspoken, as though the two wills could not coexist.

Sky Teacher set aside the planting stick and stared at his brother, into the fiery, sky eyes so unlike his own, even though some claimed they could not be told apart.

"You have decided, then?" Sky Teacher said, breaking the silence.

Topiltzin nodded.

"And Father?"

"He threw my ball equipment into the plaza."

Sky Teacher thought of trying to explain, but then, there was nothing he could say that, somewhere, Topiltzin did not already know.

"Sky Teacher," Blue Prince had said quietly, "my brother, I will most probably be gone for several seasons and . . ." He paused. He couldn't say what was inside him, but Sky Teacher could have finished the sentence for him. The two of them could always read each other. Perhaps that was one reason words were so few between them. Topiltzin's sentence would have finished something like: ". . . and I want you to take my place—be what he wanted me to be. I want you to be our father's son." Those were the words in his eyes, but not the words he spoke.

". . . and I meant to say . . . farewell."

K. MICHAEL WRIGHT

"How long is 'several seasons,' my brother?"

"Years, I suspect."

"You go to learn the rubberball game?"

He nodded. "There, in the Southland, they have perfected it. They are the greatest players, and we . . ." His voice broke off. "We shall learn from them."

Sky Teacher might have tried to talk him out of it, but he understood how his brother's passions worked. Since he was young, passion had spilt from Topiltzin like fire and smoke. He would find even simple things and become possessed of them, burn with them, for months. Once it had been the lakes of Tollán, and the taking of silverfish from skimmer boats. Topiltzin had learned to use an atlatl as though it were an extension of his fist. Another time it had been war, and Topiltzin had trained at the camps of the warlords as though he were pitting himself against time and fury.

Now it was to be this game. But the game was more than simple obsession. Choosing to play the rubberball game would leave the Blue Prince a wandered one—like the wolf of the plains, tied to no one, given to no law but his own. Topiltzin was running, not just from Tollán, not just from the Dragon's shadow, but also from himself. There would be a cost to running. Sky Teacher believed to every man there was given inner light, a strength borne by stars. The day would come when Topiltzin would need that light, when he would bleed for it, even weep for it. Such a moment came to all men, but it would come to Topiltzin in heavy rain, like spears.

Sky Teacher settled down in the grass of the hillside next to Eslabeth and attempted to go back to sleep, but there was no sleep. He simply laid there, his hands folded behind his head, thinking of the past few days and of Eslabeth. His heart had been troubled of late, for he knew something was turning, he felt the terror breathing down upon them. The only balm had been Eslabeth. How could things go wrong now? He had finally found her, kindred, someone he had searched for all his life. Surely, God would give them time, a space to know each other's hearts.

328

TOLTECA

They had been traveling ten days, and midmorning tomorrow, they would finally take the narrow pathway that led west. There, they would travel along the foothills of the northern mountains, passing not far from the north passage. Among the foothills of the west were caverns, and in them were the plates of gold and brass: the carvings, the records, the whisperings of the dead. This was where Sky Dragon would be, beneath the earth, in the stone catacombs of the ancients.

The last few days had been wondrous and Sky Teacher kept each memory carefully set aside. The shadow over them, the haunting he felt, seemed to make it necessary he press each moment with care and store it away like precious things kept in stone boxes from thieves. Sometimes he would be laughing with her, lost in the smell of her, when suddenly sadness would grip him. It was a panic he would lose her, for Sky Teacher could not shake the feeling time was turning, that a shadow stretched across the sky like blood on the moon. He would be ever grateful to see his father. He could hear himself plead, "Father, take my fears, help us, save us—give us time."

Two days ago in the village of Jaco, they had watched children, all young girls, dance the Flower-Song. Sky Teacher was sitting against an adobe hut, holding Star Skirt beside him. She had laughed and pointed.

"There, the third girl from the end—that was my part."

"You danced in Chalaco?"

"Oh, yes. I love dancing."

"I wish I could have seen that—the child Eslabeth, dancing."

"Oh, but I was only Star Skirt then."

"No, you were always Eslabeth."

As the dancers wove, younger children followed at their side, throwing flowers, and Eslabeth had caught a rich, red rose. Sky Teacher had reached over and set it into her hair. Later, the elders asked Sky Teacher to lay a blessing on the children of the village, and he had gathered them 'round, encircling him and Eslabeth, the parents watching from the hearth fires of the market plaza. He had noticed Eslabeth looking over the children just before he prayed, how her eyes were sparkling and so filled with life. He wondered what children she would give him—how that would be, in old age, with time worn and memories rich, to gather their children about them, like this. Yet something inside him knew they were never going to taste old age. He had taken both her hands before he prayed on the children, and he had not closed his eyes, but watched her as he spoke.

"Ahman-om-Amen, the flesh of men and the wings of God, Serpent Plumed, take these, the children, give them strength, bless them, honor them, and protect them. Look upon these, our children—their hearts are pure, their faces shine with the Light Whose Name Is Splendor—look here, gaze upon the work of thy hand, thy glory, and let Heaven sing this night."

Later, the next day, as they walked and the road grew long and flat, Sky Teacher had said to her, "Dance then, Eslabeth. Show me the flower dance."

"Here?"

"As we walk."

At first, she shook her head, and they walked on. She smiled and hummed the song, moving her feet—lightly at first, dancing before him along the road. Eslabeth moved with perfect grace, weaving, turning. When she spun, arms tucked, Sky Teacher laughed, clapping.

"Excellent!"

She continued spinning until she was near. He caught her and then she was in his arms and Sky Teacher kissed her. She looked up and he took that moment, her eyes, all alive and sparkling, and put it away like a picture in a fanfold plate.

"I knew I liked you, Sky Teacher," she said quietly. "I knew that you excited me, but being with you, I believe . . . all that you've told me of kindred. I know I love you now, but I also believe we have loved before. Yet in this life, I have never tasted anything like this— I've never tasted love."

"Nor have I."

"How would that be, never to taste it?"

"Terrible. Lost."

"Forever lost. Thank you. For finding me . . . thank you."

They slept each night beneath rich stars, Eslabeth always beside him, sometimes her hair against his cheek, sometimes her hand on his arms, and sometimes he wept. He wasn't sure why, but his mind was fevered.

On this night, weary from the day's journey, he found a hillock matted with yellow grass. The plains here were wide and flat, nearly empty, here and there the skeletal offering of cactus, or the fat-leaved corpuscle of a maguey plant. He had been pressing hard the last few days, feeling ever more desperate to see his father. Sometimes he even felt the urge to run, but it was too hot for that, the distance too far, especially for Eslabeth.

They were still following the merchants' route that eventually led to the Petén. Though it was well traveled at all times of the year, in the past few days it had been strangely quiet. They had not passed a single caravan, a single merchant; and in ordinary times, this close to the southern passage, caravans should have been plentiful. Yet, the road had been empty of all but scampering lizards, and though he had said nothing to Eslabeth, this worried him. What could have choked the only passage south?

That evening, before they found a place to rest, Sky Teacher noticed the southern sky was heavy with storm. In this country, where the land was low and flat, one could see for miles, and the storm looked far to the south. Still, Sky Teacher had noticed the odd look of it, almost as if they were not clouds; as if, somehow, the sun was being darkened and the sky had begun to boil.

As night fell, Sky Teacher gathered a simple meal. He sat next to Eslabeth, cutting cinnabar root with his knife, laying it on dried banana leaves.

"You have been so quiet today," Eslabeth said, rolling one of the banana leaves tightly in her fingers. "Why?"

He glanced to her, his sky-blue eyes lost in thought. He turned and sliced another white root down its center. "Tomorrow, we shall start west, toward the coast."

"Does that trouble you?"

"No, it will be a relief. It is this road that troubles me."

"In what way?"

He shook his head. He offered a slice of the sweet root. She sucked on it, looking at the skies.

"The stars . . . they seem so bright here."

"There are no city lights, and the land is very flat. My brother, he loved such stars as these. He longed to sail them."

"Sail the stars?" She chuckled.

"I remember, when we were boys, how once Topiltzin asked our father—as though it were merely a simple, ordinary question—what it was like to sail . . . *up there*. When Sky Dragon looked uncertain, Topiltzin explained: 'Up there, the stars—what was it like to sail them, Father?' He seemed so disappointed when Sky Dragon replied that men did not sail stars, merely seas, lakes, rivers—never stars. Topiltzin was crestfallen."

"I would like to meet him, this famous ballplayer."

Sky Teacher almost assured her that someday she would, but he did not feel it in his heart. He wondered if ever he would see Topiltzin again.

After they had eaten, Sky Teacher lay back in the grass, feeling unusually weary, tired. He could sleep for whole days. She had lain down opposite him, and he turned his head, reached out his arm. Their fingers touched.

"I love you, Eslabeth," he whispered.

"And I love you, Sky Teacher."

"There is something you should know."

"Yes?"

"When our father seals it—it shall be more than marriage you have seen in your villages."

"More? I don't understand."

"He is the Dragon. He has gifts, powers. He shall speak it for all time. We will be wed not just here, but in that place we remember, the place of kindred."

"All time," she whispered. "That sounds so comforting."

Her fingers curled through his, they squeezed tight. In later times, when he became the wanderer, when he became the traveler of far lands, high into the north where snows came whole seasons long—later, when Sky Teacher would become known by a different name, he would often remember this night and it would always seem the last peace he would ever know.

Dawn struck. When Sky Teacher opened his eyes, the illusion was that seconds before it had been night, with stars strewn wide and clear, and now the morning sun was warm upon him. He was surprised. They had slept later than usual. Sky Teacher then became aware something more than the sun had awakened him. The earth had awakened him. It seemed to be shivering, trembling. At first he thought it was a quake, for there was often shifting of earth in this part of the land; but then he realized, with a faint whisper of fear, that this was very unlike a quake. It came with a sound, a steady drum, a rumble.

Sky Teacher glanced to Eslabeth. She lay in troubled sleep. He turned and scrambled up the hillock quickly, to the summit. It was no more than a bump, a small knoll, the only interruption in the wide, flat plains they were crossing. When he reached the top, he lay down on his belly, looking over its edge, between the fat, knife-blade leaves of an aloe plant. His breath caught in his throat. His eyes stung with the sight, and a cold panic stabbed through him. He turned onto his back. For a moment, he could only lie there, unable to move, an odd, sickening fear in him. "Please no, please God, no . . ." he whispered.

They covered the very earth. They stretched far to the east, far to the west. They marched in segments, roughly squared. They were close enough he could see the sun glint dimly off colored shields, close enough their footfall, their march, seemed like coming thunder. They were not Tolteca, and he could feel their hearts. They had suckled; they had taken blood sacrament, the one taste that changed men's souls forever. They were flesh eaters.

He searched, panicked. There was no place to run. To either side—the left, the right, even straight north—it was all flat and offered no protection. Sky Teacher slid back down to where Eslabeth lay. His hand stretched to wake her but paused, startled at his inclination. For a moment, he considered taking his knife and letting her continue to sleep through all that was coming, through the storm. Yet he could not do that.

She opened her eyes, sensing his shadow. Seeing his face, she sat up quickly. She searched, hearing it, and started to get up, but he quickly grabbed her wrist, pulling her back. They she turned. She saw the fear in his eyes.

"What . . . what is that?"

"The darkness."

"What do you mean? What are you saying?"

"We must run, Eslabeth. I can think of no other path through this. We must run north, as hard, as fast . . . as long as we can."

"Run?"

"But we'll never make it." He closed his eyes against his thought, "Oh God, give me strength!"

"Please, I don't understand. What . . . ?"

"There are armies coming. Warriors. Thousands."

She gasped.

"But we're near the passage, the southern garrison . . ."

"The Tolteca of the garrison are dead, Eslabeth. And these who come . . . they have eaten the flesh of the fallen."

Eslabeth paled. She clasped his hand tight, her eyes searching desperately. "Then you are right, we outrun them. We can run north, we can . . ."

He watched her, certain now, through sudden tears. He shook his head.

"Then . . . then what?"

"Take my hands, take both my hands—now Eslabeth, take my hands."

She nodded, her own tears spilling freely. She crouched before him and clasped his hands tightly, desperately.

He swallowed against fear and said carefully, "Remember how I told you that when my father sealed us he would do it with gifts—with powers."

She nodded. "For all time," she whispered.

"I too have these gifts. We . . . we must do this, now, Eslabeth. Are you ready? Is your heart ready?"

"Yes," she whispered, though she could hear them, the clank of armor, voices, and then a scream, like animals were coming as well as men. "I am ready, Sky Teacher."

He closed his eyes, lowered his head. "In the name of the great Father, by the word of the Son, through the spirit of the one Mother, the Light Whose Name Is Splendor, I seal us—under sky, in the whisper of morning, with witness of the Heavens—I seal us for this life, this breath, and for all of time."

Eslabeth shook with tears. He opened his eyes, and even though there was terrible fear therein, terrible sadness, there also, somehow, seemed to be joy . . . even peace.

"Kiss me, Eslabeth," he whispered.

She fell into him, into his lips.

There were howls, screams not of beasts but of men dying, of torture. She felt his arm move past her hip, he drew something from his belt, then suddenly shoved her back, pinning her to the ground. He lifted his knife. She took quick, shallow breath, waiting. Sky Teacher bared his teeth. He screamed between them, his hand shaking, but he did not plunge the knife; he just closed his eyes and lowered his head.

"No," he whispered, "I cannot, I cannot."

Eslabeth reached both her hands forward and clasped his knife-holding wrist. When his eyes opened, hers looked back without fear, and though a tear spilled free, when she spoke her voice was firm and unshaken.

"You said something once, Sky Teacher, you said that faith is belief in what is . . . in things that are, but are not seen." She waited, watching him carefully. "I believe you, Sky Teacher! I believe everything, all you have ever taught me. You must do this—and I will see you—there, I will wait for you—there . . . I will wait for you, kindred."

His mouth fell open and he cried out in sorrow. He looked to the Heavens as though pleading help.

Over his shoulder she saw them, she saw them coming, like scattering wolves, shadows moving; some of them seemed to cross the ground on all fours.

She turned her eyes, locked on his, only on his. He clenched his teeth, and he tried; but it was Eslabeth who had to pull his hand down, hard and quick with both of hers.

Eslabeth did not feel the blade. Something else had touched her. Through the dark, the fear, and the tears, pure light had taken Eslabeth like a mother's tender touch.

CHAPTER THIRTY-SIX
TIKAL

Hueloc leaned across the counter of the chief merchant's hut, just outside the city of Tikal. The merchant's name was Black-Turtle-Grease-Crier; he was skinny and dark skinned with rabbit eyes. Hueloc had dealt with him before; in fact, Hueloc made his first profit at the hands of Black-Turtle-Grease-Crier, who purchased two pack-loads of white agate gem Hueloc had mined out of mudflats along the coasts of Utzlampa. But this time, Black-Turtle-Grease-Crier seemed to have lost all interest in the one interest of his life: bartering. He was busy packing what treasures he had into wicker back-carriers. The people of Tikal were fleeing. Panic was evident; debris littered the streets. Hueloc had left the girls in the jungle near one of Tikal's principal rivers, telling them to keep low. He left Paper Flower with his long knife, earnestly bidding her to trust no one.

He had run most of the way from the river to the hut of Black-Turtle-Grease-Crier, which was difficult considering his wounds were hot pain riddling his already infirm body. Blood loss had left his head light, left reasoning difficult. Now all he could wrest from Black-Turtle-Grease-Crier was panic.

"But, for the love of God," Hueloc exclaimed, "even if the city is being evacuated, certainly there are still a few shrewd buyers!"

"Not for women," Black-Turtle-Grease-Crier said, shoving a gold statuette with turquoise eyes into one of his wicker back-carriers. "Jade . . . maybe gold . . . maybe. Women, impossible. Do you not see with your eyes, Hueloc? Everyone is fleeing for his or her lives!"

"Gods, women have legs!"

"Does not matter, Great Gut. *They* are coming. They are without number; they are uncounted as are the stars."

"I have heard this already. But even so, someone, some rich Lord, who is going to reach Uxmal or Chichén safely, without fear . . . certainly he might wish to have along companions."

Black-Turtle-Grease-Crier only shook his head. "Impossible."

Great Gut paced a moment. He paused, glancing out the hut's window. Several priests were scurrying quickly down a paved artery of one of the main grasslands, followed by an ant trail of baggage carriers loaded until their backs hunched. Priests! Hueloc spat to the side. It was said the Night and the Wind were coming against Tikal. Even the priests were fleeing. Hueloc had observed in the past that in times of panic, there was profit for those who were less inclined to lose heart. He pondered a moment what objects of value would be left behind. Black-Turtle-Grease-Crier would pack his most precious possessions, but even he had only bothered with four wicker carriers. Valuables would still litter his hut. Perhaps what Hueloc needed here was not a rich lord to purchase women-flesh, but fifteen or twenty wicker carriers to be mounted on the girls' backs. *He* could at least reach Chichén safely, and from there, by boat, Tollán, and with each of the girls carrying a load of fine goods. Double profits. Besides, he had grown fond of the girls. He had even decided to keep a few. Since he was about to become a rich lord, he could afford to keep a few.

"Tell me something, Black-Turtle-Grease-Crier, how long before these dreaded Shadow Walkers arrive?"

"I should know? What do you believe me to be, Great Gut? A reader of sacred books, a speaker of stars?"

"What is it that makes you so certain they are coming at all?"

"Survivors who come from the jungles. Like you, Great Gut. Are you to say to me, without wincing, you have seen nothing unusual in the jungles of late? Ah? Well?"

Hueloc gestured puzzlement.

"There, even you—Hueloc, the Brave! Ha!" He fingered an obsidian and gold-inlaid figure of a Chac god, then tossed it aside and reached for something else.

"And where will you go, Black-Turtle-Grease-Crier? Uxmal? The coast, perhaps?"

"Perhaps."

"You are not telling me? Is it a secret?"

"Times are frightening. Best to make careful wagers in such times, Great Gut. Surely you would be the first to understand that."

Hueloc stroked his beard. If the Shadow Walkers were coming, he and the girls had kept ahead of them so far. It shouldn't be that difficult to just keep outrunning them. Direction would be the gamble—to choose a direction. "Very well . . . if I cannot convince you . . ."

"You cannot. You are quite insane, you realize, coming here at a time like this. The whole city is in a state of panic, and you come to me trying to sell women-flesh! Only a lunatic like you would attempt that, Hueloc."

"Goodbye then, Black-Turtle-Grease-Crier. I wish you well."

"I wish you well also, Great Gut. But if I know you, you will never get out of here alive. You are too greedy." Hueloc noticed as he said this he was cramming a jade idol hard into a wicker carrier filled to bursting.

Hueloc was about to step out the door when he had to back away to make room for a Mayan lord. This was one of the disfigured ones, one of the Maya who called themselves high lords. Hueloc liked to call them melon-heads. This one was very rich. His clothes were pure silk-cotton and his robe was lined in splendid scarlet macaw feathers. The lord wore an amber-tube lip plug with gold dust inside, and large earplugs of carefully worked gold parrots. His sandals were alligator skin, his wrist bracelets gold and jade. He was too rich to be a magistrate, and in fact, Hueloc thought he recognized him. When he noticed the train that waited outside the hut—a gathering of servants and women, twenty or more warriors in full battle dress—he realized this could be none other than Parahon, the chief high judge of Tikal. With him was a tall Mayan warrior dressed in peccary armor. The mind of Hueloc turned quickly. What would the governor be doing here, in the outskirts of the city, in the hut of a greedy merchant like Black-Turtle-Grease-Crier? Whatever the reason, it would be worth discovering. Hueloc eased back into a corner.

"Are they prepared?" Parahon said in a shrill voice that seemed out of proportion with his face. The Balam was speaking to a commoner and not even bothering with sign language! Something big was happening here, something very curious. The Balam paused, turned his oval head to gaze at Hueloc through one tight, squinted black eye.

Hueloc made it appear as though he was just leaving. He stepped out the doorway and started off, muttering to himself as if occupied in thought. He quickly swung around and brought himself up near a side window. He eased up near the opening and pressed his ear to the side of the hut, but hearing movement, he turned and nearly jumped out of his skin. It was Paper Flower, standing right next to him, eyeing him with an angry, dark gaze.

"Mother of whores! You should not creep up on a man like that!" he hissed. "Nearly stopped my heart—"

"You were going to sell us! You are no great warrior, you are a merchant! You guileless frog, you were going to—"

He had clapped a hand over her mouth. "Quiet!"

She started to murmur, but paused when Parahon's resinous voice sounded.

"Are they ready?"

"Everything is ready, prepared, my lord," Black-Turtle-Grease-Crier answered feverishly.

"Precisely to my instructions?"

"Precisely, my lord!"

"Where are they?"

"Just south toward the coast, where the river grows deep, where it curves into a small bay. Within the recesses of the bay is a large rock cove. You have been there?"

"No."

"It is easy to find, simple. It is just east, and west of the bay. It is not difficult to find. But it offers very good cover. And the ship is within. It is hidden there, my lord."

"One? Only one?"

Black-Turtle-Grease-Crier paused, a nervous glitch. "Ahhh . . . yes. One. One ship."

"A ship . . ." Hueloc muttered, surprised. He glanced at Paper Flower. His hand was still over her mouth, but he could tell by the shift in her eyes she was listening as keenly as he was.

"I ordered seven!" Parahon's voice rang out. "You bloodthirsty insect! One is *not* seven."

"My lord, it was impossible to obtain seven," Black-Turtle-Grease-Crier said hurriedly, nervously, obviously a lie. "The shipwright, you see, he believed to have seven, but six were stolen by thieves in the night."

There was a long pause. Even Hueloc could see through the lie, even without the benefit of Black-Turtle-Grease-Crier's pained expression or weak half-smile. He had obviously hidden the other ships for himself or for sale to other greedy, desperate, rich lords. Black-Turtle-Grease-Crier was a shrewd businessman, but he underestimated the power of desperation.

"Kill him," Parahon said. "Leave his hair hanging on his hut wall."

"My lord, I swear! I promise! On the head of my children, there was nothing I could do. But the ship, it is a good ship! A fine ship!"

But Parahon had already turned, was already leaving.

There was a squawk. Hueloc pressed back against the hut wall, holding Paper Flower's arm. He heard the sound of bone snapping. Paper Flower gasped, but Hueloc motioned for silence. He slid carefully to the edge of the hut, watching as the melon-head came out, approaching his train.

"Return for my wives. Our supplies, gather them, bring them here, assemble them. I shall meet you."

Most scattered quickly, but two of the tall, muscled warriors remained. These were white, Tolteca. Parahon, after all, could afford the best. "Go with them," said Parahon. "See my women are safe."

"And you, my lord?" one spoke, watching the Maya suspiciously.

"Arrangements—alone."

The Tolteca nodded and were thus dispatched.

"He is up to something," Hueloc whispered. "The city in panic, the rich fleeing, wolves and thieves out in abundance, and the Lord Parahon is going somewhere alone." He glanced to Paper Flower. "This should prove interesting."

He crept to the other side of the hut. From where he crouched, he could see Parahon's peaked head starting down a narrow trail that led into the trees, toward the jungle, due west.

"Come along," he whispered and started after the governor, keeping to shadows. Paper Flower crept along at his side.

"So, you had your money invested, did you?" she said in an intense whisper. "Invested in us! You bastard."

"It is not as you might think, Paper Flower," Hueloc muttered, turning about the big trunk of a cedar. The high judge was easy to follow; from his bald, peaked head, crimson macaw feathers were hung, swaying as he walked, like markers.

"Please, do explain, Great Gut," Paper Flower whispered. "Tell me how it is not as I think."

"My plan to sell you, it was for your welfare—yours and the girls'."

"Not to mention *your* welfare."

"This is not true. I had only you girls in mind."

"Explain how it is our welfare to become slaves and harlots."

"Look around, people are fleeing, everywhere. And why are they fleeing? Because they are terrified. And why are they terrified? Because this is war. War is a terrible thing. I have seen situations such as this before, and I know: only the rich get out alive. Naturally, I planned to sell you girls to the rich. After all—no one else could afford you. So you see, then, it was for *your* welfare."

He ducked low a moment, pulling her down beside him. Parahon had paused, glancing back, suspicious. He then continued on, looking like a big, strutting bird.

"Damn fool," Hueloc whispered.

"I am no fool," Paper Flower responded.

"Not you, him, coming out here alone. If you were a thief, Paper Flower, a cutthroat, and you saw that crimson head dress, what might be your reaction?" He glanced at her. She peered past him at Parahon's plume.

"Why does he do this?"

"There can be but one reason." Hueloc squatted, walking awkwardly behind bushes, nearly on his knees. "Avarice and greed."

"Where is he going?"

"Just keep your voice low and we will find out shortly, elder sister."

"Is that because you yourself are a thief?"

"Not ordinarily."

"You're not a Dragon Lord either, are you?"

"No, I am not. And proud not to be. Most of them are boring, wholly devoted to the state and God—no time for anything else."

Hueloc caught the sleeve of his tunic on a branch and struggled a moment to free it. Paper Flower reached up and plucked it loose. They continued.

"I still cannot believe you were going to sell us," she said.

"Use reason here, Paper Flower. Where best would you and your sisters be? Safe in the hands of the rich, that is where. But it no longer matters. I have decided not to sell you after all. I have decided to keep you. All of you."

"Keep us? How do you mean that?"

"Well . . . er . . . that is, if you wish to stay. You see, Paper Flower, I myself am about to become rich—momentarily."

"By stealing?"

"By taking advantage of a business opportunity."

"And you assume, now you are about to be rich, that we will want to become your servants?"

"Well, no. Actually, I can hire servants."

"Then what are we to become? Your vassals?"

"Vassals? No . . . I thought more as though . . . you might become . . ."

"Concubines?"

"Companions! Yes. That is all, just companions—all the girls but for you, that is."

"I am an exception?"

Hueloc realized he was fast getting in over his head. "Yes."

"And what am I to become?"

He paused a moment, surprised at himself. He had been about to tell her it was breaking his heart to think they would be parted, that for God knows what reason he had fallen in love with her and he intended to keep her forever—even, God forbid, marry her. "You would become . . . elder companion."

"Elder companion? What is an 'elder companion'?"

"It is . . . a companion . . . who is . . . older than the other companions."

She offered a suspicious glance. She was keeping close to him as they crept through the brush, close enough he could smell her. Paper Flower, even in the jungles, seemed to smell of some perfume, a soft, alluring scent. The night he had lain with her, holding her while she slept, he had stared for the longest time at her face, eyes closed, the long lashes, the smooth skin, the high cheekbones, the silken dark hair. Something had swept over him, like an ache or a fever. The others he cared about, but it was a feeling like one might feel for a sister, for a daughter. With Paper Flower, it was different. He had awakened that morning—for the first time in his miserable life—in love. Of all people, he had awakened in love with Paper Flower, the she-bitch. He had decided that even if he were forced to sell all the others, he would at least keep Paper Flower. Then, of course, Hueloc had not really taken into account the fact she might not wish to be kept. It had always been that way; women came, women went; they laughed, they sang; they all liked the fat merchant Hueloc, they smoked blue smoke with him in taverns, sat on his lap, stroked his beard. Yet none of them ever stayed, none had ever loved him.

The Mayan had stopped, and Hueloc held out a hand, touching Paper Flower's shoulder. They were well into the jungle now. The hut of Black-Turtle-Grease-Crier had already been on the outskirts of the city, near the forests, and this far in was well out of anyone's traveled path. Parahon was rolling aside a stone. The stone was overgrown in moss and vine; whatever was hidden behind it had been there a long time. Paper Flower pressed close to watch, and for a moment, he glanced at her. She caught the gaze, looked up. *Could you . . . possibly . . . ever, feel for me, Paper Flower?* He thought *at* her, shivering. She might have heard him, for she studied his eyes intently before looking away.

"Look there," she whispered. "What is that?"

Hueloc squinted. Parahon was lifting two large, fat, net bags. They were filled with the finest jade he had ever seen. It shimmered, even in the distance, making Hueloc's skin quiver like a whore had walked fingers down his back. "That, Paper Flower, is our future."

"Our future? How is it *our* future?"

"There are times, elder sister, when you must seize the opportunity, take the turkey by the throat, when you must cast discretion aside. This is one of those times. He is rich like a filthy dog. He has never in his life shed kindness; and now we are going to take his jade. And then we are going to take his ship."

"We are going to steal the ship of the governor of Tikal?"

"Exactly. If the jungles are going to boil over in madness, I say let us go sailing. What do you think? You, me, the girls. Eh?" He grabbed her without waiting for an answer and jerked into a half-run, keeping low, dodging trees.

"But Hueloc, this is outright theft!"

"The sweetest kind, Tender Heart. Outright theft of the rich."

"What . . . did you just call me?"

He winced. "Nothing. Nothing."

They ran down a short glen and quickly up its side. Hueloc was aware, distantly, that his side was burning, and he was fairly certain it was bleeding again, but all that would have to wait. She paused, pulling him back, pointing.

"Hueloc . . . look!"

He looked up. Over the tips of the trees could be seen Tikal's high temple towers of the Nonaloca Maya, for they rose into the sky like mountains, thrusting through the forest canopy. Now they were framed against dark smoke that curled, lifting in billows. Hueloc could hear screams; they were distant, far, and they swam through the trees like a haunting. He winced. It was true then. The Shadow Walkers had come to Tikal. "Lord protect us," he whispered.

Hueloc pulled her back into a run, quickly through the trees. He drew up short. There was a tall willow here, with stout branches, drooping its tendril leaves over the trail.

"This will do. Stay here."

Hueloc leapt, catching a lower branch and hoisting himself up. He worked quickly, climbing hand over hand. When he was high enough, he cut loose a smooth *liana* vine. He slid out precariously on a branch and found a limb that had just the right bend, tying the vine to its tip. He quickly climbed down, pulled the vine taut, setting the spring action, and using a cord of leather, staked the vine to the ground. He fashioned a slip tie, then looped the loose end of the vine over the narrow footpath. He quickly hid it, scattering leaves. In the bushes, he got down on his belly, pulling Paper Flower down beside him. Then he waited with the loose end of the leather tie in his fingers.

"I do not like this, Hueloc. It is not moral. If we steal his ship, he could possibly die, and his wives too."

"This is war, Paper Flower. It is a matter of him, or us. I prefer us. We are better people. He is a pompous, melon-headed frog. Now be still."

The Mayan came up the path clutching his two massive net bags of jade in fat hands. It was almost too good to be true. The chief Judge had calculated that everyone, every good citizen, even every thief, would be fleeing toward the coast. No one would be coming in this direction.

Parahon's alligator-leather sandal stepped directly into the center of the vine, and Hueloc jerked the stave loose. The upper branch sprung and Parahon uttered a panicked *glurp* as he was sucked upward into the air. One net bag of jade went flying, scattering jade along the path, but the greedy bastard held onto the second with clawed hands. He now hung upside down, swaying slowly, his big head with its stretched eyes searching, incensed, furious. Hueloc stood up. No one was sweeping the path before the Mayan now, no servants scurrying, afraid to meet his eyes. He was hanging by one leg like a fat woman, his robes and jeweled belts hanging down over his belly, his white loin wrap exposed to the sky. Hueloc stepped out of the bushes, walked around the swaying vine, and tipped his head, meeting the upside-down chief judge eye for eye.

"It is a bad season, my friend," Hueloc explained. "All manner of vermin in the jungle these days, eh?" Hueloc snatched the bag of jade, then danced back as Parahon groped for it, muttering, sneering, spitting. Parahon was so filled with rage Hueloc wondered if his melon head might pop. Hueloc shoved the polished jade rocks that had scattered on the trail into the second net bag and tied the two together with a leather cord. Parahon watched, swaying gently, the tree creaking as he did so. Hueloc glanced to Paper Flower, who had remained in the shadows. He looked around and calculated that if they continued to press west and north they would reach both the girls and the bay holding the ship Black-Turtle-Grease-Crier had described. Things were falling into his lap. He had never had such luck as this.

"Let us leave, Paper Flower," he said, staring down the trail.

"Hueloc!" she shouted, coming out of the bushes. He paused, looked back.

"For love of God, Hueloc, you cannot leave him here like this.

He will die!"

"What do you want me to do with him? Take him with us?"

"Cut him down, let him go."

"Oh, yes, let him go. Within a blink, he will be back here with twenty Toltec warriors!"

"I will not leave this man here to die hanging from his foot, Hueloc. Perhaps we can be thieves—just this once—as you say. It is war and we must make harsh decisions. But I will not bloody my hands with murder."

Hueloc grunted. "Paper Flower, we *truly* do not have time for this!"

She stared back defiantly. He glanced at Parahon, who was looking from one to the other. If he was worried, or if he was concerned, the stretched, beady eyes offered no hint. Their deformation left Mayan lords without emotion. They looked in a state of permanent disdain.

"Hold these, woman," he said, shoving the bags into her hands and stepping past her. He drew his knife and shinnied up the tree. He groped for the vine once he was sufficiently high, but it was just out of reach.

"Swing him a little!" he shouted.

Below, Paper Flower started toward Parahon, then paused, withdrew. She laid aside the net sacks and picked up a fallen tree limb, and used it to start him swinging, pushing it against his fat belly. Hueloc chuckled as he caught the vine. God, but she was a quick little bint. He cut a notch in the vine and shinnied back down.

"That will eventually fray out and break," he said, shoving his knife back in his belt. "When he falls, he can run off and save his greasy buttocks. We will start him swinging here, and soon the vine will break."

"How soon?"

"Long enough for us to get out of here, but not long enough for his head to pop from too much blood. Satisfied?"

"I suppose."

Hueloc grabbed Parahon and pulled the chief judge back, then let him go. Parahon swung directly into the trunk of the tree with a *thud*, his head banging with what Hueloc swore was a slightly hollowed sound.

"Sorry," Hueloc said, "my mistake." He grabbed Parahon a second time and started him swinging in a crosswise direction. Parahon was hissing and spitting, spewing rage. Hueloc grabbed Paper Flower's arm and started running.

The screams were closer now, floating eerily into the jungles. They were horrid. They were not the screams of warriors locked in battle, but of dying, of cutting. The sacred city of Tikal was surely being bathed in blood.

CHAPTER THIRTY-SEVEN
THE SERPENT PLUMED

Plume Gum searched the clearing beyond the trees where she and the others crouched, where Hueloc had hidden them in bushes, huddled together in the shadow. Something was going wrong, and Plume Gum's heart began to beat in her throat. There were screams, and they seemed to float through the air, like spirits drifting in dull wind. And there was smoke. It came in lazy, slow curls, like a great beast snaking tendrils through the trees, searching them out. She met the eyes of her sisters, of Night Jasmine across from her, of Jade Skirt, crouched behind tall fronds, Jewel Twirler who kept near, searching the forest, fearful. Where was Hueloc? Where was Paper Flower? Plume Gum noticed the sun, distant in the west, sinking behind the line of the mountains. The dull mist of smoke had bathed it red, a blood sun. Plume Gum was not certain what was happening toward the city from where the screams and smoke drifted, but she remembered well the village in the jungle. She knew this would be a night of horror. Several times she thought she heard the trees and bushes behind them shiver, and she feared at any moment they would bristle with warriors. The Shadow Walkers were close.

Not far away, a man screamed and screamed again, and again, until quite suddenly the sound was obliterated. The girls gathered tighter, hushed, eyes wide in terror. Jewel Twirler, shivering, wept with quiet tears. Plume Gum fought the voice within that promised the Dark Lord was not dead, but was looking through his mirror into the jungle, searching for them.

TOLTECA

Tikal was about to fall to the armies of the Smoking Mirror. The outlying villages, the huts of reed, the houses of adobe, and the corrals, all these were burning. The only defense the city had left was a hastily thrown up rampart of dirt and wood manned by the armies of Parahon, those called the Foxes, fierce fighters, honed and deadly, but numbering only seven hundred.

Smoking Mirror studied them from a temple tower in the jungle. The tower was built high enough that he could view the whole valley before him, including the great, rich city with its limestone, its temples, its palaces, all painted red, all shining. From his high point, Smoking Mirror lifted his hand, and with this signal conch shells sounded that would send the ten thousand warriors of Red Skull against Tikal's pitiless ramparts. Below, warriors sprang forth, sprinting, their war cries lifting to the Heavens. Some of the Maya, seeing what came against them, began to run, to scatter, but others stood fast and prepared to die.

Smoking Mirror made a second motion, with his left hand. Conch shells called, and the warriors of Serpent Slayer began a slow sweep about the east flank of the city. They would cut directly into the lines of refugees that made ant trails outward from the city. The Shadow Walkers would scatter them, consume them, and close on the eastern edge of Tikal, enveloping it.

Smoking Mirror lifted his right hand and clenched it into a fist. Conch shells sounded, and the warriors of Sun Ray began a sweep toward the west, toward the western rivers whose currents opened to the sea along the southern ocean. The armies of Sun Ray moved like an arm coiling. The trees, the undergrowth shivered as they came.

Smoking Mirror could feel all his armies, as if they were appendages, as though they were his tentacles, curling, sweeping. While the frontal attack of Red Skull overran the shallow ramparts and spilled into the central plaza of Tikal, the people, the lords, the merchants, the rich, the fools—they would scatter like seeds spewing from crushed fruit, but the great arms of the Smoking Mirror would curl inward, collecting them, gathering them. This night would be a harvest to the Lord of Youth, Mocker; this night would sustain *him*, offer *him* blood and flesh in abundance.

A guttural moan caught his attention and Smoking Mirror turned. At his side crouched Nagali, the sorcerer, the Filth-Eater. He had crawled here, or flown here. Filth-Eater came only in such moments when he had something choice to offer his Lord; and the little magician smiled, his teeth, his hands, and his feet stained with blood. He had been engaged in killing, feeding. He was crouched, still half in the form of a cat, and his voice had a certain snarling hiss to it when he spoke, as though he was unable to shed himself of his animal familiar.

"I have . . . I have found him, my lord," he whispered.

"Found who?"

"Fat Merchant," Filth-Eater announced with pride, grinning, "and his women."

The Smoking Mirror was stunned. He had been expecting some offering, some bit of news, but not this. He had, in fact, purposely forgotten the fat merchant. When Flower Weaver had not returned, Smoking Mirror had begun to fester from anger. It was filling him, consuming him like toxin. This pompous Toltec had made a mockery of him, and had fled with his virgins, nursing victory. That left a taste so bitter that Smoking Mirror had forced it from him, shed himself of the thought, for it was breaking his power. Now anger flooded him once more, and this time it came with sweetness, for Filth-Eater was never wrong, never stupid, but always sly, always the cunning one. If Filth-Eater said he had found the fat man, then Smoking Mirror could already taste the Toltec's blood. Taking the jewel of the Nonaloca that was Tikal was like drinking power, getting drunk. It wasn't the fat man, besides. Smoking Mirror glanced down at Filth-Eater and let a smile curl.

Seeing a spark in his master's eye, Filth-Eater chuckled slyly. His back was still thick in cat hair, and the stub of a tail that curled from his buttocks began whipping, excited.

🙶🙷🙶🙷🙶🙷🙶🙷🙶🙷🙶🙷🙶🙷🙶🙷🙶

"Wait here," Plume Gum whispered to the others, "I will return quickly."

Night Jasmine touched her shoulder. "Paper Flower said we were to stay together."

"Yes," Plume Gum whispered, "and she may be dead. I must discover in whose path we lie. If the Shadow Walkers descend, Night Jasmine, we cannot wait like sparrows before the hawk." She turned and sprinted into the trees.

As she left, Night Jasmine, who was now eldest sister, motioned for the others to gather close. She watched the figure of Plume Gum slip into the trees.

Plume Gum knew the jungle, knew the forest, the fronds, the trees, the soft, moist earth. She had grown up in such places, and she kept the red sun at a certain angle, mentally marking the pathway back. She ran, keeping measured breath, dodging about trees, past the ferns and bush. When she reached a part of the jungle that was thinner, where the bush was lower to the ground, she chose the highest tree, a tall, splendid oak that stretched its crown into the smoked, purple sky. Hastily she climbed, pulling herself hand over hand, until she was high, until the ground was a dizzying speck below her. She shaded her eyes and searched, squinting, holding her breath.

They were not hard to find. A whole line of them was coming through the trees, making no sound, parting foliage as they came. Here and there, she could see the glimmer of a weapon, the glint of a shield face, the shadow of a body. They stretched far to the west, far to the east. They seemed to fill the whole jungle.

She felt a stab of fear numbing her as she climbed down, but not surprise. Rather, she would have been surprised at anything else. She had been on the mountainside that day not long after they were captured. Taken from their village and led to the City of Thieves on the crest of the mountains, she had looked back. She had seen the armies of the Shadow Walkers filling the valley, the jungle, the coasts, filling the whole earth, and far campfires flickering like the star skirt, like the night sky. Now they were coming against the cities of the rich Nonaloca Maya. Plume Gum and her sisters, if they waited, if they paused at all, would be swallowed into a beast that ate the hearts of living beings, which feasted on the flesh of the suffering. They would cry with the souls of the lost, forever.

She sprinted back through the trees at a swift run. She had not panicked when she saw them, for there was still time to run. Then she realized there were sounds behind her, that the jungle was whispering after her. She looked back over her shoulder.

Plume Gum was being pursued. They must have been scouts, ahead of the main armies, and they had spotted her. They were runners. She could hear the quiet pad of their feet, hear them swishing past the jungle as they closed, coming for her. Now panic stabbed; it closed off wind in her throat, it shivered across her skin. They were running much faster than she was, for they were Slayers, coming like wolves to a scent.

◨◧◨◧◨◧◨◧◨◧◨◧◨◧◨◧◨◧◨◧◨◧

The hairy worms in the bowl seemed to writhe about each other as Topiltzin watched. The bowl was fashioned from a hollowed-out gourd, and the masher Coyotl was using was a blunt palm stem. He rammed it down, twisting, and the worms were mashed into a brown, gooey paste. To this Coyotl sprinkled bits of chopped mushroom.

"I picked these days ago," Coyotl muttered, not looking up, "near that river we first crossed. I hoped these might come to some use, but I never imagined this would be it."

Topiltzin watched Coyotl add a tarantula, pulling it from a palm-leaf wrapping and letting it crawl along his arm under his hand,

354

TOLTECA

flicking it into the mixture, where it was smashed, legs groping and body popping with a squirt of white liquid. Coyotl also added stems and long, white petals from a flower, all of which had been ground between his fingers; and fungus mold, which he had scraped off in paper-thin strips.

Coyotl paused and looked up. "This I will add for measure, Topiltzin: that I am there with you . . . in spirit, in heart." Coyotl slit open a small vein of his wrist. He squeezed out drops of his own blood into the mixture.

He used a fire drill he had fashioned from old wood, twirling the spindle swiftly, igniting a small flame which he used to light a little bundle of weeds and sticks. He held the gourd over the flame, heating it, black streaks of smoke searing the wart-filled surface of the yellow gourd skin.

Topiltzin watched Coyotl with a detached feeling, almost as though he were somewhere else, as though this could have been a dream and he only a watcher. There was sadness, weariness inside Topiltzin since he had awakened, just past mid-sun. It was something that settled over him, like the evening sky settling over the white heat of day—sadness, a longing.

Coyotl rolled his preparation into paste balls, of which he made six. He arranged them upon a pattern he had etched into the brown dirt with powdered lime, forming an image of a star with five points. This was the signet of the ancients, of the ancestors, the kings of the Nephalli. At the outer points of the star, he laid the paste balls. He then paused, easing back on haunches, looking to Topiltzin. Topiltzin noticed how Coyotl's burn, along the right side of his face, had hardened into a red-black mold. He had jammed cotton in his socket, tying it in place with a bloodied strip torn from his hip belt.

"You will need to shed yourself of clothing," Coyotl said.

Topiltzin loosened his belt, tossed it aside. He withdrew his loin-clout and chamois and tossed these aside. He pulled the crimson tie from the braid of his hair. He knelt on both knees before Coyotl's star.

"How do you feel, Topiltzin?" Coyotl asked.

"Distant. Dead."

"When you do this, when you partake, you must let it fill you, let it into you like the fever of the game. Imagine you hear the screams of the crowds that have gathered, and then . . . become, fix on an image . . . and become it. Remember but one thing, my prince, let not fear choke you—not for an instant, not for a second. Fear, it if comes, shall steal you away, take you swiftly down, deep into the land of the dead. Like a stone dropped into the sea, that is how you will fall. They will attempt to take you there—demons, dancing, with high steps and fire, coming for the spirit, the heart of Topiltzin, and you must not fear them. Look in their eyes and spit. That is all I know to tell you, my brother, all I know to say. Are you certain, then? Are you sure of this in your heart?"

Topiltzin did not answer; he only leveled a hard gaze.

Coyotl swallowed. He reached out his hands, and Topiltzin clasped them in his. Coyotl squeezed hard, and there was a crack in his voice when he said, "Remember me, my brother, as I shall remember you. We shall keep each other in our hearts."

He looked away, and Topiltzin wondered if these were the last words he would ever hear from his friend, the sly one, the quick one, Coyotl. How many years had it been they had known each other? Since they were young. Since they were foolish, since they were immortal.

Topiltzin half closed his eyes and laid his hands on his thighs. He let out all his feelings, his anger, his fear. The heavy sadness, he let it from him, like pouring out water from an urn, let it spill over the ground, and he felt the calm, the same harnessed, waiting calm he felt before a game. He barely breathed. His heart beat slow, steady; his skin simmered in a certain, waiting fever.

Coyotl smashed the paste ball set to the north nodal point first, mashing it into a strip of palm leaf, then lifted his finger and smeared this across Topiltzin's forehead, in three quick streaks. Coyotl whispered to himself as he did this, low, garbled. Topiltzin realized it was a prayer, possibly the only prayer Coyotl knew. Ironically, it was the prayer they had both been taught in the Calmecac schools, the prayer of offering, of sacrament. A second paste ball Coyotl crushed and smeared across Topiltzin's navel. Two more he smeared over either breast. He then took the last, the smallest, warming it in his hand and lifting it. Topiltzin opened his mouth, letting Coyotl place it on his tongue.

It had a harsh, gritty feel, an angry taste as Topiltzin squeezed it between his tongue and upper palate, mashing it into his teeth. It numbed out his gums; it left a slightly bitter, acrid taste. For a moment his body tried to heave, gagging, but Topiltzin let nothing through, he simply swallowed the paste down, then fixed upon an image. The image he chose was from the marketplace of Tollán. It was the basalt image of his father, the Dragon—the Serpent Plumed.

It did not take long for the mixture to take effect. It first seized his gut in a knot of pain, but he let the pain feed him, let it bleed through him. Topiltzin's eyes were half open, half closed, and a part of him could see the jungle, the face of Coyotl waiting. Vision suddenly sharpened, as though everything was now cut in crystal painting, the colors fired into edged fury. Quite suddenly, it all looked to be melting, as though rain were sweeping, washing, leaving the face of Coyotl watery and uncertain. Coyotl's hair and eyes loosened, about to dissolve. The world began to lose form. It seemed to come apart like a woven cloth unraveling, wriggling, melting.

Topiltzin could feel the dance, the high, singing dance—all around him, air like fire dancing, licking at his skin. He could feel his flesh, like water, like running acid. He could taste himself . . . melting.

They came for him—the dark. Like a beast they came, inhaling, sucking him into waiting jaws. The world was shredding, and a void was rushing forward, screaming without sound, coming, coming, then it enveloped him. It took him. All was dark, all was lost, and he realized the small, distant glimmer—that far light he could see in the distance—was his soul and his entire world. He was dissolving. The light was spinning away, farther, farther. He tried to hold, to move toward it, somehow knowing the very spirit and fiber of Topiltzin, all his world, all he had ever been in all of time, was slipping away. It was existence: there was light, and there was dark; and the dark, the fear, the empty space of the sky, was the death of those who fell from hope. It was the end of all knowing. Topiltzin choked in panic. In the last moments, he tried to scream the name of God, but his world dissolved and God no longer had a name. The blackness sucked the spirit out of Topiltzin like fingers closing over flame.

Fire Serpent crouched on one knee, weary, feeling his head light, feeling blood loss. He held fingers against a wound in his side. Warm, dark blood trickled between them—the wound was deep. He had lost his shield and had taken two other wounds, though these were bearable, one to his shoulder, where a heavy, copper-bladed stone axe had sheared through his leather corselet, and one to his forearm. He had also lost half his men.

It seemed the Shadow Walkers had come out of nowhere, through the trees, full run. When their war cries had sounded, it was already too late. Fire Serpent had been running just ahead of them. He knew their strength, their size, but he still hoped beyond hope he could reach Tikal and gather the people into the marketplace. The high walls might have protected them. He was close; he was almost to the outskirts of the city when Fire Serpent, the lord of the jungle, the protector of the weak, had been taken by surprise. His vanguard troops were slaughtered like fatted animals. They came, Shadow Walkers, and they kept coming, waves of them, like the sea itself was rolling in. Fire Serpent's men had formed a solid front, swinging about, locking shields, but they were soon outflanked on both sides, and would have been outflanked to the rear had he not managed a hard, pressed retreat to a deep river which offered a temporary barrier. The retreat had cost him perhaps two hundred men, taken quick, scattered across the jungle floor, left like droplets of blood; but once their rear was protected, the Slayers of the Fire Serpent were able to turn back the slaughter, they were able to hold them off, if only for a time.

Twice Fire Serpent had moved to the fore, stepped into full battle, and was stunned at the power of it, the fury, the rage. The Shadow Walkers were prime warriors, the look in their eyes wholly fearless, if anything, craving death, fierce as leopards, muscled, hard, their weapons wetted in blood. It was madness, the nightmare of prophecy, and there was a terrible hopelessness to it all. Only when they reached the river had his captains been able to draw in flanks, tightening. They fought there, died there, for a full degree's shift of sun. Now, finally, the Shadow Walkers had withdrawn into the trees, re-gathering. It was a temporary stay. Fire Serpent knew they would soon come for the kill, and this time, there would be no escape. One last thrust and the Slayers, the Sons of Helaman, would be swallowed into time, would be no more.

The sky had massed in gray clouds that seemed to leave it colorless, empty. The jungle here was a thick, darken green, smoldering, shifting in mist.

The river behind him was wide, slow, and bordered by mangled growth. Near its shore were the wounded, the dying, some resting on the hilts of their swords, or against the battered edges of their shields, some dead. The thick brown waters were edged in crimson like the lining of an expensive cloak.

Farther down the same river, due south, where it curved toward the ocean, was the bay described to Parahon by Black-Turtle-Grease-Crier. Although neither he nor his warriors would ever know it, Fire Serpent had given Hueloc and the sixteen virgins a moment longer to live, for if he had not been there to swallow death, to temporarily snag one of the armies of Sun Ray, Hueloc and the girls would already have been overtaken.

Obsidian Sword, crouched beside his prince, looked in Fire

Serpent's eyes. Fire Serpent guessed his first captain could see the wound he held closed with his fingers was mortal. This would be the Fire Serpent's last battle.

"They come for hearts now," Fire Serpent said. "They believe they have hewn us down to the chosen. They will now try to take captives. We shall disappoint them, Obsidian Sword, we shall offer them only moonsteel, only our dead. Let us take up arms, bind our wounds, and prepare."

Obsidian Sword motioned with a fist to his shoulder, and runners, waiting to spread Fire Serpent's command, turned, sprinted, keeping low.

Fire Serpent looked to the line of the forest where the enemy waited like shadows boiling.

Seven of them came out of the trees, into the clearing, into view. They danced, high steps, twisting, ducking, drums sounding, trumpets calling. These were sorcerers and had dressed themselves in human skin, the skin of captives taken from his own men. Fire Serpent stepped forward, parting his warriors, until he was at the front. Obsidian Sword followed.

"Bring me a longbow," Fire Serpent said.

"They are out of range, my lord," answered Obsidian Sword.

Fire Serpent did not respond, and at a signal, a longbow was brought. Fire Serpent chose a light, moonsteel arrow. He lowered himself to one knee, and drew the bow back, held it, then slowly, carefully took aim. He took his time. It was a difficult shot. He first aligned dead bead on a center dancer, then brought the tip skyward, measuring out the distance. He released. The arrow spun, in silver gleam, a high, slow arc. Fire Serpent knew by its path that he had taken mark, and he watched it drop, like a bolt from Heaven. It struck. One of the dancers spun in a twisted leap, and fell into the grass.

Fire Serpent stood. "My atlatl," he said. His shield-bearer produced it, loaded. "Pull my corselet tighter, hard against this wound."

Pain knifed through him as they cinched the tie straps tight, but he welcomed it—with the blood he had lost, pain was the only thing still keeping him conscious. "Tighter!" Fire Serpent hissed, and the shield-bearer set his boot against Fire Serpent's back, pulling harder. For a moment Fire Serpent thought he would pass out, for his vision had grayed. He glanced down. The corselet bit into his wound.

He looked to Obsidian Sword, into his eyes. Obsidian Sword understood the look. His own gaze hardened, his eyes narrowed.

Fire Serpent turned to his men, and shouted, his voice strong, still their Lord, still their captain.

"Each man, each sword, all we are, we shall now die, bury ourselves into them like spears. If we do not die by their sword, then we shall die by our own daggers, through the heart, the throat. We shall give them no flesh to offer their God; we shall give them only death."

Two captains turned and sprinted, spreading word.

Fire Serpent chose several moonsteel atlatl-darts from his shield-bearer and wedged them into belt notches, anchoring them against the back of this corselet. He pulled free his helmet and cast it aside, shook out his hair. He lifted his atlatl.

Then he screamed, wild, a war cry, echoing into the sky like the scream of a cat, and the dancers in the clearing, paused, turned.

The Slayers of Fire Serpent sprang forward, singing the song of war, lifting on haunches and coming like leopards. Fire Serpent sprinted at the fore. All his life was being sucked into the effort, his blood was spilling out of him, but he still brought the atlatl over his head and launched its dart. It *whunked* dead center through a mirror breastplate, and one of the Shadow Walkers, a captain, whom Fire Serpent had chosen by his mantle, crumpled like a bird felled from a tree.

None of the Shadow Walkers had expected attack. They turned in their shadowed trees as the atlatl-darts of the Slayers flashed into them, scattering the first of them. The warriors of Fire Serpent then lifted thrusting spears, anchored to belt hinges, and they continued at full run, screaming, hair whipped back in the wind of the flight. They tore through the trees like raging beasts. Flesh scattered before them.

Fire Serpent took two more wounds before he finally dropped to his knees, his atlatl-darts spent, his thrusting spear buried, and his sword broken. He spun there on one knee and opened a throat with a quick upper slash of his dagger. They were going to try to take him alive. They were surrounding him cautiously. Nevertheless, it was useless. He laughed as he sliced through a soft belly, for Fire Serpent was already dead. He had spent his life in the clearing; it had sucked through him at full run, long before he reached the trees. All that was left in him now was death's shadow. He shared it with them until he fell forward and the light went out from his eyes.

All about him, his Slayers fought in fury, savage, spending their life in full blood rites. And none were taken alive.

🔲🔲🔲🔲🔲🔲🔲🔲🔲🔲

A panicked sweat broke against Plume Gum's forehead, and she realized that if she ran farther, she would simply be drawing them toward the others. She decided to lead them in a different direction, but just then she ran past a dark figure waiting behind a tree. She caught the form only from the corner of her eye, and had almost screamed, but then she realized who it was. She spun about, looking back.

"Keep running," Hueloc hissed, "Join the others! Go!"

She paused, but Hueloc had turned away. She realized how close they were, her pursuers. She saw them—three, no, four, closing, whipping through the trees, weapons drawn. Plume Gum backed away, stumbled, then turned and ran. Hueloc was, after all, a Dragon Knight, and these were but four. She sprinted for the others.

🔲🔲🔲🔲🔲🔲🔲🔲🔲🔲

Hueloc stepped from behind the tree, atlatl angled. He chose the closest. He had once been on the west coast, near the desert in the Northland, and one night, kneeling on a ridge, he had seen wolves moving through the brush, low and swift, almost as though they were gliding. The Shadow Walkers struck him with the same image as they came at him through the trees. Hueloc kept his blood calm and slung the atlatl about his head, dropping to one knee, bringing it in a half-circle, then angling with his wrist, launching the short spear. It dropped a lean, savage warrior whose long dark hair whipped behind him, whose dark-bladed Toltec sword hugged his chest. The warrior kicked back as thought he had run headlong into a tree, Hueloc's atlatl slamming through his neck.

Hueloc ducked hard to the side, letting a javelin spin past, feeling its wind against his shoulder as he reloaded his atlatl. He whipped it, once full circle, then a second time, taking aim. The short, heavy moonsteel dart launched like a bolt from dark clouds, the metal watery, glimmering, and it *thunked* into the chest of a second runner.

There were two left, closing quickly. Hueloc ripped the buckler from his shoulder and brought it up to catch a flint knife just as it was flung. It hit the wooden shield at its edge and was deflected, spinning wildly into the bush. Hueloc dropped his atlatl, drew his heavy, doubled bladed Dragon sword. It felt good in his hand and he smiled, even generating a low, harsh chuckle as the runners closed the final distance. He braced himself, back onto one bent leg, angling the sword. The first was like spearing a fleeing tapir. The warrior came past, thrusting spear angled. Hueloc deflected the spear's tip with his buckler and ripped open the runner's abdomen.

The last attacked full run, and Hueloc couldn't get clear. He threw both his shield and sword aside and caught the runner by his chest armor, dodging the slash of a ripple-bladed knife. Hueloc rolled, going down on his back, and heaved the man into the air. He continued rolling, over his atlatl, snatching it, and when he came to his knees, he slammed his last moonsteel dart into the atlatl's trough. The man had hit a tree trunk, but was rapidly regained his feet, jerking free a spear that had sunk into the ground near him. It was a matter of close timing. As Hueloc whipped the atlatl over his head, the warrior lifted the spear. The Shadow Walker grunted as he was pinned to the tree through his soft parts, the guts below his ribs. He flung his throwing spear, but the effort was weak enough Hueloc caught the shaft, grinning, and spun it about in his hand before planting it into the man's chest. The feet kicked in spasm.

Hueloc stilled, listening. A kind of sickness turned in his stomach, not from what he heard, but more from what he could feel— the earth below his feet. The jungle itself seemed to be trembling. He glanced back, into the trees, shadowy in dusk. There, through the silent husks of the forest, he could barely make them out: far shadows coming, moving slow and ponderous. Hueloc winced. An entire army was bearing down from the north, not at a run, but in a steady sweep, and the weight of them was like a mountain coming. Hueloc felt himself chill. Time had narrowed, squeezed in upon him. He grabbed his sword and ran toward the bay, where he had instructed Paper Flower to take the others.

He told himself there was still time, the river was to his right, pooling slowly, and it curved off ahead behind an outcropping of rocks. On the far side of those rocks, which stretched through a grove of strangler figs, was the bay, and the ship. There was time to reach it if he ran, to launch it, to let currents take it swift toward the southern sea, but Hueloc, instead of feeling confident, felt a cold dread. He somehow knew in his heart he would never make it. It was suddenly a dream, a nightmare run. Even though he fought the illusion, his breath came hard, panicked.

Paper Flower dropped onto a natural rock ledge where the warm waters of the wide, shallow bay lapped, and peered into the shadow of a cove. A large, overhanging rock stretched over the waters like someone had wished to construct a roof. There, within the darkness, was the hulking, silent form of a great reed boat, its prow-and-stern structure forming half-moon arcs, its oars laid back. It floated in the water like a fat, yellow bird.

TOLTECA

"I will need help," Paper Flower shouted, and started forward, wadding into the waters. The water was body temperature, warm. Though beyond the rock ledge of the cove there were smooth flowing currents, here the water seemed to pool about itself. Moss tickled her legs as she made her way to the side of the ship. She saw where it was tied to a wooden stave that had been hammered into a crack in the rock and she brought her sword up and slashed through the hemp. The big ship rocked with the motion as though being awakened, and immediately the current slowly sucked it into the deeper part of the lagoon.

Four of the others were making their way to her. Paper Flower saw rope ties looped about the edges of the big, fat bundles of reeds that formed the top of the ship. She had to claw her way up the side in order to loosen them; as she did so, the boat turned slowly, slipping away from the cove. She tossed ropes out to the others.

"Hold it back! Pull it alongside the ledge!" She took one and dropped into the water herself.

Soon five of the girls were pulling the big boat about, hauling it through the water, and keeping the lines taut as it strained to sink deeper into the lagoon. When she was at the top, Paper Flower had looked down, into the ship's belly. She had seen a mast laid in a wooden assembly, a sail of coarse maguey hemp lashed about it. There were jars and wicker carriers stashed against the stern assembly. There was enough space in the great hollowed bottom for all of them.

◨◧◨◧◨◧◨◧◨◧◨◧◨◧◨◧◨◧

Plume Gum waited for Hueloc. She was at the edge of a sandy strip of land that curled around the length of the lagoon. Behind her, the yellow ship slowly emerged from the rock cove. She had followed the others here, all of them running, close, Paper Flower in the lead. Now she watched, letting the others run ahead, searching for any sign of Hueloc. The warriors coming for her had looked

365

cunning, swift. She feared Hueloc had been cut down, that he was lying somewhere dying in the jungle, and the thought pierced her with sadness. He was a good man, the Great Gut; he was kind, he was noble, he should not die here. When she heard a rustle beside her, she felt relief. She turned, smiling, and looked into the eyes of the Smoking Mirror. They were like a cold, ice wind striking. She tried to scream, but his hand seized her throat, her windpipe, the fingers curling sharp, breaking through the skin. She tasted her own blood.

⛭⛭⛭⛭⛭⛭⛭⛭⛭⛭⛭⛭⛭⛭⛭⛭

Coyotl lay nearly dead, half conscious. His head felt to be burning, and he guessed it was blood spilling out into the dark, rich earth of the Petén. More blood had spilt in the Petén than on the whole of the earth. The Petén drank blood, it fed on blood. Its forests were nursed on blood.

Topiltzin was gone. He had vanished.

At first, Coyotl thought Topiltzin was dead, and perhaps, in fact, he was. The Blue Prince went into a seizure, his eyes rolling into the white. Coyotl leaped forward, realizing the teeth had clamped down on Blue Prince's tongue and that blood was squirting out between them. Topiltzin's arms were flipping, spasmodically. Coyotl grabbed his shoulders, shaking him.

"Topiltzin! Hold onto it! Hold on! Don't die! God, Lord God, don't let him die!"

Darkness descended. Night was close, it was true, but this darkness was beyond night. It came swift, as though some beast had dropped from the sky; and in fact, Coyotl was the first to look up, thinking a shadow had fallen over them. Yet the darkness was not falling, it was sucking inward as though the air had taken on a sudden, hard density, and Coyotl had been seized. The sensation suggested he had been flung back from Topiltzin so hard that his knees bent beneath him and snapped like tinder. He felt the bones give, heard them crack when he slammed into the earth. He could hear screams, a thousand screams that echoed far and away. Coyotl struggled for breath, unable to move. His chest seemed to be collapsing, the bones, the muscles, straining. Coyotl was being driven downward, into the earth. For a moment, he blacked out. How long it was, he could not be certain, but somewhere he heard a warrior's cry, piercing, a scream that lifted to the Heavens, of rage, of fury, and only then did he manage to draw breath.

After the scream, the dark had dissipated. Coyotl lay for a moment dazed, then slowly rolled to one side. He spit out gobs of blood, sucked at the air. There seemed a mist about him, a scattering of smoke, as though the darkness had been shattered and was left to linger in pockets. He rose painfully to his elbows. Topiltzin was gone, and so, too, his sword.

Coyotl heard movement, someone coming through the trees, perhaps a scouting party, perhaps a wing of the army of the Shadow Walkers, perhaps demons. It really wouldn't matter, because Coyotl collapsed, onto his side, then onto his belly, facedown in the dirt.

▨▨▨▨▨▨▨▨▨▨▨▨▨▨▨▨

Hueloc saw something coming for him, but he could not believe what it was. He thought it a shred of madness, a hallucination. He was almost to the edge of the forest, to the cove where waited the girls, the ship, freedom—life. It was all there, just beyond, the glimmer of white sand, just within reach. Yet it seemed miles away. Hueloc was good at many things, but he was no distance runner. The sprint from the woods had left him nearly spent; his lungs were burning with labored breath. Had his grandmother been present she would have told him it was all that blue smoke finally robbing him of air.

Then he saw the monkey, a red monkey, coming directly at him mostly on its back legs, but then on all fours, face drawn in a snarl, baring fangs, its eyes furious, insane. Hueloc braced himself though he could not believe a monkey was going to attack him, but when it was too close to deny, he saw the eyes, pitted, furious, and he felt his heart jump, for they were clearly human. It was another shifter! The monkey leapt to the side and rebounded off the trunk of a tree, landing on Hueloc's neck, wrapping about his head.

"Mother of whores!" Hueloc screamed, circling, groping with one hand for the beast, managing to clasp a fist of red hair. He felt teeth sheer into the side of his neck. He drew his dagger, and slashed, dizzily, over his shoulder. A clawed hand clapped across his forehead and the fingers dug, they sunk into his right eye. The pain stabbed through the back of his skull as the monkey's finger scooped into the eye socket. Hueloc felt his eyeball burst. It was a hot, quick stab of pain, but Hueloc still managed to seize an arm. He wrenched the thing off his back with a scream and slammed it into the ground. That should have ended it, but instead, the beast seemed to suck onto his leg, and the teeth bit into his kneecap, cutting through tendons. Hueloc's knee gave out with a pop, and he dropped, but even as he hit the ground on his shoulder he shoved his sword into the hairy body.

The little beast screamed, twisting wild. Hueloc came to his good knee and stabbed deeper, his mind swimming in the nightmare image he was murdering Grand Prince. He then stood, staring. For a moment, he couldn't take his eyes off it. It wasn't a monkey any longer. He wondered if it ever had been. It was, instead, a shriveled, godless, deformed little man; his limbs were gnarled and twisted, nothing but flesh and bone. The back was curved and lumpy, the legs stumpy. It was a monster, and Hueloc might have guessed it to be a child, but the face was a man's. Hueloc set his sandal against it and wrenched his sword free. He turned and lurched into a half-run, dragging one useless leg. He might still make it. The white sand of the cove glittered just ahead, like jewels scattered. He even caught sight of the prow of the yellow reed ship, and his heart leaped with hope.

Behind him, somewhere, moving slow, were sounds, the whipping, numbing, soft thunder sound of the coming of the

Shadow Walkers. Still, he just might make it. He no longer cared about riches or bathhouses. All Hueloc wanted now was simply to live, reach the ship, and corral the girls. Let the jungle boil in death and agony, let the whole of the world sink into a pit of blood. *Just get me through this, God; just this last bit and I promise, my word as a Toltec, I'll change my ways.*

He reached the edge of the cove, reached the border of the white sand, and stepped drunkenly past the body. At first, that's all it was, a body. Then, almost as an afterthought, the face hit him. It was Plume Gum! He spun about on his good leg, and stood, gaping, holding his bloodied sword, feeling a cold, numbing rage. Her throat had been torn away, to the back of the neck bone. Plume Gum's dark eyes stared blankly skyward.

"Hueloc! Hueloc, run!"

He realized the voice was Jewel Twirler. He looked up to see the little one running toward him across the sand.

"Hueloc!" she screamed. "Look out!"

He turned, sensing the figure before he ever saw it. Hueloc came about in a low crouch, wielding his sword, but the blood drained from him, and fear sucked away his breath.

The Smoking Mirror slowly moved toward him. His hands were bloodied. He didn't seem to be walking, he seemed to be gliding, and the eyes, those silver eyes, just sank into Hueloc, freezing him.

"All mine, fat man," whispered the Smoking Mirror. "Your heart, your flesh . . . your soul."

"Hueloc!" Jewel Twirler screamed, still running for him. It was her voice that pulled him out of the trance, and he glanced back at her. She was coming right for them.

"No! Get back, little sister!" Hueloc screamed, and shifted to meet the Dark Lord, lifting his sword, letting a slow growl through his teeth, ready for battle. The Smoking Mirror was suddenly directly before him. Hueloc's body jerked, stiffened. A pulse of hot pain cracked in his chest. His back arched in spasm and the sword flipped out of his hand. He saw Smoking Mirror arm-deep, completely into his chest; then it wrenched out, with a sucking sound, like a foot being pulled from mud. Before the light left his eye, Hueloc saw his own heart, still beating, held in the fist of Smoking Mirror.

Paper Flower had leapt to the side of the rock ledge and now she called to Jewel Twirler, but the girl had stopped; she stood wailing, her tiny hands in fists. Paper Flower then saw the Dark Lord for the first time, his crimson-lined cloak, his long, silvery black hair. He was holding Hueloc, and Hueloc's body was shaking in spasm. The Smoking Mirror tossed him back. The big Toltec fell like a stone. Paper Flower felt a stab at her heart, felt her eyes mist, even over the fear that caught in her breast.

Smoking Mirror turned. Jewel Twirler dropped to her knees, her screaming had broken into wailing sobs.

The eyes of Smoking Mirror first rested on Paper Flower; they searched her out across the distance, sunk through her, then they calmly shifted. He started toward Jewel Twirler.

"Nooo!" Paper Flower screamed. Her protective instinct overrode her fear, and lost in sudden rage, she ran forward.

"Paper Flower! The ship! We can't hold it!" screamed Night Jasmine. The girls clutched at the stay ropes, but the reed boat's weight was pulling it into deeper waters, into the currents of the bay. One of the girls was wrenched from the rock ledge, splashing into the waters.

Smoking Mirror was in no hurry; he walked slowly. Jewel Twirler didn't try to flee. Paper Flower sprinted the distance, her feet slipping occasionally in the soft sand. She reached them and threw Jewel Twirler behind her. "Go to the ship! Run!" she screamed.

Jewel Twirler did not; she only looked upward, stared into the sky. Her mouth fell open. She gasped.

Smoking Mirror backhanded Paper Flower so hard her head

was snapped to the side; a numbing grayness passed through her as she was flung back, airborne, hitting on her back, sliding in the sand. She saw him grab Jewel Twirler by one arm, whipping her as though she were weightless. She saw him reach for her head, his hand wide, as though he meant simply to clasp it, to dislodge it.

Smoking Mirror paused, his hand poised, and for a moment he stilled. He looked skyward. Paper Flower saw a shadow pass over the ground and looked up herself. There was a piercing scream, a terrible eagle's scream that ripped through the air, sending a shiver over her. Above them, descending, was a sky serpent, plumed wings spread, shimmering in red sun; and in its talons, it clutched a darkened, moonsteel Tolteca sword.

In the end, it was not darkness he had suckled; Coyotl had been wrong about that. In the final moments, when Topiltzin knew that to descend any farther would mean death, light reached him. It came to him, almost a memory, the face, the eyes of the Sky Dragon, his words when Topiltzin was still young—too young to know he and his father would never be one, still innocent enough to believe his father was close enough to a god to be one. His father had once told him of fear, that fear was never light, only darkness. And Topiltzin remembered. He whispered the word, and the Light Whose Name Is Splendor shattered the void.

He was . . . moving, unfolding. Suddenly he saw, suddenly he understood all things. It filled him: light, like fire blossoming in a crystal. Light, as though he had looked into the face of God.

Topiltzin twisted, took hold of his sword with the claws of his feet, then looked skyward through different eyes, eyes not his own, but crafted, shaped, formed of his heart, his soul. Then, with a flex of what once were arms, he lifted, and the ground fell away. Topiltzin understood wind, air. He felt almost as though he could continue, lifting, as though he could steal the light of the sun, take its fire.

He was no longer Topiltzin, no longer the ballplayer. For a moment, an instant of time, there upon the wind and the blue sky he was something else; his mind, his thoughts, moved in a different pattern. Only his heart remained the same. It was as if he had given himself over, loaned himself to another being—and this being understood one purpose, one single object of pursuit. This being searched through narrowed, fiery eyes.

The ground below unfolded like a painting bathed in red hue, the jungles, the rivers, as passing beneath the shadow of a serpent. This being caught, heard the sound, the smell of the Dark Lord, like the smell of acid mist. It turned on a wing, then sailed the purple sky effortlessly, a clean, simple, swift movement, a pump; a beat of mighty wings drove through the air as though they were great oars against water. The creature he had become screeched, a hollow, terrible sound, the very promise of death, and then it turned again on its wing and curled inward, tucked, pulled its talons close, and soared downward. Below, Topiltzin saw a half-moon curl of white sand; he saw dark waters, and a ship, a huge, well-crafted ship of reeds such as he had only seen in pictures.

He saw the Dark Lord, turning on the sand, holding a girl. To-piltzin screamed a war cry, a terrible shriek that chilled his skin, and dropped. He unfolded out of the light that had swallowed him.

Paper Flower came to one knee. She believed it was a god who descended from the air, and she knew his name. It was Quetzalcoatl, in resplendent brilliance: Serpent Plumed, the soul of the Tolteca. She winced at the sight, the scaly skin of the serpent tail as it curled, sheathed in red-gold feathers. The wings, great arched wings of shimmering quetzal green, folded back against the creature's side as it screamed once more. Then it seemed to roll, to tuck into itself, doubling up, becoming only shadow, and it dropped onto the sand a man—a man with golden hair, a naked Toltec warrior of fair skin who lifted the moonsteel sword that had been clutched in the creature's talons. No sooner had he touched earth than the Toltec spun forward, tight, a movement that reminded her of a ballplayer, and the sword flickered, opening a wide swath of the Dark Lord's side, blood spilling rich.

Stunned, Smoking Mirror screamed, he howled. Snarling like a jungle cat, he threw Jewel Twirler aside as though she were nothing. The Dark Lord then ripped his own sword from his belt and attacked. For a moment the two were locked in solid combat, swords flashing, muscles quick and powerful, sand spinning about their feet, the metal of their weapons ringing in heavy, thunderous blows. Perhaps it was illusion, but the earth seemed to tremble, shiver, as though giants fought.

Paper Flower scrambled, half on her knees before she could get to her feet, and dashed for Jewel Twirler, barely stopping when she reached her, just grabbing her arm, pulling her to her feet and into a staggering run.

From the jungles came the sound of conch shells, of drums hammering. She could hear them, the Shadow Walkers, approaching. The jungle bristled; it was about to burst.

Paper Flower reached the ship, throwing Jewel Twirler to the others. "Get in and launch it!" she cried. All of them, all thirteen of the girls on the edge of the bay, were occupied in holding the stay ropes, and even then the big reed ship was dragging them into the waters.

"But we cannot sail it!" Night Jasmine shouted.

"We will be slaughtered otherwise! Quickly! Into the ship!"

Paper Flower glanced back at the two warriors. For a moment she considered leaving him here, this Great Lord, a god who had descended, for he seemed then very much a man. Already he had taken two wounds, one to his side that was deep enough to spill blood across his naked hip. She shuddered.

Topiltzin's first cut had been a wide, slicing swath through the soft section of the High-Blood's belly, and he had given it his full force. If not for the thick leather corselet and the outer sheath of moon-steel armor Smoking Mirror wore, it would have halved him, left him squirming in two pieces. But even with them, it cut deep enough for a flush of dark, rich blood. Topiltzin had at that point closed for the kill. He had taken such kills many times in the jungles: first a deep slice, and with the shock of it, a thrust or a cleaving strike to the neck. Amazingly, Smoking Mirror had blocked this death-stroke with his forearm. Topiltzin's sword grazed off the edge of a studded leather bracelet. The Highborn had drawn a weapon. Rather than sucking air against the crippling wound, he had attacked with the force and fury of a jungle cat, and it was Topiltzin who was taken unprepared.

The blows came heavy, relentless. Unbelievably, Topiltzin was being driven back. As he attacked, Smoking Mirror kept a low snarl in his throat, and the wound in him seemed to fire his eyes; they burned, furious. Topiltzin took a cut to the side, swift through naked flesh. Topiltzin screamed, twisted sideways, and slammed his foot into Smoking Mirror's stomach, into the Dark Lord's wound, kicking it inward. Even the inhuman High-Blood staggered from pain. Topiltzin came again for a death-stroke, but again, Smoking Mirror blocked.

The Highborn's sword hummed, hard and heavy. Topiltzin was staggered. A thrust tore open his shoulder, slicing through his skin as clean as a surgeon's cut. Topiltzin saw a death-stroke descend, the dark metal of the High-Blood's sword a blur. The ballplayer spun, dropping low, and his sword met the High-Blood's with a *whang*, the two blades momentarily locking.

Topiltzin met his eyes. They seemed not the eyes of a human; they were swallowed, and he saw there the face of the dark, the same face that had nearly taken him before the transformation.

Topiltzin was heaved back. He hit the sand, sliding.

Smoking Mirror drew a dagger with from his belt and flung

it. Topiltzin tucked and rolled. The dagger whispered past his ear and buried into the sand. The Blue Prince rolled over it, making it appear as though he had taken the blade in his neck. He cried out, as if wounded, and tucked into a ball, checking the shadow of the High-Blood, waiting. The Smoking Mirror was fast, moving in for the kill—but the feign had given Topiltzin a breath of time, and that was enough.

Topiltzin twisted, springing to his knees. He had moved too rapidly even for the High-Blood. With a scream in his throat Topiltzin slashed, gripping the sword with both hands. It hit the leg of Smoking Mirror just above the ankle, and the bone only tugged as Topiltzin's blade sliced through.

Smoking Mirror careened to the side. His severed foot dropped in the sand, and the High-Blood hit on his side. Topiltzin sprang forward with his sword angled down, gripping the hilt; and it seemed he had struck home and his blade had slammed into the skin of the thorax, piercing through. But the chest mirror the Highborn wore was as hard as rock and so solid Topiltzin's sword cracked at the tip, deflected.

Smoking Mirror brought his sword over one shoulder and Topiltzin could not clear it. It *whunked* into his face on the left side, near his eye. It jammed there, wedged into Topiltzin's cheekbone, into the bone of his forehead, like an axe wedged in a tree, and Topiltzin screamed. Blood spilled, flushing out vision. He ripped away the blade and reeled back. Topiltzin desperately wiped the blood from his eyes, seeing the Smoking Mirror rise, sitting up, reaching his sword, and dragging it with him, crawling.

The High-Blood was winded, finally feeling his wounds, and he moved slowly, but with certainty. Topiltzin crouched, for he was dying.

Smoking Mirror screamed, bringing his sword from the side in a death thrust.

With his last moments of consciousness, Topiltzin twisted hard, spinning. One last play, one last move in the rubberball game. He ducked past the hiss of the dark sword and brought his elbow in hard, centered, angled. Gripping his wrist via a double-arm blow, the rubberball became the head of the Smoking Mirror. Topiltzin slammed into it full weight. The nose bones and jaw of the Highborn cracked, his head jerked hard, and Smoking Mirror went down.

Topiltzin hit the sand. He tried to come again to his knees, but could only crawl. Desperate, clinging to consciousness, he searched for a sword. He had to make sure, to take off the head. Consciousness waned. Topiltzin's mind was numbing out, but still he forced all his will to maintain his grip. He found what he thought to be the hilt of the Dark Lord's sword, clasped it, drew it up, but then paused, for it was only a stick. He held it, staring down . . . at it, then finally fell forward, and felt the light slip away.

Paper Flower stared breathless, almost numb. She had seen the two grappling, and now they lay, separated, both bloodied, both still. The Smoking Mirror was twisted to the side. The last blow had knocked his sword from him. His ankle puddled blood into the sand, the white stump of a bone showing through the muscle.

The other one, the Toltec, lay facedown, and he was bleeding badly. He looked very dead, lying there, blood spilling. He must be dead. But he had fought for them; he had given them this chance. Most of the girls were now on the ship, and it was slowly easing into deep water.

She turned. There were screams. The edge of the forest blossomed, like a flower opening to the night sky. The Shadow Walkers had reached them. They burst from the trees, lifting weapons, swords, spears, coming at full run.

"Night Jasmine, help!" Paper Flower screamed as she sprinted forward.

"No!" Night Jasmine cried, but seeing Paper Flower was not turning back, ran after her.

TOLTECA

Paper Flower reached the Toltec warrior and grabbed his arms, pulling him in jerks across the sand, leaving his blood in a swath. But he was heavy. As his body turned, she saw his face. She winced, for it was sliced open, the cheek laid back. She could see his tongue, his teeth. The white bone of his forehead was cracked, and blood spilled. He was surely dead, but then . . . he was also a god.

An arrow whizzed past her, singing.

Night Jasmine was at her side now and they pulled the dead warrior in a half-run, jerking him onto the rock and staggering backward, both of them, dropping off into the waters of the river.

The ship was pulling into the deep, but at its edge, one of the sisters threw a long line and Paper Flower leapt to catch it. Taking hold, the weight of the ship in the current jerked them forward.

Night Jasmine swam alongside, helping Paper Flower loop the rope under the Toltec's arms and tie it about his chest. A spear skidded past them. Warriors ran to the rock ledge and dove, clutching knives in their teeth.

"Pull!" Paper Flower screamed. "Quickly, pull us in!"

The rope was hauled hand over hand, and the three of them were pulled forward in jerks. Paper Flower glanced behind. They were coming, swimmers, plying through the waters like caimans.

When they reached the ship, Paper Flower gripped an edge of reed bundle and pulled the Toltec against her.

Night Jasmine had started to climb up the side; she was half out of the water. Paper Flower heard the arrow take its mark and cried out, seeing Night Jasmine gasp, arching her back.

"No!"

Night Jasmine dropped past her. She reached for her, but the ship was fast spinning around, the currents pulling it into swift water. Blood pooled about Night Jasmine's body as it swirled, facedown. An arrow emerged through the black hair, coming out of her neck.

The ship was sucked about, swinging wide, and Paper Flower climbed up its side, guiding the body of the Toltec as the other girls pulled up on the rope. Blood still spilled down the front of him, and his head fell limply to the side. She realized in a way she had traded him for Night Jasmine. It was something that would haunt her for many years. Once she reached the top edge of the reed boat she turned, crouched.

"Hand me a bow," she said quietly. The ship had been well stocked with provisions. Jewel Twirler lifted on tiptoes to hand her a longbow, an arrow against its shaft. Paper Flower crouched and drew the arrow taut. She took her time, for the ship now fast outdistanced the swimmers; it swiftly glided into heavy current. She drew a bead on the closest of the warriors and put a shaft through his back.

CHAPTER THIRTY-EIGHT
THE SKY DRAGON

Boaz—The Northern Plains before the City of Tollán

They had stripped Sky Teacher of all but his breechclout. They lashed him to a pole and first beat him until consciousness was a bare, thin line. They passed thick marine stingray spines through his sides, his feet, his hands.

Sky Teacher never spoke or gave any words. Neither did he cry out, even when they slowly pulled off two of his fingers, taking them by the base joints, breaking the bones back, and twisting, shearing skin and tissue. A muscled giant had done this. His face was blunted, flattened, his eyes narrow slits, inhuman.

It was clear they knew who he was. Perhaps captives had told them, perhaps there were spies among them, but the Shadow Walkers knew he was a sky speaker. They shackled his outstretched arms to a heavy wooden shoulder brace. He carried it throughout the day. The cross beam had been weighted at the corners with stones where his wrists were lashed and the journey had nearly left him spent, but if ever he slowed, the Shadow Walkers would torture the captives who marched alongside, so Sky Teacher had forced himself to keep pace, long into the afternoon sun, until his legs were weak and rubbery.

The Shadow Walkers had taken the city of Boaz like plucking a stone from the ground—but close to the city walls, they had met stiff resistance. As Sky Teacher was led across the battlefield, he saw the Tolteca who had fought here left the path of their retreat a literal field of dead. Bodies trampled into muddied earth, shields, swords, flesh, all twisted in carnage. On the fallen shields, Sky Teacher recognized the insignia of the Eagle; but once or twice, he saw another graphic: the feathered wings of the dragon, which symbolized his father's personal guard, warriors earmarked Sky Dwellers. He guessed at least a division of Sky Dwellers had fought here. He gauged they were the reason the armies of the Shadow Walkers had been slowed earlier that day.

Sky Teacher quietly noticed each fallen shield of a Sky Dweller was littered with prime kill. This battle held the mark of a high captain who had cautiously gauged his retreat. Whoever he was, the Sky Dweller had sacrificed his prime very carefully. He was slowly drawing them north, and most probably would make a stand in the hillocks beyond Boaz, where there was better cover and a steeper grade against the opposing armies.

It was a wise move; it would allow the armies of Tollán to join with the Sky Dwellers when they made their stand. The city of Boaz had fallen, and it had been taken too quickly for even the Sky Dwellers to evacuate the innocents. For those left behind terror was unleashed without mercy.

The Shadow Walkers brought Sky Teacher to the Temple of the Sun, the highest level of the city, and he felt his will simply fail as they forced him up the steep stairway. The stairway was coated in a thick, glistening sheen of blood. Once Sky Teacher reached the high platform at the top of the temple, they anchored his shoulder brace to a tall pole where he was forced to watch as the sacrifices continued. He couldn't fathom how many had been sacrificed; perhaps a thousand or more innocents throughout the day and deep into the night.

When it was late, the fires of the Shadow Walkers burned white with cinnabar leaving the city bathed in an eerie mock daylight. Conch shells sounded, signaling the last hour of night, when the sun was deepest in the belly of the serpent. It might have signaled the end of the sacrifices, but Sky Teacher knew the worst was yet to come. Singers and dancers, many of them naked, paraded in the plaza below, spinning, high-stepping. It was a mocking imitation of the flower dance of the youth. The flute and the emerald drum sounded. The voices of the Shadow Walkers' women lifted with a haunting, airy sound that seemed to float surreal through the smoke of the blood fires.

It went on for hours. Each time Sky Teacher's head sagged from weariness, they jabbed his broken ribs. They had thoughtfully chosen which ribs to break and where, for they were masters of pain. When they jabbed his side, he jerked upright, sucking for air. If ever his eyelids began to close, tiny lancet slits were cut into them. A priest with the stink of dried blood matted in his hair had whispered to him that should he choose to close his eyes and not open them, they would cut off his lids, and the last images he would see in this world would be forever burned into his mind. He kept his eyes open and watched.

How long he was held there, he wasn't sure. It seemed time stilled, that the stars somehow stopped turning in the sky as blood continually spilled across the sacred stone of the temple-tower stairway directly across from Sky Teacher. This was the Pyramid of the Creator, built on the eastern edge of Boaz, where it faced the rising sun. For many years, it had been a sacred place, knowing only peace, only the prayers of the Nonaloca, but on this night, small streams of blood ran to either side of the stairway. The Shadow Walkers brought the victims up in parades, in ceremony, with flowers thrown before their feet. The drugged victims followed the dark-robed priests without resistance, walking in an eerie daze. Once their white chests were opened and their still-beating hearts swiftly plucked, the bodies were rolled down the limestone stairway. At the base of the temple, they were harvested. Blood on the market plaza below glistened in diamond sparkles as it dried and runners periodically lifted sections of thigh, ribs, or upper arms, sprinting for the fire beds. Screams occasionally floated lazily across the night air amid the song and dance, but it seemed oddly quiet most of the time.

But numbers alone were not a climax. The Shadow Walkers had saved the best for last. Sky Teacher was nearly unconscious when he saw excitement growing in the plaza below. Then they came—the little ones, the fairest, the most perfect offerings the Shadow Walkers had been able to gather. There were perhaps twenty. Sky Teacher's mind lifted from numbness. He felt his skin shiver in a quiet rage. The children, looking lost and confused, were being herded into the center of the plaza. Sky Teacher knew this was the reason they had kept him alive through the night.

"No . . ." he whispered.

They pushed the children onto a platform of wickerwork overlaid with dried corn stalks. Once they were in the center, dancers wound lines of oiled hemp about them, then slowly forced them tighter, crowding them together. Some panicked. Sky Teacher noticed one girl lift an infant into her arms, trying to comfort her. Her image blurred out of focus through his tears.

He hissed through tight teeth. "Not this . . ."

With a soft chuckle, their high captain, the one who called himself the Hummingbird, drew near. The warlord's face was painted in diagonal blue stripes and his eyes were dark stone. His hair was shorn, his arms, his legs were stained blue, as were his weapons. They called him Blue Hummingbird, and Sky Teacher had chilled a bit when first he heard the name, for he was one of them: those who had been foretold, the Nomads, the ancient princes of the highlands. His appearance was dread, but his voice, oddly, was high pitched and soft.

"Where is your God now, Priest?" he whispered.

"My God would prefer my blood over theirs."

"Why is that?"

"They have not sinned."

"But does not that leave them pure?"

"He will make them his own; you gain nothing by their sacrifice. My blood, though—from the sight of you, my blood runs hot. Take them, you gain nothing. Take me—you drink my soul."

The man called Hummingbird only smiled. "No. No, I think not. I would rather watch you save them. You are a sky speaker. You can command the sun and the wind."

Sky Teacher did not answer. He let no emotion through his eyes. He simply watched the face of the Hummingbird, and, as it had been with the demon he faced so long ago in Eslabeth's brother, he offered neither fear nor pride.

The Hummingbird spit in his face, but Sky Teacher did not flinch.

"Or perhaps it is true what they say, that the God of the Tolteca no longer hears his people. Like your king, the Sky Dragon, your God no longer walks with you. He leaves! He goes the way that he came. He delivers us the Tolteca like suckling. Even these, your children."

The Hummingbird turned; he raised his hand high, fingers spread wide. It was a mockery of the sign of the word. The conch shells sounded, and for a moment, the drums and the singing ceased. Only the flicker of firelight and the soft whimpering of children broke the quiet that followed. Gathered about the perimeters of the platform were the parents, the children's elders—held at the tips of spears. About the wicker platform waited dark priests with torches of burning resin, black smoke curling.

"Behold your prophet, Tolteca!" the Hummingbird screamed in his high-pitched voice. The priest behind him grabbed Sky Teacher's hair and lifted his head to look over them.

"I bring you your prophet!" the Hummingbird screamed again. "That he can call on your God."

Sky Teacher could not make out their faces through his tears, but all of the children had turned to gaze up at him.

"Call to him, children!" screamed the Hummingbird, so shrill his voice cracked like a woman's screech. "Call on your priest! Surely he will save you!" The Hummingbird curled his hand into a fist. It was a signal. Below, his warriors lit the edges of the platform, and tendrils of flame licked and surged through the wicker. The children started screaming.

Sky Teacher did speak to his God, but he did so quietly. *Take them Lord. Dear God, take them quick, yours—forever.*

"Here is your prophet! Surely, he will not let your children burn! Call to him, Tolteca!"

Sky Teacher *did* hear his name being called. Some of them called him prophet, some Sky Teacher, but there were others who used his priest name, the sacred moniker given by his father. He heard his own voice moan from his throat as the fire quickened about the children. The corn stalks laid on the wicker were dry, but also they had been soaked in resin that brought the hot flame up through the edges of the wicker mat. Sky Teacher tried to turn his face, but the Hummingbird grabbed his chin and snapped it back.

"You will look on them," he hissed, pressing his cheek hard against Sky Teacher's, his breath foul with the blood he had tasted this night. "You *will* watch them burn, Priest."

Tears streamed across Sky Teacher's cheeks. As flesh burned, a black smoke rose.

A small girl had broken free of the restraining ropes and ran, streaking across the plaza, but it was too late—she was just a little ball of flame, until she fell, kicking. The heads of the elders were hewn off by axe-stroke even as they wailed, until there were no more voices, no more screams, only the flame licking.

The naked dancers below wove strings of flowers, letting them float upward where they shriveled as they caught the searing heat.

Finally, Sky Teacher screamed. His head dropping back, he screamed, shaking, and his cry echoed into the night.

"FATHER!"

***

Blade Companion, the first high captain of the Sky Dwellers of Tollán, stood watching the plains of Boaz, its fires casting the night sky behind it a bronze hue. The screams reaching across the distance had been continuous throughout the night, but now they had suddenly ceased, cut off. That chilled him even more.

Blade Companion's wounded right arm was wrapped against his side with maguey cloth bandages. His men, the chosen protectors of the Dragon, those called the Sky Dwellers, had gathered at the summit of a hill. They had pulled in their weary, their wounded, and had thrown up ramparts around the perimeter of the hill's base. He had lost that day warriors he considered immortal, men he had believed could never die by the sword. None were taken alive and the Lords of the house of Turquoise had made the cost of their retreat very dear to the enemy.

The sudden battle had raged from early dawn until near dusk. Only when he saw the armies of Boaz outnumbered and outflanked him had he begun the retreat. It was a careful, practiced retreat. The warriors of Blade Companion slowly gave way their center, letting the Shadow Walkers take ground. At his flanks, divisions of Eagle Knights held a solid ring of shield-bearers. The Sky Dwellers retreated in shifting movements, sometimes quick, sometimes turning to take kills before withdrawing farther. Blade Companion knew he could have held here longer, he could even have chosen it as a dying field, but the cost would be terrible. Boaz could be evacuated, but the city of Tollán would have been left without protection.

Blade Companion drew the Shadow Walkers into a long, slow death march as his men pulled back from the city. He left his path littered with dead like a planting of crops, but he was not going to leave the plains before Tollán and Cholula exposed. He had sent his swiftest runners ahead to the high cities, and once they reached the plains, he called full retreat. For the first time in their history, the Sky Dwellers turned to run. The enemy had cheered behind them, but they did not pursue the day's lesson had taught them that pursuit would mean death.

On the hillock, in the dead of night, Blade Companion briefly wondered a moment about his old friend Fire Serpent, the Chichimec—what he had faced in the jungles of the Southland. The warriors of Fire Serpent had fought two hundred years in those jungles, but they had surely been overwhelmed by now. Blade Companion had no hope the Southland had been spared. Even here, in the north, the Shadow Walkers easily numbered more than two thousand, and scouts had warned him that flanking divisions were already sweeping west toward Cholula.

Hours ago, when the Shadow Walkers took the city of Boaz, a great cry went up and he chilled at the number of innocents he had been forced to leave behind. Through the night, as he heard their screams, Blade Companion drank damnation to his soul, but he did not let his men attack. He waited, he wept, and now the silence left a dread in him that could not find any comfort. More than anything, he wanted to stride though this night and answer this blood.

He had sent the Eagle Knights north to Tollán, but the Sky Dwellers remained here. They were now only six hundred strong, and many of these were wounded. As weak as they were, it was still enough to make a stand here, where the hillock offered them advantage.

A runner was brought to him from below, a scout who had lingered near the city of Boaz long after it had fallen. He was sweaty and soot-stained, still breathless from his run. Blade Companion saw only fear in his eyes. He could not guess what this man had seen, but he would not want to share it.

"They drink, my lord," said Frog Runner weakly. "They are drunk, but not with wine. They are drunk with the blood of our women, our children!"

Blade Companion paused. One of his high captains, Stone Slayer, actually seemed to growl, looking back toward Boaz. His hand grabbed Blade Companion's shoulder in a tight grip.

"They sacrifice children!" he snarled at Frog Runner.

"Hundreds, my lord."

"Mother of whores, this will not stand, Blade Companion!"

"We hold here till dawn," Blade Companion said grimly, but his muscles flinched at his own command.

TOLTECA

The scout, a young warrior named Frog Runner, who had come from the deserts to join the Tolteca, even though his blood was Chichimec, stepped closer. "My lord, Blade Companion, let me take a hundred—fifty, give me fifty Sky Dwellers! In the name of God, let us take vengeance this night!"

"I will go with him," said Stone Slayer. "Say the word, my lord. Give me the command. I will take my knights. I will cleave heads, by my beard, and in God's holy name!"

Blade Companion lowered his head. "If we thin ranks, and they come in the night, they will take Tollán with the dawn. You wish the innocent of Tollán to coat the temples of the Creator with their blood as well?"

"Then give me ten!" Blade Companion bellowed. Seeing the resolve in his captain's eye, he spat to the side. "By God, we are Sky Dwellers!"

Blade Companion tightened his jaw, but shook his head. "I need you, Stone Slayer."

"I have followed you many years, my brother," said Stone Slayer. "But this is not right. We cannot stand here and leave this blood unanswered."

"No. But it shall be answered another day."

Stone Slayer threw his head back and screamed with his hands in tight fists.

Hearing Stone Slayer, many of the warriors stood; many gathered weapons. They were not ordinary men. They stood with fire in their eyes. Blade Companion realized Stone Slayer was weeping in rage. Blade Companion felt the earth sucking him downward. He turned to stare at the glowing embers of the distant city.

"We stand," he whispered, fearing his own voice might break. "I need you all. We stand."

Then he noticed the sky. Clouds were gathering, rolling in out of the south, the east, the west, like billows of great smoke, boiling, coming swift. Frog Runner, the scout, gasped openly. It was more than storm. The night sky rolled in clouds like waves crashing.

Veins of dry lightning snaked across their dark surface.

Frog Runner pointed. "There, my lord!"

Blade Companion felt a shiver. He searched the plains Frog Runner had indicated, but with the sudden cloud cover the night was dark, so swallowed by the sky he could see nothing. A *crack* of lighting touched somewhere close, so close he could smell the light of the air. It ignited the slope of the hillock, and *he* was there. He was coming out of the plains—alone. His hair was wild, frayed out like snakes coiling. His robes and cloak billowed in the sudden winds that had seemed to walk with him. The old man was making his way slowly up the hill, using his staff. Blade Companion felt his mouth dry; his skin pimpled in shivers. When again the thunder ignited the plains in blue light, he was close enough that Blade Companion could see his face—a face he had not seen in seven years. Seven years he had abandoned them. Seven years he had turned away. Now, the Sky Dragon of Tollán returned.

Frog Runner fell to his knees, bowing his head, chanting, as though God himself had stepped from the night. Blade Companion knelt on one knee, lowering his head, as did Stone Slayer, as did all the high captains, and in a breath, the entire army—all of them knelt there on the crest of the hill. The old man stood in silence a moment looking over them. A thunder blast of lightning struck overhead and Blade Companion felt its touch sting across his forearms. He finally looked up, lifted his gaze. Sky Dragon seemed older, his hair and his beard, where it fell across his chest, were both white as driven snow, but his shoulders were still massive, his arms still thick, his eyes still fires of gray stone.

"My lord, Sky Dragon," Blade Companion whispered.

"Speak only my priest name this night."

Blade Companion paused, then nodded, "My lord, Mormon. What would you have us do?"

"I would that our people had turned from this moment. I would that you had remembered always his name alone. But that hour is lost to us. Stand, all of you. You shall for a time longer stand as Sons of Light."

The Dragon of Tollán lifted his staff, and this time the sky responded. With a thunderous *crack*, quick fingers of blue lightning spilled over the hillock, all around them, and for a moment, the Sky Dwellers seemed to swim in perfect, brilliant light.

CHAPTER THIRTY-NINE
THE PROPHET

In the city of Boaz, there had been no ramparts erected; there had not even been guards posted. Blue Hummingbird felt it was over here; they had fled before him, and with the dawn, he would begin hunting the rabbit that ran. He wore one of their splendid cloaks, the broad shoulders silvered in feathers that seemed metallic as they reflected the dull, far blood of dawn soon to spill over the temple tower of the Toltec city of Boaz. It was the last moment of night, and Blue Hummingbird intended to savor it, like licking the fat and drippings from the thigh of sacred meat.

It was said the Tolteca of the north were the greatest warriors known. It was said they were voyagers, that they once came not only from across the far sea but also from across stars. As long as their God walked with them, they would never be destroyed, for it was spoken even in Aztlán. Just as Smoking Mirror had promised, the Fourth Sun—the time of the Tolteca—the time of the God Speakers—was ending now. They had lost their vision. He had proven this night that not even their high priest held power. The prophet now sagged against his arm-cross nearly drained of spirit, his blood dropping in splats mixed with his tears. He had done nothing, even when the Blue Hummingbird had unleashed the melting of their children.

Here, in the morning mist, from the tall temple mound of Boaz, he could see a far distant line of smoke and that marked the place the Tolteca called Smoking Mountain. Blue Hummingbird remembered all the stories, and he knew that beside the Smoking Mountain was White Woman, always with a cap of snow. He had never seen snow, and he could only imagine the wonders of it, as he could wonder of the riches of the mighty city of Tollán.

Boaz was only a small city, but even here, the Toltec lords bore cloaks of splendid quetzals. This night their women were beautiful as visions as they danced naked up the slippery temple stairs, linked by the flower tendrils, giving song to the Night and the Wind. They were tall and lithe, and some had red hair that made Blue Hummingbird feel he was sweating just to look on them. He had found others whose hair was full and wondrous white-gold, and Blue Hummingbird thought these hearts would be like red poppies, sweet and rich. He had taken three of these for his own, and once the winnowing of night was done and the lords of the house of Aztlán lay drunk, after the last sacrifice, that of the hollow priest they called Sky Teacher, Blue Hummingbird would find his way alone to the chamber beneath the temple where he would himself taste them, lick them. There would be in that moment hot blood and quick pulse and the fluttery feel of skin freshly peeled from muscle, and their sex would touch with the smooth, wet flower lips of virgins. Occasionally, throughout the night, he had let his mind play with such thoughts, let himself get more exited, feel himself hard. This night he stayed awake by eating the white knotted buttons of the peyote, and now, just before dawn, the bloodstains made the sacred Toltec temple—after having tasted so many hearts, so many tender flowers—look like a living, silvery tendril that lifted to feed the milk stream of the earth mother's tit.

He sniffed the air. The bitter smell of drying blood mixed with the musk of mesquite fires and the sweet of the rain mist of coming dawn made his skin tingle as though it touched his own blood. It was time—the last station of night had come. The lords of night would soon leave and even now grew sleepy.

"Bring him," said Blue Hummingbird to his captain. "Bring the prophet to the slaying stone."

"My lord," Night Speaker said and turned.

Blue Hummingbird stretched his palms to the last of the night.

The sacred butterfly knife in his hand had a strange, fantastic power now. If the night before it had begun as only polished obsidian, it now beat with life, as a heart. It was more than stone; it was living tissue now. The spirits of the night lords circled, ready to ascend with the last breath of dark. They would give him such strength he would swell like a god and this last one, the heart of the prophet, would be like eating gods' fire.

They brought him forward, feet dragging, head hanging. He had been cut anew by each station of the night; and his chest was like the gill of a shark, slices of skin hanging, blood coating his torso and legs. It was the way of the slicing. When Smoking Mirror had first shown them the slicing, he had used the Old Teacher, the first Toltec, and Smoking Mirror had cut each layer like thin tissue, and the slicing of the old man had taken days, with the pain of burning renewed each hour as new muscle dried and crusted. The slicing would have been Blue Hummingbird's preference for this one, this prophet with no power, but at the moment, his heart was more important. Hummingbird had told the Blood Gatherers to keep the prophet's eyes. He wanted to look into the blue irises as he used the blade of the butterfly tissue. The priests had used careful lancet cuts throughout the night on the prophet's eyelids, but they had been careful never to cut deeply enough to dry the eyes. Marvelous, for each cut had been a razor slice that should have made the prophet scream. The prophet hadn't screamed; he had only wept, and his tears were blood tracks down his cheeks. He was still conscious, and now, having witnessed the fairest of his people offered as Flower-Song, his heart would be succulent, swollen, like the sweet, tender meat of the orchid.

As he waited for the last ember of night, with the prophet hanging limp and leaving fine drops of blood about his feet, Blue Hummingbird remembered Aztlán, the mother's lake, that far summer when Smoking Mirror had come to gather them. At first, they had not known who he was. No one knew the man with the lightning eyes who had walked from the desert, and the old grandfathers had laughed when he claimed God spoke to him, whispered in his ear. They called him Auca, homeless one, to which the Smoking Mirror had only smiled and said he was indeed homeless, he was poor, he was wretched, and he called himself Filth-Eater, and he chuckled at the grandfathers. Everyone said Auca was crazy, possessed, and if they dared listen to him, they would wither with disease and excrement would fill their mouths. Those had been lies—Blue Hummingbird was certain of this now—the grandfathers had lied, they knew nothing.

One night the Smoking Mirror had walked among them naked, and he had danced, his member swollen, and everyone thought he was crazy, so no one dared go near. That was the night he had taught them the Flower-Song. He taught them first with the skin of the grandmother, the tissue of her lips, and then he had spoken with the voice of the whisperer, the Mocker, the Night terror. Blue Hummingbird had never been filled with such horror and wonder, but when he had tasted the tissue of the grandmother, he understood, and *the knowing* swelled in him even now, on this far dawn. Now he, the blue Hummingbird-of-the-Left, had wrought terror before the Tolteca unlike what they had ever before seen. Surely, he had become the Axe of Night himself. Surely, the changing of Blue Hummingbird was not far.

Even the sky, even the stars were different, everything rich and woven by the Sky Makers into images constantly fantastic. The mandrake mushrooms, the peyote, it kept the Star Artist working the skies feverously throughout the night. Each heart he had opened, each flower he had tasted, had given him a different strength. A woman's heart had a taste that was sweet and utter madness: it flushed him; it brought climax. That night, just by opening the flower of a red-hair, just by letting her warm down his throat, he screamed at the edge of the temple, hands clenched, and jettisoned his seed, spewing it into the womb of sky. His sex was with her, Coatilcue, the earth mother—who was so terrible to look at she could turn men's flesh inside out.

K. MICHAEL WRIGHT

Blue Hummingbird believed he had seen wondrous prophecy this night, but he had saved the best for last. Not only did he plan to savor the white-hair virgins and sleep the dawn in their silk-skin blood, but now, at the very last heartbeat of night, he was about to take the orchid flower of the Priest Speaker, the one they called Sky Teacher.

They set the Teacher's mesquite wood cross into the temple's mount and lifted him up for the last time. Blue Hummingbird grabbed his yellow hair and turned the Toltec's face where he could look in the blue eyes when they opened. Surely the prophet would look back into Hummingbird's eyes and see the power that swelled in him, the souls that swam here, the tender sweetness of children, the young white skin of their women—the screams of their mighty warriors, all this power swimming in him now.

Sky Teacher's face was almost comical from its many lancet cuts, as though he were a fish being filleted for a morning meal.

"Morning comes, Teacher. You have the honor of suckling its final breath."

The lancet cuts of his eyelids had dried enough that, though they were swollen, the Teacher could still lift them; and when he did, when he opened his eyes, Hummingbird could see the blue irises. Yet the Teacher did not look at the Hummingbird; instead, he looked past him. He saw something, for his face flinched and a shadow fell.

"Now?" the Teacher whispered quietly, even sadly. "Now you come?"

"Who comes?"

Blue Hummingbird paused, turning on the balls of his feet, feeling sudden quick fingers of fear he could not explain. The armies of Tollán had run the night before, like rabbits—all of them. The Tolteca had fled, their armies already crushed. No one could be returning from the desert! Yet there were sounds, and Blue Hummingbird saw them coming, sprinting, scattering, moving across the plain as though they had wings. As he leaned forward, catlike at the edge of temple tower, he could not believe

394

his eyes. They were returning, brilliant, filled with some kind of terrible light. Hummingbird wondered a moment if perhaps it was the peyote, perhaps the drunkenness of the night's feasting, but it appeared their skin had absorbed the moonlight, as though they hurtled like comets in the predawn, coming like star streamers.

"This cannot be," he muttered, grabbing the shoulder of his priest. "You see there! What comes!"

"Dragons," the priest answered. "They are plumed dragons, my lord."

"No, this is only madness! Take out the armies. Stop them!"

"Yes, my lord," the priest shouted as he turned to sprint their stairs for the plaza where most of the Shadow Walkers still celebrated, drinking, and singing—unprepared for battle.

Sky Teacher tried to focus, though his sight was blurred from the cuts against his eyelids. The images of the night had mercifully left him so weak he could no longer process thought. He seemed to be floating, slowly spinning in dark water with no current, no wind, just the still sky drawing down its stars. Sky Teacher had believed by morning his flesh would find peace, but not his soul. His soul would never know peace for he would always remember the lives he had watched snuffed this night, the children's screams, the cries of their mothers—it would walk with him forever. It was finally over; dawn was near, and Sky Teacher knew if he willed it, he could draw last breath and leave his flesh—yet something held him here with the thin, flower tendril of a dancer—perhaps it was the flower tether of Eslabeth. That had been the single image he let play in his mind through the smell of the night's blood, the imagined memory of the young Eslabeth's flower tendril as she danced as a child, her tiny feet spinning, a laughing sparkle in her green eyes.

Now, with morning, when his life should finally have passed—now they came. When it was too late to save a single child—now they came. With his eyes blurred, they looked like eagles, moving so close to the ground it was as if they were running. Already in the courtyards below there were screams as the Sky Dwellers of the Tolteca ripped through the porticos and into the square. Shadow Walkers were dying. He could see they were inspired; they fought with the spirit of the Eagle—somewhere his father had spoken and his sworn protectors were slaughtering the warriors of the Hummingbird where they lay drunk from the night's terror.

The tears in Sky Teacher's eyes washed into the blood on his cheeks. "Not now, Father, for God's sake, let them take me first." But it was not to be; the Shadow Walkers were being scattered like leaves. Sky Teacher would live.

"What is happening?" Blue Hummingbird seized Sky Teacher's throat in his claw hand.

Sky Teacher's eyes slowly turned to look upon the Blue Hummingbird and he found a far, quiet sadness still living in the man. The fear in the warrior's eye had left something exposed, and Sky Teacher was able to look through to his soul, a lost but once tender part of him, a young boy who had rowed onto the lake in his father's reed boat, who had dreamt of catching the carapace of a sea turtle and riding its back to the magic island where the corn maidens danced.

Blue Hummingbird staggered away from the priest, stricken. "What . . . what did you just do to me?"

"Reminded you," whispered Sky Teacher, "of who you were."

Blue Hummingbird gasped. His eyes were suddenly watery with tears. He was remembering things! The tender face of his sister, the smile of his mother so long ago, so far from here, so far he had thought them forever gone.

"No!" he screamed, his voice cracking with panic. He lifted the killing blade, the obsidian knife, but before he could move to kill the prophet, he was spun by one shoulder, thrown back against a pillar. The sacred butterfly knife slipped from his fingers, dropping away. Blue Hummingbird snarled, ready to attack, but instead he froze, unable to move. He knew this old man from legend, the white hair and beard; he knew the image almost as though he had seen these great stone eyes all his life. This was none other than the Sky Dragon of the Tolteca, the man who had looked on the face of God. To Blue Hummingbird, the Dragon's eyes were the most horrible sight he had witnessed; they were white fires, like burning stars.

"Dead," the Hummingbird whispered, "you are dead."

The old man didn't answer. Beside him, Toltec warriors in great, splendid feathered cloaks were unlashing the Teacher; they were going to save him. In fact, Hummingbird realized his own captains on the temple platform had already been killed. They lay scattered about him, in their own blood now. He was amazed, for he hadn't even seen them fall. The Tolteca had retaken Boaz so swiftly it was only a whisper, over in moments.

"What . . . ?" he said warily. "What are you going to do with me?"

He glanced to the Teacher, hoping for something, as though they were friends, but the priest's head had dropped forward limply; he finally fell unconscious. The Blue Hummingbird was to be left alone before the Dragon of Tollán.

The Hummingbird could not bear to look in the terrible eyes of the old man. He sensed them, as though the stars of the night sky spilled through them, but he spoke looking down at the Dragon's shadow.

"What are you going to do with me?" he repeated.

The Dragon's voice was deep, creviced, and he understood why they called this one the God Speaker. His voice, even spoken quietly, was touched with the sky.

"I will have you take your lord a message," Sky Dragon said. He was not speaking the language of the Tolteca; he spoke the tongue of the Shadow Walkers as if he had been born to them.

Hummingbird continued to stare only at the robes of the old

man where they fell at his bare feet. The king of the Tolteca wore simple cotton weft. Even the bottom of his staff, where it touched the stone of the temple platform, was plain and unadorned.

"Look on me," said the Dragon.

Hummingbird shook his head. He tried to turn away, but the voice would not let him; he had to turn, he had to look.

The old man's skin was worn; his great beard, where it fell across his chest and his hair were the color of white fire. But his eyes were terrible. The eyes of the Dragon bore into the Hummingbird like the heart of the sun.

"You will run through the land of the *ceiba*," said the Dragon. "You will find this lord you call the Smoking Mirror, and you will tell him Sky Dragon has called gathering."

Blue Humming felt such a terrible dread he could not even train his thoughts. "I do not understand gathering," he stammered.

"He will. Now go," said Sky Dragon. "I give you strength to run."

With that, the Lord of the Tolteca lifted his arm, and Hummingbird turned. He no longer controlled his own movement; he turned and followed the pointed finger. Hummingbird was amazed, for he ran and leapt from the side of the temple, soaring high over the trees, and he should have fallen, he should have been crushed, yet he seemed to swim down through the air. When finally his feet hit the ground, he found he was running as never he had run before, like he *was* the very wind. He could not have stopped even if he tried. He was being carried without will of his own, and that was madness; but what seemed even more terrible was that as he ran, he felt sudden tears in his eyes—and at that, Blue Hummingbird wept. He wept continually, for he so wanted to be again that boy who could catch the turtle shell and hold until he reached the magic island where the corn maidens would dance and sing, where he would laugh and run with them until the welcoming sun rose. He would spread his fingers, welcoming the light, welcoming life. Yet the Blue Hummingbird knew he would never dance again. He knew in his heart that in time and all of time, where it stretched forever and away into the stars; never would he again see light. When this run sucked away his life, he would die, and when the flesh of Blue Hummingbird failed, he would cease to be. He would simply become the Utter Dark that never burns. He thought he had practiced terror, that with the Smoking Mirror, he and his brothers had become the masters of the Night and the Wind and had been given the sacred power, but now he knew, now he understood—they had only been Mocked, and even the face of the Night Axe was not as terrible as what he saw in his mind's eye. There was no face more terrible than "never."

CHAPTER FORTY
THE FATHER

Sky Teacher wasn't sure how long he had slept in the tent of his father; he was not sure if it had been one night or many, but when he finally stared up at the peccary hide of the tent, warmed from its hearth fire, he first heard his father speaking low. He lifted his head and saw his father kneeling by the fire, watching as one of his high captains, a man Sky Teacher knew as Blade Companion, traced a map on the ground before them. He realized the herbs to treat his pain left things dulled and Blade Companion's voice came in and out of focus.

"They move swift on the western plain," Blade Companion was saying, tracing the line of an army's path in the dirt with the tip of his sword. "But if we run, we can still cut them off here, and then here. We would be pressed hard, my lord, but the armies of the Cholulans, led by Scarlet Macaw, are even now moving south to meet us."

Sky Dragon nodded. He touched Blade Companion's wrist guard. Upon seeing Sky Teacher's opened eyes, Blade Companion stood for a moment and paused. He bowed, brought a fist to his heart, and left the tent.

Sky Teacher didn't look on his father for a moment. He felt tears; they came without invitation, and the light of the fire blurred. The tears stung into the cuts of his face with sharp pain. When he felt his father's hand touch his shoulder, he closed his eyes.

"Why?" he whispered. "Why come so late? Why let me live?"

Sky Dragon took his time in answering. He sat on a wooden stool near Sky Teacher's mat, and for a time, there was only the sound of the fire softly licking.

"Did you not notice they no longer cried out when you prayed for them?"

Sky Teacher thought about it. Yes, he did remember that as the flames licked about the youth, though the parents and elders continued to scream, the children were silent. He had thought it was the smoke.

"I noticed," the Dragon said. "I heard your prayer answered, my son. I heard them stop screaming, and I watched as their spirits cut a path through Heaven. Lifted by the voice of a singer, they were taken in gentle hand. You need weep for them no more. They are home."

Sky Teacher opened his eyes, slowly, painfully. "Seven years," he said, looking into the stone eyes of his father. "You have been gone seven years."

The Dragon nodded. "It is finished now; the work is done. Only one task yet remains."

"What?"

"Cumorah."

Sky Teacher knew the answer already, but he felt that word lick with the ice of fear. He had not let himself think of that name in years; almost he had hoped if he didn't remember it, it would never happen. "Father, take me with you. Give me time to heal, let me lead your lords into battle. I need that now. I need it!"

For a time Sky Dragon merely watched the fire. He seemed calm, but Sky Teacher knew he was merely resigned.

"Why?" the Dragon asked.

"For them . . . the children, the innocents. And for her."

"I'm told her name was Eslabeth."

"Yes. We were coming south to find you. I had hoped to have your . . . your blessing."

"And you believe you will find this girl at Cumorah? You saw her eyes when she left you. Do you really think that is the path she chose?" The Dragon sighed. His hand, where it rested on Sky Teacher's shoulder, tightened softly, carefully, since the lancet cuts still stung, even through the wrappings.

"When I was young," the Dragon said, "only ten and six years, we fought them once—Shadow Walkers. They had sent a foraging army so far north they were months from their homeland when they reached us. They were perhaps five hundred strong, and a priest who followed the ancient pathways on his own led them. He knew our writings; he had found the maps. They overtook several villages before we were able to reach them. I was able to feign an ambush, and I lured the core of their army into the Valley of Sidon. The jungles there were thick enough to keep our armies concealed. I watched from an outcropping of rock—letting them pass through to my chosen killing ground.

"Seeing them, my heart failed me. They were too few. These were not the ones of whom my father spoke. I realized they were only a splinter group and that in fact, by now they had even lost contact with the mountain people they left months ago. I let them walk into my trap and I coiled my armies about their flanks soundlessly before launching even the first atlatl. That night we burned them. I watched as the smoke of their souls lifted to the dark, and I begged, I begged with all I had that this be the end of it. That day I begged God to spare me in this hour that has now finally come."

The Dragon turned his gray eyes on Sky Teacher. "Do you know how few there are left, my son? We were once teachers. We once built temples, not ramparts. We were the singers! We were so many! How I wished I could have lived in ancient times, shared it with them, tasted anything other than war. How I longed in my heart..."

Sky Teacher swallowed past a knot in his throat.

"It is written," the Dragon said, "that we answer the blood of innocents, and when it is spilled, we each time follow that command of the ancient one. Each and every time. Though the words of the One True Singer have been made covenant by his flesh and blood, in men's hearts, we remember only the command of the ancient one. Never will the sons of men leave the blood of innocents unanswered."

He closed his eyes, tightened his jaw. "On the morrow I go where you cannot follow."

"No. No, you must give me time to heal!"

The Dragon shook his head. Sky Teacher tried to sit up, but his father's strong hand did not let him. The Dragon's eyes merely turned to study Sky Teacher with tenderness.

"This is goodbye, my son."

"No, Father—"

"You must not follow me."

"No!"

"It is given me than I must lead them one last time," said Sky Dragon sadly, "just as it is given you to write their last song."

CHAPTER FORTY-ONE
SKY DWELLERS

The Northern Plains of Tollán, near the City of Cholula—seven days later

The man who was called Terror Speaker, the second high captain of Smoking Mirror's northern armies, led his one thousand warriors into the wide plain of Cholula with confidence. He came in pomp and glory, his standard-bearers lifting their gods on their backs, his warriors fanned wide to either flank. They filled the plain, and with them came the singers and the tumblers. Drums kept a slow steady beat, for Terror Speaker was not afraid to let it be known he walked here, in the great sweeping northern plains of the Tolteca. This was given him. It was his land now. After breaking through the southern passage, he had separated from the Blue Hummingbird, his brother of Aztlán, known in their homeland as Hummingbird-on-the-Left. The Hummingbird would move due north. He had been given Tollán as plunder, and that was fitting; he was elder to Terror Speaker, and his kills were all great warriors.

But Terror Speaker had heard many things of the land that lay in his path, and he knew although Cholula was a sister city, it was also a trade route and was swollen more with riches and women than Tollán itself. And they were close. He had studied carefully the ancient maps and he knew this plain, seemingly empty and dry, bordered the southern edge of the city. In fact, once he reached the hillocks just north of them, no more than an arrow's flight longer, he would be able to view his plunder for the first time.

TOLTECA

He believed the Tolteca fled before him. That morning they had reached a city that was uninhabited, but the Tolteca had left behind their silver and fine feather-working, their lapis lazuli and precious jade. They had left the armies of Terror Speaker all but flesh. But their flesh could not outrun him much longer. Even the Tolteca could not outrun the night, and that is how Terror Speaker came to the northern plains, as the Night and the Wind. Surely, there had not been time to evacuate the great city of Cholula. He and his armies would feast this night. He lifted his fist in the air, and Blue Mouth, his first captain, called a halt. The drums stilled and the armies of the Shadow Walkers drew up in array.

Blue Mouth, a dark-skinned lowlander with a square head and tiny pits of dark eyes stepped beside Terror Speaker and scanned the plains. It was not often lowlanders were chosen as warriors, but Blue Mouth had fought the Shadow Walkers and had taken so many kills that to honor him, he was given the sacred meat and the blood of offering and invited to join their ranks. Blue Mouth did not merely eat and drink, he drank his soul, he let the whisperer fill him, and so now, he marched with the greatest warriors and had become Terror Speaker's right hand.

"Why do we pause, my lord?" said Blue Mouth. "I sense nothing ahead."

"We will draw breath, smell the mesquite and the dry wind. Here we will prepare ourselves."

"Yes, my lord."

"Have we word from the Hummingbird?"

Blue Mouth shook his head. "Nothing, my lord."

Hummingbird was to have sent seven hundred to join him on the seventh dawn, which was today. Terror Speaker had expected the Hummingbird's runners to reach camp the night before, but when the blood of the morning sun had spilt from the east, there was no sign of the armies of the Hummingbird. The plains to the southeast, from where they should have marched, were silent.

"Shall I send a runner in search of them?" asked Blue Mouth.

Terror Speaker shook his head. "They are all drunk. They have fattened themselves on the spoils of the cities behind us. All the better, I say. They leave Cholula ours alone. Do you have the slingers placed well in the rear?"

"Yes, my lord."

"And your shield-bearers, they are ready? Well prepared?"

"All are ready, my lord, all is prepared. The offerings have strengthened them. We could slay dragons."

"When I give signal, we will close on these hills at double march in case the Tolteca have laid an ambush. It is good ground for an ambush, hills to all three sides. I would welcome one, let them test their strength. These last days all our warriors have done is march, and it is due time we let them feed."

"I agree. Yet, we are still only a thousand strong. Should we not wait longer for the Hummingbird's warriors?"

Terror Speaker drew his lip back in a snarl. "You question me?"

"Never would I question you, my lord. I merely offer counsel."

"We have not crossed this flatland to eat more dust while the Hummingbird's fat warriors catch up with us. There is nothing to fear. They are weak, these Tolteca. They flee each city we approach. Perhaps here they will come out to meet us; surely they would not lay bare their city of whores, the place they name Cholula. I've come into this plain spread wide, my flanks exposed. Perhaps that will draw the cowards. I want these men to fight before feasting this time. I want to see these Tolteca lift a sword."

Suddenly Blue Mouth grew pale, his eyes wide. "My lord," he gasped, pointing. "There! Who is that?"

Terror Speaker turned. Blue Mouth's voice had cracked in panic. What could possibly have left his first captain panicked? Terror Speaker felt a shiver cross his own skin. He was not sure why, for on the center hill before them stood but one old man, yet Terror Speaker felt his skin crawl, felt a spike of panic in his throat. It was impossible—madness. His fear angered him.

"Who is he?" Blue Mouth screamed. "It is him! We are doomed!"

TOLTECA

Perhaps it was the lowland blood in Blue Mouth's veins; he was shrieking like a child. Terror Speaker turned sharply and grabbed his captain by the breastplate. He struck Blue Mouth with the back of his hand. "Hold your tongue, fool!" he snarled.

"But, my lord—"

"Hold your tongue! That is only one old man."

It was amazing, Blue Mouth seemed not even to be hearing, his eyes lost in panic, like a rat who had been spotted in the night by owls.

"We must run," muttered Blue Mouth. "Must run, we must flee—"

"Swallow your fear before these men, Blue Mouth, or I shall open your throat like a fatted offering."

Blue Mouth blinked, still crazed.

"It is *him*," whispered Blue Mouth.

"What do you mean by *him*?"

"That is the one they speak of. It is the Dragon."

"Impossible."

"That is the Dragon of the Tolteca! We must flee, my lord."

"That is no more than a barefoot old man!" Terror Speaker screamed. "He is just a wizard. Order your archers to take him out! Now!"

Blue Mouth finally seemed to find his wits. "Archers!" he cried. "Archers to the fore!"

The shield-bearers parted to let the archers pass. They came at a sprint and instantly assembled before Terror Speaker. Some scattered dust as they slid in the dirt on their knees, lifting their bows, others took positions in staggered lines. Seventy archers were soon waiting in tight formation before Blue Mouth and Terror Speaker. Shafts were fitted to the sinews, bows yawned tight. Terror Speaker watched the old man. He was slowly moving through the tangled brush of the hillside, as though he was going to crush them all with nothing but his staff.

"Kill him!" screamed Terror Speaker.

"Fire!" Blue Mouth commanded.

A shadow of arrows rose into the plain swiftly, arcing, then closed in on the old man like birds of prey. They struck the side of the mountain with fury. For a moment, they seemed to obliterate him. Yet the old man continued walking steadily, slowly, as if he had all day. Murmurs ran through the troops.

"This is priest-craft!" shouted Terror Speaker. He stepped back, facing his men. "It is wizardry! You will not panic! They deceive us! They mean to unnerve us with tricks! Hold your ranks!"

Blue Mouth gasped. He had even staggered back a bit, as if something had struck him.

Terror Speaker whirled about. The old man's staff lifted into the sky; and with the motion, the hillocks blossomed. The banners of the mighty Tolteca fluttered against the horizon. To the west, the entire ridge massed with shields of rich, feathered tapestry, and curling along the low mound to the east were row upon row of helmed warriors. They were splendid, their shields and cloaks were a fantasy of color. In the center hillock, the tassels of their standard fluttered quietly in the sun. The signet looked to be alive, as though lifting its dark blue, flashing quetzal wings into the air. Its diamond eyes caught the sun like lightning and the silver streamers below coiled like great talons. This was the signet of the Serpent Plumed, and gathered on the ridge before Terror Speaker and his warriors were the fabled Sky Dwellers. It was as though the old man had spawned them.

"This is not possible," Terror Speaker whispered. "We had runners search these plains; there were no armies here! And him, the Dragon, he does not live! Smoking Mirror would never have deceived us!"

"The Dragons of the Tolteca live," said Blue Mouth. "And we have been made fodder for their knives."

The white-haired old man spoke and Terror Speaker froze. The old man's voice peeled out like heavy thunder, and it seemed that surely he was calling down the fires of the sun. He spoke only three words. They were words Terror Speaker had never heard before, and yet they cut through him with a kind of recognition, as though once they had meant something.

"Ahman-om-Amen!" the Dragon roared.

The Tolteca surrounding the armies of the Shadow Walkers screamed, they roared from the hillsides and descended like eagles, swift, closing on all sides at full run. The very ground beneath Terror Speaker trembled. He realized what looked to be wings were banners riding on the shoulders of bearers, but the quetzal feathers of the standards flashed like silvered feathers in flight.

The ranks of the Shadow Walkers broke and his warriors fled, dropping their shields, their weapons, fleeing—warriors who had marched for two years drinking the blood of innocents, warriors bred from youth to fight to the death against the very face the dark—yet they fled like rabbits.

"Turn back, you filth!" Terror Speaker screamed, his face red. "Turn and fight!" Even Blue Mouth had dropped his flint-edged sword and was running, parting his own shield-bearers, throwing off his armor for speed.

Terror Speaker snarled, curling his hand about the hilt of his dagger. He, at least, would spill blood this day. Yet, when he turned for the kill, even Terror Speaker screamed, like a child might scream in the night, because the old man was there, right there before him. The Toltec king lifted no weapon, not even his staff—there was no need because as Terror Speaker watched, the fires of a distant star spilled from the eyes of the prophet.

CHAPTER FORTY-TWO
GATHERING

The Coast of Anáhuac, the Year One Death, the Season of Flaying—
six months later

Sky Dragon drew his troops up alongside the slow-moving river of the Sidon. Here mangroves spread lazy canopies; willows trailed their limbs in the warm water. Occasionally a caiman slithered through the grass and slid into the river. The day was dull, hard. A white-hot sun beat down upon the land of Anáhuac, and it seemed to dry the earth, to steal souls.

Across the river, the Shadow Walkers slowly assembled wearing leather corselets, disk chest armor, carrying atlatls, bows, thrusting spears, and, of course, Tolteca swords. Only the Tolteca knew the source of the moonsteel, the mountain where it was mined. Ironically, that source lay along the coast, in the marshlands and swamps, near the ancient cities of Xibalba. In Xibalba as well was the thunder-mountain men called Cumorah, the Place of Burning, the name given it by the Death Lords when they were once flesh.

The Shadow Walkers who had been sent to the northern plains against the Tolteca had been destroyed, but in the south, beyond the narrow passage, there were many old enemies of the Tolteca. Once the cities had fallen, the armies of the Smoking Mirror owned the jungles, leaving the Tolteca of the north vastly outnumbered.

The Dragon and his Sky Dwellers alone had been allowed to cross the southern passage into the lowlands.

The king of the Shadow Walkers, the one who called himself

the Smoking Mirror, was carried before his armies in a litter whose canopy was red silk-cotton, whose dark, wicker frame was inlaid with gold. The wicker carrier was borne by warriors who went naked. They did not set him upon the ground; rather the warriors knelt to one knee and continued to hold him, as pedestals.

It grew silent. This meeting had been agreed to, arranged, and there would be no bloodshed this day. The high captains of the Shadow Walkers and the sworn protectors of the Dragon regarded each other warily across the wide, slow-moving waters. They had all descended of the ancestors, the four brothers. The Shadow Walkers were descendants of the two eldest, the Tolteca and Nonaloca were descendants of the two youngest. For eight hundred years, they had fought each other, like the ebb and flow of the ocean against sand, and now, finally, the end had stretched its fingers from the beginning.

Smoking Mirror was dressed in a blue cotton tunic. A silver diadem curled through his night-black hair. Sky Dragon noticed the Shadow Lord's left foot was missing. In its place had been fashioned a mirror disk of polished obsidian, attached to the ankle by a tight band of silver. There was something about it, something that whispered, and Sky Dragon understood—this was mark left of Topiltzin. Somewhere his son had met the Dark Lord in combat. Topiltzin had tried, of course, to turn time, to change prophecy. Sky Dragon attempted to feel through the Smoking Mirror if Topiltzin was still alive, but he could not pierce beyond the lightning eyes of the young prince. What Sky Dragon did sense in them was brilliance still living in the blue-white eyes, a fascination and wonder, but beneath the surface there was something far more powerful, something far beyond the blood of a Highlander. This youth might once have been a singer, but instead he had tapped the very vein of the Utter Dark. Though his eyes were still lightning and quick, he had become his namesake, a mirror that could flash brilliant in the sun, but when turned would offer back a misted reflection beneath the smoked obsidian. The very face of the Mocker was there, across from them, close enough to touch. Sky Dragon had an impulse to panic, but he turned it back and calmly offered the face of the Utter Dark neither fear nor pride. He would speak only to the mirror's surface, for though the Mocker breathed in this skin, the youth was still there as well. He was a once-brilliant soul left flickering like a candle beneath a storm cloud.

"We, the Tolteca," Sky Dragon said, "are honored you have agreed to this meeting. I thank you, Highlander."

The quick eyes flashed. Sky Dragon knew the boy had not been called Highlander since before a time he no longer remembered, but he knew as well it would strike a far chord.

"You are welcome, worthy Sky Dragon," the youth answered. "I have heard many things spoken of you. They say you are a prophet who has gazed openly into the face of God. I seem to have waited a lifetime to look in your eyes."

"As I have feared a lifetime to look in yours."

This seemed to amuse the youth. But it was not the youth; it was the Mocker who chuckled, a sound Sky Dragon tried to shut out.

Sky Dragon continued speaking, quietly, calmly. "Here, in the land of the Fourth Sun, it is already dusk. Our day is near an ending. We—the Tolteca, the Nonaloca, the kings and priests, the merchants, the artisans, the common people—we understand this, for it is written of in our sacred texts. Therefore, we call gathering before the lord who names himself the Smoking Mirror."

Smoking Mirror leaned forward. "Yes, Sky Dragon. I have heard you might call gathering. As you well know, my commander Blue Hummingbird spoke this to me before he died."

"And you understand the gathering, Highlander?"

"Yes, I learned of it from the grandfathers of Aztlán. There the Old Ones still spoke of a time long ago when our people and yours, rather than lay waste to the land, chose instead to gather for the final killing without fortifications or siege. It began at dawn and continued through the night, and when the sun came the next day from beneath the earth, only one army was left standing. Since then, you have been kings and priests of this land, and you have built great cities. But time now comes full circle. The Shadow Walkers stride once more. You may have swallowed the armies of the Hummingbird and crushed Terror Speaker's fine song, but we are still legion! If I marched from the south, you would fall before me like the dry stalks of corn you are. Tell me, Sky Dragon, why should we agree to a gathering? Why not take you where you stand in your cities and your temples?"

"For me, the gathering will spare innocents. For you, it will spare time. Your proposed siege of the north will not be gentle. We can withstand you for years. I know you care not of innocent blood, but you do care of time. We both, then, have our reason to allow a gathering."

"Yes. But my men will ask me, Honored Sky Dragon—what of the riches of Tollán and Cholula?"

"Is that what you have come for? Riches?"

"As you well know, riches feed the hearts of men. After all, we are here for only a short time, but a flicker, and only riches can make the shortness sweet."

"You may tell your men they can take comfort that the dead will claim no riches. Our cities will be left open."

Again, the knowing chuckle, not from the youth but a deeper and whispery chuckle, and once more, Sky Dragon had to force himself calm.

"What is your answer then, my young prince?"

The Lord of the Shadow Walkers smiled. "We accept," said the youth. "We accept! Let there be a gathering. One of us shall live and become lord and king of all he sees, and the other shall inherit the kingdom of Xibalba."

"The kingdoms we each inherit, my lord Smoking Mirror, will be those we have ourselves sown."

"You are quick, wise one," answered the Dark, no longer bothering to disguise his voice in any way, the firstborn of God, the lord of the fallen, the very dark that burns at the end of the universe. "You speak careful words. Have you not yet learned to fear me?"

Sky Dragon answered with measured breath, "I have feared you since the day I was born, and I will fear you in the hour of prophecy, but never will I offer you grace."

"So be it. Use your tongue to sing your gathering, God Speaker. Name now your dying place."

"It is you who has granted a gathering; let the killing ground be your choosing."

"It shall be there, in Xibalba. As your prophecies have always promised—I name your killing ground Cumorah."

Sky Dragon nodded. The Smoking Mirror first chuckled harsh and whispery, but he then laughed aloud. Sky Dragon felt himself chill as the laughter faded and the face froze, watching him, the eyes opening to the dark of the Night. It unfolded slowly, but then reached swiftly across the waters of the river, coming for his heart. For a moment he almost cried out, for in all his days, he had not felt as close to panic as he did in this moment. But the Dragon held himself in check, he stared back, he did not blink when the heart of the Night and the Wind swept through him.

"Impressive," the voice whispered in his ear.

The Smoking Mirror lifted his hand, and his bearers were instantly on their feet, turning to carry him away. He did not look back. Once their king was safely in the jungles, the warriors of the Shadow Walker withdrew.

When they were gone, Sky Dragon felt himself finally breathe, but the chill did not leave him. He felt weak, immensely old, as though he had long outlived his years and they rested on him as heavy as stone. He turned to Blade Companion, who stood near his side.

"Leave me," Sky Dragon said quietly.

Blade Companion nodded, then stepped back. At his silent command, the Sky Dwellers of Tollán withdrew from the riverside, moving almost soundless through the trees.

Sky Dragon waited until he was alone on the banks of Sidon; he waited until he could no longer feel the hearts of his captains—

the hearts of Slayers. It had become necessary in this world that such men be fashioned, that there be Slayers, men of pure heart, refined of blood's fire until they held no feeling before the kill. It was necessary. They would not be damned; they would be honored in Heaven as warriors. They would be killer angels. Ones he had never known.

Alone on the banks of the river he had once called home, the Dragon prayed that somewhere, in some distant and far day, the children of men would find the truer path before the hour when all time came to an end.

When his prayers were finished, he looked on the waters of the river Sidon and for a moment let his thoughts turn to Zarahemla, when it was his homeland, in the time when he was young, when the city was so beautiful. In that day the fair, the young, the glory of the Nonaloca, was like a precious stone, glittering with light from the eyes of its children. Light that seemed able to turn even prophecy. They had once been kings; they had once been the teachers, singers. In this land, they would now only be remembered as the Nephalli. They would become the Many Dead.

▱▱▱▱▱▱▱▱▱▱▱▱▱▱▱▱▱▱

And they left their cities. They departed. The fair, the wise, they gathered their books, their works, their metal castings; they lifted their children, and they began toward the south, toward the marshes. The Tolteca marched into the land of Xibalba. And Tollán burned. For seven days, she burned. The houses of the nobles, the temples, the palaces, the streets of Heaven—all burned.

The Tolteca followed the voice of their prophet: the women, the children, the old men—all left. The fair ones departed. They had always been strangers to this land, even as rulers and conquerors, for always they had lived in the shadow of this day, this prophecy, the final gathering.

There were those who remained in Tollán, the Oaxacans, the

415

Mixteca, and many of the Chichimeca who had lived and worked in the city. Many were artisans and masons. Others were obsidian workers. They remained behind in the outskirts of the gutted city. And they stilled, watching the Lords of Tollán depart. It would seem to them, in the stories they would tell their children, the great bearded ones left as flesh, as men, but in their leaving, they became legend. In their leaving, it was said, they joined with the gods. Thereafter, Tollán would be known as Teotihuacán: the City Where Men Became Gods.

CHAPTER FORTY-THREE
CUMORAH

Through the thick of the jungle foliage, Smoking Mirror studied the top of the Mountain called Cumorah. It had been quiet that morning, a dark, stone finger rising through the trees, a dead cone. Somehow Sky Dragon had brought it to life, and now plumes rose from its side to spread fingers across the pink skin of dawn. Every now and then, it shook the ground about Smoking Mirror.

The fighting had gone on through the night, and though Smoking Mirror had always used night as his weapon, it seemed even to him a night of madness.

It had begun to turn first in the swamps where the eastern finger of Cumorah cut a dark swath of black stone into the jungle. The swamps were oily and stretched for miles, but amazingly, the prime of the Tolteca had chosen this spot to make their strongest stand. It seemed a weak place to defend, for the ooze was difficult to move through, and there was no retreat up the steep slope of Cumorah should they wish to turn. The Smoking Mirror had sent Blood Gatherer and the prime of the Shadow Walkers, the children of Aztlán, to move against them in full force; and at first it had seemed the Tolteca were utterly sundered. Their center had broken, and mired in swamp they began to die; but as they did, they slowly pulled the armies of Blood Gatherer deeper. The burning began. The smoke of it was like ink against the night, but its heart was a blinding white fire. Soon the smell of burning flesh mixed sour and sweet with the smell of blood. The screams were insane. The Tolteca had burned their own prime, but they had also closed on

Blood Gatherer's flanks, blocking any retreat. It had been a trap.

The marshes were still smoldering, and the sight of them, the bodies there, had unnerved even the coldest Aztlán warriors. Only then did Smoking Mirror realize what was happening. Of course, it was too late to turn.

With the armies of Blood Gatherer destroyed, Smoking Mirror had lost his left flank, though it never really mattered. Nothing came through the swamp fires to challenge him but the smell of death. Runners soon brought more news from the south. There, the Tolteca had drawn them deep, but each time, just before it seemed they were exhausted, the warriors of Tollán had turned and begun to slay. It did not seem to matter to them how many they lost, and only later, when night was long, did Smoking Mirror realize the true meaning of Sky Dragon's gathering.

Smoking Mirror waited as Serpent Slayer made his way through the warriors guarding the prince. The Smoking Mirror stood in a field of bodies that had left the ground matted with blood as though it had rained from Heaven. The Sky Dwellers, the Dragon's chosen protectors, had fought here and for each Sky Dweller who fell, as many as twenty warriors of the Shadow Walkers died as well. The Lords of Tollán had left a mat of bodies that led up the muddy slope of Cumorah. They were splendid killers. The Sky Dwellers, as they retreated, had cut mortal wounds, but wounds that took life slowly, the spleen, the vitals; and throughout the night, the jungle was filled with the screams and moans of the dying. It turned out the Shadow Walkers were not the only warriors well versed in terror.

Serpent Slayer was bloodied and out of breath, having just returned from the front, somewhere beyond them at the base of the mountain. The sound of battle was sometimes near, sometimes far, it seemed to ebb like tide, but also it swam in a fantasy of madness.

Serpent Slayer had lost his helmet; his peccary-skin armor was slashed as though a cat had shredded it. Serpent Slayer knelt before his prince and lowered his head.

"Have you reached their women yet?" asked Smoking Mirror.

"My lord, they have already killed their women and children."

Smoking Mirror was not surprised; nothing surprised him any longer. "Explain."

"They were fierce, those who guarded the innocents. The closer we got, the more men we lost, the Tolteca fought like caiman, there was no turning them. Still, when we finally thinned their rank, when we reached their women, we found the Tolteca had taken their own innocents—they let them sleep by potions, and when we drew near, they opened some throat of the mountain. Running rock, molten, it came like a river and took the bodies of their innocents before we could carry them away. It has also taken almost all the warriors of Departer. I saw Departer himself melt, I saw him scream in the molten river with its fire-runners swimming up the sides of his face."

"How many of the Tolteca still stand?"

"Only a core of the Sky Dwellers remains—directly to our south. We have heard nothing from the east or the far north. I have sent out runners but they do not return."

"And your west flank?"

"My lord, the armies of the Sun Ray moved against the west when the moon was mid-sky during the night. None of them have returned. My runners tell me the bodies of the Tolteca are scattered throughout the jungles there—but also, Sun Ray and all his warriors gave up flesh. They are no more, my lord."

"And the armies of Flower Prince?"

"We have heard nothing from them. They were to the north, beyond the burning marshes, but there has been no word—they are utterly cut off; no one can find a path through or around the burning marshes. I fear, my lord, we have been tricked."

Smoking Mirror nodded calmly. Indeed, the old man had tricked them. Still, he asked his captain, "Explain this, Serpent Slayer. Tricked in what way?"

"When the Tolteca gathered on the killing fields, they knew our strength, that we outnumbered them. They were prepared to die, but what we did not foresee—they fully intended to take us with them. After they burned Blood Gatherer and his prime, they began to thin us no matter the cost to themselves. Throughout the night, they would fade into the jungle only to reform and close for more killing. The closer we have gotten to their mountain, the more we have lost. Here at its base, they have welcomed death; but also, my lord, they have welcomed us in the embrace. It is done—we are no more!"

Smoking Mirror turned back to the plumes of black clouds sweeping the sky above the cone of the mountain. He wanted to feel angry, he wanted to feel his blood hot and scream, he wanted to let the whisperer fill his flesh, but the whisperer had not spoken to him throughout the night. He had been alone.

"How many men are still with you, Serpent Slayer?"

Serpent Slayer kept his head lowered. "My lord, the warriors of Red Skull only. I have sent runners elsewhere, but I fear the jungles everywhere are silent now."

"Go, take Red Skull and press the last of them, these so called Sky Dwellers. Ensure they will not see the dawn."

"It will be done, my lord. And you? How many do I leave with you?"

"You do not see, Serpent Slayer? I stand here in my kingdom. My lords are everywhere." He lifted his arms and smiled, "They surround me."

Serpent Slayer stood. Smoke drifted past them.

Serpent Slayer lifted his fist in salute. "My lord," he said, then turned and with a scream ran into the jungle toward the shadow mountain, his men falling in at his flanks, lifting weapons for their final run.

Smoking Mirror was left alone. He heard the whisperer speak one last time, though not in his head, not whispered in his ear; this time the Utter Dark was all around him, playing through the shadows. *All men were fools, and none of them understood, none would ever learn—this is the day that was promised, this is the changing that awaits them all.* As the dark closed upon him, the youth, the Highlander who had led his people from the far fingers of the southern mountains, thought how he had crafted terror his whole life—but in truth, he had never imagined the taste of true terror that now filled him. True terror was nothing. Nothing at all—forever.

Blade Companion was forced to fall back. His arm could no longer lift the war hammer. The last of the Shadow Walkers had come from the jungle at full run and time was marked, the shields of the Sky Dwellers would soon break. As he stepped to the rear, a bloodied warrior took his place and Stone Slayer, whose priest name was Helaman, after his ancient ancestor, took Blade Companion's arm and knelt with him a moment as Blade Companion caught his breath.

"It is over, my lord," said Stone Slayer. "Sky Dragon has asked that you return now."

Blade Companion looked up. He saw the rearguard lift the tasseled shields and fan outward to hold the flanks against the last of the night's spawn.

"My leg," said Blade Companion, "I don't believe it will take my weight any longer."

Stone Slayer nodded. The big man helped to lift Blade Companion to his feet. He wrapped Blade Companion's arm about his shoulder, taking the weight off his leg; and they turned together to walk up the steep edge of Cumorah's southern spur. The sounds, the screams, and the constant clash of weapons faded slowly to quiet, almost like snow melting away, like a wind passing, and as they rounded a heavy outcropping of rock, a thick silence seemed to envelop them. It seemed the first silence he had heard in many, many days. As they moved through the drifting smoke and shadow, he noticed the sky above Cumorah's ridge. Dawn was coming the color of bright blood through the plumes of smoke from the mountain's cone. The ground trembled; rocks and dirt spilled past their boots.

Blade Companion paused a moment when they were quite high, turning to scan the jungles below them. There, nothing moved. Shadows painted the bodies, as though the blood and flesh had been sculpted into twisted, tangled, watery stone. Tolteca and Shadow Walker embraced like lovers. The only sound emanating from the jungles was the trickle of the stream flowing between the rocks; the water ran red as it curled past fallen warriors and into the sea.

Blade Companion had to pause a moment for breath. A dart was buried deep in his chest. The wound was mortal, but the dart remained too close to the heart to be pulled.

"I could try to carry you, my lord."

"You are as wounded as I, my friend."

Blade Companion looked up the stone pathway that led closer to the summit. He could see the Sky Dragon's white standard fluttering, its white feathers catching the ray of dawn, silvery and quick. He pressed on and finally, with dawn's first light breaking, he reached the side of his Lord. He knelt at the side of Sky Dragon. Stone Slayer dropped to the ground, his strength spent. Blade Companion nodded to Sky Dragon's manservant, and let them lower the king's head against his own strong shoulder. Together they watched dawn's fingers slowly bring the jungle below to life, but there was no life with this dawn; it was a field of death as far as the eye could gaze.

"It is done, then?" Sky Dragon asked.

"Yes, my lord. It is over."

Sky Dragon finally let himself weep. Throughout the night he had watched, silently, quietly ordering the battle. There had been no emotion, but now, finally, his chest heaved as Sky Dragon's stone eyes stared across the field of dead to the edge of the sea, where the blue-green waters washed red against the bodies on the shore. He slowly lifted his hand, perhaps to touch them, and whispered his last command.

"Come forth, earth shaker, earth swallower, come, O Lord." Sky

Dragon's hand closed into a fist. The mountain rumbled in answer.

"Take this, our final harvest."

Blade Companion lowered his head, closed his eyes. There was a hissing sound, like a rushing of waves. Behind them, the mountaintop ripped upward in screaming thunder. Stone Slayer, Blade Companion, his king, along with the last of the warriors of Tollán, were vaporized in a blast of wind and fire that swept outward, in all directions—the breath, the last word of the Dragon.

Sky Teacher turned, hearing the explosion. He was inland, near the mountain passage, far from Cumorah's peak, but the plume that reached into the sky was easily visible, even from here. *It is the Valley of Sidon!* the Heavens were screaming. He watched, amazed, as the trees and vegetation in all directions from Cumorah were stripped away. From the distance, the fire blast flashed in a wave of searing earth, sweeping everything from its path, and when it spilled through the jungles and finally played out, blood rock continued to rain from the peak like hail pelting.

Sky Teacher shivered where he stood, even this far from the eruption. In way, he was thankful not to have seen the carnage. He had witnessed enough death to last him eternity. His father had left a vanguard of warriors with him, but the night before, Sky Teacher had ordered them to leave him, and when morning came, he was alone. He knew he would be alone for many years to come. He wrapped his cloak tighter; kneeling, watching as the dawn sky darkened, slow at first, but then more quickly. Behind it, the sun glimmered a blood red, and then faded as the shadow plume spread outward, like the very hand of God. A single dot of light seemed to remain on the horizon, glimmering. It was the Morning Star, and it looked to have spawned from the heart of the mountain.

How long Sky Teacher crouched there, head lowered, searching his soul for strength to continue, he wasn't sure, but when he finally stood, it was so dark it was difficult to mark a path ahead. He shouldered the wicker carrier, heavy with the golden plates, the writings, and started north. That was where the spirit called him, north. And Sky Teacher understood this would be a long journey.

This land, this valley, once filled with promise, would now be swallowed. It was ended. The Tolteca had passed from the earth and for a thousand years, God would turn his face.

PART III

THE FIFTH SUN

CHAPTER FORTY-FOUR
REBIRTH

The Jungles of the Land of the Ceiba, *576* AD—*fifteen years after Topiltzin's return*

When Coyotl first saw them, his breath caught in his throat. He had not believed the stories being told in the Southland, stories that had filtered from the coast and the outland cities, stories that finally reached even the small village where Coyotl lived with his wife, his many daughters, and his many more grandchildren. He thought at first they were merely old tales resurfacing, the kind Coyotl used to hear during the years that followed the smoke of Cumorah's ascendance. At first, when the cold and the dark swept over the Southland there were stories Sky Dragon would return, that they would return, the Tolteca. They would come, choosing their day carefully. For a time, everyone seemed to wait. Coyotl knew better, but he never spoke his feelings, he never talked about them, or Tollán, or the rubberball game, ever again. He let himself meld into the jungles until no one would guess he had once been famous.

As the years passed, people finally accepted that the Fourth Sun, the golden age of the Tolteca, was lost forever, and the dark settled over the land of the *ceiba* like a long, cold winter. A winter without sun. A winter without gods. It was to last many years.

Most of the Mayan tribes had survived Cumorah. Sky Dragon had decreed that no one was to be compelled, and the Maya held back. A few leaders joined the Tolteca, but most had stayed behind, in the villages and cities, and when it was over, these survivors wandered in the dark of the storm like lost children. Some asked, *Who do we pray to, who will protect us?* They believed the Tolteca had taken their God and their sacred writings with them, their metal castings, their books—they left nothing behind. Therefore, the elders of all the tribes of the land of the *ceiba* gathered and made a journey to the north, to the ruins of Tollán. And there they prayed a new God would show himself. They sacrificed pigs and dogs and turkeys, but finally, one of the highland Maya stood and offered to sacrifice himself. He stepped into the fire, and the legends say that because of him, the whisperer came—the people now had a new God. He taught them the new way, the suckling, and the crumbling city of Tollán became a sacred place and the people thereafter called it Teotihuacán, the City Where Men Became Gods. And then it started just as it had a million times before, the sacrifices, then the blood wars—everything such that there was no other way, that nothing had been learned from the blood of Cumorah.

Coyotl had moved deeper into the jungle, then deeper still, until he finally found a place so miserable, so thick with vermin and crawling things he guessed no one else would want it. There he found a tribe of quiet Chontal-Maya who had probably lived here long before any empire. If Coyotl were to walk backward in time until he was past all known history and myth, he would find these same people—living high much as they did now. The deep of the jungle was a place where things never changed and he decided to grow old here, to enjoy what was left: simple things, quiet things.

But this morning, seeing what he did, for the first time since Cumorah he wondered if it might be possible—the tales they would return. He wondered if perhaps some of them had survived.

Coyotl was cautiously crouched on a hillock that overlooked one of the old Toltec roadways. If one wanted to plan a robbery, this was a choice vantage point. Of course, Coyotl had not robbed Mayan merchants in many years—that was a time of long ago. The only reason he had come this far out of his jungle was to find new seeds for the tobacco plants that had been lost in the heavy rains last season. He had decided not to venture into any of the Mayan cities, since he didn't want trouble. Despite the fact he had let his skin darken under the sun for many years, people still now and then noticed his face, the cut of his eyes, and asked from where he had come.

For that reason, he had decided to just wait by the side of the road here and spot any merchant who might be traveling with seeds to offer. He had been here for hours before he saw them coming, and now, suddenly he had forgotten everything. He crouched in the shadows, breathless, watching through the foliage as a caravan lumbered through the jungle passage. They were dressed as Pochteca, the ancient merchant-warriors of Tollán. They were lean, healthy Chichimeca, but they wore the feathered mantles, leather armor, and chest disks that bore the symbol of the seashell cut through the middle. That was the sacred spiral of the Nonaloca. It was the signet of waypoint, given to all warrior-merchants who traveled the caravan routes. Coyotl shivered. He had not seen that symbol since he had played the rubberball game so long ago. He moved in closer and near the roadway, he watched, amazed. It had to have been some kind of cruel illusion—Pochteca escorting a merchant shipment from the north. He stood there, mute and frozen, until one of the merchants almost knocked him off the road.

The young merchant paused. "Old man," he said, "you should not stand in roadways."

From the backpacks of one of the carriers, Coyotl touched a fine, feathered mantle, quetzal green. "This mantle, where did you get this?" he asked.

"Fine, is it not?" The merchant pried his fingers away. "But not for you, old man. We seek the cities of the Maya farther south."

"But where?"

"Due south."

"No, no, where are you from?"

"We come from the City of Serpents, the place called Tula."

"Tula? *Tula* is the Chichimec word for River That Runs Nowhere.

There is a river of that name. It lies not far from the ancient city of the dead, near Teotihuacán. Is this the place where one would find your City of Serpents?"

The merchant exchanged glances with the others and chuckled. "Where have you been living, old man?" he asked Coyotl.

"Me? Well . . . I live west of here. There, some leagues west."

"Nothing in there but stinking jungle."

"That and a few villages."

"You should leave your swaps more often, old man. Things have changed. You have not heard of our lord, the Serpent Plumed?"

Coyotl felt his skin crawl with quick fingers. He could have told them that not only had he heard of the Serpent Plumed, but once the dark shadow of its wing had crossed his face.

One of Coyotl's grandchildren, the small one, Turtle Runner, who had simply refused to stay behind, squeezed between Coyotl's disfigured legs to stare up at the merchant through his round, brown face, amazed.

"Who are they, Father? What are they?"

Coyotl didn't answer; he couldn't take his eyes off the smooth, well-made quetzal mantel. No one else made cloaks like that, not with that kind of stitching or the padded shoulders of refined cotton.

The young merchant chuckled. "We must move on, old man. Unless you wish to barter?"

Coyotl shook his head.

"I did not think so. Go back to your jungles and take your children with you. The roadways are too busy for you these days."

Coyotl nodded. He might even have made an offer for the cloak, but the only thing he could barter with would have been dirty brown grandchildren. He took Turtle Runner's hand, and both of them watched as the merchants passed.

That night, Coyotl sat in the hut of his eldest wife, staring blankly at the flame. He hadn't spoken all afternoon and she watched him, troubled. Emerald-as-the-Sky, full-blood Mayan, had been his wife for thirty and nine years, and she was still healthy and fat with pretty brown eyes.

"You are troubled," she said.

Coyotl looked up, his brow furrowed. "I must leave, good woman. I must go north—see of what this youth spoke, this place they call Tula. There were no cities in that place; it was desert land. Now they say a city lies there, with its lord. Merchant caravans with Pochteca passed this day through the jungles not far from us."

"Yes, I know. They are only stories. I have heard them myself."

"Why would anyone make up such stories?"

"Tricks. Merchants out to make money."

"Where have you heard these stories?"

"The village. They have been speaking of this fable for months now. You can even trade for trinkets—incense burners, bowls, cups. I have seen them. Even toys with little round feet."

"Wheels . . . toys with wheels. Why have I known nothing of this?"

"Because you never leave the house or the cornfields, Coyotl. You never go anywhere. The only people you talk to are your grand-children. How then should you know about things in the village?"

"You didn't think to tell me?"

"I did."

"Good woman, I would have remembered if you told me these things."

She stared at the fire, sadly. "I meant I thought about it. But I did not tell you."

"Why?"

She went on stirring the pot. "Because of this, because of this look in your face, because of what you are going to do now. Because, Coyotl, you would leave us should I tell you of these fables. You would go chasing after them!"

"Of course. But I will come back, Emerald-as-the-Sky. You are my life here, I have no need to chase dreams—all my dreams have been answered. But I must see this! I must at least see for myself what it is they speak of."

She nodded, but her eyes remained sad and distant.

He carefully touched her shoulder. Her face was old now, wrinkled up like his, yet these were the same young eyes that had helped him stay alive all these years.

"Emerald-as-the-Sky, you know I love you."

"I know, Coyotl."

"You know I would come back."

This time she didn't answer.

"I couldn't leave and not come back!"

"If you leave, Coyotl, they will take you. They've been waiting these many years for you. I thought . . . only in the last little while, I thought . . . perhaps they had forgotten you."

"Who?"

"The Nephalli. The Many Dead."

He pulled back, staring at her, feeling a light shiver across his skin.

She returned to lift the mortise stone to grind the corn. "I have packed dried fish and seedcakes," she said. "And some cocoa drink. Your favorite. You can find them in your old haversack."

He leaned forward and kissed her cheek, but Emerald-as-the-Sky just kept working.

<hr />

It had taken him thirty days to get through the jungles, moving as quickly as he could with his staff and knee braces. Coyotl's knees had been broken the day he last saw Topiltzin, but he had learned to move quickly with leather-and-wood braces, sometimes with the help of his unadorned staff, wreathed at the top in peccary leather for grip. When he was younger, he had forced himself to move at a run with his braces on, ignoring pain, and eventually the scars and gristle and bone in there had hardened, and he was able to hunt once more. Coyotl could still surprise an enemy that assumed he was no longer quick. He had kept his wind, kept his body hard and toned.

On this journey, he traveled through the jungles alone, following one of the old Toltec roadways. In the beginning, the roadway was broken and dirt-filled, but then he reached a crossroads beyond which the roadway had been repaired, the stone reset. He was able to make quick time to the passage of Manti. The last time he had seen it, the stones of the fallen garrison were such rubble it was difficult to scale, as though the canyon walls had caved in, sealing up the Northland forever. The garrison had not rebuilt, but the old Toltec highway had been cleared through the center of the debris.

Coyotl was careful not to let himself get excited. He just told himself all he needed to do was confirm his suspicions—that the desert remained a desert—and then he could return to his well-made hut and the soft red dirt floors and his many brown grandchildren. Live out the last of his days playing bean games with the village elders.

Coyotl stared in awe. He had reached the top of a manmade temple platform far enough north of the passage and high enough to provide a decent view of the Northland. The sky was blue and cloudless, and there was little wind. Coyotl had only one eye, but even as an old man, he could see farther than many of the young pups who hunted with him in the jungles.

The mighty plains of Otumba lay before him. The lake was still there, though it seemed to have moved. The lower beds that had once thrived on the outskirts of Tollán were now dry, merely patches of white sand, but farther north Coyotl could see the edge of the lake's green-blue waters shimmering. He could see the edge of islands that had to have been *chinampas*, for they were rich and green, yellow and orange. But what took Coyotl's breath the most was the far, faint image whispering from the ancient river the

Chichimeca called *Tula*—the River That Runs Nowhere. No longer, it seemed. He could make out the tips of columns. New stone. Someone was building a city. The rows of colonnades glittered, standing like sentinels in the plain. From a distance they looked like a stone army. For the first time since Cumorah, a city was thriving in the plains of Otumba.

He wandered down the slope of the temple mound and began walking along the wide, well-swept roadway. The sight left him dazed. How could this be? They had all been killed; they had been swept from the earth by the very hand of God.

Coyotl was so deep in wonder he barely noticed the sound of heavy footfall behind him; he went on walking until he was shoved out of the way.

"Move aside, old man, make way!" a strong voice commanded.

Coyotl stepped back from the road, then froze, watching them file past—an army marching toward the city in division rank, four abreast. They were returning from a far battle; they had been on the road many days. Their cloaks and armor were coated in dust. This was no small band—they stretched far up the hill in an ordered line. Yet what truly took his breath, what shook him to his marrow, were their breastplates, their cloaks, and the ensigns of their divisions, especially the foremost. It was high in the sun, riding on the back of a standard-bearer. Whitish gold in color, it was unfurled in silvered feathers whose streamers curled with the talons of the Dragon. That was nothing less than the very signet of the Sky Dwellers of Tollán.

"Oh, dear God," Coyotl heard himself whisper as if he were no longer in his own body.

They were splendid! They wore the breastplates, the helms, the feathered mantles of the protectors. They bristled with atlatls, with fine, burnished swords—not moonsteel, but deadly nonetheless, swords whose edges glinted from rows of razor sharp flint. Many of the warriors bore feathered headdresses, the signets of high knights, captains, warlords. Every so often, he caught sight of a manicured beard of war. Beards! He had not seen a beard in twenty-four years.

TOLTECA

So . . . they *had* returned. The Tolteca had returned to the Valley of Tollán, as though Cumorah had yielded her dead. A tear stung his lash, for in all his days he had never seen one survivor. Not one, not a single soul.

"Tolteca!" Coyotl suddenly shouted, beside himself. "Oh, Dragon Lords—mighty Sky Dwellers! Welcome, my brothers!"

One of them paused. Coyotl had expected that, for how many desert beggars knew the sacred names of the ancient dragons?

The warrior who stepped from the ranks bore the feathered plume of a captain. This was a division commander, and Coyotl shivered, for beneath the wood-and-bone helmet—which was fashioned as an eagle, with crafted silvered wings—were blue eyes. Blue eyes! And wasn't that a fine, carefully manicured black beard? The captain looked at Coyotl, wary. He bore a cloak of finely wrought quetzal feathers. From his shoulder pads, the talons of the Eagle coiled rich in quetzal feathers. He was shorter than the others, but well muscled, well fleshed.

"You speak the tongue of the ancients?" said the warrior, surprised. "How is this?"

"It is because I have spoken it from birth!" came the proud exclamation.

The captain narrowed a brow. "From birth, you say?"

"I speak it, noble captain, because it is my native tongue. Who are you? Where have you people come from?"

The warrior did not answer straight away. He first removed his helmet. Tangles of long, brown hair fell over his shoulders. It was the straight hair of a Chichimec, but the eyes, the beard . . . they were not Chichimeca—this was no less than the son of a blood Tolteca. The warrior was more than thirty years in age, which meant it could have been the son of someone Coyotl might have known personally. He had played many royal courts in his day.

The Toltec captain studied Coyotl carefully, noting his white hair, his single, green-blue eye. Coyotl had long ago stitched up his other eye, letting the eyelids grow together. He would never set

435

another glass eye in his head as long as he lived and still shivered from the sight of idols that bore them, particularly those of the Smoking Mirror, which now were everywhere.

"Nephalli," the captain whispered, "are you Nephalli?"

"That I am, my boy."

The warrior turned. "Summon Huemac!" he shouted. "Bring him, quick!"

One of the warriors stepped from rank and sprinted forward. The captain turned and lifted a finely crafted sharkskin flask from a shoulder sling. "My name is Sky Hawk," he said, prying open the polished gold lip and extending it. To see a captain's personal wineskin left Coyotl speechless, for one would never find such manners among the warriors of the Maya. He was getting more and more excited. Curiosity was now a fever in him.

"Care for a drink, my lord?" the polite captain said, since Coyotl simply stood there like a deaf mute. "You look weary, elder."

Coyotl's hands were tremulous as he reached for the skin. "Thank you," he muttered, then lifted the skin to his lips to drink. It was cactus wine, the *pulque*, but this was light, carefully blended Tolteca wine. The taste brought back memories of Tollán, of the high market of Night Butterfly.

"Tell me," Coyotl said, handing back the skin, "who is your lord? Who is king in this city you have built by the river that men have named Nowhere?"

"You do not know?"

"I travel from the far south. I have not seen this valley in many years. Once, long ago, it may have been my home, but I am now a stranger to these lands. People who have spoken of this city have told me only that the Serpent Plumed rules it. Is this true?"

The youth dropped the skin over his shoulder. "Yes, there are those who call him that name. Many also call him Son of the Morning."

Coyotl wondered what that could mean. He did know that on the morning after Cumorah there had been a single star in the sky, the planet-star—red as blood. Cumorah's plume covered the lands for many days, a long night of darkness that lasted almost a month, and it seemed the only star in the sky that whole time was the planet-star.

"As to myself," Sky Hawk added, "I just call him 'Father'." He smiled.

Four others fast approached. Coyotl saw by their bearing these were all commanders, though of differing dress. Only one of them was Tolteca, the rest wore the distinctive mark of Nomads, desert wolves, though their leathered armor and net-cloaks were far richer than ordinary wanderers' were. In front of the Nomads walked nothing less than a Toltec warlord. He was broad shouldered and somehow his gait seemed familiar. When the warrior was close enough to see his eyes, Coyotl felt quick fingers run down his back. Perhaps he had traveled too long, too far, perhaps he was hallucinating—everything, all of it might be just a dream, a comeback fit of too many mushroom voyages in his youth. That would be far easier to believe than what he was seeing now with his one good eye.

Long ago, when Coyotl was just a boy, in the company of his grandmother, he had once seen the Sky Dwellers fight. He had crouched, like a fox, well hidden in the bushes, and watched, breathless. He saw the gleam of their silver moonsteel swords; he saw the lightning streaks of their atlatls, screaming as the hollowed tips ripped through the air. They were flashing, terrible to behold. But what left the greatest impression on Coyotl's mind was the image of their commander, the young Sky Dragon, who was then king of all the Tolteca. Coyotl would not meet Topiltzin for some years, but on that day the Dragon of Tollán had stepped directly in front of Coyotl and for a moment, merely a second, he had looked into the bushes and cunningly met Coyotl's eye. His gaze was solemn, perhaps a bit surprised to find him, a small boy, looking back, and even though battle raged beyond, the Dragon smiled slightly before moving on.

Now, as Coyotl watched the warlord of these new Tolteca approach, he felt his breath catch in his throat, for this was the very countenance that had looked down on him that day. The warlord wore a brilliant, silver breastplate wrought with the Dragon's personal signet—the cross, painted blood red—the symbol of a Toltec king, a symbol feared by all who opposed the Voyagers, the Turquoise Lords, the sons of the One True God who was creator of all things. The warlord's light net-cloak fell from heavily muscled shoulders caped in brilliant, priceless blue-green quetzal feathers. He drew up before Coyotl, and the Nomad warriors spread at his flanks to stand at the ready. One of the Nomads was a tall, muscled killer who watched Coyotl with steeled indifference—this one, obviously, was the king's protector.

"What is this?" the warlord asked. "Why call me here, Sky Hawk?"

Coyotl truly questioned his sanity, even searching his memory: had he perhaps taken mushrooms recently? Could some *pulque* have been laced with the meat of the gods that he hadn't been aware of eating? Because it was all too insane. This voice, the words that came out of this young warlord, it was deep and gravely, it was the very voice of the mighty Sky Dragon, the seer who had warned his people from the Hill of Shouting when Tollán was empire. Surely, what had happened this day was that Coyotl had simply lost his wits. He shivered as if a cold wind had crossed him. The warlord who looked like Sky Dragon arched one heavy brow.

"You bring me for this? A wrinkled old man? He can barely stand up. What is your intent, Sky Hawk?"

"This old man is an elder speaker, Huemac! This is a Toltec, a Nephalli."

The warlord remained skeptical. "He is brown. Bent over. He looks Mayan to me."

"That is only his dress, Huemac. Look in his one eye, his good eye—see there? This is no Mayan."

Huemac leaned forward, studying Coyotl's eye, then stepped back and glanced to the other. "Very well, it is an old brown, wrinkled, bent over Tolteca. Should I dance about now? Run about waving my hands in the air? Sweep the path before him?" He snorted a guffaw. "You are such a dreamer, Sky Hawk—even if this beggar were Nephalli, what should it matter? We were bound to find one eventually."

"We have been fifteen years in this land, Huemac, and this is the first Tolteca we've found. Does that not excite you?"

Huemac shrugged, glancing again at Coyotl. "Depends, I guess. Who does he say he is?"

"My lord," Sky Hawk said, addressing Coyotl respectfully, "this is my elder brother, our Lord, Strong Hand. Excuse his abruptness, for I assure you he is as honored as I am to meet a true Nephalli. He means no disrespect. But if it would please you, elder Nephalli, we would like to know your given name and where you are from—where you were born."

Coyotl paused a moment, troubled. His mind raced. He suddenly realized even the one called Sky Hawk had a certain cut to his cheek, a certain angle to his chin that was unmistakable. Just now, the way his lip had curled in a half-smile, even the subtle jest in his words—it was all too familiar. The possibility of what he was seeing left Coyotl speechless. And their age—both of them close to thirty. Coyotl felt a flush of emotion.

"Dear God," he whispered, weakly, only to himself.

"What did you say?" Sky Hawk asked.

Huemac snorted and shoved Sky Hawk's shoulder, grinning. "The poor man can barely speak, Sky Hawk!"

"No, no wait. He speaks. Tell us, honored elder—speak your name and where you were born."

"Yes, do speak up, old man," demanded Huemac with a raspy growl. "The sun draws low in the sky! My army wishes to reach Tula while we are yet young!"

"I am Coyotl, son of Seventh Star. My home, once, was there, below. The city of Tollán."

Sky Hawk gasped. "Bite your lip, Huemac! His name is Coyotl! Coyotl of Tollán!"

Huemac tipped his head to one side, studying Coyotl curiously now, and that movement was one Coyotl had seen before, the expression, the scrutiny of his eyes.

"Tell us, Coyotl," Sky Hawk said anxiously, "did you—there in Tollán—did you play the rubberball game?"

Coyotl noticed they were all attentive now—waiting, poised, even some of the warriors still in rank had turned to watch. Asking that question—that question in particular—settled any lingering doubt. Coyotl understood with certainty to whom he spoke. He looked in the blue eyes of the one called Sky Hawk and a fresh shiver snaked beneath his skin.

"No," he lied, "I was a simple man, a plodder . . . a chili farmer, as was my father."

Sky Hawk was visibly disappointed. Huemac turned without saying another word and walked away, two of his Nomads following, but one of them, the protector, paused. The warrior lingered to study Coyotl a moment longer. He was quick, this one, this lean Chichimec killer; his job was to protect his warlord at all cost, and he had not missed a beat; he knew Coyotl had lied, but all he did was give Coyotl a warning glance before turning after his lord.

"Come to Tula," Sky Hawk said, still smiling. "Chili farmer or mighty warrior, you were once Tolteca! Our city is your city, by blood rites!"

Coyotl continued to shiver with emotion. He wanted to embrace the boy. How he wanted to tell him! But he only offered a weak smile.

The boy set a strong hand on Coyotl's shoulder. "You will be welcome; you will be honored, noble elder. When you get there, come immediately to the court of my father. Tell them you come as a guest of Sky Hawk."

He pulled a quetzal feather from his shoulder pad and set it in Coyotl's hand, curling Coyotl fingers about it in case he was too shaky to hold it.

"Use this if they doubt your word. Make your way to the palace of kings and ask for me."

"Why?" Coyotl stammered.

"Because I believe my father would like to meet you. It has been long since he has heard Nonaloca spoken by any but his sons—it would fill his heart to meet a blood Nephalli. You need not be afraid, he is kind really, quite kind. People do not understand him. Forget all these stories you hear. So then, elder Coyotl, my brother, good journey to you."

He patted Coyotl's shoulder warmly and turned.

"You must make him proud, Sky Hawk," Coyotl said in the last moment. The warrior paused. "Your father, I mean."

Sky Hawk smiled. "I try, old man." He left, his cloak flaring as he ran ahead to join the ranks, and when he was out of sight, Coyotl felt his heart sink a bit.

For a long time, Coyotl watched the warriors of this new Tollán pass—line after line of them, all fitted with shields, leather-and-cotton armor, cloaks, helmets. The foretold end of time—the resurrection of souls—would have left him no more speechless. Near dusk, he also watched a line of captives pass. Lengths of hemp bound them to each other, and though their legs were shackled, they were forced to walk quickly. He recognized them. They were Maya of the midland cities. Many were all dark priests, priests of the matted hair. In his life, Coyotl had never seen a Mayan Blood Gatherer hobbled. The new Tolteca warriors were not an illusion; these captives meant they had conquered the cities of Manti, which meant they now controlled the trade routes to the south—and that meant one thing, one certain and inescapable outcome. War. It would soon spread through the jungle like fires through dried brush. War was come. Blood had already begun to water the jungles of the Southland, and when it was done there would be enough to fill a lake. Coyotl shivered at the thought.

He turned to gaze at the city. It looked like a jewel in the valley below: white, polished stone and gold, glittering beneath the dying sun. Topiltzin had returned. He had built a rich city in the ancient valley, and had stocked it with warriors as deadly as those who had died at Cumorah. He had learned . . . nothing.

CHAPTER FORTY-FIVE
TULA

It was a night of celebration. Coyotl guessed the reason without hearing it: the armies of Tula had returned as conquerors. It was easy to learn what was happening; there was talk everywhere. Coyotl did not even need to ask questions, he simply wandered the streets and the marketplace, quietly walking through the plazas, listening.

The armies of Tula had destroyed the proud Maya of the midland cities that lay south of the passage of Manti. They had been called "midlanders," residents of the three cities that controlled all trade through the Petén. There were stronger cities of the Southland, the powerful Olmeca, the deadly *Itzá* mercenary warriors of Zarahemla who owned the jungles, and the night-stalking secret covenant of Gadianton Highlanders. But the midlanders had controlled the plains of Manti since Cumorah and it was hard to believe they were shattered. Yet, Coyotl saw spoils of war that left no doubt. He recognized gold and silver artifacts for which midlanders would have sacrificed their children, such was their value. There were also slaves. In a southern corner of Tula's market plaza, on platforms, Coyotl paused to watch a huddled group of what had days ago been Mayan royalty, the children and women of governors and high priests, now offered for bidding. A young Toltec warrior, his beautiful, dark-eyed Chichimec wife watching on, opened one girl's mouth to check her teeth as a greedy merchant watched with a broad smile. The warrior tore away the cotton blouse to measure the market value of her breasts.

He could only imagine how maddening, how utterly terrifying

it must have been for the greed-sodden midlanders to see this army of fresh, resurrected Tolteca in full colors marching out of the rubble of the Manti passage. As terrible as the coming of the end of time.

Yet the children of Tula were more than resurrected Tolteca. They were different. They were young, deadly, terrifying Tolteca—struck in the image of their namesake, but overlaid with the cold blood of predators.

In the marketplace were dancers. They moved with poetry; they flashed; they spun. As everything else here, they were a rich, fascinating imitation of the rites of jubilee that had once been practiced in Tollán. It was a brilliant adaptation, so skilled and crafted Coyotl almost wanted to weep. They were splendid. Naked, oiled bodies, moving through the night with cunning grace, with torches whose streaks of flame flashed like swords.

Everywhere there were warriors. Coyotl walked among them, dazed. The entire city was saturated with youth. There were very few old people, very few working citizens or laborers—this was a city of warriors and their women. Most were hard, lean, muscled Chichimec youth, some shorn, all bearing the signet of their knighthood, all carrying weapons, even in the city, atlatls slung over their backs, the ever present grim razor-swords. Coyotl could only imagine how such swords would work in battle, lined as they were with their teeth of surgeons' scalpels. Who had thought these up? They were terrifying even hanging from leathered hip sashes, and it appeared the custom was not to wash blood from the black obsidian blades.

Still, the prospect of seeing Topiltzin again brought a good feeling, a warm feeling. He almost wanted to run for the palace, wave his arms, and shout for Topiltzin. It had been so long. Why did he hesitate?

He wandered down streets and alleyways without deciding on a course of action, and found himself on the edge of a courtyard. Once again, he stared, amazed. This plaza was filled with platforms—rows and rows of racks, all of them lined with heads. Skull racks. The heads, without exception, all bore the matted, unkempt black hair of Blood Gatherers. Why did he feel his skin crawl? Surely this was just reward for the years of terror these priests had wrought, combing the jungles for children and young girls, taking them in cages, peeling their skin inch by inch over nights of horror unspoken. Yes, Topiltzin, yes, teach these bastards, teach them well. Let their stinking skulls dry here in the sun for all to see! Yet perhaps Coyotl had changed over the years, no longer the person who played the rubberball game and spent his days in taverns bedding whores and wagering on bean games, maybe something had weathered inside Coyotl. Standing here, he felt disheartened and weary. Because when would it end? When would it ever be finished?

The only thing left to do now was to get drunk. Coyotl found a *pulque* seller, a strange man with fat lips and beady eyes. The seller seemed so gleeful and there was something suspicious about him, but what did it matter? Nothing here was as it should be. It could all have been an illusion, the work of wizards. Coyotl procured several sharkskin bags of wine—expensive bags of wine that cost him every cocoa bean he had, but Coyotl didn't care about anything else, he needed only to ensure he had enough hard drink to get good and fatheaded. He found an alley where he was able to prop himself against a stone wall and there proceeded to drain each skin, one after the other.

Just beyond the alleyway was a fabulous palace. Night fires lit its frontal façade in brilliant streaks. Within, he could make out even more of the tall, painted warrior columns that were everywhere in this city—the sentinels of Tula. Chill your bones, they did. Pray your skin sticks to you in this place, by God.

Coyotl knew the building beyond the alleyway must be the royal palace, and somewhere inside its marbled hallways would be his old friend, Topiltzin.

"I suppose someone had to do it," Coyotl muttered, feeling warm enough in his skin, drunk enough after two full wineskins to speak aloud, even though youth passed by. None of them even gave him a glance.

"Someone had to shame these godless Blood Gatherers. Just wish it could have been someone else but him. Don't know why. Maybe it's because we all did enough. We died! Love of frogs, we all died, damn it! Isn't that enough dying for one God? Well?" He glanced to the sky. "Don't you think? Eh? Well, have your fine, new city. Who I am to question things? Muddled now, old and muddled. Brains dried up inside this thick-boned head long ago— so pay me no mind. No need to bother with what I say up there in your bloodied thirteenth Heaven."

Coyotl shook his head sadly. He turned and held his *pulque* skin upward, toasting the splendid palace.

"So be it, then! 'Mothers of whores' and all those cheeky grins—you show them! Piss on the desert! Piss on the sky! Piss on the moon!"

He stared a moment, breathing heavily through tight teeth. He wanted to scream. He wanted to stand and scream and shake his fists, but all he did was stare until the anger settled and sadness filled him.

"But Heaven light your shadow, Topiltzin . . . old friend," he finally said. He drank, tipping the sharkskin upward until the container was empty and he could cast it aside with the other two.

One left. One stinking skin of thick wine left. He tore off the lip plug and tossed it, littering the fine, clean streets. The well-swept streets you could eat off and still feel proud. When he sucked a long drag off this skin, it came 'round like being slapped in the face with a dead fish. This was strange *pulque*. In this city, who knows what they might put in their *pulque* wine?

"And who cares? Eh?" he said, almost shouting. "Who gives a rabbit's ass?"

Two youths, a lean warrior and his starkly beautiful wife were passing by and both chuckled at his musings. Coyotl toasted them as well.

"To youth! To not giving a pig's end-hole what tomorrow brings us!"

The warrior pretended to cover his wife's ears, but chuckled, looking over his shoulder as Coyotl drank heavily, squinting back through his one good eye.

He reeled, everything spinning now. He decided that tomorrow he would begin the journey back, return to the thick of his jungle, to the red dirt, the heat, the simple thatch hut and little wooden fence, the herds of turkey and peccary pigs, his dirty naked grandchildren, his hairless dogs, and most of all, Emerald-as-the-Sky. She was right; he shouldn't have done this. The only proper thing to do would be to return to the stinking jungle and let its peaceful night skies roll past day after day until old age settled through him like winter snow; until he started to soil himself; until the day he could stagger off with spittle on his fevered lips and find a place to watch the stars wink out came. Much easier just to die stupid.

Something *thunked* against the side of his head. He looked down. A brick. Coyotl went down on his side. Half conscious, he was dragged into the shadows of an alleyway. He looked up, vision blurred. Children—they were going through his robes. They had plucked the cocoa bag from his belt, realized there wasn't a bean left in it and tossed it aside, but before leaving one of them kicked Coyotl in the ribs as a farewell.

CHAPTER FORTY-SIX
THE SERPENT KING

I n the great stone palace of the Butterfly Dragon, Topiltzin watched as the priests and kings who ruled the midland cities south of the Manti passage were led before him. Their journey registered on their faces in fatigue and awe. Fatigue because they had witnessed the fall of their walled capitals at the hands of an enemy they thought was long ago laid to waste. Awe because they had just been led through Tula, down its streets, past the marketplace, through the wide Avenue of the Blue Stars, beneath the great serpent lintels into the palace of lawgivers. They gazed, stunned by the colonnades of warriors. Some of them even fearfully glanced at Topiltzin, where he sat upon a throne placed on a stone platform at the end of the hall. He was an unexpected king of such a splendid city. He wore only the garments of a priest, as his brother had done, the white robes, the simple, maguey cloak. The only signet he carried was the plain, unadorned staff Turquoise Prince had fashioned for him on White Woman's Mountain passage.

Topiltzin watched the midlanders shiver before him, but that is what they had brought on themselves. Months before, Huemac's scouts brought word to Topiltzin that their temples were so encrusted with putrid blood the smell filled the whole valley beyond the passage of Manti. In answer, Topiltzin unleashed his darkest passion. He had sent them his wrath. He sent them Huemac.

As the midlanders' king and a handful of advisors and princes were forced to kneel, Huemac stepped onto the platform and took position on Topiltzin's left, his skull helmet tucked beneath one arm. Topiltzin only glanced at him briefly. Huemac didn't expect more.

K. MICHAEL WRIGHT

Huemac spent his life on campaigns. He rarely slept a single night in the stone city his plunder had fed. In fifteen years, few words had passed between Topiltzin and his second-born son. Formal ceremonies, such as this, were the only times they were even in the same room.

Next to Huemac, Sky Hawk took his place as counselor. He pulled off his captain's headdress and shook out his tangled brown hair. Both he and Huemac had come directly from the march.

On Topiltzin's right was Turquoise Prince. Turquoise Prince no longer marched on campaigns, nor did he fight with the warriors of Tula. Instead, he guided every aspect of the growing city. He had begun the planning of the schools, the Calmecacs, fashioning them after the schools of old Topiltzin still remembered. He had overseen the building of the Temple of the Creator, even the training of its priests. If Huemac was his wrath, Turquoise Prince had become his artisan and priest.

The Lords of Tula were assembled, and it was time for judgment.

Topiltzin studied the king of the midlanders. He was a young Mayan warrior with long, dark hair, wearing a lip plug and gold earrings. Even bound, even beaten and taken in bondage, he still held himself regally. But then, the Maya were never lacking for pride. The midlanders were pureblood Mayan, descended from the ancient lowland tribes and they would have learned from their ancestors that no other race on earth was more pure, more filled with divine grace.

Among the captives were seven high priests, Sun Speakers, Balams, and they came with hair matted in blood; they came dirty, still dressed in the dark robes of their priesthood.

"First, the priests," Sky Hawk said. As counselor, it was his duty to oversee the judgments of war.

The captains of Huemac's Nomads prodded the captive priests to kneel before the throne. Huemac had oddly left his Nomads much as he had found them—desert warriors. They wore leathered armor, carried light shields of hardened wood and peccary skin

448

strapped to their backs. In fifteen years of bloodshed, they had become lean, powerful Slayers whose blades ever dried with the blood of their enemies.

One Nomad wrenched back on a priest's matted, blood-encrusted hair, forcing him to look up at the Lords of Tula. Topiltzin was always amazed at the eyes of these priests—always a cold, empty gaze.

"Your wish, my lord?" Sky Hawk said quietly, deferring to Topiltzin.

"Deliver them their souls."

It was quick work. Each neck was cut through with a singing backstroke of a Nomad's razor-sword. The cuts were smooth as planed wood. The Nomads turned and strode from the hall, taking the heads but letting the bodies drop lifeless to the stone as blood pooled from rhythmic spurts in the severed necks.

The eight Mayan nobles were prodded forward. They were openly terrified, most of them trembling, for they were left standing directly over the still bleeding humps of their priests' bodies.

"My lord," said Sky Hawk, "the governors of the cities of Manti."

Topiltzin looked upon the king and his governors. "Cut their bindings," he said quietly.

Expecting to be slain at any moment, the Maya watched amazed as Nomads instead cut the ropes binding their wrists and legs.

"There comes a new law to your land!" Topiltzin shouted in their native tongue, startling them as his voice echoed in the marbled walls. "No more shall you suckle the Night and the Wind! No more shall you spill the blood of innocents! From this time forth, you will offer only flowers, only butterflies, you will share the seedcake and the cactus wine, with these alone shall you honor our Creator. No other gods, no demons, no idols can stand beneath his shadow. From this time forth, those who do not bend knee to the Creator will die as the priests you see at your feet. Do you understand all I tell you?"

Topiltzin waited, It took them a moment to realize he was expecting an actual response, and after glances shared, all bowed their head in supplication.

"It seems proselytizing is not as difficult as they say, Father," Sky Hawk said behind Topiltzin's shoulder.

Topiltzin spoke quietly. "You have been brought as captives, but now you will walk free. The Serpent of Tula grants you life. You will be led to the gates of the city and released to return to the Southland. Once in your jungles, you are to spread my word. Tell all your peoples the Serpent Plumed, the Son of the Morning, Ce Acatl Topiltzin Nacxitl dwells here, that you have seen him and have heard his voice, that he has sent you to bring all the Creator's children a new covenant."

Even staring downward at the bloodied stone beneath his knees, the face of the Mayan king remained proud and stern, but the eyes could not betray his fear. Probably this man had never feared anyone in his life; it was a new feeling swimming through his veins right now, alien and strange.

Sky Hawk stepped forward. "To help you remember your visit to our city," he announced, "our lord brings you gifts."

The Maya waited, nervous. The Nomads who had beheaded the priests returned to offer each dignitary a severed head placed in a wicker cage with rope handles. The Maya were left holding them like children who had been disappointed at a celebration.

"Consider these precious gifts of our lord Topiltzin," Sky Hawk said. "Cherish them. Carry them with you wherever you go. The warriors and captains of my brother Huemac, Strong Hand, Lord of Tula who has leveled your cities, will always remember your faces. He has many eyes and his memory walks many days, never forgetting. If any of you are seen without our lord Topiltzin's precious gift, you will be slain. Go now. Take your gifts and return to the Southland. Proselyte. Spread the word: a new age has dawned; a new sun comes to the land of the *ceiba*."

They were led out. The king, the proud one, backed away, his eyes fierce, but when he turned, he looked utterly defeated, clutching his priest's head like a beggar's cup.

Topiltzin stood. The smell of blood in the room weakened him, left him weary and strained. Sky Hawk set a hand on his father's shoulder.

"I'm sorry, Father," Sky Hawk said. "One other matter to which you must attend."

"What matter is this?"

"I understand it is a civil judgment," Sky Hawk said, then motioned. "Bring her."

Concerned, Topiltzin sat back in his throne and waited.

This time it wasn't Nomads who walked into the hall; it was four city sentinels, the protectors of Tula trained by Turquoise Prince. Wearing the cloaks of Eagle Knights with red shoulder feathers, the sentinels were as devoted to Turquoise Prince as the Nomads were to Huemac. They ushered in a young woman.

She knelt gracefully. She wore tatters, her skirt ragged, her hair wild, but even so she was beautiful. She was Chichimec, no more than eighteen, with high, sharp cheekbones. She reminded Topiltzin a bit of his queens. He had not taken a companion in this new land, and each time he saw a young Chichimec woman, he felt such lingering sadness he always looked away. He missed them terribly. There were mornings when all he felt was the piercing emptiness of their being gone.

"What is this?" Topiltzin asked. "Why is this woman before me?"

"My lord," said Sky Hawk, "she is here at the request of one of Huemac's captains."

Sky Hawk motioned and one of Huemac's Nomads stepped from the back to stand near the woman. He removed his helmet and bowed to one knee.

"My lord," the warrior said quietly.

Topiltzin recognized him. He was one of the original Nomads, the youths who came from the deserts and had fought in every campaigns of the Northland. Topiltzin knew the man was at least a shield-bearer. He bore six quetzal feathers that hung from his shoulder, all confirmed kills of enemy captains. Topiltzin guessed he had been brought for some honor or decoration.

"Do I know you?" Topiltzin asked the shield-bearer.

"This is Salamander Dog," Sky Hawk answered. "He is second captain of the seventh century of Nomads. He serves you with honor and blood, Father. He is a noble warrior. This woman is the woman of Salamander Dog. Yet this woman was found with another. Even as her husband was at the fore of the battle, yielding his own flesh to the enemy's spear, at home, this woman lay with another in mortal sin. We have brought her before you for judgment."

Topiltzin was stunned. The blood of the midlanders was dark enough; he had not expected this as well. For the first time he noticed the girl's wrists had been bound so tightly that the ropes cut into her flesh.

Salamander Dog stood and looked up. "My honored lord, Serpent Plumed," he said, "I ask the judgment of your word."

Topiltzin noticed the young warrior's eyes did not turn in the direction of the girl. "Do something, Sky Hawk. What am I to say here?"

"Father, you have told us that should a woman commit adultery, should a woman bring shame to her husband and her family, that woman should be stoned."

Topiltzin was horrified.

"I said this?"

"Those are your words, Father."

Topiltzin knew that often he quoted as best he could the writings of the Old Ones, but surely he never said this. Topiltzin could no more have this girl stoned than he could stone one of his own daughters. It struck him that all his words, even careless ones, were being recorded—memorized or written down in the priests' glyphic, deerskin folios. Every word he spoke was law. He shivered. He collected himself and slowly leaned forward, studying the warrior and his young wife. They could not have been wedded long. Salamander Dog was a veteran, but his wife was no more then ten and six years. They were newlyweds.

"Salamander Dog . . ." Topiltzin said.

"Yes, my lord?"

"Do you want this woman stoned?"

The warrior did not immediately answer. It was enough hesitation to give his heart away, and his eyes had darted ever so quickly to the girl and back again.

"Yes," he said weakly. "It is law."

The girl began to cry softly.

Topiltzin turned to Huemac. He could no longer guess his son's thoughts and there were times when he was thankful he could not. He had spared Turquoise Prince the horror of bloodshed, but Huemac had taken the sins of his father without question and now bore the eyes of a stone killer, unflinching, as dark and empty as the night sky. Even Huemac, certainly, would not stone this girl.

"Huemac, he is your officer—what would you have me do with this woman?"

When they turned to him, Huemac's dark eyes left a faint chill through Topiltzin. "Why ask me this?" Huemac said, his voice washed and resinous from shouting orders. "You have given us a law. It is simple. If justice is to be served, then law must be answered. Otherwise, why do we behead the priests of the Maya? If we turn aside this law, then what others should we choose to ignore? Where would you have me draw the line, Father?"

Topiltzin stood from his throne and turned his back on the hall. He didn't want anyone to catch emotion in his face. What had he done? Not only his words, which hung over this poor couple, but also the eyes of his son. For a moment he studied the great stone wall behind the throne, painted in bas-relief, brilliant blues and reds—butterflies, all the butterflies that could be found in Paradise. One of his sons had painted it. Some of his sons were artists, others were Slayers.

"Turquoise Prince," Topiltzin said without turning. "What do you say?"

Turquoise Prince sat studying the warrior and his woman. Topiltzin knew if anyone could save the girl it was Turquoise Prince, who had a silvered tongue as gifted as his own. Unlike Huemac, Turquoise Prince took his time in answering.

"Our brother, lord Huemac, speaks true," said Turquoise Prince. "It is law. It was written in the days of our ancestors— adulteresses should be taken to the marketplace and stoned until dead, crushed."

Topiltzin slowly closed his eyes, waiting, praying.

"However . . . we are kings, and it is given that a king can allow mercy."

Topiltzin finally breathed, grateful. He turned to look at the warrior and his young wife. The girl's head was lowered, but there was a small spark of hope in the warrior's eyes.

"Sky Hawk?" Topiltzin said. "You are counsel. How shall this be judged?"

Topiltzin knew Paper Flower's second son was far too clever to have missed Topiltzin intentions.

Sky Hawk studied the two in the hall carefully. "Let us suppose Mercy answers this law. What should be done? The woman could not go unpunished. Perhaps she could be sent out from among us, banished. The priests and the people could gather along the Avenue of the Blue Stars, and she could be paraded, stripped of all but her undergarments. She could be spat upon, palms fronds could whip her, and she would leave Tula, never to look back. She would ever be exile, but would live another day. Sadly, though, I fear such judgment does not rest with us. Our lord Turquoise Prince speaks true, we can allow mercy—but we cannot grant it."

The warrior looked alarmed. Sky Hawk shook his head in emphasis.

"Mercy can be proffered of you alone, Salamander Dog. Otherwise the law must stand. Do you understand this?"

Salamander Dog nodded, though clearly he was struggling with Sky Hawk's words. "Yes . . . yes, I understand, my lord."

"Very well. You must speak your will."

He paused, his eyes briefly darted to Huemac, but Huemac did not move or blink.

"Salamander Dog," Sky Hawk pressed. "Do not look to your warlord. He has not brought this woman to the palace of the lawgivers. You must look to yourself. Which do you choose: mercy or law?"

"I . . . I choose to grant mercy."

Sky Hawk nodded to one of the sentinels. "Mercy it is. Take her away."

As the sentinel took the girl's arm, Huemac stood. He glanced at his father.

"My work is done here, Father, I will take my leave. Unless you would have me clean the blood off these stones and affix the heads of these priests back onto their shoulders."

Topiltzin hardened his gaze, but Huemac ignored him, brushing past his shoulder, dropping from the throne platform and striding across the hall, his cloak billowing. Topiltzin glanced to Sky Hawk.

"No worries, Father. He thanks you."

"Really? How do you arrive at this?"

"I know him. He did not want that girl harmed."

Topiltzin glanced to Turquoise Prince.

"Sky Hawk speaks true, Father," Turquoise Prince agreed, though his eyes did not confirm such. "Huemac knew his Nomads were watching. He needed to be strong."

Topiltzin nodded. "Well, I am not strong, I am weary. Goodnight, my sons." He took up the staff and turned to the back hallways that led to the inner palace.

☙☙☙☙☙☙☙☙☙☙☙☙☙☙

No sooner had Topiltzin left the great hall and started down the long pillared hallway toward his chamber than the little hunchback, Coxcox was at his side. Topiltzin guessed Coxcox had been standing in the shadows, listening to every word.

"I thought you were tending to the money changers this day," Topiltzin said.

"I have been," Coxcox said. "I've just come from there. Money changed hands, and then changed again, and so it goes."

Topiltzin smiled, shaking his head.

"Judgments are over now?" Coxcox queried. "It is done now?"

"Yes."

"Hard this time, all this. Hard, these things."

"Indeed."

"My lord, I have seen the marketplaces. Slaves there, many slaves. I know they are examples made, that it is necessary. It is true, then? The cities of Manti are no more? Has this happened?"

Topiltzin nodded, the dread of it settling over him. Even before Huemac had returned victorious, night after night Topiltzin was haunted by an old dream—the white eyes of the witch who had tended his poisoned wound so long ago on the celebrations of Night Butterfly of the last ballgame. In the dream, just before he would wake in sweat, the witch's raspy, whispery voice would echo in his head: *Do not journey to the land of the* ceiba, *Topiltzin Nacxitl!*

Now it was done. The gates had been thrown wide, the passage of Manti gaped, its fangs glinting with fresh blood. The Southland would soon spill its shadows across the plains of Otumba like a dark storm.

With a quick shuffle, Coxcox circled about his king until he was walking in front where he could cock his head back over his shoulder. Coxcox was a hunchback, and his left side was partially paralyzed. It left him dragging one foot, and even though he could move quickly when needed, his deformities made him—like Topiltzin—a monster.

"You are troubled," Coxcox puzzled. "Your brow is so heavy. What can I do? There must be something. Just to talk perhaps . . . just speaking of your worries will help. You think?"

"I should have never let him do it. The Southland can keep its shadows. I should have stopped him. I should have ordered him to stand down."

"But, my lord, you forget who he is. He has mastered war! You were a revered ballplayer, I know, and a knight; and even you were the king of Tollán! However, your son . . . why, your son has become the mightiest warlord to walk the land, there has never been a warlord as powerful as Strong Hand. He is cunning and practiced. He is able and swift. Perhaps we should trust him."

It was surprising how often Coxcox said things that took Topiltzin unaware. "I hope you are right, Coxcox."

"But I am right!"

Topiltzin just sighed, slowly shaking his head. "Before I left Paradise I told Paper Flower I would show them the way home. She made me promise that. She wasn't talking about the island. She was speaking of their souls. I have so tried to understand things . . . but I have let it go too far. I have failed her, Coxcox. I have failed them as well—I have even failed you."

"You cannot speak this way, my lord!"

Topiltzin glanced at him and smiled. "Never mind this, good friend. Just melancholy. Just a hard season in me, pay no heed." He stopped to stare at the entrance to his chambers. "Maybe all I need is to be alone for a while."

"You once told me when I was deep in despair that the light will never find those who hide in shadow. To find the light we must step out of the caves and dark places into which we crawl. The Creator will never come to these dark places. He waits for us to first come to Him."

Coxcox was wringing his hands; it was an old tic of his, wringing his hands as though he was busily creating something.

"Goodnight, Coxcox."

The little man nodded, turned to go, but then paused. "My lord . . ."

Topiltzin waited, his hand on the chamber door.

"You cannot save everyone. You cannot take sin. Teach them well. It is all you can do. Teach them light and hope and faith.

457

Those are your words. Maybe you need me to whisper your words back to yourself now and then. I will be close if you need anything. Goodnight, my king."

Coxcox turned and shuffled away.

Inside his chambers, Topiltzin quietly closed the heavy doors. He did not light any of the braziers, but it wouldn't have been necessary. Light from the fires of the celebrations danced on the walls as they spilled through the open portico. Topiltzin thought of drawing down the bamboo shades, making it dark, but they seemed to fit his mood, these fires. They were a little bit savage. He stared across the opening to the third steppe of the Temple of the Creator. Turquoise Prince had built it carefully, using the exact dimensions of the temple in Tollán. The lower tiers of the temple were already sheathed in gold. He wondered if Turquoise Prince had the talent not only to build a temple, but to find a Creator to dwell in it as well.

Topiltzin was suddenly drawn out of his daze by a small, soft melody, so sad and lost that it matched perfectly his heart, and turning, he saw the dwarf, the girl named Moon Child, playing her flute. Two of them had come sneaking into Topiltzin's chambers, perhaps had been watching him all this time. He guessed this was Coxcox's idea, sending them. With Moon Child was one of the dancers, Topiltzin's favorite, the little cripple named Widow Woman. Like Moon Child, Widow Woman was tiny, though she wasn't a dwarf, she was just small, as though she stopped growing when still a child. Her face was almost perfect, with a fawn's brown eyes, framed in long curls of black hair, and her tiny body was without flaw except for her legs. Widow Woman's legs were like sticks, so thin they were only bone, and it seemed impossible they would carry her, but they did. Widow Woman seemed always as if she were falling, but the little legs still carried her, wobbly, and she could dance like no one else. She came up to Topiltzin now, lifted

458

her arms.

He extended his hands and she took his fingers. Widow Woman turned slowly and together they danced to Moon Child's sad tune, a melancholy waltz about the chambers of the king.

CHAPTER FORTY-SEVEN
THE PRINCES OF TULA

Huemac left the palace and hurriedly stepped into side streets until he was sure he was alone. The affair in the hall of judgments had left Huemac angry, though he wouldn't have changed what happened. He was grateful the woman would live. So why did he want to smash his fists against the stone of the apartments here?

He had been heading to the western gate, where the high captain of his Nomads, Second Skin, would be waiting; but oddly, he found himself drifting. He paused to watch a woman as she rolled flatbread on a white stone. Something about her calmed the storms swirling. She was Chichimec, simply dressed, quiet and careful in her work. She was possibly older than Huemac, but her long, glistening, night-black hair that brushed her thigh as she worked left the illusion she was much younger. It left another illusion as well, the far sad memory he had held closest to his heart all these years.

Behind the woman was a stone fire where tamales were roasting. She was a vendor; a clay plate filled with cocoa beans sat in payment. Huemac pulled off his helmet and sat on a stone pedestal beside her. When she looked up, she paused a moment. It was clear she recognized him and she bowed her head, startled.

"I know you," she said, eyes lowered. "You are the prince. The one they call Strong Hand. Huemac."

He nodded. "Yes, but I have already filled my duties as a prince this day. I think I will be common for now. Just ignore my cloak and weapons. What is your name, good woman?"

"Wild Flower."

"A pretty name."

She slowly looked up, drawing a hand through her hair with a calm smile. "Thank you, my lord . . ." She paused, uncertain, then simply turned back to her work. This pleased Huemac. Women like this were not ordinary.

"Would you like a tamale?" she asked.

"No. But if you do not mind, I should like to watch you make them."

"You are saying you simply want to sit here, watching me make tamales?"

"If you do not mind."

"Well, no, I do not mind." She turned back to rolling the flatbread. "Though it cannot be much to watch."

He merely smiled. He was grateful she was mature enough to go on working, that she was comfortable even with silence. He couldn't help but stare at the curls of her black hair. When she leaned forward, doing her work, he could even imagine it was she.

"I have heard there will be much celebrating," the girl said as she worked.

"There will be. You should move your oven near the market. You will sell more that way."

"No. I like it here."

"Why?"

"It is a long story. You might not have time for it."

"I will make time."

She glanced at him and turned back to her work. "Well, I grew up near Tollán. When I was very young, only four, I used to come each morning with my mother to the artisan barrio. This part of Tula, it reminds me of those days, of my mother."

He stared past her. It was true, the murals of the apartments here were strikingly similar to ones he had seen fading in the ruins of Tollán.

"More," Huemac urged. "Tell me more, Wild Flower."

K. MICHAEL WRIGHT

Wild Flower did not know what to make of this, the Prince of Tula asking her to talk of ordinary things. She was hardly anyone to play court to royalty, but his voice seemed calm and even kind, so she kept working and continued her story.

"Well, for me they were bright days, those days—the smell of corn in the stone fire, seeing the same faces each morning. My mother called them familiar strangers, the people you see each day but never know."

She glanced at him. He was just sitting there, staring sadly at the sky, but he seemed to be listening so she continued talking.

"Then one day my mother and I came to Tollán and found it burning. When she heard that gathering had been called she dropped everything and ran for our village. I ran too. My legs were small, but I somehow managed to keep up with her. When we reached the village, she found my father had already left. He was half-breed, but he was Nonaloca by faith and he left with them. He never came back."

The prince's eyes seemed to darken. "He died with the Tolteca?"

"Yes. It was a hard time in those days—afterward. The fields dried, the canals no longer fed the *chinampas*, and it seemed it just stopped raining everywhere until by the next year there was only dust blowing. Many died. So that is why I come here each day. It reminds me of the times when my mother and I visited the familiar strangers."

"What happened to your mother?"

"She went after him."

"After your father?"

Wild Flower nodded, worried now she might say the wrong thing.

"You lost them both?"

"Yes. My father, my mother, my four brothers. I lost them all."

Something in his eyes changed; they darkened.

"That is a sad story," he said.

462

"I suppose we all have sad stories, my lord. Most of the people here, they will have sad stories. Why is it you ask me to tell you of these things? Your warriors are now celebrating throughout the city and you come to listen to sad stories of a tamale vendor?"

"You remind me of someone."

"Really? Who?"

"Someone I knew. Someone who will ever own my heart."

"And what was her name?"

He paused, reluctant to tell her, as if the name were sacred. "Obsidian Snowflake."

He stood, then pulled his leather pouch from his belt and dropped cocoa beans near her on the mat. It was far more than anyone would pay for tamales.

"But this is too much, my lord, and you have not even taken a tamale."

"These are not for your tamales. These are for memories." He studied her a moment longer, his jaw tight. "I will avenge them, good woman. I will answer their blood like an eagle taking a serpent; I will descend on them with all the fury of Heaven."

She was thankful when he finally turned and made his way through the streets toward the west gate. Still she shivered, because she knew he would deliver on his promise—she knew this because even as he walked away, shadows seemed to fall in at his wake. The blood of thousands walked with him. It was the blood of the Many Dead.

ᒒᒲᒒᒲᒒᒲᒒᒲᒒᒲᒒᒲᒒᒲᒒᒲᒒᒲᒒ

Near the western gate, Second Skin waited, alone. He calmly watched Huemac approach. He checked the shadows around them, ensuring no one watched. Huemac stepped up to his side and for a while said nothing, he just stared out over the desert beyond the gateway.

"Are the troops making ready?" Huemac finally asked.

"They are. They assemble now. If we moved in the night, we

could take and hold the southern gate of the city without bloodshed. It might give you a stronger position come the dawn."

Huemac continued to stare at the open plain a moment.

"No," he said finally. "No overt threats. When the sun rises, I want the Nomads waiting in the southern crossroads in full battle array. I want them where they can clearly be seen from the palace. But make no move, do nothing. For now, all we will do is let my brothers know the armies of the Nomads stand ready but a stone's throw from the city walls."

Second Skin quietly saluted with his fist to his shoulder, then turned and started his run into the desert to join his men.

◙◙◙◙◙◙◙◙◙◙◙◙◙◙◙◙◙◙◙

Sky Hawk had been searching the taverns of Tula for his brother, but without success. Back from a campaign, Huemac often dressed like a commoner and went with his hair unbraided so he could drink at the city's taverns and listen to ordinary lives—forget about bloodletting. His men would celebrate after returning home, but never Huemac. Each time they returned from campaign Huemac would descend into a darkness that was often frightening, and Sky Hawk had been always careful never to leave him alone the first night.

Earlier, when Huemac had stormed out of the palace of the lawgivers, the dark was quickly gathering in his eyes and Sky Hawk was desperate to find him. Huemac had effectively slipped into the shadows. Something was weighing on him like never before.

It had been much the same after the last campaign, fought in the lowland deserts. Sky Hawk searched for hours before he managed to track Huemac into the foothills of Smoking Mountain where the warlord had made camp, alone. Huemac tolerated Sky Hawk, let him remain, but said very little. Sky Hawk was fine with silence; he just stayed near his brother, tended the camp, caught a few rabbits for braising. It was three whole nights before Huemac spoke.

Huemac sat stirring the fire, prodding dying embers to life.

"Sky Hawk, what have you been thinking all these nights? You do not speak at all."

Sky Hawk shook his head, smiling. Of course it was Huemac who had not spoken, and they both knew that. Yet, Sky Hawk at first tried to avoid the real reason for Huemac silence.

"I have been troubled," Sky Hawk said.

"By what?"

"Age, I guess. It seems we are getting so old."

"This is impractical. Why worry of that?"

"Thirty and one years. I never imagined I would become this old."

"You keep your face behind a beard, how would anyone even notice?"

Sky Hawk touched the corner of his eyelid, pulling on it. "Here, look: wrinkles." He pushed his finger against the middle of his brow. "And this one, this one especially."

That should have brought a laugh, at least a smile, but Huemac only stared at the campfire. The sadness in him seemed to cut like spears.

"God, Sky Hawk, they were so young. They were boys. We killed boys."

Sky Hawk glanced down. In the outland days before, they had pursued a desert band of sorcerers. The priests were fast. They moved with the speed of blood eaters; they were swift and shadowy.

Huemac, Sky Hawk, and seven carefully chosen Nomads, the lean, cunning Second Skin among them, paced themselves, tracking, always at a steady run—never slowing, crossing the long, flat deserts with its deadly bitch sun. Soon, they had shed their armor, shields, everything but their swords and water skins, and they ran without stopping for three days before they closed on a canyon where the wizards were trapped.

The priests and their protectors outnumbered Huemac's small party six to one, but without pause, Huemac had his men spread out, blocking any escape.

"Submit or die!" Huemac commanded, even though they were sweated and exhausted. The weary Tolteca must have looked easy prey.

The sorcerers attacked with fury.

Huemac eased back onto one leg and began to slay. At his side, the terrible sword of Second Skin sang like a bird of prey. Blood sprayed like rain. The Tolteca fought until none of the sorcerers or their protectors were left standing. Only then did anyone notice who they had been fighting. There were seven dead priests. The rest were boys, some no more than ten and three years. Most probably, they had been slaves. Their lives had been short, they had served the terrorist cult, they had been forced to submit to humiliation and torture; and now, instead of being freed by the Strong Hand, the Prince of Tula, they had been slaughtered by him. Huemac stared in horror.

That night, sitting near the campfire in the foothills of Smoking Mountain, Sky Hawk could remember the terrible weight of sadness in Huemac's gaze as he stared across the fire. The eyes of Huemac were so often fierce, deadly. Before combat they were as black and empty as a winged predator, but there were times, kept only to himself and a few trusted, when Huemac's eyes were like this, filled with pain beyond bearing.

"There was nothing you could have done," Sky Hawk said. "They looked as grown warriors, it was sorcery. You cannot take this blood on yourself, Huemac. It was not your fault."

Huemac tossed his stick into the fire. He had never spoken of it again, but Sky Hawk knew he had taken it deep, as he did all the blood of innocents, whether they had been caught in crossfire or trapped in burning cities. Somewhere inside Huemac, the blood of innocents constantly wove a dark and terrible web.

And this time, they had returned from a heavy, blood soaked campaign beyond the narrow passage in the jungles of the Southland where Huemac had left no less than three cites laid waste and burning to the ground. Nothing was left of them, no children ran in their streets, no merchants plied their wares, no priests suckled the blood of sacrifice.

Sky Hawk continued through the streets, weaving among the

celebrants, searching for Huemac until it was deep into the night, until it was nearly dawn.

Sky Hawk finally climbed onto the parapet of the southern wall, the wall that faced the lake and the *chinampas*. It was a night of new moon and the sky was dark. Cloud cover left it even darker—this was what Sky Hawk called thick night. It seemed Huemac always returned to Tula on a thick night. Either he timed everything carefully, or, what Sky Hawk guessed was more likely, the skies, the air, nature herself somehow connected with his spirit. When Huemac returned from battle, the sky would sizzle in fingers of dry lightning under cloud cover that was always thick and slid through the night uneasy. And not without cause. Huemac and his Nomads had become leopards; they were supreme hunters and now wild, nothing like the city's builders or artisans.

Peering through the night, Sky Hawk saw something. Movement. He shivered; he knew what it was. Nomads could move in thick night like the dead, like shadows in shadow, but Sky Hawk had learned to see through shadow. This was the reason Huemac could not be found. He had ordered the Nomads to assemble. More than that, he had ordered them to gather at the southern crossroads, not far from the city. He knew what this was, what Huemac meant. It was a challenge, it was a spear broken and thrown into the dirt.

Chilled, Sky Hawk turned and climbed down from the wall, dropping the last few feet to the ground in a crouch. When he stood, he was shocked to find Huemac there, alone, watching him coldly. It wasn't easy to take Sky Hawk by surprise, but Huemac had acquired the very shadow of the night. Sky Hawk studied his brother's eyes.

"You will either be with me or not," Huemac said. "I leave it your choice."

Sky Hawk stared back, troubled. "I understand."

"I can do this with the Nomads alone. You decide if the Wind Sign Knights, the Shark Knights, the Eagle Knights stand with us. I do not know if they would follow me without you. I doubt it, but that will not change my resolve. It is done, it is decided."

Huemac studied him a moment longer, then turned and strode away. That last look had almost been a plea; it was as close to asking Sky Hawk to join him as Huemac would come.

Sky Hawk shivered. He didn't want to see the future right now; he didn't want to know what would happen, what would become of them. In fact, Sky Hawk had stopped wanting to know the future from the time they had first stepped foot in the jungles of the Southland. Up until that point, Sky Hawk had always been sure of himself, certain of his path. It seemed simple, it seemed the laws were written and the words were spoken plainly, and he had filled his life with them. By following law, even the killing of those boys in the canyon was justified. It was sad, it was a sick feeling to see them lying there slaughtered, but it was law. Law held true path. But the day they crossed the narrow passage into the jungle, everything changed. Sky Hawk had tried to fathom it; he had searched his soul for an answer. There were no answers, there was nothing tangible to see, there was no more than a whispering wind. Yet everything was different. Law had just stepped sideways.

Sky Hawk noticed the cloud cover was moving; dark lines of it now streaked past the few stars still visible. It was restless—connected like blood and flesh to Huemac's spirit.

෴෴෴෴෴෴෴෴෴෴෴෴෴෴෴෴෴෴

Coyotl awoke with the worst headache of his life. He pulled himself to his knees and leaned against the stone beside him. It took him some moments to place himself. Everything was strange, every sound, every smell. Worse than that, pain pulsed though his head with hammer blows. Only as an afterthought did he remember where he was. The city of warriors, built on the River That Runs Nowhere. His fingers tested his skull. He remembered being robbed, the children of these predators with their well-aimed stones. Coyotl determined the hammer blows of pain were nothing to do

468

with the children. It was the *pulque*. Such a strange, thick *pulque*. He had drunk a good deal of it as well. Too much *pulque*. So much it wanted to pry his head open, split it like a coconut, and spill his brains all over the street.

He wanted to puke as well, puke into the gutters, puke all over himself, and it welled up, almost to his lips before he forced it back. Coyotl had maybe become a febrile old man, but he damn well was not going to puke it. He still had some pride. When he looked up, he was surprised it was not even dawn yet. These were the fingers before dawn. The only reason it was so dark was the cloud cover, like a storm, but lacking wind. It seemed strange.

Surely the celebrants had gone home to have sex or had passed out, or had been beaten senseless, like happened to him, but the city was uneasy, left with a strange, methodical quiet, a kind of hushed apprehension. The streets were oily with it. If he had been pressed, Coyotl would have said spirits walked here, the Many Dead, legions of them.

He gazed down the alleyway and saw the far torchlight of the palace, and only then did he remember his sadness of the night before. The melancholy that had overcome him was still with him, though this strange feeling over the stone city left him oddly curious.

That was nonsense, of course. It was still prudent to head back. Best even to start out while it was still dark, get at least clear of the city before the sun bore down on his headache. That would be merciless. The only salvation was going to be a lot of walking and a nice sweat working that could cleanse the thick *pulque* from his blood. Best he get on with it, so he pulled himself to his feet and grimaced. His knees throbbed. Coyotl had learned all these years to ignore everything and plod on, and that is what he did. He made his way through the hard stone streets, not even thinking about Topiltzin in his palace because that would trouble him deeply. Coyotl just fixed upon one task, a simple task: to remember the way out of this damned cunning, cruel city. He was passing row after row of apartments here. He hadn't seen this much dressed stone in thirty years, and it smelled of living people. It should have made him want to dance, but it just made his heart that much heavier.

Finding his way out took longer than he expected. He had wandered into a twisting street that left him disoriented. In Tollán, the streets were carefully matted across the desert in patterns of straight lines, north to south, and west to east. The cities of the Maya were similar, cousins, because many of the artisans who built those old cites were the same who had traveled with the Tolteca north to create the city of reeds by the lake. Tollán was precise; its streets mirrored the stars. Here in this west end of Tula the streets curled and twisted like a serpent. That was somehow fitting for Topiltzin's city.

When he finally reached the long wall that spanned the city's gateway, Coyotl had already walked so much the ache had been worked out of his deep bone, into the tissues of his knees. It had turned from throbbing pain to shooting pain, but that was something of an improvement. Life was all about pain: dealing with pain, living pain, making pain, and making pain go away. Coyotl paused a moment, wondering if he should perhaps snag a few hot drinks before starting out.

Then he noticed something. Movement, a lot of movement. For this time of morning, just before the actual dawn, in the last breath of darkness, and after a long night of unabashed celebrations as he had witnessed the night before, a city like this should be slumbering almost in a stupor. It would have been a good time to attack, if that were an objective. The main gate of Tula was active with swift, calculated movement. What was strange about it, what puzzled Coyotl, was its quietness. Listening, one might think the morning was ordinary. Something was up. Perhaps he should not be in such a hurry to move on. Perhaps it might be better to disguise himself and just filter into whatever was going on beyond the gate. He already guessed it was an army forming, and armies were complex animals and Coyotl was not without his old tricks. It wouldn't be difficult to become one of the baggage carriers, one of the workers, one of the vanguard merchant attendants. He could be a whoremaster, a procurer of sour wine; he could be virtually *anything* and no one at all would notice him, for Coyotl was just a crippled old man who would generate no interest.

Coyotl cleared his head as best he could, and though the headache still hammered, though his legs were still stiff, he nonetheless straightened himself up and walked purposefully up the street toward the activity at the gate. Coyotl knew exactly what he was doing. There was hardly a trace of the limp in his legs; his back was straight as though he had gained some fifteen years in a blink.

▩▩▩▩▩▩▩▩▩▩▩▩▩▩▩▩▩

Topiltzin had not slept. He knew. He had known since the Nomad armies returned from the passage of Manti. Dawn was not far, another degree of the sun at most, and yet it might have been the darkest hour of night beyond the portico. He had killed the fires in his chamber long ago and had for a time stood in the dark, studying the plains near the southern crossroads. He didn't need to see through shadows to know what was out there. He should have forbid any contact with the Southland. It should have been the first law he uttered, the first thing written, unbendable: never restore the narrow passage. Leave the garrison of Manti slumbering in its dark, burnt-out ruins.

He felt Turquoise Prince enter the room. He didn't even turn, just continued to stare into the night as Turquoise Prince moved up near his shoulder.

"My father once showed me the ancient books," Topiltzin said, "the writings that came from the Land of the Red and the Black. I touched their plates of gold, and eventually I learned to read them. They amazed me. The very blood and spirit of everything we were had been pressed into sheets of gold as thin and whispery as dried leaves.

"In one of these ancient books I read of a great sky speaker. He was legend, he was mighty and he led his people out of slavery—he

471

gave them purpose, he made them great. Once, to show them true passage, this sky speaker lifted a brazen staff that bore the image of our people: a serpent with wings. It spoke to each soul who looked on it. For some, it was a healing hand, a touch like a comforter, a light that filled them with awe, giving promise. Yet to others, it was the serpent's whisper of death, as quick and as absolute as stepping into the sun. And whether a person saw the healing hand or feared the sting of death was not determined by this sky speaker, this prophet, as holy as he was, neither was it determined by the staff he lifted above his people—it was not even determined by God. What each person saw was the light of his or her own heart.

"I fear that is what is going to happen now, Turquoise Prince. What comes next will be like what happened when the sky speaker lifted his staff over the heads of his people. I do not fear the staff, but I do fear what is in our hearts, what we will see when it is lifted."

Turquoise Prince stared into the darkness for a long time, reflecting on his father's words. "We can stop him, Father," he finally said.

"You really think he can be stopped?"

"With a word. Your word. He listens to you. I think he listens to no one else any longer, but he still listens to you."

Topiltzin tightened his jaw and shook his head. "You must confront him. Alone. Without me, Turquoise Prince."

"But, Father, if this troubles you so, if it leaves you such apprehension, how can you possibly trust what I might say?"

When he turned, Topiltzin was shaken by the fact that nothing was left in the deep blue eyes of Turquoise Prince any longer of the small child with the shock of white hair who used to run from his mother and chase the curls of waves. The little boy was gone, he had finally and truly gotten lost in the waves, gone forever now.

"My lord," Turquoise Prince said, "you are still king here."

"No. I was never a king—even after they made me one. You go, Turquoise Prince. You be there in the hall of judges when he comes."

"And what would you have me do? If I stand against him, Father, there may be blood in the streets of Tula this day. Civil war."

"You must do what is in you, my son. You must speak from that place where the sprit and mist of your heart lives. And I know you; I know you could never do otherwise, for you bear the heart of Paper Flower."

Turquoise Prince stared past Topiltzin's shoulder to the desert. The sun was spilling into the morning sky and Huemac's Nomads covered the plain. The deadliest army to ever walk the desert was now coiled beyond the road that led to the southern gate.

"This is your land now," Topiltzin said. "My time ended long before we journeyed to this place. But know well your choices. If you choose to stop him, you must do it now, this day. The cities of Manti will be forgotten. They were greed merchants, despised by all; their deaths need not be avenged. But if Huemac turns his armies south once more, time will shift and nothing we do will ever turn it back."

Turquoise Prince looked one last time in his father's eyes, and turned with a flair of his cloak. He had made his choice, his resolve was firm, but Topiltzin could not guess what it might be.

⊡⊡⊡⊡⊡⊡⊡⊡⊡⊡⊡⊡⊡⊡⊡⊡⊡

Outside of the palace, four of the firstborn, all Sky Dwellers, were waiting for Turquoise Prince. They bristled arms and armor. One of them was Moan Bird, who watched Turquoise Prince approach them from beneath a plumed helmet.

"Has everything been prepared?" Turquoise Prince asked.

"As you instructed, the second army of Tula is assembled before the southern gate. The sentinels have secured the city streets."

Turquoise Prince nodded and kept walking. The other three fell in behind as Moan Bird walked at his left side. They made their way toward the palace of the lawgivers in the center of the city. Civilians watched them in awe. By now, there were no secrets; everyone knew the two Princes of Tula were about to clash.

"When he comes," said Turquoise Prince, "he will come with

few of his warriors. He does not fear us. I want you to seal the route behind him, move sentinels in place to block the streets and once he is inside the hall, surround it."

"But surely he will realize he is walking into a trap."

"I would lay no trap for him, Moan Bird. He is my brother."

"Then why hem in his flank?"

"As insurance."

As they turned one corner, a corn vendor scampered so quickly that his stand overturned and corn rolled beneath the boots of the Sky Dwellers as they passed.

Coxcox had known something was wrong all night. He had tried to watch Topiltzin closely, but Topiltzin had withdrawn to his chambers.

That was not all, however. As the sun rose, Coxcox quickly learned the two armies of Tula, the Nomads and the Sons of Topiltzin, now faced each other at the southern serpent gate. He hurried quickly through the city streets, keeping to himself, keeping to the shadows. Inside the city, the sons of Topiltzin, the Sky Dwellers, were everywhere, as were the sentinels of Tula, the enforcers of law.

Coxcox realized what was at stake. This was to do with the passage south; this was to do with the ancient homelands.

Coxcox was descended of very superstitious people. But the old ones never lied. Everything the witch speakers told him had come true. One thing they had always promised: the Southland was death for the Tolteca; it always had meant death.

Coxcox shivered as he hurried for the palace of lawgivers. He had seen the protectors move into the great hall. They were the personal captains of Turquoise Prince, named after their ancestors: Sky Dwellers. The hall was filled with them. Now Coxcox saw Huemac striding toward the palace. Huemac came not with a hundred, not with fifty; he came with only his first captain, the lean hunter named Second Skin, and two others, both of them tall, deadly Slayers.

Huemac walked through the streets of Tollán with only three warriors! He walked with purpose and intent, as if he owned Tula, as if the shadows themselves should flee the echo of his boots. City dwellers scattered, running. Panic was spreading, but the sentinels and the warriors of the second army were everywhere, and Coxcox noticed how they had quietly closed off the path behind Huemac, sealing him in, leaving him separated from his loyal Nomads.

Though sentinels surrounded the hall, Coxcox was easily able to slip through them. He could have walked up and demanded entrance—Coxcox was well respected. Topiltzin had not just made him a manservant; he had given Coxcox almost the full powers of a governor. He also knew Turquoise Prince and should he have asked, it was possible he would have been turned away, told this was a meeting of the Council of Seven alone. Therefore, Coxcox simply did not trouble himself with asking permission. Instead, he slipped beneath the cave-like tunnels that laced the underground of Tula and made his way toward the underbelly of the great hall. Hurrying like a rat, moving at a brisk crawl with his bad leg catching up, in little time Coxcox emerged under the throne platform. Here small porticos had been hollowed, so small a normal-sized person would have to crouch, but just right for Coxcox. He was able to climb onto the hollow portico of the upper platform, and from there, he had a perfect view of the great hall. The sound would be superb, for the acoustics were marvelous. He couldn't have gotten a better view if he was had been riding the shoulders of Turquoise Prince who now stood in the center of the hallway. The prince's warriors, the Sky Dwellers, and all the firstborn were gathered as well. They lined either side of the hallway, nearly as imposing as the great stone statues that faced east painted in their brilliant colors and casting long shadows from the tripod braziers.

Coxcox watched, breathless.

Huemac entered the hallway. As he walked into the center of the chamber, the only one who followed was his first captain, the one named Second Skin. The other two halted at the palace entrance, standing there as though they were hemming in the rest, even though they were only two, even though sentinels had closed rank in front them.

◊◊◊◊◊◊◊◊◊◊◊◊◊◊◊◊

Huemac felt oddly calm as he entered the great hall of judges. Everyone now knew the Nomads had assembled in the plains south of the city. The city was thick with Turquoise Prince's army, as well as city sentinels. He briefly wondered how long the Sky Dwellers would last against the Nomads, but didn't let himself think of it. It was impossible that could happen. Surely, no one here was foolish enough to challenge him.

Inside the chamber, Turquoise Prince and his Sky Dwellers watched silently as Huemac made his way through the colonnades. In the center of the hall waited the Council of Seven, Turquoise Prince standing in the middle. Sky Hawk, one of the named Seven, stood off to the side. He had not taken position by Turquoise Prince, and that said something; it did not reveal his hand, but it at least spoke reservation.

Huemac drew up directly opposite Turquoise Prince. Second Skin had dropped back, taking position behind Huemac's flank, paying respect to the firstborn. Second Skin rarely spoke three words at a time, but his countenance did not need elaboration. His face was chiseled, rough, the long braids of his black hair dropping over his muscled shoulder. Unlike the splendid cloaks and feathered armor of the Sky Dwellers, Second Skin wore battle-scarred peccary leather.

Huemac knew there were formidable opponents in this hall. He knew his path out of it had been blocked. Though he did not believe they would oppose him, briefly he wondered how many would be left standing if this turned wrong. The games of Paradise were a far memory, but even then, none of them had been able to topple Huemac. He put such thoughts aside. That would be impossible. It could not happen here.

Huemac briefly caught Moan Bird's eye; there seemed uncertainty. That was curious. It meant Turquoise Price had not revealed to them what he intended to do here. Sky Hawk had revealed nothing to anyone. All of them, it seemed, were keeping their choices to themselves.

Turquoise Prince watched Huemac calmly, then finally spoke. "I noticed this morning that the Nomads were gathered in full force beyond the city gates."

"And I noticed the Sky Dwellers and all of the sentinels have gathered within. Not to mention our brothers in this hall. It seems we have a situation."

"It does, my brother."

Huemac tossed a fanfold map onto the floor before them. Turquoise Prince paused before he looked down and when he did, he scanned the painting only briefly. Huemac had spent years finding the map. He doubted Turquoise Prince even understood how rare it was. Few of Huemac's brothers knew that Huemac could even speak the Mayan tongue, let alone that he had learned to read the glyphic scripts. Huemac drew his sword and slowly placed its tip on the map, over the sacred symbol of the city of Zarahemla. It was near the coastline of the Yucatan and its symbol was a plain cross, the tip pointing downward. The symbol supposedly represented the Star Cross of the night sky. The Maya called it the Homeland Star.

"Zarahemla," Huemac said.

"I noticed."

"The city of our fathers, of our ancestors. Our home."

"Not our home, Huemac, their home—the home of the Tolteca. We were born on an island, east in the sea where our mothers still wait for us. That is my home. It is yours as well, in case you might have forgotten."

Huemac narrowed his brow, but had no words.

"Now, this sacred city, this Zarahemla, have you noticed how it lies far from the narrow passage? That it lies deep in the Southland?"

"Of course."

"Then, if you intended to reach it, that would mean crossing through the heart of the jungle, through the lands of the Olmeca and the Lords of *Itzá*."

"You grasp of geography is impressive."

"And are you telling us you still intend to take this city in one single campaign?"

"I will take it, and I will need only one season."

"Without having any idea what might be waiting for you in these unknown jungles? How many armies, how strong the Mayan nations are going to be once you draw them out?"

"They are divided."

"That is not what my scouts have told me. My scouts are merchant-warriors, Huemac, Pochteca. Their lives depend on knowing these jungles; they do not make mistakes."

"Have they told you the armies of Tikal covet the trade routes along the coast? Or that the highland Maya routinely sack their jungle caravans? Or that Zarahemla relies on mercenaries who honor an uneasy alliance with the Olmeca? All of them, these 'Mayan nations,' as you call them, are allied by one thing: *greed*. Not blood, not land—greed, pure and simple. When I break the back of the Olmeca, the jungle mercenaries and the Highlanders will fold like spanked children."

"So you say. But remind me, Huemac, just once more—the Olmeca, they have how many men who can be deployed against your thirty thousand Nomads?"

"Numbers are not significant. They never have been. The battle, my brother, belongs to God."

"And He answers to you now?"

Huemac tightened his jaw, trying to keep his temper in check, even though it flickered at the surface like fire running through oiled water. "Tell me, good prince," he snarled, "how many times have you led men in battle? Tell us all how many armies you have destroyed! How many cities you have crushed!"

TOLTECA

Turquoise Prince briefly glanced at Second Skin. Second Skin had not so much as blinked; he could have been stone, he could have been one of the colonnades. Huemac felt his anger rising. Then, oddly, something in Turquoise Prince's gaze softened. Turquoise Prince paused to look down at the map and this time he actually studied it, looking not just at Zarahemla, but also the passage north, the coastline with its ring of Mayan cities.

"These jungles," Turquoise Prince said, "even on your maps they are dark, Huemac, even the artisans have chosen dark ink. I believe I know why: it is because something lives in here, something waits. I am told there is a place you can hear it, like a heartbeat."

"What is your point?"

Turquoise Prince drew his own sword, and as Huemac had done, touched its tip against the map, but in a different place than Zarahemla—he touched it to the center of the jungle.

"Cumorah," Turquoise Prince said, and when he looked up, his eyes flashed.

Huemac was stunned.

"Am I right, Huemac? Is this Cumorah?"

"Yes . . ."

"These people, these Maya—they watched our grandfathers die there. They watched them die and none of them lifted a hand, not one tribe."

Huemac shivered. He realized that all of them, the Council of Seven, even the Sky Dwellers—all of the firstborn were watching him, but now with something altogether different in their eyes.

"Go then, Huemac," Turquoise Prince said. "I send you to answer the blood of our people. This beast whose heart still beats in the jungle—find him, slay him. He has a name. They call him Smoking Mirror."

Turquoise Prince turned and strode out of the hall. Several of the Seven went with him, their cloaks billowing, but others—Sky Hawk, Seven Macaw—stayed.

"We march," Sky Hawk said. "The Eagle Knights, the Seashell

479

Knights, the Wind Sign Knights, we join you."

Huemac felt himself trembling. He hadn't known what to expect this day; he had come here for at least a bitter argument. Now, when he turned to the rows of the Sky Dwellers, they had all lifted their fists to their shoulders. They were one with him, and almost it left him uncertain, it left him feeling a shadow of doubt.

CHAPTER FORTY-EIGHT
BLACK WATER

In the season of the owl, when the moon was in its second quarter and the morning star ran herald of the rising sun, the armies of Tula crossed through the deep gorge of the narrow passage into the Southland. The Toltec garrison, which once spanned the passage with a thirty-foot-high rampart of stone and wood, lay in ruins. The heavy gates of priceless thick mahogany that had been shipped from the southern jungles were ancient hulks of charred coal. Here and there, the stone heads of warriors that were once the carved façade of the battlement lay on their sides or facedown as though they might have been the very Toltec defenders who died at the hands of the sorcerer named Hummingbird on the Left. That was thirty years ago. Now the thirty thousand of Huemac's Nomad army, along with the three divisions of Sky Hawk's knights, passed in cover of darkness and turned sharply westward, cutting across the foothills.

Moving at quick march, they skirted the edge of the swamplands, and by the fourth day they had reached the edge of the jungle known as Black Water. At its edge, Huemac had his armies set camp, each division quickly erecting temporary shelters and rampart perimeters.

Huemac assumed the Maya would know he was here. Surely, runners had quickly spread word the armies of the Tolteca had returned. That wouldn't matter, because the target he most wanted to strike with surprise was below him, the jungle itself. Cities he understood. He had mastered siege. In open warfare, only fools fond of dying would dare his hand. But here, this jungle, this was an alien world. Perhaps here, finally, something could oppose him. He was eager to meet it, see its face, look in the eyes of the dread shadow he had felt all these years.

"I have come," Huemac whispered. "Welcome death."

A macaw screeched in answer, mocking him. Huemac wondered of it, but dismissed it. He noticed how the Toltec highway, once well-fitted stone lined with manned outposts, crumbled before ending in a stump at the edge of the jungle.

He thought about its age, this jungle, that it was a million years ancient. Scanning its treetops, Huemac tingled. It was magnificent, like nothing Huemac had ever seen. Vast, almost like an ocean, it stretched below him in a dark green canopy that covered the entire valley. It was rich, alive—birds fluttered, an ocean wind moved through it like gentle waves rolling. He found it breathtaking.

Over his shoulder, he noticed a scout approaching. There was something about this one, this odd scout who had joined them—an old man but toned and quick, sometimes limping but other times, like now, striding.

Several days ago, as they approached the passage of Manti, Huemac had sent runners ahead to find scouts. Several Maya had volunteered for the job, but Second Skin came to him with an old man, a man with bent and crooked legs skillfully sheathed in leather buckling. Second Skin said the old man had been waiting for him in the ruins of the Manti garrison. Huemac would never have chosen this wrinkled old man who grinned slyly, but he trusted Second Skin's instinct, and the scout had been traveling with the armies ever since. He seemed swift and capable, although there was something about him Huemac could not figure out. Perhaps it was the way the old man's single good eye, which was two colors, both green and blue, watched Huemac as if he already knew him. That single eye in him was very clever, deeply intelligent. He seemed to know many things; in fact, he seemed to know everything. He was more than a scout; his disguise did not fool Huemac.

As Huemac turned back to the jungle, the old scout stepped up beside him. He just stood there. That was another thing, the way he didn't keep to his place. He made assumptions—he seemed to think he did not need permission to speak with Huemac. The little scout approached the commander of thirty thousand Nomads, the deadliest army to ever march, and without inquiry or even a bow stepped up and scanned the jungle as if *he* were the commander and Huemac was merely a boy. Huemac wanted to be seriously irritated; but oddly, there was something he liked about this scout.

"I suppose you know this place," Huemac said.

"Oh, yes. Everyone knows this place."

"I must cross it using the quickest route. Can you guide us through?"

"I can guide you in there, but crossing will not be simple or quick. They will be waiting for you. A jungle like this makes good killing ground if you know how to move in it, and the Maya know the jungle very well. They know whole armies have gone in there and never reappeared. Men used to say it is why this jungle is so rich—blood of the dying."

"Well, I am not going to die in it. I am crossing through it—directly south. And I will kill whatever waits for me."

"Aw," the scout mused, as though they were in a tavern pondering a bean game.

"Does that mean you are going to take us through it?"

He looked up with his one good eye. "What do you want me to say? I am telling you it is a trap. I am telling you they will be waiting for you. But that does not make any difference to you, does it? Traps for you are just an invitation."

"I do not think you know me that well, old man."

"No? Am I wrong, then? I'm telling you they have been watching since you crossed the narrow passage and this is the place they will come for you. But you are going in anyway. Am I wrong?"

"You are not. But you do make assumptions."

"Not really," the old man said with a sly smile.

"What do you mean by this?"

"I knew someone very much like you once. I will go in, scout the borders. When will you be ready to move?"

"Once my men have rested. They rest quickly, these men. They need little sleep. A few degrees of the sun will be sufficient."

"Then I will come back for you in a few degrees of the sun," the scout said. He paused, grinning, and added "my lord" before vanishing into the trees, moving rapidly with his leather-bandaged legs. He had said *my lord* not like a servant or even like a scout, which he was supposed to be—he had spoken it lightly and without reverence. Then he was gone.

Sky Hawk walked up to Huemac as the scout vanished into jungle.

"He is a strange one," Huemac said.

"Who?"

"That scout. The old man."

"Ah, yes. We met him, you know."

"Met him? Where?"

"Coming from the passage, the march home after the cities of Manti were taken. He was standing on the roadside, watching us. He is a Toltec. He lived in Tollán."

"You are joking."

"No, I'm not. His name is Coyotl."

"Coyotl, like the ballplayer?"

"Yes, but he claims he was only a farmer. You were there when he said this. You don't remember?"

"Perhaps. Yes, I suppose I remember that. You are sure this is the same old man? He moves differently now."

"He is the same one. I saw him in the city as well. He came to Tula on the night of celebrations. I think he made the mistake of buying *pulque* from Jade Frog. He is lucky he was able to walk the next day, let alone keep up with us. Jade Frog sells his victims the *pulque* and sends his children to rob them when they are falling down."

"You are saying this scout followed us all the way from Tula?"

"Yes. He had no choice."

"But Second Skin found him in the ruins of Manti waiting on a rock, as if expecting us."

"I guess he moves fast for an old man. Still, when we spoke to him, he did say he was a simple man, an ordinary plodder."

"A simple man who is very sly. I am not sure I trust him."

"We've other scouts, Huemac."

"Not like him. He is clever."

"Then why don't you trust him?"

"Because I fear he is too clever." Huemac glanced at his brother. Sky Hawk was turning a small stone in his fingers, a smooth piece of obsidian carved into the shape of a dolphin, its back arching.

"What is this?" Huemac asked.

Sky Hawk paused; he clearly had not meant Huemac to see the object and slipped into his belt. "It belongs to your nephew."

"Silver Feather?"

Sky Hawk nodded. Huemac turned back to stare at the jungles. Again the macaw called from there, his cry echoing, once more as if it were laughing, mocking them. Huemac dismissed the sensation with a sneer.

"How old is your boy, Sky Hawk?"

"Almost ten years. He's good with carving tools. That was one of his carvings. It has a name. It is called *The Dolphin Prince*. He got that from you."

"Me?"

"Yes. Your story, I understand. The ten dolphins who led the golden knights through the deep of the blue-green sea."

Huemac didn't say anything for a time, but then corrected him. "Seven dolphins."

Sky Hawk chuckled. "Seven—my mistake. They memorize them all, you know. All of your stories. You are good with children. Has anybody told you?"

"How could I be good with children? They are children."

"I can't answer that. But whenever you come, they run for you, skipping. They don't seem to realize at all you are a feared warlord.

Someone should tell them, I guess, so they don't come skipping, abandoning everything. Even if we told them, it would do little good. I've seen you hiding the ball from them, you know. So has Purple Sky. She wonders why you have no children of your own."

"We are marching into that jungle below us as soon as that clever scout returns. He tells me armies have gone in there and never reemerged. There should be other things on your mind right now, Sky Hawk."

"You think so? I'll tell you something, Huemac. Whenever I find myself at the edge of battle, I think always about them. I think about my boys, I think about Purple Sky, picture her face. Someone to come home to after this madness is done, or the one I die for if death is my path. What other thing should be on my mind?"

Huemac didn't argue. The sons of Sky Hawk held a special place in his heart as well. Children. Huemac had always wanted children. Desperately sometimes, though he carefully kept this secret hidden. There were nights of which only Huemac knew; they were secret. Thoughts of the children he might have had with Obsidian Snowflake danced with him, and he knew all of their faces. He could hear their voices. There were always lost children in his dreams, haunting him. But he remained true to her. Huemac remained true to all his promises, and the promise he made to Obsidian Snowflake that night on the beach was as strong in him as the promise he had made to fulfill his father's dream—his kingdom, his empire, the Tolteca—all they ever were. Huemac was almost finished in that promise. Only the Southland remained.

He realized Sky Hawk was watching and he glanced at the belt pocket where Sky Hawk had slipped the small carving.

"You carry that with you always?"

"Ever since he gave it to me."

Huemac nodded. He thought a moment of how Silver Feather had Sky Hawk's brown hair that was lighter with youth, as his father's had been. It all seemed so far removed, so out of place, these thoughts. Below him waited blood and stink and screams, but here, just in this quiet moment, he could smile that young Silver Feather had remembered the fantastic story of the golden knights. He grinned with the thought, then took a breath and drew himself serious.

"Well . . ." he muttered, turning.

"You know," Sky Hawk said, "This idea you have. About saving your heart . . ."

Huemac paused. "What are you talking about now?"

"Obsidian Snowflake."

Sometimes he wondered if Sky Hawk could read his mind. He had let none of his thoughts out through his eyes, he was sure of it, yet Sky Hawk says something like this. Huemac gave him a warning glance. "No," he said firmly. "We are not speaking of her, Sky Hawk. Not now. Not here. In fact, I recall you gave me your word we would never speak of her again. We have an agreement."

"Wrong, Huemac. You agreed, but I never did. All these years, all this time, and still you hold to this strange idea your heart belongs to Obsidian Snowflake—whom logically you will never see again! How can your head be that thick? She was only a girl, and even then, she never meant that night to be a curse on you. She just wanted to say goodbye and didn't know how."

Huemac gave Sky Hawk a deeply serious look, one that would leave no question as to his mood. Sky Hawk just looked back with his half-smile.

"I am preparing myself," Huemac growled. "Down there is an alien land, and it is not a place in which we have previously fought. You choose your thoughts; I will choose mine. No more talk of trivial things."

"Trivial?"

"Yes, trivial. I am getting some sleep now—I will close my eyes and I will rest my mind. My Nomads are in their tents, they know to get sleep when they can. So should you. Get some sleep, Sky Hawk. I will need you in there."

Huemac turned and headed for his tent. He tried to ignore the feelings Sky Hawk had stirred up and he cursed his brother soundly.

That was Sky Hawk's way: he was always speaking of life as though everything were ordinary, as though it were simply another sunny day and here they were. He did this even at the edge of a jungle that whispered for their souls—the darkest battle of their lives breathing down on them and Sky Hawk, ever the dreamer, starts talking about a girl Huemac had not seen in fifteen years. Yet despite himself, and thoroughly cursing Sky Hawk, Huemac still whispered to her. No one would know, but Huemac always whispered to her, especially on the eve of battle. This battle, however, he knew would be different. This was the end of battles. This was the hour she had seen during the beach-night conversation; his heart would be tested this hour. So this time Huemac whispered from his soul, certain his words would travel across the waters, certain she could hear. *I will fight for you now, Obsidian Snowflake, because this is why I have come, this is why we pledged our hearts: that I may live this hour. For you. For him, for our father. For our children. The ones I see in dreams. For wha ever we could have been and for what now we must become.*

When Huemac lay on his sleeping mat, he closed his eyes and his body shut down. It was a deep sleep. Usually, when he shut his body down, he did not dream. But this time it was different. It was a strange dream. As he slept, he dreamed not of Obsidian Snowflake, but of their smallest child: a little girl with blue eyes, bright blue eyes and dark, dark hair that fell about her fair skin in tangles. And such a quick smile. This was his favorite. She called him Poppy.

꒰ꑬ꒱ꑬ꒰ꑬ꒱ꑬ꒰ꑬ꒱ꑬ꒰ꑬ꒱ꑬ꒰ꑬ꒱ꑬ꒰ꑬ꒱

Coyotl moved only in shadow. It wasn't difficult. The jungle was thick and shadow was not hard to find. Since the old Toltec stone roadway stood in this jungle the ground had shifted, leaving most of it under water. When Cumorah died, it shook the land around it; it changed the face of everything. The jungle was named Black Water since the vast swamps were always as dark as cocoa. Most of the jungle was swampy, always a stink to it, but patches were peppered with islands of dark, rich dirt that spawned fronds, moss, and mushrooms.

As Coyotl crouched and stealthily navigated the cold water and its slime-choked mud, he alternated between slow and quick movements. His path was unpredictable. He had learned how to hide. It is what had kept him alive after Cumorah, when death squads hunted the jungles from the eastern coastline to the highland mountains of the Gadiantons. During that time, Coyotl had learned to move as one with the shadows and he had developed a sense that never failed him. He knew when he was being watched. He could feel eyes on his skin as if they were fingers walking.

Here, surprisingly, no one watched, at least not in the outskirts of the forest. Nothing. No roaming hunters, no squadrons preparing for ambush—the jungle seemed empty of all but slitherers and crawlers. He had not expected that. He had fully expected to find the Olmeca or their mercenaries—they had to be here somewhere. Coyotl knew if he could find the Maya, all he needed to do was to guide the Nomads in like trained wolves for the slaughter. He had seen the work of the Olmeca, and fate could deliver them no better end than these young, cunning warriors of the desert could. The jungle was quiet, passive, indifferent to him. He finally eased up against the flared buttress roots of an old cypress and slid to a crouch where he remained as still and breathless as the cloistered air. A dense tangle of *liana* vines snaked about him. One of them, a Monkey Ladder, soared straight up into the mushrooming canopy.

Coyotl closed his eyes and listened carefully to each sound, frogs, the occasional bird call, slithering sounds, then a splash from the west—a caiman wading into the black water and gliding through it. He spotted the caiman's scales as they parted floating grass. Then he paused—something in the thicket just beyond where the caiman had passed. Whatever it was, he felt it had been there all along, playing the game just as Coyotl, moving shadow between shadow, and now it simply waited. Coyotl held his breath, he became the cypress, but it did not matter. Whatever watched was cunning, confident; he could feel the fingers of its eyes touch his face and he could almost hear it chuckling over his surprise.

Coyotl finally stood and moved to open ground, not hiding any longer, stepping into a shaft of sunlight that cut through the jungle canopy to leave a yellow stain across the swamp waters.

"Come ahead, you cunning bastard," he said calmly. "Here I am, here I be, let us get introduced."

Something answered. Nothing he recognized, just whispery words, running past him like a wind, then gone. He realized with a start he now saw eyes. When he had spoken, they had quietly opened—eyes watching from the darkness, tiny beads of light glimmering off pupils. They could easily have been the eyes of a puma, but they weren't. He sensed they were human, although not ordinary. After all, these eyes had outsmarted Coyotl at his best game and now simply watched him, unafraid.

Coyotl shifted his weight back slightly onto his heels. The eyes blinked. He had moved, it had moved. Coyotl smiled.

"So that is how it is," he said. He spun into a blur, twisting to a low crouch as his fingers plucked one of the silver daggers from his side sheath and flung it. The small blade streaked through the fronds and swamp grass and vanished into the dark without a sound. The eyes winked out. Coyotl wondered if he had taken mark, but he had little faith in that—rarely was there such a thing as a soundless mark. He waited, crouched. Briefly, he toyed with the idea of going in there to check, maybe even getting his dagger back, but the cautious Coyotl in him, the one who had kept his skin all these years, reasoned he had plenty more daggers and the dark of that mangrove looked as empty as a starless night right now.

Suddenly, he heard the whispery words, this time distinctly human, though oddly, it sounded like a child, like a little girl running past—and this time the sound had not come from the mangroves, it was directly behind him, in the opposite direction. Coyotl spun, still crouched, just in time to see cycads fronds wavering as though someone might have just trespassed. He searched the trees there

490

thoroughly, angry—nothing could move past him this way. It just couldn't be done. An owl hooted, but nothing else stirred. He already knew it was futile to go over there and check for tracks. This was a cautious game, and Coyotl was being outmaneuvered. He told himself there was more than one; he refused to believe anything had ran from the mangroves to the thicket behind him without giving itself away, a sound, a shadow, something, and Coyotl had lived too long in dark places to be easily fooled. Whoever they were, they were good.

One of the reasons Coyotl decided to dog the tracks of the armies of Tula when they left the city—the reason he had been waiting for them at the passage of Manti, offering services as a scout—was that he knew this was a prime season, that the wind of promise was in the air, and something was closing in on these sons of Topiltzin. He didn't know what. Since Cumorah, the world had slowly simmered into a dark and heartless landscape where blood was valued only as sacrifice. Terror—simple, stark terror—ruled here. The terror of skinning, the terror of burning, the terror of lidless eyes. Terror had driven Coyotl to make his home deep in the jungle in red dirt that no one could envy.

Topiltzin had obviously chosen not to hide. He had returned, he had roared like a cat in the night, he had built a stone city in the desert, and now he sent his sons to challenge the terror. What they didn't know was the terror had been waiting for them, waiting patiently, ever since Cumorah. Coyotl was determined to find it first. He was determined to at least give these well-honed warriors of the serpent city an edge.

He stood, purposely remaining in the open, letting himself remain a target, but he knew he wouldn't be bothered. Coyotl was not the target here. The shadows had only flirted with Coyotl, daring him to bring them in, and if he were a true scout he would go back and tell Huemac to take his armies anyplace but here, take the coast, take the midland highways, march along the mountain footpaths to old Tikal and then swing west, anything but cross the ancient land. Yet, the army camped in the lowland hills above the swamp was no ordinary army. True, they were desert warriors, but the smell that came off them, their eyes, the way they moved, even in march, it had left Coyotl wondering if perhaps this might be the deadliest blade ever fashioned. It was one thing to flirt with Coyotl, an old, half-crippled bean farmer (or at least that's how he let the people of the Southland see him)—but the lean, cunning desert Nomads—flirting with them would be a lethal courtship, even for clever jungle shadows.

He glanced up at the position of the sun. In a few degrees movement it would be time to lead the hunters in, but right now, there was still enough time to get a nap, so Coyotl found a huge, felled banana tree and laid down on its spongy bark. He couldn't have found a nicer bed if it had been stuffed it with quetzal feathers. He closed his eyes and was instantly asleep.

Resting on haunches, Sky Hawk studied the jungle below. He was sweating, but he let the sweat spill off his face because below him the jungle was sweating as well; steam came off it, tears of steam dripped through the canopy of green. Movement down there, beasts stirring.

He had been unable to rest. Sky Hawk knew how vital it was to sleep whenever possible and he had tried. He had lay on his sleeping mat, determinedly closed his eyes. He had long ago trained himself to sleep no matter what bore down on him. A warrior sleeps—it is a matter of life and death—either your edge is honed and sharp or you die. A warrior sleeps in rain; he sleeps in the mouth of death. But this time, he purposely stayed awake. Because the jungle was watching him, smiling back, mocking him. He seemed to hear it breathing as well—careful, measured breath, and each time it exhaled, the air crawled over his skin like ants. It was alive. Sky Hawk knew if he slept, the jungle would send dreams. It had looked into his mind, he felt the eyes there, felt it reading him. What kind of being was this who could effortlessly wander Sky Hawk's mind?

He couldn't take his eyes off the roadway. Sky Hawk did not believe that spirits roamed. He believed even those who die in terror or sadness still moved on. If the terror or sadness was great enough, their spirits left a shadow of tears. This roadway, crawling into the jungle, its stone breaking apart, swallowed by overgrowth, this road was covered in tears. Somewhere down there, deep within this same jungle, was the mountain of burning where thousands, tens of thousands, more, all had died, and though some must have fought to the death swearing down their enemy, there were certainly others who died shivering. There were children who died never knowing why. There were women who died with a prayer on their lips. The tears of their spirits were part of the sweat that dripped in this jungle and nothing had ever left him feeling so unnerved, so terrified.

He set a fist against his heart and prayed. He prayed to them, the ancestors, the Old Ones who had walked here so long ago, he prayed not just for their help—though he did, he asked they give him strength, protection—but Sky Hawk also prayed to tell them he was sorry. He was sorry they had to die, that this was a world where even the innocent bleed.

When he looked up, he noticed Second Skin had drawn up beside him. Second Skin was pulling on the snakeskin gloves he used to keep a tight grip on his razor-sword in battle. The razor-sword rested against Second Skin's hip. It had tasted so much blood, by now it was alive. It spoke always and as Second Skin stepped close, Sky Hawk could hear the blade whisper.

"You must put it aside, my friend," Second Skin said quietly. Sky Hawk knew fear did not touch Second Skin like it touched other men. He felt it just as they did, but when he felt fear, he simply welcomed it. He had learned to feed on it.

"And where do I put it?"

"You kill it. There is nothing that cannot be killed." Second Skin looked up and calmly pointed south. "The scout comes. Soon we will meet whatever makes our skin crawl, Sky Hawk." He smiled and turned to walk back to the camps. With a harsh cry, he stirred his Nomads to life.

Sky Hawk turned to watch the old man. Sometimes he seemed crippled, but now he came swiftly through the brush. For some strange reason, the sight of the scout gave him hope. When he reached the rock where Sky Hawk waited, the scout paused. Huemac was right—something about this one. Not an ordinary scout. He understood blood and shadow. Sky Hawk noticed the scout had started to grow a beard. Coyotl was Nonaloca blood; he hadn't lied. He had known the Tolteca who passed through here thirty years ago, and Sky Hawk wanted to ask him why he hadn't died with them, and he would, but not just yet.

"What did you find?" Sky Hawk asked.

"Shadows. Not that it would matter."

Sky Hawk studied him, ignoring the sounds behind them, the shouts of Second Skin, the army stirring.

"You knew him, didn't you?" Sky Hawk said.

"Ah?" Coyotl answered, as though he hadn't heard, but he had heard, he was too quick to miss anything.

"You knew my father."

Coyotl paused a moment, staring right into Sky Hawk, and the look made Sky Hawk shiver a little. This was he. This was the ballplayer. It had to be.

"When we reach the jungle, keep moving," Coyotl said as though he had never heard the question. "Remember that. Whatever happens, keep them moving. If I were planning to kill these Nomads, I would slow them because if I could slow them, I could spend my time killing them. It would be the only way."

"I will do my best."

Coyotl nodded and laid his hand on Sky Hawk's shoulder before moving on, as if they known each other a long time.

TOLTECA

Once the jungle named Black Water had swallowed them, the armies of Tula moved steadily through it, cutting their own roadway. To the front, razor-swords cleaved a pathway continuously. When one warrior was weary, another took his place, just as in battle. Where the marsh was too deep or unstable, bamboo and palm fronds were bundled and laid out as temporary bridges.

Huemac left no flank exposed. Shield-bearers ringed all sides and even the rearguard had been ordered to move as though always in retreat, shields covering their path.

Coyotl stayed near Topiltzin's two sons. Huemac wondered of it. He had expected the scout to range, and indeed Coyotl had ranged far in the days they had been in the Southland. Now he stayed close. The scout kept his eyes on the shadows, his fingers never far from the hilts of his throwing daggers.

Half a day passed. Other than trees, swamp, and stink, the jungles seemed empty. The dark waters rippled with the footfall of thirty thousand, but no one approached them. At this rate, they were cutting through jungle fronds almost as quickly as they might move through open desert. The scout had told them to use the trace outline of the old Toltec roadway as a guide.

None of them talked; hardly a word had been spoken since entering the thickets, no words, just the steady sound of blades cutting through the trees. Snaps. Chunks. Huemac noticed how Second Skin's dark eyes constantly searched the trees as they moved through them.

Huemac usually walked in the lead, but this time Sky Hawk had insisted they remain behind the front, deep enough he would be well protected.

"Get through these jungles," Sky Hawk had said, "then you can harvest whatever kills you wish—but while we are in there, you will let your Nomads take the bite."

Huemac had agreed, but he guessed he would do what he pleased if they were attacked. If these jungle Maya could fight, he intended to measure the cut of their flesh.

Huemac had placed the three divisions of Tolteca knights in the rear of the Nomads. First was Silvered Leaf and the Wind Sign Knights and behind them the Seashell Knights of Flower Prince.

The jungles soon forced them to spread out into a long column. Both the rear and front could hold off a direct attack, but the center, with flanks to both sides, was weak. This was not a worry, however. In fact, by exposing the flanks, Huemac invited the Mayan to taste flesh. Let them come for the underbelly, the center where the army was thinnest, and to lure them, Huemac had placed the Eagle Knights, using their brilliant feathered cloaks as bait. Scarlet Macaw, a firstborn, led them. The Eagle Knights were skilled killers, savage in attack, but they were also methodical; they worked a battle as if it were craft, which made them as deadly in defense as in attack. During one campaign, Crimson Companion and his Eagle Knights had held the Valley of Fire against outland raiders four times their number. The shields of the Eagle Knights had never been broken.

At the front, on point, Huemac had placed the elect of his Nomads, captains all—any one of them as deadly as ten ordinary warriors. They moved through the jungle ten abreast, the width of the old Toltec roadway. The front was maintained as if the jungle itself were an enemy. The captains swiftly cut through frond and sapling, but their shields were kept always at the ready.

When the day grew long, Huemac was surprised how swiftly the dark was descending. He wondered if he had misjudged the time. It seemed the sun just slipped from the sky as thick shadows crawled through the undergrowth. Glancing down, he swore the shadows moved like fingers, curling about his ankles, creeping as they went. Huemac searched the trees. Everything had changed. No longer the crusty hulks of ancient trees, this was young growth: lush, green, and damp. The feel of the air, the hot sticky way it clung to his skin, that had not changed at all, but the plants were richer, fuller. The *liana* vines snaked across the smooth trunks of trees like vessels beneath skin. There had been no rain that day, yet everything here was damp, the moss and lichen dripping. For a second he swore it was blood dripping there, but of course that was imagination whispering and he dismissed it.

The sun was fast falling, and it was time to find a camp. He knew the journey through the jungle's heart would take days, and he did not intend to exhaust his men on the first leg.

Despite its glistening, reddish sheen, the area actually looked promising. Though much of it lay beneath ankle deep water, there were broad islands of red-black dirt. Rich dirt. The jungle canopy was so thick, it stifled growth from the ground, and the almost-bare dirt of the islands reminded him of freshly prepared *chinampas* on the lakes of Otumba. Some of these islands were even laced at the edges by rock—as if buttressed. The rock was black as pitch, and the moss covering glistened, moist. This, then, was the reason he thought of blood: the lichen and moss were red, coating everything, gathering moisture until it left things looking slick, resembling muscle after the skin is peeled away.

He guessed the rock was lava—it was chunky, broken up here and there like parched mud baked by sun. Sometimes, the breaks were mild, other times violent, even spiking out of the water like claws. They passed beneath one spar of lava that jutted so high, it was like a curved blade arching, swamp grass clinging to it like tendrils that brushed his shoulder when he passed. An eerie place, but the teeth of this lava rock lacing the islands was perfect for creating a defensible camp.

"Good ground here," he said to Sky Hawk. "We will make camp, erect ramparts. Second Skin! Call halt!"

"Wait," Coyotl cautioned, but Second Skin's command was already echoing through the lines. The Nomads at the front stopped cutting. Those carrying packs had started lowering them to the ground, but the scout was staring about as if he had just seen the ghost of his mother.

"What is it, old man?"

Coyotl looked behind, then to the side, his boots splashing as he turned. "Can't be. No, this can't be . . ."

Huemac was growing irritated. "Sky Hawk, discover this man's problem!"

"What is it, friend?" Sky Hawk asked.

Coyotl merely stared, aghast, scanning the trees, the water, the shards of lava rock scattered; and then, spotting something—he froze, as if he had been slapped. Huemac traced his glance. It was a stone, not a natural stone, but flat and rounded, carved. A death stone—a grave marking.

"Mother of God . . ." Coyotl muttered.

"Speak your problem, scout!" Huemac ordered.

"How did we get this far south? When did we turn south?"

"For the love of frogs, you are the blessed scout! You tell me!"

"We are not where we were moments ago."

"Are you mad?"

Sky Hawk was searching the jungle with alarm, irritating Huemac further because the scout's apprehension was spreading.

"Explain yourself," Huemac demanded. "What are you telling us?"

"I am telling you we were following the Toltec highway but moments ago. It's gone. This is deep jungle. We've been shifted—we are no longer where we were."

"Good God!" Huemac moaned. "A whole day into this stinking, motherless swamp, and you wait until now to tell us you have lost your wits! Second Skin—the others, the Mayan guides, where are they?"

Second Skin was searching. "They were right behind us. Gone, my lord. I suspect they've fled."

Furious, Huemac was about to lay hand on the scout, perhaps knock some sense into him, but he paused, caught by the way Coyotl was staring at the sky. Huemac glanced up through the dense canopy. Darkness was unfolding. It wasn't dusk settling—this was unlike anything Huemac had seen, it was like a hand closing on them. His skin pimpled with a chill. He swore under his breath. All day, keeping himself poised for battle, muscle tensed, searching every sound, every nuance, and now this, night inking from the blessed sky, trees that dripped like blood.

"This is a trick of light," Huemac declared, "nothing more."

"We have to keep moving," Coyotl said.

"What?"

"Keep moving. We have to get out of here!"

"Nonsense. Over there is good ground for ramparts. Farther on we'll most probably find more soup and I do not intend to make camp in a soup!"

"We can find ground," Coyotl said, "but not here, not this place!"

"Give me a reason, old man!"

Coyotl glanced up to him, his good eye set firm. "Because this is the killing ground. This black rock is all that is left of Cumorah."

"Impossible, Cumorah is two days into the jungle!"

"Cumorah is beneath your feet. We are in the spell of a shifter, a very powerful one. Powerful enough to open time and draw us here."

"There can be no such power," Huemac growled, but the scout's words had sent a chill through him. Even Second Skin was searching with alarm.

"Mark me, Prince; there are powers you dare not dream. You wanted to force his hand, spring the trap. Well, this is his trap. He has brought you to Cumorah."

Fresh shadow swept over them, as if in testament of Coyotl's words. The jungle shivered. Something rustling, shifting. Movement. Huemac looked up, tingling. In the closing darkness, shadowy forms stepped from the trees, the rocks; it seemed they even rose out of the swamp. In but a breath, the Tolteca were surrounded.

"Lock shields!" Second Hand screamed.

The Nomads swiftly closed ranks, shields swinging 'round, *thunking* into a protective wall. Huemac could not believe his eyes. Their skin was painted black and their armor, weapons, and shields were burnished. They had gathered with hardly a sound, and even now were hard to see, being so effectively concealed by the darkness.

"Shadow Walkers," Coyotl whispered.

"Impossible. They were destroyed. No Walkers live."

"I didn't say they were alive."

Huemac wondered if the taste in his mouth was fear—damn this scout, was he trying to unnerve them?

The jungle warriors hadn't moved; they simply stood there, watching. Their eyes glinted beneath shadowy helms, their weapons glimmered, licking the dark, but none of them moved, none attacked.

"When it comes," Coyotl warned the Nomads, "measure your strikes. Some are shadow, no more than mist, but others are shifters—flesh and blood. You can kill the shifters, but take care not to spend your strength against shadows."

Second Skin turned. "And how is it we tell the two apart?"

"Cut them. If they are flesh, they will bleed."

The jungle warriors still did not attack, they waited, and the night continued to close like a veil drawing down.

Huemac unsheathed his sword. Sky Hawk reached over his shoulder to withdraw slowly his killing axe. The shield-bearers dug in, preparing.

It wasn't like darkness had fallen, it was more like the air was turning back light, tightening until the glint of their eyes winked out, until everything melted to pitch black.

"God help us," a Nomad muttered.

Huemac could see nothing; he couldn't see his hand inches away.

Then fire flared. It was Coyotl; he lifted a torch high, tossed it to a Nomad captain, and with a flick of his striking stone brought another to life, tossing it as well. In the torchlight, Huemac caught a glimpse of archers moving into position—some were kneeling, others standing. They were not shadow, they were real and about to fire directly into front lines.

"Brace for missiles!" Huemac cried.

Arrow and atlatl came screaming with hollowed tips, missiles that tore through shields, shredded cotton armor. All along the front, shield-bearers were thrown back as the hail of darts ripped through them, but when the shower passed, the Nomads closed rank without ceremony, stepping over their dead to lock shields before the shadow warriors could rush the breaks. The jungle warriors hit hard and heavy. Coyotl was right, some were wraiths, some passed through shields and armor and bodies to simply dissolve into the darkness. Yet others were all too real. There were screams and confusion, and in the inked black, it was impossible to tell how many were coming.

Huemac saw one Nomad simply heaved into the air, blood flying—it appeared a beast had split him in half and hurled him at the trees. What could possibly be that strong?

Second Skin shouted commands, striding behind the front like a panther, and his men held fast, though at any moment it appeared the line might shatter completely.

As more torches were passed, pockets of the inked night washed in a watery glow. The Nomads had not faltered; on all sides the front was solid, but beyond them raged pure madness, a frenzy of screams and weapons. Impossible blows, coming too fast, too hard, pummeled the Nomads' shields. The pitch black beyond every torch's flicker left everything framed in godless nightmare. There were sounds Huemac had never heard. One of them was a heavy, continuous growl, like a wolf shaking the necks of rabbits, but deeper there was a rhythmic grunt that soon became a chant. It was a timed beat, and the weapons of the jungle warriors slammed and surged with its rhythm; but rather than become predictable, each chant made the next more terrifying. When the chants were strongest, despite their years of facing everything from savage outlanders to the heavily armored warriors of Cholula, despite being the most deadly warriors on earth, the Nomads fell. Some spun back, blood whipping. Others were jerked into the line, pulled into the enemy as if being stolen. Huemac saw the legs of a Nomad being jerked beneath a line of shields and then saw his body lifted high and carried into the night. For a brief second he saw the man's face caught in a flicker of torchlight. He was screaming. The jungle warriors were not just slaying; they were taking captives.

Huemac snarled. He gripped his razor-sword in both hands and started for the front, but with a savage lunge, Second Skin caught his shoulder and threw him back.

"No!" Second Skin screamed. "You will stay back, my lord!"

Second Skin turned swiftly, spotting something to the side. "Reinforce the left!" he shouted, the muscles in his neck straining, "The left, to the left! Now!"

Huemac realized the left flank was being shattered. Bodies were dropping, shields fell, and the enemy was boring in like wolves tearing flesh. He had seen fronts give way, but never from this side, never from the receiving end. No enemy had ever broken a Nomad line. Huemac lifted his sword, stepping forward, but this time Sky Hawk planted himself directly in front of Huemac, blocking his path. Before Huemac could move farther, Nomads had surged to Second Skin's cry, and reinforcements slammed into the weakening line. The dark-armored Maya were driven back so hard some even turned to flee. The Nomads did not follow; they stepped back and locked down, digging into the mud. They knew enough not to pursue.

Directly to the front—the strongest point, Huemac watched in disbelief as one, then two immortal Nomad captains dropped. It appeared they had been torn to pieces. They spun, shields dropping, and through the opening in the front, four dark warriors poured in from the night. They seemed inhuman, overwhelming everything that closed on them. One fought with nothing more than a huge, spiked cudgel, its blunt end worn from use but still frayed with the bark of the tree from which it had been cut. The cudgel smashed heads, shattered helmets, caved in breastplates. It struck a hardened Nomad in the shoulder and Huemac saw the bone split through the crushed leather armor. Once more, Huemac moved to counter, and once more Sky Hawk blocked his path, this time turning to shove Huemac back with both hands.

"Damn you!" Sky Hawk screamed above the din. "You will not take this bait, Huemac!"

"You want I should hide in the mud?"

"I don't care, as long as you stay back!"

Second Skin himself took out the big Mayan, who was the only one left of the four. As Second Skin closed on the big warrior, his Nomads cleared ground, leaving a small circle where a brief, single combat waged. It was quick. The cudgel whispered over the torn shoulder strap of Second Skin's leather armor, but Second Skin's razor-sword first sliced through the black cotton armor, then in backstroke opened the Mayan's torso almost to the spine. The Mayan's eyes flew wide as he dropped.

"How many are there?" Sky Hawk muttered, watching stunned as another rhythmic chant sent a surging blow that staggered the locked shields.

"There appear many," Coyotl answered, "but most are shadow. The *Itzás* fight with more than sword and shield."

The little scout held his torch high. He searched the darkness like a hunter.

"You believe they are *Itzás*?"

"Yes, shifters, all of them. They are probing, searching."

"Searching?" exclaimed Huemac. "For the love of God, they are all over us!"

"They haven't come for Nomads—they've come for you!"

A body splashed into the water at Coyotl's feet, and the scout let it pass, not looking down. Huemac did. Just before the black water of the swamp closed over him, Huemac saw the face of Seventh Sword, twisted to the side, teeth tight in grimace.

"I will stand no more," Huemac screamed, furious. He threw Sky Hawk aside, lifting his sword, but this time, surprisingly, it was Coyotl's hand that slammed against Sky Hawk's chest, stopping him.

"Stay back!" Coyotl shouted in a commanding voice. "Don't you understand? They search for you! When they find you, it will be over!"

Coyotl stepped away, moving quickly; the torch whipped. He dropped to a crouch, his free hand a blur as it ripped a dagger from his side belt and flung it. Huemac was amazed to see it sink into the throat of a Mayan warrior who dropped facedown into the water, almost at Huemac's boot.

Coyotl snarled. He had to cast his torch aside this time. The water snuffed it as Coyotl leapt upward. Midair, he caught a dark, sleek form. It had soared over shoulders and heads of warriors at the front like bounding off rocks and then stretched, claws glinting—green slitted eyes coming straight for Huemac. Coyotl caught the big cat; they tumbled and splashed down, Coyotl on top, his dagger arcing through its throat, flinging blood. Coyotl held it fast until the struggling stopped. Huemac expected it to melt. Though he had never encountered one, shifters were said to die human no matter their form, but in the water remained only a bloodied mat of fur. It was just a jaguar. Coyotl stepped back. He glanced at Huemac.

"It saw you," Coyotl said. "I think they've found you. They will come for you now, prepare."

Coyotl backed to a crouch at Huemac's right while Sky Hawk circled on his left. With a spark of his flint stone, Coyotl brought another torch to life. Huemac wondered about the torches' origin. He saw a quiver of them over the scout's shoulder.

Briefly, even in all the madness, Huemac wondered of him. He was no mere scout; he was more than even a hunter. Coyotl was a stone killer. The battle had not shaken him at all, and yet it was like nothing Huemac had seen; it had already left more men dead than had fallen in ten years of campaigns.

"What are we looking for?" Sky Hawk said, searching.

"Anything. Everything."

With a scream, Second Skin took his turn at the front just as it was again being shattered. Maya died as they met Second Skin's razor-sword. It never stopped moving, slashing, then ripping upward, then crossing sharply down—each strike a kill.

Coyotl cursed himself. Somehow the shadows had shifted, deceived him, and instead of guiding the armies of Tula through safely, he had walked them into the heart of the killing ground. The power here was so strong that living night had crawled down from the sky, and it was going to take whatever it wished. If Coyotl had any say in it—not without a fight.

Though the battle was furious, Coyotl believed it was nothing more than a ruse. They had thrown everything against Huemac's point, the most impenetrable part of Huemac's army and the Maya were far too clever to exhaust themselves against the terrible blades of the desert warriors. If they had wanted to cripple the army, it would have been far better strategy to stab for the underbelly, the center. The night that came against them wasn't interested in the army of Tula; it had come for Topiltzin's sons alone. What Coyotl didn't know was which son had been targeted. Was it Huemac or Sky Hawk? If he were the night searching, which would he take?

Coyotl had already pressed his broken body to its limit. Pain surged with each heartbeat, but he let the pain fuel him, let it keep him sharp, focused.

Then something changed. He wasn't sure what it was; at first, he only sensed it. He passed the torch over the waters. They were strewn with body parts—the cocoa-colored water swirled with the blood of death, almost in a froth. As he held his torch up and passed it before the front line, it lit macabre faces. He wondered if the Nomads even saw them. One figure that raged in fury against a desert warrior bore a skeletal face—it was stark, pure bone at the cheeks, but flesh where the eyes burned. It wasn't paint; it was his face. This warrior had cut the skin from his cheekbones and chin.

Coyotl realized what he was sensing, what had changed. The rhythmic chants had stepped up, but there was another sound now. It was growing. This sound was a steady, constant hum. It was like a million insects. He realized it had started the moment the jaguar spotted the sons of Topiltzin behind the frontline. Water Wizards might be pressing against them in fury, crushing in from all sides, but the hum that closed now was the jungle itself. It moved quietly. Slowly. Methodically. He could feel it against his skin. Eventually the noise would grow so loud, it would swallow even the rhythmic grunts and thrusts of the Maya, thrusts almost like sex—thrusts that were coming to a climax.

He wasn't going to be able to stop this. Everything he was, everything he could be, it wouldn't matter. Coyotl felt helpless—too strong, too powerful. He wondered how such power could crawl through the air, why the Creator allowed it. It was power enough to crush them all with a single flick, and the only reason it came slowly was to savor its moment.

Coyotl was suddenly aware of eyes on him. As always, he first felt their fingers on his skin, this time the skin of his neck. He whirled, looking behind, and then he gasped. Up. Straight up. Something was moving the canopy of the trees above them.

Sky Hawk had noticed the scout whirl. He followed the scout's eyes and saw them at the same time—shadows, literally dancing across the leaves and branches, swift as bats, but these were no bats, these were warriors, sleek, swift shapes flirting with the sky. Something about them, the way they moved, chilled Sky Hawk worse than the heavy caiman warriors who were slamming against the shields of the Nomads. These were dancing as they came, they moved like feathers in a wind, like children playing.

Their cadence of the battle was now merging to a steady, deadly scream.

Sky Hawk pointed, but it was Second Skin who cried out first.

"The trees!" screamed the Nomad. "Archers! Hit the trees! Now! Now!"

Whatever they were, they came falling through the sky. Some looked like flying squirrels. Their screams were high-pitched, piercing shrieks that cut through even the roar of battle. So many, there were so many. As they dropped through the night, a hail of Nomad arrows ripped upward, tearing at leaves and branches, shredding everything. Many of the dark assassins twisted as the missiles took their mark, killed instantly, but others dropped straight and true, as though they could easily out-dance the deadly strafe of arrows. The night was theirs; they were the night.

Sky Hawk had no time to move for Huemac; two were coming for him. If he ignored them, he would die. He twisted, but the first dropped onto his shoulders, rocking him back, and the second came for his face with a cry that chilled to Sky Hawk's bone. He saw the obsidian blade, the butterfly knife. There wasn't time to counter.

ظ©ظ©ظ©ظ©ظ©ظ©ظ©ظ©ظ©ظ©

Huemac killed the assassin above Sky Hawk. His razor-sword halved the creature midair, just above Sky Hawk's face, inches from it. Behind Huemac, something dropped onto his back with a *thud*. A knife slashed through Huemac's backplate armor, through the reinforced leather, the cotton, piercing with a hot sting into the muscle of his back. Huemac snarled, whipping around, his very weight discombobulating the assassin. Without breath, another one caught him. Hands that seemed claws slashed for his face, but caught the edge of his helmet instead. The helmet strap broke and the assailant sailed past him, clutching the helmet as though it were a prize. Huemac arched his back with a snarl, reaching for the dagger. He could hear Second Skin screaming, slaying as he waded toward Huemac. He found the hilt and wrenched it from his back just as another dropped onto his chest. Huemac never saw the face.

Huemac cast aside the razor-sword. He twisted in a full circle. A dagger had arched quick and Huemac fed it the skin of his fore-arm, blocking the stab as he reached with his other hand for his atlatl quiver. He ripped the assassin off him with his right hand. The body seemed amazingly light as Huemac slammed it into the water with a heavy splash and then brought a briarwood atlatl hard into the sternum. The bone cracked. The arms flailed a moment, then stilled.

Huemac realized the rhythmic thrusts of the battle had ceased. In fact, when he finally looked up, everything had stilled. The Maya were gone. They had melted back into the jungle as suddenly as they had appeared. The Nomads at the front were still tensed, still searching, standing amid mounds of body parts and dying men, but nothing came from the trees now, only the dark of the jungle. It would have been quiet but for a hum, a strange steady sound that seemed to be coming from the air, even the ground, the trees, everything seemed to be humming.

The assassins who had dropped from the forest canopy had all been killed. It had happened so quickly. It had seemed they were terrifying, but now there were just scores of small bodies in the water—they had all be slain. They littered the ground about Second Skin like leaves strewn, cut to pieces by the deadly scalpel blades of the terrible sword that hung from his dripping hand. There were also bodies in the water around Coyotl. Coyotl's cheek was slashed open, his shoulder, his forearm. Still, amazingly, no one seemed to have been killed. Huemac noticed how Coyotl was watching him. Coyotl's look was odd, worried—concerned. Huemac glanced to Sky Hawk who was crouched over a figure beneath him, studying it through the black-blood water. Sky Hawk slowly stood and looked to Huemac.

"What?" Huemac said. "What is it?"

"Children. They're all children, Huemac."

Huemac's lip drew back in a snarl. He looked down. An ice chill spilled through him. In the water at Huemac's feet was a youth, no more than eight or nine, a child, no armor here, just a black cotton tunic, a tiny dagger belt. No wonder the attacker had been so light. Huemac reached into the water and lifted the body by its tunic. The head hung limp, long hair trailing. The eyes blinked open. Huemac gasped. It was a girl and the eyes were not Mayan, they were large, blue eyes. Bright blue eyes and dark, dark hair. The little, cupid's mouth was whispering. *Poppy.*

It was her, it was really her; out of some madness she had been thrown here, and it was real. It was she. He had somehow, out of all sanity, just slain his own daughter. Huemac roared. The girl's body dropped back into the water. Lips still moving, the small, round face floated on the surface a moment before sinking into a swirl of its long, curly hair.

"You son of whores!" Huemac screamed.

Second Skin stepped to Huemac's side. "Calm, Huemac, careful . . . best let this be."

"I will not!" Huemac screamed back, not so much at Second Skin as the jungle itself. The hum was growing, steadily, slowly—like something moving, but with great calm. "You motherless bastard! Come at me! Come ahead, come take me!" Huemac turned in one direction, then another. "I am right here! Come take me! You piss-drinker, you shit-eater! You cunt! You piece of filth!"

Sky Hawk reached for him, but Huemac violently twisted away.

"You find killing children is easy, well, come kill me!" he wailed, splashing through the water, slamming his fist against his chest with a heavy *thud*; then again, and again. "You father of all whores! Twice you kill children with my blade! Well, come kill me! Here is what you want! This is what you have waited for! Come take me, you motherless bastard!"

The hum surged. It moved, it slithered closer.

Coyotl was searching every corner, panicked.

"Drink my blood, you whore!" Huemac ripped out his dagger. "Drink my blood!" He slashed open his forearm and turned his fist to the night, exposing the slashed vein. "You drink the blood of children, well, come drink mine! You unholy bastard of creation! Mine! Drink mine! I offer my blood!"

The Nomads couched behind their shields, searching, for though nothing moved in the jungle, it seemed everything moved— it seemed at any moment the night itself would roar to life.

"You coward! Huemac howled. "You shit-eating piece of filth!"

Coyotl glanced at Sky Hawk. "Do something! Calm him down!"

"I smell you, shit-eating filth!" Huemac tore off his leather breastplate, snapping the shoulder hinges to fling it aside. "Face me! Come taste my flesh, bastard!"

The humming surged again.

"Huemac," Sky Hawk screamed, "remember the words of our father! Neither pride nor fear! Neither pride nor fear!"

But the rage in Huemac had no place to go; it could rip him apart. Though his eyes were dark pits of stone, the face of the little girl had left tears streaming down Huemac's cheeks. Her face left him trembling; he wanted to tear his own flesh, rip out his own heart. She was dead. She was gone. She was ever gone. He screamed at the jungle once more, and this time it finally screamed back. Like witches, like a hundred wolves. Then the humming ceased; it stopped dead as abruptly as if a blade had severed it.

Everything that happened next unraveled as though it had occurred a hundred times before.

The scout saw it first. Coyotl spun, dagger in his fingers; he moved more quickly than Huemac had ever seen anyone move. But not quickly enough.

This time the night did not come from the trees or the sky. It was in the water. Amazed, Huemac first thought it was Coyotl's dagger slithering toward him in a ripple through the dark red water; but then he realized the hilt had embedded itself through the flat head. The head turned to the side with flashing silver-green scales and Huemac saw an eye. It flicked open, looked onto his, and as the torchlight glinted off the glistening black mesh, Huemac saw the Dark that waits at the far end of the universe.

Coyotl lunged past Huemac, savagely stabbing at the water, but the serpent vanished with a quiet ripple of the red-black water.

All Huemac had felt was a sting at his heel, like a mosquito, nothing more.

Sky Hawk watched powerlessly as Huemac went down. Second Skin had leapt forward; he was even there to catch Huemac, to pull his head into his lap. Huemac's body shivered in spasm, his back arching, his teeth clenched, but he was no longer conscious.

"No!" Second Skin screamed, lifting Huemac up against his chest.

Coyotl scrambled to their side. He ripped a dagger from his side belt and took Huemac's limp hand.

"He's not breathing," Second Skin hissed through tears. Sky Hawk was stunned at the hard Nomad's tears—they streamed freely.

"He's trying to breathe, but he's choking," Coyotl answered as he slit open Huemac's wrist. "It's an allergic reaction; the swelling has closed his throat." He wrenched a small leather pouch from his belt and tore it open with his teeth, then poured the medicine into the open slash and closed Second Skin's hand over it. "This is powdered mandrake and nightshade; it will counter the swelling, but it will also leave him in a near coma. Hold the cut tight."

Sky Hawk stepped closer, watching. Second Skin's big hand curled over Huemac's wrist and squeezed. The effect was visible. As Coyotl's powder mixed with his blood, Huemac seemed to relax. Beads of sweat had broken across his forehead, but he finally started breathing again, shuddering at first and then going limp—his bare chest rising and falling. He looked asleep, but pained, as though the rage in him was still burning.

Coyotl backed away and wearily dropped against the buttress of a massive cypress root. Sky Hawk noticed Coyotl was trembling; and for a moment, he looked old, frail, and broken. He was massaging one leg desperately. He looked up to meet Sky Hawk's eyes.

"I tried," he said, "but just like before, I couldn't stop anything. I was useless."

"Before?"

Coyotl glanced at him, then away. "Your father."

Sky Hawk gasped. He all but knew, but even so, he shivered a bit. This was the ballplayer. "Is Huemac going to die, Coyotl?"

"I don't know. I do not know what poison is in him. But there is no reason for him to be alive at all; many poisons would have killed him in seconds. Perhaps that leaves hope—whatever the jungle wanted, it wasn't his life. Not yet, anyway." Coyotl hung his head moment. He looked completely exhausted.

Sky Hawk stepped closer. "Are you all right?"

"Just pain. Sometimes I endure considerable pain." He took a breath and looked up. "I am going to go for help."

"Help? Who would help us now? The armies of the Maya have certainly realized at this point that we bleed. If anything, they now know we can be killed."

"It is not an army I'm after, just a witch. This is the jungle of the Petén. There are no finer healers to be found in the world then those who practice medicine in the villages south of here. I will run south."

"You look so weak, Coyotl."

"Yes, but my looks haven't counted for much in years. I've had to pay for sex like everyone else." He grinned, but turned serious. "They will come again. Your brother mentioned the Olmeca, but these are not Olmeca. These are *Itzás*, water wizards." He looked around at the others, the Nomad captains, including Second Skin. "Do not believe anything you see. Trust your swords, your shields, but never your eyes." He reached down and tightened the leather leg bracings, cinching them down though he grimaced with the pain it caused. "I wasn't sure who they would go for," he said as he worked, speaking only to Sky Hawk.

"What do you mean?"

"Whether they would choose you or your brother."

"Why should they go for me?"

Coyotl caught his eye. "Because you are the strongest."

Despite his pain and exhaustion, Coyotl stood, testing his weight against his leg. He tore open another small bag from his belt pouch, but this time he put the contents under his tongue. He laid his head against the tree behind him and sucked it down. "I will find a healer," he said though his teeth, his eyes closed a moment as the medicine worked. "I will send one back. You have my word."

"Alone? You are going alone?"

"Being alone is what has kept my skin these many years." He looked up, his gaze almost fatherly for a moment. "In your city, I first thought he was wrong—your father. He'd learned nothing. But I do not think that anymore. His sons are sons I would call my own. If by chance, Sky Hawk, if somehow I was not to make it back . . . tell Topiltzin I still believe. All of it. Everything for which he has lived. If anyone can bring them back from the dead, you can."

Coyotl turned, walked to the front line where Nomads were still holding shields against a possible attack, then, just as he reached the shield-bearers, he dropped into a run and vanished into the night.

Sky Hawk glanced back at Second Skin. "Move to ground, set ramparts."

Second Skin nodded. Nomads gathered about Huemac and gently lifted him.

CHAPTER FORTY-NINE
UTTER DARK

Night three. Silvered Leaf turned slowly, trying to see through the shadows of the jungle surrounding them. He was going to die this night. A son of Topiltzin had not yet fallen in battle, not in all the years of fighting in the north, but that was about to change. Silvered Leaf could not explain how they had been interceded. He had fought in many campaigns; he had stood with Scarlet Macaw in the passage of the Valley of Fire where the Eagle Knights of Tula held off many times their number while the Nomads caught up to them. He had learned to keep his front strong, to rotate his warriors; he had learned to bring fear to the hearts of those who came against his sword and never fear to his own. This night, as he searched the shadows, though fear was not in him, certainty was. They had been sectioned off the main force like a branch cut for pruning; it had happed too quickly to understand. It seemed the jungle had twisted, enveloping itself, that it had literally taken his men and spit them out somewhere else—so far from the main army he could no longer hear the shouts of captains or the moan of daylong battle. The one thousand Wind Sign Knights of Silvered Leaf suddenly found themselves alone, feeling they were a small ship in a calm sea about to turn rogue.

He heard nothing, the jungle was dead, silent, it could have been an illusion of sorcerers it was so quiet, but Silvered Leaf had learned to feel the enemy. He didn't need sound, he didn't need to see them coming, he could feel the air brush against his skin, he could smell a wind gust before it stirred the dirt.

"Circle!" he screamed. He gritted his teeth. He clenched the leather-wrapped hilt of his sword tightly in his fists. It had been hard enough holding three fronts. As a circle, they would die. He braced. "They come!" he shouted.

The air screamed to life, thick with missiles humming through the trees, clipping leaves and branches, shearing fronds and sapling as they came, a wave of missiles, like insects boring. Silvered Leaf swung and placed himself behind his shield, crouched, but he was stunned at the impact. Armor was ripped away. Shields were shattered like sticks. Men screamed as they were hurled through the air. The missiles seemed to have been launched from atlatls like gods had thrown them from the sky.

Without a beat, without a second's pause, the jungle warriors rushed the shattered front on all sides, from everywhere. As he came out from behind his shield and slashed open a warrior's chest, he wondered how they had done it, how they had shattered a front line that had held against a hundred armies before this. With the front broken, the Mayan warriors, clad in dark armor that left them shadows in shadow, swarmed into the ranks. Blood and chaos were everywhere. The Wind Sign Knights of Topiltzin Nacxitl who had fought a hundred battles, who had trained on the very sand of Paradise, who had never flinched or taken but trivial casualty, were now being torn apart like rabbits pinned beneath the claws of pumas.

꒷꒦꒷꒦꒷꒦꒷꒦꒷꒦꒷꒦꒷꒦꒷꒦꒷꒦

Second Skin heard the screams of men dying. It was far behind them, too far, somewhere in the flanks where none of his armies should have been. He had not heard slaughter like this unless it was that of the enemy, but though the sound was similar, Second Skin knew these were the Wind Sign Knights. Many of them were sons of Topiltzin, men Second Skin could not imagine falling in battle. But he could not think of them. He could only think of his own flank now.

Not far from him were mounds. Many were his own men. The

rest were the warriors of the dark, too many to count, too many to know. He had realized these past three nights that sometimes they were flesh and sometimes they were smoke. Some of them were not there at all. The mounds of bodies strewn through the jungle, shadowy heaps now, had all been flesh, but the smoke had drained them as well. Phantasm was as terrible as blood sometimes. As they closed after each killing, drawing back, there had been no time to bury or burn the dead. When the fighting calmed there was only time to retreat farther back—retreat, tighten the lines, and hold. He pulled back because each time, after hours of fighting, when it ended, their numbers were fewer and the perimeter of the camp tightened. Second Skin was not interested in holding ground any longer, he was only interested in keeping flesh on his men, so he pulled back, even if it meant throwing up new ramparts. He wondered what their numbers were now, how many left, but he hadn't let anyone think of it or count survivors. To those who asked, he replied numbers did not matter; if they were down to ten they would fight no differently.

Surely, the armies of the Maya that came against them were thinning. Second Skin could not imagine how many men he had killed over the past nights; they were all a blur now. They were countless. It seemed they had just been endlessly killing. The few moments he was able to sleep, in short spurts, his mind would dream kill, flesh cutting and cutting and cutting.

He had tried to keep his armies tight, but it was difficult, and he no longer knew how well the rear or far-left flanks were holding. He did know the enemy kept coming at them from different areas of the jungle, always looking to carve out pockets and destroy them. On the second night, he had pulled the army into one large circular camp; he had thrown up ramparts of dirt, mud, and bamboo. The bamboo was cut to spikes and pointed outward everywhere. In the desert, nothing would have breached them, but here, with nightfall as black as ink, the darkness simply swallowed everything. It was insane, sorcery, no night could settle that heavy or that dark; it took everything, every color, every trace of moment. Torches burning and yet even the night eyes of Second Skin, the hunter, could see only a few hands in front of his face. As soon as each night fell, as soon as the unholy darkness thickened, it started. It had been this way for so long it seemed never to have been otherwise. He had been fighting here for eons, and it had become a common thing: the night turning to soup and the mothers of the dark spawning to hurl against them.

Sometimes he wondered if they were going to die here, but he dismissed it. Dying was not a problem.

Tonight, the jungle had been watching him for hours, but as the death screams of the Wind Sign Knights slowly died down, he was certain they would come.

They did.

Second Skin breathed slowly, letting fear out through his fingers, letting it settle deep with rage, screaming in him, screaming through his skin.

"Come ahead, you bastards," he hissed through his teeth, and then spoke for Huemac who no longer stood with them. "Welcome death."

But when he expected impact, nothing struck. Instead, this time they ran, they ran in circles. Through the trees, splashing in the swamps, moving too fast to be human, but sounds of them whipping, screams that came and shot past, screams that literally rippled though the air and then scattered away into the trees. The pace grew faster, they were running with millions of legs now, running around and around, and, it seemed, peering through the darkness, there were only legs out there, just legs, running madly. The night started laughing now, laughing as though something was hysterically funny—perhaps that they were only legs, millions of legs. The laughter was sometimes close, then suddenly far, then close again—then it shrieked right into his ear, for an instant a stark white face against his cheek that vanished when he turned.

Second Skin focused and ignored them. There was nothing he

could do.

The first night, Second Skin had watched as his men poured arrows and atlatls into the screaming shadows without effect. He had learned quickly. Battle was always about learning quickly. Second Skin decreed that anything killed must be done close in; anything slain now would be sliced or stabbed by reusable weapons. Thus, the Nomads waited and watched as the night laughed insanely all around them, a big joke. Second Skin knew even his veterans, though they were swearing through their teeth, were becoming unhinged.

Something soared overhead. Sometimes there were flying things, screamers, and looking up he saw one, the sound of it like a wailing torture victim. Also a ripping sound, as though skin were peeling—indeed, it was skin—only skin, the skin of a man, all flayed out with holes where its eyes should have been. It whirled madly though the air above them, shifting, wobbling—shrieking madly.

Then, right before him, in his face, a growl, down low in the throat of a beast, a heavy, certain, fearless growl.

Stone Killer, Second Skin's first captain, shoved a bolt into this atlatl thrower and locked it in with a click. He had managed to retrieve the same bolt seven times now because he only launched it dead into the faces of the assailants.

"They've about finished dancing now," Stone Killer said. "Maybe they'll get on with it."

Suddenly, no more laughing. Second Skin saw eyes, hundreds of eyes flickering in the torchlight. The way the eyes reflected light left Second Skin thinking of wolves; the watery flicker of light captured in the night eyes of a wolf was the exact light he saw moving in the jungles beyond them. They were low to the ground, moving slowly inward, creeping as wolves creep—but they wove in and out of themselves as if there were only eyes, no bodies, just hundreds of wolf eyes able to growl. Their growling seemed to run about them everywhere, a scattering of growls.

"Bastards!" Stone Killer howled. "You want my blade, come taste it!"

TOLTECA

Second Skin lowered himself into battle stance, curling his hand tightly through the straps of his shield. Stone Killer took position on his right. The staggered front of the Nomads settled and steadied itself with a sound of shields locking. The jungle still toyed with them, the eyes moving slowly, creeping in and out, always close but never closing. A huge shape rose up, light glinting off claws, eyes reddened like fires, far larger than a wolf. Even Second Skin gasped; it was monstrous, and it lunged, but the thing was only shadow and it passed right through them, scattering afterward into the night air.

"What in God's name was that?" Stone Killer muttered, as angry as he was disturbed.

"Ignore your mind's eye. Focus your fear. Anything flesh can be killed; anything shadow cannot kill us. Focus."

Another scream, so close it was right in his face, so close he smelled the foul breath of the thing and this time Second Skin screamed back, he screamed into its face with equal terror, gripping the hilt of his sword tightly, but not wasting his time with shadows. They were good at shadows. Second Skin had already learned to save his strength for the flesh that would soon come seeking.

To the left were howls and then a rushing, things moving swiftly across the ground, a weight to it, a feel in the souls of his feet. Second Skin looked down the ranks. He saw them folding in on the line of warriors, hurling through the air, and they looked like wolves. The lines were staggered, but held, men screaming as they fought. The wolves were flesh and blood. The killing had begun.

"They come!" shouted Stone Killer.

Second Skin turned and braced but the beast that rose up before him hit so hard he was staggered. It swiped again, this time with such a powerful blow his shield was ripped from his arm, out of his grip, tearing off the leather handle. It was a shifter. He had killed them on nights before. They would wither to dead naked bodies once they fell. A second blow swiped for Second Skin's chest but he spun back with a war cry and sliced with the razor-sword. He couldn't see what was in front of him, but he could feel flesh as the

519

razor-edged sword cut through, catching bone, tugging before the thing dropped. Second Skin did not look down to see it shrivel to a human, he just kept fighting. He moved in a blur, never still for an instant or a second, he continued spinning, slicing. As he did often, he flung his shield and fought with both hands. His shield became his weapon, always moving. He ignored completely his mind's eye. Naked bodies were all around him. He saw one man, a head, an old man's head, with ancient withered flesh on him. How could an old man have fought here?

Silence now. Second Skin looked up. Everything was gone again; the Maya had melted back into the jungles. He ached to pursue. If only this were open ground. If only he could see more than a few hands past his face, he would track them, hunt them, and give them no time to pause or regroup. But this was Utter Dark and to step into it was to vanish.

He looked to Stone Killer who was panting, body parts littered all around him. Blood was dropping in splats from Stone Killer's forehead, but it wasn't Stone Killer's blood.

There are places where demons walk. In these places, though your heart is true, though your spirit is strong, the night is stronger. God has turned His face—yet the Mocker strides, walking openly. Sometimes he is an old man, sometimes a young woman, sometimes simply shadow. It does not matter if you believe in him or not. He believes in you. In these places, there are names that should never be spoken, words that should never be whispered, thoughts that should never be entertained. Cumorah had become one of these places. Coyotl wondered if it would let him go. When he left the sons of Topiltzin and the Nomads three days ago, he had run through the trees making himself pretend it was an ordinary jungle. Nothing at all followed. The jungle simply let him go. Now he understood why. Leaving was not the problem. The problem was reentry.

TOLTECA

He had found a healer, a man with magic strong enough to inspire awe in even Coyotl. He was old. He was so old there was no count to his years. Coyotl guessed he had lived far beyond years of mortals; he had sustained himself, he had cheated death and though his skin was fissured and hung from his face like old, worked leather, though his eyes were only stabs of dark pits, this old Mayan knew more about magic than any being Coyotl had encountered. He had no name. Yet when Coyotl came, no name and no words were needed. The old eyes looked up and the shifter nodded. Of course, he had guessed Coyotl would come for him.

The run back through the jungles would have been impossible for the old man. But he had shifted. He had become young and he ran naked but for a breechclout, he ran with lean, tight muscles, sweating, panting. He was dark, handsome, striking, his hair was no longer gray and thin, it was thick and black and streamed behind him like a wolf's mane. He ran with the power of the wolf, the spirit of the wolf, he ran with padded feet, as though he were four-legged.

They entered the jungles and though Coyotl knew the path, he grew more and more uncertain the closer they came to Cumorah. He had timed everything, his run, his distance, his rest, all timed to ensure they reached the heart of darkness in daylight, but it had been no use. The daylight failed, the night swept the sky. The jungle turned time; it moved, shifted, did anything it wanted to, and Coyotl had a sinking feeling, even with the powerful shaman beside him.

He heard the wolf grunt, as though something had struck him. They had been running for a full degree of the sun, both of them nearing exhaustion, and sweaty, but pacing themselves, keeping their breaths careful. When Coyotl turned to help, all he could do was watch. The shifter was hanging a few feet off the ground. His arms were uplifted as though he were impaled, but there was no staff, he was just floating, slowly turning. His eyes were open; he looked upward, into the sky. He was possibly trying to reach the sun. If his spirit could have found the sun, he might have saved himself.

He turned, slowly. His body started whipping; it became a blur and blood shed from flesh—a rain of blood, splattering everything. It was because the shifter was spinning so fast his blood could not stay in his skin; he was simply being pulled apart. And then he stopped, he hung for a moment, most of his skin stripped off, most of his muscles torn from the bone, and then unceremoniously he was dropped to the ground as though he were no longer of any interest.

Coyotl took a step back. He briefly prayed the shifter had somehow found the sun. The old man's heart had been pure, his spirit strong. Coyotl felt eyes on him. He was next. Coyotl began his last run, not letting himself even think of a direction so nothing could outguess him. He could shake off fear, ignore it. He was Coyotl, he had lived these long years, and he could outrun even the night. If only he believed.

━━━━━━━━━━━━━━━━━━━━━━

Huemac gasped for breath as the peccary hide of the tent spun into view above him. He seemed to be on water, on a raft, slowly spinning, everything moving. Yet when he was fully conscious, he realized he was lying on solid ground—the movement had been an illusion of the fever that had gripped him for what seemed to be an endless number of days. He found Sky Hawk nearby, sitting with his back against a wicker chest, his helmet beside him. Sky Hawk was in full armor, blood splattered from whatever battle he had last fought. He had taken wounds. A gash across his cheek glistened from fresh blood. His head was down, for he was sleeping. Huemac could remember that each time he had awakened Sky Hawk had always been there, always nearby, sometimes holding him, sometimes sleeping beside him, but always there.

A native woman, a Mayan who never spoke, sat across from him and wiped Huemac's forehead with a cool, wet towel of maguey fiber. Huemac remembered her doing this throughout the nights and days that were now just blurred memories, always dabbing at his heated skin, carefully wiping him down with the cool water. The fever left his skin feeling like he had been decapitated, as though his muscles were drying—and then, in a wave, he would be iced and shivering.

Sky Hawk lifted his head. "You're awake," he said, moving to Huemac's side.

"How . . . how long have I—?" A spasm of coughing cut off his words.

"Two days this time. Here, drink." Sky Hawk lifted him up to pour cool water down his burning throat. "Drink as much as you can, Huemac, as much as you can."

It was work, drinking; it was toil, since each swallow took much effort. Finally, he pushed the skin away, exhausted. It wasn't water, something else, some herb in it. Huemac dropped back; he had to suck air a moment or two before finding strength to speak again.

"How many?" Huemac said, his voice sounding like someone else's, all washed out, scratchy, weakened.

"Two days."

Huemac stared out the tent flap into the night. It seemed he had not once awakened to daylight, as though in this place it was eternally night. Just beyond the tent was a carved stone, slightly tipped to the side, leaning drunkenly, half buried. The top was smooth, having been hand cut and rounded at the edges.

"What is that?"

Sky Hawk glanced at the stone. "One of the markers," he said. "They are everywhere. Carvings. Most of them are single warriors. Bearded warriors."

"Tolteca?"

Sky Hawk nodded. "Coyotl was right. This is the killing field, the place of final gathering."

"Cumorah . . . are you saying we haven't moved?"

"You've been too sick, Huemac. I fear even a litter. I dare not move you, not while you are this sick."

"Sky Hawk, you cannot stay in this place!"

"No. And I cannot leave without you. Whatever it costs, I don't care anymore. None of us do. We did not come to the Southland to see you die in it. We will not leave you, Huemac."

Angry, Huemac started to respond, but choked, coughing, and Sky Hawk held him, again pressing the sharkskin with its silver rim to Huemac's lips.

"Drink, keep drinking. The old woman drips this mixture into your mouth constantly; otherwise, you will die. You have to drink when you are conscious."

Huemac tried to push it away, he had to speak, but Sky Hawk forced it down him and once more Huemac worked at drinking, swallowing past knots that seemed to have been scraped raw down the back of his throat. He finally pushed the skin away.

"Damn it, Sky Hawk," he heard his old man's voice rasp.

"Nothing we can do about this until you get stronger."

"The Maya? The Olmeca?"

"They are not Olmeca. Coyotl called them *Itzás*—water wizards. They do not fight like anyone we've known. I think they are shifters. They come at us each night. Second Skin is out there now—they come in waves, wait, and come again."

As weak as he was, Huemac seized Sky Hawk's wrist. "If you stay in this place they will pick us off like turtles in the sand!" he rasped in a harsh voice.

"I do not argue that point."

"Move west, due west—the coast. Ocean. Ocean at your flank!"

"I agree. As soon as we are able to move you."

Huemac forced himself to focus, even though the fever dulled sound and pulled him back into its sweat. "You listen to me, Sky Hawk," he hissed through teeth gritted against the pain, "This is a command! Get out of this swamp. Now!"

"You gave that command yesterday," Sky Hawk answered quietly, with a slight smile as though something in all this madness could still be a joke. "And the day before that as well."

"Damn you, I will not have these men die for me!"

"Oh, they would easily die for you, in fact your Nomads wouldn't leave if I drove them at spear point. But the point of it is, the rest of us are your brothers. We are kindred. None of us are going to leave you, Huemac."

"This is a trap!"

"We know that—you knew that."

"Leave me!"

"No. If we die, then we die. They can leave us stones like they have left our grandfathers. But not yet. I hold out hope still for the scout."

"What?"

"Coyotl."

Huemac had to think, he had almost forgotten the old man, the scout. It seemed the last thing he remembered were the eyes of the scout before he slipped into the place of shadow from which he now could only struggle out of for moments, and this one was almost complete.

"The scout?" Huemac rasped.

"He is the real Coyotl, Huemac. You sensed that secret in him. He is Coyotl, our father's Coyotl. He has gone to find a healer, and I have faith in his return."

"But days, you said it has been days—"

"He's not dead. I don't feel that. Not yet."

Huemac knew he was fading; a wave of numbness left his thoughts scattered. Sky Hawk's face momentarily grayed out, then refocused, but Huemac was still gripping his sleeve.

He thought he was talking, shouting, telling Sky Hawk to leave him, take the men, get out of this jungle, but then, with a shiver, he realized he wasn't even awake any longer, he wasn't speaking at all, for the fever had dragged him under. It was like falling, like dropping backward into a pit, a feeling of cold, gray hands pulling him down. Each time it happened, it was like dying, as though he were letting go, as though if he didn't struggle he would simply die. With the fever, Huemac kept dying over and over and over.

K. MICHAEL WRIGHT

All fabric of time and things had unraveled here. This is the place between the light of breathing things and the end of all thinking. Beyond here is the place called Utter Dark. Nothingness. Here it is shadow: smooth, empty, soundless. Shoal: Shadow Land. That is the name of this place. The place that comes before nothing.

Huemac was clinging to a thin veil by focusing on the smells. Smells of dying. Of sickness. They were desperate, revolting, but they were not the Utter Dark, they were the last tendrils of life, sheathed in the burning skin of his own body somewhere.

"Huemac," a voice whispered. It was far, but close. He has heard this voice before, a soft voice, like a tender wind. It seemed each time he heard it, the voice somehow softened the hot, searing feeling that his skin had peeled off, that—exposed to air, screaming in anguish—his muscles were slowly drying. Each time he heard the voice, it was such balm he could sometimes even sleep. This time, however, he sensed the voice was searching for him—and suddenly, quite suddenly he realized whose voice it was. Obsidian Snowflake. When he knew her in Paradise, she was only young, only a girl, but even then she spoke wisdom far beyond her age. He had given her his heart. All these years.

He was not crazy, and he wasn't dreaming: she was real. Somehow, in all the madness, Obsidian Snowflake had found him. He was amazed she had such courage to come to this place, to venture so close to Utter Dark, where there was no more thinking, no more being.

"Here!" Huemac called. "I'm here."

"I see you, oh God, yes, I see you."

He turned and Obsidian Snowflake was there. He swelled with hope and fear: hope that she could reach him, a terrible fear she might not. She was coming toward him as if a current carried her, as if they were all underwater. He wanted to move to her, but if he were to fall, she would never reach him. If the Utter Dark drank his soul he would be nothing forever and for all of time because there would be no time, no thinking, no being.

Somehow, she came, she guided herself—so carefully, so very carefully. He realized as she grew closer she was light, pure light. It was only light coming toward him, slowly feeling through currents that brought her ever nearer. She was right before him; her face was right before his own. He felt her touch his hand and openly wept; he did not care about weeping, for this place was so terribly alone.

"Huemac!" she whispered excitedly.

"Is it you?" he said. "Are you really here with me?"

"Yes, my love. I am here. It is me."

He just stared at her face. She was hard to see; the underwater of the shadow land was thick and everywhere. Anything he saw turned to shadow and nothing unless he concentrated with all he had in him—but she had found him! He marveled because she had aged, much older now; it surprised him, how she was no longer a girl. As a woman, she had a quiet, simple beauty that seemed to come from everything she was: her eyes, her skin, her heart. She was so pure. Huemac understood that was how she had managed to find him. He could never have done this, he could never have reached her—even if she were desperately in trouble, as he was. It was she. She had to come searching, and she had found him.

She smiled, as someone who loved him deeply, who had dreamed of him long nights and now was close. She grew deeply serious and studied his eyes. "I knew you were in danger, such danger. Oh, what has happened to you, Huemac?"

"She died. I killed her. Oh, dear God, forgive my hand, but I have killed her, the little one, her perfect blue eyes . . . our little one . . ."

"No, Huemac, it is a trick. Only a trick." Her hands somehow reached up to move over his cheeks, caressing his face as if this were the only way she could stay—as though she were holding on this way.

"But it was her," Huemac said, his heart bursting. He had tried to keep the little girl out of his thinking. From the moment he saw her eyes there in the water, when he lifted the small, crushed body, he knew it was her, the Lord of the Utter Dark had somehow delivered Huemac his own daughter; she was real and she died in his hands. Their little girl. The little girl with the bright blue eyes.

"Her eyes," Huemac said, "it was her eyes, her little soul in there!"

"I know her eyes, my love, I know them so well. But that was not her. Oh no, no, no." Whenever she moved, it seemed so hard for her. "Someone has tricked you, Huemac. It is just a trick. She is here—she is with me, I promise! She is someday, and that is what I call her: Someday. Now I understand. This is why I needed to find you, because your heart is breaking. But it was only a trick. She is with me; we are here. We are here."

"But it felt so real, so real . . ."

"Only a trick," Obsidian Snowflake promised. "Your heart is not being broken, it is only tricked and you must take it back, you must draw strength. This place, here where you are—you need all of your heart, Huemac."

"I must be lost somewhere. Just beyond us . . . there is a place . . . I know its name."

For the first time she moved quickly, just her finger over his lips. "Do not speak its name!"

He nodded, feeling chills crawl though him.

"Do not speak it here—do not speak it anywhere. Never speak its name," she whispered. She looked around, her hands against his face, holding to him as though the current were pulling at her stronger. "Oh, dear God." She shivered. "Oh, God be with you, God protect you! Oh, Huemac, such dark here, such dark as I never imagined there could be!" With difficultly she looked back into his eyes. "You must leave this place! You cannot survive if you stay, not even you, not even all your strength can prevail here."

"I know that. Sky Hawk is somewhere, I feel his touch, he holds me, keeps me somehow, but I cannot find him."

"Yes . . . yes, Sky Hawk. He has used magic. I feel something . . . something he sent with you—swims not far from here, watches you.

A dolphin. I think it is a dolphin." Her fingers against his face pressed tighter. "Listen to me, very carefully . . . listen to my words."

"Yes, I listen."

"Make whole your heart and no longer give this place your fear. Make whole your heart and believe. That is how to walk from here; it is the only way out: *the knowing*."

He was finally able to touch her face. He had been trying, but his fingers hadn't moved. Repeatedly he lifted them, but they had not lifted. Finally, they did. They touched her skin—it was smooth and delicate, he touched pure light, it tingled slightly and he dared not press against it, so he simply let his finger gently trace her cheek—it was like touching a butterfly. "Seeing you," he whispered, "knowing how you have found me, Obsidian Snowflake, I can believe. I think I can find *the knowing*."

"You touched me—you already have found it. I am the way, I am the path. Listen now, for my time is thinning. I cannot hold much longer."

"Don't leave me, Obsidian Snowflake, it is so terrible here alone." Briefly it flashed in his mind, for he knew. He understood there were those who came here and never left, always alone, ever and ever without time—and the terrifying thought filled him with an awful dread.

"Look at me, look in my eyes," she whispered, focusing him, pulling him back. "I will never truly leave you, I am there, in your heart, keep me there, hold me there. Do you understand?"

Huemac nodded.

"Hear what I say. Your time comes soon, Huemac, and you must know direction. When it comes you must know the way, the path, the crossing." She spoke hastily, as though she was slipping—and she was, her light had dimmed.

"It will come in a place of butterflies; it will come. In an hour, when you are looking elsewhere, it will come. The number of the place is seven, and the hour of the place is the high hour of stark death, the last hour of night sky. When it comes, you must hold to that thing which is *the knowing*, you must hold to it with all your strength, Huemac. If you are lost in that hour, remember our love, remember me—my face, my eyes. I am the way. Remember me and come home! Come home, Huemac."

She was fading quicker now. The touch of her had failed; she was only shadow. "Obsidian Snowflake!"

"I cannot hold, my love. I cannot. Remember what I've told you. In the hour that comes, find me! I am home!"

He wept inside, he didn't want her to go, but she was already gone.

He looked about in the smooth, lifeless black, shuddering. The whisperer chuckled. It did not care what she had told him. It was always confident.

⊡⊡⊡⊡⊡⊡⊡⊡⊡⊡⊡⊡⊡⊡⊡⊡⊡

If he had to, Coyotl could run. He had learned, he had trained his legs, and running had kept him alive, and now he ran with all his strength. The fronds, fingers, and branches of the jungle whipped and scratched at his face as he ran. He was panting, out of breath. He dodged, keeping his path jagged and singular before doubling in on his own route, like the rabbit, turning quickly to outmaneuver, and in his mind, he never let his path be certain. That is how he was able to outrun the jungle for so long. He had little hope of reaching Topiltzin's sons, or the Nomads, but he thought he might be able to clear the heart that beat in the killing ground.

Ahead of him the ground leveled out, the trees thinned, it looked deceptively like a clearing, but Coyotl knew it was a *cenote*, a sinkhole. It was as though the earth here floated over the black water for which it had been named, and in places, the crust of the land sunk inward through circular openings that suddenly opened to deep wells. The Mayan claimed some had no bottom, that they reached forever into the night, into the place where the sun swims beneath the earth, and to keep the sun from drowning they had thrown hundreds of thousands of victims as offerings. They had done it for so long, so many centuries, the *cenotes* became fonts of power. As he ran, he briefly thought how the dark would not expect him to go there, yet the only current chance of survival would come from doing what would never be expected. It wasn't far; he took a course through the thinning jungle as though he hadn't seen it, as though he were pretending there was a clearing ahead. He wondered how deep the sinkhole would be. Some were shallow enough that the drop to the surface of the water was not enough to kill a victim, but others were death holes.

He measured his breath as he came out of the jungle, past the last trees. He saw the far side of the *cenote*'s circular wall. It looked like someone had poured hot acid in a puddle that eroded through the rock leaving rings of the earth's crust as it ate downward. He leapt before he reached the edge. He knew *lianas* always snaked into the wells, and in the moments before he leapt he had chosen one that trailed over its edge. He could only hope it was strong, that it crawled deep enough to let him slide down and was thick enough to hold his weight. He sailed over the edge, snatching the vine in the last second.

As he fell, he first let the vine slip through his hands loosely before taking hold. He swung into the side, into a fissure of rock, and Coyotl twisted to let his back absorb the blow. It hammered his weary spine, sending fresh arcs of pain through his neck and shoulder, but the *liana* held. He was spent, out of breath, and he momentarily hung there, slowly swaying back and forth. He looked down. The water was a dark, dark green, as though the jungle itself had melted in here. The water was too far to let go. He might be able to drop that far and survive, but he wouldn't want to try it.

Coyotl listened carefully for anything that had followed him. Maybe he had lost the shadows. It was possible. Anything was possible here. Above him, there were only ordinary jungle sounds. Somewhere far a howler monkey screeched. Insects hummed. He looked up. The sun, blunted by cloud cover, left the jungle sky in a hot, misty haze, but the sky wasn't night, and because of it, it looked to Coyotl as clean as a fresh blue sky dotted with puffs of perfectly white clouds. Nothing seemed to be following, and Coyotl wasn't sure why. He cursed himself already for not being able to turn it. If you didn't believe, it could not take you, or so his grandmother had taught him.

He decided to climb back up. Perhaps whatever was following had been outmaneuvered. Perhaps it could not come here. The *cenotes* were filled with strange powers and not all of them were dark, although when he looked down at this one, he was certain it would gladly let him join the many victims on the bottom.

Coyotl used the uneven spurs of rock that jutted from the round rim of the *cenote* to walk up its side, but for a moment he paused— a long, low wail sounded from above and he wondered of it, then realized it was the wind twisting its way downward, moaning as it passed through the crevices of the rock. Looking up, the sky had changed. The clouds were not gray or black; they seemed purple. Staring at the upper ledge of the *cenote*, he cursed himself—a strange fear was eating at him. Something waited.

He let his head fall forward, resting a moment on a patch of soft lichen, hanging from the vine. He could feel his heart beating as if it were the last moments of his life. As if this were going to be the end.

He had so wanted to help them, to save them. He had known Topiltzin's sons such a short time, but they seemed somehow his sons as well, they held such true hearts. But it was no use; Coyotl was powerless. It was the same with Topiltzin that moment in the forest before the sky spirit lifted its bright, silver talons—he had wanted with all his being to give Topiltzin faith, but he had failed. The dark had crushed him, and now it was going to crush him again. It wasn't going to let him reach Topiltzin's sons. It was taking them. He felt tears close, thinking of this, but pushed them aside, because he couldn't stay here. He was growing tired of being afraid, and his legs throbbed like motherless whores. If he didn't keep them moving, they were going to swell and stiffen. If the motherless bastard wanted him, Coyotl was ready to have it done.

He started climbing, hand over hand. He swore between his teeth. The wind started ripping above him, howling over the *cenote*. His hand gripped the top ledge, where the vine curled over the side. He paused; just for a moment his heart failed him. He wasn't ready to die. He wanted to see his little brown grandchildren again, see them grow old, teach them all the magic things. He wanted to see Emerald-as-the-Sky just once more.

He pulled himself over the top of the *cenote*, sliding on his belly and then coming to a crouch. The wind stopped instantly. The insects stopped humming as everything evaporated into a dead silence. In the field he was facing, a stone's throw away, an old witch was sitting there, watching him. Her eyes were white, but they seemed focused on nothing but Coyotl; they stabbed like picks of ice, and they could look through to his soul. They terrified him even though he forced terror to the side. He didn't move, he didn't know what was going to happen; he froze where he crouched, one hand forward.

"You lost your healer, Coyotl," the old woman said. Her voice was a harsh, strained whisper, but floating over the gravel of it was a gentle woman's voice, as though she might once have been young and beautiful. Coyotl had no doubt the being he saw was flesh. She had once been a living witch, gifted, pure—but that was long ago.

"Don't worry," she added, "I will heal the Strong Hand. I will heal him for you. In my own way."

"Why do you bother? You have all you want."

The chuckle. He had heard that only once before; it seemed such an ordinary sound.

"Oh no, no. Not yet. But I will soon."

He hated how she seemed somehow familiar—almost, although the thought was revolting—almost it could have been his grandmother there, her face, the skin leathered, a dark pale, sitting there, watching. He tingled. She had just read his mind, and she smiled a warm smile, like Grandmother.

Coyotl's mind raced with all the things he could do now, twisting to throw a knife; he could move fast, he could fling it before she could flinch—or dropping back over the edge, either dive for the dark green waters or grab the vine. He could run—behind him the jungle was thick, maybe his legs could keep moving, he might still find an escape route. Yet Coyotl knew none of these things would work; he was caught. He was not an insect, and she was following his every thought, she was reading everything and she tipped her head to the side, bemused.

"I will tell them you sent me." Her voice played with him, soft and human. "And then I will say how you ranged in the jungles to find me, how you ran until your legs were broken all over again, until lungs gave out, and then—just as we neared, so close we were, almost to the killing place—and you suddenly slipped. I will tell them how you fell into the sinkhole, Coyotl, how you were lost." She lifted her hand. "Goodbye, clever one."

He blocked her cast, forced the fear from his mind, and insisted she had no power over him and could not control him. He did not believe. *I do not believe in you, I give you no power; I give you my spit.* He felt his leg braces tighten. He heard the bones he had nursed all these years snap as they were crushed once more. He cried out. The pain surged so livid, so white hot, all Coyotl could do was scream. As she chuckled over him, she flung him back, spinning, tumbling into the thin air of the *cenote* as if the victims it had swallowed over the many years were pulling him to them—welcoming him.

◙◙◙◙◙◙◙◙◙◙◙◙◙◙◙◙◙◙◙◙

Sky Hawk came awake with a start, with a jolt. He thought someone had slapped him, thrown cold water on him, but the dark night with its sticky moisture crawled back over his skin. He turned and laid a hand on Huemac's chest, thinking it was his passing that had jerked him so suddenly awake, but Huemac was still breathing. His face looked calmer than it had. Sweat beaded off his forehead and the

534

Mayan girl wiped it with the towel. He glanced at her.

"Is he all right?"

"He dreams," she said in broken Nonaloca. "Dreams in his eyes."

Sky Hawk nodded, turned back only to have his breath caught in his throat. He almost screamed seeing the old woman standing there in the open flap of the tent, but then she smiled warmly and he had a strange feeling he knew her; she was like a grandmother, her eyes opaque and empty—a blind woman, but her gentle smile calmed him.

"Do not be frightened, child," she said softly, though her voice had a strange whispery sound that left him uneasy. Her Nonaloca was perfect; she spoke it like a first tongue. "Coyotl has sent me. We have work to do."

In Tula, a runner had come every few days since Huemac had left for the jungles. It was a pact Turquoise Prince made with Sky Hawk, and Coxcox waited always at dusk, near the southern gate, watching the plains that stretched west of the lakes.

But the runners had stopped coming. This was the third day and he searched anxiously. The plains beyond Tula were as empty as if no souls remained out there. With his heart beating in his chest, he noticed warriors assembling beyond the serpent arch, a century of them, runners all, swift and light. He knew Topiltzin had told them to gather, and he guessed Topiltzin was not going to send them to the jungle alone.

Coxcox started hurrying back, but when he reached Topiltzin's chamber in the palace, the king was already assembling his weapons. He looked up, seeing Coxcox, then returned to his tasks. He laid out a worn, polished atlatl. It was an old atlatl of Tollán with dark, rich wood and wrapping of gilded leather worn from use.

"We should wait," Coxcox suggested. "We should wait one more day."

"We?"

"But my lord, I would not stay here without you. Of course you know this. I can hire my own runners if I must, as fleet as yours."

"Can you?"

"Certainly. My place is with you. My place has been with you since the Scorpion Valley. Of course you know that. Really, we need not even speak of it."

Topiltzin paused; his cold blue eyes studied Coxcox briefly. "I suggest you pack lightly," he said.

Coxcox shivered. Topiltzin really was planning to leave for the Southland. When Topiltzin did something, he did it simply. Once he had gathered his weapons, the king would walk down the corridor and swiftly through the streets to the city gate. Coxcox did not know how to stop him. He *would* follow, naturally, but he was deeply terrified of the Southland. He had spent enough cruel years in that place. Going there would be a terrible, terrible thing. Coxcox wrung his hands about each other nervously. What was he going to do? What was going to happen?

He heard footsteps coming. His heart leapt. Yes, it was Turquoise Prince and only just in time. The prince was a quick as Coxcox. The prince had found the century of runners beyond the gate as well, and he most certainly *had* reached the same conclusions as Coxcox.

"Stop him," Topiltzin said, not even looking up.

"My lord?"

"You heard me."

"Yes, my lord." Coxcox measured his cross to the door; he paced himself so it appeared he barely had time to step aside as Turquoise Prince came in. With Turquoise Prince were three Sky Dwellers, heavily armed. Their broad-shouldered cloaks always brought a feeling of order and purpose, and Coxcox was desperately thankful to see them this time—though he put a frown on his face that suggested Turquoise Price had spoiled everything.

"Father," Turquoise Prince said calmly when Topiltzin did

nothing to acknowledge him.

Topiltzin continued to ignore him. The king rolled a belt of daggers in their leather wrap and cinched the tie. He tossed it aside where it lay next to his atlatl quiver, already with silver-coated spears that had dark blue feathers. The spears were the talons of the Serpent Plumed.

"You will not do this," Turquoise Prince promised.

"Since when do you tell your king what he will and will not do?"

Topiltzin buckled on a light leather corselet.

Turquoise Prince circled to where his father could not avoid him. He finally slammed both hands on the table, and this time Topiltzin looked up.

"For God's sake, Father, this is madness. I will take my knights and reach the passage in half the time it would take you! I will go in there with Sky Dwellers. Do you think you can travel faster?" Topiltzin seemed not to be listening. "My lord, you are the king. You are too important. I cannot let you be placed in harm's way."

"Too important," Topiltzin said, lifting his cloak, "or too old?"

"You know I cannot let this happen."

"Coxcox," Topiltzin said calmly, latching the silver shoulder pin. "We are ready."

"Yes, my lord."

Coxcox turned to go gather his things, but Turquoise Prince stepped to block their exit.

Topiltzin stared at his son, angry but focused. "Stand aside, Turquoise Prince."

"I will not. The risk is too great. I cannot stop you as the Prince of Tula, but I can stop you as your son. And I will."

"I told you to stand aside," Topiltzin said, underscoring his calm with threat.

Turquoise Prince met his father's eyes with equal strength; he did not flinch, and he did not blink. He stared Topiltzin down and slowly shook his head. "No," he said flatly.

Coxcox was getting worried. He feared what would come next.

K. MICHAEL WRIGHT

Then he heard the pad of running feet. Yes, they were far down the palace, they were in fact too far for any of them, including himself, to actually have heard them. It was *the knowing* that discovered them, but Coxcox spoke nonetheless because he could not bear to see the father and the son face each other down. He simply could not tolerate it.

"A runner comes!" Coxcox belted out.

For a moment, Topiltzin's gaze remained locked on Turquoise Prince, but then shifted to Coxcox. Topiltzin already knew what Coxcox was about to say.

"This runner brings news, my lord. This runner comes from the narrow passage."

Though Coxcox rarely displayed *the knowing*, he had never been able to hide it from Topiltzin. Topiltzin had learned his gift those many years ago when the king had first come upon the abandoned circus and led the cripples and little ones out of the Scorpion Valley. Coxcox would of course never forget that day. The slavers, the owners had fled—they ran, they had seen him coming and though he was only a single man walking through the deserts alone, they fled from him, terrified. Coxcox later learned this was the time Topiltzin had gone to the far deserts alone—without food or water he had wandered the scorched earth cleansing his spirit, searching for his God. For that reason, he was very powerful the hour he happened upon the camp of the Mayan slavers.

Their hearts were dark; they feared they would burn if his eyes were to look on them. And they would have. Oh, yes. In their haste, the owners left their wagons, torture boxes and prison carts behind, abandoned like trinkets strewn. When Topiltzin came out of the desert he looked down at Coxcox, then at the others—Widow Woman standing there, holding the hard, wooden door of her cage; Moon Child peering at him from the narrow slit in her small box. Seeing them, Topiltzin wept. He had looked in their hearts; he had seen all of their many years—the cruelty, the terror, the shame. He took them back to Tula and by the time they reached the serpent

538

city, Topiltzin knew them all. The whole way he had them tell him their stories; he talked with them as if they were children he had lost somewhere. Topiltzin, without questioning him, had guessed Coxcox's gift—that he saw things not seen, that he could peel the future back ever so slightly and read the shape of things coming.

Topiltzin stared at Coxcox now with a troubled gaze. "And what is the news this runner brings?"

Turquoise Prince looked surprised. He glanced from his father to Coxcox. For once, Coxcox did not care if someone might discover his gift—he hoped—but he did not care; he just spoke and did not make any explanations.

"He has been found, my lord. Huemac has been found. They are alive, they are well."

Topiltzin's eyes seemed relieved, but almost they were disappointed and Coxcox knew this was because Topiltzin wanted to go. It had not been without reason Topiltzin feared for Huemac—for any of his sons in that dark place. Topiltzin knew better than anyone what waited in the Southland.

Topiltzin turned away from Turquoise Prince. "Leave," he said.

"Father, I—"

"I will be alone now, Turquoise Prince."

Turquoise Prince nodded, stepped back. Only when he turned for the chamber doorway did the runner find them, a Chichimec scout, naked but for a breechclout, breathless and nearly exhausted from his long run.

"My lord!" the runner gasped, seeing Turquoise Prince and Topiltzin. "We have word! I come from Boaz and we have word! They are alive—many Nomads die in the jungle, but the prince and lord Sky Hawk—they live!"

Turquoise Prince had glanced at Coxcox then, just a passing glance. Coxcox shrugged; it was nothing, he said in his expression, just a guess—he had heard these footsteps coming and guessed—that was all. Nothing more.

Turquoise Prince took a breath and left the chamber, his Sky

Dwellers with him. Topiltzin had not even turned to the messenger; he stepped to the edge of the portico and looked out at the southern sky. Coxcox shooed off the messenger and turned, folding his hands in front of him. A disaster had been narrowly averted.

"Better I had gone," Topiltzin said.

"Of course, my lord. But now there is no need."

Topiltzin glanced behind. Coxcox waited calmly.

"Did I not say I wanted to be alone?"

Coxcox bowed as he stepped backward out the door.

CHAPTER FIFTY
KUKULCÁN

Everything had changed—smells, the feel of the air against his skin, sounds—everything was different now. Quickened, made alive, the sun, the sky, the sea—they breathed and swam and screamed all about him. Huemac had never felt so strong. He walked down the beach and strode into the crest of a wave, letting it shatter into his chest as he felt each singular drop, each with its own kiss. Everything fresh now, everything clean. The sick smell, the smells of dying things, the sweat, the urine, the dribble smell of diarrhea, all were washed—gone. He was cleansed.

As he waded out of the water, Second Skin stood watching, troubled, but Huemac strode toward him smiling. "Sing!" Huemac ordered. "We sing tonight! I want the Maya to know the Tolteca have emerged from the jungle alive. We will sing through the night."

Second Skin nodded, studying Huemac with alarm. "My lord—you are all right, then?"

"I am good!" Huemac shouted. "I am great!" He slapped his hands against Second Skin's shoulders, startling him. "I have never felt better! And how are you?"

Second Skin winced. "Good . . . weary, but alive."

"By God, we are alive! And damn weariness! No more weariness! We are going to sing! Understand me?"

"I do hear you, my lord."

"Then why are you standing here? Go make them sing! Build great fires that burn on the beach like stars! And no ramparts! Lay unprotected in the sand—bare your glorious member to the night, Second Skin! Let them know we fear nothing. We are Tolteca!" Huemac arched his back and screamed at the sky now. "We fear nothing!"

He paused, grew serious. "Make them sing, Second Skin," he said, more quietly. "I am perfectly serious. Tonight, your Nomads must sing the moon into the sea."

Second Skin brought his fist to his shoulder and nodded, stepping back.

Huemac turned and strode up the sand toward his tent, which he had erected at a cliffside overlooking the sprawling sea. He knew Second Skin was watching him, troubled, and it made Huemac laugh. Second Skin's face as he stood there on the beach: what a fine joke.

Sky Hawk had been watching. He stepped up to Second Skin carefully. Second Skin turned, nodded in acknowledgment.

"You look worried," Sky Hawk said.

"The things we saw those nights . . . now this." He glanced at Sky Hawk. "What did the witch do to him?"

"Other than healing his fever? I wish I could tell you, old friend, but I know not."

"Where is she now? This old woman?"

"Gone. I do not believe there is any use trying to find her."

"Mother of pigs!" Second Skin swore. "What are we to do for him?"

"Seems simple enough, Second Skin. We sing."

Second Skin stood a moment, breathing heavily. "He has gone mad, hasn't he? No ramparts. Night fires like stars in the sand. Sing all night—he forgets where we are. This is still the Southland." Second Skin narrowed his brow. "Tell me now, Sky Hawk—tell me he has not gone mad."

Sky Hawk thought it over a moment. Second Skin watched him carefully. "No," Sky Hawk answered. "No . . . he has not gone mad, Second Skin."

"But . . ."

TOLTECA

"Tell your Nomads to build big fires and sing like they've never sung before. Huemac is with us—he is strong. When has he ever failed us? Any of us?"

Second Skin nodded, though troubled. "At least go up there and talk with him."

"I will."

Second Skin took a breath. "All right, then. I suppose I shall . . . go sing."

As he turned to walk for the tents, Second Skin's eyes suggested he had been staring into the face of demons for nights without number, and Sky Hawk guessed he had.

In the end, they had emerged from the jungles unopposed. The attacks had stopped when Huemac recovered and they simply walked out. It was oddly the same as when they had slipped into the heart of the jungle; they were cutting through the thick of it when suddenly the jungle ran out and a stretch of sand opened to bright ocean. There was no explaining it. The jungle that had held them facedown in the mud—bled them for days—it had simply let them walk out, let them run to the sea.

Sky Hawk turned to look up at Huemac's tent, and wondered if it was over yet. He felt a strange uneasiness crawling. He wasn't sure what had happened to Huemac. He remembered the old woman kneeling there, remembered her whispering, close to Huemac's ear, speaking into it—telling him things no one else heard. She seemed so kind, so careful in her ways. Sky Hawk wanted to believe Huemac was cured, but he trusted nothing. He did not even take comfort in the smell of the ocean, a smell that always brought warm memories of Paradise.

॥॥॥॥॥॥॥॥॥॥॥॥॥॥॥॥॥

When the stars of night were zenith, Huemac was pleased to find the campfires of the armies of Tula spread across the white sands with abandon. High tide brought the welcome sound of breakers

543

crashing, a mother-giving sound to Huemac's ears.

Cocoa was brewed, its smell mixing with roasted duck and iguana—the night was rich with smells. And there was singing. The Nomads were the strongest. They sang with a kind of rage, an invitation for anyone to challenge them. Huemac smiled.

The first of the images stung him. It took his breath—spilling through his mind as if the seams of reality had begun to ripple. Whispering images—moving quickly, a flood of them. High-stepping, laughing, mocking—faces he had never seen, nude flesh, pieces of women, things impossible, all writhing in his mind like snakes.

He opened his eyes, touching the edge of the tent for support. The images stopped, the night folded back in, the singing from the beach resumed. Huemac angrily clenched his fist. He was here— they had reached the ocean, and nothing was going to steal this moment. In the past few days, Huemac felt his heat beat like a young jaguar—the brief hallucination was no more than sweat left of the fever and he would let it dry up, like puddles of a thunderstorm when the sun breaks.

Huemac turned. He smiled, seeing Sky Hawk walking up the white sand beach toward him. Surely, Sky Hawk would dispel any lingering madness. He was struck with a far memory of when they were young and Sky Hawk had captured a mud toad. Grinning widely, he had brought it to show Huemac, and as he held the creature up, it suddenly squished out of his fingers and soared into the air over their heads. When finally they looked at each other, Sky Hawk started laughing and soon they were both falling down with laughter—all over a simple mud toad. He paused, startled. Had tears just stung his lash? He furiously wiped the back of his hands over his eyes, cursing once more. What was happening?

Sky Hawk had just taken a swim; and when he reached Huemac, he shook out his wet hair and dropped his washed armor on a tuft of sea grass near the tent. He was quite handsome, Sky Hawk. He had married a darkly beautiful Chichimec, intelligent and even somehow kind, a virtual prize—but Sky Hawk could have had any woman in the world. It wasn't just his looks. He could speak with them. He somehow understood the strange minds of women. Everything came so easy for him.

"It's good to wash the stink off every once in a while," Sky Hawk said.

"That is why I struck for the sea. We are its children. The sea will heal us."

The crashes of the breakers below seemed to echo in answer. Huemac reached into his belt pouch and pulled out the object he had found there several days ago. He spun it in his finger. A carved, back-arched dolphin.

"The dolphin-prince," said Huemac. "It seems he somehow found his way into my belt pouch."

Sky Hawk nodded. "It was all the magic I could find in that dark place. I sent him after you—wherever you were those nights— I told him to keep you from leaving us. Do you remember anything about them? The nights you sweated there?"

Huemac puzzled, contemplating if such memories were too far away with which to be bothered. He shook his head. "I remember little."

"Perhaps that is good."

"Do you want him back?"

"No. You keep him. And if the dolphin-prince whispers in your ear, listen carefully."

Huemac slipped it back into his belt. "You do realize where we are, Sky Hawk?"

"That is the western sea. To the east . . . somewhere is the jungle. I know that much."

Huemac turned, pointed. "North. Home."

"We're going home?"

"Yes. We will cut our way through."

"What do you mean?"

"Olmeca. We are south of their city. It now lies between us and home."

Sky Hawk looked north in alarm. He shook his head. "The city of the Olmeca is walled. It is a fortress. The garrison armies surrounding it would alone be twice our numbers."

"Numbers will not matter."

"Huemac, these men . . . do you realize what they've been through? Do you know? No one has counted, but we've easily lost ten thousand. We still haven't heard from Silver Feather—the Wind Sign Knights are still lost in there. Huemac, the Olmec capital is far too strong. It is impossible."

"So . . . we do not go home? Is this your advice?"

"We will have to find another way. I remember the maps as well as you. If we circle farther south and then swing east, we can find the midland highway."

Huemac simply shook his head. "We go north; we pluck the city of the Olmeca as our gift."

Sky Hawk paused, worried. "What did she say to you?"

"Who?"

"The witch. She spoke to you, whispered things to you. Do you remember any of them? Anything?"

"No . . . wait. Yes, I remember this. She said she once looked in our father's eyes, and through them, she saw us. We were the reason she healed him once. Because she wanted us."

Sky Hawk stared at him, amazed. "Why would she tell you that?"

"I do not know. Perhaps she knew our father. Perhaps she mothered him, nursed him. As she did me."

Sky Hawk shook his head. "No . . . something is wrong in this, Huemac."

"In what?"

"In this! All this! Suddenly we are free of the jungle? Suddenly you are as strong as an eagle? Now the city of the Olmeca is our gift? Whatever she was, Huemac, I do not trust her, and whatever she did to you you need to understand it was not a motherly thing. We must walk careful now. We must . . . pray."

"Yes. Always pray, Sky Hawk. You pray, I will pray. And tomorrow we will kill the Olmeca like killing rabbits." Huemac tightened his jaw. "If we walk all the way to the south, go searching for the midland highway, not only will we be strung so thin and so weary that birds can walk over and pick our bones as we shuffle past, but also we will be destroyed utterly. So it is a simple thing; we take out the Olmeca and go home."

"It's another trap."

"Why bother with traps? They had us already, Sky Hawk. They killed ten thousand Nomads! Silvered Leaf is not lost; he was slaughtered. They were torn to pieces."

Sky Hawk shivered. It was true, he had denied it, but Silvered Leaf was dead.

"We have lost men," Huemac said, "but we have not lost our way. Home is north. And while moving north, I will cut out the heart of the Olmeca and take it back to our father." He slapped Sky Hawk on the shoulder. "Now, go get some rest. We will march with the sun this time. We will drink strength from the night and kill with the day."

"Huemac—"

"No more!" Huemac said warningly, shivering in sudden rage. "We march in the morning. Now go. Get sleep. I have a battle plan to blueprint."

"In the past, we planned battles together."

"Yes—but this one is mine."

Sky Hawk stared at him a moment longer, then lifted his armor and turned to walk down the sandy hill toward the fires that burned below like villages aflame.

Huemac kicked the body of a fallen Mayan warrior from the top of a rock and spread out the painted-bark parchment that had been brought to him. He used stones to anchor its edges and studied it by the light of torches stabbed into the dirt to either side.

The last of daylight was only a purple glaze left in the western sky. There was still open fighting to the north, but the outlying armies of the Olmeca who had tried to hold the jungle's perimeters about the city were destroyed. The Olmeca had fought to the death, but most were no more than fodder, cut like felling trees. The deadliest Olmec warriors had pulled back behind their city walls. Perhaps they were cowards. Huemac guessed they were survivors. The Tolteca were masters of fighting in open ground; the only chance they had was their city. Huemac would make it their tomb. None of the other Mayan tribes came to their aid, but Huemac knew there were many eyes in the trees, runners who would track every move he made swiftly to the narrow neck of Zarahemla, throughout the lowlands, even to the highland mountains of the Gadiantons.

Sky Hawk came out of the night, weary, a smell of sweat and blood to him. The killing smell was like no other. Huemac thought for a moment how over the years it had become an ordinary smell.

"What is this?" Sky Hawk asked.

"The city. You were right—a citadel." He touched a dagger to the map. "Ramparts of dirt landfill faced with smooth limestone. They will be difficult to scale."

"A good reason to let the Olmeca rot inside them. The path north is open, Huemac. Nothing stands in our way."

Huemac ignored him. "Second Skin tells me you found a step pyramid back there. He said it stank. He said the hearts about the offering stone were like flowers all dried up and tossed aside."

"I don't care if they have stripped more flesh than Mictlan. Taking that city will cost us everything. We'd need twenty thousand men."

Huemac smiled as he studied the map. If only Sky Hawk knew. "I guessed this—see, they build their streets in straight lines, always from the west to the east." Huemac turned, searching the jungle behind them. "Second Skin!" he shouted.

Sky Hawk glanced at the map. "Who drew this?"

"A captive."

"You trust a captive?"

"No. But he knows if we find he has deceived us, he will carry his sister's head in a wicker box."

"Huemac, tell me you are not going to take siege."

"I do not have time for siege."

"Then you agree—we leave for the north?"

"A lot of thatch—we could burn them. But if we did that, the tribes watching us would see it as the act of cowards. We would gain nothing."

"I suppose you would prefer they watch us die instead."

Second Skin joined them. His peccary-leather armor was matted in blood, but the killing in the jungles was over. Ordinary night sounds, even crickets, had replaced the screams of dying. Second Skin pulled off his helmet.

"You asked for me, my lord."

"How many dead—and how many are inside the city walls?"

"I have no count of how many we killed in the jungles this day, but there were whole divisions that have fled into the jungles and the forests. Those we killed were suspiciously easy prey. I believe their best warriors are inside the walls. Perhaps fifteen hundred, perhaps two thousand. All of them prime."

"And all of them nicely gathered in one place. We will take them right before dawn."

Sky Hawk closed his eyes a moment, shook his head. "Huemac, you must know that is impossible. It would take days, months. We would have to defend all flanks against the Olmeca regrouping from the jungles and lay siege of their city walls at the same time. We do not have enough men. Even if we did, we have been pressed to our limit, we could not endure."

"Relax. We will take this city before the sun is mid-sky."

"How?"

Huemac left the map on the rock and used the tip of his sword to draw its rough outline in the moist dirt. "This is the capital, looking east. Two gates, a small gate to the north, the main gate here on the eastern wall. It opens to the coastal highway and it is wide. Opened, nothing could stop us from sacking the city." Huemac knelt, pulling an arrow from his quiver. He broke the arrow into three pieces. "We come at them from three directions." He stabbed the tip of the arrow into the dirt. "First: the eastern wall. The Nomads and every division except Crimson Companion's will circle and take up formation near the sea. They will wait until the sunrise is at their backs before engaging. Archers, slingers, and atlatls will harass the towers above the gate while squadrons advance under the cover of long shields. We should bring along two or three rough-cut timber for rams."

"My lord," said Second Skin, "with respect, these gates will not be challenged by rams. They are massive."

"Agreed. The rams are a ruse. I want the Maya to think we are dumb enough to try."

"And of course," Sky Hawk mused, "we are not."

"Of course. Better to open it from the inside. Before that, however, the Nomads must move in under cover of shields close enough to ram. When it opens, the gate must open very quickly— seconds will count. Once close enough, the Nomads will sink grappling rope into its face. Ten ropes for each half of the gate. Second Skin, have your men make these ropes thick, well knotted, strong enough twenty men can pull on each line."

Second Skin glanced in Sky Hawk's direction, raising a brow.

"Huemac," Sky Hawk said, "how do you suggest we lift the crossbeam and open this gate?"

"I am getting to that. First we will talk about the second thrust." Huemac stabbed the middle piece of his broken arrow into the ground. "From the cover of the northern forest, Crimson Companion and the Eagle Knights will launch a full attack on the smaller gate."

"Another ruse?" asked Second Skin. "The gate there is as massive as the eastern."

"Yes. The gate itself is of no interest to me. Crimson Companion will convince the Maya that our assault on their eastern wall was to cover our true target, the smaller northern gate. That is it. That is the plan. Except for us."

"Us?" questioned Sky Hawk.

"You, me, Second Skin, chosen others." Huemac planted the last piece of the arrow, with its white feathers. "This is the southwest edge of the city. I am told the wall here is irregular and built of stone that is more ancient. The limestone is not flush—gaps are left where the mortar is soft enough to anchor grappling lines. We can use atlatls launched from the ground to secure them. Afterward, it should not be difficult to scale."

Sky Hawk looked closer. "We go over the wall?"

"Yes. Scale to the top, then down the other side undetected."

"How are we undetected?"

"Because we are small. Like the children who dropped from the trees, we will be tiny to them. With an army at the sea and a second at their northern gate, no one will be watching this corner at all. We take in three and twelve, sacred numbers. The three are you, Second Skin, and I. The twelve are chosen shield-bearers and rangers."

"Fifteen men?" Sky Hawk chuckled. "We are going in with fifteen men?"

"Yes. But think only of three and twelve. We need magic. Three and twelve: sacred numbers."

"And when the three of us and the other twelve are inside the Olmec city, what then? A bean game? Put on a play . . . die, perhaps?"

Huemac sighed and finally gave Sky Hawk a hard look. "Have I ever let you down, Sky Hawk?"

"No, you have not. It has always been and still is my role to temper your strength with wisdom—and right now I am very worried about the wisdom part of this plan. We would be dead in a heartbeat of the sun. The few of us drop over the wall into the back of a city filled with two thousand fresh warriors?" Sky Hawk let his point rest.

"Numbers do not—"

"Here they will matter! My God, Huemac. Have you lost your mind? Fifteen—"

"Twelve and three."

Sky Hawk sighed in frustration. "Twelve and three—against two thousand!"

"There is a backstreet of the city here," Huemac said calmly as he drew a line in the dirt with the tip of his dagger. "It runs along the edge of the temple platform. It will give us cover all the way to the ceremonial plaza, here. From that point we must stun them, surprise them—a direct thrust from the corner of the plaza straight through to the eastern gate." Huemac cut a deep line in the dirt with his dagger, leaving his dagger in place near his first arrow tip on the eastern wall. "We must be swift, we will move and not stop moving, we will shock them by moving so quick and so suddenly they cannot think what to do. Then it is over. When we reach the eastern gate, we turn and hold. That will be hardest, the moments we must hold at the gate. They will no longer be surprised. On the other hand, we need only hold long enough to drop the crossbeam. With the grappling lines, the Nomads will wrench the gate wide. The eastern sun will pour into the capital along with all the armies of Tula."

Second Skin had tightened his jaw, but his dark eyes now studied Huemac's sketch with interest. Sky Hawk stared silent for a long time.

"As to the twelve," Huemac said, "choose carefully, Second Skin. Three of them must be ranged fighters, atlatls and bow—they will keep a pathway open as long as possible. They will certainly die. Two must be shield-bearers. Seven must be Slayers. Seven, two, three: all good numbers." Huemac eased back on his haunches. "In the end, the plan is quite simple."

Huemac stood and looked to Sky Hawk.

"I just don't think you have made it impossible enough," said Sky Hawk. "I think we should all go in with one arm tied to our backs."

"That is just your mother speaking, Sky Hawk. Paper Flower— always the clever one. No, we should use both hands."

Second Skin didn't look at either of them; he stared at the map for a long time with his stone killer eyes. "At least we will die quickly," he finally said.

𝕎𝕎𝕎𝕎𝕎𝕎𝕎𝕎𝕎𝕎𝕎𝕎𝕎

Before dawn, Huemac, Sky Hawk, Second Skin and twelve Nomad warriors moved into place in the shadows of the jungle with the tall, ancient wall of the old city before them. The mortar in the stone was easy to spot since mold had left it darker than the limestone finish. They waited first for the far sound of the conch shell from the east before quickly and silently sprinting from the jungles. Second Skin was the first up. He spun and dropped to a crouch to whip his atlatl for a high thrust. His launcher fired the heavy dart with it grappling line and when it came taut, he went up the wall as swift as a spider. On top, he pulled himself over the edge and squatted, searching for any manned towers. There were none; no one watched the back wall of the city.

Second Skin could hear commotion from the east. His Nomads were closing on the gate. Within the city, they would be running, everyone running like ants all stirred up by a stick.

Second Skin worked speedily. Using his war hammer, he embedded atlatls in the stone cracks and then dropped heavy lines over the side. As soon as they dropped they were seized, and the others were all soon crawling up to join him. He heard the second conch shell, far to the north—the signal for Crimson Companion to attack the northern gate. From where he crouched, much of the city was visible. There was commotion down there everywhere now, some running for the main gate, some to the north. They were all terrified. Thus far, Huemac's plan had worked perfectly. Of course, the difficult part had not been attempted—yet.

The next to reach the top was Huemac; he pulled himself over then rolled to Second Skin's side. They were all keeping low, squatting. The twelve chosen then gathered, one by one. The rangers said nothing when they reached the top; they busied themselves loading atlatls and checking equipment. The last over was Sky Hawk, who had been covering their flank in case they were spotted from the jungle.

On his belly, Sky Hawk crawled to the edge and surveyed the plaza below. He silently pointed out marks, warriors in positions who might possible spot a descent inside the walls. Second Skin motioned and his archers crouched beside Sky Hawk, where they took swift and deadly aim. When Sky Hawk motioned the plaza was clear, Second Skin threw the grappling ropes over the inside face of the wall.

Huemac went over first, the others following, all of them letting the ropes slide through their palms, moving swiftly, soundlessly, almost flying down the face of the stone. They dropped onto the hard, red dirt inside the Olmec city. They were behind the temple; they were in shadows.

Sky Hawk led them, crouched, running. They were moving quickly, the alley between the ancient temple platform on their left and the old city wall to their right. Huemac had been right—the passage here was narrow and dark. This was the largest temple in the city and its platform was huge, offering perfect cover until they reached the plaza. They ran as fast as they could, slightly crouched. Once they reached the far corner of the temple, Sky Hawk motioned them to halt.

He carefully scanned the market plaza in front of them to the right. There were buildings, well-placed brick walkways, glyphic heritage slabs known as *stelae*, and ancient trees that had been left to spread canopies of natural shade. The plaza was rather well manicured; it appeared peaceful and calming. The Maya were skilled artisans; the buildings were all etched in painted bas-relief with fantastic images and symbols of red and black. The stone of the buildings was, though brightly painted, weathered, a far different look than the clean stone of Tula. In places, natural ivy and vines snaked over the stone, giving the building a natural look.

TOLTECA

It was a beautiful city. Even the Olmeca, the tall, proud Maya who were everywhere in the plaza beyond, were regal, stately. Many were lords, their heads purposefully misshapen and elongated.

But most of the Olmeca in the plaza were commoners. There was a lot of movement. The two attacks to the east and north had sent warriors running and left women scampering with children. The people were hushed and murmuring, all aware of the shouts and screams coming from the gates, and most would be terrified the Tolteca had even dared to attack the city. It seemed outrageous to try, especially to launch a full assault against the massive, heavily fortified gates, but the Tolteca were unlike other armies, and the people obviously feared them as if they were supernatural. Panic had broken out. Magistrates and military commanders were trying to keep the panic from spreading, but it must have confusing, even to the warriors. Groups of warriors were rushing to the east or to the north. No one was scared of the shadows near the ancient temple.

From where he stood, Sky Hawk could see past a building across the plaza to glimpse a high corner of the ornate eastern wall. Huemac was right; his dagger could cut a deep straight line to that gate. Yet here it looked far away. It just as well could have been an ocean away. It was filled with warriors—mostly closer to the gate—but even in the plaza, they were scattered everywhere.

Sky Hawk glanced back at the others. "Huemac, if we were to move due south, hugging this wall, we might have a chance to circle around and beneath the gates."

"No," Huemac said. "No time. There is only one path, the truest path, directly through the plaza."

"I was afraid you were going to say that," Sky Hawk sighed, "a true path directly into the heart of the entire standing army of the Olmeca."

"If ever you were swift, Sky Hawk, be swift now." Huemac glanced back to Second Skin. "Have your archers drop back and take out as many as they can for as long as they can."

Sky Hawk glanced at the three archers. They were heavily

armored to allow them to stay alive as long as possible, even against spears and darts. In the shadows, he could barely see their eyes beneath the helmets, but they looked unafraid. Second Skin had chosen well.

"Spare women and children," Huemac told them, "but open the best killing path you can maintain to either side of us."

The eldest archer slapped his fist to his shoulder. They knew they would die here. They were probably all about to die, but even if Huemac's plan were to succeed, these archers would be left in the rear, alone. They carried no swords; they would spend out their atlatls and arrows until they were overtaken—and they carried obsidian daggers to cut their own throats. Sky Hawk watched Huemac meet each of their eyes.

"If this hour is remembered," he said to them, "then your names will be spoken first."

Sky Hawk was readying his weapons, unlatching the thigh brace of his dagger, dropping back the loop that held his war hammer over his shoulder. He drew his razor-sword, curling his hands through the leather wrist strap and then tightly about the sharkskin hilt. "Of course you realize this is still impossible," he whispered to Huemac.

"Of course," Huemac whispered back.

Huemac himself reached to either side and withdrew two modified razor-swords. Huemac had trained himself to wield two of them at once. The swords had special vertical hilts that allowed him to grip them sideways. They became extensions of his arms, rings of flashing silvered obsidian.

Sky Hawk eased himself loose, limber, quickened his reflexes. "And of course you realize it is utter madness to even attempt reaching that gate?"

"Crossing the ocean was madness. Leaving Paradise was madness. All we've known since coming here is madness. Why bother with change?"

Huemac took measured breaths, preparing. He latched his

cheek-guards into place. He looked about at all of them, Sky Hawk, Second Skin; he met the eyes of the twelve chosen.

"Everyone ready, then?" Sky Hawk asked.

Huemac let a long slow breath out and the muscles in his arms seemed to swell.

Sky Hawk noticed a shield-bearer muttering a quick prayer into his helmet and waited for him to look up.

Second Skin lowered his head slightly—a nod, *let's go.*

Sky Hawk crouched and leveled his sword at the plaza. "Go!"

"See you on the other side!" Huemac said as he turned the edge and sprinted into the open sun.

Sky Hawk, Second Skin, and the chosen nine warriors fell in at Huemac's flanks. Behind them, the three rangers stepped out of the shadow and quickly spread out, running toward the steps of the temple. When they reached it, they dropped back to take up positions along the temple's base, lifting their spear-throwers, their bows, and spilling piles of atlatls and arrows about their feet. Immediately they fed arrows into the gut-strings of their bows— swiftly choosing targets.

At first, the Maya were unaware. All of the Nomad rangers' marks were kills. Warriors dropped soundlessly. Eventually it was noticed that here and there warriors were spinning and slamming into the stone. Even then, the Maya were still slow to realize where the fire originated. One woman started screaming. She was holding an infant tight to her breast, staring down at a Mayan warlord whose skull had been cracked by an atlatl shaft. She continued screaming until she crumpled with a *gluk* as an arrow took out her throat. The baby, wrapped in a colored blanket, rolled away. A warrior noticed, turning in utter amazement, but as he reached for his spear, arrows peppered him and he unceremoniously dropped to the stone.

Mayan warriors came to life; they turned, searching, weapons clearing sheaths—but they still hadn't comprehended what was happening. Just as Huemac had promised, it was madness to them. Most warriors were still looking to the eastern gate or running for the northern wall thinking the wall had been breached. None of them realized the deadly spray of arrows ripping one after the other without a second's pause came from the very steps of their most sacred temple.

Surprisingly, in the confusion, few even noticed Huemac coming like a heavy, charging caiman, hurtling silently toward them. The feathered streamers of his shoulder pads flew behind him and his boots were heavy as they padded across the stone. In years to come many would tell the story that he came with thunder feet—that each of his running steps shattered stone.

To Huemac's left, as shield-bearer, was Second Skin, and to his right Sky Hawk. Behind the three, the remaining nine Nomads moved at full run in tight formation, all of them with mantles streaming, weapons bristling. They may have come silently, but their colors flew—the crimson headbands, their feathered shoulder streamers—they looked like shooting stars. They tore across the plaza like panthers closing on flocks of geese. At first, those they collided with were thrown aside; others, seeing them coming scattered, terrified. As they closed on the more crowded area of the plaza, their formation tightened into a wedge, a phalanx, a spear point about to drive inward. The tip of the spear was Huemac's scalpel-edged swords, spinning in brilliant flashes. No one had ever seen anything like them, and at first, Huemac achieved complete and utter shock.

The Maya in his path fled. Huemac's fantastic spinning swords made him look like a specter. Even hardened warriors turned and ran. But not all. One Olmec warlord screamed a war cry and pushed through the crowds leading a group of heavily armored Slayers. Huemac kept running, not even bracing because though they had spotted him, they had yet to comprehend the deadly swarm of arrow shafts buzzing everywhere.

The Nomad rangers had cast aside their atlatls and used only bows—bows that blurred with arrow after arrow, swiftly taking their mark with deadly selection and precision.

TOLTECA

As the first group of warriors closed to block Huemac following the lead of their charging captain, their flanks were quickly stripped and then their center hollowed. They didn't even get close. It left a bizarre effect. As the warriors fell against the deadly spray, Huemac appeared to be slaying from a distance, as though warriors were dropping dead from his approach alone. Many Olmeca truly feared a warrior god had spawned that day. They would name him Kukulcán: Feathered Slayer.

Huemac drove always forward, never looking back or to the side. Nor did any of the Toltec warriors behind turn. They all drove at full run for a single target. The Tolteca kept moving. You could mark their path if you wished—a straight line of felled bodies, from the temple platform across the ceremonial plaza directly for the eastern gate—much like the deep cut of Huemac's dagger the night before. Ahead, the massive mahogany lintels of the gate were a dark, polished silhouette against the morning sun, which now was blinding the archers in the towers and battlements as they tried to fire down on the solid mass of shields closing against them from the sea.

Within the plaza, the spray of arrow fire for the longest time continued to give Huemac and the others an advantage. Just as a spear lifted against them, the warrior would grunt, staggering. It kept attacks thinned. Those who did reach the Tolteca were delivered an even swifter death of razor-swords that flayed them open like gutting fish. For a moment the small band of Tolteca moved through the forest of warriors and civilians in the plaza like a shining obsidian wind, scattering people like leaves, cutting flesh in broad, savage slashes, leaving blood splayed in a wide swath behind them.

Now, finally, they were about to close on the prime of the Olmeca, the city's protectors. The closer they got to the eastern gate, the thicker the warriors became. Huemac and Sky Hawk were about to thrust directly at the heart of a gathering frontline formed of Mayan warriors hardened of battle and grizzled by death. By

K. MICHAEL WRIGHT

now, the Maya had realized that as amazing and swift as they were, the Tolteca tearing across the plaza consisted of only a handful of warriors. The protectors closed rank to snuff them.

Huemac came low, boring into them—spinning, circling as his swords to either side sliced flesh almost continuously, ripping to bone in swift, clean arcs. It was as though flesh had become cotton or silk, cut to strips. There were unholy screams. Maya rushed to block him, but Huemac had become a death of whirling, spinning blades. Sky Hawk saw them drop from all sides of Huemac—warriors who had simply been flayed and thrown back.

Deeper they moved. Harder, boring into them.

At first strike, even the protectors were tossed and scattered before Huemac, though they tried to close on him. If they came at Huemac's left, the deadly, living blades of Second Skin welcomed them. To his right, the swift cuts of Sky Hawk. Everywhere, the razor-swords of the Tolteca flashed. It seemed impossible, something out of nightmares. Blood whipped as surgical cuts sheared through armor, flesh, bone—nothing mattered, the terrible flashing blades just hummed.

Inward. Deeper still.

᳁᳁᳁᳁᳁᳁᳁᳁᳁᳁᳁᳁᳁᳁᳁᳁᳁᳁

The archers who had remained at the base of the temple platform continued to fire; but by now, the armies of the Olmeca had folded in behind Huemac and the others, enveloping them. It would no longer be possible to help. But it didn't matter. The archers had been spotted. From all sides, Maya came at a run. The archers did not flinch—their constant fire simply shifted to train on the advancing squadrons. The gap was closing, bodies marking their path. At close range, warriors spun wildly, backs arched, knees buckling; but then it was over.

Seconds before he was overwhelmed, the first archer cast aside his bow and as his hand drew back, his own dagger opened his neck

560

beneath the chin, shearing the windpipe with a *chunk*.

🮥🮥🮥🮥🮥🮥🮥🮥🮥🮥🮥🮥🮥🮥🮥🮥🮥

Now only momentum could save the Tolteca thrust. They were completely enveloped. And they began to die.

There was such frenzy in the last moments, Sky Hawk could barely distinguish earth from sky. There were warriors hurtling at them from every side.

To Sky Hawk's rear he briefly saw a war hammer shatter Second Skin's helmet, but Second Skin did not drop; he spun in a tight circle and coming out of it, his blade lobbed the top of the Mayan's head back as if it were a drinking cup.

Directly behind Sky Hawk one of the shield-bearers arched his back as a hardwood spear *thunked* through his shoulder. With a flick, his razor-sword cut the poltroon to a stump. With gritted teeth, the Nomad continued fighting, continued moving, beheading the Mayan who had wounded him.

Somewhere to the rear, a Nomad screamed. Nomads died with death cries. Their fall could be marked above any battle din. From a corner of his eye, Sky Hawk saw the warrior drop, saw Maya swarm over the fallen body like snarling wolves.

Now they were ten. Still moving, driving.

Sky Hawk fought blindly. He did not waste time with "targets"; everything was a target. His only mark of direction was Huemac's scream to his left front—as well as the screams of those dying at his blades.

As he moved, Sky Hawk was slaying sideways to hold the flank.

Seconds now. Only seconds left to live. Sky Hawk's heart failed him—they could never win this. An axe slashed through his shoulder, deep enough he felt the hot sting of the cut. A spear tip lanced his chest, impossibly sharp. Its blade ripped through the leather corselet and Sky Hawk's own blood splattered across his face, in his eyes. He thought he was going down when his backplate was seized from behind.

It was Huemac.

"The gate!" Huemac screamed, hurling Sky Hawk to collide with the wooden buttresses. They had reached the gate. Through the blood in his eyes, he saw arched ramparts framed against the blue sky that had somehow remained serene.

"Throw the bar!" Huemac cried.

Panic clawing at him, the frenzy behind him a roar of utter madness, Sky Hawk scrambled up the stanchions, leaping for the crossbar. Without volition, Sky Hawk screamed his mother's name. "Mother, help me!" he shrieked like a boy whose foot had been caught and was being braced by the last stanchion's edge. His hand pushed against the crossbeam's squared buttress.

"Hold! Hold!" Second Skin's harsh cry ripped above the din.

As he heaved upward with everything he had, Sky Hawk briefly caught sight of them. Their backs against the gate, Huemac and his Nomads fought the most impossible battle of their lives. They held a sheer killing zone of obsidian razors that washed everything in such blood the Mayan defenders slipped on the limestone. It might have been the only thing that saved them.

Sky Hawk heaved, everything straining. He could never lift this beam, it would have taken three men, but the terror and fury in Sky Hawk felt as if it would rip him to pieces against it should it refuse to budge, so he screamed, he shoved his whole shoulder into the bar. It moaned. It lifted off the brace.

He was aware of Nomads dying. From the corner, he saw Purple Sand twist to the side. Mortally wounded, the big warrior flung himself into them with a furious battle cry—launching into spears, hammers, and axes that ripped and smashed him into a bloodied hulk.

Another Nomad roared as a heavy spear impaled him into the gate, sundering his right shoulder. It had nailed him back into the heavy wood. He continued to fight with his left, sharing death as his life spilled out his blade. Weakened, he became fodder. One spear impaled his chest and another the center of his face, through his helmet.

Five left holding.

The beam moaned as it painfully slid upward. It ground against the bracing as it moved. Sky Hawk was going to pass out, but the beam continued lifting. He was giving everything he had—his scream sucking away the last of his wind. An arrow ripped across his back, just beneath his armor, strafing from shoulder to shoulder. The beam crushed back down on him, falling—but a Nomad from below leapt to the stanchion, catching it. As Sky Hawk fell, the Nomad heaved upward with his whole body.

The crossbeam cleared the bracings. The second it was free, grappling lines seized the gate from behind and wrenched it open like the jaws of a beast.

Sky Hawk hit the ground on his back, ground cleared by the huge gate as it was wrenched open. Barely conscious, he somehow knew to scramble out of the way. He didn't know if Huemac or any of his warriors survived. He couldn't see anything and the screams of fury as Nomad warriors cut into the Mayan protectors swallowed everything, including Sky Hawk's consciousness.

CHAPTER FIFTY-ONE
NAMED

The healers had sealed their wounds with the flat edges of obsidian daggers fired to a white-hot sheen. It was painful, but quick, and when the message came, Second Skin stared at the messenger a moment feeling a chill. Second Skin nodded and the messenger turned and walked away, stepping over bodies that littered in his path.

Second Skin walked over to where Huemac sat against a tall, standing stone. It was a Mayan *stela*, though the line of kings it spoke of had ended.

The ocean behind them calmly washed against the white shore that bordered the capital city's eastern wall. Over Huemac's shoulder, beyond the city gate, whose massive mahogany doors still gaped wide, fires calmly licked the sky. They were quiet now, but for hours, they had raged.

"*Itzás,*" Second Skin said when Huemac looked up.

Amazingly, Huemac had few wounds, none of them serious. It turned out very little of the blood that soaked him was his own. He was virtually unscathed.

"What about them?" Huemac responded.

"They ask for sacred council. Twelve of us, twelve of them. They wait in the jungles west."

Huemac nodded and pulled himself to his feet. He had shed himself of all but a loin-clout. Though the blood had been washed off, the thick hair of his chest was still oiled in sweat.

"Should I waken Sky Hawk?" asked Second Skin.

"He needs to recover from his wounds. He has lost too much

blood. Gather ten captains to accompany us."

"Crimson Companion among them, my lord?"

"Only Nomads."

"As you speak."

"Have the servants bring my armor."

⊟⊟⊟⊟⊟⊟⊟⊟⊟⊟⊟⊟⊟⊟⊟⊟⊟

They waited, in a grove: twelve *Itzás*. They did not move when Second Sky, Huemac, and the Nomad captains entered the grove, but they did watch warily.

Second Skin had never seen Maya like these, High-Blood Maya, each of them with their heads purposely misshapen, reaching backward to peak, deforming their eyes. Their robes were black, but from their shoulders, the rich plumage of their mantles was a fantasy of color to rival any Tolteca dragon cloak. Their hair was the color of night and their eyes as they watched the Tolteca enter were cold—they held no fear, no fear—no feelings, no emotions. The oval, almost almond shape of their heads left the illusion they were not human, and indeed, it was said that of ancients the Water Wizards had come from a far place not of this world. Second Skin knew they were nothing like the Olmeca who hung now from a forest of poltroons lining the edge of the western sea. The grove they waited in was almost like a cave, hollowed into the jungle.

When Huemac and Second Skin's ten captains reached the middle of the grove, they stopped. Second Skin took up his position on Huemac's left flank, one step back. His captains fanned out behind them. When one of the *Itzás* caught his eye alone, Second Skin nodded his head slightly, an offering he gave very few enemies. The wizard did not nod back.

Huemac faced down the king of the *Itzás* in a cold stare. Second Skin noticed how the mirrored edge of one of Huemac's razor-sword rippled in the watery torchlight, unwashed of the Olmec blood.

Yet it was not the *Itzás*' king who spoke. In fact, he wasn't a king at all. The tall, dark-haired figure who stood in the center moved aside. Behind him, sitting on a dark red mat, was the old woman. Her head, of course, was not as deformed as the others were. Instead of the tattered gray threads she had worn when she came to the camp to heal Huemac, she wore flowing black silk robes, her stark white hair and opaque eyes in contrast. Impossibly, the haggard old woman now looked . . . regal. Powerful. Dread. Second Skin felt a shiver crawl under his skin.

"I have called you forth," she said, her dead, blind eyes staring only at Huemac. "Now I will give you a name. You are Kukulcán: Feathered Slayer."

The old woman's voice had lost all trace of kindness; it was edged in a harsh, grainy whisper that unnerved even Second Skin.

"By what right do believe you can name me, old woman?" Huemac snarled.

"Careful. You may be God's wrath, but trust me—*He* seldom bothers with his chosen. I am ancient. I am many. By my own right I name you."

Her bony hand lifted. The tall one Second Skin had first thought was their king stepped forward. When the light of the torches struck this one's face, Second Skin was amazed. He was only a youth. He was beautiful, perfect. His eyes were the cold, dark blue of deep water. He lifted his hand. In his delicate fingers was a small, silver cylinder.

No one moved. The youth calmly waited.

"He has something you seek," the old woman's raspy voice urged.

Huemac motioned Second Skin. Tingling, though not displaying a trace of his disquiet, Second Skin stepped forward. When he was close, he felt an energy playing about the youth. It bothered Second Skin deeply; it was passion, licking his skin as he reached for the scroll. Second Skin had killed men for feeling this kind of passion, and disgust welled in his gut. He wanted to stare the *Itzá* down, but he had no desire to look in those eyes up close.

In the youth's fingers was a fantastic cylinder with rich, silver swirls and intricate jade insets. Second Skin tried to take it, but for a moment the youth's finger held tight, forcing Second Skin to remain close. His breath on Second Skin's cheek was cold. Second Skin had no choice but to look up. The young wizard's eyes were quick, the irises a shining blue, but the pupils were so dark they seemed to open into the night—as if Second Skin could look through them and see stars. The youth finally released the cylinder and Second Skin was able to turn away.

Second Skin held any emotion from showing his face. As he passed Huemac, he handed over the cylinder. He took up his position at Huemac's left, but the eyes haunted him, as though they had followed at his back, as though if he were to look at the face of the youth there would be only empty sockets. But Second Skin didn't look. His stare focused on Huemac's fingers as they turned the cylinder and broke the blood-red wax seal.

Out of the silver cylinder spilled a rolled parchment the size of finger. Huemac unrolled it, spreading it against his palm. Second Skin was amazed. It was wondrous—only a small piece of parchment, but worked with tiny feathers in brilliant colors with edges lined in golden foil. It was a signet—a cross, the top facing downward. This was the symbol of the southern star.

"The talisman of *Tomoanchan*: Zarahemla," the old woman's voice whispered.

Huemac looked up, startled.

"It was crafted many centuries ago in a time when there was only water and sky. It is holy and untouchable."

"Why give it to me?"

"A gift," she said. "My gift—both the signet and the city that bears its name."

The old woman lifted her hand and all of them, all but her and the tall youth, bowed before Huemac, their pointed heads lowered.

"The Tribute of a Thousand Hearts," the old woman said. "That is a name once given *Tomoanchan*. Now it is yours to do with as you wish, its riches, its lineage, its blood . . . even its hearts, I suppose—

all yours now."

"How can that be?"

"We are ancient. We decide who shall be named in this land. Even in your grandfather's day, though the dragon was feared in Heaven as he was on earth, we were the ones who named our lord. And in this hour, we name you."

Slowly she lifted her hand and extended her finger. At the motion, the youth walked over to silently take position at Huemac's side—to his right. Huemac looked at the old woman, puzzled.

"He goes with you now. If you wish him to serve you, he will. If you wish his heart, he will cut it out for you. If it you want his flesh—it is yours."

The *Itzá* around the old woman ow lifted her platform. It rode on golden handles to the height of their shoulders. "When you reach the north," the witch said, "go to your father, the one they call Serpent Plumed—go to him and tell him who has named you king in the land of the *ceiba*."

Then she was gone; they turned with her and it seemed they simply melted into the dark of the jungle. Just as they had turned away, Second Skin noticed something about her left foot. It was silver.

CHAPTER FIFTY-TWO
THE NIGHT AXE

Huemac stood upon a balcony of his father's Butterfly Palace staring out at the city of Tula. The fires from the plaza etched the mural behind him in soft, shadowy light that made its images seem almost to move. Huemac watched as the singers and musicians wandered the streets, weaving a spell over the city. He wondered how many understood the full measure of what they celebrated.

He closed his eyes and waited. Almost instantly, the Night and the Wind flooded the backs of his eyelids. Blood this time—writhing bodies moving with the many types of blood that covered a battlefield: blood as it melts between the lacerations of mangled flesh; blood as it runs clean and quick about the edge of freshly cut bone; clots of the thick, black blood of dead organs.

He opened his eyes and let the firelight and songs of celebration slowly burn out the nightmare though its afterimages, the screaming in his ears, lingered to remind him he had not slept. He had not been able to sleep a single night since the old woman had met his eyes in the jungle grove.

He lifted a tremulous hand against the Creator's Temple, washed in firelight across from him. He spread his fingers in the sign of the word. His mother, the small, light-haired Jewel Twirler, had taught him this sign. Then, in the days of his youth, faith had spilt from his mother's eyes like the milk stream of Heaven. He was only four when she taught him this sign. She had placed her fingers over his and lifted them both to the sky, and when her soft, whispery voice spoke, it left tingles through him, as though he needed to remember this, as though a time would come when nothing else would matter but her words on that single day. *The sign of the word, little one— given in a time so old it has no age, in a place remembered only of the Star Voyagers. Here speaks the Light Whose Name Is Splendor!*

But even the memory of his mother's faith failed him now. Huemac's hand, though held in the sign of the word of God, just trembled like a drunk's until he finally pulled it back and curled it into a fist. He pressed it against his thigh and forced it to stop shaking.

Hearing the pad of feet approaching, Huemac turned. He watched Coxcox coming down the hallway. The little man strode with determination, his bright eyes quick and alive. How odd; the sight of Coxcox actually calmed him slightly—as if there were a chance here, some slim forgotten chance still to turn time. The songs, the stories, the legends of their ancestors, it could not end like this. There must be salvation. There had to be. Strange he would find such thoughts in seeing the little cripple.

◧◨◧◨◧◨◧◨◧◨◧◨◧◨◧◨◧◨◧◨

When Coxcox first heard that Huemac had been asking for him, he felt hopeful. Over the years he had gotten to know almost all of Topiltzin's sons, but Huemac was always distant from them. Huemac let no one close. Coxcox had never been able to reach him. Perhaps this was finally his opportunity. Perhaps he could find a way through to the soul of Topiltzin's dark-eyed son. He sometimes felt a person's spirit, as if he could look beneath flesh, and Coxcox had been surprised to find such a childlike, almost gentle spirit in the broad-shouldered, heavy warrior who spawned terror by simply walking through the streets of Tula.

Just beyond, Huemac was an imposing figure standing on the portico. His great dragon cloak fell from his broad, muscled shoulders like dark wings. His tangled, night-black hair was wild, unwashed. The silver band on his arm glinted from the night fires. Coxcox could not help but feel a shiver for Huemac had truly

570

become the Warlord of the Tolteca; he had absorbed his damnation and fueled it into fear that bled off him like the heat of the sun. Despite his anxiety, Coxcox entered without hesitation. Coxcox bowed three times before speaking.

"My lord Huemac," he said, "you have summoned me?"

Huemac almost smiled. Just in case, Coxcox made sure he smiled back. The warlord's eyes were heavy, and there were storms in them, storms flashing in terrible night. It was difficult to look on them, but Coxcox did—he remained hopeful, he wanted to look beyond the storms and somehow find the quiet soul who breathed in those eyes, the child. Coxcox looked into those dark eyes, searching, but instead of finding the quiet one, something screamed at him.

A sharp chill shot down his back, something terrible here, some-thing very dark in these eyes. What could be wrong? Where was the boy? The quiet one? Coxcox's left hand clasped his right hand in front of him as if they were friends meeting in a dark hour, and despite himself, he felt a sweat break across his brow.

"What is it you need, my lord?" Coxcox pressed, still smiling. He could not understand why suddenly everything inside him wanted to scream. Something terribly wrong here, something that could swallow him in a second, all his world, all their world, something that could swallow light itself. His mind raced.

"How have you been, Coxcox?"

The voice of Huemac was calm, but Coxcox had to force his concentration. *Focus, try to look composed.*

"Me? I have been well, my lord, yes, I have been well." Feeling suddenly desperate, Coxcox just kept talking. "Yes, it is has been a good season here in the North. Exceptional orange fruit from the coast this season—did you know? Exceptional. Also, the markets here in Tula have been thriving. I saw gooses. Gray gooses and white gooses as well, all barking like little hairless dogs, except these had feathers. Ha. I mean, gooses barking like dogs!"

Huemac had not smiled. Quite suddenly, Coxcox realized what was wrong, what was crawling through his skin. They were not alone in this room. It might appear there were only the two of them, the dread warlord and Coxcox, but that would be wrong; that would be a most deadly error.

"I need to speak with my father," Huemac said. "My father and no one else, not even you."

They were moving all about the prince, everywhere. Oh, but, oh God, Coxcox could not even count the shadows that moved about him!

"Did you hear me?" Huemac asked with a slight underscore of irritation.

"Yes, my lord. Yes. You were saying . . . saying you wanted to speak with Topiltzin. Alone. Yes, I understand." Inside he was feeling raw panic. "When would you like this to happen, my lord?"

"Now, if possible."

"Yes, I see. Right away, then? If possible?"

"Yes."

He realized that though Huemac seemed aware of the shadows, they had not yet overtaken him. Something there, some small thing between them and the Prince of Tula. Then Coxcox realized what it was. The child—the quiet heart of innocence still beating in the warlord's chest, belonged to someone. It had not been taken because it was already owned, given to another. There was a far hope, because as terrible and clever as these shadows were, Huemac's heart had not yet let them in. It was someone else's property, and Coxcox sensed a spirit fighting there, holding against the dark and this spirit had the strength that could only belong to a woman. That seemed so odd. Coxcox had never even seen Huemac with another, had never known the warrior to bond with either a man or a woman. Yet a woman owned his heart. The dark eyes were watching. If he remained any longer, more than the warlord's eye would discover him, and so Coxcox bowed quickly as he backed toward the door.

"Are you . . . are you going to wait here, my lord?"

"Yes."

"And should I mention a topic?"

"I have not mentioned one."

"Yes, yes, of course. Ha. Very well. Good, then, I will return in short time."

He bowed once more and turned to walk briskly down the hall. He walked as quickly as he possibly could without running, his lame leg hurrying to catch up. He would have run his shuffling run, but he did not want them to sense his apprehension. Even the thought horrified him—that they might be following, the dark ones, the Terror Speakers—and so he quietly whispered the magical poem his grandmother used to sing whenever they traveled the high roads at night and especially when they neared the crossroads where the dark and the shadow always waited for unsuspecting travelers.

"Yellow bird, green bird, blue bird, black—rabbits run away but rabbits come back."

He glanced behind. Far down the hallway, Huemac's brooding figure had turned to stare over the plaza. None of the shadows had followed. Coxcox swallowed and kept walking. He was not certain how he was going to warn Topiltzin, but he must think of a way.

꙰꙰꙰꙰꙰꙰꙰꙰꙰꙰꙰꙰꙰꙰꙰꙰꙰

Sky Hawk stood in the ceremonial plaza of Tula watching the balconies of his father's palace. Fire dancers spun past him. One of them, a woman, leapt high through the air; her glistening thighs tightened into a nimble spin while arching flames traced her path against the night sky. It was a savage dance—the fire dance. It was in imitation of the dances of old, of Tollán and the ancestors. He had seen his sisters perform this dance on the island, but there they had traced their path using the tendrils of flower cords. But the Nomads had added fire, and the simple dance of his sisters became fierce, like the dance of a screaming cat. Something else screamed as well. The night itself. Something was coiling. They had returned victorious, and these were celebrations as before, as always when they returned; but on this night, something was different. The air against his skin left chilly fingers running.

Sky Hawk carefully searched the shadows of the porticoes. Was it possible Huemac was up there? Huemac never went to the palace; he avoided it as though it was cursed, and yet Sky Hawk had a feeling he had done just that—that he had gone into the Butterfly Palace. To face their father. It seemed almost impossible.

Huemac hadn't been the same since the fall of the Olmec city. Huemac had hardly said a word the whole march. Several nights before, when they came out of the Southland passing through the ruins of the Toltec garrison in the passage of Manti, Huemac had stopped, nearly blinded. He had even fallen to his knees. Sky Hawk, recovering from injuries sustained in the taking of the Olmeca, was still traveling in a litter, but he stopped his carriers and climbed out. He crouched before Huemac.

Huemac just knelt there, muscles tensed, eyes closed tight. He was trembling. Second Skin and as many as nine Nomad captains circled him, ready to protect him against anything that might step out of the night, but Sky Hawk could see the thing which tore at his brother's heart was not going to come from the night. It was inside Huemac, it was coiled in him like a serpent waiting beneath a rock.

"Can I help?" Sky Hawk said.

Huemac suddenly seized Sky Hawk's wrist tightly, squeezing. When his eyes opened, Sky Hawk saw he had been weeping. He had never seen tears in his brother's eyes. Whatever Huemac fought, it circled them both that night in unseen winds like those that sometimes reached down from the sky in a funnel and sucked everything into their vortex. Sky Hawk pulled Huemac into an embrace, but Huemac finally pushed away. He stared at Sky Hawk a moment longer and stood, breathing heavily.

"Go back to your litter, Sky Hawk," he said. He motioned Second Skin to keep the army moving and walked away.

Watching him stride into the night, Sky Hawk tingled, noticing the strange Mayan youth following. He had followed that way ever since they left the jungle, always at a distance from Huemac, never close, but never far. The youth had kept to himself, the cowl of his cloak drawn to hide his face. As the Mayan passed by his litter, Sky Hawk gave him a warning glance, but the youth did not glance in Sky Hawk's direction, as if Sky Hawk were nothing to be concerned with, as if he were unimportant.

When they finally reached the city, Sky Hawk spent his first few hours with Purple Sky and his four sons. He told Purple Sky to prepare a meal especially made for Huemac with all his favorite dishes, just as he had promised Huemac in the jungle. He knew his brother carried a heavy weight, but if he could get him here, with his nephews and nieces, with laughter and bright eyes, he knew he could help. Sky Hawk had brought banana leaves and fresh limes from the market. Silver Feather had danced excited hearing his uncle was coming.

As night drew on, Huemac did not come and finally Sky Hawk went searching. Even Second Skin had not known where to find Huemac. Sky Hawk found the Nomads' camp outside the southern gate. In the cities, there were celebrations, song and music, but the camp of the Nomads was somber, silent. They had lost too many in this campaign. The Nomads would not celebrate this night. Instead, they honored their dead, many of Topiltzin's children among them.

In the center of the camp, Sky Hawk was taken to Second Skin's tent. Inside, the captain sat in a wicker chair, staring at the hearth fire, his eyes deeply troubled. He had barely looked up, barely answered Sky Hawk's query.

"His orders are that no one follows," Second Skin said, and his eyes were sad, as if he had lost a friend.

"And you ignored them, of course."

"Not this time," Second Skin said, looking up. "He forced me to promise none of my men would follow."

"He is out there alone, without guardians?"

"Not quite alone," broke in Second Skin's captain, a lean killer named Stone Slayer. Second Skin glanced at his captain, but didn't press him. Sky Hawk realized what he meant.

"The Mayan?"

He waited, but neither Nomad responded.

"He is with the youth who followed us out of the jungle? My God, what were you thinking!"

"I was thinking when I am given orders that strong, with that kind of resolve, then I am compelled to do as my lord commands. That is what I was thinking, Sky Hawk."

Second Skin set his jaw tight, his dark, cold eyes watching Sky Hawk. Perhaps he wanted to say more, but Second Skin would always be as loyal to Huemac as the Morning Star to the falling sun. Sky Hawk shifted his gaze to Stone Slayer who had no trouble voicing his concern.

"We trust that Mayan pig no more than you do, my prince," Stone Slayer promised.

"What happened back there?" Sky Hawk asked. "After the battle, when I was unconscious. You went with Huemac into the jungles, alone. What happened there, Second Skin?"

Second Skin did not answer, though his eyes betrayed a kind of dread at the mention of it. Sky Hawk suspected Second Skin felt the same shadows crossing the night sky as Sky Hawk did, and that he too felt this night coiling like a serpent ready to strike.

"Perhaps you should give us an order," said Stone Slayer. "Perhaps we should hunt down this Mayan . . ." He paused, cut off by Second Skin's hand against his arm.

"Find him, Sky Hawk," Second Skin said quietly. "He did not order you not to follow."

Sky Hawk nodded. "Keep your troops here, outside the city. Watch the plains."

"You feel it also, then?"

"I don't know where it is going to strike, but I feel the battle did not end in the jungle."

"No," Second Skin agreed. "It has followed. We will wait for it, my lord."

Sky Hawk searched the city on his own, a whisper of panic

moving through him. Whenever they returned from campaign, Huemac was ever troubled, pensive, but this was the first time he had disappeared. Sky Hawk moved quickly through the city, following only his instinct, his sense of things, and finally had ended up in the shadow of Topiltzin's Butterfly Palace. It seemed impossible Huemac would have gone there. He always chose the deserts—several skins of *pulque* and the quiet of the desert night. That he had gone instead to their father's palace seemed far more troubling.

Sky Hawk stared at the palace, its front façade lit by the fires of celebrants and the cinnabar torches of the city streets. The Southland was far behind them, and he wanted to believe they had left it behind cognitively, but this time the terror had come with them. Sky Hawk guessed it was somehow connected to the shadowy eyes of the Mayan youth, and decided then he would find the Mayan. He would track him down and when he did, Sky Hawk intended to look in his eyes and if he did not find them to be human, Sky Hawk would kill him.

He turned to find Turquoise Prince at his side. He was surprised. Rarely did people sneak up on him. Turquoise Prince wore his mother's dragon cloak, his sword, even the arch of his bow, carved long ago in Paradise, lifted over his shoulder. He might have been readied for battle instead of celebration. Turquoise Prince must have shared the same uneasiness. In the years they had been in this land, all of them had learned to read the shadows, to feel the approach of a threat long before it materialized. Such sense had kept them alive these fifteen years.

"I've been watching you," Turquoise Prince said carefully. He glanced to the portico of the palace Sky Hawk had been studying. "What is it you search for?"

"Huemac. Have you seen him?"

Turquoise Prince lifted a brow, surprised. "You don't know?"

"Don't know what?"

"He has asked for a sacred council."

"What?"

"Huemac came to me. He has called sacred council. With first light of dawn we are to gather beneath the chamber of the temple."

Sky Hawk felt a shiver down his back. "He said nothing to me. Are you sure?"

Turquoise Prince nodded.

"But why?"

"I thought you of all people might have that answer, little brother. I have been searching for you to ask just that question."

They both knew Huemac would have fretted over speaking with his father, brooded over it, gotten drunk long before approaching the Butterfly Palace, and certainly, he would have come to Sky Hawk to seek counsel.

Turquoise Prince glanced at the bandages wrapped about Sky Hawk's shoulder. "You are bleeding, Sky Hawk."

Sky Hawk glanced at his arm, surprised. His wounds had been slow to heal, and the worst was the spear through his shoulder. It was wrapped in cotton weft soaked in brine dried brittle. It ached this night, but Sky Hawk thought it had closed days ago. This was fresh blood.

"It is nothing. I'll have Purple Sky stitch it closed later."

Turquoise Prince studied him. "What happened, Sky Hawk? In the Southland, in the jungles? What happened?"

Sky Hawk shook his head, troubled. "If I were a singer, a sky speaker, maybe I could try, but even then I doubt I could find the words." He stared at the fire dancers a moment, the way they turned and twisted in the ancient dance, laced with streaks of fire that seemed to feed off the restlessness of his spirit. "Remember before we left, in the hall of princes—remember what you said to us?"

"I said many things."

"Yes, but you ended by speaking his name. The one who would be waiting for us there, at Cumorah. You called him the Smoking Mirror." Sky Hawk felt his skin tingle saying it because he knew it was an ancient name, that it was a name spoken in this land long before any Tolteca had ever set foot here. It was the name of a prince as ancient as the stars. "He found us." Sky Hawk paused, lifting his eyes to Turquoise Prince. "The sacred council, you must call it off. You can't let this happen. You have to call it off!"

"I share your apprehension, but what would be gained by calling off the council?"

"I am not sure, but I do know if we gather in the sacred caves, he will come for us there. I don't believe we are ready for him, Turquoise Prince. Call off the council. Let me find Huemac first. Let me talk to him."

Turquoise Prince looked up at the stars. "Already the last hour of night closes on us. If you can find him before dawn, do so. Otherwise, come to the council. Reason with him there. We will all reason with him, as brothers, as firstborn. I know you have a bond with Huemac the rest of us do not share, but if we are to truly confront him, perhaps it is best we do it together. That is the way our father taught us."

"This is different. What if . . . ?"

"Yes?"

"What if it is a trap?"

"You think it has gone that far? That Huemac would betray us?"

"Not Huemac . . ."

"Then who?"

"The demon. The one who has followed us from the Southland."

Turquoise Prince raised a brow, surprised. "Demon?"

"I can think of no other thing to call him."

"Well, if there is a demon, where better to face him than the heart of the temple? And who better among us than Huemac? If you walk to the ends of the desert, people there will know the name of Strong Hand, the son of the Serpent Plumed. They won't know your name; many will not even know mine. Huemac has ruled here longer than we realize. Perhaps we are in his hands now. His hand is strong."

Turquoise Prince squeezed Sky Hawk's shoulder in reassurance and turned to find the others. Watching him leave, Sky Hawk felt no comfort in his words. His panic only spread deeper.

Sky Hawk looked to the sky. Turquoise Prince was right; the

last hour of night was closing on them. Sky Hawk could not shake the feeling that everything here had already been written, as if they were only memories, as if they were already becoming shadows. Cumorah's dark and mist had circled on them since they had come to this land, it had followed them, and through the years, they had tried to change it, to rewrite what happened, outrun the shadow of the Tolteca. But it was like trying to outrun the night.

Coxcox waited for Topiltzin to stir before speaking. At the foot of Topiltzin's mat stood Moon Child. She had been lightly playing a flute, but seeing Coxcox's eyes, she stopped. She knew there was trouble. Topiltzin lay on his mat naked and facedown, one arm over Widow Woman, who lay next to him on her side. When the sad notes of the flute stopped suddenly, Topiltzin glanced over his shoulder.

"What is it?"

"Your son, my lord," Coxcox said.

Topiltzin glanced at him, surprised. "Coxcox?"

"Yes. He asked for me and I found him but—"

"Who are we speaking of?"

Topiltzin had been drinking most of the night. It was not only the news of Silvered Leaf that set him to drinking, it seemed to have come over him after watching the long trail of slaves. Most of them were children. Coxcox knew they would be better off as slaves in Tula than left in the jungles where their cities burned, but Topiltzin's mood had darkened, as it always did when Huemac returned. This time, Topiltzin had taken his two favorites, Moon Child and Widow Woman, along with several skins of hard *pulque*, and withdrawn to his bedchamber.

Widow Woman sat up and pulled a woven blanket up to her chin, staring at Coxcox with alarm.

"It is Huemac," Coxcox said. "He . . . he wishes to talk with you, my lord."

"Huemac? Here? In the castle?"

"Yes."

Topiltzin winced and sat up. "Why?"

"He does not say. But . . . you should know . . . something you should know . . ."

"Speak it, Coxcox."

"Huemac . . . he is . . . there is darkness near him. Many shadows, too many to count. They twist, they dance. They dance."

Most men, hearing such things, even from Coxcox, might have dismissed them, for how can demons dance?

"The Night and the Wind," Coxcox added. "It walks, my lord. It stirs about him. Perhaps you should not go there. Perhaps . . ."

Topiltzin was on his feet. Of course he would go. Coxcox knew his king had faced this dark before, that Topiltzin would walk into it without hesitation, especially if it concerned his son.

"He is here," Coxcox said, "the east portico. He waits."

Moon Child hurried over to give Topiltzin his robe and waited with his sash and cloak. Widow Woman had not moved at all. She watched Coxcox over the edge of the blanket, her eyes terrified. She had seen the Night and the Wind herself; she knew its face.

࿐࿐࿐࿐࿐࿐࿐࿐࿐࿐࿐࿐࿐

Huemac touched his belt. The knot where the dolphin-prince rested against his hip was still there. He wanted to believe the dolphin-prince was immune to the nightmares, immune from the sadness and the terror—from a different world, a different place than this. He slowly lifted it from his belt and stared at the smooth, polished stone, still left with the whittle marks. He pictured the face of Sky Hawk's youngest, the boy named Silver Feather. As he stared, breathing heavily through his teeth, he tried to let the dolphin-prince whisper to him, call his name, tell him what he must do. But it was silent. It was just a carved stone and Huemac with a snarl hurled it into the air. He watched it turning as it fell; saw a glint of it before it vanished below.

He turned and stared at the firelight playing upon the wall mural. The mural was an ocean scene with fish swimming and cormorants, like the ones that had circled in the bright blue sky when the seven ships of Topiltzin first reached the shores of Tollán, when the Sons of God returned. It struck a memory. The young face of Obsidian Snowflake as she spoke to him the night before they left the island. *Tell me that in your heart, time will just stop turning and you will never forget me, and that we will always be together there, in that place, a place known of stars and written of in the Heavens where love is spoken. Would you say that to me, Huemac?*

Something in the mural struck him. It was the pathways, painted to represent their crossing. The seven caves through the sea. *The number of the place is seven.* As he stared, trying to understand what stirred in him, the mural oozed with a smooth coating of thick, slow-moving blood that slowly inked across its surface, even pooling onto the polished limestone floor of the portico. The madness was pushing him to act, willing him, but he did not know what it asked. He just stared, terrified, as the blood reached the tip of his boot.

Sensing someone watching, he turned.

Topiltzin stood in the arched doorway, his figure shadowy, bathed only by the dim glow of the celebration fires. Huemac suddenly felt weak. Part of him wanted to go to Topiltzin—run to him. He saw a shadow of himself doing that, but the shadow that threw his arms about Topiltzin's neck was only a boy, and Huemac had not been that boy for a long, long time.

"Father," Huemac said quietly.

Topiltzin stepped into the room. Huemac noticed the shadow of Coxcox hesitating from the doorway. Topiltzin also noticed.

"You did say alone. I was to speak with my son alone, Coxcox?" the king asked.

"Yes. Alone, yes," Coxcox answered from the hallway.

"Then you may leave."

"Very well, my lord."

TOLTECA

The shadow stepped back slowly until the shoulders and head retreated into the hallway. Huemac almost wished he had asked Coxcox to say.

Topiltzin walked forward until the light of the braziers fell over him. It struck Huemac how he had aged. Topiltzin's beard was white where it fell across his chest. His hair was silver. His father's eyes were still strong, still an intense, dark blue.

"What it is, my son?" he said cautiously.

Huemac realized it had been years since he had spoken alone with his father. He wondered how many years. Twelve, thirteen, he had lost count. What had happened? When did it all begin to turn? Once, the stories of his father had seemed filled with light. His songs could reach all the way to Heaven, touch the star stream of the sky, and the Tolteca were the brightest stars to be found there, blue and shinning like ice. Now Huemac had restored their kingdom. The shadow of the Tolteca crossed the narrow passage to fill the lowlands, the jungles, even Zarahemla, the city named *Tribute of a Thousand Hearts*. The kingdom of the ancestors was about to lift out of the ground and shake off its dust. When this night was over, the Tolteca would live forever. Why then did sadness strike him like a rain of spears as he looked into his father's eyes?

"I have something for you, Father."

Topiltzin waited. Huemac lifted the cylinder in his fingers. He held it up. Topiltzin stared at it, surprised, then walked over to Huemac and slowly took it. Standing close, his father smelled of sweat and *pulque*, smells an old man might have, though they were masked by some kind of perfume. Something deep inside Huemac felt a shiver of revulsion for what Topiltzin had become. *He is weak now*, some voice whispered; *he has forgotten all the songs of the people; he is old; he will not understand the gift. The years have stolen his breath and plucked out his eyes. Only you, Huemac, only you now. It is you alone who has been named.* Huemac shivered. How could such feelings crawl in him?

Once Topiltzin had broken the cylinder open, he paused to stare at the small parchment that spilled into his palm. He narrowed his eyes, as if he were looking into the night. He said nothing. He just carefully rolled it back up and returned it into the container. Finally, his eyes lifted to Huemac, troubled.

"Where did you get this?" Topiltzin asked.

"It was given to me . . . as was the city."

"Zarahemla? Given?"

"Yes. It is mine. A gift, an offering. The homeland once again belongs to the Tolteca, Father. I bring you kingdom." Huemac motioned with his left hand. Behind him, from the shadows, the youth took two steps forward. He did not come fully into the light, nor did he look at the king. His face was hidden by the cowl, and his gaze was at the floor.

"What is this?" Topiltzin said, wary. "What have you done?"

"All the way from the Southland I have struggled with my thoughts. There are cities that lie before us—thousands of people, Father. Thousands of souls. Zarahemla, Tikal, all the cities of the jungle, all the cities of the narrow neck, even the highlands. Their eyes look up to mine. Their voices whisper my name. They have become my people. This is my offering to you."

Topiltzin stared back, astonished, his lips slightly parted. Huemac paused now, unsteady. The next words seemed not even to belong to him; they came out of his mouth, but it was almost as if he hadn't spoken them.

"The *Itzás* stand with me," the voice declared, and Huemac first felt frightened, but then he swelled with its promise. Had he not delivered his father everything? Had all their dreams not been spoken?

Topiltzin's dark blue eyes tightened; they flashed with quick anger.

"The *Itzás* are mine," the voice in Huemac repeated. *If this were Turquoise Prince standing before you, your father would not look on him with astonishment and shame; he would embrace him, honor him. But see the eyes of your father now?*

"What are you saying?"

"The Southland already belongs to us," Huemac said. "There

will be no more wars, no more blood. We will not lose anymore of my brothers. No more of your sons will fall. We will become one people, as once long ago there were one people in this land, as once there was one blood. Can you not see the wisdom, Father? Do you not understand what I am offering?"

At that moment, the youth looked up, as if he had been given a cue. Huemac wanted to tell him to stand back, to look away, to remain staring at the floor, but instead the Mayan lifted his head. Though his face remained in the shadows of the cowl, though his eyes were hidden, still he looked directly at Topiltzin, watching as if they were not strangers, as if they had faced each other before.

"We have shed blood for eight hundred years!" Huemac pleaded, feeling desperate because Topiltzin wasn't listening. "But now, if we allow the *Itzás* to stand beside us, nothing on this earth can turn from our shadow! Our strength will be like the sun, leaving nowhere to hide. And why could we not live together? Why not try to learn what they whisper, even if it seems to be the very wind of the night? We can do this, Father. We can end the spilling of blood."

Huemac could see this clearly in his mind: a world where Topiltzin would once more gather at the hearth to sing the songs of old, the songs of the Tolteca, those who addressed each other as *My brother* and *My sister*, those who worshiped the one true God, the Sons of Light, the Turquoise Lords.

For a moment, nothing happened. The sounds from the city drifted lazy. Huemac felt his heart beating hard in his chest. Was it wrong? Was it really betrayal? The voice had whispered him things, and yet—even though Huemac understood this was the darkness and the night, a shadow voice—he wondered if there were not some secret here everyone had missed. It spoke against everything he understood, and yet, strangely, he felt there was possibly an answer here, a different way.

Topiltzin slowly curled one hand about the cylinder. He stared at Huemac, his jaw tight, and without warning struck Huemac with the back of his hand. The blow was startling, and it staggered Huemac, forcing him to take a step back. Huemac felt the sting, felt the numbness of the strike. Something in him crouched, snarling. A trickle of blood spilled from the cut in his lip. His hand curled into a fist, but he forced himself to stand and even to await another blow.

"You are a fool," Topiltzin said.

The word sent a vapor of rage though him, and Huemac thought he heard a chuckle. Was it the youth? Had the Mayan laughed at him?

"Always I am a fool," Huemac said. "Always him you listen to, the other, and never me! Do you not understand that I bring you kingdom? I bring you empire!"

"We did not come to this land for empire! It was never about empire! If you allow this to happen, do you not realize what that does to the blood on our hands?"

"Our hands? *Our* hands, Father! This blood is on *my* hands! From the beginning, from the start of all this! *My* hands! What would you have me do? Peel back my skin to wash it from me? I offer you a way past blood and as always, you turn away in shame!"

"Not until this moment have you brought me shame."

"I have been your shame since we came to this land."

"No. No, Huemac. That is not true."

"Then why do you never meet my eyes? Why do you always turn from me?"

He noticed something change in Topiltzin, a shadow crossing. *It is the* pulque *in him,* the voice whispered, *the old man smells—his weakness.*

"You don't understand, Huemac."

"Perhaps that is because I am such a fool."

Fool. Fool. He is no longer your father, this reeking farce of a king. Let him go. Turn away. You are king now.

From somewhere far, a place he had almost forgotten, he heard her whisper his name as if it were a lost memory floating through the night. Obsidian Snowflake. She was the only one ever to love him, to love him without question, without conditions. She might

586

have been only more madness. Perhaps her voice was no more than imaginings, perhaps he needed the comfort of her touch, and so his mind produced it; still, its warmth, its tenderness seemed as real as the blood in his veins. *Find me, Huemac; find me now, for this is the moment I spoke of! I whispered this hour to you.*

"Huemac, listen to me." Topiltzin's words threatened to shatter any thoughts of Obsidian Snowflake as though a stone had been hurled against fragile ice.

Still she tried. *Huemac, I am here, I am with you. Come to me. Find me!*

Huemac felt a tear fall, but he ignored it. It was a lone tear, forgotten. It was not even a part of him now; it was the tear of a shadow.

Topiltzin stepped forward, reaching for Huemac's shoulder, but Huemac brushed his hand aside roughly.

"Save your kindness for your firstborn."

Topiltzin's eyes were sincere, but Huemac did not feel any pity for them. Rage continued to crawl though his skin.

"If only you knew," Topiltzin said. "If only I could bare my heart, make you understand what I could never show you. I had to hold it back. You had to be strong, Huemac. You had to be strong enough to need no one. I hid all that I felt for you, but in my heart, always . . . always I have loved. It was always you, Huemac—I loved you more than any of them.

"That is why I have had to turn away. It was never shame. No. I have turned away because I loved you too much to watch you change—to see what this had done to you. One of us had to be strong; one of us had to be the law of God, unflinching. You were my strongest, and that is why I had to choose you, but, Huemac . . . it has broken my heart."

Huemac swallowed past a tight knot. Deep inside, the shadow part of him wanted to let go, let whatever burned with rage peel off into the night and allow him once more to become only the child who could run to his father's arms. But that part would ever remain shadow now. The fires rippled too deeply. They were stoked and raging.

They were too strong. They had their own voice, their own tongue.

"You should have told me, Father. You should have taught me these things. It is too late to speak it now. I cannot hear your words; they are too far away."

Topiltzin looked stricken a moment longer.

See, his footing is unsure. A drunken old man. Incapable of love for a son. Incapable of knowing a wise man from a fool.

The Mayan took a step forward. Topiltzin turned to him and Huemac saw the kindness leave his father's eyes.

"Tell him to leave, Huemac."

Topiltzin waited, but Huemac said nothing.

"Do as I say!"

Who is he to issue commands to you, Huemac, as if you were a servant or a dog?

"Tell him to return to his jungle!"

A servant or a dog or a fool?

"Huemac! Tell him now! There may still be time to set things right, but first you must tell him he has no place here."

Though the powerful, deep blue eyes trained all their authority on him, Huemac slowly shook his head. He was finished with listening.

"In the jungle I looked into their eyes," Huemac said. "And they looked into mine. For once, someone honored my name; for once, someone claimed me. He stays, Father. He is what you have crafted. These many years, I have waited for you to look at me just once, to realize and to acknowledge what I have done for you, what I have given up for you—just once to look on me as your chosen. Now I am finished with waiting. I brought you empire, and you spat in my face." Huemac offered his father a bitter smile. "No, you slapped my face. This time I will speak our future—not Turquoise Prince, not even you. *I* will speak it because I have given my soul for it. It is come. The seven rivers and the three oceans, the four winds and the five directions—all will bow before me. I lay it at your feet, Father. *Fool* that I am, I brought it as a gift. I have honored your word with my life and my blood and the blood of my brothers, but you slap my face as though I were some insolent child. You have no idea of what I have sacrificed for you. So this night, I will not ask that you honor me. This night, I no longer care."

Topiltzin's brow narrowed. He glanced at the cylinder in his hand, then stepped back and hurled it from the portico into the night. Huemac once would have felt his heart sink, as if part of him were falling through the polished floor. He once would have believed he could spill away like rain. He once would have wished he had never survived, that the fever of the jungles had taken him. But that Huemac was a portrait of disgust to this Huemac. He felt strangely calm. He felt absolutely nothing.

Topiltzin turned and strode across the room. There was a long table with a bowl of fruit, and on the wall above it were crossed spears. When Topiltzin reached the end of the table, he snarled; he spun to rip a spear from the wall, then turned and flung it, straight and true with a scream.

The heavy spear soared across the room. It kissed the cowl of the youth as it passed over his shoulder and shattered against the stone of the wall behind him. The youth had not flinched; he had not so much as blinked. He stared at Topiltzin, unaffected.

Topiltzin looked to Huemac. "Take your disciple and get out of my sight," Topiltzin said coldly.

Huemac welcomed the smoldering anger that flared.

"Go!" Topiltzin shouted, his dark eyes flashing. "Leave my house. Now! I can't bear to look upon your face."

Huemac turned with a flare of his cloak and strode from the room.

Behind him, the youth remained a moment longer, watching Topiltzin. He slowly stepped back into the shadows, and as Topiltzin watched, he dissolved into them as if he might never have been there at all.

K. MICHAEL WRIGHT

Huemac moved though the crowds of the marketplace staggering as if he were drunk, consumed by an unfamiliar combination of sadness, rage, and a strange euphoria. He was not drunk; he was spinning like a pebble being washed down a river melt, out of control. Yet he fully intended to get drunk; he intended to drink until he could not stand, until he could fall on his face. Perhaps, if he drank quickly enough, choosing the strongest sour *pulque* the old bastard Jade Frog could sell him, perhaps he might fall down and never wake. That is what he really wanted. The emotions were a torrent through him, sadness like the thick storms that sometimes came off the desert without warning, like the storm you could watch cross the plain with a wall of rain almost as strong as a waterfall. And beneath it boiled the fires of anger swirling, dancing, a high, wild dance, and the demons that were walking with him, they knew this song well; they came high stepping and singing; they came with drums and fire wands, and their song screamed in his head with a voice of winds.

For a brief moment, Huemac considered ending this pain. He could take it with his own sword, but there was no honor in such a death. He had never listened to the priests of his father or any other supposed holy men, but all of them, even the dark priests of the Blood Gatherers, all said taking one's life never lifted pain, for the dead would wake in a world far worse than the one they left, and Huemac could picture that world. He had seen it before, in the fever of the jungle—Shoal, the empty place, the shadow land, where there was no thought, no speaking, no futures, where everything was nothing and nothing filled the universe without end. To take one's own life was to step into that terrible place and never return. He knew that; he understood it, and yet still he longed for it.

His fingers fell over the hilt of his dagger as he strode through the marketplace unaware of the celebrants, the fires, the flutes, or the singers. He walked alone, and the hilt spoke to him softly. The voice of this thing, of taking one's life, it was whispered with the intoxication of a woman. It seemed a familiar voice; it said, *Come now, lay with me. I will take all your cares, all your troubles. You can bring with you . . . these demons who dance with their high steps, singing all the way. You can bring them down into the shadow land, and they will scream until their mouths are empty. You will finally hear the song of silence.*

Huemac stumbled into a stack of vendor cages, knocking one of them over, and suddenly his anger turned on the cages as if they were people, as if they had stepped in front of him. They were filled with geese, and the birds squawked, terrified as he lifted a cage and hurled it into the night. It crashed onto the stone, splintering, breaking open as geese squawked and beat their wings to run, terrified, across the plaza. Of course they could not fly. Their wings had been clipped. They were intended as offerings of sacrament for the high hour of night, and flight had already been stolen from them. He watched them running, trying and trying to lift into the sky, but held to the stone by a curse they could not fathom. He understood well how they felt. The vendor, an old, withered Mayan, stepped forward to shout his complaints, but when Huemac turned his eyes on the old man, the vendor gasped a stifled cry, then staggered back from the warlord, turned on heel and ran, just like his geese, terrified. Huemac snarled at the small crowd that gathered.

"Get out of my way, move!" He pushed a woman and a young warrior aside. "Move, I say!" They cleared ground about him, stepping away, watching him stride into the plaza with frightened glances and whispers shared.

Huemac kept going. He found the squat hut of Jade Frog and paused to take several old, withered sharkskins that promised to have the strongest *pulque* in the city. Jade Frog crawled out of his hut and watched Huemac, worried.

"What is it, old man?" Huemac sneered. He noticed on one shelf of Jade Frog's hut were a line of balls, a paste wrapped in pig intestine.

"Your brother searches for you."

"Which brother?"

591

"The young, handsome one. Sky Hawk, he told me—"

"Tell him you never saw me. Tell him nothing, you understand?"

"Yes, my lord."

"One of those," Huemac said, pointing to the balls.

"My lord?"

"What is in them?"

"Venom of the sea cucumber. But you do not want these, my lord, they are for—"

"Give me one. Now!"

Jade Frog noticed the warning look in Huemac's eyes. He offered it, and Huemac snatched it. He had heard of these. Some used them for sex, to gain the ultimate climax, and when it was used, sometimes they lived and sometimes they died. He did not plan to have sex, but when he was drunk enough, taking the venom would be a little like gambling, and this night he felt like gambling.

"Here." Huemac ripped off his coin belt, tossing it. It broke open to spill its contents of cocoa beans across the planking and onto the ground beneath Jade Frog's feet. "Be happy, old man," said Huemac. "Enough there for you to retire!"

He turned and made his way to the darker shadows of the tenement dwellings that lay off the southern end of the plaza. He would find an empty back alley. A place no one would ever search for him. He could end this madness in his head with Jade Frog's wine, and when he was drunk enough not to feel the emotions pouring through him any longer, he could let God roll the dice to determine the outcome. He knew with that much wine, the nectar of the spiny cucumber would most likely be deadly—but perhaps not—and in that, he could say he wasn't really taking his own life. He was leaving it in God's hands. That was all. Heaven would decide.

He paused, startled. It was the Mayan, the youth, standing at the edge of a painted apartment with its sweep of limestone stairs and its cluttered windows opening to blackness. It should not have surprised Huemac that the youth had guessed where he intended to go; the Mayan was a sorcerer. Huemac knew it.

Huemac snarled and closed on him, though the Mayan did not react, even when Huemac's big hand shot out to catch the Mayan's throat. He squeezed, shoving the youth back against the wall, glaring into the youth's dark blue eyes, eyes like deep cold water, eyes that watched back unaffected, distorted by the high deformation of his peaked skull.

"I'm going to deliver you to your God, you scurrile bastard," Huemac swore, pushing the Mayan hard against the painted abode. "And you will not complain, because it is my choice? Is that not true? Well?"

He waited, but the cold eyes with their arched brows watched him with nothing more than a mild curiosity, even though Huemac's hand pressed his windpipe closed. It was as if the Mayan didn't require air to breathe.

"Anything I want of you," he reminded the youth. "I can take anything I want. I can take my dagger and peel the skin off your face if I wish."

The eyes continued to stare back with perfect calm.

"Before I crush your throat, sorcerer, I demand you tell me how to quiet these screams, how to make it stop! How do I silence the madness in me! Tell me how to still these demons following my shadow! Tell me!"

He released the pressure on the sorcerer's throat. The youth studied him a moment, slightly narrowing his eyes. In answer, he nodded his head toward a far edge of the marketplace. He lifted a finger, pointing.

Huemac turned, searching. The plaza was crowded, people milling about, but Huemac immediately found the youth's target. The chill of the many voices inside his head picked up their whispered cadence. Huemac's eyes were drawn to an old man. It was as if the old man's face moved through the crowds and bore down on Huemac with such presence he could smell the stink of his unwashed body. Huemac was left breathless. The old man knowingly grinned, the top front teeth all missing, and the bottom had been filed to points that leaned like broken stakes.

"Huemac," the old man whispered. Even though he was far, the whisper was right there, in Huemac's ear. Seeing the effect of his cunning, the old man cackled, amused. He was squatting on haunches beside a pavilion as if he were a merchant. The pavilion was a skin seller's, and all about the old man hung weary skins. Some seemed to be rabbit, or dog, but others had indistinct shapes, and Huemac thought they might even be human. All of the skins were a sick yellow color, looking like they had been peeled from days-old, already-rotting corpses. He turned, but the youth was gone. He had simply vanished, and when Huemac looked back to the plaza, it seemed all the people of the marketplace had become smoke and drifted away leaving only the two of them in the entire city, just Huemac and this old man who seemed to have some joke he wanted to share. He was cancerous with age, his skin crusty and wrinkled, and he was naked, squatting, one hand playing idly with his member.

"Closer . . . come closer," the whisperer said, and Huemac was compelled; he couldn't turn away. He crossed over to the plaza, up its steps, then to the very edge of old man's pavilion, next to a ragged piece of blotched, yellow skin stretched over two poles. Hands stretched there, several hands with fingernails still intact.

The old man smacked his lips to catch spittle as it drooled, and when Huemac turned, he was chilled at the eyes. They were dark as stone—empty eyes, as if they might have just been holes in his head. Huemac had the feeling that if he looked closer, he would see the night spill through them; he would see the stars at the far end of the universe.

"How do you know me by that name, old man?"

"I know all your names, for you have many—some not yet given—names that will become legend, names far beyond the mere son of Jewel Twirler you once were."

No one but his brother's could speak of his lineage. The sons of Topiltzin had always kept their mothers' names sacred, written and kept, but to everyone else secret, as was the name of the Queen of Heaven, so no man would ever defile them. The old man seemed pleased with his little surprise, watching Huemac with mischievous delight, grinning through his few spiked, crooked teeth. The old man's skin was dark and leathery, as if it had been baked in the sun for so many years it was left no more than leather hanging off his bones. It sagged in folds at his breasts where wiry, stiff gray hairs stuck out like curled thorns.

"How do you speak my mother's name?" Huemac demanded.

"Ah, the little Jewel Twirler," he said with a different voice, not whispered, instead a high, quick voice. "Eyes like emeralds and the freckled skin of a child, ah yes, her."

"Who are you?"

"You know who I am, Feathered Slayer."

Huemac tightened his jaw, trying to maintain a sense of what was real and what was unreal. "Where are your clothes, old man?" he said, speaking on purpose of ordinary things. "It is not allowed here—your nakedness. It is not allowed in Tula."

"But *I* allow it," he said in whisper, chuckling at his joke. "And I am the only one that matters now." Shadows crossed the empty eyes. "You can stop this," the quick voice said.

"What?"

"The madness in you."

"What are you saying?"

"Come closer. You would not make an old man get up, would you?" He lifted his hand from playing with his member and waved the bony fingers, motioning Huemac forward. "Closer . . . here, by my lips. This thing I must whisper to you."

"What thing?"

"The answer to your question: how to silence the screaming winds in your head. How to still the demons that walk this night. You come seeking answers, do you not? Closer, and you will have them."

Lured almost hypnotically by the waving of the old man's bony fingers, Huemac stepped forward, closer, but the old man wasn't satisfied; the bony fingers motioned toward his lips, and Huemac lowered to one knee, leaning to where the old man's dry lips and sour breath brushed against the warlord's cheek. At first Huemac could not understand any of the words; they came and went, just confused whispering, but as he listened, the mumbled, songlike gibberish turned to words.

"At the crossroads, the four corners, he comes, he strides. He walks the night! You can hear him. Go there, listen, hear the sound: an axe striking a tree. In the night it comes. There, the crossroads! It thuds, it strikes. Look quick and see the heart! There it beats, glistening, wet. Take it! Taste its meat. If any man swallows the meat of the heart of the Night Axe, there is nothing he cannot become, nothing he cannot do. He can command the night and whisper the very sun into the void!"

Huemac gasped and staggered back. He stared at the old man, amazed. The noise from the plaza slowly returned, as if it had been running to catch up. The stars spilling through the old man's empty eyes seemed to dim. He finally looked away. He pulled himself to his feet and hobbled off. Huemac noticed his left leg dragged behind him; the foot was not flesh, it was some kind of shiny metal, tacked to an old wooden foot. He had seen something like it before, but he couldn't remember where. The old man moved on, naked, into the marketplace, his shriveled buttocks hanging like leathered piles as he shuffled away. Huemac watched, amazed as the old man paused before a girl. She was young and beautiful, one of the dancers, with long, silken hair and a supple, toned body, and she let the old man, as horrible as he was, in all his nakedness, pull her forward and slip his bright red tongue into her mouth—into it, licking, sucking. Instantaneously he was gone. He had taken the girl and vanished into the crowd.

Huemac knew of what he spoke. A night, long ago, his mother had told him of the Night Axe. Jewel Twirler had always been superstitious. She had fantastic stories of shape shifters, bats whose scream could turn one to stone, wolves that were shadows—but none of her stories chilled him more than the Night Axe.

"If ever you see him, do not look in his eyes! If he comes to your door, do not let him enter. If you hear his sound, the axe striking a tree in the night, do not listen! Never, never believe! Do you hear? Never believe he is there. Even if you hear it, ignore the sound, pretend it was nothing more than a twig snapping. Even if you see him walking the crossroads, tell yourself it is only shadow. Never believe because if you believe, Huemac, he becomes real."

Huemac turned, staring across the plaza to the great serpent tails of the southern gate where they lifted into the sky. Huemac felt his heart beating in his chest like that of a frightened bird. Outside that gate, past the city, just beyond a hill that still bore trees of the ancient forest that once covered the Valley of Otumba, was the place where the roads to the southern passage and the roads to the eastern and western seas overlapped. It was said that in such places the five directions came together, creating a sacred cross whose center always lifted to the night sky. In such places, the breadth between this world and the smoke and shadow of souls from beyond would sometimes grow thin. On nights like this, when the stars were covered and the moon was slivered to nothing, the veil became so thin that shadows of the other world spilled through, and when that happened, he came. He walked; he strode the night.

Huemac did not leave by the southern gate. There were too many people that way, including Second Skin and the army of the Nomads, who were camped just outside the city walls. To avoid them, Huemac dropped into a measured run—through the unlit backstreets of the barrios. He made sure no one followed. When he had to cross open ground, he did so as a warrior, moving with stealth, quick and low to the ground.

He flew over the last hillocks before the crossroads, a ghost whipping through its trees until he finally crouched, instantly still, hidden in the twisted bark and braches of a mesquite tree. He looked to the sky. It was what he and Sky Hawk called a thick sky, the moon no more than a thin sliver and clouds masking the stars.

The plains beyond were flat and empty but for the pale lines of the worn, windswept crossroads. Seeing it, the madness inside suddenly stilled—the screamers in his head, the visions of blood, the pain of his father's words—all were silent.

He heard wings and looked up. A white owl streaked overhead, stark against the night as its talons snatched a smaller bird midair, feathers flying.

Thud. It was a sudden sound, and it jolted through him. He looked toward the crossroad, his breath caught.

Thud—louder now, closer.

"Here!" Huemac screamed. "Here I am! Come for me, you motherless bastard!"

It turned and began walking toward him from the center of the crossroads. Naked, no clothes, naked flesh, thighs wet and glistening, feet bare. There was no head.

Thud. The Night-Axe: it was like the sound of a striking tomahawk, but muffled, resembling the noise a severed limb might make were it slapped against heavy tree bark.

Huemac stepped out of the shadows. "Here!" he shouted, the veins in his neck taut. "You want me, come take me!"

Thud. The sound was made by the ribs. They yawned open before slamming shut. This was the ribcage of a sacrificial victim, torn open by the rippled blade of the butterfly knife.

He was caught by a sudden gust of the corpse's smell. It was horrid, sweet, and rotting. It struck him so violently that despite his defiance, he was on his knees, vomiting in the grass.

He snarled and wiped the back of his hand over his mouth. When he looked up, the Mocker was no longer in the crossroads, he stood directly over Huemac, but Huemac did not scream with fear, he screamed with pure and utter rage. He screamed with all the fury of man who had lost everything, his long black hair streaming as he came off haunches to ram his fist into the chest cavity.

The ribs slammed over his forearm and curled inward like the fingers of a great hand. The sour sweet smell was overpowering, but Huemac ignored it. He would have stared it down, he would have watched its eyes, but all he could do was scream his rage. His fingers seized the hard, muscled heart.

The creature panicked. It flailed at Huemac—like a child who didn't know how to fight, the arms blindly slapping his head and face.

Huemac wrenched his arm free. It burned like fire as the rib's teeth shredded his skin, leaving his forearm sheathed in blood. When Huemac stepped back, he held a dark clot of muscle in his fist.

He heard a thrashing noise and looked down to see the body had fallen, landing on its back. It was moving crab-like, circling quicker and quicker. A high-pitched shriek filled the air. It was like the cry of a dying rabbit, like a terrified child—a girl, it was a little girl's scream and for one last time he heard the name, Poppy. With tears of rage streaming down his cheeks, Huemac bit into the heart of the Night Axe.

⊡⊡⊡⊡⊡⊡⊡⊡⊡⊡⊡⊡⊡⊡⊡⊡⊡

Coxcox found Topiltzin in a small antechamber of the palace, alone, sitting on the floor, his back to the wall, one knee bent, a flagon of *pulque* at his side. Topiltzin had already been drinking, even before he had gone to speak with Huemac, but he did not seem drunk sitting there; he just seemed sad. He stared out over the portico into the night with his head against the painted mural of the palace wall. He hadn't even looked at Coxcox. Coxcox quietly walked over to him; and then, since his king was sitting on the floor, Coxcox did the same, sitting at Topiltzin's side, leaning back against the wall just like his king. For a long time nothing was said, but Coxcox was comfortable with the silence, and he felt the sadness of it; he shared the heaviness of Topiltzin's heart. The room had high ceilings, and it made Coxcox feel that both of them were small—that the world had forgotten them.

"I must go find my son," Topiltzin said. "I need to tell Huemac it does not matter, nothing matters. He is alive. He came back; that is all I care about. We can find a way. I will listen to his words, find a way."

Coxcox felt his own heart breaking. Tears ran down his cheeks, and he made no effort at all to collect them; he just let them drop onto his robe.

"I tried to tell him I loved him, but he no longer believes me, Coxcox. Perhaps that is because the last time I told him I loved him was before the ships—before any of this began."

They gathered. First Moon Child, with her small, round face that might have belonged to a doll, the way the eyes were so carefully set. Then Widow Woman, walking delicately across the floor, her small legs moving her along like a stumbling dancer. The rest, all the servants of Topiltzin, the monsters, the cripples. They gathered with worried faces. Widow Woman was softly crying.

"What is this?" Topiltzin said. "In the streets they dance and celebrate and in the palace we are all so sullen. No more of this. We need to sing, we need song. We need to remember God. Did any of you bring instruments?"

Comes Spinning pulled a flute out of his robes. He was a blind dwarf, but an exceptional flute player; his melodies were unlike any Coxcox had heard anywhere, and he began to weave a gentle tune that was neither sad nor happy.

Widow Woman took one of Topiltzin's hands, Moon Child the other, pulling him to his feet.

"We dance," Widow Woman said in her small voice.

"We dance," Topiltzin answered.

He spun around the room with the two small women. The others danced as well, and even Coxcox pulled himself to his feet and stepped sideways and back in the only dance he had. The antechamber became a ballroom and Topiltzin lifted Widow Woman so high she forgot all her tears.

CHAPTER FIFTY-THREE
THE FIFTH SUN

At dawn, the city of Tula was finally quiet. Litter was scattered in the streets, and in places, drunken warriors lay sleeping. The markets were mostly abandoned, but many of the tents and pavilions, many of their frames, still remained. Shadows stretched long fingers. A low fog drifted aimlessly in windless air across the stone of the central plaza and the ball court. Sky Hawk was crouched on the wall, near the serpent gate, searching. Though he had searched the whole night, he had not found Huemac, so with the morning's first light he was here, searching the flat, empty plains, the mesquite and dog-brush, the borders of the great lakes.

When the sun began to lift out of the earth, boiling but cold, far in the distance, Sky Hawk noticed a lone figure. Huemac was emerging from the desert. The red sun was at his back; it seemed he was walking out of firestorm and fury. Yet there was something about his walk, something Sky Hawk had never before seen. He was no longer moving like a warrior. He moved like a king.

∎∎∎∎∎∎∎∎∎∎∎∎∎∎∎∎∎∎∎

Topiltzin returned alone to his chambers, intending to find his cloak and then search the city for Huemac. As he knelt to open his wardrobe chest, he suddenly felt someone watching. He stood, turning quickly only to stare amazed. It was a girl. She stood just near the portico, watching him. She was beautiful, the kind of beauty that shivers the skin. She did not move when Topiltzin looked on her; she just watched him shyly, eyes a performance of fear. She was strangely familiar. He had seen her before, he was almost certain, and he searched for the memory.

"Who are you?"

"You do not remember me, Blue Prince?"

No one had called him Blue Prince in many years.

"How did you get in here?"

"I have been here all along. I have watched you from the beginning."

She moved as though she were shadow-stirred by wind. When she was close, he could smell her—tender, soft. She had almond dark eyes and satin jet hair. Her skin was the color of ripe, crimson berries, smooth, perfect. She half lowered her gaze. Her fingers touched his chest where the edge of his robes parted. The touch was cold, but he could not turn away.

"What . . . do you want?" he said, quietly.

"You," she whispered. "You are all I have ever wanted."

Her hand slid up his chest, curled about his neck. Topiltzin felt his breath caught in his throat as she lifted onto tiptoes. Perhaps it was a spell cast, but he could not resist; he allowed her lips to meet his. Her tongue slid over his lower lip and then—a quick sting. She had bitten him with tiny, sharp teeth, like a cat's.

She quickly lifted the little finger of her left hand to draw her nail over the blood on his lip. Topiltzin drew back, and she spun away. He touched his lip, puzzled. Some poison had left the side of his face almost instantly numb.

She danced, spinning low and sleek. The dark veils of her dress seemed to wave like the wings of a dark butterfly. Then he remembered. It had been so long ago, so far in time. The ancient ball court of Tollán's lakeshore—she was the girl with the poisoned paper rose.

"He comes," she sang lightly. "A shadow, a Mocker, whose face is darkness."

Feeling dizzy, Topiltzin lowered himself to one knee. She crouched just in front of him, her cat eyes glittering. From her blouse she withdrew a mirror, a polished obsidian plate, its surface smoked. She held it up, angling it in the light.

"Look, my prince! Look on your face."

Topiltzin recoiled from what he saw. He looked more than old; he looked savaged by age, his skin leathered and wrinkled. The old scar cut through his forehead, through the white beard. He was a monster.

"You are old, Topiltzin . . . sooo old." As she spoke the words, his face aged even more, wrinkles running through his skin like fresh cuts.

¤b¤b¤b¤b¤b¤b¤b¤b¤b¤b¤b¤b

Turquoise Prince walked through the cavern hollowed out beneath the Temple of the Creator. Its surface was smooth, unblemished, and at intervals torches were set into the walls.

Beyond was the stronger light of the cavern's heart, the room where all seven caves intersected. The temple masons had cut the caverns square; they had smoothed the sides and even carved brass brackets to hold torches. Turquoise Prince's boot echoed as he walked down them, following the steep decline that snaked deep into the black rock. He had always thought it would be cooler beneath the ground, that the rock would leave the desert air behind, but instead, it was often hotter. The chamber was natural and was cooled by an underground stream the masons had tunneled to intercept. In the center of the Chamber of the Heart, as it had been named by the priests, was a choc mol, carved of black basalt just as the one found deep beneath Tollán.

It was here the seven firstborn sons of Topiltzin gathered before each campaign, and, as they did on the eve of their first battle in this land, they would share the covenant of first blood.

Turquoise Prince bowed as he passed beneath the last lintel, carved in a triangular arch as was said of the temples of the ancients. He stepped in to find all of the firstborn gathered about the choc mol, except for Huemac and Sky Hawk.

Moan Bird nodded when his brother entered. Moan Bird had been playing soft music as they waited and now lowered his flute.

The braziers burned with a soft mixture of cinnabar. The walls bore images of the sacred island that had once been their home, the birds and fish of Paradise, the seashell, the curl of waves, and the frond and tall palms.

"We will wait," Turquoise Prince said. "Prepare ourselves quietly. Huemac was deeply troubled last night. When he comes, let us hold our hearts outward. Let us welcome him. If ever we have loved our brother, we must do so now. He needs us as never before."

As the blood of dawn washed over them, Second Skin realized the sky had changed. Dust was whipping through the air in bloodied streaks. The first division of Nomads was in the desert, far from the city gate. Second Skin knew Huemac was intending to meet with his brothers, but his last order had been to place themselves far from the city. Whatever he intended to say, he had intended to do it alone.

A sandstorm was coming. He was studying the red-brown sky when Stone Slayer stepped to his side.

"You see it, then?" said Stone Slayer.

Second Skin nodded. What Stone Slayer might not have known, this was a sorcerer's wind, and it was going to overtake them in seconds.

"Gather in," Second Skin said. "Prepare for battle."

"Battle? But there is nothing there!"

"Order them to take up shields and weapons, now!"

Stone Slayer turned, shouting commands. The winds continued to build, so swiftly his cries were swallowed. Second Skin watched the sandstorm pour over the hill above them like a river breaking its banks. Behind him, the Nomads were grabbing shields and weapons, but Second Skin knew it was already too late. Shadow sand. It slammed into them, swallowed them, but did not sting or bite.

"Gods!" screamed Stone Slayer above the howl. "What could this be?"

"Take up shields! Brace yourselves!"

They came, just as before. They lifted from the shadow winds as if spawning, just as they had done in the heart of Cumorah. Shifters—*Itzás*. Second Skin turned, alarmed. This time the Nomads were surrounded, this time they were scattered. Most had been drinking.

Turning to Second Skin to search the gloom of the desert, he saw archers crouching, saw bows yawning.

"Missiles!" he screamed.

Arrows whizzed through the air, came in a heavy rain, straight into the Nomads who were still lifting shields and moving for the front. Second Skin's warriors, honed on a decade of war, were everywhere dropping to the ground. Second Skin tore his sword free and screamed defiantly as arrows ripped through him, taking his shoulder, chest, stomach, throwing him back to land beside Stone Slayer's riddled body.

ⴷⵃⴷⵃⴷⵃⴷⵃⴷⵃⴷⵃⴷⵃⴷⵃⴷⵃⴷⵃⴷⵃ

Turquoise Prince hadn't heard Huemac enter, though he had felt something, a chill that settled through him. He looked up in alarm, his hand even falling across the hilt of his razor-sword. Huemac was watching from the shadows of the entrance.

Huemac's eyes had always been dark. In battle, they were like black stones. But whenever he returned to the city, when he stood in the judgment chambers or came here, beneath the temple for sacred rites, the warrior seemed to retreat from Huemac's eyes, and there was an awkwardness; Huemac showed a restless spirit, a little untrusting and even a bit unsure of himself.

The shadows were gone. Huemac's eyes were focused—fierce,

so strong that if not for Huemac's broad face offsetting them, he would not have recognized his brother. Turquoise Prince found himself lost for words. He had meant to start with an embrace, then speak the words he had rehearsed all night long, ignoring sleep, but now he just stared, alarmed.

"My brothers," Huemac said, opening his palms to great them, "once more the sons of Topiltzin gather as firstborn."

"Not fully gathered," said Turquoise Prince, surprised it was he who felt self-doubt this time. "Sky Hawk is—"

"Sky Hawk comes just behind me, but because he brings a sacred, holy offering, I have come first to ask we speak covenant and share the ancient ceremony of our father."

"Without Sky Hawk?"

"Not without him, my brother, but rather to sanctify what he brings. Trust me in this, son of Paper Flower. All will be made plain."

Turquoise Prince was startled to hear Huemac speak the name of his mother.

Huemac stepped into the chamber and laid a fresh amaranth seedcake and a white, shark-leather wineskin. Turquoise Prince tried, tried to speak, to voice his concern, but strangely, the eyes in Huemac looked up so sharply his words were lost.

"Our elder brother," Huemac said. "Will you honor us with the words?"

Where was Sky Hawk? Turquoise Prince tried to contain his panic. He tried to reason with his fear, tried to tell himself this was Huemac, this was the mightiest warrior alive. There could not be anything to fear; it was impossible.

"This we do in memory of the Singer," Turquoise Prince said. "Who, though he was a god, walked once among us in the skin of a man . . ."

"In the skin of a man," Huemac added. Turquoise Prince turned, startled.

"What is this?" he said carefully. "Huemac, what is this you do?"

"We will take covenant. We will remember him; we will speak

in his name." He broke the seedcake and lifted the first piece to Moan Bird. For the first time, Turquoise Prince noticed Huemac's forearm was wrapped in cotton weft from the elbow to the wrist, a bandage, blood seeping through it in places. Yet no one spoke of it. Did they not see? Why was everyone so quiet?

"Serpent Plumed," Huemac said as he continued passing the seedcake.

"And for this we give unto his memory our best seedcakes—that it becomes like his flesh."

Now it was Turquoise Prince. This close, he could not stare into these eyes. They were terrifying, something had happened to Huemac that was terrifying beyond words. Turquoise Prince took the seedcake and ate, trying to believe this moment was all a dream, that he hadn't waited up the whole night after all but must have fallen asleep. Nothing here could really be happening. Huemac remained close a moment to study him. When Turquoise Prince finally looked into his eyes, he realized they opened to the dark of the universe.

"We have just shared the Meat of Heaven. Welcome the new covenant, welcome the Fifth Sun."

Turquoise Prince could not move, could not scream. This was the drug of the sacrificial rites; when a victim was forced to eat it, he would dance even while ascending the temple. Beneath the strange, intoxicating euphoria it produced was absolute terror.

Sky Hawk finally entered the room. The Mayan, the youth who had returned with the Nomads from the Southland, walked at his side; it wasn't until he turned Turquoise Prince saw it was only his brother's head. Swirls of fresh blood still spiraled down the pole upon which it was mounted. The youth slipped the pole into a slot meant for banners. He examined the offering stone of the choc mol.

"Sky Hawk's gift," Huemac said.

As still fresh blood oozed, the youth ground the meat against the offering stone with his palm.

"Come, then, sons of Topiltzin. It is time your temple was

dedicated to the one true God of man."

Turquoise Prince did not compel his body to follow, but it did. His body would do whatever it was commanded.

꙰꙰꙰꙰꙰꙰꙰꙰꙰꙰꙰꙰꙰꙰꙰꙰꙰꙰

Coxcox scanned the street below the portico, waiting for Topiltzin to join him. They would go down and search for Huemac, make things right. He had been hopeful, just waiting. Behind him, scattered everywhere in the antechamber, the others had all fallen asleep. It had been a hard night, so confusing, and when Topiltzin had left for his chamber, they settled down, some holding each other, many of them drunk. They had fallen asleep as if they were leaves littering a forest.

Only as an afterthought, as though he had just remembered something, did Coxcox realize what he was seeing in the streets of the city below. It was as if his eyes had been watching but not speaking, as if his mind kept secrets from him. It was quiet, but there were warriors everywhere, moving quickly, but these were shadowy. He watched with a shudder as a division of warriors passed beneath the gate, entering the city like conquerors. They were warriors of the Southland—Maya, but not just any Maya, these were *Itzás*—shifters. Their armor was blackened leather, their faces were painted, and even their weapons were burnished. The hidden ones, the Shadow Walkers.

Coxcox looked at the others, but he knew nothing would be gained by waking them.

Coxcox backed away from the portico, his mind reeling. How many times had he awoken sweaty and flushed with an icy panic after dreaming of the end of all things, of the sky boiling, of blood running through the streets like heavy rain? How many times? He would wake, and the terrible dread in his heart would dissolve as he realized that, of course, everything was fine, it was a normal day, an ordinary day. The end wasn't coming; it was far; it was distant.

Yet this time, Coxcox was awake; this time the horror was real and walking toward the palace.

Coxcox ran. If he could reach Topiltzin, perhaps he could help him escape. He knew the underground of the city. He could lead them through the caverns below, old caverns that ran beneath the buildings of Tula; caverns that few were even aware existed. He could find Topiltzin and spirit him and the others out of the palace, and together, if they were clever and quick, they might even outrun the dark.

In his panic, however, Coxcox ran blindly. He did not try to feel the hallways or listen to *the knowing* inside him; he just ran, down one hall, around another, and then he turned down the last hallway that led to Topiltzin's chamber. Here he slowed, stricken. The path to Topiltzin's chamber was blocked by two tall sentinels who stood near a pillared arch of the hallway. Coxcox decided to try something, for anything would be better than standing in the hall screaming, although that was his internal impulse: just to stand there and yell because everything had ended now, everything was over. Instead, he steadied his pace and walked with purpose and authority toward the tall sentinels.

"Stand aside," he ordered.

"We cannot let you enter, Lord Coxcox. It is denied."

"By what authority?"

"The king of Tula."

"The king? The king's chamber is behind you, impudent fool! His orders have not been given!"

Hearing footfall, Coxcox turned. A maniple of dark warriors approached—*Itzás*, their weapons burnished red and black, their armor stained to look like smoke, and their eyes the dark stones of wizards. They were deadly predators that had no place here; they were of a different world, a world he had prayed every day to remain in the past. One of the warriors was a lean youth dressed as a sorcerer. He had terrible, flashing blue eyes. At his flanks were dread warlords of the South, but what most struck Coxcox was the figure who strode in the center of them. Coxcox could only stare, stricken with horror. Coming toward him was the harbinger—the herald of a new sun. Xipe Totec. The Flayed Man.

Coxcox screamed. He turned for Topiltzin's chamber and attempted to break through the legs of the guards, but one of them grabbed Coxcox by the arm and first slammed him against the hard stone of the hallway, then threw him sprawling. Coxcox landed on his back. He still scrambled, tried to get up to run for Topiltzin, but a guard kicked him in the side of his head and Coxcox went down.

⟐⟐⟐⟐⟐⟐⟐⟐⟐⟐⟐⟐⟐⟐⟐⟐⟐

Topiltzin shivered. The room was melting. The walls seemed to drip, seemed to spill liquid into the floor. The girl was dancing high, laughing, her hair whipping. Topiltzin could hear the music she danced to; it was wild and mocking, as though fires had been built about them, weaving a terrible song.

She turned, her eyes watching him carefully, and as she stared her youth fell away. Her skin changed; fissures cracked into the skin and snaked across her cheeks and down her neck. Her skin wilted into folds beneath her arms. Her hair shimmered from jet black to silver, then white, thinning. Her eyes masked into the opaque film of a blind woman.

"You are such a fool," the shifter said. "You always were. To-piltzin, the dreamer. How could you not understand it ended here long ago? You come praying, making your offerings. You even built temples!" She laughed and then spoke in a harsh whisper, "What a fool you are, Topiltzin. For whom are these temples? What God has ever smiled on you?"

She tore open her blouse. Her breasts were long, hanging, shriveled, the nipples black knots, useless. She lifted a finger; and with it, she scratched a lesion across her chest, making it look as if she had been savaged. She walked past him, and he wondered about the sound: one foot padding, the other a metallic clink. Her left foot was silver, attached to the stump of her leg with screws that sank into the bone. She threw herself onto his sleeping mat, then pulled her skirt up around her legs, then threw her legs open. She laughed, watching Topiltzin.

"We still have time. If you are quick!"

Someone stepped into the doorway of the chamber, and Topiltzin turned to find a hooded figure. He wore the robes of a sorcerer, a shifter, and at his flanks, warriors wearing the smoked armor of Shadow Walkers took positions at the chamber entrance. The shifter slowly reached delicate, long fingers to drop the hood. It was the youth, the same who had stood beside Huemac. He turned slowly to look at the old woman through the stretched slits of his misshapen eyes.

"Mother," he said.

"What have you done to her?" the youth asked. He turned. "Priest!" he shouted. "We need a priest here!"

The warriors at the doorway parted to let a shaven priest step into the room. He was a priest of Turquoise Prince's temple. He was clearly terrified, shaking.

"Exam her, Priest. Determine if she has been touched."

The priest turned to the old woman. She stared back with white eyes. He stepped forward, knelt.

"Look closely," the old woman hissed. He did. He leaned forward, studied her, and drew back. He kept his face calm.

"Well?" asked the youth."

"Yes, lord. She has been touched."

The youth nodded and turned to the city sentinels who had been ushered into the room.

"Sentinels of Tula," he said, speaking unbroken Nonaloca, "you see this woman here—my mother. She had been touched. You are witness. This priest is witness. I have heard there is a law decreed in this land, spoken of the Serpent Plumed. What is done with adulterers in this city? You, Priest, speak me this."

"They . . . they are to be judged," the priest answered.

The youth glanced at the old woman who had crawled back against the wall and watched everything with a calm amusement through her dead, white eyes.

"Mother . . . we need a judge."

"A judge," she hissed. "Who is judge here? Ah, yes, I know. Favored son. Bring the favored son."

Topiltzin moaned, seeing him walk into the room. All his life drained between his fingers—his heat shattered. He wore the skin of a flayed victim, laid over him like a costume, over his face like a mask, over his arms and legs, over his fingers like gloves, over his feet like sandals—even the toenails intact. The face of Turquoise Prince was ragged, ringed in tired locks of yellow hair. The mouth had been cut in a wobbly oval to reveal a man's lips beneath. The eyes were holes through which someone watched Topiltzin.

Topiltzin dropped to his knees. He cried out.

"How shall we judge him?" asked the youth.

"He should be stoned," answered the flayed man.

Hearing the voice, Topiltzin looked through the holes in the mask to see the eyes beneath the flayed man. They were the dark eyes of Huemac.

"No," Topiltzin moaned. "No, not this . . . please, not this . . ."

"By the law of our ancestors," the flayed man continued. "He should be taken to the marketplace and stoned until he lies dead, crushed. Or . . . we could grant him mercy."

Topiltzin thought of going for the old woman, for her throat, but he simply did not have the strength or the will any longer to fight.

"The priests and the people will be gathered along the Avenue of the Blue Stars, and he will be paraded, stripped of all but his undergarments. He will be spat upon, and palms fronds will whip him, and he will leave Tula, never to look back."

"Bind him," commanded the youth. Two *Itzá* warriors stepped forward and pulled Topiltzin's arms back, tying him to a beam.

"No," said the youth, "use that . . . the staff over there."

They lifted Topiltzin's staff, the one Turquoise Prince had

handed him when first he looked upon the valley of Otumba after crossing the seas, the day he had first seen the ruins of Tollán. He was lashed to the staff by his wrists.

The youth looked to the old woman. "What do you choose as his fate?"

The old woman stared at them all. She looked at the flayed man, then at the youth, then the sentinels. Topiltzin watched the opaque eyes finally turn to him.

"Mercy," the old said quietly. "Topiltzin Nacxitl, I choose to grant you . . . mercy."

When midnight bled full, Huemac, who had taken his brother's mantle and was now called the Great Red Hand, was inaugurated the king of Tula. In celebration, in honor and covenant, a thousand hearts were given to the sun, and the first of these were those of the sons of Topiltzin, those who had crossed in ships.

Amid the celebrations, as the dancers spun and the priests' fires lifted to Heaven, Topiltzin was driven from his city. Striped to his loin-clout, his arms lashed to the staff of Turquoise Prince, he was led by his servants—the cripples, the dwarfs, the hunchbacks. They pulled him through the streets by flowered tethers. They were whipped if ever they slacked the ropes, so they kept the lines taut. Leading them was Coxcox, though his face was swollen and it was difficult for him to see his path. As the king and his monsters passed, the people who lined the road spat upon them.

Behind them, the temple of the Creator glistened with the blood of firstborn, and the new dawn blinded with the brilliance of the Fifth Sun, a sun that would burn for a thousand years, a sun whose terror would ever be unmatched in the history of men upon the earth.

CHAPTER FIFTY-FOUR
EXODUS

It had begun to snow. It was light at first, but then the winds funneled down the passage that lay between the two peaks beyond the Valley of Tollán—Smoking Mountain and White Woman—and snow began driving against them in sheets. It came head-on, whipping against Topiltzin and his servants as they attempted to make the crossing.

They had rested little since Tula. Topiltzin had kept them together, moving slowly. Those who could not travel well, particularly the crippled one, the little dancer, Widow Woman, he sometimes carried upon his back, like a child. They had spent one night about a fire, not far from the ruins of Tollán, and most of the servants had wept continually.

Moon Child would have given them music, but she had lost her flute, and seeing tears fall down her round, red cheeks, Topiltzin pulled her close and reached out, gathering them in until they were all huddled near the fire.

"We shall continue east, until we reach the coast," he said to them, "and when we do, I shall take us back to Paradise."

"What is Paradise, my lord?" asked Coxcox, though his lips were so swollen from his beating it was hard for him to talk.

"It is a place of deep blue sea and endless sky, a place where my queens and my children shall welcome us, and all the rest of our days we shall sing and dance."

"There really is such a place?" asked Widow Woman.

"I promise."

"And you will take us?" said Moon Child.

TOLTECA

"If I must carry you all myself."

Coxcox was staring across the fire at the darkened outline of the ancient city. "Do you hear them?" he asked.

Topiltzin turned to the far shadows of Tollán.

"They weep for you," Coxcox said. "The Many Dead, the white owls that wait, watching: they weep this night."

⊡⊡⊡⊡⊡⊡⊡⊡⊡⊡⊡⊡⊡⊡⊡⊡⊡

The final ascent of the mountain passage had been difficult. Topiltzin helped them as best he could; but by nightfall, they were exhausted. He had hoped to make it over the passage to lower ground, but as the sun slipped from the sky, he realized he had only reached the top, where it would be coldest through the night. He thought about turning back, but the wind was gaining strength, and what at first had been light, cold rain, was now a growing blizzard. He searched for shelter, but this high between the two peaks, there was little offered. The temperature had dropped with the wind, and they were all shivering now, all looking lost and frightened. Topiltzin wore his loin-clout and a blanket-cloak Coxcox had gotten for him from a village, but the dwarves and cripples were not dressed for cold weather; none of them had been expecting it; most wore only cotton, the light, multicolored dresses of the palace.

Topiltzin pointed toward Smoking Mountain's peak. "That way, Coxcox!" he cried against the wind. "There is a cave in that direction. Keep everyone together. When we reach the cave, I will build a fire!"

However, once they were off the roadway, the snow and wind become furious, a virtual ice blizzard. Topiltzin could not even make out the shadow of the mountain against the sky any longer; there was only a blinding sheet of cold pelting them. It caked on one side of his face and left tangles of his hair frozen. It seemed time moved as frozen as the wind, and though he said nothing, Topiltzin soon realized he had lost direction.

"We've lost Widow Woman!" Coxcox suddenly screamed. He cupped his hands. "Widow Woman! Where are you?" There was no answer.

Topiltzin turned, searching. The little cripple would not last long in this, and all Topiltzin could think of was her smiling face and her quick, trill laughter. He recalled that on the road, she had been huddled with the others, and one of the dwarves had for a time carried her on his back, but now she must have gotten separated. He was stunned at the severity of the storm. He had never known storm like this.

"You wait here, Coxcox," Topiltzin said. "Keep together, huddle for warmth. I will find her!"

"Together," Coxcox said, stretching out his arms, "everyone together!"

"I'm cold . . . so cold," shivered Moon Child through clenched teeth.

"Do not worry," Topiltzin told them. "We will find the cave. Stay together, stay warm." He lifted his cloak to hand it to Coxcox. "Cover yourselves."

"No, my lord! You need it to find Widow Woman. We have each other for warmth."

Topiltzin hesitated, holding the blanket. Though they were holding each other, still they shivered, but Coxcox was right; if he didn't have some protection, even he would not last long.

Topiltzin turned and strode through the storm, the blanket covering his shoulders and face. The cold stung against his bared flank and legs.

"Widow Woman!" he shouted. He was trying to follow tracks, but they were fast disappearing; all that was left was a mild depression in the snow. "Widow Woman!"

He heard a voice, lost somewhere amid the wind, small and distant. It seemed to be on his left, and he made his way slowly, carefully.

"Widow Woman!"

"I am here," she said finally, and he turned, surprised she was so close, just to the right of him, almost lost even then, curled in the snow, shivering, her arms wrapped tightly about her thin legs. Seeing her, a tear stung his lash. Topiltzin swept her up. Widow Woman was so cold, her skin so icy.

"Forgive me, my lord," she said weakly. "I got lost."

"It's all right; we'll be all right."

He pulled the blanket about both of them and turned.

His own tracks were gone. He struggled forward and the snow drove against him, stinging his skin. He wore deerskin sandals, and as it had gotten colder, he had wrapped them with weft, but his feet and toes were already numbed.

Topiltzin paused, searching. He thought he had tracked his direction, but now a panic gripped him, for every direction looked the same. He could no longer tell if he had turned north or south. Widow Woman was tight against him, and though he held her close, her skin was like holding ice.

"Coxcox!" Topiltzin shouted, pushing forward, but his voice was swallowed in the whine of winds. Topiltzin tripped against a rock and dropped to one knee, still clutching Widow Woman tightly. For the first time since snowfall, Topiltzin wondered if they were going to live through this. It seemed it took all his strength just to get back on his feet. But he did, he kept moving, turning in the direction he most trusted to be Smoking Mountain's summit, remembering dimly a small thicket of evergreens and a shallow, rocky cave he had visited in his youth. It was their only chance.

"Coxcox!" he cried again, as loudly as he could. He thought he heard an answer this time and angled toward it. He could no longer see more than a footstep or two distance, and the cold was making its way through his blanket. The skin of his chest, where he held Widow Woman, was numbed and icy.

Then he sighted them; the wind had shifted, and for just a moment, he had seen through it. In the distance, they were all but buried in snow, hugging each other. He made his way toward them, but the storm strengthened once more, and their images vanished.

"Coxcox!"

Widow Woman had stopped trembling. Topiltzin paused. Her face was still, the lips blue, the eyes clamped shut. He felt for breath. There was none. "Widow Woman!" Topiltzin shook her, but there was no reaction. "Oh, God!" he moaned. A lump swelled in his throat, choking him.

In all the days Topiltzin had been upon the land of Tollán, since he had left Paradise, he had prayed. He had constantly lifted his voice, searching. Even in the most heartfelt moments, there had been no answer, but now Topiltzin lifted his voice from the very depth of his soul. He fell to his knees and looked to Heaven, holding the icy body of Widow Woman against him. "Not this!" he swore, angry. "Not my little ones!"

Then, quietly in answer, the storm slowed and died. The sheets of ice slackened to flakes slowly drifting. He turned, searching. His breath caught short, and he stared, stricken.

Coxcox was in the center of them. There was a sheet of ice over the little man's head and arms where he held two sisters against him. Ice had covered his still open eyes, and though they were now white and crystal, Coxcox looked still to be searching through them, hopeful. The others, heads lowered, clinging to each other, were a careful, white sculpture of children in the night; frozen, perfect.

CHAPTER FIFTY-FIVE
DEPARTURE

The ocean looked as blue and calm as the surface of a jewel. Topiltzin stood upon a sand dune, sea grass whipping against his leg, and smelled it, smelled the ocean and remembered. He pulled a chain locket from the pouch of his belt. Still there, after all this time, in his hand lay the tiny seashell of Jewel Twirler, the one she had given him that day so long ago in Paradise. He could still hear her words, *you will return to us!*

He did not know how long he had been walking, but there was no longer anywhere else to go. He had reached the seacoast and the scent of the ocean touched him like balm. He wore tattered, gray robes, but no shoes. His hair was as white as his beard. He was thin, almost wasted by the journey across the dry lands of the north. Had he died, he would have accepted death without question, but he had not died; he had reached the east sea. He started slowly down toward the ocean, using Turquoise Prince's wooden staff for support. He hardly noticed the villagers gathering. There were only a few at first, seacoast Chichimeca who had noticed him from a distance, but soon there were many, soon the whole village was gathered, and when Topiltzin finally paused, looking around, he was startled to see so many of them, lining the dunes, watching him. One of them, a young woman with long, black hair and beautiful eyes, approached him slowly. She seemed to study his face as though it were a puzzle.

"Are you . . . him? The one?" she asked, almost whispering.

Topiltzin paused, uncertain.

"The one they call Sky Teacher," she added.

K. MICHAEL WRIGHT

Topiltzin felt a shiver pass. He had not heard his brother's name spoken in a very long time, so long it was a shadow memory from the past that now brought a mist to his eyes.

"We have heard," said the woman, "from those who come out of the north that the Teacher still wanders. He leaves his word wherever he goes, and he blesses the people, especially the children. Please, if you are he—and we believe you are, for you look as he has been described: your robes, a priest's; your eyes, blue; your hair, white—please, would you then, bless these, our children?"

Topiltzin wondered a moment of her words. Was it possible? Could Sky Teacher still be alive? She was not speaking of Topiltzin, for he could hardly be called a Teacher. He realized these villagers had gathered their children upon the beach. A huddle of brown faces gazed at Topiltzin in wonder. The woman waited, perhaps puzzled why Topiltzin took so long in answering. Finally, he looked down on her and smiled.

"Bring them closer, then. Yes, bring your children."

She motioned, and several other girls helped herd the children around Topiltzin until they encircled him. The villagers, for the most part, kept at a distance, watching. And Topiltzin let the sound of the ocean fill him as he laid his hands upon the heads of the two nearest, and he looked up, into the sky, into its clear, crystal blue, its scattered, cotton clouds, and he opened up his heart.

"Hear me, O God," he said, quietly, but his voice nonetheless carried in the light wind from the sea—and then, strangely, the words he had forgotten came easily to his lips. "Amen-om-Amon. Bless these, the children. Keep them from the shadow, from the dark. Protect them, O God, from the Night and the Wind. Make them strong that they will never forget, that they and even their ancestors will always this day remember the Light Whose Name Is Splendor."

In that moment, for the first time in his life, the hand of God touched Topiltzin. He felt it, warm. It was only a whisper, a far, soft touch, and yet it moved through him like fire. Tears fell into his beard as he looked up, past the children. He looked into the faces of the villagers, the women, the warriors of the tribe, those gathered.

"Hear me, all of you. Hear my last words! Take them to all the people! See that they are scattered like seed upon the wind. I go now; I depart to that land whence I came. But I shall return, and in that day, I shall answer the blood of the innocents and scatter the lords of shadow. And I will tell you the day, the hour in which I shall return that my people may know when I come that they are delivered. Mark, it shall be in the year of my birth, the year One Reed, and it shall be in the day the rabbit runs."

He watched, and he knew by their faces each word he had spoken would be remembered. They would take them back to their village, they would memorize them, and they would carry them out from their village as song. He backed away slowly until he felt the lick of the tide against his heel, and raised his staff into the air.

A wind built around him, and he felt what was happening; he understood, for he had somehow commanded it.

Murmurs built among the villagers. They pointed; they gasped, amazed. Long they would tell the story. Many of them would tell it until they were old, how the serpents had come from the sea, from all directions. They had gathered, tumbling, swirling all about the Teacher, hundreds of them, until they knitted together. Like reeds they entwined, forming a patchwork, a raft, and they stilled as would things no longer living. The Lord Quetzalcoatl stepped upon their backs and knelt. He lifted his staff and was carried into the sea until he was out of sight, until it seemed the sky had swallowed him. Left upon the horizon, white and shining, the morning star glittered like a jewel.

EPILOGUE

Emerald-as-the-Sky was working over the corn grinder, taking comfort in its rhythm as she quietly made the evening meal. Coyotl's grandchildren were all in the eastern field, playing. It had been a year since Coyotl had stripped the forest there and burnt it, then planted their crops. They were yielding now, Coyotl would have been pleased, and the crops were more than they needed, bountiful, plentiful. But sadly, much of it was going to waste, Emerald-as-the-Sky no longer had the will to gather this harvest; her heart had simply been broken too long.

She heard the children screaming and looked up. Frog Runner came skipping over the hill above her, laughing, almost dancing as he came. When he reached her, he grinned wide.

"What?" asked Emerald-as-the-Sky. "What is it? What is your joke, Frog Runner?"

He waited and then pointed a dirty finger, looking to the hill with a wide smile.

Emerald-as-the-Sky turned her head and felt her heart leap. He was there, holding himself up on crutches fashioned of bamboo sticks. His legs were bent, almost hanging from his body, but it was he. From the distance, he offered a weak smile. Emerald-as-the-Sky dropped everything. The grinding stone was even knocked over when she rushed forward, up the hill until she could sweep him up, pull him into her arms, and hold him fast against her.

"I'm afraid I've broken my legs again," he said, stroking her hair. "But you always knew I would come home, didn't you, Emerald-as-the-Sky? You always knew."

623

THE
DREAM
THIEF

HELEN A. ROSBURG

Someone is murdering young, beautiful women in mid-sixteenth century Venice. Even the most formidable walls of the grandest villas cannot keep him out, for he steals into his victims' dreams. Holding his chosen prey captive in the night, he seduces them . . . to death.

Now Pina's cousin, Valeria, is found dead, her lovely body ravished. It is the final straw for Pina's overbearing fiance', Antonio, and he orders her confined within the walls of her mother's opulent villa on Venice's Grand Canal. It is a blow not only to Pina, but to the poor and downtrodden in the city's ghettos, to whom Pina has been an angel of charity and mercy. But Pina does not chafe long in her lavish prison, for soon she too begins to show symptoms of the midnight visitations; a waxen pallor and overwhelming lethargy.

Fearing for her daughter's life, Pina's mother removes her from the city to their estate in the country. Still, Pina is not safe. For Antonio's wealth and his family's power enable him to hide a deadly secret. And the murderer manages to find his intended victim. Not to steal into her dreams and steal away her life, however, but to save her. And to find his own salvation in the arms of the only woman who has ever shown him love.

ISBN#1932815201
ISBN#9781932815207
Gold Imprint
US $6.99 / CDN $8.99
Available Now
www.helenrosburg.com

erin samiloglu
DISCONNECTION

There is a serial killer on the loose in New Orleans. Someone is branding, stabbing and strangling young girls. Their mutilated bodies are being found in the depths of the Mississippi River.

Beleaguered Detective Lewis Kline and his colleagues believe the occult may be involved, but they have no leads. And the killer shows no sign of slowing down.

Then Sela, a troubled young woman, finds a stranger's cell phone in a dark Bourbon Street bar. When it rings, she answers it. On the other end is Chloe Applegate. The serial killer's most recent victim.

So begins Sela's journey into a nightmare from which she cannot awaken, a descent into madness out of which she cannot climb . . . as she finds herself the target of an almost incomprehensible evil.

ISBN#1932815244
ISBN#9781932815245
Gold Imprint
US $6.99 / CDN $8.99
Available Now
www.erinsamiloglu.com

SIREN'S CALL
MARY ANN MITCHELL

Sirena is a beautiful young woman. By night she strips at Silky Femmes, enticing large tips from conventioneers and salesmen passing through the small Florida city where she lives.

Sirena is also a loyal and compassionate friend to the denizens of Silky Femmes. There's Chrissie, who is a fellow dancer as well as the boss's abused and beleaguered girlfriend. And Ross, the bartender, who spends a lot of time worrying about the petite, delicate, and lovely Sirena. Maybe too much time.

There's also Detective Williams. He's looking for a missing man and his investigation takes him to Silky's. Like so many others, he finds Sirena irresistible. But again, like so many others, he's underestimated Sirena.

Because Sirena has a hobby. Not just any hobby. From the stage she searches out men with the solid bone structure she requires. The ones she picks get to go home with her where she will perform one last private strip for them. They can't believe their luck. They simply don't realize it's just run out.

ISBN#1932815163
ISBN# 9781932815160
Gold Imprint
US $6.99 / CDN $8.99
Available Now
www.sff.net/people/maryann.mitchell

THE LUCIFER MESSIAH

FRANK CAVALLO

Sean Mulcahy answered Uncle Sam's call. In the autumn of 1917, he left his home, his friends, and the girl he loved. On the killing fields of the Western Front, he vanished without a trace.

Thirty years later his best friend Vince Sicario is a broken man. Split from his wife, run off the NYPD, his world swirls in the bottom of a bottle. Until Sean comes clawing at his door. Bleeding. Delirious. And looking not a single day older.

Vince turns to the only person he trusts, his wife Maggie — the woman Sean left behind three decades earlier. Together they hit the streets of Hell's Kitchen, seeking answers to Sean's disappearance . . . and mysterious return.

But others are on the same trail, and something terrible is lurking in the dark alleys and dirty corners of the West Side. Wise guys are disappearing. Mutilated corpses are turning up. The cops are baffled and gangsters are running scared. Rumors abound of strange gatherings in the shadows, of ancient horrors reborn, of blood feasts and pagan rites rekindled. Some say the savior of the damned has come.

Sean may be in terrible danger. Or the greatest danger of all.

The Lucifer Messiah.

ISBN#1932815163
ISBN# 9781932815160
Gold Imprint
US $6.99 / CDN $8.99
Available Now
www.frankcavallo.com

FOREVER
will you SUFFER
g . a . r . y f . r . a . n . k

Unsuspecting Rick Summers had simply gone to the cemetery to visit the graves of his mother and sister, killed in a car accident years earlier. He had the cabbie wait for him. But when he got back into the taxi, he didn't have the same driver. His new chauffeur was a re-animated corpse. And he was about to take a drive into hell.

The doors to hell open in the house of his ex-lover, Katarina, where he is delivered by his not-so-sweet smelling driver. Rick learns that Katarina is missing and has been recently plagued by a stalker. That's just the beginning of the bad news. When the house changes right before their unbelieving eyes, taking them somewhen and somewhere else, a horrifying mystery begins to unfold. At its heart is unrequited love. And Rick Summers.

It seems that several lifetimes ago, Rick, then Thomas, spurned a woman named Abigail. Not a good idea. Because Abigail's great at holding a grudge, some of her best friends are demons, and she's dedicated to keeping a promise she made to Rick long, long ago. "Forever will I remember; forever will you suffer . . ."

ISBN#1932815694
ISBN#9781932815696
Gold Imprint
US $6.99 / CDN $8.99
Available Now
www.authorgaryfrank.com

K. MICHAEL WRIGHT

K. Michael Wright grew up near an Assinaboine Indian reservation in Montana where he first gained a deep appreciation for Native American culture which later led to extensive travel and research into Mesoamerican myth and history. After picking up a BA in History, he earned a Maters of Fine Arts degree in Creative and Critical Writing from Brigham Young University during which time he won the Kennedy Center Award for Excellence for his play Outrun the Night. After graduating, he moved to LA and worked in production companies and as a screenwriter. He also wrote scripts for the Canadian Broadcast Company in Vancouver. He eventually "did time" in New York as a consultant and technical writer for companies like Comedy Central and Bank of New York. Tolteca is his first novel. Mr. Wright lives in an historic 1630 house in New England and also spends time in Utah. Among his hobbies are building wooden model ships, online computer gaming and karate (SKA).

For more information

about other great titles from

Medallion Press, visit

www.medallionpress.com